DAKOTA WILLOWS

A STORY OF VOLGA DEUTSCH IMMIGRATION

Gerald Thompson

"The German is like a Willow. Bend him in any direction and he will take root."

—Alexander Solzhenitsyn

For Wendy

with

Thanks to Gail Tyndall

TABLE OF CONTENTS

Part I: The Great American Desert

The Volga Germans 2

The Betrayal of Catherine's Manifesto 13

Wohin und Worum: 'Where to' and 'Why' 23

Saratov to the Sea 32

The Poorest Passengers Make the Best Cargo 59

America: God's Promise Fulfilled 81

Kansas: I Never Saw a Finer Country 95

St. Anne's: An Intentional Community 116

Merchants and the *Schullehrer* 143

Summer: A Season of Tending 156

In Death A New Life 173

Winds of Change 192

Prairie Winter 200

Part II: Margin to Monolith

Casselton 220

Seeds of Expansion 239

A Secure Winter 266

The Great Dakota Boom 292

Prosperity Means One More Year 318

The Lean Years: Harvesting on Credit 337

Economic Collapse 362

Golden Age of Agriculture 386

Lost Homestead: The Final Years 422

A Less Troubled Path 447

Duplicity 471

PREFACE

Late in the nineteenth century, my grandparents immigrated to America from the village of Pfeifer, on the Russian Steppe. They set out for Kansas to avoid conscription, find land sufficient to support their expanding numbers, and escape the growing sanctions imposed by the Crown—the latter designed to make their villages more Russian. *Dakota Willows* charts that immigration and a subsequent move to the Dakota Territory.

The exodus to America was preceded by a similar migration a century before when the Schmidt family and others left the Landgraviate of *Hesse-Kassel* (now Germany) at the invitation of Catherine the Great, who sent emissaries promising free land, remuneration, and exemption from taxes and military service. The Czarista's desire was to expand the secure borders of her vast empire through colonization. She found willing participants in Germania, whose people had endured famine, religious persecution, and political chaos in the decade following the Thirty Years' War. More than seven-thousand souls accepted her offer, making the treacherous journey, under sail, across the Baltic Sea from Luebeck to the Russian city of St. Petersburg, then overland to Saratov.

As a child, I had no understanding of why these migrations took place. My mother and father lived more than six hours from our extended family. We saw them twice a year on weekend visits, spending as much time traveling as in their company. The visits were understandably fleeting, and family history was rarely discussed. I knew my grandparents were immigrants, but nothing more.

Most of my recollection surrounds grandfather. He was a kindly man devoted to his children and grandchildren. He never mastered English, but "conversation" still took place—I smiled when he smiled, laughed when he laughed, and tried to look serious when it seemed appropriate. We managed to communicate. I trailed him around the basement, fascinated by his tools and curious as to why he swept a dirt floor. We spent time in the garden that occupied much of his yard, and each visit included a walk to the candy store.

In later years, the visits became less frequent. I left for college and, absent my mother's encouragement, visited only once in five years.

Grandfather attended our wedding—his contagious enthusiasm was something of a disruption. No one complained. Two years later, he was dead. With his passing, a valuable cache of history was lost.

Thereafter, the only time the family got together was on the occasion of a funeral. Before and after the ceremony there was a time to "catch up." At some point, genealogy would enter the discussion. Russia and Kansas were mentioned, but most often followed by "I'm not sure." After the passing of an uncle, I decided to learn something of my heritage. With elders gone, firsthand reconstruction was difficult. I was able to form a sketchy outline based on vague recollections of family members, but relied heavily on studies of the *Volga Deutsch* undertaken by countless others, notably Fred Koch.

Writing *Dakota Willows* was an exercise in learning. I have a new appreciation for my own course in life, and better understand the sacrifices made by my ancestors who, twice in the span of a century, undertook a treacherous journey across continent and ocean. They colonized the Russian Steppe and joined the teeming masses who settled the American West. Their migration was not wanderlust, but testimony to their fierce desire to protect family and preserve tradition. This book is a tribute to their courage and tenacity.

ABOUT THE AUTHOR

Gerald Thompson was born in a small lumber and fishing town on the coast of Washington state. He graduated from the University of Washington with honors, and spent thirteen years as an executive with American Telephone and Telegraph in Seattle, Spokane, and New York City. In 1978, he joined the cabinet of then-Governor Dixy Lee Ray as Secretary of the Department of Social and Health Services, Washington state's largest agency. He left government in 1981, joining a firm engaged in General Management Consulting. The last twenty-seven years of his working life were spent as owner-operator of a Puget Sound marina.

Gerald and his wife 'Wendy' now make their home in Jupiter, Florida.

LIST OF CHARACTERS

Schmidt Family

Gerold Schmidt: Among First Volga Deutsch Colonists
Jacob Schmidt: Elder, Father of John
—Helena Schmidt: Wife of Jacob
——Ada Schmidt Reuter: Daughter of Jacob
——John Schmidt: Son of Jacob
———Maria Schafer Schmidt: Wife of John
————Morgan Schmidt Lowry: Daughter of John
—————Britton Lowry: Husband of Morgan
——————Spencer and Alexandria: Children of Britton and Morgan
————Clara Schmidt Bergmann: Daughter of John
—————Robert Bergmann: Husband of Clara
——————Alecia: Daughter of Robert and Clara
————Calvin Schmidt: Son of John
—————Victoria Mccutcheon Schmidt: Wife of Calvin
——————Gavin: Son of Calvin and Victoria
————Tavendar Schmidt: Son of John
Frederic Schmidt: Brother of Jacob

Schafer Family

Ewald Schafer: Early Volga Deutsch Colonist
Peter Schafer: Elder, Leader of Schafer Party
—Melina Schafer: Wife of Peter
——Albrecht Schafer: Son of Peter
———Hilke Weber Schafer: Wife of Albrecht
——Maria Schmidt Schafer: Daughter of Peter, Wife of John Schmidt
——Freidrich Schafer: Son of Peter
———Agnes Morehead Schafer: Wife of Freidrich
————Sophia: Daughter of Freidrich and Agnes
——William Schafer: Son of Peter
Hermann Schafer: Brother of Peter
—Wendelin Schafer: Wife of Hermann

Members of Schafer Party

Peter Schafer: Leader
Felix Austerlitz
—Rachel
——Helmut

CONTINUED—BACK OF BOOK

PART I: THE GREAT AMERICAN DESERT

"Mingled in the swelling streams of immigration from Russia ...was a strain of people whom officials generally classified ... as Russians. But they were not Russians ... their ancestry was wholly German."

—Fred Koch

Chapter One:
The Volga Germans

Three days of *Kerbfest*, the annual celebration marking the end of harvest season, were nearing their conclusion. Jacob Schmidt asked his son John to take some of the children home on this last night of festivities. The scarred wagon floor was now occupied by eight youngsters whose parents were left behind to restore the village of Pfeifer to its pre-festival state. As always, the children and young adults reveled in the festivities, while the enthusiasm of the adults waned with each succeeding day. One of those adults, Uncle Frederic, joined the children on the floor, feeling the effects of too much *Brahnhtevhynh*, a favorite vodka drink. Frederic often left family gatherings and festivals in the same condition. John didn't care how he left as long as he made it home without getting sick, another unpleasant custom attached to his uncle.

"The 1874 harvest will long be remembered," Jacob told his son. "There have been few better."

"I know father," John dutifully responded.

Jacob continued intent on making this a teaching moment.

"Such bounty cannot always be expected."

John did not need a reminder. He recalled the disappointing yield of two years previous caused by heavy rain and hailstorms late in the summer. The deluge left them with few sacks of grain hanging in the barn and almost none available for market. Even the usually prosperous Brodbeck and Moser families were forced to borrow from the village storehouse to supplement foodstuffs and acquire seed for spring planting.

John had expected his father to carry the discussion, as he often did, back to his ancestors, the first *Volga Deutsch*, who came to *Russen* a century before under the reign of Catherine the Great. They suffered unimaginable hardship. He meant no disservice to those early colonists and the privation they endured, but John preferred to enjoy the festival rather than hear, yet again, of their travails.

Thoughts of harvest were not foremost on John's mind. Twice during the festival, his father and Peter Schafer met to discuss the long-anticipated courtship of Peter's daughter Maria—the third born and only daughter—of seven Schafer children. Maria had always been a part of John's life. He was smitten as a boy and his attraction grew over time. Maria was taller than her peers and well framed. Her fair skin and calm demeanor gave the illusion of timidity, but Maria possessed a self-assurance, acquired from her father, not often seen among the young women of Pfeifer. She had once asked Father Nicholas, during a lesson on Confirmation, if he could prove the existence of God. The question brought an audible gasp from the other students. The priest was capable of answering—but stumbled—given clergy was never challenged, least of all by a young woman. No malice was intended. Maria simply wanted to know.

John and Maria had been friends for as long as either could recall. They were the same age and attended *Volksschule* together. Studies were spread over six years, with lessons beginning after harvest and ending with spring planting. *Volga Deutsch* education was designed to prepare the student for the Sacrament of Confirmation. Instruction beyond this rite of passage was random, with a curriculum designed to fit educator rather than student. Reading, writing, some mathematics, and a rudimentary understanding of the *Russische* language may or may not be included. The subject matter was designed, not for scholarly pursuit, but to maintain church, farm, and household.

Maria completed her full six-year term alongside John. Peter Schafer resisted the temptation to withdraw his daughter immediately following Confirmation. An early departure from school was common place among young women. Fathers saw little value in educating daughters, who would soon marry and join their husband's family.

The parish school was a welcome respite from grueling fieldwork, but student and parent alike understood that the farm took precedence over education. The skills necessary to succeed on the Steppe could not be acquired in the classroom. Under the tutelage of their parents, young men toiled in the fields or learned the family trade. Their sisters watched over siblings, cared for animals, and helped their mothers with household chores. By the time they reached the age of fifteen, an arranged marriage was not far off.

Well before the onset of puberty, John began to see Maria as something more than friend and playmate. Womanhood had changed his childhood companion. No longer a tallish, awkward girl, Maria was a comely woman, one with features young men found attractive. She understood the effect her womanly attributes had on John and was not beyond engaging in flirtatious behavior. He responded by planning, often clumsily so, chance encounters. Since Maria was a willing participant, his efforts bore fruit. In their most recent tryst, he returned from fieldwork to find Maria gathering the last of the apples in the Schmidt *Hinterhof.* She was in an area screened from the courtyard by the barn and granary. John made his way to the orchard, and the two engaged in blissful experimentation. His mother finally called to him, sure the couple was doing more than collecting fruit.

John's understanding of womanhood came, not from his father, but from his association with Maria. He more than once confessed what he supposed were mortal sins, all having to do with Maria and sexual fantasy. After one such revelation, the priest had assigned a lengthy penance. His mother, Helena, questioned the reason for the atonement.

"Why so many prayers—what have you done?"

John was understandably reluctant to share the content of his confession.

"Father Nicholas thought it too long since I last sought absolution," he answered.

Helena gave her son a curious look, but chose not to question him further. For his part, John was certain Maria's name would never again be mentioned in the confessional. His peace with God would be made in some other way.

Both families understood that John and Maria had progressed beyond friendship, and the time for courtship had arrived. Tradition held that John's uncle, or perhaps godfather, would seek approval for the courtship to begin. Peter would acquiesce, though he believed his daughter could do better. In his mind, there were no worthy suitors in Pfeifer. Maria's mother, Melina, was certain to approve as John had always been a favorite.

4

Except in those few cases where a young woman disgraced herself, the events preceding marriage were cumbersome. Banns must be read and lessons conducted by the parish priest. Father Albin was new to Pfeifer and the ecclesiastic anchor to three other villages. He was struggling to gain acceptance in a community devoted to his predecessor. He had the misfortune of following Father Nicholas, a legend who ministered to the village faithful for over twenty years. Father Albin's approval was seen as a formality since Peter Schafer and Jacob Schmidt were leaders in the community—Peter as *Vorsteher* and John as an elder. The final step was to present John and Maria to the *Gemeinde*. In time, the couple would belong to each other, but for now their proposed union was captive to decades of tradition.

Maria's attachment to the Schmidt family went far deeper than her association with John. Over the past few years, she had become a friend and confidant of Helena, who was frequently ill and easily fatigued. Helena could not work in the fields, tend the animals, or manage the courtyard garden—the latter a task she loved. Her treatment consisted of a bewildering array of herbal remedies proffered from every corner of Pfeifer. Any relationship between these concoctions and relief from her suffering was mere chance. There had even been a suggestion to call upon the *Braucherin*, who promised to draw out evil by simply "lying hands on" the afflicted party. John reminded his father that the witch lost a husband and her firstborn— hardly evidence of mystical powers.

Jacob was profoundly disturbed by his wife's illness. There was neither explanation nor relief. Though he expressed it to no one, he was bothered that Helena could not simply fight off the malady. Stubbornness and determination were his defense, but Helena seemed unable to mount a resistance. Jacob was especially thankful for Maria's assistance, since the Schmidt workforce consisted of just him and his son. A daughter had married and left the home, and Helena had not blessed him with any children since John's birth. Maria's help in the kitchen and field was a godsend.

Jacob considered ending his son's education when Helena began to fail. Aside from the time spent with Maria, John would not have been disappointed. It wasn't because of the lessons, but rather the confinement. He enjoyed tending the animals, the smell of freshly tilled earth, and the satisfaction of a full barn at harvest. He was happiest when outside, and felt as one with the Steppe. Most of the children felt as John did. The world beyond was a mystery. Aside from the trappings of the occasional nobleman, there was little to want or envy. The *Volga Deutsch* led a simple life. They expected to marry, raise their offspring, and die within steps of their birthplace. Families were large. Children meant more hands and young, strong backs. Male children, in particular, were integral to the success of the family, and basic to the accumulation of wealth.

Pfeifer practiced the *mir* system of land tenure where each male, regardless of age, received an equivalent *dusha,* or plot of agricultural land. There was some adjustment in the size of *dusha,* dependent on quality of land and distance one traveled to tend his ground. An acre of fertile ground close to the village might be equal to an acre and one-third of less desirable land some distance away. Other designated lands, such as potato fields and woodlands, were looked upon as common. The assignee worked the *dusha,* but title was held by the village, and could not be conveyed. Leasing was acceptable. Upon death, the *dusha* reverted to the *Gemeinde* for redistribution. Most agricultural lands were separated from the village, and families traveled to their allotted plot for fieldwork. The complex division of land was managed by the *Vorsteher* and elders. Assignment of the *dusha* did not take place upon birth of the male child, but periodically at the discretion of community leaders and the *Gemeinde.*

The village itself was made up of walled, contiguous courtyards, individually owned by the family. The design was intended to fend off unwanted intruders. Inside the enclosure were the home, small barn, equipment shed, granary, space for the animals and a garden. The courtyards were adjacent to one another and neatly arrayed in a rectangular pattern with church and school centrally located.

Young men brought wealth to the family through the accumulation of land. The Schmidts managed two *dusha,* the second assigned to John four years earlier. The Schafers had four under cultivation, one for Peter, and three assigned to his eldest sons. Additional *dusha* would be assigned to the younger Schafer sons when redistribution took place. As *Vorsteher,* Peter was assigned prime land.

The first *Volga Deutsch* colonies received a generous, but fixed allotment of land. As the village began to grow and prosper, fertile ground became increasingly scarce. The Crown responded by creating "daughter" colonies—a resettlement occupied by inhabitants of the initial village. Jacob was not sure when the Crown last created a daughter colony, but it had been some time. Land shortages were becoming critical, with individual *dusha* reduced from fifteen *desyatina* to fewer than six. Larger families, once a source of wealth, now became a burden. Young men were beginning to leave Pfeifer in search of employment, most often in Saratov, which was quickly becoming an industrial and transportation center.

The last redistribution of Pfeifer land left the Schmidts with a smaller plot—adequate, since they were just three. For growing families, successive redistribution brought smaller *dusha* and frequently, hardship. Peter appealed to local administration, seeking a Neu-Pfeifer, but the plea fell on deaf ears. Some within Alexander II's inner circle resented the success of the colonies, and questioned *Deutsch* allegiance to the Crown. Restricting access to new land was an effective means of containment.

John was back to sifting through children in search of the next to disembark. He had spread blankets on the floor, and the children wrapped themselves in those as well as each other. They seemed to be enjoying themselves mimicking the unusual sounds made by Uncle Frederic, who was still reeling from his consumption of vodka. The children were comfortable with John, and most any adult in the village. Communal farming, social events, church and school bred familiarity. There were no strangers in Pfeifer, and the children were expected to follow the direction of all adults as if they were parents or grandparents.

Two of the children would be spending the night with Helena. Pfeifer was a community where seven to nine children were the norm. Helena had only John at home, and was often called upon as a surrogate mother. She did not object. Caring for children was an emotional elixir for her illness. She sometimes imagined they were her own, and the illusion eased the guilt of not carrying out her promise to Jacob, a *fruchtbarer Weinstock,* filling the home with children. Helena's eldest, Ada, had recently married and moved to Katharinenstadt, where her husband, Ehren Reuter, was employed by an uncle in a tobacco processing plant. Uncle Mirko's children were much older and had long since left the household. Ada and Ehren moved in, a circumstance that pleased the aunt. She had both company and assistance in caring for the household.

John was the second child born to Jacob and Helena. The pregnancy had been difficult, once reaching the point where Father Nicholas was summoned to administer last rites. She was bedridden for three months and never fully recovered. Jacob wanted a larger family, but since John's birth, two children had been lost, and Helena's health steadily declined.

The Schafers were more typical of the *Volga Deutsch* family. Melina delivered seven children and hoped for more, but that was a decision for her husband. Peter Schafer was the family patriarch and descendant of Ewald. There were few decisions in his family or in Pfeifer that Peter did not influence. He was unusually tall, with a stern countenance. He rarely smiled or changed expression, making conversation difficult. John was sure he enjoyed the discomfort he created in others. Peter was accustomed to getting his way, both in the community and with his children, though he found Maria less compliant than his sons. She would occasionally challenge her father, but knew her limits, retreating when he became annoyed.

The Schafer family had always been a part of community leadership. As *Vorsteher,* Peter was called upon to decide on the addition of common facilities, matters involving the church, disputes among members, and disciplinary action, when necessary. As an elder, Jacob Schmidt often allied with Peter. The two were good friends. Their shared history had long placed the Schafer and Schmidt families in positions of authority.

Hermann Schafer was Peter's only brother, four years his junior, He owned a large farmstead on ground purchased from *Russische* nobility. The Hermann Schafer farm was equal in size to all communal lands held by Pfeifer residents. Kirghiz tribesman provided security for the farm, and Hermann relied upon *Deutsch* laborers from the village and a few *Russische* peasants. His wealth came from an inheritance. The great-grandparents of his wife were driven from what was then a large and very prosperous *duchy* in *Hesse-Kassel.* Through marriage and a benevolent successor Duchess, the land was returned to its original owners. Restitution left the disputed property with Hermann's bride.

The land was sold and Hermann became a wealthy man. His first step was to leave the Pfeifer community, abandon his communal plot, and purchase his own estate. Except for his older brother, few had visited the Hermann Schafer farm. He was often seen in the village and easily recognized, largely by his own design. His horse was bred to ride, not work; his family traveled by carriage; not by farm wagon, and his clothes were akin to those of a patrician. Hermann was an anomaly—singular *Deutsch* nobility among the titled *Russische*. He was known to be less than generous with his money, but did purchase statuary for the church and had provided funding for an addition to the parish school, which doubled as a community center. Hermann also made the occasional loan to Pfeifer merchants, although it was said there was no evidence of charity in this regard.

A similar distinction in status existed between the Pfeifer community and the *Russische* peasant. The serfs, until emancipation, were bound to the land and effectively treated as chattel. Freedom had not resulted in prosperity. They struggled to gain an economic foothold, while the *Deutsch* immigrants fared much better. The distinction was not lost on the Crown, and gave rise to the Czar's reluctance to provide land for daughter colonies.

Tomorrow would be an early start for John, leaving before daybreak with his father and Uncle Frederic. Their destination was the twice-yearly auction held at Volmer. John had never attended the auction, although the event was often frequented by his father and uncle, the latter said to be somewhat of a livestock expert. John wondered about his uncle, who claimed a wide array of skills, but displayed few. Jacob's purpose was to secure another horse to replace an aging mare. The farm now had three horses, a rarely used ox, a cow, and several smaller animals. Jacob had pared down his livestock knowing Helena, who was expected to care for the animals, now required assistance. He and John were already behind on their fieldwork and had come to rely on others, notably Maria, for help with Helena's chores.

A second horse would be purchased, but not for the Schmidts. Almut Berger recently lost her husband working in the fields. He was using a borrowed horse and sled to remove stones when he momentarily lost control of the animal. The line snapped, sending the iron harness back in his face and making contact just above the eye socket. It was a ghastly wound, taking the eye and leaving a four-inch cut exposing the skull. Angela Rupp was the only one in Pfeifer with some understanding of medicine, but the injury exceeded her skill. Karl lingered for a day, then died. A young man was immediately dispatched to Volmer, home of the nearest *medizinisch*. He arrived in time to join Father Albin in praying over the body.

John was sent by his father to help the Berger family following the accident. It was time away from chores the family could ill afford, but Karl had repaired a harness for the Schmidts a few days before the accident and Jacob felt obliged. A number of villagers had done the same, but in comments after the funeral, Father Albin singled out the Schmidt family and John for stepping in so quickly. Karl's funeral was not John's first, and he had developed an intense dislike for the process. He found the festive mood following burial to be discordant, a pathway marked by despair and grief that led to celebration. John had a hard time with the transition and left post-burial festivities as quickly as he could. The Schafers attended as well, and John hoped to steal away with Maria, but she, under the watchful eye of her father, stayed close to the family. They spoke briefly and arranged a tryst for later in the evening.

The horse to be purchased at auction for Almut was a replacement for an animal that broke a leg just before Karl's accident. The borrowed, more spirited horse, likely contributed to his demise. The farm needed a work horse, and Almut had neither the means nor understanding to make the purchase. Her eldest son was only ten and lacked the experience to select a good animal. Since Jacob was planning to attend the Volmer auction, it was decided he would buy the horse. The Berger family could pay later, if at all. Peter and the elders approved the purchase.

Life had been a struggle for Karl and Almut Berger. The subdivision of communal farmland left the family with an adequate, but small *dusha*. A more committed farmer might have succeeded, but Karl was anything but. The family had come to Pfeifer long after the village was settled. They were artisans—leatherworkers, but found opportunities in their profession wanting. Like many tradesmen, they took up farming, not by desire, but by necessity. Karl continued to ply his trade, mostly at fairs throughout the region. Whatever he gained in the sale of leather goods he lost time and again in neglect of his plot. Despite advice to the contrary, Karl persisted in his effort to make leatherwork pay. His untimely death left Almut with little to show for their years in Pfeifer.

The Bergers were beset by tragedy. Their eldest daughter, at age fifteen, had been assigned as an apprentice to a local seamstress—an unpleasant mating following on the heels of a troubled childhood. Gisa Berger had since disappeared. She was known to walk alone far from the village, and there was talk of kidnapping. Some contended Gisa had simply run away, the result of a contentious home life and ill-suited apprenticeship.

Not long after, she was seen with a group of bandits who worked the nearby roadways. The outlaws were *Russische* peasants who found thievery, rather than farming, a quicker path to riches. They were cunning and, at times, ruthless. If Gisa had taken up with the outlaws, she was likely secure in her new profession. Local authorities had neither the means nor the desire to pursue lawbreakers.

Karl's death placed the Berger farm in the hands of a ten-year-old boy, his two younger sisters and a distraught mother. John, at the direction of his father, continued to help Almut bringing in the last of the field crops and planting a small area in winter rye, although probably too late. He did so with the help of several neighbors who, in the tradition of the village, continued to assist. Help came even though Karl was something of an out-sider—a reluctant participant in community gatherings. The elders knew Almut and her three children could not manage their *dusha*. The Berger farm needed attention and Almut a husband.

The Schmidts left for the Volmer auction much later than planned. Frederic, suffering from the effects of too much drink, experienced difficulty getting out of bed. Jacob was annoyed and unwilling to engage in conversation. John knew this behavior—best to just leave him alone.

When they arrived, Jacob scolded his brother, "The best horses are gone."

"I think not," Frederic mumbled.

By early afternoon, the rift was behind them and the brothers able to purchase two horses and a young pig.

The auction provided an opportunity for merchants to display their wares. A blacksmith had set up a display of farm implements in a nearby barn and Jacob was drawn to a plow offered for sale. The blade had an unusual entry that appeared to add strength and perhaps stability. Jacob was a skilled woodworker, as were his father and grandfather. He and

Stephan Haus, Pfeifer's only blacksmith, were collaborating on a plow that looked much like the device he was now studying. With minimal adjustment, their blade could be adapted to match the plow offered for sale. He was eager to share the design with Stephan.

Chapter Two:
The Betrayal of Catherine's Manifesto

"You have no duty to Russische Army. We are Deutsch. We will always be Deutsch and will never be Russische."

—Volga Deutsch elder

Helena had prepared a lunch of sausage, rye bread, and a large quantity of dried fruit. Frederic, feeling much better, purchased *kuchen* from one of the booths near the auction. They decided to eat while underway, but Frederic saw two men he knew from previous auctions. Jacob was eager to get started, but Frederic was out of the wagon before he could protest.

John noticed another group gathering just outside the entrance. He motioned to his father and the pair drifted toward the growing throng. A young man, perhaps 18, had just taken to a wagon bed. He was discussing conscription, and held the rapt attention of the crowd. Over the past week, he had traveled through the Norka region where he saw several postings declaring all men, sixteen through forty, were required to register for military service. There was no distinction based on ethnicity—the *Volga Deutsch* were included. This was not the Czar's first call for mandatory enlistment. A similar edict had been issued three years before, but included a grace period of ten years for descendants of the first *Deutsch* colonists. This Second Edict, according to the young man, was different—calling for immediate registration—the grace period no longer existed.

The young man paused, and then said, "Your children will soon be soldiers."

Someone from the crowd shouted, "The Czar will make concessions for our villages."

"Not likely," he responded. "My family is joining a group from Rothammel. We're bound for America."

Jacob knew what John was thinking. Conscription meant, at best, six wasted years and, at worst, a death sentence. *Russische* military units were commanded by noblemen from the surrounding area. The more conscripts a nobleman brought to battle, the higher his military standing. Young men of *Deutsch* descent would be the first thrust into battle. The noblemen would return—title and regalia intact—their conscripts not so fortunate.

Jacob and his neighbors knew further intrusion by the Crown was inevitable. The designs of Catherine the Great, a century before, had borne fruit. The Steppe had blossomed largely due to the skills and dogged determination of the colonists. Her grandson, Alexander II, recognized the contribution of the colonists, but was suspicious of their autonomy. Conscription was but one means to force the "intruders" to become more *Russische*; the decision to limit availability of additional land for daughter colonies was another.

The *Volga Deutsch* were caught in a trap of their own design. The increasing number of adult males and constant redistribution of scarce communal farmlands resulted in plots too small to support a family. The system of land tenure adopted by the *Deutsch* settlements had left the authorities with a ready means of control. The Crown need only cease land grants to starve the village.

Unrest was also growing among the *Russische* populace, particularly former serfs. Though ostensibly freed by Alexander II, the serfs were mired in the lowest level of society with little chance of escape. They questioned why native *Russische* were denied benefits provided Germanic immigrants. The Crown took note of this unrest, while growing weary of villages that jealously guarded their culture, spoke *Deutsch*, taught *Deutsch*, and practiced a religion brought with them from their homeland.

Frederic's visit with his friends was brief. When Jacob and his son returned he was already astride one of the horses, the other tethered to the wagon. The brief encounter with the young man from Rothammel left Jacob with more questions than answers. As an elder, he was concerned for the future of the community, but more so for that of his son. Until recently,

John's path, like generations before him, was easily charted. He would live out his years in the village. The Steppe, once non-productive grassland, was now the world's cornucopia, and the *Volga Deutsch* had found what their forebears had sought—a simple, cloistered life free from the entanglements of external forces.

Now a century of colonization was threatened. Political turmoil and a desire for a better life had driven their descendants from the Hessen States to the lower Volga. Perhaps a new sanctuary must be found. The Czar's Second Edict provided impetus. Jacob knew the stories of America. Broad reaches of inexpensive, fertile ground waited, but travel and resettlement were daunting. His son faced a more immediate concern—service in the *Russische* military, which could easily result in serious injury, if not death. Jacob knew his son would gladly stand in harm's way for family and village, but not for the Crown.

John was full of questions, but Jacob had few answers and even less desire to engage in conversation. His thoughts drifted back to the first *Volga Deutsch* colonists. A century before, they left farms and villages to escape forced servitude, conscription, and famine in the aftermath of the Thirty Years' War. Their homes had been razed, reconstructed, and razed again— pawns in wave after wave of conflict.

Jacob's ancestors left the *Landgraviate* of *Hesse-Kassel* in 1763, following the Schafer party already en route. The families were drawn by the promise of a better life offered by the *Russische* Czarista, Catherine the Great, who assumed the Crown the year before. Catherine desired to colonize the land on either side of the Volga River south of Saratov, a frontier outpost. The land was thought to be fertile, but uncharted and often lawless. Efforts by Catherine's predecessors to colonize the region and develop its agricultural promise had failed. Early settlements were threatened by *Kirghiz* tribesmen, who periodically ravaged the poorly defended farms and villages. Catherine understood that a successful farm economy was fundamental to the extension of secure borders. The Czarista, herself of Germanic ancestry, sent emissaries to her ancestral homeland to entice settlers to farm and develop the Steppe. Similar colonization efforts had borne fruit elsewhere in Eastern Europe. She was of the belief that the Germanic people would succeed where the *Russische* peasants had failed.

Her first Manifesto inviting Western Europeans to the Steppe was issued in 1762 and modeled after an initiative proposed by Empress Elizabeth Petrovna a decade earlier. The Manifesto was vague and attracted few settlers. Her second, issued one year later, included a more careful expression of privileges, among them freedom to practice religion, thirty years of tax exemption, immunity from military service, and interest-free loans for the purchase of agricultural equipment. An accompanying document to the Second Manifesto stipulated a food-and-boarding allowance for immigrants reaching Hamburg and Luebeck—the point of embarkation. Thereafter, transportation was by sea at the expense of the *Russische* government. Although Jacob's ancestors and those of Peter Schafer had no concept of their destination or the distance involved, they were among the first to respond to Catherine's promise.

Ewald Schafer led a group of sixteen families. They traveled overland from *Hesse-Kassel,* enduring hardship and the threat of marauding bandits. They reached Hamburg tired, but with the party intact. A second, somewhat larger party, set out fifteen days behind, led by Gerold Schmidt and two of his brothers. Although their route was the same, the Schmidt party was set upon by a rogue warlord. Six in the Schmidt party were killed, among them Gerold. When they reached Hamburg, they found that the Schafer party had already departed. They were provided a meager stipend and boarded in makeshift shelters barely able to withstand the elements. After twenty-one days of privation, the party sailed from Luebeck crossing the Baltic Sea. Their destination was Saint Petersburg, passing through the *Russische* seaport of Kronstadt, then on to Oranienbaum. They arrived in the closing months of 1763. The two parties were reunited, grouped with others of similar religious preference, and provided tent-like structures as their only shelter.

The colonists, while being processed, discovered the first of what would be several betrayals of Catherine's Manifesto. It was not the Czarista that failed the colonists, but rather a duplicitous bureaucracy. The *Tutel-Kanzlei fuer Auslander* or *Kontor* was created to manage and care for arriving immigrants, but the distance between the Crown and the *Russische* Steppe was great. Local administrators seized upon the Manifesto as an opportunity to enrich themselves and routinely twisted Catherine's intent—siphoning funds for local government or personal use. The Manifesto promised crafts-men "to settle where each shall decide" and pursue "diverse useful trades." The Schafer and Schmidt parties included artisans, but local authorities were unwavering. Craftsmen, like all others, were destined for the lower Volga and the yolk of agriculture.

After wintering in Saint Petersburg, they undertook a waterborne route, rafting the Neva River to Lake Lagoda, then down the Volkhov until it reached Lake Ilmen; from there, over land to the headwaters of the Volga, then 1000 miles downriver to the distant city of Saratov. Frequent stops to bury the dead were commonplace as the party made their way south. Upon reaching Saratov, the colonists were provisioned, and four additional Cath-olic families, originally assigned to a Protestant group, joined the combined parties, now under the direction of Ewald Schafer. Each family received the necessary components of a wagon, to be assembled prior to departure, and two small horses. They were given primitive implements for working the soil, a small selection of hand tools, cooking utensils, and six cows. When Ewald questioned the quality of provisions, he was told to take what was given.

A week later, the colonists set out for the foreboding Steppe heading toward the *Bergseite* on the western side of the Volga—their ranks swollen by artisans with no experience in farming. Each day the settlers scanned the horizon for signs of the village they were told awaited their arrival. There was nothing. Early on the fifth day the *Kapitan* rode ahead leaving Ewald Schafer and the members of his party to rest. He returned near midday, reformed the group, and continued south toward an outcropping of trees in an otherwise grassy plain. When they reached their destination, the leader raised his hand and commanded the party to step down. There were no homes, construction materials, or source for water. With an admonition to stay or face punishment, the *Kapitan* told the party he had fulfilled his obligation.

The first nights were spent in the shelter of their wagons. Lacking the materials to build above-ground shelter, the settlers created *semlinkas* hollowed out of the ground and covered with thatch. These were often shared by two or more families. The Ewald Schafer party, now apparently abandoned, survived on limited foodstuffs provided before departure, supplanting their diet with wild fruits and berries. Before leaving Saratov, each family was given a few *rubles*. They quickly exhausted this currency purchasing dried fish and grain from curious local peasants attached to large estates owned by absentee *Russische* noblemen. Game was available, but the means to kill wanting.

After three weeks, the *Kontor* appeared. He brought seed, but too little and too late for planting. There were no tools to replace those already shredded by the Steppe's impenetrable soil, and just enough currency to sustain their agony. The colonists were left to their own means to survive, the promises of Catherine's Manifesto unfulfilled.

Fertile ground was everywhere, but the task of breaking sod difficult. Makeshift implements broke and seed quality was poor, leaving the party with a harvest that barely returned the seed invested. They were able to establish contact with other settlements, but found their circumstances to be the same. The *Kontor*'s visits became less frequent, and the suggestion the party abandon the Steppe was met with threats of imprisonment. The colonists had no way of knowing they were in an unusual cycle of drought that left the soil parched. For almost a decade, Catherine's design on colonizing the Steppe hung in the balance. Each year the settlers faced eradication. Poor growing conditions and a treacherous bureaucracy left the experiment in constant jeopardy. To escape the cycle of subsistence required a surplus. To compound matters, each winter saw the return of typhoid, diphtheria, and smallpox, for which the families had no remedy save potions and prayer.

Finally, the drought broke, and the Steppe returned to a more familiar weather pattern. The Czarista discovered her colonization plan had been thwarted by greed and sent her own emissaries to manage the experiment. Local government was purged of its worst offenders. The *Kontor* provided quality seed on a timely basis and the colonists were given proper implements. They were blessed with an abundant crop and fields were expanded. Logs suitable for construction were floated down the Volga and painstakingly dragged to the village. The settlers emerged from their dugouts. With secure housing and the stability offered by a surplus of grain, the settlers took their first steps toward the creation of autonomous villages.

Their fierce desire to succeed in the face of staggering obstacles would grow in the coming years. Many followed Ewald Schafer and Gerold Schmidt, but none would experience the suffering and hardship faced by the early colonists. The Czarista's experiment proved successful. With the barest of essentials, the *Volga Deutsch* persevered. Little by little, decade after decade, the settlers built vibrant communities and turned grassland to fields of wheat, barley, and rye. By the mid-nineteenth century, the area south of Saratov became a world leader in grain production, and Saratov itself a center for distribution.

Jacob knew the story well. His ancestors had risked everything to protect their livelihood and family. He was sure, if necessary, their descendants would do the same. The Czar's most recent edict was certain to trigger a migration to America and elsewhere—an exodus no less daunting than undertaken by Ewald Schafer and Gerold Schmidt a century before. He was eager to meet with Peter and the elders to discuss yesterday's experience at Volmer, and to learn what they knew of the Czar's action.

First, he needed to take stock of his woodworking backlog. In the past month, he had fallen behind on commitments shared with Stephan Haus, the blacksmith. Fieldwork had intervened as did meetings with community leadership and, of course, *Kerbfest*. One delivery was critical to the partnership. He and Stephan were paid in advance by a *Russische* nobleman with a large estate east of Pfeifer. The order was for six plow assemblies. The nobleman was uncompromising and held anyone beneath his class in disdain. Jacob considered rejecting the contract, but knew its successful completion would bring additional orders. In the past few years, repairs and fabrication of farm implements brought a substantial addition to family income. Woodworking was more profitable than tending fields, and Jacob had assigned his son full responsibility for the family's *dusha*.

John spent the next morning preparing the root cellar for winter storage. His next task was to deliver the horse, purchased at yesterday's auction, to the Berger farm. Almut would experience some difficulty working the horse, but she was capable of providing daily care. John expected to spend the remainder of the afternoon assisting Almut as necessary.

Today would mark the end of Schmidt charity. There was plenty of work for John at home. When he arrived at the Berger courtyard, John was surprised to find Sepp Vogel, a recent widower, and two of his sons helping

Almut. They were engaged in a number of chores, and preparing to visit the Berger *dusha*. John had the clear impression he was an unwelcome addition. He noted a marked change in Almut's behavior. She seemed to have recovered from her grief, and was enjoying the attention. The skills of her deceased husband, at least as a farmer, were often called into question, but Almut was thought to have the attributes of a good wife. Sepp needed a wife, and it appeared that a marriage of convenience was likely. Almut had all the help she needed. John released the horse to Sepp, acknowledged Almut, and took his leave. He was not sure his father would approve of his early departure, but he saw no purpose in staying on.

By noon, Jacob had rescheduled his woodworking tasks and met with Stephan. The pair decided, in the interest of time, not to incorporate the blade design Jacob had studied at the Volmer auction. His next stop was the *Schulhaus*, where he hoped to find Peter Schafer or one of the elders. Instead, he found Father Albin. Jacob asked if the *Kontor* had recently visited Pfeifer and, if so, had there been any discussion of the Crown's Second Edict. The answer was yes to both queries. The *Kontor* and, what Father Albin believed was an official from Saint Petersburg, had arrived by military wagon and posted the conscription notice. They were escorted by a small group of Cossack riders. The official spoke briefly with the priest, but Father Albin understood little of what the *Kontor* said. Jacob decided further discussion with the priest was futile. The more the he recounted the conversation, the less Jacob understood. One thing was clear—Father Albin had been intimidated by the experience.

Jacob found Peter at the Schafer home. The *Vorsteher* had seen the conscription notice, but had no additional information. Peter's brother Hermann had arrived just before Jacob. The *Kontor* had visited his farm as well, but to what end he was uncertain. The official had questioned Hermann regarding the size of his farm and how it was acquired. Hermann's understanding of *Russische* was limited, but he was sure the official was annoyed by a *Deutscher Bauer* with landholdings equal to those of *Russische* nobility. Hermann could sense the disgust, even if he didn't speak the language. The encounter was threatening. So much so, he was relocating his wife and children to the village. For the moment, they would be staying with Peter's family.

Jacob and Peter set out to find Frida Geist. She was working at the school during the *Kontor's* visit. They learned, as expected, that the conversation with Father Albin had been one-sided with the government official controlling the dialogue. The priest had struggled to understand, while Frida, who spoke some *Russische*, remained in the shadows. She thought the official read from a manuscript, telling Father Albin to expect changes in curriculum, and a new instructor for the parish school. *Russische* was to be the official language, and the language of education. She also believed there was some discussion of a more active regional administration in Saratov and a government presence in Pfeifer. Frida was sure the official asked to speak with Peter, but Father Albin, likely confused, had sent the *Kontor* in the direction of the Hermann Schafer farm instead.

Hermann left almost immediately, still shaken by his encounter and concerned for the security of his farm. Much of his angst had to do with a commune recently established by former serfs that adjoined his property to the south. A stream passed through Hermann's property before moving on to that occupied by the commune. Hermann had diverted the stream to provide water for newly planted tobacco fields. He had done so as the commune was coming together. The dam cut the flow of water by more than half. He was approached by the leader, who insisted the dam must be breeched. Hermann dug a bypass to increase the flow, but he was sure the serfs would still be unhappy. A second visit from the increasingly belligerent leader was certain to come. The serfs did not prosper by emancipation, and most complained taxes paid the Crown following their liberation far exceeded the toll paid former landlords. The unrest was widespread, and Hermann feared his farm could be a target. He knew the commune to include a lawless element and, if threatened, he could expect little help from the authorities.

John had not spoken with Maria since his return from Volmer and was eager to do so. The events of the past few days had cast their marriage, indeed the future, in an entirely different light. Finding Sepp Vogel at Almut's home was a blessing and allowed him to take leave sooner than anticipated. He set out for the Schafer courtyard and immediately came across Albert Wetzel, a close friend and classmate.

"What do you know of a call to military service?" John asked. He went on to describe his experience at the Volmer auction.

"I've heard nothing," Albert said, then added, "We have no allegiance to the Crown."

Albert's father, Bernard, was a long-time resident of Pfeifer and his family was deeply rooted in the community. He had five sons, all subject to conscription.

Albert knew his father's mind. "If the choice is compulsory service or leaving *Russen*, father will choose the latter."

When John arrived at the Schafer home, he was surprised to find his father talking with Peter. The reverse was also true.

"You should be helping the widow Berger or working our *dusha*," he said.

John told his father, "Sepp Vogel has the chores well in hand. Almut has no further need for our help."

Jacob understood what drew John to the Schafer home and gave him a look reserved for a miscreant. John was unfazed. He was there to see Maria. His father's momentary displeasure would pass.

John asked, "Is Maria here?"

"Collecting vegetables in the Brobeck courtyard," Peter answered. John hurried up the street and caught Maria just as she was completing her task. The two decided to walk toward the church rather than settle within ear-shot of the adults. Maria was aware of the conscription notice, and imme-diately told John they could not begin their life with military service and a six-year separation. It was Maria's desire to marry immediately and, if necessary, start a life elsewhere. If the family or Father Albin objected, there were ways to accelerate the process.

John blanched at the suggestion. He expected Maria to be reluctant to leave family and village behind. Instead, he found his intended bride planning their departure. She had found a handbill belonging to her father that extolled the virtues of the American prairie. Like the young man in Volmer, she was ready to leave. Once Maria recognized that John was of similar mind, she began to quiet. The two agreed to talk individually to their parents, and to await a meeting of the elders. Time was not their ally.

Chapter Three:
Wohin und Worum
('Where to' and 'Why')

*"Here in Russia it's no good to live. We must our
men as soldiers give. And now as soldiers we must
stand. That's why we leave the Russian land."*

—*"Auswanderlied"*

Peter Schafer called for a meeting of elders to be held on Sunday following midday mass. A message was sent to three nearby villages inviting their leadership to attend. He and the elders believed it was too soon to convene the *Gemeinde*. The government's intention seemed clear enough, but if the past were any indication, concessions may be forthcoming. Alexander II had called for conscription once before, but faced with mounting opposition, had agreed to a grace period. The elders, Peter Schafer, Jacob Schmidt, Nicholas Geist, Noah Adler, and Felix Austerlitz planned to meet with eight to ten families in advance of Sunday's gathering to acquire some sense of community reaction. Jacob immediately began his counsel. He could easily have stopped after the first contact. Families with young men of conscription age, or soon to be so, were deeply concerned. Military service put their sons in harm's way and could threaten the family's *dusha*. Jacob found only one family willing to bide their time. The others were contemplating the unthinkable—leaving the village to protect what they saw as the community's greatest treasure—its children. As expected, he found no allegiance to the Crown or *Russen*. Catherine the Great would always be held in high regard, but not her grandson. The villagers felt betrayed. Whether their families had come to the Steppe in the past decade or were among those who had suffered the hardships of a century before, they believed the Manifesto to be sacred. Alexander II had turned his back on the *Volga Deutsch*.

Jacob and his colleagues never held themselves above the *Russische* peasant, but their fierce desire to remain autonomous made it seem as if they did. The Czar's inner circle traded on the resentment. The Second Edict was proof. A century of toil and tradition was at risk. Hoping for a change or concession was a dangerous ploy, and one the elders could not in good conscience recommend.

Helena had heard of the posting from her neighbors. She knew what it meant, but could not bring herself to face reality. Surely there must be some relief. She was sweeping the summer kitchen when Jacob called.

"Come to the table mother," he said. Helena continued as if able to sweep away the inevitable conversation. Jacob called again and she took a seat next to her husband staring blankly at the darkening sky.

To Jacob's surprise, John began the discussion. "The Czar has issued a new edict. I will be called to military service."

Helena knew what was coming and bent forward, head in hand.

"Maria and I wish to start our life in America."

Helena began to weep. "I wanted only to grow old among children and grandchildren," she said. "Ada is gone and now I will lose my son."

"Would you have John die for the Crown?"

Jacob's response was callous, but he was concerned that John, to appease his mother, would choose to remain in *Russen*.

"I would not," she said.

Helena's gaze returned to the gathering clouds.

"God help us," she said.

The next morning John found his mother standing alone in the garden. She turned to embrace him. Helena told John she understood his decision. Her whispered remark was unquestionably prompted by Jacob—not wanting to burden his son with the guilt of leaving the family. Helena stood silently for a moment as if struggling to find something lost and perhaps gone forever. When John tried to continue the conversation, she simply pointed toward the kitchen and a list of chores to complete.

Peter Schafer, in his capacity as *Vorsteher* of the host community, presided over the meeting of elders. He began with a discussion of the Crown's effort to insert itself in the affairs of the *Volga Deutsch*, notably the Second Edict and conscription. Peter described what he and others learned from visits to individual homes in Pfeifer, each report similar to the one before. A few families were already planning to leave *Russen*, with most pointing to America as their destination, although there was little understanding of distance or method of travel. Their decision was influenced by agents traveling the Continent representing the Kansas Pacific and Atchison, Topeka and Santa Fe Railway. Aware of the unrest in Eastern Europe, the agents lauded the American prairie citing free land, long growing seasons and rich soil. The railroads were awash in land, occupying more than one-sixth of Kansas in 1870. The land grants were designed to spur western migration, but newly laid tracks required tonnage. The railroads needed farmers.

Arne Schwab was asked to attend the meeting. He had some knowledge of the American prairie, as his cousin was among the Balzer delegation, fourteen in number, which traveled to Kansas, Iowa, and Nebraska as *Kundschafter* a year earlier. Their purpose was to determine if railroad handbills were accurate or if the prairie was closer to what some skeptics called "The Great American Desert." The scouts reported finding good land at attractive prices. Their summary was consistent with the accounts of early immigrants already scattered throughout the prairie.

Arne was also an associate of the Reverend Wilhem Staerkel, a Norka missionary, who spent time in Kansas and Missouri a decade earlier. Reverend Staerkel had since returned to the Steppe. He was impressed by the religious, political, and personal freedoms common to the new world, and cited the recently enacted Federal Homestead Act that provided land to all who applied. Schwab also referenced a second delegation spawned by a large meeting in Herzog. From this gathering, a second, five-person delegation had been sent to America. Like their predecessor scouts, they were asked to assess the suitability of the American prairie for settlement. Schwab was uncertain when the group would return.

Peter Schafer motioned to Jacob to stay on after the meeting. "Our family will leave the village in the early spring," he said.

Jacob responded, "John will be joining you. He and Maria will not be separated."

"I know," he answered. "John is welcome to join the Schafer party and our family."

Unless there were objections to his appointment, Peter planned to lead a group of sixteen to twenty families including Hermann, his wife and children. He felt this to be the optimum size. Kansas was the probable destination. The Schafer party would travel from Pfeifer to Saratov and then on to Bremen, with departure by steamship for America. Peter would begin recruiting like-minded villagers within the week. One concern was foremost on his mind. Given the potential for conscription, families were understandably eager to leave. Some would do so even if they lacked the resources necessary to establish themselves upon arriving in America. The fear of losing a son to the *Russische* military displaced the consequences of a hasty departure.

Peter understood the motivation, but knew that without adequate funds, success would be difficult in the new world. He wanted to establish a *Volga Deutsch* community in Kansas. To achieve that goal, members of the Schafer party must arrive with funds held in reserve. Anything less would force them into servitude. Jacob was sure Peter would ask him to join the party, perhaps as an assistant. The thought was appealing. He wanted nothing more than to follow his much-beloved son. He also knew it was a journey beyond Helena's capacity. She was simply unable to withstand the rigors of travel.

Winter brought a period of normalcy to Pfeifer as families prepared themselves and their livestock for the bitter cold. Vegetables, bags of wheat, and other grains were hung in storage sheds and barn rafters. Shelters were girded from penetrating winds and root cellars were checked and rechecked. Animals fattened during the summer were butchered, and ice would soon be gathered from nearby ponds to maintain winter foodstuffs.

Hermann Schafer rode his southern boundary more frequently, but for the moment, tensions between him and the adjoining commune had eased. The parish school opened for lessons with residents reluctantly acting as educators. Father Albin was beginning to better speak and understand *Deutsch*. As he did so, he captured at least some of the stature once held by his predecessor.

The end of the year was also an encouraging period for Helena. She no longer found it necessary to rest in both the morning and afternoon, and actively participated in lighter work. Maria still lent a hand and the two became even closer. Jacob viewed this growing fondness with mixed emotions. Their time together brought happiness to Helena and lifted her spirits, but he knew Maria's visits would soon come to an end. John and his bride would be leaving in a few months.

For Maria it was a period of anxiety. Her father was deeply involved in planning for departure, and she worried that the courtship process, already cumbersome, could be delayed even further. Maria saw the turmoil as reason to advance the wedding date. Courtship was too heavily laden with tradition. Why not adopt an abbreviated schedule similar to that used by couples hurried to the altar by unwanted pregnancy? John thought it a good idea, as did his father. Peter Schafer did not. He held to custom and was adamant there be no deviation. Maria felt just as strongly, citing the uncertain future to support her argument.

Melina Schafer, who rarely contested her husband's view, sided with her daughter.

"Maria should marry in Pfeifer," she said, "not en route or in a hastily built chapel in an unfamiliar land."

"There's not time," Peter protested.

After a contentious debate, Maria and her mother prevailed. Planning for the marriage on a much shorter schedule began immediately.

Before her father relented, Maria, at her mother's behest, had taken a wagon to fetch an urn left at the family *dusha*. She asked John to ride along, since the urn was heavy and awkward to lift. Maria's real purpose was to advance the marriage on her terms. When the couple arrived at the *dusha*, she ran to a small shed the family used as sleeping quarters during harvest.

"I'm inside," she called to John.

Thinking Maria had located the urn, he pushed the door aside and saw that Maria had removed her tunic and unbuttoned her blouse. His first instinct was to retreat.

"It's time," she whispered, pulling John through the door.

"But Maria," he said in disbelief.

They tumbled together onto the straw bed. With Maria as the

instigator, John lived the fantasy he had once confessed to Father Albin. The pair engaged in passionate, if clumsy, intercourse. For John, it was over almost before it began. He briefly feigned resistance, but was caught in the ecstasy of the moment. John lay there stunned by what had just happened. Not so Maria—she was pleased with herself. Fornication was marriage. The ceremony with all its formality was secondary. John was her lifetime companion and she saw no shame in her actions. If the tryst produced a child, it would be early in their marriage, but within reason.

Peter was true to his word—the wedding date was set for January 1 to honor Maria's namesake, Saint Mary, Mother of God. As Maria desired, much of the preliminary tradition was omitted. Father Albin insisted on lessons. They included lectures by a celibate priest to a couple now regularly intimate. John and Maria came to appreciate his sincerity, and the three of them laughed as he struggled to discuss marriage in a language he had yet to master.

Events leading to the nuptials would be held at the home of the groom and typically consumed three to four days. Maria and her mother, careful to include Helena, had begun planning, along with help from the women of the community. The two families were among the first *Deutsch* to settle the lower Volga, and Peter and Jacob were elders. Most of Pfeifer would attend, as would several guests from nearby villages.

Peter took little interest in wedding preparation, citing his obligation to the party he would lead to America. Twelve families had committed, with at least seven still weighing their options. Kansas was confirmed as the destination—a daunting goal given they must first traverse Eastern Europe, a foreboding ocean, and finally one-half of the United States. Money remained Peter's greatest concern. He knew the edict would push some families to risk travel without sufficient resources, a foolhardy choice with consequences to the family and others in the party.

Jacob was thinking of the future as well. He had begun construction on a small space adjoining the blacksmith forge. His partnership with Stephan Haus was common knowledge, and the backlog of woodworking projects was growing. Four of the six plows had been delivered to the *Russische* nobleman, and the remaining two were nearing completion. Additional orders were expected.

The elder Schmidts had decided to give up their bedroom to John and Maria, moving to what had been Ada's room. It was quieter and allowed for a view of the courtyard. Maria arrived midmorning to help. She called to Helena, but got no response. A heavy, wet snow had fallen during the night, the first of the season. She knew John was helping a neighbor, but had no idea where Jacob might be. The door to the summer kitchen was ajar, unusual given the weather. Maria moved to close the door and saw Helena lying face down on the snow-covered steps. She ran to the street and found the Haas twins playing in the snow, pleading with them to get help. The boys sensed the urgency and ran directly to the nearby Wetzel home. Albert responded immediately. He arrived at the house to find Maria cradling Helena's head. Helena seemed alert, but in a great deal of discomfort. Any contact with her left side resulted in obvious pain. Albert's father was right behind, and the two were able to move Helena to the shelter of the summer kitchen. One of the neighbors set off to find Jacob, while Albert was dispatched to locate Angela Rupp. She eventually determined that Helena had broken one of the bones in her lower left arm just above the wrist, and suspected cracked ribs as well. The bone could be set, but Helena would first have to consume a healthy dose of vodka. Jacob arrived just as Angela was completing her work.

The night before Helena's fall, Jacob had invited three of their neighbors for an afternoon and evening of sausage making. It was a tradition carried out each winter. Families gathered together to prepare and pack sausage as they had done for decades. The Wetzel and Haus families joined the Schmidts, as did John and Maria. Thomas Amacker was a skilled butcher and presided over the festivities. His reward was a large string of freshly made sausage. Helena was in good spirits. She had missed the informal gatherings of *Kerbfest*, and sausage making offered something of a proxy. Now Jacob wished he had sent his wife to bed earlier. The festivities lasted much longer than planned, and Helena, rather than turning to Maria for help, had done far too much. He was uncertain what caused Helena to fall. The snow contributed, but Jacob could not rule out the possibility that she was overtired. The bones would heal in time, but the fall meant an even lesser role in the wedding. She would be the host in name only. Preparation was left in the hands of the Schafers. Helena also understood that her son's last days in *Russen* were fast approaching. So much was happening and she was relegated to bed rest.

An old *Deutsch* proverb suggested that a thorough cleaning purged the home of unpleasant thoughts. Jacob was not about to clean house, but he was committed to a brighter holiday. If only for a week, the worries of what tomorrow might bring must be pushed aside. Christmas was a time to celebrate—to come together with family and friends. Maria decorated the Schmidt home with native plants, festooned with ribbons and paper chains. The village was now covered in a blanket of white. Horse-drawn sleighs moved quietly through the streets—their bells tolling the season. Even Helena was caught up in the moment, cautiously moving about the house. Mass would be held Christmas Eve in the parish school. The church was too difficult to heat in the winter with its tower and high ceilings. Everyone attended, including those whose age or illness kept them from weekly mass. Following the service, the families mingled briefly in the cold, then returned home to prepare for a visit from *Christkindche*—a young woman selected from the community, veiled to hide her identity, and dressed in white. Children were given small toys, clothing, and candy, but first had to attest to their good behavior. On Christmas morning, the village returned to the *Schulhaus* for celebration of the Savior's birth.

Jacob's role in planning for the wedding was insignificant. He fussed around the courtyard and spent time at the blacksmith shop. Once guests arrived, he would be expected to entertain male relatives and elders visiting from nearby communities. The real burden fell to the women. They welcomed the task as a joyful alliance. There was one disappointment for Jacob. He hoped Ada could attend, but his son-in-law believed travel from Katharinenstadt was simply too dangerous. Outlaws, although fewer in number, still roamed the highways.

Jacob and Helena chose not to attend the annual New Year's Eve celebration. Maria's wedding was just hours away, and Helena needed her rest. John and Maria attended, but left in the early evening. Revelers understood that in a few months many of their neighbors would be leaving for America. The night offered one last opportunity to celebrate together. Guests had come from the surrounding villages for the Schafer-Schmidt wedding and the salute to the new year lasted well into the night.

The next morning males in the groom's party gathered in front of the Schmidt home calling for the bride to come out. Pretenders came to the door asking for the bride's hand until John finally appeared. The couple then joined the others in a procession to the church. It was a bright, clear day with temperatures well below freezing. The ceremony took place in the parish school. Maria wore her mother's dress and a veil worn by Helena and Ada. The parents sat in the front row, delighted the families were now linked together through marriage. Father Albin was ready, and fell back on his native language on only one occasion. His fondness for the young couple, borne from their lessons, was evident.

A celebration followed the wedding and began with music and dancing. Money for the bride and groom, rather than gifts, was the norm. For the privilege of dancing with the bride, the men pinned money on Maria's dress. Hermann Schafer pinned a sum that turned out to be more than all the others combined. He made sure everyone recognized his generosity, placing the large pouch where everyone could see. The guests then moved to the home of the groom where Helena, keeping with tradition, welcomed Maria to the household. Food was spread on tables and drink was plentiful. For some, the celebration would last another day, particularly those traveling from other villages. The Schmidt and Schafer homes were open to all throughout the festivities. Blessedly for both families, there was an end.

Maria's frequent visits to the Schmidt household in the months leading up to the wedding eased the transition to her new home. She was considered part of the family even before her marriage to John, and quickly became woman of the house. Helena was delighted with her new daughter-in-law and the household seemed more vibrant than it had for years.

Arne Schwab attended Maria's wedding as a guest of Peter and Melina Schafer. He had committed in the fall to contact Peter when the Herzog *Kundschafter* returned from its exploratory visit to America. During a break in the festivities, he took Peter aside. The delegation had submitted its report and found conditions, particularly in Kansas, to be favorable. The soil was fertile and land attractively priced. Communities akin to those of the lower Volga could be established. Peter was grateful to Arne, but the Herzog report had no effect on his decision. Departure was a certainty.

Chapter Four:
Saratov to the Sea

"Peril, loneliness, an uncertain future, are not oppressive evils ... so long, especially, as Liberty lends her wings and Hope guides us by her star."

—Charlotte Bronte

J acob was working in the blacksmith shop when he saw Peter and Nicholas Geist hurrying through heavy snow. They were carrying a leather pouch that he assumed held something of significance to the elders and community. His presumption was correct.

"The Crown has directed all males, sixteen to forty, to present themselves on the first Saturday of March," Peter said. "An examination is planned, and anyone judged to be eligible is subject to conscription."

"Does the document include a specific date?" Jacob asked. He was concerned John could be called to military service before the Schafer party left for America.

"No," Peter responded, "Conscripts are simply subject to call, but the call could come immediately."

"The Ministry of Education will visit at the same time," Nicholas added. "A new curriculum will be introduced, with the *Schulmeister* chosen by the Crown. *Russische* is now the language of education."

Peter was still scanning the document and anxious to share his discoveries.

"The *Kontor* plans an extension of his office in Pfeifer," he read. "Decisions by the elders on taxation, discipline, and division of land will be subject to oversight by the local office."

"Have we no opportunity for comment?" Nicholas asked.

"I see none," said Peter.

The *Gemeinde* was convened four days later and Peter announced that he was stepping down as *Vorsteher*. The Second Edict demanded the undivided attention of leadership, something he could not provide. His every waking hour was consumed by planning for departure. Jacob Schmidt and Noah Adler were suggested as Peter's replacements.

Jacob knew his name would be placed in nomination. He was inclined to defer, but Peter requested he not do so. He won easily on a voice vote. The path ahead for leadership was fraught with obstacles. Conscription and a more active role for the *Kontor* in the affairs of Pfeifer left no doubt that authorities were committed to elimination of Catherine's Manifesto. Jacob and his counterparts would have difficulty preserving village autonomy and tradition.

Presiding in his new capacity, Jacob found the *Gemeinde* surprisingly docile. A few suggested the Czar might delay implementation of the proposed changes, but Jacob counseled against this outlook. Unrest among the former serfs and anti-*Deutsch* sentiment suggested the Crown was unlikely to waiver. Resistance was futile, and opposition was likely to bring additional constraints.

The meeting was adjourned with Jacob asking members of the Schafer party and anyone interested in emigration to remain in the parish hall. Most of the *Gemeinde* stayed on. Peter had again spoken with Arne Schwab and better understood the findings of the Herzog delegation and earlier scouting trips to America. He was prepared to take questions on travel, soil conditions, cost of land, how settlers were received, and whether a communal system of farming could be established. The number and intensity of questions gave both Peter and Jacob pause. The Schafer party might be the first to depart from Pfeifer, but it would not be the last.

Peter had now amassed fifteen families and expected two more. Seven single men would also be joining the party. He was contacted daily by members of the Pfeifer community, and resisted the temptation to expand, though he could have done so easily. Peter insisted on two conditions—good health and sufficient funds to survive for at least six months after arrival. A year would be better. Arne Schwab favored the latter requirement, citing immigrants who failed did so because they lacked resources. Peter's concern went beyond putting food on the table. His desire was to create a new-world Pfeifer, a colony with *dusha,* shared ground, and common structures. The dream could not be achieved if members were scattered in distant homesteads or forced to seek employment for survival. He even considered the possibility of having two or three wealthy families purchase a large block of land, then dividing it for resale to members. This would keep the party together and also allow expansion to accommodate new-comers. Peter believed contiguous parcels promoted interdependence—the foundation of community.

One couple's financial condition troubled Peter. He allowed Karl Sei-gler to join the party, largely at the behest of Melina, who knew the family and interceded on their behalf. Peter now saw the addition as a mistake. Karl was just eighteen with a wife and two daughters. They made their home with Karl's parents. He had yet to receive a *dusha* and was dependent on his father, himself deeply in debt. Melina pressed for Karl's inclusion, knowing he was a certain target of conscription. The Seiglers were a liabil-ity, but casting them aside at this point would be awkward.

The Kalb family, by contrast, was the picture of stability. At forty-three, Denzel had five children—three boys followed by two girls. The two eldest sons were both allocated a *dusha* and built their own homes. The youngest Kalb son still lived with Denzel and his wife. They had accumulated some wealth, and the sale of personal possessions meant their future in the new world was secure.

Frederic Schmidt was a late and surprising addition. His inclusion was not one Peter favored, but came as a result of a sordid affair. Frederic rarely missed a celebration, and often left having had too much to drink. Jacob did not like his brother, nor did he approve of his behavior. Rumor had him involved with Peter Schafer's youngest sister Margret—the two having allegedly met on several occasions. When confronted by Peter, Margret, a married woman, admitted to the disgusting affair. Although Peter had mis-givings as to the wisdom of including someone with Frederic's history, it did provide an opportunity to put a dark episode in the Schafer and Schmidt families behind them. Frederic could have refused, but saw Kansas as a welcome escape from what was fast becoming an untenable circumstance.

The situation was already an embarrassment to all concerned. Aside from a convenient subterfuge, Frederic saw the new world as adventure and a chance for a new start. Whatever his reasons, he was leaving Pfeifer and few would mourn his loss.

John and Maria were as well prepared for the journey as anyone. Jacob had given the couple a share of profits from his woodworking projects. John called it a loan. In addition, Maria was jealously guarding the money collected as part of the marriage ceremony—including the substantial gift from her uncle and a smaller sum from her father. Despite their solid financial condition, Peter often spoke of having their daughter and son-in-law stay with them upon arrival in Kansas, a course of action John disliked. His intention was to someday strike out on his own. His father-in-law was committed to a system of land tenure that John believed was destined to fail in America. Communal living was the antithesis of freedom. John would participate, but only for so long. He wanted no part of the *mir* system or his father-in-law's experiment.

Hermann Schafer briefly considered staying in *Russen*. His wealth would protect his sons from conscription, but might also encourage retribution. He saw a growing anti-*Deutsch* sentiment in his association with *Russische* landowners—noblemen as well as serfs. In the past, the relationship had been passive. Now it was strained. The same tension could be felt in his occasional interaction with the *Kontor* and other representatives of the Crown. A *Deutsch* landowner with extensive farmlands was not welcome. His wife, Wendelin, was deeply concerned for their safety, and Hermann made the decision to join his brother's party. The family would travel with the others to Saratov where they would secure first-class accommodations for the remainder of their journey. He sold his farm and most of his personal belongings through a third party. It appeared the farm would end up in the hands of the same *Russische* nobleman he purchased it from a few years earlier. If so, the nobleman would realize an unexpected windfall, since Hermann was selling for less than what he paid, though still a substantial sum.

The experience in Pfeifer was repeated throughout the Steppe as worried parents developed their own plans for emigration. Some community elders saw a passing benefit attached to the exodus. Fewer young males meant more

35

land for distribution and a larger *dusha*, but those who understood what lay ahead knew that the benefit, if any, would be short-lived. The Crown's expressed intent was to cripple, not enrich, the colonies. Unintended consequences, should they work to their advantage, would be quickly reversed. There was simply no relief from the government's desire to break the autonomy encouraged by Catherine's eighteenth century manifesto.

Smaller groups had been gathering regularly throughout the community to bid farewell, knowing a parent, child, or sibling may never be seen again. The pain was eased by the inevitable discussion of how soon those left behind would join family members in the new world. The sentiment was expressed to brighten the spirit, but most knew there was little chance of reuniting. John was one of those. He understood his mother's poor health meant relocation for his parents was impossible.

As the Schafer party closed on the departure date, there was contact among members almost daily. Most found that the sale of personal possessions raised far less income than anticipated. *Versteigerungs* were common place as families, desperate to raise funds, sold heirlooms at a fraction of their value. Peter was unmoved, steadfastly maintaining his position that members arrive in Kansas with sufficient funds to purchase land.

For some, it was circumstance, not funding, which stood in the way of passage. Hersh and Anna Schneider had the resources, but were faced with the sudden illness of their youngest child. After some discussion it was decided that Anna, if necessary, would stay behind until her daughter was well enough to travel. Hersh and their three sons, one of whom was subject to conscription, would depart as planned. Anna and her daughter would then join the next party led by Ludwig Bruener, who was a neighbor of the Schneiders.

Peter was also keeping close watch on Gustav and Luise Kunkel. Gustav was among the first to sign on, but his wife, while feigning support, did nothing to ready the family. She questioned the destination, timing, and even its leadership. Peter understood the party was only as strong as its weakest link. Luise was a threat.

The departure plan called for an advance party to reach Saratov six days ahead of the main body. Their purpose was to purchase rail tickets, investigate steamship passage, and arrange for temporary housing. Peter believed there would be far less confusion if these tasks were completed before the main party arrived. The group was to be led by Werner Geist, the son of Nicholas, an elder for more than twenty-five years. They would travel, like the main party, by wagon and horseback. Peter was aware there were tickets providing passage from Saratov through to Kansas. Payment was required in advance and he did not favor this approach. If some phase of transport proved unsuitable or was canceled, there was little recourse for travelers. Even with this concern, Werner was instructed to evaluate all options. He was also told to gather information on methods of travel and their destination. Arne Schwab had told him there were representatives from American railroads vying for the attention of each party as they arrived in Saratov.

Werner's advance party was made up of seven men and scheduled to leave before sunrise on March 15, 1875. John was a late addition made at Werner's request. They hoped to reach Saratov in one day—an ambitious goal. Since travel after sunset was unwise, provision had been made for an overnight stay in Balzer. There was also a planned first stop in Kamenka to resolve a problem with Ida Kalb's travel papers, thought to lack a required signature and stamp. Werner was told that the *Kontor* recently established an office there and could assist with paperwork. If not, Saratov would be the next, and perhaps last, opportunity for resolution.

Pfeifer was quiet on the night before departure. For most in the advance party, it would be the last meal taken with family and friends. At the Schafer home, Helena busied herself checking John's trunk and finding ways to pack more food. She included mementos—so many that John secretly gave some to his father to hide. Jacob did so, but Helena stumbled on the cache. The discovery provided some momentary humor. The family talked late into the evening recalling treasured memories, but avoided, as best they could, any discussion of tomorrow's departure.

Jacob encouraged Helena to retire, but she was understandably reluctant. Her son would likely be gone when she awoke.

"You need your rest," Jacob told his wife.

Helena embraced John for what was surely the last time.

Stepping back, she carefully studied her son, committing every feature to memory.

"God be with you," she said. Then, after touching Maria's cheek, slowly withdrew to her room.

John was struck by the moment. His instinct was to go to her, but a discouraging look from his father changed his mind. Helena was losing a son. There were no words to mitigate the loss. Suddenly, his adventure seemed less significant. He turned to Maria. The night was cold, but he felt a need to walk through the village one last time.

The morning of departure saw a small group on hand to send the advance party on its way. Helena was up in time to glimpse Maria and John as they walked toward the *Schulhaus*. She sat staring at the empty street long after the couple slipped from view. Father Albin hurried from morning mass in time to pray for safe passage, then gave the advance party a final blessing. Jacob, speaking for the community, wished godspeed, then passed through the group sharing a last word with each of the members. With that, the advance party took its leave.

They reached Kamenka well ahead of schedule. Werner Geist was able to quickly locate a clerk at the *Kontor's* office to assist with the Kalb papers. A signature had simply been omitted, but it carried a heavy price. Werner, not anxious to antagonize officials or draw unnecessary attention to the party, paid the fee. The group resumed their journey, but the diversion, albeit short, meant Saratov was beyond reach in one day—an overnight stay in Balzer was now certain.

Two hours after leaving Kamenka, the party reached an unexpected obstacle. A swollen stream had surged beyond its banks, damaging the footing of a makeshift bridge. Upon inspection, it was clear the damage was purposeful and caused by something other than the torrent. Werner was immediately suspicious. Before he could sound the alarm, the party was encircled by a group of heavily armed men, each carrying a military-style rifle. They were on foot and appeared instantly from the brush. These were not the once-feared Kirgiz marauders, but rather *Russische* bandits known to seize freight. The advance party froze.

Suddenly, Helmut Austerlitz, partially shielded from view, made a clumsy move toward a firearm resting on a nearby wagon seat.

Werner shouted, "No Helmut."

It was a foolish decision—one which could have put the entire party at risk. Helmut backed away just as a large, dark-skinned man with a jagged scar through his eye socket emerged from the underbrush. Unlike his band, he was mounted, and wore a long fur coat.

"You wish to fight?" he said, riding slowly toward Helmut. He drove his rifle into Helmut's chest forcing him to the ground. "Perhaps you'd rather die?"

Helmut tried to slide away, but his tormentor followed, continuing to jab at his prey.

"Open the trunks, Yaroslav," he said, pointing to the lead wagon.

Kurt Haus, the blacksmith's son, recognized the man as a former serf employed by Hermann Schafer—perhaps the reason the bandits had anticipated the party's arrival.

"We're farmers," Werner pleaded. "We carry nothing of value."

"But you do," the leader responded in perfect *Deutsch*. He continued to prod Helmut, "One of you has a large sum of money. Perhaps we'll find it in the trunks?"

Just then a woman appeared crossing the torrent upstream from the bridge—she was dressed entirely in white and riding a horse of the same color.

She called to the leader, "*Lass den jungen.*" The leader gave Helmut one last shove before returning his rifle to its scabbard. She then turned toward the wagons and shouted, "*Aussteigen.*" The bandit assigned to break open trunks immediately retreated.

The woman was dressed for riding, but in the clothing of nobility. She rode directly toward John, the sun's brilliance framing her body.

"You are John Schmidt?" she called.

He slowly nodded wondering what might come next. As she drew closer, John recognized her—Gisa Berger, the young woman who left her apprenticeship in Pfeifer and seemingly disappeared. He remembered her to be plain, but his memory was flawed. Gisa was a striking woman. She continued toward him, her gaze never wavering. Gisa paused for what John thought an eternity, eyes still fixed on him, before riding toward the dark-skinned leader. They spoke briefly. It was clear the leader was annoyed. He glanced toward the wagons as if to consider what might have been, then waved a hand and the bandits faded into the landscape as quickly as they had appeared.

Gisa turned and rode across the stream. For a moment, no one from the advance party moved or said a word. They stood in stunned silence, not fully understanding what had just taken place. Was Gisa's action based on some attachment to her birthplace or recognition of what John and others had done for her family? How had she acquired such power? The advance party could only be sure of one thing—they were free to continue on their journey. A certain return to Pfeifer, or perhaps far worse, had been averted. Werner inspected the path taken by Gisa and found it safe to ford. The party harnessed the wagons and remounted. Their plan had nearly been thwarted until Gisa Berger's godsent intervention. Just why was unclear, but the group was grateful.

The advance party reached Balzer in late afternoon where they planned to spend the night in a barn belonging to Werner's cousin. The soon-to-follow main party would do the same, with the option for women and children to overnight in the Balzer Parish Hall. The cousin knew the local *Kontor* and strongly urged against reporting the encounter with bandits. Drawing attention to their departure was unwise.

Following the evening meal, the party received a surprise visitor, Johann Houfner, whose brother and four cousins had settled near Topeka in 1873. Johann had specific knowledge of Kansas through letters received from his family. He was a wealth of information. Johann's insights on travel, geography, and the people of America captured the attention of the advance party.

He told the members, "You will not be alone. Others—many others—are beginning their journey, bound for the port cities of Bremerhaven and Hamburg."

John asked, "Will the *Volga Deutsch* become nothing but a memory?"

Johann did not believe so. "Some families are unaffected by conscription or willing to take the risk," he said. "Others have deep roots in *Russen* and believe conditions will improve."

Johann maintained there would always be *Deutsch* farmers on the Steppe. For those choosing to stay behind, departures could result in additional land for redistribution, but Johann was quick to point out any benefit would be fleeting. The Crown was committed to contain the *Volga Deutsch*. Emigration remained the best course of action.

Travel resumed the next morning. As the advance party closed on

Saratov, the party overtook a group from the village of Merkel also bound for the rail station. One of their wagons had broken an axle and repairs were just underway. The wagon carried five children, all standing precariously alongside the roadway. Freidrich Schafer, Peter's second eldest, recognized the Merkel wagons were overcrowded, and agreed to take the children with him. He was accustomed to youngsters and produced treats. Freidrich immediately won their allegiance.

Most of the occupants of the Pfeifer and Merkel wagons had never visited Saratov and were awestruck by its size. The city had experienced exponential growth, ironically fueled by a population the Crown now wished to suppress. The wagons pulled to a side street to close ranks and allow leaders to better understand their location. Traffic was everywhere, and teamsters had no concern for the uninitiated. Werner had a crude map prepared by his cousin the night before, but was already confused. Rather than push on, he decided to use a nearby *Wagenbauer's* stable as a base. The Merkel group, joined by the damaged wagon, continued on.

Kurt and Freidrich were directed to find lodging. Werner and John set out for the train station. The remaining members stayed at the livery. After a few wrong turns, Werner and John reached their objective, but were disappointed to find no agents from American railroads. They learned an agent from the Kansas Pacific Railroad, one of the carriers offering single-ticket passage from Saratov to destinations in Kansas, would be available in the morning.

The station was crowded, and Werner learned three large parties were scheduled to arrive within the next few days, all seeking rail tickets for the same destination. He was immediately concerned for availability of passage. A day's wait could result in a delay of a week or more. Since Peter was only curious about single-ticket passage, and Johann Houfner counseled against it, Werner decided to immediately purchase tickets for Bremerhaven. He knew Peter would have liked to compare through passage to buying each leg independently, but waiting, even for a day, could result in an expensive, uncomfortable stay in Saratov. The less time spent in the city the better.

After a long wait and a certain amount of jostling, Werner and John were able to secure rail passage departing late on the evening of March 22nd. Their path would take them to Smolensk, Eydtkuhnen, Berlin, and eventually Bremen and Bremerhaven. For those accustomed to traveling overland by wagon, it was a journey of unimaginable distance.

Timing was critical. Peter and the main party must depart Pfeifer no later than March 21, spending overnight in Balzer, then continuing to Saratov, arriving in time to board the train that evening. The schedule was unforgiving, but consistent with Peter's desire to spend as little time in Saratov as possible. John and Werner returned to the *Wagenbauer's* barn and found Kurt and Freidrich waiting. The group would spend the night in a two-story hostel with twelve rooms and bathroom facilities in an adjacent building. One room was suitable for the party's brief stay. The proprietor told Werner the only steamship line that maintained a local office was *Norddeutscher Lloyd*. This was not the company Peter Schafer favored. There were frequent reports of unexplained route changes, long delays, cramped sleeping quarters and unsanitary conditions—not uncommon on transatlantic sailings, but reportedly worse on this carrier. Early the next day Werner and John set out to find the steamship company, locating the office after wandering about an industrial area for an hour. The agent struggled with Deutsch and knew nothing of passenger bookings. Werner's difficulty understanding *Russische* left little room for effective communication.

"Your reputation is not good," he told the agent. "Steerage passengers are treated badly."

"They are not," the agent objected. "The unfavorable reports come from a single sailing of the *Ohio*."

A second agent, who spoke near perfect *Deutsch*, appeared and repeated his colleague's claim.

"Food is good, sleeping conditions are improved, and more deck space has been provided for steerage."

Werner had little choice but to take the agent at his word.

The list of sailings was consulted. The steamship *Neckar* was scheduled to begin its seaborne journey three days after the party's expected arrival in Bremen. The timing was good, and the purchase of tickets included food and lodging while awaiting embarkation. Werner and John booked passage for the Schafer party. They were now ticketed for travel from Saratov to the port city of Baltimore. Their task completed, the two returned to their lodging to rest and enjoy the last of the vodka brought by Helmut Austerlitz.

The next morning five of the advance party set out to return to Pfeifer. Once there, Werner Geist, George Breit and Kurt Haus would join the main body and return to Saratov. John and Freidrich remained in the city to gather information from the Kansas Pacific representative and anyone else with knowledge of the new world. The group bound for Pfeifer left the hostel well before dawn, eager to begin what was sure to be an arduous trip. Rain had fallen for much of the night, and there appeared to be no letup. A young man serving as an apprentice slept in the stable and arose early to hitch wagons and ready mounts. He offered a word of caution—the deluge and heavy traffic would make their passage difficult. The advice was appreciated, but there were no alternative routes. The encounter with Gisa Berger and the bandits cost them a day. There was no longer any margin for error. They must reach Pfeifer before sunset so the main party could return to Saratov and their train connection two days hence. Timing was critical, but Werner was confident that Peter would have the main party ready for travel.

The warning by the apprentice proved to be well-founded. The road was a quagmire. Heavy rain made passing oncoming traffic difficult, and wagons that moved too far from center line became stuck, or worse, tipped over. Midmorning saw a respite as the downpour began to moderate. Traffic was slow, but moving steadily. Werner calculated the group would make Pfeifer by early evening.

Conditions continued to improve until they reached the stream where bandits had set upon them a few days earlier. The watercourse was still out of its banks and the damaged bridge had completely dislodged from its footings. The path upstream was passable, but blocked by a wagon close to tipping over. The driver was busy trying to secure his load, much of which was already scattered downstream. A lone rider had a line on the wagon and was trying to steady the horses. Werner maneuvered his horse alongside the wagon and convinced the owner to let his load go and mount the team. A second line was then secured to the wagon. With the team and two horses, the wagon was pulled to shallow water. At any other time, Werner and his group would have stayed on to help, but not today. Jurgen Winkler immediately moved his wagon across the stream, as did his brother Simon. George Breit's horse, pulling by itself, balked at the water's edge, but with a quick snap of the whip, it was safely across.

It was now midday and Werner was concerned. The party should have been much further along. Any further delay would mean arrival in Pfeifer well after dark—not only dangerous, but too late to ready the main party for a morning departure. His solution was to divide the advance party. Werner sent the wagons to his cousin's barn, where they overnighted en route to Saratov. He and Kurt set out for Pfeifer on horseback. Absent the wagons, they could reach their destination before nightfall.

Peter Schafer and Jacob Schmidt had been waiting for the better part of two days expecting some or all of the advance party to arrive. They began to worry that Werner had experienced difficulty. Peter sent the elders into the community to remind members of the main party it may be necessary to leave on very short notice. He had no idea what arrangements Werner had made, but was certain a quick turnaround was likely. The lateness of the hour suggested that another day was lost. Disappointed, the two were about to give up their watch when they heard hoof beats.

Werner and Kurt had finally arrived, exhausted by their eleven-hour ordeal. Peter whispered a prayer of thanks, which he considered retracting when he learned their train would depart Saratov in two days. The party had only sixteen hours to prepare for departure. There were many things Peter wanted to discuss with Werner, but notification of the main party came first. All should have received the notice to be ready, but none expected turnaround in less than a day.

Kurt was directed to care for the horses, while Jacob set out to advise the travelers of the new schedule. Peter was eager to talk with Werner, but first there was an unresolved matter involving Hersh and Anna Schneider. The couple had made a decision to travel separately—Hersh and his three sons with Peter and Anna in a group now scheduled for a May departure. The planned separation was due to the illness of the couple's daughter. Anna did not believe the child was well enough to travel, but staying on put their eldest son at risk of being called to military service. Sadly, the child had died two days before. Anna, though still grieving, had decided to join her husband and the Schafer party, but tickets for her passage had yet to be purchased.

When Peter returned to the parish school, he found Werner waiting for him. He explained the rail connection in more detail and discussed his selection of the *Norddeutscher Lloyd* steamship *Neckar*. He also told Peter there was simply not enough time to research the single passage from Saratov to Baltimore. Peter was disappointed with selection of the steamship company, but it served little purpose to question the decision at this point. The advance party's experience with outlaws came as a complete surprise. Peter was aware of bandits in the area, but thieves that answered to Gisa Berger were beyond imagination. Werner's message was clear—the main party must be prepared for confrontation.

The two separated, each to their own tasks in preparation for tomorrow's departure. Peter was annoyed with two families, one late in joining the main party, the other poorly organized. He visited both and found the first ready—the latter in its usual disarray. Luise Kunkel continued to be a source of concern, resisting her husband's attempt to liquidate personal effects, and leaving the family with too many possessions and too little funds. Now departure was imminent. There was no time to sell household goods and no room for an additional trunk.

"I will not leave," Luise told her husband.

"*Du sturer hund*," Gustav answered, pushing his wife against the wall.

"Perhaps she needs encouragement," he told Peter.

"Do what you will," Peter answered. He agreed with Gustav's assessment of Luise. "Just be ready."

"The children and I will be there."

Peter arrived at the parish school early the next day to find more than half of the wagons already in line. The first two, belonging to the Schafers, led the group, Peter and family in the first—the second occupied by four men, each armed with a rifle. In the center of the caravan was another armed wagon. Their weapons were antiquated and most in the party were poor marksmen, but the main party was at least ready to defend itself. Members continued to arrive one or two at a time. By midmorning all were ready for travel. There were eighty-five souls, seventy-six in wagons and nine on horseback. Most of the riders would tether their mounts and return with the wagons to Pfeifer following the main party's departure. Peter glanced down the line and saw the Kunkel family. Luise was seated in the back of the wagon. She obviously suffered through a very long night.

Hersh Schneider made a decision to ride ahead, hoping the extra day in Saratov would allow him to find tickets for Anna. Peter asked Kurt Haus to accompany him. A single rider was at far greater risk, and Hersh might need help at the rail station. Peter was reluctant to let either go, but the sooner Hersh arrived in Saratov, the better the chance of finding a ticket.

Hermann Schafer took up the third and fourth spaces in line. He and his family were in a farm wagon much like the others, but hired a second teamster and wagon to carry what Peter thought to be an excessive number of trunks. Hermann was excused from limitation since he would be traveling, on the train and aboard ship, in first-class accommodations. Wendelin wanted to travel to Saratov by carriage, but Peter believed it would draw too much attention to the group. A young peasant girl was in the second of Hermann's two wagons, no doubt to assist the family in its journey to Saratov and perhaps beyond. Hermann strutted through the assembled wagons acting as if he held some preeminent role in planning. His wife remained aloof. Jacob Schmidt, in his new capacity as *Vorsteher*, was on hand, along with Father Albin. This was not a time for speeches. Even the priest, never one to miss an opportunity to pontificate, simply moved among the wagons, quietly talking with each occupant as he passed. He was now considered "their" priest, and conversations were often accompanied by a blessing and clasp of hands.

As departure drew closer, a crowd formed around each wagon for one last expression of sentiment, one last prayer, and one last embrace. Maria arrived, having spent her last morning with Helena. It was a tearful departure. The two had grown very close, and Helena was increasingly dependent on Maria for help. Her mother-in-law was in obvious distress, and Maria had a hard time pulling away. When she arrived at the wagons, Maria went directly to Jacob, telling him to return home as Helena seemed to have taken a turn for the worse. It was not good for her to be alone. She embraced Jacob. They prayed for safe passage and a time they could be together again. Maria was no longer able to hold back the tears. Jacob kissed his daughter-in-law and turned for home. Maria took her place alongside Peter in the lead wagon. As they made their way through the village, each traveler studied courtyard and crossing knowing that neither would be seen again. Family members and friends walked beside the departing wagons until they reached the edge of the village, then watched as the caravan slowly fell from view. The journey had begun.

Most in the party would see their first train and knew nothing of steamships. They could not conceive of a body of water so large it took twelve to fifteen days to transit. Then came America and a world of which they had even less understanding. Facing sadness and uncertainty, they remained steadfast in their decision. Their forebears had survived a similar journey and emerged better for the experience. With God as their companion, the party would take root in the new world.

Peter was equally sure God was watching over them, but decided to take protection a step further. Beyond the two heavily armed wagons, weapons were randomly placed throughout the caravan. Peter's first reaction was to not share the advance party's experience with Gisa Berger and the outlaws, but he had second thoughts. Secrets were never well kept in Pfeifer and rumor would soon outstrip reality. The event must be disclosed. Just before departure, he and Werner shared the advance party's encounter. Like Peter, the members had a hard time understanding how Gisa found herself in the company of outlaws, but were thankful for her intervention.

The main party made good time, helped by a firm roadbed and absence of precipitation. For most, the sadness of leaving family and friends behind gave way to curiosity and a concern for their safety. There was one brief stop to balance the load on a wagon experiencing axle problems. A planned second stop to care for horses took longer than anticipated. People and horses had been on the road for six hours, and neither was in a hurry to start again. Peter moved through the group gently pushing the stragglers to capture children, secure loads and get in line.

Finally, after a few unpleasant encounters, the party was assembled and underway. They stopped short of the stream where Gisa Berger had given the advance party a reprieve. Four men rode ahead, but found nothing amiss. The water level had retreated and the bridge footing temporarily secured. Werner Geist had the uneasy feeling Gisa was hidden in the woods, watching their every move. If that were the case, she and her ruffian friends were content to let them pass. The main party arrived in Balzer, later than anticipated, but with an hour of daylight remaining. By any measure, their first day had been a success—no wagons strayed and travel was uneventful. Werner's cousin was there to greet them, along with the Winkler brothers and Freidrich Schafer, the three having arrived the day before with their wagons. The men turned horses to pasture and set up camp in the barn. A handful spilled over to the courtyard of an adjoining neighbor. A few women, particularly those with young children, spent the night in the Balzer Parish Hall.

A carriage was waiting when the party arrived to carry Hermann Schafer and his family to the estate of Hartwin Kastner. Like Hermann's family, the Kastners were wealthy *Deutsch*, having left their village and communal farming years before. They were frequent visitors to Hermann's farm, and the stopover to Balzer gave Hartwin a chance to reciprocate. Wendelin Schafer was delighted. She was uncomfortable with the Pfeifer women and not accustomed to spending the night in a public place. An overnight stay with the Kastner family allowed her to avoid both.

Johann Houfner was among those waiting as the main party arrived. His intention was to cover topics similar to those discussed with the advance party a few days earlier. Interest was keen. Johann was addressing a group who left farms and families behind and carried all their worldly possessions in one or two trunks. They knew Kansas was their destination, but little more. Anyone with knowledge of America had their rapt attention. They discussed steamship travel, homesteading, and soil conditions. Since the party must begin farming upon arrival, availability and cost of land were paramount. For a few, notably those with limited resources, employment opportunities and the health of the local economy were equally significant. Johann said nothing to discourage members of the party. He did caution that the first few years would be difficult. The Steppe was a cruel master. The American prairie would be the same. Johann was confident they would succeed. Of course, he favored the traditional *Volga Deutsch* village, where families lived and farmed together. Sounding much like Peter, he warned that striking out on your own or in small groups increased the risk of failure. Peter tried to gauge the reaction to Johann's admonition. He knew a few members had discussed separating from the party, one of those his own son-in-law. A few departures were likely—Peter hoped John and Maria were not among them.

Finally, the questions began to slow. Some of the women had delayed their departure to the community hall, wanting to hear more of what

Johann had to say. The hour was late. Peter called for an end to the gathering. He took Johann aside to question him on two topics. What could the party expect from immigration officials in Baltimore, and what alternatives existed for rail travel to Kansas? Johann told him what he knew of the immigration and inspection process, suggesting denial of entrance was uncommon. With regard to transportation, the party should expect two or more railroad agents offering some form of discounted transportation. Rail travel would start with the Baltimore and Ohio Railroad and ultimately connect with the Kansas Pacific Railroad or Atchison, Topeka and Santa Fe. Agents for both would be on hand when they arrived.

There would be others promoting passage to various locations throughout the United States. Some offers would include free transportation and even housing with contract work in mining or manufacturing. Johann warned against agents eager to dispatch unsuspecting immigrants to squalid labor camps or others whose objective was to separate immigrants from their money. The members should be advised to leave travel and their ultimate destination to leadership.

Peter had purposely drifted away from the group to conduct his conversation with Johann. When he returned to the barn, he found Frederic Schmidt arguing with two players in a just-completed game of *Schafkopf*. He apparently had lost money, and having too much to drink was in a foul mood. Frederic's habit left him disconsolate and often belligerent. Tonight found him angry, drunk, and looking for trouble. Peter's efforts to calm Frederic earned him nothing more than a flurry of insults. Before he could respond, Frederic had stormed from the courtyard and toward the fields, carrying nothing but his container of alcohol. His departure eased the tension, but Peter suspected there would be more trouble. He hoped Frederic would behave, at least at the onset of travel. He had already proven himself a liability less than a day into their journey. Four to six weeks of arduous travel lay ahead, much of it in close and uncomfortable circumstances. The emotional health of the party was important to Peter. The last thing he needed was Frederic's disruptive behavior.

The next morning saw a quick and orderly assembly of wagons. There was a brief delay waiting for Hermann Schafer and his family to arrive. Wendelin was purposely late, making a display of exiting the Kastners' carriage. Frederic was nowhere in sight, and Peter was not interested in finding him. Perhaps, Peter thought, Frederic had decided to return to Pfeifer. That would be a disappointment to Jacob, but not to the party.

A few members of the Balzer congregation gathered at the church and provided each wagon with a selection of *wurstchen* and *brot*. Within an hour of sunrise, the party was on its way to Saratov. Traffic was decidedly more active on this leg of the journey, with large commercial wagons unwilling to give ground to what their drivers considered a nuisance. Despite the crowded roadway and menacing looks from teamsters, travel continued without incident. Two stops were planned to water and rest the horses. After the second, the party overtook a small group of wagons from Kratzke. In limited conversation, Peter was able to learn they too were headed for the rail station at Saratov. The party was bound for South America via Hamburg to join others from their village who had left *Russen* a year before. The two parties traveled one behind the other until within sight of the city. There each took a different course—the Pfeifer wagons to a large field, while the Kratzke party continued on. Peter's greatest concern was the separation of wagons in the confusion of Saratov traffic. Local teamsters had no patience with the deliberate pace of farmers unaccustomed to city travel. An accident or wrong turn could easily disrupt their already tight schedule.

Saratov had grown immeasurably and was no longer a far-flung military outpost, but rather the distribution center for the world's breadbasket. Streets were congested and traffic was controlled by those least likely to give way. Peter signaled the others to slow their pace, closing the distance between wagons. He could only hope there were enough members of the advance party scattered throughout the wagons to guide them to their destination. Werner, who found the station a few days before, joined Peter in the lead. The effort started out well enough, but quickly fell into disarray. Four of the rearmost wagons were overtaken by traffic and unable to follow Peter's lead. A subsequent turn carried them to a street with no through passage and ultimately to what appeared to be a livestock yard. They were hopelessly lost. Among the group was Elma Wetzel, who sometimes taught at the Pfeifer Parish School. She spoke enough *Russische* to ask one of the yard workers for guidance to the rail station.

The lead group, following Werner's guidance, found its way to the station without difficulty. Upon arrival, the trunks—which represented everything the travelers had left in this world—were unloaded and moved to the baggage area. Peter was quick to dispatch two of the men to stand guard. He located John, along with Hersh Schneider, who was successful in finding tickets for his wife's train and steamship passage. The two had cleared a large space in one corner of the station and the Pfeifer group began to gather there. Peter caught a glimpse of his brother, Hermann. He had located a porter to care for his trunks and was on his way to an area set aside for first-class travelers. It was the last he would see of Hermann for some time. Frederic, much to Peter's disappointment, had found his way to the station and was conversing with the others in the waiting area.

Peter had begun to form a search party to locate the lost wagons when the group finally arrived. After some wandering, they managed to find the station based on the instructions provided. Their trunks were unloaded and the group was reunited. John immediately set about handing out tickets, while Peter and Werner went in search of the station master to determine when their train might arrive.

* * * * *

In comparison to European standards, the Saratov station was modest in size and utilitarian in design. Elements of the Crown had been slow to embrace railroads, particularly on the western frontier. Expansion relied on private capital with tepid loan assurances from the government. Growth was modest, and the railroad was late in coming to Saratov. Two factors brought a change in outlook. The first was algebraic increases in grain production that outstripped the ability of river transport to meet demand. The second was the realization by military leaders that rail provided for rapid deployment of troops and equipment. Alexander II saw both factors as reason to expand railroads, but passenger travel remained an afterthought.

* * * * *

The station master had seen nothing on the tracks—passenger or freight— for more than eighteen hours. He had no idea when their westbound train might arrive, nor could he hazard a guess. The trains were often eight to ten hours late, but Peter was told to keep the party close. Communication was poor and there would be little notice before arrival. Both Peter and Werner had the impression that the station master was apologetic, as much for the delay as for the travel conditions they were about to experience.

When the pair returned to the ticketing and reception area, they found the party in a circular encampment a short distance from the tracks. Their trunks were still awaiting transfer to the freight shed, and some in the party were rearranging belongings and pulling out additional clothing and blankets.

John and two others had left to purchase food at a stall seen as they approached the station. As was his habit, Frederic had simply disappeared, probably to locate supplies more to his liking. By late evening, all in the party were settled in. John and Maria had found a secluded corner where they could enjoy some privacy. Frederic had returned choosing a space some distance away, but close enough to monitor activities. Peter positioned himself near the ticketing area where he could easily be contacted by the station master. The other passengers gathered in small groups, either asleep, or engaged in quiet conversation. The party was reconciled to spending the night on a cold station floor.

Just before sunrise, the party was awakened by a locomotive pulling ten freight cars. It stopped long enough for the engineer to talk with the station master. He told Peter a slide had damaged the roadbed. Repairs had been made and their train should arrive within two hours. The Schafer party quickly formed a queue, hoping to occupy two third-class cars, one behind the other. Four hours later the train pulled into the station. Fewer than a dozen passengers were on board, and none were traveling beyond Saratov. The Schafer party occupied all available space in cars three and four. Two passenger cars were ahead, and three freight cars followed.

Stepping aboard was both exhilarating and worrisome. Only a few in the party had experienced rail travel. The locomotive's size and power were intimidating. Periodic bursts of steam and sudden hissing sounds suggested a terrible force held against its will—but there was another emotion attached to leaving Saratov, deeply felt by each member of the party. Departing by train was an irrevocable decision. In a few days, they would have traveled an unimaginable distance, far from family and friends. The

SARATOV TO THE SEA

simple act of taking a seat aboard the train sealed their future—there was no turning back.

The torrent of emotion diverted notice from the filthy conditions within the car. Seats were covered with a light coating of soot, and attachments to the floor were encased in a muddy substance—the combination of dust and leaky overhead. Some daylight penetrated the moldy windows, but illumination was dependent on candles.

For more than an hour, the train sat motionless in the station, with no advice from the station master on expected departure. Suddenly, there was a violent jerk, and the train slowly began to move. One-half hour of cityscape gave way to endless countryside with its predictable monotony. The novelty quickly wore off and the party turned to readying the space for the long journey ahead.

The cars were partitioned with families toward the center, each arrayed in a circular pattern. Neighbors in Pfeifer had now become neighbors in adjoining rows. The front of each car was reserved for men to play cards with a small area set aside for sleeping. At the opposite end, women brought their needlepoint and gathered around Ella Seigler and Herta Berg, the two who most often hosted *kaffeeklatsch* on summer evenings in Pfeifer. The discussion immediately turned to former neighbors and became more pointed with each mile the train traveled west. Felix Austerlitz moved through the cars playing the *Zimbal,* although the sessions became less frequent as Felix seemed to enjoy them far more than others in the party.

John and his new bride were content to sit together, having no interest in gossip or games. Hersh and Anna Schneider commonly joined them. The couples discussed their destination, and talked of independence and opportunity. Both shared a common dislike for a system of land tenure that stressed commonality at the expense of individual initiative. Others in the party held similar views, but Peter was a strong man not given to tolerating opposition. He steadfastly maintained that the *mir* system had served them well on the *Russische* Steppe and would do the same on the Kansas prairie.

Frequent stops at towns and villages with unfamiliar names offered a welcome respite from the cramped and increasingly malodorous railcars. Facilities on board were woefully inadequate. The *Russische* third-class cars were simply not designed for overnight travel, or for the number of travelers in the

Schafer party—twenty families, all sharing a single toilet. Occupants raced for the facilities at every stop, only to find nothing more than an open pit.

The conductor was rarely seen. It was not uncommon for the train to stop in area without a station or any sign of development. Passengers were never told the purpose for the stop. The only way to locate the conductor was to step off the train. He would then instantly appear directing the adventurous passenger to reboard. In one desolate area, the locomotive uncoupled leaving the cars behind. The conductor then passed through each car shouting something unintelligible before disappearing. The locomotive returned four hours later backing two newly acquired freight cars. A connection was made, and they were again underway. A published schedule was displayed at each station, but it bore no resemblance to reality. Arrival and departure times were struck through with no replacement entered. Westward progression was all the party could expect.

The modest enthusiasm displayed when the party left Saratov was quickly waning. Officials gave them little information on their whereabouts, and schedules made little sense. The *kaffeeklatsch* had broken up, and there were few players for the card games. Passengers had begun to feel like cattle, penned up and prodded by their master. Then, on the third day, the conductor advised Peter they would reach the border by midmorning. He continued through the car repeating *"Deutschland"* as he passed each row of seats. The announcement brought an immediate change in outlook among members. Crossing the border was an important step in their journey toward America. *Deutschland* also meant a return to their country of origin and a culture they steadfastly maintained in *Russen* for more than a century. How would they be received? Would they be seen as *Deutsch*, or would decades of life on the Steppe and their peculiar experience cast them as outsiders? The answer would not come until midafternoon.

The train came to a halt at the *Russische* border city of Verzhbolovo. Four uniformed guards, who left no doubt they were *Russische* Border Patrol, immediately stepped on board and took up positions at the exits of each car. The passengers were advised to gather all personal belongings, leave the train, and line up along the platform. One of the guards made a final pass through the cars casually throwing out a few miscellaneous items left behind. Then, in single file, the passengers were led across a small bridge to take their first step on the soil of their forebears. They were met by a much larger contingent of soldiers, and instructed to form three lines in front of the station. The commands were delivered in a militaristic fashion. It was a language they more or less understood—different, yet familiar. They had reached Eydtkuhnen.

Each passenger was required to show authorization to leave *Russen,* rail tickets to a port city, and evidence of steamship passage. Having done so, they were allowed to enter the station, but told—quite directly—not to exit. The rigid formality of the process suggested a further inspection, but none was forthcoming. The authorities were surprised at the party's mastery of *Deutsch,* thinking them to be *Russische.* Peter tried to explain, but it was clear the soldiers were more interested in process than history. Their first encounter was encouraging. There was regimentation, but it was designed to show military acumen, not to harass.

As the passengers awaited entry to the Eydtkuhnen station, they could see their trunks moving across the border and toward a baggage-handling area. This was all part of a change in trains necessary to accommodate the *Deutsch* gauge. Those who could observe the transfer of luggage strained to see their belongings. They brought very little, but what they had was treasured.

Peter asked "May we check our baggage?"

"*Nein,*" the guard said.

"*Bitte, ein minuten,*" Ida Kalb pleaded.

"*Nein,*" the guard repeated. His tone made it clear there was no room for discussion. Sadly, there was just enough distance from their position to the baggage-handling area to make identification difficult.

The cursory review of necessary papers took more than two hours, with each traveler permitted entry to the station immediately following inspection. Once inside, they were quickly relocated to a separate room at the west end of the building. Facilities were much improved over what they had recently experienced, with multiple toilets and clean water. In addition, a folding door was opened to expose a food stall. A few travelers made purchases, but most were reluctant given their confusion on exchange rates.

Four hours after the party's arrival in Eydtkuhnen, the train backed into the station. The first cars to appear were the so-called immigration cars, similar to the *Russische* third-class, but reconfigured to fit the new and growing class of traveler. Conductors assisted the first- and second-class passengers in boarding the train, while the Schafer party watched from their separate room. Workers brought small quantities of food and drink on board, but none were available to third-class passengers. Their cars were blocked from access to the rest of the train.

At last, the emigrants were permitted to board. It was obvious that the interior of the cars had been recently modified. What appeared to have been compartment walls had been removed, and seating capacity increased. Gas lamps were installed and the windows made much larger. The most welcome difference was cleanliness and the number of facilities provided.

As the train pulled away from the station, the conductor called out a number of stops, none of which were familiar except the last three—Berlin, Bremen, and Bremerhaven, the latter their port of embarkation. Travel to Berlin would take twelve to fourteen hours. Third-class passengers were not allowed to leave the train unless released by authorities. There were no further announcements, and the conductor disappeared.

Now on *Deutsch* soil, there was again keen interest in the countryside. Farms were small and each appeared to be independent. The adjoining courtyards so common among the *Volga Deutsch* were nowhere in evidence. There was also industrial development, even in communities not much larger than Pfeifer. At each stop, boarding passengers recognized the immigration cars, and strained to catch a glimpse of the occupants. Emigrants were a curiosity. With darkness, the passengers drew back from the windows. Only the children slept.

The train continued at a steady speed on tracks far quieter than the poorly engineered *Russische* equivalent. *Deutsch* reunification had significantly spurred rail development. New tracks had been laid and the network expanded. During the night farms gave way to more intense development. Lamps were commonplace, defining streets and storefronts in every direction. The train was approaching Berlin. Travelers again gathered around windows. Two more stops and the train entered *Gorlitzer Bahnhof, Deutschland's* railway center. It was staggering in its size and grandeur. Trains could be seen in every direction—an intimidating sight for anyone, let alone farmers from the *Russische* Steppe.

The conductor suddenly appeared reminding them they were not to leave. The command was almost welcome given the frenzied pace on the station platform. He returned shortly thereafter, instructing them to gather all belongings. They exited the train and gathered in a large room that appeared to have been a freight holding area modified by the addition of benches and a few tables. Facilities were available only a few steps away. The group was advised that the train would leave for Bremerhaven in ten hours and proceed directly to the port city. This represented a change in plan since their tickets indicated a three-night stay in Bremen with travel to Bremerhaven on the day of steamship departure. Peter asked for an explanation, but was simply told the change was requested by *Norddeutscher Lloyd*. They were again advised to remain in place.

An hour later, an *Offizier der Reichsbank* and uniformed *Polizist* visited their holding area. The purpose was to acquaint them with nearby services, and caution them against wandering too far from the station.

The *Offizier* told them, "There is a bank within easy walking distance. Funds may be exchanged at the official rate. A market is also close," he added.

Now it was the *Polizist's* turn. "Approach all merchants with caution," he said. "There are thieves among them."

Ida Kalb asked, "Are we safe?"

"Yes," he said. "But your movements will attract attention—some perhaps unpleasant."

After a brief discussion among themselves, a group of fifteen left the station. A few visited the bank, while others set out to find the market. Most were reluctant to leave, intimidated by the multitudes, frantic pace, and the *Polizist* warning. Peter did not favor any excursion, but said nothing. Ella Seigler and her youngest daughter managed just a few steps before returning to the sanctuary of the terminal. Berlin was simply too busy, too big, and, curiously, too foreign. No one from the Schafer party was accustomed to these circumstances. Their experience began and ended with the *Russische* Steppe and villages much like Pfeifer.

The city was incomprehensible. Cathedrals, government buildings, commercial wagons with eight-horse teams, elaborate coaches, and men and women dressed in fine clothing—all compressed so as to occupy every inch of available space. Fifteen bewildered *Volga Deutsch* stood amidst a cacophony of sounds and boundless activity. The women dressed in thread-bare garments, and men with heavy beards, all showing the effects of too many days in third-class travel. The Berliners stared at them, intrigued by their appearance and curious as to their origin.

Maria was uncomfortable. She wanted to escape the throng that seemed to ridicule, but John and the others convinced her to continue the excursion. They walked through the city for more than an hour, always keeping the train station in sight. When they returned, Peter was conducting a head count. The only one missing was Frederic, who disappeared as soon as permission was granted. Frederic was all but disowned by the membership. He behaved himself after the first night in Balzer, but was roundly disliked by his traveling companions.

Peter managed to speak briefly with his brother Hermann, who arrived three hours behind the main party. He and his family were now scheduled to reach Bremerhaven just before the ship departed. There was no reason to worry about Hermann's itinerary. His money ensured a timely arrival.

By noon, the Schafer party, including Frederic, had returned to the station. They spent the afternoon in their makeshift quarters, a few of the more adventurous again stepping out. The train for Bremerhaven was ready in late afternoon. It consisted of four immigrant cars and at least the same number for first- and second-class. There were passengers already on board including a *Volga Deutsch* party from the villages of Kamenka, Husaren, and Grimm. The immigrant cars were the last to load. Their movements, while not tightly controlled, were closely watched.

The party was again struck by the size of Berlin—so large it took the train more than an hour to escape its boundaries. Bremen was the next stop. Here, most of the first- and second-class passengers left the train. Only a few boarded. Judging by their dress and manner, they were also emigrants. The train followed the course of a river. The ground appeared marshy, and there was an occasional glimpse of barge traffic. The rail segment of their journey was coming to an end. The next and last stop was Bremerhaven, where they would board the *Neckar* for their transatlantic crossing. But before that, each member of the party must submit to a mandatory health inspection. Failure to pass meant a prolonged stay in the port city, family separation, or even return to Pfeifer.

Chapter Five:

The Poorest Passengers Make the Best Cargo

"The bosom of America is open to receive not only the opulent and respectable stranger, but the oppressed and persecuted of all nations and religions"

—George Washington

The train slowed as it crept onto the Port of Bremerhaven pier. The conductor boarded, announced their arrival, and told them to gather possessions. They were directed to exit the car and line up alongside the train. In the pre-dawn shadows, the party could see the outline of an immense ship. Ella Seigler fingered her rosary, and Hersh Schneider wondered aloud what body of water required a vessel so large. Most of the travelers simply stood in awe.

Their wonder was short-lived. The party was directed to proceed to a large building near the foot of the pier, where trunks were being off-loaded. This would be their only chance to access personal belongings. After identification, the trunks would be tagged, fumigated, and transferred to the cargo hold. The travelers were released fifteen at a time to identify belongings and grab what necessities they could.

The Schafer party, occupying the first two cars, was the last group allowed entry to the baggage area. Almost immediately, Anja Metz, a young mother, became agitated. The family's trunk and a small wooden box could not be located. She began frantically moving through what remained. It became obvious the family's only possessions were not on the pier.

Anja fell to her knees and began to sob uncontrollably.

"Where are my things?" she cried.

Her husband begged a worker to jump aboard the baggage car.

"Can you look, please?" The train had already begun to back off the pier.

"The car is empty, *nichts.*"

Anja, still kneeling, cursed the Lord, "*Verdammt du Gott.*"

A supervisor told Anja Bremerhaven officials would replace what she lost from belongings left behind by travelers whose possessions exceeded weight limits. It was little consolation. Anja's link to the past was gone—a stark reminder how fragile their existence had become. A matron arrived to guide the party to their lodging. She took Anja's arm, comforting her as they left the pier. It was the first gesture of genuine compassion anyone in the party had seen since leaving Pfeifer.

* * * * *

Bremerhaven was among the first of *Deutsch* ports to promote their city as a point of embarkation. Officials provided guidance to travelers, kept a watchful eye on extortion, checked for overbooking, and required vessels to be clean and free of disease—actions borne of an enlightened appreciation of their own self-interest. If discrepancies were found, port officials ordered the ship remain at berth until violations were corrected. The city's efforts included construction of a large hotel-like facility, the *Auswandererhaus.* It was built prior to the extension of tracks from Bremen to Bremerhaven, when the only means to reach the port city was by barge on the river Weser. Tides, wind, and persistent silting combined to make for an uncertain arrival. The *Auswandererhaus* offered comfortable lodging for those already in port and awaiting their shipmates.

* * * * *

Bremerhaven was temporarily overrun by emigrants and the Schafer party would make its home, not in the *Auswandererhaus,* but in a group of two-story frame houses located a quarter mile from the pier. Bathing and bathroom facilities were located in an adjoining building. Guests were segregated, with mothers and young children on the first floor, along with single women. Fathers, their sons, and single men were housed on the second. The dining area was located on the main floor. Housing was paid for by the steamship company, which was also responsible for providing meals.

Each house had a *Hausmutter* whose charge was to make sure traveler needs were met. Her first obligation, which she promptly executed, was to acquaint visitors with the rules and schedule. There was to be no alcohol. Men and women were required to sleep, without exception, on their assigned floor. They were also encouraged not to miss any meals. A number of other, less strident, rules were posted in the dining area. The Schafer party had few demands, having just traveled, over 1,900 miles, on third-class railcars.

The first scheduled event, a document inspection, was slated for the next morning, followed by the dreaded medical inspection. Sailing was now scheduled on the tide two days hence. Aside from these obligations, the travelers were free to come and go as they pleased. The Schafer party took the opportunity to bathe and wash soiled clothing, something they had been unable to do since leaving Pfeifer. They were mindful of their pending document and health inspections, but rejoiced in the comfort of their boarding house and the freedom to wander the streets of Bremerhaven. They drew little attention as the number of emigrants often equaled the local population. Those awaiting embarkation could be found day and night in the pews of *St. Petri Dom*—the new world with all of its challenges reason to seek the Lord's blessing.

In anticipation of inspections, Peter, with John's help, contacted each member of the Schafer party. Only one, Herta Berg, appeared to be ill. She began to feel sick after eating *Lebkuchen* in Berlin. Others in the party had also eaten the honey cakes and experienced some discomfort, but only Herta was still suffering. They could only hope the symptoms would pass before the examination. Inspectors had varying degrees of medical training and were known to misread symptoms. An ailment that appeared in any way to be contagious was reason to deny boarding. Given the schedule, failure to pass likely meant that the ship would leave without them. A number of remedies were suggested to Herta, but it was thought that rest was the best antidote. The *Hausmutter* aroused the party early the next morning, and after breakfast led them to an area just off the main reception room of the *Auswandererhaus*. The document inspections would be conducted under the direction of *Norddeutscher Lloyd*. Exit permits from their country of origin, claim tags for baggage, and boarding passes all must be verified. The Schafer party was first in line. John and Maria passed without question, as did several others.

When Anna Schneider handed her documents to the agent, he asked, "Where was this ticket purchased?"

Hersh intervened, "In Saratov, from a young man willing to delay his travel. I paid extra."

The agent signaled to a uniformed steamship official, who studied the ticket.

"Your passage is valid," he said, "but not for the *Neckar*."

Peter joined the discussion. "Surely, a vessel the size of the *Neckar* can accommodate one more passenger?" he asked.

"Absolutely not," the official responded. "We are overbooked, and the inspectors are threatening to remove a dozen passengers."

Peter continued to plead the Schneider's case, while Hersh and Anna anxiously observed. The *Norddeutscher Lloyd* officer was unwavering.

Suddenly, Frederic Schmidt pushed his way forward, "You can have my ticket. I'll trade with Anna."

Frederic's offer caught the *Norddeutscher Lloyd* official by surprise. He temporarily suspended inspections and left the room returning in a few minutes. The steamship line, eager to escape an unfortunate circumstance, was agreeable. Replacement tickets would be issued. Anna and Frederic would simply change places.

Peter was dumbfounded. Before he could express his gratitude, Frederic told him, "Spirits are not permitted in steerage. Until I find a way to make the trip enjoyable, I'll wait."

With that, he walked out of the *Auswandererhaus*. There were no further complications.

Following document inspection, the travelers moved to a much larger room. At the far end were uniformed steamship employees, one doctor and what the emigrants would later come to know as a consul from the United States, on hand to observe the inspection process. The consulate and *Norddeutscher Lloyd* both shared a common interest in the health of the travelers. The United States had no desire to admit sick, indigent, or diseased emigrants. For the steamship company it was purely a matter of economics. Seriously ill travelers arriving at the point of entry were subject to return to their port of embarkation, with the expense borne by the company. Thorough examination before departure was important to both parties.

The angst could be seen on the face of each traveler as they approached the inspector's bench. All understood the consequences of failure. Even the children were quiet, not sure what was taking place, but aware of their parents' unease. This was the last hurdle. Acceptance meant certain access to the ship and passage to America.

There were six lines, with an inspector located several steps from the foremost point of each queue. The travelers were carefully observed as they were called upon to move forward. A visual inspection for signs of infectious disease was followed by a series of questions. Herta Berg, sick to her stomach the night before, passed without incident. The remaining members of the party appeared to be doing well until Meta Gerber approached the inspector's table. Her two children had already passed, and her husband, Wilfried, was immediately behind her. Meta walked with a slight limp, the result of a farming accident as a youth. A small infirmity was rarely cause for rejection, but suggested a more careful review.

The longer Meta spent with the inspector, the more anxious she became. Finally, the doctor was summoned. Meta was a step away from passage and her children waited just beyond the table. She sensed the possibility of rejection and became agitated. Her husband stepped forward to calm his wife, but was directed to return to his place. Meta was taken to an examination room, where a matron joined her and the doctor. The children were returned to their father. After a few moments, Meta emerged from the room in tears. She had failed to pass the examination. Wilfried looked for help from the inspector, but it was clear there would be no reconsideration. The American consul moved closer, studied the papers, then simply backed away.

The family was directed to an anteroom where they were faced with several unpleasant alternatives. They could return to Pfeifer. Wilfried still had his *dusha,* but his home, animals, and equipment had all been sold. The family would have to start anew. They could also separate—Wilfried and the children making the passage and waiting near the port of entry for Meta to arrive. Of course, there was no assurance that she would pass the medical inspection in the future.

Meta's rejection was based on the suspicion of a mental defect, her anxiety so great that she had forcefully tried to pull away from the matron. She and her family were joined by a *Norddeutscher Lloyd* official and an employee of the *Auswandererhaus.* They proposed a third alternative. The family could take up residence in Bremerhaven, and after a period of quarantine, try for passage later. The Gerber family would then join the Schafer party in Kansas. By midafternoon, all medical inspections had been completed. The Schafer party was relieved, but their collective joy was tempered by the knowledge that one of their group would not be joining them. Most of the party spent the remainder of the day wandering through Bremerhaven, making a few small purchases and taking time for a last visit to the cathedral.

Steerage was to board in midafternoon the following day, with the ship set to sail sometime before midnight. It was a restless night. All were up early; aimlessly rearranging their few personal belongings and engaging in activities designed to waste time rather than improve their readiness for travel. The Gerber family looked in on the party to say goodbye. They had decided to remain in Bremerhaven and try for passage on the *Strassburg,* scheduled for departure two weeks ahead. If Meta did not pass, the family would then return to Pfeifer.

Just before noon, the party took their last steps on European soil, making their way past the *Auswandererhaus* and onto the pier. Each adult carried a mattress and selection of tinware purchased after inspections were complete. First- and second-class passengers were already on board sampling spirits offered by attentive stewards and gazing down at the hapless souls about to enter the bowels of the ship. Some were still boarding, and it was apparent that steerage would be kept waiting until all the above-deck cabins were settled.

Peter caught a glimpse of Hermann and his family looking down from their perch high above the pier. Hermann did not wave, but rather acknowledged Peter with a slight nod, not wanting his fellow passengers to know of his relationship to anyone occupying the lower decks. The convivial feeling on the upper decks was not replicated among the waiting steerage passengers. Their thoughts were occupied by rumors of cramped, unsanitary quarters, barely palatable food, and an overwhelming stench. The wait seemed interminable. All the while the more fortunate upper-deck passengers continued their pre-departure frivolity.

Finally, steerage passengers were allowed to board, leaving solid ground for what would be several days of uncertain footing. Heavily laden with bundle and mattress, the passengers made their way up the gangway and on to the forward deck. From there, they passed through a large hatch and down stairs more properly described as a ladder. They did so with little or no assistance from the crew. Once on the steerage deck, they found row after row of adjacent bunks stacked in tiers. The bunks were hammock-like and divided by an iron bar. Absent that division, inhabitants would tumble one onto the other. Sleeping quarters served as bunks, closet, and pantry. The only light available came from portholes located high above the steerage deck and small lanterns gimbaled to swing with the ship's movement. There were three sections. The first was reserved for single men. Married couples and families were placed midships. Single women were located aft—as far from the men as possible.

Canvas partitions represented a futile attempt to create privacy. Nearly 240 passengers were berthed in forward steerage, with a similar compartment aft. The women's area had a matron assigned. On each side of compartment were four toilets. A similar number were located above deck. A queue had already formed at each toilet. It was a line that would persist throughout the voyage. Buckets filled with salt water were positioned on either side of the toilets. Fresh water was not available for personal hygiene, washing clothes, or cleaning decks. *Norddeutscher Lloyd* and other steamship companies operated under the assumption that steerage passengers would sleep in their clothes and would not bathe for the duration of the voyage. Bunks had been assigned, but the travelers began to trade so that friends and family could be berthed together. Ida Kalb managed to get her youngest son alongside only to be advised, at twelve years of age, he was required to take a bunk in the single men's section. She immediately protested and was told if accommodations were not to her liking, she could leave the ship or contact the purser for an upgrade.

At the center of each partitioned area was a long dining table with benches. The first meal was served soon after boarding. It was delivered in large urns and carefully ladled into passenger tinware. The meal consisted of salt pork and potatoes. A salted main course would become a staple—whether pork, beef, or fish—occasionally replaced by soup and often coupled with either potatoes or rice. After the meal, John and Hersh climbed above deck to inspect the space reserved for steerage passengers, while Maria and Anna struggled to establish some semblance of privacy in their communal sleeping area. A few others joined John and Hersh, but were sternly warned to stay clear of the rail and hatches. The *Neckar* was still receiving cargo, and deckhands were busy preparing for departure.

The open deck space assigned to steerage was limited. John wondered how even a quarter of the passengers could be accommodated. An officer took note of the growing numbers and directed them to return to their below-deck accommodations. They were told to remain there until they heard a single, long blast of the ship's whistle. On the decks above, large numbers of first- and second-class passengers lined the rails still attended to by stewards, and free to wander as they pleased.

The *Neckar* left Bremerhaven just after midnight on the outgoing tide. John, hearing the long blast and sensing movement, returned to the above-deck area just as the ship slipped from its berth. Given the lateness of the hour, there was ample space to observe. John's exit from the berth had awakened Maria and others, but none wished to join him. There was far less revelry among first- and second-class passengers, and John found himself next to an older man with a keen interest in the activities of the ship's company. His attire suggested he was a city dweller. The two stuck up a somewhat awkward conversation. Both spoke *Deutsch*, but there were striking differences in dialect.

Valentin Krause introduced himself. "Bremen was my home," he said. "A mapmaker by trade, but I've made this passage twice before as a young sailor."

John told him he was traveling with a party from *Russen*.

"But you speak *Deutsch*."

"*Volga Deutsch*," John responded.

Valentin continued, "I'm on my way to Wisconsin to join my son and three grandchildren I've never seen."

He explained that once they were clear of the Weser narrows, the *Neckar* would enter the North Sea, then the English Channel making its way to Southampton in the British Isles, where the ship would take on additional cargo and, quite possibly, passengers. John was intrigued since he had no understanding of their route.

"I'll show you a chart tomorrow," Valentin said.

As they talked, the ship continued down the Weser. Valentin explained the navigational aids the *Schiffemaster* relied upon as he made his way to open water. The conversation lasted more than an hour until Valentin expressed a need to ready his bunk space. John took a moment to look back at the fading lights of Bremerhaven and then followed his new friend below deck.

The first night aboard the *Neckar* confirmed the worst of their fears. Restless passengers found the slightest movement awoke bunkmates, and well before sunrise, lines had formed at the toilets. The number of passengers and their proximity to one another rendered steerage a most uncomfortable experience. John and Maria quickly made their way above deck hoping the cleansing effect of the ocean breeze would act as an elixir. For those below deck, the only relief was the movement of air through the open portholes, but not enough to mitigate the stench. Even the food seemed to take on the smell, driving many to reject the morning entrée. Some were fortunate to have purchased food in Bremerhaven, and took it above deck to escape the unpleasantness below—a welcome, but short-lived solution. Upon reaching the outside deck, they were disappointed to find that the few available benches had been rearranged. Partitioning was now complete. Upper-class passengers could only glimpse their less fortunate traveling companions. John asked the steward if the benches could be returned to their original location to provide more deck space. He was told that was impossible. The steward looked upward, indicating the decision came from above. Peter entered the conversation, and the two, careful not to offend the steward, continued to plead their case.

The discussion came to an abrupt end when the steward noticed a disturbance caused by a woman begging to get off the ship. Seas were calm, but a heavy fog had settled in. The woman came on deck and saw no land—nothing but gray. She was claustrophobic, frightened by what she perceived as a suffocating blanket. The woman became increasingly agitated, screaming, "*Off Schiff! Off Schiff!*" while pounding on her husband's chest. She could not be restrained and ran toward a stairwell where two stewards, responding to the commotion, forced her to the deck using an apron to tie her hands. She was dragged up the stairwell through an unmarked hatch. At this point, she appeared to have lost consciousness. One of the stewards returned and advised the husband that his wife would be escorted off the ship in Southampton. In her ranting, she had suggested the ship would falter, and there was no means of escape. An officer had observed the incident. Challenging the ship's seaworthiness and master was a threat to security. He ordered confinement and release to authorities when the *Neckar* made port.

After their fruitless conversation with the steward, John told Peter of his discussion with Valentin Krause. Peter was surprised by the intermediate stop at Southampton, and eager to learn more of their anticipated route. Both went below to find the mapmaker. He had already drawn a crowd. Three charts were laid out on the end of the dining table—one of the Atlantic and two of the United States. On the Atlantic chart was a small figurine marking the *Neckar*'s current position in the southernmost waters of the North Sea.

Valentin moved the figurine slightly. "We'll pass through the Strait of Dover tonight and should make Southampton late tomorrow or early the next day."

"Will we take on cattle?" an observer asked. He had heard that some ships did so, and located the animals in close proximity to steerage.

Valentin answered, "No, the configuration is wrong, and the hold nearly full."

Peter was more interested in their final destination—Baltimore. He asked the mapmaker, "How long a voyage?"

"Absent storms, twelve days," he answered. "Maybe fifteen if we encounter bad weather. If it's more than twelve days, the voyage will be unpleasant."

While Peter and the mapmaker discussed the crossing, John was drawn to the comments of a small group of men contemplating their planned destination—the Dakota Territory. He understood the need to support his father-in-law upon arrival in Kansas, but once Peter's colony was established, he planned to move on. He was intrigued by homesteading as well as inexpensive railroad land. Maria joined her husband, pointing to an area marked "Indian Territory." She wondered if settlements there would be ravaged as the early *Volga Deutsch* had been by the *Kirghiz* tribes. John, with no foundation for his comment, assured Maria that Dakota was far more civilized. John and Maria moved above deck to continue their discussion. Peter had managed to pull Valentin from the crowd. The two were discussing potential routes from Baltimore to Topeka and farther west toward Colorado.

The officers and crew of the *Neckar* saw nothing unusual in their first two days at sea. Even the outburst from the woman now in confinement was not unexpected. The emigrants saw it differently. There was nothing ordinary in the disagreeable task of adjusting to shipboard life. Sleeping was impossible, necessities in short supply, privacy was nonexistent, and confrontation brought on by crowding was inevitable. They were hopelessly imprisoned. Passengers in first- and second-class could look to stewards for relief—not so their counterparts in steerage. The ship's company barely tolerated those trapped below. Intimidation was commonplace, and pleas for assistance met with a contemptuous stare.

Near dusk the lights of Southampton came into view, and the *Neckar* slowly made its way up the estuary, gently slipping into its berth. A persistent, heavy rain forced all but a handful of passengers to take one last breath before heading below. John stayed on deck, interested enough in the ship's work to ignore the inclement weather. He marveled at the skill of the *Schiffemaster*, his crew, and the dock workers as they effortlessly moved from hawser to loading cargo. The process was momentarily stopped as the woman confined earlier was escorted from the ship by two uniformed policemen—her husband already on the pier with two young children sitting quietly amongst their meager possessions. John wondered what would become of the family. Charges were unlikely, but the family would be left alone in a strange land with few resources; their dreams of a new life in America all but gone. Cold and tired, John made his way below. As he did, he noticed Valentin, wrapped in oilskins, still among the observers.

Early the next morning, John and Maria hurriedly made their way above deck. They had discovered that toilets there were cleaner and came without the unpleasant smell and queue. They also learned it was best to access wash stations after breakfast. The stewards changed the water as breakfast was being served, and waiting meant a chance for untainted seawater. Valentin was in his customary position along the rail. He told John that departure would likely come sooner than expected.

On the dock below, a group of men were lined up in front of the gangway and appeared ready to board. Their mattress and tinware identified them as steerage passengers, but John had no idea of their nationality. Valentin thought they were Welsh, probably miners. The men numbered near twenty and had a manner about them suggesting they were best left alone. John went below to watch as the Welshmen made their way to the section reserved for single men. The only available bunks were in the foremost section, more susceptible to the ship's movement. They secured an area together—a few bunks simply "taken" from existing occupants. No objection was voiced.

Soon after leaving Southampton, a pattern surfaced and quickly became a ritual. Between meals, the men found their way to the open deck to smoke, play cards, and talk among themselves. The women spent much of their time below deck caring for children, dispensing the small amount of food brought on board, and doing their best to keep their sleeping space tidy. Even with the help of daughters, they had little time to themselves. If they did complete their tasks, the women joined husbands on deck, often festooned with laundry pinned to their skirt and coat since on-board rules strictly prohibited hanging of laundry within sight of upper-class passengers.

The families gathered in small groups, with little exchange between ethnicities. Language was a problem, but so too suspicion borne of unfamiliarity. Valentin was the exception. His counsel was sought by everyone, and his knowledge provided common ground for interaction. John did his best to understand Valentin as he spoke with the group of Swedes headed for the Dakota Territory. The northern prairie was appealing. Maria was not as sure, still bothered by the large area designated as "Indian Territory."

On most evenings there was some form of entertainment. A few instruments made it on board, and this often gave rise to singing and, on occasion, dancing. Noise was not a problem since first- and second-class passengers were comfortably situated in their salons. The Welshmen quickly became a favorite with their large repertoire. They had also managed to bring a substantial quantity of whiskey on board. The stewards were not fooled, but chose to keep their distance.

They were two days out of Southampton when the *Neckar* encountered swells and began to pitch fore and aft. There were no sailors in steerage and the ship's rhythmic motion quickly took its toll among farmers, miners, and those who tended shops. *Seekranheit* became commonplace above and below deck. For some, it was an uneasy feeling and loss of appetite, but little more. Time above deck offered relief. For others, nothing could be kept down. Some tortured souls would remain sick throughout the voyage. They found no relief in their bunks and even less above deck. The smell was overpowering. Saltwater was used to scrub down decks, but only once daily. The cleansing provided some relief, but was short-lived. Anyone who could took their meals in the open air to escape the odor. Even the Welshmen, who had created their own segregated berthing section, had taken to sleeping above deck. Among the Schafer party, sickness was particularly acute for Anna Schneider, Ella Seigler, and Felix Austerlitz. The movement of the ship was not extreme—only the occasional shutter as the vessel breached larger swells. Yet Anna, Ella and Felix could do nothing more than move from bunk to toilet.

The ship's doctor made an appearance on the afternoon of the second day. His duties were those typically associated with doctoring, along with keeping a sharp eye for infectious diseases. On this occasion, he came below deck to distribute ginger pills to quell the *seekranheit*. The doctor did not want to be in steerage, and his behavior suggested as much. Near the end of his visit, he paused to look quickly at two children in the family section. He called for a matron, and a more thorough examination was conducted. The doctor and matron returned to the upper deck. Early the next morning they returned with two officers. One of them announced that inoculations had been ordered. Most in steerage had only a limited understanding of the term, but they did understand *Pocken* or smallpox, the suspected affliction.

The passengers recoiled at the sight of needles. Mothers sheltered children and were unsure whether to console or hide. Finally, an additional officer and steward were successful in calming the passengers, who by now had pushed as far away as possible from the doctor and his suggested remedy. The Welshmen were the first to submit, which drew an unexpected, but approving nod from the doctor. Next came the leader of a group en route to Arkansas, followed by Peter Schafer. The others quickly fell in line. After a few hours, the ordeal was concluded. Two mothers and sixteen children were pulled from common berthing and quarantined. Steerage would never see the doctor again.

John was one whose *seekranheit* fell short of real discomfort, though it affected his appetite. Valentin noticed and recommended he remain above deck and focus, to the extent possible, on the horizon, rather than on some part of the ship. He told John the ship's movement against the backdrop of the sea accentuated the feeling of instability. The suggestion seemed to work. By late evening, he felt well enough to eat some bread from the small stock Maria purchased in Bremerhaven, but not well enough to sample the evening meal of salted fish. The other passengers seemed to have improved as well. There was still discomfort, but the number of those visibly sick declined—Felix Austerlitz was the exception. His *seekranheit* reached the point where family and nearby bunkmates slept on benches. He could manage his sickness as long as he stayed in the bunk, but gagged the minute he took to his feet. The steward contacted the doctor, who simply recommended more ginger.

Just after the evening meal on the fourth day, there was a disturbance near the hatch leading to the engine room. Two stokers, still blackened by coal dust, were half carrying, half escorting a young girl, perhaps fifteen, from a passageway that led below. The stokers were coming off duty when they saw the girl and an older man engaged in sexual activity in an adjacent cargo area. She was the oldest daughter of Gustav and Luise Kunkel, and suspected of promiscuous behavior in Pfeifer. Peter responded to the commotion and found the daughter defiant, refusing to accompany her mother to the family section. Gustav arrived, and after a brief discussion, slapped the girl with enough force to send her tumbling into an iron bunk support. She sat stunned, with blood flowing from her nose and mouth. Peter tried to calm Gustav, while Luise picked the girl up from the floor. The steward saw the melee, and bolted up the ladder in search of his superiors. He returned with two officers carrying sidearms who questioned the girl and the two stokers. The man had run from the scene toward a passageway that led to the galley, but was intercepted and held there by crew members. He now appeared in constraints escorted by a third officer. The three conferred, and the man was pushed roughly through steerage. He stumbled and was pulled to his feet by the hair. The message was clear—behavior of this sort was not tolerated.

Reports from earlier sailings had suggested women were mistreated on *Norddeutscher Lloyd* crossings. The steamship company was committed to changing that perception. Passengers would find later that the man was *Deutsch* and part of a group from a village outside of Bremen. He would spend the rest of his voyage in the ship's brig, a six by six-foot compartment with three small slits above a solid door. Upon arrival, he would be released to the Baltimore authorities. The punishment for the Kunkel girl was equally harsh. She was released to Gustav. Despite pleas from some in the Schafer party, he continued to beat his daughter throughout the voyage. The young woman endured lurid glances from male passengers and looks of disgust from females.

John was past his discomfort. Whether it was Valentin's suggestion or simply adjusting to the ship's movement, the sickness was behind him. He and Maria could be found most evenings sleeping above deck. They found a place alongside cargo brought aboard at Southampton. The wooden containers provided shelter from the wind and some protection from the dampness. On clear nights, the sky was brilliant. There was little privacy, and the *liebesnest* provided at least the illusion of being alone. The space was discovered midway through the voyage by an officer making his rounds. He was tall with a weathered face and intimidating gaze.

"*Ehemann und ehefrau?*" he asked.

John answered apprehensively, "Ja."

The officer studied the couple for a moment,

"Enjoy your evening," he said, smiling as he turned aft.

The next morning the couple awoke to a ship that seemed to be crying in agony. The wind had freshened overnight, and there were persistent groans, as if every fastener was struggling to break free. It was a terrifying sound to passengers, who felt certain the ocean might swallow them at any time.

John saw Valentin in the breakfast queue.

"A storm will soon be upon us. I expect a force ten."

John looked at him quizzically, not sure of the definition.

Using his hands, Valentin described the distance between wave crests.

"A short, deeper trough brings much sharper seas," he said. "Winds will be stronger, perhaps in excess of fifty miles per hour."

Anna Schneider overheard the conversation. She and Ella Seigler had recovered from their *seekranheit* and spent the pre-dawn hours above deck in the blessed, cleansing wind. The same could not be said for Felix Austerlitz. He was still uncomfortable and had little to eat or drink since leaving Southampton. Hope for improvement was now lost to the impending storm. By noon, both wind and seas had risen, and black clouds stacked on the horizon began to tumble forward. The farmers on board the *Neckar* recognized the signs. If still working the land, they would have sought shelter for family, animals, and equipment. Aboard the *Neckar*, there was but one refuge—their wretched compartment. The crew moved with a sense of urgency securing hatches and lashing cargo. The officers, rarely seen in steerage entered the below deck space checking on preparations. They said nothing to the passengers, but their appearance in numbers spoke to the severity of the expected weather. Near midafternoon, the steward announced that the evening meal would be served early consisting of dried fish and heavily crusted bread—nothing more.

Among the passengers there was a curious mix of muted excitement and anxiety. Valentin was unusually somber, having experienced the fury of Atlantic storms. Even the Welshmen, who regularly faced death in the mines, lost a bit of their swagger. They moved about cautiously, fearful they would be cast into the abyss. With few exceptions, steerage was occupied by church-going Christians, mostly Roman Catholic. Ella Seigler formed a prayer group endlessly reciting the rosary. Some prayed for deliverance, while others sought forgiveness, convinced the storm was punishment for past indiscretions. John thought it strange that the God-fearing faithful prayed to the same Deity that placed their lives in jeopardy. Frida Geist was among the most terrified. She moved about the compartment fueling even greater anxiety. Her husband, Nicholas, reminded her that a woman was confined for similar behavior. He was sure the crew was in no mood for hysterical passengers. Frida quickly decided the prayer group was the better alternative.

In the midst of storm preparation, a young woman appeared below deck and began speaking with Noah Adler and Werner Geist, her attire in stark contrast to the unkempt emigrants. The steward took note of her presence, but paid little attention beyond that. The woman had spoken earlier with Ida Kalb and Peter's wife, Melina, introducing herself as a *Shriftsteller* for the *Fragende*, a magazine with offices in Berlin. Her intent was to publish a story on the plight of emigrants, why they were leaving, and their experience en route to America. The storm offered insight into the travails below deck under the worst of conditions. To confirm her employment, the young woman brought an introductory letter from her publisher, which few understood, and several copies of the magazine. One night was spent in steerage, but deciding that the story did not warrant the deprivation, she found accommodations in first class. She had since spent part of two days wandering the steerage decks, and took a particular interest in the *Volga Deutsch*. They left the German Federation for *Russen* a century before. Now they were bound for America. She had spoken briefly with Peter, a good source of emigrant experience—both past and present—but he found her shallow empathy to be boorish. The *Shriftsteller* showed little interest in what had been achieved on the Steppe, nor the reasons for leaving the fruits of their labor behind. Her interest was in the conditions on board and nothing else. Even this was tempered by an obvious desire to cast *Norddeutscher Lloyd* in a favorable light. Thankfully, the weather forced her to return to the comforts of her cabin. She was not seen in steerage again.

The steward announced that passengers with personal belongings above deck should bring them below. Even the Welshman complied, returning a few hidden mattresses below deck. John reluctantly gathered the blankets he and Maria had arranged among the crates. All passengers were confined below deck until further notice by the *Schiffemaster*, their welcome respite from the unpleasant smells of steerage no longer available. Nothing of the storm could be seen, but much could be felt and heard. The *Neckar* was struggling through very heavy seas. The ship shuddered as it pitched forward into each crest. The noise of shifting cargo and twisting fasteners was increasingly disconcerting. For some, the cacophony and dim lighting were almost unbearable. John glanced at Valentin, who was sitting at the dining table writing in a small tablet. He was calm, showing no signs of alarm.

Moments later, the first splash of seawater came through the rearmost porthole. This was followed by a cascade of seawater from the forward hatch tumbling down the ladder and setting the area around the toilets awash. The steward lashed the hatch shut and secured all portholes. Seawater began to drip through the deck. Whatever was on the floor, including the vomit of an increasing number of passengers, now found its way through the compartment. Movement was difficult, and a fall meant that woolen clothing, already soiled, was fouled by the unpleasant accumulation of ejecta. Bunks were the only safe haven. With hatch and portholes closed, there was no visible opening to the outside. The passengers were not only below deck, but below the water line. Some felt trapped, convinced the ship could not withstand the onslaught. Gimbled lanterns, true to their design, were extinguished by the violent movement, adding to the perception of being entombed. Strangely, despite conditions worsening through the night, the level of anxiety appeared to ease as passengers came to realize that the ship was capable of absorbing the worst the Atlantic had to offer. Several times during the night, John glanced toward Valentin. He dozed off for an hour, then returned to pencil and paper.

By morning, most passengers had put their fears behind them and prayed, not for survival, but an early exit from their confinement. Their petitions were answered midmorning when the steward opened the hatches and portholes, and announced that shortly after the noon meal passengers would be permitted above deck. Even the hint of fresh air provided relief from the suffocating conditions. Passengers quickly realized just how disgusting their surroundings had become. With some help from the crew, sea water was used to scrub and wash down squalid surfaces making sure the acrid residue found its way to the bilge.

Finally, the steward allowed the passengers to escape. Every soul, man, woman, and child made their way above deck. They were greeted by bright sunshine and a stiff breeze. Never was exposure so refreshing. The passengers studied the now familiar deck and found that the only evidence of damage was a single broken crate, its contents lost to the sea. The women extended their stay as long as possible, then retreated to wash clothes and put sleeping areas in order. In an unusual departure from shipboard practice, the *Schiffemaster* announced that items washed could be hung, but only until noon the following day. Within the hour clothing was everywhere—hung from stabilizing wires, tied to rails, and spread over crates. The outlook among the passengers had changed immeasurably. Questions regarding the ship's durability had been answered. Even Frida Geist, driven to near hysteria a few hours earlier, walked the decks with the assurance of an experienced seaman.

Valentin, with a bit of mysterious dead reckoning, now believed they would reach their destination four days hence. They were closing on the end of the voyage. Peter decided it was time to gather the party to discuss travel from Baltimore to Kansas. A meeting was arranged for the following morning. He purposely avoided discussion of medical inspections or any other steps that might be required by authorities upon arrival. In truth, he was unsure of what to expect. Instead, he focused on their destination, probably Topeka, staying there long enough to evaluate the suitability of land for settlement.

John wondered if everyone understood Peter's intent—a new Pfeifer. No one in the party dared question Peter while in *Russen,* but with the promise of America days away, the bonds of tradition were breaking. Kurt Haus wondered if the *mir* system would function in America. How could title, the lynchpin of ownership, be held or transferred when property was owned in common? Anja's husband, Sander Metz, expressed his interest in homesteading; a small investment meant nearly 200 acres of land with no obligation to share with the *Gemeinde.* Others questioned Peter's choice of Kansas as their destination. Some of the *Neckar's* passengers were bound for Colorado and the Dakota Territory, where land was more readily available, less expensive, and every bit as fertile. One member even suggested they postpone their decision until they heard from employers in Baltimore with offers of housing and advance wages.

Peter was offended by the challenge to his leadership. He saw talk of alternatives to his plan as naïve, uninformed musings. John had questions of his own, but at the behest of Maria, chose not to challenge his father-in-law. Peter was shaken by the sudden show of independence. Talk of separation threatened his utopian dream. He lectured the party at length, reminding them hardships awaited and they would be happy to have neighbors and community.

Later that same day, a steward brought a note from Hermann. Peter was surprised to learn that his brother would not be joining them in Kansas, at least in the near term. Hermann had met two businessmen. They were returning from England after negotiating contracts for the sale of wheat in the British Isles and the Continent. Transocean shipment of wheat was fraught with difficulty, but Hermann's new partners had developed the means to ship bulk grain without significant damage. The men owned a large mill in St. Louis and planned further expansion through Missouri and beyond. They had reason to believe that Kansas, Nebraska, and the Dakota Territory would one day lead the world in grain production, with much of the ground turned by Eastern Europeans. The men needed someone who could relate to the newcomers.

Hermann's wealth and ancestry were the attraction, not his business acumen. He planned on meeting with company financiers before joining his partners in St. Louis. Hermann was not sure when he would reach Kansas. Peter was disappointed. He never expected his brother to be an integral part of the village, but was counting on him as a lender of last resort. Peter knew some members would reach Kansas lacking the funds to purchase land—fundamental to inclusion in his commune. Friends and relatives were the first option for borrowing, then banks, but immigrants with no resources were unlikely candidates for a mortgage. If they did qualify, interest rates often approached ten to twelve percent. Hermann was the last alternative. That opportunity was lost with his brother's decision to establish a home in St. Louis.

The remaining four days of the voyage were uneventful. Calm seas prevailed, and each day morning clouds gave way to afternoon sun. Everyone's outlook improved. Good weather was a blessing, but proximity to American soil far more important. Late on their eleventh day at sea, a crew member somewhere high above steerage saw faint lights on the horizon. Word quickly spread, and before long, most passengers could be found on deck. As always, Valentin drew a crowd. He advised they were approaching Chesapeake Bay and would reach Baltimore by tomorrow afternoon—his small figurine advancing to the point where it touched the shores of America.

For many, it was a sleepless night. Their first step in America was reason for angst, but so too was the specter of facing immigration officials. Rumors of denied entry raced through steerage. Physical deficiency, feeblemindedness, contagious disease, political views inconsistent with those commonly held in America, or low moral character were reasons cited by inspectors to deny passage. Whether real or imagined, it took just one chalk mark to require further examination and possible rejection.

Passengers were advised that medical examinations would be conducted on board and above deck. They were told to remain below until otherwise directed. Land was now visible on both sides of the ship, and the *Neckar* moved easily through calm waters. Shortly after breakfast the ship slowed, and a smaller vessel pulled alongside. A group of ten uniformed officials boarded the *Neckar*—eight inspectors, one matron, and one officer carrying a sidearm. Stations were set up above deck and passengers were brought from steerage in groups. Single women were first, followed by mothers with children, then single men. The physical inspection took less than five minutes, and consisted of a series of questions followed by an examination for evidence of trachoma. All members of the Schafer party passed. As each returned below deck there was a small celebration. Against the backdrop of joy and relief, there were passengers who failed to pass, four from a small Polish village. The reason for denial was unknown, but the disappointment obvious. Friends and family tried to console the rejected. At best, they would be detained at the Port of Entry and subjected to follow-up testing. For an unfortunate few, failure meant an immediate return to their port of embarkation.

The passengers were held below for more than two hours after inspections were complete. When finally allowed above deck, they were astounded by what they saw. Ships of every size and description plied the harbor, some much larger than their own. Smaller vessels darted in and out of piers. Industrial development covered every inch of waterfront, as did the acrid haze which hung just above the entire scene. The *Neckar* slowed to a point where movement was barely discernible, and two small vessels came alongside to assist with docking. Steerage passengers were permitted to remain on deck to observe the process. First- and second-class passengers were preparing to disembark, and the pier filled with dock workers, porters, and those waiting for friends and relatives. The Schafer party and their counterparts were once again reminded of their lowly status—held until all passengers on the upper decks and their baggage were off the pier. Finally, it was time to set foot on American soil. Several members of the Schafer party, led by Herta Berg, dropped to their knees to thank God for their deliverance.

Chapter Six:
America: God's Promise Fulfilled

*"Give me your tired, your poor, your huddled masses yearning
to breathe free, the wretched refuse of your teeming shore. Send
these, the homeless, tempest-tost to me, I lift my lamp
beside the golden door."*

—Emma Lazarus

T he *Neckar* was docked at Locust Point, a joint venture of *Norddeutscher Lloyd* and the Baltimore and Ohio Railroad. The ship was berthed at Pier One which held the Reception Center. A second pier housed the railroad terminus and a boarding house. The tracks ran directly onto the second pier and were sheltered by two large sheds. The immigrants were directed to the Reception Center and asked a few cursory questions, including destination and how much money they were carrying. They were also given the opportunity to exchange currency. Immigrants met by family, friends, or perhaps an employer moved on to a holding area to await their party. Those traveling by rail were simply directed to the Baltimore and Ohio terminal. Their trunks and other containers could now be claimed.

John could not help but contrast the sacrifice, hardship, and time required to reach America with the few minutes it had taken to gain entry. It was a contrarian thought. The travelers were just happy to be in America and had no desire to engage in further deliberation. Peter, Noah Adler, and Denzel Kalb started toward the Baltimore and Ohio ticketing area, while the others collected personal belongings.

Suddenly, an Immigration Officer stopped all movement. The matron assigned to steerage had collected the young Kunkel girl caught in sexual promiscuity and was taking her to a room near the front of the building. Luise Kunkel was pleading with her daughter not to go, but the young woman seemed relieved, if not anxious, to be separated from her family. She had been subject to abuse at the hands of her father throughout the voyage, and the matron apparently decided that separation was in her best interest. Peter watched, but could only hope that the matron's motives were honorable. Luise started toward the girl, but was immediately restrained. Gustav said nothing, and Peter saw no reason to intervene. Decisions made in the Reception Center were the exclusive domain of authorities. Protestations by those seeking entry were not welcome, and could lead to detention and a return to *Deutschland.*

The three members of the Schafer party continued toward the Baltimore and Ohio terminal. The path was blocked by a large number of agents waving handbills offering employment opportunities in mining, timber, and manufacturing. A few were in Baltimore, but most in cities with odd-sounding names. Free transportation and guaranteed housing were among the enticements. None of these options were of interest to Peter and his colleagues. Their intent was to locate representatives of the Kansas Pacific Railroad, which proved to be a difficult task amidst the sea of immigrants, agents, and peddlers.

Finally, they located a helpful Baltimore and Ohio agent. He produced a Kansas Pacific Flyer written in *Deutsch* and pointed toward the rearmost section of the rail shed. Peter read the flyer as the trio made their way toward the indicated section. It described rich farmland suitable for grain production. The price per acre ranged from $3.50 to $5.50 dependent upon the amount of land purchased. There was also a map showing a vast stretch of land on either side of the Kansas Pacific right-of-way.

* * * * *

The impetus of the United States Government to populate the "Great American Desert" was not unlike that undertaken by Catherine the Great to populate the Steppe one-hundred years earlier. Both governments wished to extend secure borders, and both required sworn allegiance. Catherine provided transportation and gave money, tools, seed, and implements, albeit late in coming. The United States offered homesteading and inexpensive land via grants to railroads. Both governments, at time of entry, disavowed conscription. In the United States, westward expansion followed the precept of "Manifest Destiny," the widely held belief that Americans possessed ordained virtues and were obliged to spread their superior culture.

There were also distinctions, perhaps the greatest the desire of newcomers to assimilate. Following their arrival in America, immigrants, while preserving certain elements of their heritage, made an effort to adopt the mores of their new country. They considered themselves Americans. The *Deutsch* colonists, upon arrival in *Russen,* distanced themselves from their new homeland and strove to maintain absolute autonomy. They were *Deutsch* and would always be *Deutsch.*

* * * * *

After some searching, Peter and his colleagues located the Kansas Pacific agent. He struggled with *Deutsch*, but Peter understood that transportation to Topeka was available at a discounted rate and personal belongings would be carried by the railroad at no charge. Noah had seen the published rate offered by the Baltimore and Ohio representative and confirmed the group would pay less if tickets were purchased from the Kansas Pacific agent. Peter was convinced the agent's offer was as good as any. He recalled the independence displayed by members four days previous. The longer members wandered through the terminal, the more the temptation to consider alternative destinations. It was time to make a decision. Peter arranged purchase of tickets for the entire party leaving at three p.m. the following day.

Their overnight stay would be in an alcove just outside the reception area. All belongings had been secured, and there were no missing trunks. Since the Metz trunk had gone missing in Bremerhaven, loss of personal belongings was a constant worry. Peter shared the departure time and the flyer provided by the agent. He expected two or three among the party to question the plan, but there were no dissenters. The reality of setting foot in

America and the journey that lay ahead quieted even the most adventurous among them. Peter was relieved.

There were two options for spending the night: the boarding house operated by a Mrs. Koerther, who received seventy-five cents per night— paid by *Norddeutscher Lloyd*—or the stone floor of the terminal sheds. Maria, her mother and Anna Schneider were blessed to find a room in the boarding house with real beds and fresh water. Most were relegated to the stone floor, but thankful for solid footing and a reprieve from the foul scent of steerage. They spent the late afternoon wandering between the two piers that made up Locust Point before returning to their alcove. The conversation again turned to their destination. The optimists saw a period of adjustment followed by prosperity. The contrarians saw late planting, low yields, and problems with acceptance. The debate continued knowing answers awaited their arrival in Kansas.

The Welshmen were their neighbors for the night, camping at the end of the pier. Somehow, they gained access to a small dock, ignoring the "Keep Off" sign. Two of the men were trying their best to catch a fish with a piece of string and hook fashioned from a nail. They were successful at amusing the small crowd, but not so with fishing. In a conversation which relied heavily on hand signals, Peter learned the Welshmen would leave early the next morning. They had been hired as a group and destined for the coal mines of West Virginia.

The Schafer party ate together, enjoying real *Deutsch* food purchased at a surprisingly well-stocked *Markt* adjacent to the Reception Center. It was a welcome change from salted fish and watery soup. John was quite sure he had lost at least five pounds on the crossing—the product of a churning stomach and tasteless diet. Werner Geist was told that the food at "Depot Restaurants" was even less appetizing than on board the *Neckar*. With this as guidance, the Schafer party purchased sufficient *roggenbrot* and *wurst* to last through a four or five-day trip. Denzel Kalb recalled asking the Kansas Pacific agent about food on their trip west. He was told there were frequent stops with access to food, but the agent seemed anxious to end the conversation without reference to quality.

Earlier in the day, Werner briefly caught sight of perhaps twenty travelers whose dress suggested they were *Volga Deutsch*.

"Have you come from *Russen?*" he asked.

"Yes," answered one of the men, "From the village of Bauer. We are five families, a childless couple, and a single man."

Werner continued, "When did you leave the village?" and was surprised to learn they departed fifty-six days earlier.

"We were delayed in Bremerhaven for several days while our steamship, *America,* underwent repairs. The ship was plagued by dysentery," he added. "Nine passengers died."

"Were any of the dead from your party?" Werner asked.

"Two dead and one, Catherine Schuler, just released from quarantine."

The party had agreed to remain at the terminal for three days, then start west if Catherine was not permitted entry. Her release meant tickets could now be purchased. The party had done so a few hours before.

Werner invited the Schuler party to visit their encampment. Several of the men, including Gabriel Schuler, husband of Catherine and the group's unofficial leader, accepted. The two parties learned they would be traveling together, at least to the Kansas border. The Schuler party would be met by representatives of the Atchison, Topeka and Santa Fe Railroad. Gabriel shared a flyer describing the land available along the Santa Fe tracks. Like most handbills, there was glowing reference to fertile lands, low prices, and generous credit terms. The name C. B. Schmidt, no relation to John, was prominently displayed on the handbill as *Generaldirektor Deutsch* of land sales in Kansas.

The *Generaldirektor* and his representatives were frequent visitors to the Volga colonies. The flyer sparked an immediate discussion as to which railroad had access to better land—Santa Fe or Kansas Pacific. No conclusion could be reached as the conversation was based on the overstated claims of both carriers. The parties did agree there was more and cheaper land the farther west one traveled.

Peter had been listening at a distance and joined the conversation,

"Land should be divided much as it was in *Russen,*" he said.

Gabriel concurred, "The *mir* system served us well," then added, "There is security in numbers."

Peter was pleased to find that Gabriel felt the same as he did on land tenure and community, but suspected his party was less committed to the old ways. Some were likely to homestead, while others may be forced into employment. Werner Geist had been quietly listening to the discussion and suggested that the two parties combine their investigation. A member of the Schafer party would join the Schuler party as it investigated the Santa Fe properties, and they in turn would reciprocate.

The approach provided for an expanded search area. Kurt Haus volunteered to represent the Schafer party, while Henry Bissing did the same for the group from Bauer. Henry was single, and the only member of the Schuler party who would continue beyond Kansas. His destination was eastern Colorado to join a brother who had homesteaded a year earlier. Henry was not from the village of Bauer, having set out on his own from Kraft. It was his good fortune to board the same railcar occupied by Gabriel Schuler and his party. Henry was immediately adopted by the group. He was happy to return their kindness by assisting in the evaluation of land. Colorado could wait a few days.

Peter didn't believe the plan would work, but the membership of both parties was excited, and he saw the scheme as harmless. What bothered him most was the display of independence. The agreement with Gabriel Schuler and his party had been reached democratically without his direction. He was uncertain of whether Werner and the others were simply caught up in the moment or his grip on the party was weakening. John observed the conversation and, as something of a heretic, believed that Gabriel better understood life in America than did his father-in-law. Neighbors and the *Gemeinde* were important, but not to the point of suffocating participation.

John found Henry Bissing's desire to homestead in Colorado intriguing, and he questioned him on his brother's experience. Henry had but one letter from his brother, and the contents were not encouraging. The summer had seen Rudolf Bissing lose half of his corn crop and a good number of vegetables to grasshoppers. The meager harvest would not carry him through the winter and he had turned to game. In spite of his difficulties, Rudolf was able to build a home and expand his 160 homesteaded acres to 220. That was America. Hardship was the precursor of success, and risk, the pathway to reward.

Maria was up early the next morning, refreshed by her overnight stay in the boarding house. She immediately set out to find John. He was not with the main body, but rather sitting at the food *Markt* with Kurt Haus. The two had been discussing John's conversation with Henry Bissing and their shared desire to leave the Schafer party. Maria reminded her husband it was time to pack their belongings for the afternoon departure. John noticed Maria was unusually animated, which he attributed to a restful night and the anticipation of starting the final leg of their journey.

When they reached the alcove, they found Peter busy checking the readiness of each member. Were necessities packed separately, was there sufficient food for everyone, and did they all understand they were to gather on the platform two hours before departure? As he listened to his father-in-law's ceaseless reminders, John noticed Valentin, standing on the platform ready to board his train. He had lost track of his mapmaking friend after their arrival. With Maria by his side, John hurried to say goodbye, and thank Valentin for his guidance aboard the *Neckar*. Valentin gave John his son's address in Wisconsin, wished the young couple the best of luck, and encouraged them to write once they settled. John agreed to do so, then realized it was time to write his parents—they would be concerned for his well-being. He had penned only two letters in his lifetime. The third was overdue. Thoughts of home momentarily saddened John. He wondered if his mother had regained her health or taken a turn for the worse.

The Schafer party watched as two trains departed, Valentin's among them. As far as they could tell, the trains carried mostly immigrants, each dutifully boarding in groups, their ethnicity defined by dress. John wondered how many knew what lay ahead and how many had succumbed to the empty promises of agents. Peter's overbearing nature was annoying to some in the party, but he could never be faulted for lack of preparation. John was sure that within weeks they would be turning soil in Kansas.

The travelers, eager to get underway, began to gather on the platform around midday. There were already a few parties hoping to occupy a car or sections of a car, but none as large as the Schafer party, its ranks swollen by Gabriel Schuler's group. Peter was able to locate a Baltimore and Ohio agent and found the cars would be loaded by gender—men in the first car, adult females and mothers with young children in the second and third. Given the size of the Schafer party, the agent was willing to load them as a group. Peter agreed to gather all tickets and ensure members were directed to the proper car.

The first car looked much like those boarded in Eydtkuhnen. Seating was side by side, and the cars rather narrow. Cars two and three, the so-called "immigrant" cars, had been converted. They were older, slightly broader, and likely to have carried first-class passengers sometime in their history. Seats had reversible backs, and windows were large, although few in number. Facilities and a stove were located at each end. Boards were available to place between the reversible benches, creating a bed. Just after boarding, the conductor slowly walked through cars two and three. His purpose was to identify and dispatch older male children who, in the conductor's opinion, belonged in the first car. Movement between cars was permitted, but all passengers must overnight in their assigned car.

The party was still busy rearranging space as the train pulled from the station. Factories lined both sides of the right-of-way, and a large number of immigrant cars were parked on either side of the two main lines. Closely built housing and some storefronts were visible in the distance. They had been underway for only a short time when the train came to a stop and began backing up, changing tracks as it did. The sudden jolt implied additional cars were being coupled. There was another pause, and the backing resumed until reaching a platform occupied by travelers whose attire suggested they were first- and second-class passengers. Some recognized the immigrant cars and tried their best to catch a glimpse of the occupants. The experience was disturbing to the Schafer and Schuler parties. They had attracted attention in Europe, but were transients. Now, they were Americans. This was their new home, but the condescending looks suggested otherwise. Peter watched the behavior of both parties, and could feel them drawing together as one, an outcome that bode well for his planned community.

They left the central Baltimore station in the early evening. Factories gave way to housing, then farms, and finally darkness. The travelers did what they could to make themselves comfortable. The immigrant car swayed and creaked much like the *Neckar* on stormy seas—sleep did not come easy. The train stopped twice during the night, once for water, and once for three hours at a bridge crossing—the only thing visible a few lanterns and the occasional shadowy figure. No one left the train.

Daybreak found them traveling through hilly terrain. Trees covered much of the landscape, except for small patches where intrepid settlers had cleared the ground. Some began to wonder when the grasslands would appear. John and Kurt Haus, having spent time studying Valentin's maps, understood that it would be another two or three days, if not longer, before they reached the prairies. Their comments offered some solace, but the travelers were impatient. Where was the ground reputed to match the black earth of the *Russische* Steppe?

Near midmorning the train stopped at a small community. The conductor stuck his head in the door and shouted, "*Speisewagen.*" There was little desire on the part of the Schafer party to eat, but it was a chance to stretch their legs and to see what a depot restaurant looked like. They would have to wait. The restaurant was closed and the city beyond very small, with a few railroad buildings and perhaps ten houses. The conductor warned, "*niche wandern,*" as they stepped to the platform. He said something else in tortured *Deutsch*, which implied they could leave without warning.

Maria pulled John along the platform toward the locomotive.

"I am with child."

"A son?"

"Or a girl," Maria quickly added.

John could only babble. He was full of questions, but unable to ask the first before the second got in the way. He wanted children more than anything and hoped this would be the first of many. John now understood his wife's giddy behavior on the day of departure.

Maria had not told anyone and was eager to share the news with her mother. They hurried back to find Melina.

She embraced Maria and turned to John without hesitation.

"You and the baby can stay in our home."

It's too soon to discuss living arrangements." Maria answered for her husband.

John did not like the idea of sharing a roof with his father-in-law, but a nudge from Maria put a stop to any protestation.

The remainder of the day was spent celebrating Maria's announcement. The married women felt obliged to share their experiences. Most spoke of motherhood as joyful, but a few suggested she had taken the first step toward a lifetime of endless drudgery. One of those was Anja Metz, a new mother who was sickly and fearful of having more children. Anja walked through life under a cloud. Hearing of Maria's pregnancy, she could not wait to share the worst of childbirth, going so far as to suggest that children would ruin her marriage. Maria would have none of it. Instead, she sought the counsel of Anna Schneider, a woman who saw children as a blessing. She and Maria had become close friends. When Maria first suspected she might be pregnant, she spoke with Anna and found her a source of strength and confidence.

To mark the occasion, John planned to buy a celebratory treat—he wasn't sure what—at their next stop. The opportunity came late in the afternoon when the train took on water. Adjacent to the coal bin was a makeshift canteen. The meager selection included bread and dried meats, but no festive items. His celebration would have to wait.

Aside from Maria's announcement, there was little noteworthy about their second night on the train. Members of both parties, by now, were seasoned travelers and had found ways to pass the time while ignoring discomfort. Mornings were often the more interesting part of the day. With daylight, travelers scanned the countryside, always in search of the promised grasslands. There were far fewer hills now, and the landscape less forested, but the vast open prairie was nowhere in evidence.

In midmorning, the train pulled into a large settlement which carried the name "Cincinnati." The conductor managed to convey in a combination of *Deutsch* and exaggerated hand signals that they would be here for at least six hours. Everyone was eager to escape confinement, but their appearance on the platform drew immediate attention. The intense scrutiny made them uncomfortable, particularly the women, who stayed close to the train. The men were less bothered. Led by John and Kurt, a small group made their way into the city. John was able to find a baker and purchased a quantity of pastries, which he guessed should be somewhat more expensive than the bread and sausage purchased at the pier in Baltimore. The baker was agreeable. The others, noting John's success, made small purchases of their own before starting back. None was in a hurry to reboard.

While the men were gone, the women were amused by a young man struggling to pull a cart onto the platform. He carried small bars of soap, straw pillows, tinware, blankets, and some food. The immigrants were intrigued, but there were few purchases. Undaunted, he pulled his cart back toward the first- and second-class cars, continuing to hawk his wares. Just before departure, he abandoned the cart and moved all of his merchandise onto the train. That evening the Schafer party celebrated Maria's announcement. John's bakery purchase was a success, and Hersh Schneider found a source for spirits, *mais whisky*, enough to make for a joyful evening. For the first time since leaving Pfeifer, the Schafer party left thoughts of the arduous journey behind and forgot, at least for one night, the uncertainty that lay ahead.

The festive spirit was quickly dashed when travelers learned that Gotthold Sumas, a member of the Schuler party, had died. He had complained of an upset stomach and soreness in his midsection. The pain became severe overnight. He lost consciousness and passed in the early morning hours. The conductor was called, but there was nothing he could do. He was anxious to take Gotthold's body off the train, but agreed that it could wait until they reached St. Louis in midafternoon. The four-hour stop was time enough to locate a priest, but little else.

Albert Wetzel volunteered to assist Mari Sumas. He and the Sumas family were to depart the train, provide for Gotthold's mass and interment, then catch the next westbound train two days later. Kansas Pacific made the necessary arrangements. The process seemed cold and rather abrupt, but given the circumstances, the customary period of grieving was impossible. Almost immediately, the women of both parties began to discuss the potential marriage of Mari and Henry Bissing. Mari had two choices— both disagreeable. She could return to *Russen* or manage a Kansas farm on her own. Irrespective of her attraction to Henry, she needed a husband and father for her children.

A few in the party ventured into St. Louis, trailed by curious onlookers. An hour before departure, an open wagon and casket pulled alongside the train. Albert was riding in the front seat with the undertaker, who seemed rather jovial given the circumstance. He was dressed in black, that being his only concession to the somber event. Mari and the children remained with the priest. The body was placed in the hand-hewn casket, and the wagon set out for the church.

During the St. Louis stopover, some shifting of cars took place, but the first six, including those occupied by the Schafer and Schuler parties, were undisturbed. An agent of the Atchison, Topeka and Santa Fe boarded the train briefly and met with Gabriel Schuler and others who would soon be traveling on Santa Fe tickets. It was an introductory visit. Company representatives would meet the travelers the following day. The agent had a large number of handbills available and was willing to discuss the railroad's land with anyone interested.

Kurt Haus took advantage of the opportunity since he had agreed to travel with the Schuler party to investigate Santa Fe properties. When the agent discovered that Peter Schafer would be meeting with Kansas Pacific representatives, he was disappointed. A large group seeking hundreds of acres meant a substantial payday. The next morning the travelers awoke to their first sight of grasslands. The sight buoyed their spirits. During a watering stop, Peter and Nicholas Geist kicked at the ground and found the soil rich in color. This was land they could work. Breaking the ground would be difficult, but with a measure of good fortune, the yield could be excellent.

The train reached the far western boundary of Missouri and the City of Kansas (later, Kansas City) in midafternoon. The Schafer party was met there by Daniel Randolph, a Kansas Pacific agent. He would be their companion and guide for the next several days. Mr. Randolph had no understanding of *Deutsch* or *Russen*, but was accompanied by an assistant, Anselm Baten, who spoke fluent *Deutsch*. The Schafer party was told to pack their belongings for transfer to a waiting Kansas Pacific train. The immigrant cars were left behind, and the party found themselves in clean first-class accommodations. The task was accomplished in less than an hour. A few curious onlookers watched the process, but fewer than before.

Topeka was less than three hours ahead. Peter was advised that lodging for the Schafer Party was on the unfinished third floor of a hotel adjacent to the Kansas Pacific terminal. Access was via the rear stairs. The travelers could use terminal facilities, but not those of the hotel. Water and containers for washing were also available—the first opportunity to truly bathe. A single meal would be provided each day at five p.m. Mr. Randolph reminded Peter that room and board came with the expectation the party would purchase land from Kansas Pacific. Peter acknowledged the comment, but said nothing of the joint investigation of Santa Fe property. He still believed the exercise to be a waste of time.

Peter was glad for the time with Mr. Randolph and Anselm en route to Topeka. He agreed with those in the party who questioned whether the system of land tenure practiced in *Russen* could be adapted to the American concept of ownership, where title was paramount. Without ownership, there was no means to accommodate taxation or borrowing. The members also wanted land they could call their own—the American dream—but the *mir* system was rooted in commonly held farmland. Collective resources were central to Peter's planned community. Absent this lynchpin, his colony was nothing more than a loosely configured group of homesteaders, any one of whom could pull up stakes.

Mr. Randolph suggested an alternative, the *Town and Grazing Company*. Farmland was held individually, but common structures, equipment, grazing land, and water resources were held jointly by the *company* and its shareholders. Membership included one share and one vote—the shared resources purchased via an assessment. The *Town and Grazing Company* offered both individual ownership and common interest, the latter strengthened by a provision that members, upon leaving the community, forfeited their share of the *company* without remuneration.

The concept held merit save for one exception. Peter wanted homes to be clustered in a centrally located township surrounded by farmland. Members would then travel each day to work their fields, just as they had done in Pfeifer. But Mr. Randolph's scheme did nothing to encourage development of a residential core. Peter feared that members may see daily travel as a waste of time, choosing instead to live where they farmed. Homes would then be scattered over hundreds of acres, and the sense of community lost.

Peter was deeply concerned that his utopian plan was beginning to lose support, particularly among younger members. Kurt Haus was already discussing a homestead in Colorado or the Dakota Territory. He was a risk-taker and his ideas were gaining traction. Peter knew his son-in-law had similar ambitions. John disliked being governed by the elders and had little use for the traditional system of land tenure. Maria's pregnancy would keep him close to the fold, but once the child was born, Peter expected him to abandon the planned community. There were others who felt as Kurt and his son-in-law did. Freedom and independence bore little resemblance to *Volga Deutsch* tradition. Departures were inevitable. Peter could only hope new members would replace those who left. Gabriel Schuler's party was one source. Other parties from *Russen* must follow if his experiment was to succeed.

The first order of business was finding suitable land. Mr. Randolph understood that the Schafer party was looking for as much as 3,000 acres, with all parcels contiguous and priced under $5.00 per acre. This placed them squarely in central Kansas, perhaps near Fort Hays. It was futile to show any land close to Topeka. The price was much higher, and contiguous acreage of the size the Schafer party desired was difficult to locate.

Nicholas Geist, Albert Wetzel, and Denzel Kalb had all expressed interest in being a part of land evaluation. Nicholas was particularly adept at judging soil condition and output per acre. His advice was often sought when soils were depleted and crop yields declined. The three men would join Mr. Randolph and Anselm, along with someone referred to as a "surveyor," who was skilled at establishing property lines. They were to meet at the Kansas Pacific station at eight a.m. two days hence. From there, the group would board a west-bound train that included a scheduled stop in Fort Hays, where at least two potential sites were available. Peter planned to remain in Topeka with John. The two had an appointment arranged by Mr. Randolph to discuss the creation of the *Town and Grazing Company.*

Chapter Seven:
Kansas: I Never Saw a Finer Country

"If I went west, I think I would go to Kansas."
—Abraham Lincoln

The Kansas Pacific train arrived in Topeka near midnight. Exhausted members secured their belongings and quickly made their way to the third floor of the hotel. The space was much as described—no partitions; one window at each end, which thankfully opened; and enough mattresses to accommodate one-half of the travelers. Lighting could have been better, but the few oil lamps allowed them to find their way. After weeks of traveling in confined, often filthy conditions, the spacious loft was more than satisfactory.

The party awoke the next day to brilliant sunshine and the knowledge their month-long ordeal was nearly over. At some point in their journey, each wondered if they would ever reach America, let alone Kansas. A few thought they should never have left *Russen*, though never openly expressing the thought. Now they were on the cusp of farming American soil.

First came a task they valued just as highly—the opportunity to bathe and wash clothes. The latter was rarely done over the past several weeks. The women immediately set to work, while the men dragged personal belongings up the back stairs. Most of the trunks survived the transit sustaining only minor damage, though fumigation had destroyed some contents. Given the distance traveled and shoddy treatment, the travelers were fortunate to have the bulk of their possessions intact.

Anselm arranged for the Kansas Pacific cashier to exchange whatever foreign currency members still held. Some had been exchanged in Baltimore, but once in Topeka, the remainder made a sudden appearance, often from unmentionable locations. The next stop was a nearby *Markt* where a *Deutsch* immigrant had recently been hired as a clerk. With an understanding merchant and proper currency, they were able to purchase food to supplement the one meal a day provided by the railroad. Some ventured farther into Topeka drawing modest attention. Topeka had seen *"Rooshians"* before. There were few whispers.

When they returned to the hotel, they found that the women had drawn some onlookers, fascinated by the furious pace of washing and clothes hanging from every corner of the building. The hotel manager directed the immigrants to take their washed clothing upstairs, along with personal belongings strewn about the grounds. He reportedly raged for several minutes, but to no avail. The women were committed to their task and understood little of his rant.

Kurt Haus watched the sunrise from the Kansas Pacific station. He was waiting for Gabriel Schuler and others from his party. The group was temporarily housed in a warehouse one-quarter mile east. Together, they would begin the investigation of farmland south and west of Topeka along the Atchison, Topeka and Santa Fe tracks. Kurt planned on just one stop to investigate property near Florence. Gabriel would continue west toward the end of the Santa Fe line. Kurt was beginning to agree with Peter's assessment that a joint review was a questionable base for decision making. Gabriel's research on Santa Fe land was sketchy, so much so Kurt wondered if it held value to either party. Peter desired to replicate Pfeifer, which required a large, contiguous block of land. The Santa Fe agent had already suggested this may not be possible along their tracks—another reason for Kurt's lack of interest.

The train reached Florence following a brief stop at Osage City. The agent took Kurt, Gabriel, and two others south along a well-worn wagon path. They passed three small farms, finally reaching an irregular area encompassing 120 acres. The price was $6.50 per acre. Gabriel liked the terrain. The soil was good and a stream crossed the western boundary, but the price was far too high. He asked about homesteading and was told fertile ground had already been spoken for. Some still existed, but much farther west, along with railroad land closer to the $4.00 per acre his party could afford. Kurt had no questions and simply listened as Gabriel and the agent discussed potential sites. He knew $6.50 per acre was beyond the means of the Schafer party. He also knew ATSF's competition, Kansas Pacific, had been granted six million acres of land between the City of Kansas and Denver and was eager to sell, particularly to anyone willing to purchase 1,000 acres or more. Kurt had seen enough. When they returned to Florence, Gabriel continued westward. Kurt waited for the eastbound train and a return to Topeka.

Their first hotel meal was a hearty beef stew served with bread and as many steamed vegetables as the travelers could consume. Much to the relief of the manager, laundry and personal belongings had been gathered and returned to the hotel loft. The space was arranged so that dining and meeting areas were centrally located. Families and single women occupied the west end, while single men settled to the east. Extra blankets were used to create separation and some degree of privacy.

Earlier in the day, Nicholas Geist and a small group ventured into Topeka spending time at a feed store. They studied plows, a planter, harrows, and other "modern" devices designed to ease the burden of fieldwork. The owner, who spoke some *Deutsch*, was excited by the number in the Schafer party. He was already thinking of the proceeds attached to this most recent infusion of immigrants. The men also found time to discover a source for *bier* and the much-coveted corn whiskey.

Peter and John missed the evening meal. The two had spent a disappointing late afternoon with a local government official discussing the *Town and Grazing Company*. Mr. Randolph had arranged the meeting and was told the official spoke some *Deutsch*. He did not. Peter and John tried to understand, but left the meeting confused. The question of how to link communal property to title and private ownership was still unanswered.

That evening John sat on the front porch of the hotel. With Maria's help, he wrote a letter to his father. The couple debated whether to include the discomfort and perils of their journey, but decided against it. Instead, they focused on Kansas and how much the plains resembled the *Russische* Steppe. John described their temporary quarters in Topeka and told his father the party was in search of land farther west. The tone of the letter was optimistic, suggesting they should have little problem locating fertile ground and space suitable for a village. John thought of asking about his mother's health, but Maria suggested not. He should send his love and let his father comment on Helena's health in the return letter. John told his parents that Maria was pregnant and the baby was due sometime in early winter. He knew they would be excited by the prospect of a grandchild, but saddened by the knowledge the child would never know the grandparents. His father would need help in reading and responding, but was sure his business associate—the blacksmith—could help.

Anselm told John he would post the letter using the railroad's Topeka station as the return address. The telegraph office acted as the postal station, and the operator had some knowledge of international mail. The letter's transit from Topeka to major European cities was possible, but delivery beyond was questionable. Mail was costly, with no assurance of receipt. At best, the letter would reach Pfeifer in twelve weeks.

Nicholas Geist and Denzel Kalb were in front of the hotel at eight a.m. eager to begin their exploratory journey. They awaited Mr. Randolph and the Schuler party's representative, Henry Bissing. Albert Wetzel had been sick during the night and would not be joining them. The train could be seen just beyond the station and consisted of two cars. The first was already occupied by individual buyers, perhaps twelve in number, and three railroad agents. Nicholas, Denzel and Henry would occupy the second car. A small contingent of Polish descent would be joining them. The train left within minutes of boarding. At Saint George, Anselm and a well-dressed man carrying a large number of maps boarded. Anselm introduced him as the surveyor. The next stop was Grand Junction. Shortly after passing through the city, the train came to a halt. Mr. Randolph and the surveyor stepped off. They hurriedly moved along both sides of the tracks, appearing to take some form of measurement and driving stakes. The surveyor returned to gather more documents before he and Mr. Randolph reached consensus.

The train proceeded to Abilene, where the Polish group was met by three Kansas Pacific wagons. They looked to be heading north. Nicholas and Denzel carefully studied the countryside. Farms dotted both sides of the track. Most were small. There was evidence of cultivation, but also large parcels untouched. All of the farms had some quantity of livestock. Shelter was primitive—*semlinkas* or sod houses and a few of wood construction, the latter most often associated with the railroad. Once clear of Abilene, development became sparse. Anselm signaled for Nicholas and Denzel to join him to study the properties they would be looking at tomorrow. Their destination was Hays City, but since they would arrive at dusk, the review would not take place until morning. They would spend the night in housing provided by Kansas Pacific. Mr. Randolph did not recommend looking at property west of Hays City. Ogallah was the next stop and known to be a lawless community inhabited by drovers and cattlemen. "Sodbusters" were uniformly disliked. Mr. Randolph planned to show the Schafer party two properties. The first was west of Victoria—adjacent to a cattle ranch operated by a wealthy Englishman—the other south of Hays City.

Nicholas and Denzel took advantage of the hotel room. Henry declined, choosing to spend the night in a railroad storage shed. He was a pleasant traveling companion, but unusually quiet, and something of a recluse. At daybreak, the party of six began its journey to scout the first property. They headed southeast from Hays City. Mr. Randolph, Nicholas, and the surveyor occupied the first wagon. Anselm and Denzel took the second. Henry Bissing rode a horse borrowed from Kansas Pacific. The track they followed was lightly used.

The visitors were immediately struck by the explosion of prairie grass, already well above the wagon hubs. They passed a few small farms, but soon found themselves alone on the open prairie. After an hour's time, Mr. Randolph pulled aside, consulted the map, and made a sweeping motion to the west. The surveyor nodded in agreement. Anselm then explained they were very near the center of 2,640 contiguous acres acquired in some sort of trade with the United States General Land Office. Nicholas wanted to see more, and Mr. Randolph dutifully steered toward the southern perimeter, with the surveyor acting as a guide.

They stopped periodically to examine the soil and found, as before, it was uniformly rich with densely intertwined roots. Their investigation continued, but the more they saw of the parcel, the less attractive it became. The land was undulating, with a few areas, perhaps as much as 600 acres too steep for farming. In addition, there were three large, heavily wooded tracts. A supply of wood was desirable, but far too much of this land was in timber. Mr. Randolph had not mentioned water. When asked, he told Nicholas there was a well on property a few miles south of their location, but he was uncertain of the depth. Nicholas was suspicious. They saw only one stream, and its size and bed suggested it might be dry in late summer.

Henry Bissing had ridden off to conduct a review of his own. When he approached the group, he summarized the feelings of Nicholas and Denzel, "*Nicht gut,*" he said.

"Don't judge too quickly," Mr. Randolph said. "There's still more to see."

"We've seen enough," Nicholas spoke for his companions. "The land is not suitable."

Anselm and Mr. Randolph conferred. The latter still believed the parcel held promise, but Nicholas and Denzel believed Henry's assessment was correct.

"We have little time," Nicholas said disgustedly. "Show us land ready for the plow."

Mr. Randolph started to protest, but Anselm, recognizing Nicholas was annoyed, quickly intervened.

"There is a parcel south of Hays City that is perhaps better suited to your needs."

On the return trip, Nicholas joined Mr. Randolph and Anselm in the first wagon—Denzel and the surveyor were in the second. Mr. Randolph made one more attempt to convince Nicholas there was value in the land just rejected.

He told Nicholas, "We are working with the government of the United States to turn parts of the prairie to timberland."

"We are farmers," Nicholas said. "We grow *maiz und weizen,* not trees."

Mr. Randolph wisely dropped his misguided sales effort and assured Nicholas he would find the next parcel more appealing. Nicholas glanced toward his host, but said nothing.

* * * * *

President Abraham Lincoln signed the Pacific Railway Act into law on July 1, 1862. He believed the act would spur westward migration, provide for the transport of western commerce to eastern markets, and in a time of great conflict, bind the nation together.

Under the terms of the act, the federal government gave the states more than 150 million acres of land to be passed on to railway companies in the form of grants. States receiving the largest grants were California (11.5 million acres), Kansas (8.2 million acres), Minnesota (9.9 million acres), Montana (14.7 million acres), North Dakota (10.6 million acres), and Washington (9.5 million acres). The grants represented one-tenth of the then existing United States. In 1870, more than one-sixth of Kansas belonged to the railroads. Subsequent amendments to the act allowed railroad companies to sell bonds, secured by the grants, and also awarded mineral rights.

The grants were tied to miles of track laid, and typically consisted of alternating sections six-miles on either side of the right-of-way. The railroads held the odd-numbered sections, with the intervening even-numbered sections managed by the General Land Office. In cases where the property was already occupied, the grant was extended beyond the six-mile limitation. Railroads were thus incentivized to lay new track, but they often did so without corresponding growth in population and tonnage. Demand for working capital led the railroads to sell land, or issue bonds secured by the government's generous handout.

Seven years after signing the Pacific Railway Act, Lincoln's dream was realized. The final spike in the transcontinental system of railways was driven on May 10, 1869 at Promontory Point, Utah. The time required to cross the nation had been reduced from several months to one week.

* * * * *

En route to Hays City, the group overtook a family that appeared to have all of its possessions in two wagons. The first was driven by the father—his wife and baby seated beside him. A young girl drove the second. Two boys trailed behind guiding livestock. The family gave way to allow the scouting group to pass. It was a curious encounter—one group apparently leaving the prairie, while another sought ground on which to settle.

Anselm noticed Denzel's quizzical look, and explained this was the family of Michael Benson. He and his brother James had moved from

Pennsylvania in 1871. Both had fought in the Civil War and took advantage of a special program for veterans under the Homestead Act. The brothers chose to settle near Fort Hays, a major source of supply to other military outposts, thinking the presence of cavalry and occasional patrols meant greater security. The first few years had been good to the brothers. Crops came in, they wintered well, and both constructed cabins.

In 1874, their fortunes changed. Grasshoppers destroyed much of their crop and then, in late fall, James, the younger of the two, was thrown from his horse while hunting. He was found a week later. His wife tried staying on, but after a month moved to Hays City where she met a young lieutenant and became engaged. Shortly thereafter, he was transferred to Washington, taking his intended bride and her family with him. With her close friend absent, June Benson felt isolated, a circumstance she could not abide. She convinced Michael to return to Pennsylvania. They were on the first leg of the journey.

Denzel was struck by just how fragile life on the prairie could be. Absent neighbors, a family was vulnerable to nature, renegade Indians, or belligerent cattlemen. Any one or all could easily force them off the land. Peter Schafer was right. There was safety in numbers, and the chance for the family to take root in this unforgiving land was far greater as part of a village.

The group took a hurried midday meal at the Kansas Pacific canteen, and set off immediately for their next destination. Mr. Randolph assured them that they would find this property more desirable. Henry Bissing, after a brief conversation with the surveyor, rode ahead on his own. They were bound for a 4,860 acre parcel created when an independent broker bought several sections surrounding the Kansas Pacific grant, but then defaulted on the transaction. The railroad bought the abandoned property for taxes owed, in addition to purchasing the intervening sections managed by the General Land Office. The result was a near 5,000 acre block of prime Kansas farmland.

The 380 acre Lundeen Ranch was just west of the parcel. The ranch and a narrow strip connecting with the larger parcel belonged to the government, but were soon to be purchased by Kansas Pacific. The Lundeen family had first settled the ranch, initially 160 acres, under the Preemption

Act of 1841. The act allowed purchase of land at $1.25 per acre if the claimant worked the land for fourteen months. An adult son had filed an adjoining claim, but intentionally misplaced the stakes, growing the claim to a total of 380 acres. In 1858, a renegade band of the Kanza tribe attacked and killed the Lundeen males, disappearing with Mrs. Lundeen and her only daughter. They were never seen again. A cousin of the Lundeens had briefly worked the land and made improvements, but left years before. The property reverted to the government and was now scheduled for sale to Kansas Pacific.

Their route took them south out of Hays City on a well-defined, improved road. The few farms they passed had a mix of *semlinkas* and wood-frame houses, some with outbuildings. Fields were neatly organized, and much of the ground was ready for planting. The land was similar to that seen earlier, but with fewer trees, less undulation, and no major breaks. When they reached the site, Henry was resting his horse near the boundary. He said only, *"Das ist gut."* Based on what little they had seen, the others agreed. A large stream passed through the property in a northeasterly direction. Henry told them an arroyo and pond were just below. The terrain invited construction of a dam. A second, smaller stream meandered through the property farther to the south. Both appeared to be year-round.

Henry carried a pouch filled with soil. It was dark and rich.

He pointed to the west and asked, "Is the limestone within the property?"

"Yes," said Anselm. "The material is excellent for construction."

Henry was eager to show the rock outcropping to Nicholas and Denzel, but neither was interested.

"We're here to study land, not limestone," said Denzel.

Anselm suggested they ride diagonally across the property. It took less than an hour to conclude that Henry's assessment was correct. This was indeed good land. They had a decision to make—continue the inspection, or return to Hays City hoping to catch a work train that Anselm thought would arrive near dusk. They chose the latter and found the train waiting. Before leaving, the surveyor marked a clean map that showed the small rise in the center of the property, the Lundeen Ranch, two streams, and the limestone outcropping. Mr. Randolph joined the group and told them he believed the 4,860 acres could be purchased at $4.00 per acre. If they were interested, the narrow strip and abandoned ranch would be somewhat lower. He reminded them that the entire transaction was subject to approval by his superiors, and sale of the ranch required government authorization. Nicholas and Denzel were in a similar position, unable to bind the Schafer party. That was a decision for Peter and the *Gemeinde*. Mr. Randolph understood. He and Anselm moved toward the front of the car to confer with their Kansas Pacific colleagues. Henry Bissing believed the property should be purchased immediately with no further visits. He did not expect to settle there, but thought the parcel to be a good fit for the Schafer party. Not many would be looking for near 5,000 acres, but Henry worried smaller groups, or even individuals, would be attracted to the land adjoining the streams. If access to water was lost, so too was the appeal of the property. Nicholas and Denzel agreed, but believed Peter would insist on a visit before purchase.

Peter, John, and Noah Adler met the train just before midnight. They listened intently as Nicholas described the property seen earlier in the day.

Peter thought for a moment then said, "I need to see the land."

"Why?" asked Henry. "You'll not find anything better in Kansas." Referring to the investigation of Santa Fe land, he added, "Nor will Gabriel."

Denzel concurred, "Mr. Randolph is continuing to show the property. If a piece along either stream is sold, the property is compromised."

Peter thought for a moment, then reluctantly agreed. A second inspection of the parcel would delay spring planting and, worse yet, could result in breakup and sale to individual buyers.

Upon his return from Florence, Kurt Haus told Peter that the Atchison, Topeka and Santa Fe line had nothing to offer the Schafer party. The railway simply lacked property large enough to establish his colony. The Schuler party required much less ground, but Gabriel had said, more than once, there was strength in community. Peter was hopeful that Gabriel, after hearing from Henry Bissing, would encourage his party to become one with the Schafers.

A meeting of the *Gemeinde* was set for that evening. An hour before, Anselm delivered a note to Peter from Mr. Randolph. Kansas Pacific was prepared to offer the 4,860 acres near Hays City at $3.75 per acre. The

Lundeen Ranch and narrow stretch of land, if available, were offered at $2.50 per acre. If the Schafer party purchased the entire parcel, the railroad would grant an additional forty acres on the north side of the parcel to accommodate a township site. Mr. Randolph understood Peter's zeal to create a town center. The forty-acre gift provided space for centralized housing and played to his desire.

The sheer size of the near 5,000-acre parcel was both a blessing and an obstacle. Breadth provided for growth, but could the membership afford to purchase the entire site? If any part of the ground that was offered went unsold, there was nothing to stop non-members from buying land within the block. This could easily result in a community divided by interlopers. To accommodate expansion and protect the colony's integrity, the land must be secured for the community.

The subject had been addressed in a private meeting including Nicholas Geist, Felix Austerlitz, and Peter just after the party's arrival in Baltimore. They had discussed the possibility of purchasing a block of land much larger than required to meet the party's immediate needs—the excess used to accommodate future membership. The Geist, Austerlitz and Schafer families were the wealthiest among the *Gemeinde*. Peter and Nicholas had come by their wealth in the traditional *Volga Deutsch* manner. Both had several male children when the allotted *dusha* was more generous. They were good farmers, and surplus generated income. Felix Austerlitz had accumulated his wealth by investing in the family's grist mill. There had been some lean years on the farm, but the mill paid off handsomely over time.

When the purchase of a large block was first discussed, Peter and the others were thinking in terms of 2,500 to 3,000 acres. A 4,860-acre buy pushed the limits of their resources. Peter shared his concern with Anselm and Mr. Randolph. Both agreed the railroad would be willing to join the three families as a principal buyer if it meant preserving the sale. Anselm agreed to draft a plan for Peter's approval. Common areas, such as grazing and timber land, would be set aside, with the remaining property distributed equally among the four principals. The surveyor would help in identifying roughly equivalent parcels. Some form of lottery would decide who among the four principals chose first. Within their block, Peter, Nicholas and Felix would select their own farmland, not to exceed 225 acres. Of the acreage remaining in each block, one-half would be available for immediate sale to the membership and one-half held for expansion. There would be no set aside for Kansas Pacific—all of the railroad property would be available for immediate sale. All parcels would be offered to members at a premium of five percent and no single member could purchase more than 225 acres—a somewhat meaningless limitation since most purchases were expected to be 100 acres or less.

Order of selection for the remaining members of the *Gemeinde* would be determined by a simple drawing. Male children of the principals would draw with the others, but the price to be paid in such circumstances was a family matter. The plan left some 2,700 acres available for immediate sale to existing membership—500 each from Peter, Nicholas and Felix and 1,200 from Kansas Pacific. Newcomers to St. Anne's could purchase land not spoken for in the initial sale or available from that set aside for expansion. All new membership must be approved by the council—fundamental to Peter's vision of St. Anne's as a planned community. Kansas Pacific agreed to sell its acreage at whatever terms and conditions were established by the other principals. Their land would simply lie fallow until sold, although Anselm thought grazing would be permitted.

The purchase of some 1,200 acres represented a substantial commitment for Peter, Nicholas, and Felix. All three planned to pay one-half in cash and finance the remainder. Balance and interest were due when the contract ended. Mr. Randolph assured them this could easily be arranged. Designated common areas would be purchased by means of an assessment on each parcel, including those purchased by the principal buyers. Future buyers would pay the same assessment.

Unless there was an objection, Peter intended to purchase the Lundeen Ranch and thirty-acre strip for Hermann, who told Peter to purchase 200 acres or more if an attractive offer arose. Peter saw the Lundeen Ranch as attractive. He also knew that Hermann's purchase would link his brother to the community—an opportunity to someday access Hermann's wealth.

On the theory that debtors made poor neighbors, none of the principals, save the railroad, would extend credit. Mr. Randolph suggested that Kansas Pacific was interested in contracts, but would also ensure other lenders were available. Interest would be paid upon transfer of title making the decision to buy on terms or outright even more difficult. Cash was king and buying on contract left the members with more resources in the early years. Anselm agreed to help in making those judgments.

The outline for the meeting was now set. Members would discuss how parcels would be allocated, the role of principal buyers, form of government, future leadership, and something they had forgotten—the township name. Finally, Peter would introduce the *Town and Grazing Company.* The last item had been explained by George Culp, a Topeka city official, in a manner Peter and John could understand. Mr. Culp had invited a young woman who spoke *Deutsch* to act as an interpreter. A much longer than anticipated meeting produced a draft charter. John thought the document unnecessarily wordy, but the draft did convey individual ownership to members, while providing a communal element through properties held jointly by the *Gemeinde.*

The afternoon was unseasonably warm, and Peter decided their first meeting in Kansas should take place in the open area behind the hotel. Before the meeting the principals had made the required division of land, leaving each with a quarter-share of the 4,860 acres, less the set aside for common ground. Peter began the meeting with a brief description of their investigation asking Nicholas and Henry to summarize their experience. He disclosed the price paid to Kansas Pacific, then explained that he, Nicholas Geist, Felix Austerlitz, and the railroad had purchased equal shares for resale to the membership. Peter could feel the suspicion build. He carefully described the reason the principals had taken the unusual step—to make certain property was available to accommodate growth. Other *Volga Deutsch* would surely follow and the immigrants would find the colony more attractive if contiguous farmland, without interlopers, was available. The purchase was made to ensure the community had room to grow. Peter could sense some understanding, but also skepticism.

"Have you taken the best ground?" Gustav asked.

"No," Peter replied. "The most desirable ground, that fronting the two streams, is still available."

"How much have you taken?"

"Less than a fifth of my initial allotment, about 200 acres," Peter responded.

"The railroad took nothing," Nicholas Geist added. "All of their land is available for resale, along with one-half, beyond the initial allotment, held by Peter, Felix, and myself."

"That makes near 2,700 acres available for immediate distribution and 1,500 for expansion." reckoned Nicholas.

Peter next tackled the premium, reminding the members that the price of land would be five percent higher than that paid by the principals—a reward for committing resources to the greater good of the community. He expected some objection, but got only a murmur. The membership understood the value of planning for the future.

A small group pled for on-site inspection. They briefly held sway, but were turned back by the compelling arguments of Henry Bissing. Nicholas Geist called for a vote on the purchase of land and method of resale. The measure passed with only three dissenters. The question of leadership was next on the agenda, along with what form the governing body should take. In Pfeifer, there had been a mayor and four elders. Werner Geist suggested the addition of two elders, but got little support.

Peter was nominated, without opposition, as *Vorsteher*. He was surprised, expecting at least one candidate to surface among the younger members of the party. Youth did come into play with the election of elders. Seven names were submitted, three of them members in their twenties. John's name had been placed in nomination, but withdrawn as his father-in-law had just been elected mayor. Each person spoke in support of their nominee. A voice vote was taken, with Denzel Kalb, Nicholas Geist, Felix Austerlitz, and Albert Wetzel elected to the council. The use of the term "elders" was abandoned, since Albert was something of a youngster. His fellow council members were much older, but Albert had shown leadership skills and planned, as a single man, to purchase sixty acres of farmland. The council took its position alongside Peter and turned to the question of naming their township. A few in the party suggested Pfeifer, but most seemed to favor a change. Three names were suggested—St. Joseph, Joseph, or St. Mary's. A majority favored the latter until Peter recalled a town of the same name on the surveyor's map. He suggested St. Anne's. There was unanimous support.

The final topic was the *Town and Grazing Company*. Peter began with an explanation of title in America and how it differed from what they were accustomed to in Pfeifer. Within seconds, both he and his audience were lost. Peter was far too deep in minutia. He paused and looked toward his son-in-law for help.

Waving the draft charter, John told the members, "Just two elements need clarification. First, buyers hold exclusive title to farmland."

Several members nodded approval—a few even applauded.

John introduced the second. "Membership in the *Town and Grazing Company* carries one share and one vote in the disposition of common assets."

He went on to explain that land held for resale by the principal buyers did not represent a share and held no voting power. That would also be the case for the Lundeen Ranch and narrow strip of land Peter intended to buy for his brother Hermann.

John was tempted to end the discussion leaving uncovered the one condition sure to bring controversy—insistence that each share include a building site within the township proper. Peter wanted St. Anne's to be the mirror image of Pfeifer with farm and residence separated. John decided to press on. He noted some unhappiness, but no challenges were voiced. John expected the residence requirement within the township would become more of an issue as St. Anne's matured as a community.

Peter quickly stepped to the podium disallowing questions. He reminded the membership that cash and credit buyers would pay the same price for land, but lenders may charge a fee for preparation of necessary papers. Peter was unable to discern if some level of understanding had been achieved, or the lack of questions was simply a desire to end the meeting. He suspected the latter.

He explained that the council would devise a lottery to determine in what order the membership would choose farmland. Their selection was to be made from the surveyor's map and subject to final on-site approval. A challenge to choosing a farm site without inspection was again raised, but was rejected, since the issue had already been approved. Peter reminded the party that any buyer judging his parcel unsatisfactory could exchange for equivalent acreage.

The members were instructed to gather at the Kansas Pacific station at two p.m. the following day. They would be met there by the surveyor and lenders from both Kansas Pacific and the First National Bank of Hays City. Anselm hoped that at least one commission agent from the Davenport family would also be on hand. The family was known to offer private financing. Term buyers could expect to pay interest of six-and-a-half percent over a period of five to seven years, dependent on lender, with interest and principal due upon termination of the contract. The lowest acceptable down payment was twenty percent.

Peter then closed the meeting with a listing of issues that still required resolution. Among them was the approval process for new members, the type of housing acceptable within the forty-acre township, whether a church or community center should be constructed, and if a well should be dug. The community must also address disciplinary action. In Pfeifer, the elders meted out discipline without participation by the *Kontor*. Major transgressions could result in the loss of land or expulsion. That would not be the case in Kansas. Here, the individual was protected under the Civil Code. Denial of fundamental rights by a non-governmental authority could itself be a crime.

As he watched the membership depart, Peter's thoughts turned to his son-in-law. John's explanation of the *Town and Grazing Company* had been well received, far more so than his own clumsy effort. Peter wished that his eldest son, Albrecht, was more willing to assume leadership. He was a follower, content to let others make the decision. Peter's next-eldest son, Freidrich, possessed the requisite qualities, but had the same devil-may-care attitude of his friend, Kurt Haus. The tenure of Freidrich and Kurt in St. Anne's was likely to be short.

The members now came face-to-face with Peter's admonition. Without adequate funds, the promise of America was as distant as the old world. The decisions facing the Schafer and Schuler parties were endless, and most involved money—*semlinka* or frame housing, one or two oxen, additional equipment or nest egg? There were countless others. Members had been told 150 acres and $600.00 were required to succeed on the prairie. Most believed that to be too generous, particularly with access to communal resources.

The Schafer party had planned well and bore little resemblance to the multitude of immigrants that preceded them. Only two families among the party had found it necessary to seek employment or accept charity. A few days after arriving in Hays City, Christian and Herta Berg were forced to take work on a nearby English cattle ranch, Christian as a roustabout and his wife a kitchen worker. Their eldest son planned to work for the Kansas Pacific Railroad laying track. The Bergs ran out of money in Baltimore, and borrowed a small amount from Burkhard Wetzel to complete their journey. Christian could not bring himself to ask for another loan, and instead hoped the family would earn enough over the next few years to rejoin their friends.

A similar circumstance faced Karl and Ella Seigler. The family found it necessary to leave the Schafer party in Topeka. Felix Austerlitz offered to employ Karl as a farmhand, but he was too proud to accept. In Pfeifer, Karl had never been awarded a *dusha*, and the family made their home with his parents. He worked his father's land, and found part-time employment in the building trades. Karl had no chance to buy Kansas farmland. ATSF needed workers to complete its route to Albuquerque and Karl signed on leaving his wife behind. Ella found work as a maid in the same hotel the Schafer party briefly occupied upon arrival in Topeka. She and the Seigler children were living in a boarding house.

The Schuler party was not as well prepared and Gabriel was experiencing difficulty keeping the membership intact. Two of the families had been forced into non-farm employment. Emil Zimmerman was employed as a handyman for a Hays City merchant, his wife a housemaid. The second family, like the Seiglers, never left Topeka.

Younger members from both parties represented a constant worry for Peter. Sons left Pfeifer and Bauer because opportunities were too few. They would leave St. Anne's because the opportunities were so many. Senior members treasured their religion and culture, but the young considered some elements of their heritage as a constraint. Kurt Haus was one of those—almost certain to abandon St. Anne's for Colorado or the Dakota Territory. Two of Peter's own family—Freidrich and John—expressed interest in starting out on their own. If youth left in numbers, St. Anne's could not survive. As much as circumstances changed, they remained the same—conscription took young men in *Russen*; opportunity did the same in America. The new council must keep its community young and vibrant. Peter was thankful Albert Wetzel, barely twenty years of age, had been elected to a leadership role.

Following the meeting, Peter went directly for the offices of Kansas Pacific. He had one more concession to secure from the railroad—temporary housing near Hays City. Lacking protection from the elements, the party would be forced to live out of wagons or take time away from planting to build shelter. He felt certain the railroad must have a building that could be made available for thirty to forty-five days while the party broke ground, their most urgent need. He found Mr. Randolph in his office.

Peter told him, "The membership has approved the sale, but we need shelter," he said. "A 5,000-acre purchase deserves that much."

Mr. Randolph feigned surprise, but his quick answer suggested he anticipated the question.

"The Army has three buildings just outside the fort. I can lease those, but only for a month."

That's all Peter needed. The pair shook hands, and Mr. Randolph instructed Anselm to begin preparation of the necessary documents.

Late that afternoon, Gabriel Schuler returned from his scouting trip with Santa Fe representatives. He found suitable land at a fair price, but there were difficulties. In the past week, ranchers had run cattle through one farm and torn out fences on another. Two months earlier, a small band of Indians set fire to a barn. The sheriff told Gabriel that anyone with plans to establish a farm should be ready to defend themselves. He had too much ground to cover and only one deputy. Gabriel called his party together to describe his scouting experience. Henry Bissing listened patiently, but like the others, found the Santa Fe alternative wanting. Kansas Pacific offered better, less expensive ground, and it came without risk. Ranchers in the area around Hays City had either accepted farmers or moved their herds west.

Peter returned to the hotel to ensure all was in order for tomorrow's distribution and sale of land. He found Gabriel Schuler and Nicholas Geist waiting for him. The Schuler party had reached a decision. With the exception of Otto Heimler, all agreed to settle in St. Anne's. Otto was yet to make a decision. He was thirty. Emma, his wife, was just sixteen. She had made friends with several of the Schafer party women and begged her husband not to move farther west. Otto finally acquiesced.

The Schuler party would be included in the drawing for property selection. Gabriel expected to purchase 150 acres for himself. He thought Otto Heimler would be interested in at least eighty. Henry Bissing and the widow Sumas had also reached a decision. Mari suggested marriage and a new life together in St. Anne's; Henry agreed with the first part of the arrangement, but not the latter. The couple and Mari's three children were scheduled to depart for Colorado in two days. The membership was sad to learn of Henry's departure. His tenure with the Schafer had been short, but his contributions significant.

Mr. Randolph and the agents were at the railroad offices at two p.m. Each member was assigned a number, which was dropped in a bucket, then drawn for order of selection. Gustav Kunkel's number was drawn first, followed by Denzel Kalb, then Hersh Schneider. The Kunkels chose sixty acres along the smaller stream, the Kalbs sixty-five acres adjoining the Schafer land. Denzel had designs on expansion and his selection provided access to Peter's unsold ground. Hersh Schneider decided on fifty acres bordering the township. If and when the Schneiders built on the township site, the family home would be adjacent to their farmland.

The process continued until everyone had selected, with each parcel noted on the surveyor's map. Some questioned how the surveyor, miles from the land itself, could identify location. He assured the membership that their ground would be staked based on the Government Land Ordinance adopted a century earlier, which created a division by section—each 640 acres. Sections were already designated and subdivisions made within each. The prospective buyers made their way to the Kansas Pacific station where Mr. Randolph had assembled agents of the railroad and the First National Bank of Hays City. Anselm was also successful in attracting two commission agents representing the Davenport family, one with a temporary office in Hays City and the other, by chance, en route from Denver to Chicago.

Two purchases required adjustment—George Breit, whose collateral did not support the amount of land desired, and Franz Hauer's, whose application was simply rejected. The Breits scaled back their acreage to a point where the bank found the purchase acceptable. The Hauers were not as fortunate. With no money, the young couple could offer only a pledge to pay. Even the agent from the Davenport family declined the application citing their age and existing indebtedness. Franz looked to his father, Eduard, for assistance, but the elder Hauers had already leveraged their fifty-acre purchase to the fullest extent. They were in no position to help. Franz and his new bride would begin their life on the prairie sharing a soddy with his father and mother.

With draft purchase agreements in hand, the new buyers gathered at Kansas Mercantile and Feed. The owner, Mr. Leopold, had seen his business shrink by one-half as a result of last year's grasshopper infestation. The company had farm equipment, sold on terms, scattered throughout Western Kansas. The newcomers offered a chance to find a home for repossessed merchandise. Mr. Leopold did not see heavy wool coats and tight-fitting head scarves; he saw willing buyers. Mr. Leopold discovered immediately that the *Deutsch* knew how to bargain. Language differences were inversely related to price—the higher the fare, the less the understanding.

The heavier equipment drew immediate attention, with steel plows and harrows of particular interest. Mindful of his experience the year before, Mr. Leopold offered none of his equipment, new or used, on terms. For John, there was a moment of sadness as he studied the plows. He recalled the Volmer auction he had attended several months earlier with his father and Uncle Frederic. A similar plow, although cast iron, was displayed there, and his father had shown real interest in the design. The moment of nostalgia was quickly forgotten as he overheard Denzel Kalb and Mr. Leopold discuss the price of a sulky plow. There was no middle ground and no purchase.

Mr. Leopold had invited a business associate who simply referred to himself as "Landry." He tethered six oxen and a number of horses in a corral behind the store, and announced there was a much larger selection of animals at his place of business south of the city. Landry also brought a small selection of wagons. He knew there was a wainwright in Hays City, and any wagons purchased in Topeka would require disassembly. His wagon stock was priced accordingly.

Gabriel Schuler and Elmer Klein partnered on two wagons, one designed to carry water and the other a stake bed with a large step on the back. They also bought two oxen. Gustav Kunkel bought a high-wheeled freight wagon, and Otto Heimler purchased a smaller version designed for fieldwork. John was interested in Mr. Leopold's inventory, but not ready to buy. Sometime in the future he would require a plow and oxen for the Lundeen Ranch, but just when was open to question. Papers were still being prepared, and he expected to toil first on his father-in-law's acreage before working Hermann's land.

Peter kept a close eye on the membership knowing money spent in Topeka meant fewer purchases from local merchants in Hays City. He wandered through the mercantile reminding members that their future was better served by trading closer to their new home. Equipment and livestock could be transferred by rail, but the council believed it was important to establish a relationship with Hays City merchants. A cloistered lifestyle in Pfeifer fostered suspicion, distrust, and resentment—all of which led the Crown to impose constraints. The same mistake must not be repeated. Trade was a universal language understood by all and essential to building lasting relationships within the community. Albert Wetzel, as a council member, was equally concerned that members avoid duplication. Shared resources worked to the benefit of all, but this required coordination—too many planters and not enough sod knives was a disservice to the community. Sadly, some were caught up in the moment, and Albert's message was disregarded.

Chapter Eight:
St. Anne's: An Intentional Community

---

*"To understand political power aright, and derive
it from its original, we must consider what estate all
men are naturally in, and that is, a state of perfect
freedom to order their actions ... without asking leave
or depending upon the will of any other man ..."*

—John Locke

T he members arrived at the Kansas Pacific station three hours before
the train's scheduled departure. They were told a mechanical problem
in St. Louis had resulted in a two-hour delay. The party would now arrive
in Fort Hays a few hours before dusk, too late to inspect the property they
had just purchased. Three freight cars could be seen parked on the siding,
just east of the terminal. Two carried personal belongings of the Schafer and
Schuler parties, along with the wagons and farm implements purchased
from Mr. Leopold. The third carried livestock. Peter was told the inbound
train had four passenger cars—the last two would carry the party on its
seven-hour trip to Fort Hays. Topeka would be recalled as the place St.
Anne's had taken form and where the party, sight unseen, had selected their
land. Tomorrow was the day of reckoning. Had they made the right choice?
A few of the younger members, notably Hersh Schneider, had pushed for
a trip to the fields immediately upon arrival. That was no longer possible.
Their arrival would be much too late and the surveyor unlikely to have

staked individual parcels. There was also freight to unload, not to mention housekeeping in their temporary quarters.

They were underway at eleven a.m. with everyone on board turning their attention to the passing landscape. The ground looked much like the *Russische* Steppe. If the prairie could support grass, it could do the same for corn, wheat, oats, and barley. Optimism reigned within the party. Their only concern was if ground could be turned before the planting season ended. Corn was not a problem, but the smaller grains could well be. Planting was their first priority.

The train reached Fort Riley in the early afternoon. The garrison was an extension of Manifest Destiny, established to protect wagon trains along the Oregon and Santa Fe Trails as well as far-flung railroad camps. Fort Riley included a depot restaurant that members had already learned to avoid. Judging by the sparse number of clients, others understood the perils of trackside food.

Their train was held awaiting a military transport that was preparing for departure. A large number of horses had broken out of the containment leading to a livestock car. The conductor came aboard to explain that the cavalry was bound for the South Platte and Fort Morgan, where a band of renegade Indians had killed eight settlers—the second attack in as many weeks. He made his announcement not understanding the audience spoke very little English. Anselm boarded behind the conductor and translated, but immediately wished he had not. Emma Heimler was terrified of Indians, certain they were hiding behind every bush. She saw "redskins" as a people who roamed the prairie setting fire to cabins and kidnapping women and children. Anselm assured Emma that the South Platte was much farther west, and the Indians near Hays City were docile. Recognizing she could alarm the children, Emma said nothing more, but remained skeptical.

The train made three more stops, boarding passengers at Ellsworth and Abilene, and taking on fuel and water in Bunker Hill. The party reached Fort Hays at five p.m. Monday, April 26. The three cars carrying freight and working animals were backed to a siding. An eight-man contingent of soldiers assisted with unloading personal belongings and drove livestock to holding pens along the tracks. The wagons and farm equipment were left on the flatcar. The military assistance was both unexpected and welcome. They were led by a sergeant who repeated as often as he could "*Willkommen im Fort Hays.*" A few in the party responded, but it was clear the sergeant's greeting exhausted his command of *Deutsch*. The effort was nonetheless appreciated.

Two merchants were on hand when the travelers arrived. The first carefully examined the farm equipment on the flat car and then distributed a flyer which showed oxen, horses, wagons, farm implements and bags of seed. His name was Daniel Nelson. His flyer also included *Willkommen* across the top and *St. Louis preise in Hays Stadt* along the bottom. Mr. Nelson was not a friendly man. He moved through the party as quickly as possible, behaving as if the exercise was a waste of time. He was gone in a few minutes. A second merchant, unlike Mr. Nelson, relished the contact. His flyer depicted household goods, lamps, bolts of fabric, coffee beans, fruit, and dried meats. The bottom of the flyer showed a farmer exchanging eggs and butter for merchandise. As he moved through the assembled group, he made sure each of the women received a small fabric bag that included tomato seeds. His name was Josef Pallitto—he knew soldiers and railroad workers alike.

Josef was an Italian immigrant whose first stop in America was the slate quarries of Lehigh, Pennsylvania. There he took a much younger bride whose family planned to join relatives in St. Louis. Eager to escape the mines, Josef and his new wife followed with the intent of starting a dry-goods business similar to what his family owned for many years in northern Italy. He quickly found St. Louis to be overrun by establishments of the type he wished to form. A friend of the bride's family told Josef the Army planned a major expansion of Fort Hays, and the area was without a general store. After some discussion, the friend, a merchant himself, agreed to sponsor Josef, and Pallitto's General Store was born.

Anselm told the members that Josef had a contract with the Army to supply eggs, butter, beef, and some quantity of milk, but was often unable to meet his obligation. John liked Mr. Pallitto and was taken by his good nature and persistent attempts to converse. He made note of Josef's contract difficulties. Perhaps there was an opportunity to put Hermann's property to work satisfying the demands of Fort Hays.

118

The party started toward the barracks, but was stopped by Mr. Randolph. He had an announcement. The surveyor and his group would require at least another half-day to stake individual parcels. If the party were to arrive early tomorrow, it would result in a great deal of confusion. The message was not well received. The disappointed party continued the quarter-mile trek to the barracks, where they found the buildings had been recently built, spotlessly clean, with cots for each member. A kitchen, including stove and cooking utensils, was close at hand, as were toilets and water. The centermost structure had two private rooms—the others had one each.

The assumption was that Peter and the recently elected council would be first in line to access the treasured privacy. That was Peter's thinking, but not so the others. Denzel Kalb relinquished his claim to Hersh and Anna Schneider. Felix and Rachel Austerlitz did the same for Otto and Emma Heimler. The remaining council members had already disavowed any right to special treatment. That left Peter as the only member of leadership with a private room. Against Melina's wishes, he retained the space, contending quiet time was needed for planning. John was not surprised.

Their first night in military housing saw the usual shuffle of children and families within buildings and from one building to the next. By now, the party was skilled at rearranging common space to suit their needs. Conditions at the fort were better than any experienced in the past month, and some families were considering making the daily trip from barracks to field and back. Peter knew that once the party dispersed, assembly would be difficult. He scheduled a meeting for the following night.

With time on their hands the next morning, the men busied themselves with a trip to Nelson Feed. They were surprised to find his selection of rolling stock, oxen, and horses every bit as good as what they had seen in Topeka. Like Mr. Leopold, Mr. Nelson had ready access to smaller farm animals, including pigs, goats and sheep. He was also willing to deliver to St. Anne's. Everything about Nelson Feed was appealing, save the owner's unpleasant demeanor. Mr. Nelson pointed toward his six-ox sod-busting team, holding up four fingers then gestured in the direction of a standard two-ox team and held up but one. The message was unmistakable. Nelson's commercial team could break sod at a rate four times faster than the two-ox team, but the cost per acre was prohibitive—two-thirds the price of the land itself.

While the men inspected Mr. Nelson's inventory, the women chose to visit Pallitto's General Store. Their sudden appearance on Main Street caused something of a sensation. Hays City had seen "*Rooshians*" before, but never this number of women and children at the same time. Mr. Pallitto was beside himself. He, like most Kansas merchants, had suffered through 1874, a year which saw many settlers abandon the prairie. His benefactor in St. Louis was right—immigrants were returning, and in large numbers. The women were awestruck by the brightly colored fabrics and strange collection of kitchen utensils. They recognized pots and pans, but simply stared at the other devices, hoping for an epiphany. Their perusal of Josef's merchandise lasted much longer than anticipated.

Mr. Randolph and Anselm had returned earlier than expected. The property was staked and ready for inspection. The party hurriedly set off for the fields, some in newly assembled wagons, others in transportation provided by the railway. Only the youngest were left behind supervised by Rachel Austerlitz and a small group of older children. After a forty-five-minute ride and two longer-than-planned stops, the party arrived at the Township of St. Anne's. Setting foot on the prairie that would soon become their home elicited a wide range of emotions. A few saw stubborn grasslands and wondered if the ground could ever be turned. Others took a moment to embrace family and friends, then bowed their heads in a prayer of thanksgiving. They were free to begin anew without government intervention, and without losing their sons to conscription.

The surveyor and his team had platted the 4,860 acres driving red-capped stakes to mark the boundaries of each parcel. Anselm spread a map on the back of his wagon and sent the families in the direction of their properties. His assistants were positioned to give further guidance. Within the hour, each family had located their farm site. Most simply stood in one corner and contemplated what lay ahead. They tried to imagine fields full with grain and a bountiful harvest. Those with a less-active imagination saw only tedium. The prairie grass was already two to three feet tall and could easily swallow a child in a few steps. The party also made another unpleasant discovery—rattlesnakes, their presence easily charted by the occasional shriek.

Anselm rode through the property and found the new owners cognizant of the difficult task ahead, but generally pleased. The quality of soil and access to water were not in dispute. He was relieved since parcels were subject to on-site approval. The lone dissenter was Luise Kunkel. She had been angry upon leaving Pfeifer, and complained incessantly throughout the journey.

"My neighbors have better property," Luise contended.

"What makes their land better?" Anselm asked.

Luise had no answer.

"I can show you other parcels," Anselm offered, but Luise declined content with her initial choice and the disruption she had caused.

The remainder of the day was spent visiting with neighbors and planning how best to approach the task at hand. There was little time and the prairie soil would be difficult to break. John wondered if their descendants had felt the same way a century before, having been abandoned on the *Russische* Steppe. Theirs was perhaps a more arduous task, but similarities existed. The success of the Schafer party was anything but assured. No grain hung from rafters, nor were vegetables or cured meat cached in root cellars. John thought of Maria and her pregnancy. His father-in-law had a boundless need for control—keeping the family under one roof was just one example. He disliked the idea, but for the short term it was best for Maria and the child she carried.

That evening the party assembled in the area between the barracks and dining hall to address questions yet to be resolved. Peter expected the meeting to be contentious. The type of acceptable housing within the forty-acre township site was the first topic. As a result of his dogged determination, Peter had managed to convince the council that St. Anne's should be created in the image of Pfeifer. Homes would adjoin one another, with courtyards to accommodate small animals and a garden. All construction within the township must be wood-frame. Earthen homes were acceptable as shelter, but only on the member's farmland, not within the township. The party knew what was coming and there was an audible stir as the meeting began. Even the council itself was conflicted.

Albert Wetzel, the youngest council member, asked Eduard Hauer to speak for those who disliked the limitation. A wood frame home was beyond the reach of Eduard, and his wife desperately wanted the security of neighbors. The membership was sympathetic, but Peter had done his homework. By a narrow majority, the *Gemeinde* supported both the separation of home and field, and wood frame construction within the township site. The core of St. Anne's would be much like their village in *Russen* with adjoining courtyards, church and community center. Earthen homes were not included in that vision.

The discussion of common facilities came next. The surveyor had set aside, within the township site, one acre for church and school, one-half acre for a community center, and five acres for commercial development. The remainder was designated as homesites—one-quarter acre included with purchase of farmland. Emma Heimler thought the first structure should be their place of worship. A church would be pleasing to God and bring blessings to the community. The council was unmoved. The church was arguably the most expensive to construct and served only one purpose. Circumstances demanded a more utilitarian building, one that provided space for worship, community meetings, and a school. After limited debate, it was decided a community center took precedence. No date for construction was set. Planting and personal shelter came first.

Peter thought the five acres were more property than necessary for commercial development. St. Anne's was sure to attract some merchants, but extensive development, without a rail spur, was unlikely. St. Anne's would always be a village. That was fine with Peter and the council. A few small towns had paid railroads to extend tracks to their location. The growth that naturally followed came with an undesirable element—transient laborers and the raucous element attached to cattle drives. St. Anne's required access to rail transportation, but a rail hub would be antithetical to the village they hoped to create. Further discussion on commercial development was put aside, though it was agreed no business should be permitted to open without council approval.

The next item for discussion was ownership and disposition of streams, two of which flowed through the property. Burkhard Wetzel had made tentative plans for what he called a "slight diversion" of the smaller stream to feed a pothole on his land. The council saw water as a common resource and had already decided that a dam should be constructed to enlarge the naturally occurring pond on the larger stream. The reservoir so created would be available for use by the *Gemeinde*. Burkhard's pond was contained within his property and inaccessible to others. He was told that until there was a better understanding of stream flow in late summer, no diversion would be permitted.

Denzel Kalb next suggested, as he had done earlier, that consideration be given to construction of four common wells, with at least two dug before winter set in. His argument got temporary support until Anselm recited the often used axiom: "Water is within 300 feet of any farm in Kansas, straight down." Drilling was costly and dangerous, with no guarantee of success. For the moment, water for home and field was dependent on nature. Peter called for adjournment, but not before Mr. Randolph thanked the party for its purchase of land. Final papers had been signed and on-site inspections completed. Speaking for the *Gemeinde*, Peter thanked both Mr. Randolph and Anselm for their assistance.

Hersh and Anna Schneider, their children, and Albert Wetzel were the first to leave the barracks the following morning. Broken clouds revealed a sliver of light as they set out for St. Anne's in two wagons, the first pulled by an ox, the other by a pair of horses. Both livestock and wagons had been jointly purchased from Mr. Nelson. Anna, pregnant with her fifth child, rode with her three boys in the first wagon. Albert and Hersh followed close behind and carried food for a week, bags of seed, a large tarpaulin, hand tools, a rifle, plow, and sod knife. The Schneider family and Albert Wetzel had adjoining parcels and planned to stay in or under their wagons until their earthen homes were complete, returning to Hays City only when necessary.

By midmorning, they had cut the prairie grass where the properties adjoined and arranged the wagons and tarpaulin to provide shelter. Anna, terrified of snakes, beat the cleared ground and found none. Hersh then became the first in the party to break sod, selecting an area on the western corner of his property. His eldest son guided the ox, while Hersh did his best to control the plow. Anna walked alongside scraping clods of earth from the steel blade. The younger boys carried water and gathered firewood. After an hour of backbreaking work, Hersh realized that even an acre per day may not be possible. He would have liked to make a second pass, but there was too little time. Seeds for spring wheat, barley and oats should be in the ground by now with corn soon to follow. The latter would take up much of his acreage. Hersh could not justify a horse-drawn planter, relying instead on a hand-held device with a pointed tube and box holding seeds on top. The tip was inserted in the ground, the handle squeezed, and a few seeds dropped in the hole—a tedious process.

While Hersh was breaking ground, Albert was busy cutting blocks of sod for each of their earthen homes. The horses struggled to break the tough prairie grass, but proved capable for pulling the sod knife. Albrecht Schafer, or more likely one of his brothers, would be joining them in a few days to help with construction.

Hersh and Albert had purchased their ox and two horses while Anselm and the surveyor were staking property lines. They were ahead of the others, many of whom could still be found at Nelson Feed. All were eager to get underway, but Mr. Nelson behaved as if the Schafer party represented an unwelcome intrusion. Peter and John were at the feed store as well. Peter's intent was to purchase one horse, a pair of oxen, and two wagons. He also planned to negotiate a contract with Mr. Nelson's team of commercial sod-busters. In a week's time, his team of six oxen and heavy sod-breaking plow could turn thirty to forty acres—two weeks work for the usual one- or two-oxen harness. Peter intended to contract for six days, but the commercial team would not be available for more than a week.

While they waited for the sodbusters, Peter's two eldest sons, with John's help, would begin breaking ground using their own team. Peter hoped to plant at least seventy acres in corn and the remainder in spring wheat, oats, and barley. A garden must also be planted in the next few weeks, large enough so that one-half of the produce could be stored in root cellars for winter consumption. Planting and maintaining the garden fell to Maria and her mother.

John accompanied his father-in-law to help transport horse, oxen, and wagons to St. Anne's. The trip gave him the opportunity to judge the quality of Mr. Nelson's stock. He would, in time, need his own oxen for use on the Lundeen Ranch. The oxen and several head of cattle were located on the adjoining ranch owned by William Grant. Some were in a fenced area, but most could be seen in the distance grazing on unclaimed land west of the feed store.

John was intrigued by the idea of raising cattle on the Lundeen Ranch. There was a broad expanse to the north that offered endless pasture. He would need a market, but that was something to discuss with Josef Pallitto, assuming he was still having difficulty meeting his contract obligations to the Army. Satisfied that good oxen were available, he returned to Nelson Feed to find Peter had already left with his new horse and wagon. John harnessed the oxen to the remaining wagon and returned to Fort Hays where he found Albrecht and his brother attaching wheels and tongue to the water wagon purchased by Elmer Klein and Gabriel Schuler in Topeka. John split the team, taking the Klein wagon and starting for St. Anne's. The other ox and wagon were left with the Schafer boys who—as directed by their father— went in search of a house builder that had been recommended by Mr. Randolph.

They found Cyrus Larsen at his sawmill. He had several logs in his yard, along with a selection of milled lumber. Peter wanted Cyrus to build a frame house and small barn on his township property. The barn may be unnecessary, since common shelter was certain to be constructed, but just when was uncertain. Better to be safe than risk the loss of valuable livestock.

The Schafer boys had anticipated some difficulty in explaining their purpose to Cyrus Larsen. They were relieved to learn that Felix Austerlitz had preceded them. The builder had a rough sketch of the Austerlitz house, and Albrecht simply drew an addition while managing to convey there would be two families under the same roof. In a few minutes, there was understanding. Cyrus told the young men that he would visit the site with a more complete drawing. They could expect completion of the home within thirty days. The two boys next made their way to Pallitto's General Store where they purchased a tarpaulin, hand tools and a small quantity of food.

The buying frenzy that was hoped for by merchants Nelson and Pallitto never materialized, but there was reason for optimism. Mr. Pallitto, more so than Mr. Nelson, believed the Schafer party would succeed. They were far better prepared than their predecessors. Sales would grow in time, but for the moment there were constraints. Some in the party had few resources and all were reticent to spend in the face of an uncertain future. Josef believed his strangely dressed *Deutsch* neighbors would see more than one year on the prairie, and return again and again as buyers. He expected a short period of inactivity as most in the party had satisfied their immediate needs, and more than one-half planned to overnight in the fields.

Luise Kunkel was not one of them. She despised sleeping on the ground and saw no reason to do so with the relative comfort of the barracks close at hand. She was happy to watch children, sew, or shop for others—anything that created distance between herself and dirt. She discovered her husband planned on living in a sod home, perhaps for as much as a year. The prospect of dirt underfoot and overhead was simply too much for Luise.

"You treat me as swine," she told her husband. "Look at Melina Schafer and Rachel Austerlitz. They have real homes."

"Our savings went to land," Gustav said. "Nothing remains for a home."

Finally, after a series of public debates, Gabriel Shuler took pity on Gustav and offered to lend him money, using the Kunkel land as collateral. Luise was momentarily pleased—a condition not likely to persist. Peter, like many others, did not like Luise Kunkel, but was happy to see the possibility of another residence within the township. That made three committed, and he expected the Kalb, Geist and Schuler families to build there as well. A village required homes, a few merchants, and a common gathering place. St Anne's was off to a good start.

* * * * *

Necessity gave rise to the sod house as primary shelter. Often, there were no logs suitable for construction and no milled lumber. Settlers had little choice but to use the only commodity not in short supply—prairie sod. Their decision was helped along by the dearth of another resource, money. Sod houses, known as soddies, were mostly alike—rectangular, sixteen by twenty feet, sometimes larger. There was usually one division within the house, and an extension to accommodate a fireplace. Windows were the only real expense, and there were few of those. The window frame was designed to float so that glass would not break as the soddy inevitably settled. If glass was too expensive, oiled paper was used as an alternative.

A typical sod house was six feet tall with the topmost blocks smaller than the base to promote strength and stability. The roof might be constructed of dimensional lumber, but most often consisted of small logs. In either case, it was also covered with sod, though much smaller pieces than those used to construct walls. Supports were necessary to prevent cave-ins. Sod houses were expedient. They could be built in five days—fewer if neighbors helped in construction. Soddies remained cool in the summer and retained heat in the winter, but there were complications— whatever was contained in each block became a part of the house. Vermin emerged from everywhere, and small bits of dirt fell endlessly from overhead. Walls were plastered with a combination of mud, lime, and sand, while cheesecloth was spread across the ceiling to catch falling particles.

A family of six to eight often called a soddy their home. In sub-freezing temperatures, the earthen home became more crowded as humans made room for valued animals. Life in a sod house represented a significant adjustment—one not considered when immigrants chose to make their home in America. Many of the *Volga Deutsch* left behind a secure court-yard, including a frame house, summer kitchen, out buildings, and shelter for small animals. An earthen home was a significant change, but not one for the better. Small wonder that aside from family security and enough to eat, getting out of the soddy was high on every settlers' list of priorities.

* * * *

Each day saw a larger number of families overnighting at St. Anne's. They brought wagons, seed, tools, oxen, and a desire to get on with the task of breaking ground. The first of the "overnighters," Albert Wetzel and the Schneiders, greeted the members as each arrived. Having made it through two nights without incident, they were now seasoned prairie dwellers.

On the third day, Hersh shot a smallish white-tailed deer, and the animal was now hung from a three-legged support to bleed out. Hersh killed the animal to determine the quality of meat if cut into strips and dried. There was no assurance that the fields would provide enough food to carry them through the winter. Game provided a ready supplement. No one in the party was a skilled butcher, but Denzel Kalb had seen it done and agreed to lend assistance. The night before, Freidrich Schafer had gone foraging and located a large patch of berries just outside their eastern boundary. It was too early to harvest, but the fruit would be a pleasant addition to their diet later in the summer.

The experience of Hersh and Albert made it painfully obvious the prairie sod would test oxen and plow alike. The members did better each day, but early on eight to ten hours were required to turn one acre. The outcome was not pretty. Rows were uneven and large clods were still much in evidence. The Kansas prairie, like the *Russische* Steppe, was proving to be a difficult master.

Gabriel Schuler, who had consistently maintained that horses could match the work of oxen, learned he was mistaken. His team stumbled and was often stopped altogether. Coaxing and the occasional switch made little difference. After an hour of exhausting work, Gabriel pulled the yolk from the horses. He needed to buy or borrow oxen. His introduction to "sodbusting" confirmed the admonition of others before them. The prairie farm was not created in days, but rather months.

Peter spent the morning with Mr. Culp. Formative questions on the *Town and Grazing Company* remained unanswered, and somehow St. Anne's had to be recorded on the state registry. Mr. Culp assured him that he could complete the necessary paperwork. Peter returned to the barracks to gather his wife, who was among the few yet to see her new homesite. He was surprised to find Melina in the company of Father Lenkeit, a Roman Catholic priest. He learned of the Schafer party's intention to create a village near Hays City on a recent trip to Topeka. The information came to him through a chance meeting with eight immigrant families, who just arrived from New York. One of the women asked the priest if he knew of any *Volga Deutsch* arriving in the past few weeks. The priest did not, but was on his way to the Kansas Pacific terminal and would ask there. He found an agent who knew of the Schafer party's plan to create a Catholic settlement near Hays City.

Peter asked the priest, "Do you happen to remember the woman's name?" He was hopeful Meta Gerber had been released from quarantine and found her way to the Kansas prairie. If that were the case, the Gerbers and those traveling in their company would be a welcome addition to St. Anne's.

"I didn't catch a name," he said. "But they were *Deutsch*."

Father Lenkeit had come to Fort Hays hoping to learn more of the

Schafer party. He was something of an itinerant, his flock scattered throughout central Kansas. A large Roman Catholic settlement was intriguing and he asked to join Peter and Melina on their ride to St. Anne's.

En route, the cleric explained that he began his priesthood in Konigsburg before immigrating with a small group of settlers to Pennsylvania. The group had dispersed, and the priest, unable to form a parish of his own, had requested assignment to the American West. Father Lenkeit was now resident pastor to Fort Riley and Fort Hays, in addition to serving the ecclesiastical needs of the surrounding communities. Peter assured him that St. Anne's would be excited to have a man of the cloth in their company. Several weeks had passed since the members last attended mass. Even in Topeka, the best they could do was a prayer service. Arriving in St. Anne's, Father Lenkeit was immediately surrounded.

"Can you celebrate the Eucharist?" Emma Heimler asked.

The priest declined. "I have neither proper vestments nor sacred vessels, but mass is conducted in the Fort Hays chapel every Sunday morning. I expect to see all of you there."

The priest then dispatched the families to their respective farm sites, where he prayed briefly with each and blessed the newly purchased land. Before he left, Father Lenkeit asked Peter if St. Anne's planned to build a church. Peter told him that a community center came first. The priest said nothing, but was clearly disappointed.

While the community gathered around Father Lenkeit, John, Maria and her mother located the two Schafer boys clearing grass from the area where their house and small barn would be constructed. Albrecht passed the scythe to Maria, much to his mother's dislike, then harnessed plow to oxen. Freidrich marked an area for the garden on what he thought would be the south side of the house. He really had no idea where the house would be placed, but was simply eager to get underway. Albrecht then took his first pass at breaking Kansas sod.

With John prodding the oxen, Albrecht struggled to divide centuries of entangled roots. Maria left her scythe and joined the fray, pushing clods from the steel face of the plow. Melina watched in horror as her pregnant daughter toiled within a few feet of a jumpy steel blade. A half-hour's work left two very uneven rows, with some of the ground missed entirely.

Melina, after watching her daughter engage in heavy fieldwork, sat head in hand, exhausted by the ordeal.

At their mother's insistence, Albrecht and Freidrich returned to the barracks. Tomorrow was Father Lenkeit's mass and Melina wanted the entire family to attend. Only the Schneiders, Breits and Albert Wetzel remained in the fields. The day dawned bright and clear. Members dug deep within their trunks, but had long since discarded appropriate dress. The chapel was available to multiple denominations, and they were delayed by a Lutheran service. Upon entering, the party found a rotted ceiling, hastily constructed pews, a single cross somewhat askew, and a work table for an altar. Peter understood why Father Lenkeit was eager to build a church.

They also found a very animated priest. This was likely the largest congregation the chapel had seen. The left side of the nave was occupied by the Schafer party, whose numbers spilled into the right rear. The regulars—a few townspeople, but most military—filled the first four rows on the right front. Father Lenkeit said mass in English, but repeated parts of the homily and Eucharistic prayer in *Deutsch*. Following the mass, he invited everyone to gather in the adjoining hall. As a courtesy to the priest, the congregation did so, although military personnel and Hays City residents quickly departed. Father Lenkeit also left, bound for his second mass of the day.

Before leaving he introduced the Schafer party to the Reinhart Muller and Paulus Richter families. Both homesteaded four years earlier, emigrating from the village of Holstein. They fared as well as could be expected, until last year's grasshopper infestation. Crops had been destroyed, and Reinhart and Paulus considered selling or simply abandoning their farms. With Father Lenkeit's help, the men had found temporary work at Fort Hays, but the ordeal cost them the money painstakingly set aside to build small frame homes. They would have to make do with soddies for at least two more years.

* * * * *

The Jeffersonian ideal of making land available to individual farmers was a long-standing goal of nineteenth century lawmakers. The movement gained momentum in the 1850s driven by the desire of both the Free Soil and New Republican Parties to keep wealthy southern planters from gaining access to public lands. The position was summarized in the words of Galusha A. Grow, a Pennsylvania lawmaker, in a February 1860 speech before the House of Representatives.

> "Why should not the legislation of the country be so changed as to prevent for the future the evils of land monopoly, by setting apart the vast and unoccupied territories of the union, and consecrating them forever in homes for free men."

Grow's sentiments took form in the Homestead Act signed into law by Abraham Lincoln in May of 1862. It has been hailed as the most enduring and significant act of the nineteenth century. Under its provisions, 270 million acres—ten percent of the United States—was given away, making it possible for any adult citizen or intended citizen to lay claim to 160 acres of public land.

The homesteader need only work the land and build a home—earthen, shanty, or frame. After five years and evidence improvements had been made, the land was theirs, secured by a filing fee of $18.00 and nothing more. The process by which title was bestowed came to be known as "proving up."

Many homesteaders, and those who acquired land from railroads or land speculators, never saw their fifth year. Among the reasons were insufficient funds, lack of farming experience, poor site selection, weather, and not uncommonly—illness or death. Some have suggested homesteaders needed more land to succeed. More ground meant a larger harvest and a potential surplus, but methods were primitive. Maintaining anything near 160 acres required a large family and willing neighbors. The window to plant and harvest was confined to a few weeks. Lacking funds and manpower, most cultivated far less.

Survival became the objective, as defined by the autobiographical sketch of Rose Wilder Lane.

> "It was a saying in the Dakotas that the Government bet a quarter-section against fifteen dollars and five years hard work that the land

would starve a man out in less than five years. My father won the bet. It took seven successive years of complete crop failure, with work, weather, and sickness that wrecked his health permanently, and interest rates of thirty-six percent on money to buy food to dislodge us from the land ..."

The technology to escape this desperate cycle was still in its infancy and, when available, beyond the means of the prairie farmer. For some, borrowing was an option, but one bad crop meant foreclosure. Faced with insurmountable odds, more than sixty percent of new farms fell short of fulfilling the American dream. The Homestead Act was not without its critics. Problems with implementation and widespread fraud and abuse were commonplace, but no one denied its impact on westward migration.

* * * * *

Peter and Nicholas questioned the homesteaders on their planting schedule and selection of crops.

Reinhart warned, "Spring wheat will disappoint," then added, "Stalks will flower early, but struggle in the summer heat."

"Corn should be your dominant crop," Paulus said. "Plant only limited quantities of the smaller grains."

Reinhart and Paulus recommended early planting of vegetables, and the purchase of at least one cow.

"Take your game in late fall," Reinhart said, "Meat is more easily preserved then."

Peter and Nicholas listened intently, this being the first opportunity to speak with anyone completing the planting to harvest cycle.

As they were leaving the parish hall, Reinhart glanced up at towering thunderheads above and absolute blackness below. He suggested they start for home, but after hearing the clap of thunder decided that travel was unwise. Suddenly, the heavens opened. Sheets of rain obscured the barracks, and tin roofing cartwheeled through the rail yard. The rain became more intense, and within minutes a wall of water from the slightly elevated fort broke through the entrance to the dining hall. The barracks were high enough to escape the torrent, but a curtain of muddy water surrounded each of the buildings. Hail began to fall, some as large as two-cent coinage. Through the din, animals could be heard crying in agony. The downpour continued, grew stronger, then, just as suddenly as it began, was over. Debris was strewn throughout the dining hall and kitchen.

The men quickly set out for the corral. The horses had broken through a section of fence, and several strayed from the compound. Two were bloodied by the hail. Canvas tops on a row of military wagons were shredded and one, the top still intact, was on its side. Severe weather was no stranger to the *Volga Deutsch*, but this storm came upon them far more quickly than any experienced in *Russen*. The deluge moved off, but the sky was still very dark in the direction of St. Anne's. The party prayed that those who remained in the fields were safe.

Gabriel Schuler and Denzel Kalb set out for St. Anne's before daybreak well ahead of the main party. Gabriel was concerned for the horses he had left tethered, and both feared for the well-being of the "overnighters." They found Anna Schneider alone with the children. Hersh and Albert were looking for animals freed by the storm. They searched well into the night before running low on kerosene.

Anna quickly related their experience. Strong winds had torn their tarpaulin from its anchors, and lodged the tent occupied by the Schafer boys in a nearby tree. Well to the north they had seen a funnel-shaped cloud touch the ground appearing to destroy everything in its path. The funnel had disappeared in the blackness followed by the rain and hail. Without a tarpaulin, they took cover under the wagons until the storm subsided. Early in the evening, they smelled and then saw smoke, but had no idea of its origin. Anna planned to return to the fort in the evening, with no desire to return until their sod home was complete. Her husband and Albert would stay on.

Hersh was first to return to camp. He had three oxen in tow and had seen two others grazing in the distance. There were still two horses to be located. Albert's arrival provided the answer. He had the two oxen and one of the horses. The second horse was a short distance away in a small depression. The animal had broken its leg, and sometime during the night was disemboweled by wolves. The carcass would require burial, since it was located close to their camp. Gabriel and Denzel helped retrieve the tent and tarpaulin, while the others, having arrived from Fort Hays, began construction of sturdier confinement for the animals.

Just before noon, Jeremiah Olsen and his commercial team of six oxen arrived. They pulled a large wagon carrying several breaking plows and an assortment of replacement parts. Peter had convinced Mr. Nelson to adjust Jeremiah's schedule, suggesting there was more potential work in St. Anne's than elsewhere in central Kansas. Jeremiah agreed, sending a smaller team to meet prior commitments. John was a half-mile behind and quickly staked the area to be broken.

Within minutes the team began turning sod with a precision built on decades of experience. One could argue that the ground had been softened by rain the day before, but that would be unfair to Mr. Olsen. He and his team were breaking sod in straight rows at a rate five times what Hersh Schneider had achieved. The commercial team stopped only to water the oxen and exchange plows. Mr. Olsen waved at the children and acknowledged the adults, who reluctantly returned to their overburdened single- and double-oxen rigs. He and his co-workers worked until sunset, then spent the night alongside their wagon, where it appeared food and whiskey were served in equal amounts. They quieted early. The others who were camped at St. Anne's were happy for the respite. The Olsen team had turned five acres of virgin prairie in fewer than seven hours.

Peter was pleased. St. Anne's was showing the first signs of becoming a colony. Albrecht and his brother finished breaking ground for vegetables. Gabriel Schuler followed the two Schafer boys and found that prairie sod once cut by oxen could be easily turned by horse-drawn teams. The Schafer garden now looked as tidy as any in Pfeifer. Melina and Maria began planting lettuce and tomatoes for fresh consumption with carrots, beets, turnips and beans destined for the root cellar. Still to be planted were cucumbers, peas, and cabbage, but this required a visit to the general store. Albert Wetzel made progress as well, cutting enough blocks with the sod knife to establish the footprint for two sod homes.

The train carrying the Gerber family and their traveling companions arrived at Fort Hays in midafternoon. Meta was told the *"Rooshians"* returned each day just before dusk. She was eager to reunite with friends last seen in Bremerhaven. The first wagon Meta saw was driven by Otto Heimler. He was not a part of the original Schafer Party and Meta wondered if the Kansas Pacific agent had been mistaken. Then came the next wagon and two familiar faces—Burkhard Wetzel and his wife Elma, followed by yet another, Nicholas Geist.

Meta was elated. She jumped from the wagon and embraced her friends before realizing she had forgotten her companions. She motioned for them to join the gathering and quickly introduced the three families. All were from the village of Neu-Warenburg. The Baumanns and Webers were among the first to have farmed their daughter colony, while Christof Acker was a miller by trade.

They began as a loosely configured group of forty-two travelers, driven by the same circumstances that brought the Schafer party to America. Two of the families had moved on to join relatives near Albuquerque, two planned to homestead in Colorado, and one remained in Topeka, finding it necessary to take employment. The Baumanns, Webers, and Ackers had followed Meta hoping to find a colony similar to that left behind in *Russen*. Meta's description of the Schafer party was so compelling that the settlers had traveled from Topeka with all of their possessions. Nicholas Geist, as a member of the council, welcomed the families and told them that there was plenty of room in the barracks. In the morning, all would travel to St. Anne's.

The membership needed a break, and Meta's arrival provided cause for celebration. Denzel Kalb happened upon a source for potato vodka in Hays City. It was a powerful drink—one the party knew well. Corn whiskey was also available, more than enough to fuel the festivities.

Meta began the evening by describing what happened to the family after the Schafer party left Bremerhaven. She was held at the *Auswandererhaus* for three days, while her husband and the children stayed in shelter provided by the *Hausmutter*. The *Strasburg* was the next steamship scheduled to sail from Bremerhaven. Unless Meta was cleared in time, she and the family would miss the sailing and almost certainly find it necessary to return to Pfeifer. Suddenly, without explanation, the American consul intervened insisting that Meta be given another chance. She was taken to a private examination room. The same questions were asked, with a few additions having to do with family history. Meta passed the examination. When she emerged from the exam room, the consul asked what her intentions were upon reaching America. Meta simply expressed her desire to farm in Kansas alongside her neighbors. The consul penned a note for Meta to carry to *Norddeutscher Lloyd*, instructing the steamship company to re-issue tickets for passage on the *Strasburg*, bound for New York. A separate document was prepared—sealed by wax and carrying an official stamp. It directed immigration officials to assist the Gerbers in finding the most efficient rail transportation from New York to Topeka.

Two days later, the Gerber family boarded the *Strasburg*. Meta's bunk was immediately behind Elise Weber's, and the two became friends, sharing stories of children and community. When Elise discovered that the Gerbers were bound for Kansas, she insisted Meta and her family join the Neu-Warenburg party. The voyage was uneventful. They suffered the indignities of steerage—cramped quarters, putrid rations, and barely adequate facilities. Blessedly, none in the party had experienced *seekranheit*, and there was no contagion.

The party arrived at Castle Garden along New York's Battery waterfront. All passed inspection. Meta's note from the American consul was treated with the respect it deserved. Authorities escorted the family to the rail terminal explaining alternative routes and assisting with the purchase of tickets. The Neu-Warenburg party followed Meta's lead, and within twenty-four hours, all were westbound on the Atlantic and Great Western Railway.

Peter was late to the celebration, having spent a disappointing one-half hour with his wife and Freidrich. His second eldest had just announced he was joining Kurt Haus and Gabriel's son, Klaus Schuler. The trio planned to leave for Dakota Territory by week's end. Peter had suspected as much, but not Melina, who was astonished by her son's decision. She begged him to reconsider, but to no avail. Freidrich's decision confirmed Peter's worst fears. Retaining youthful leadership would be a challenge.

Melina was in no mood for celebration, but Peter dutifully made an appearance. He introduced himself to the newcomers taking the Gerbers and their companions aside to explain the *Town and Grazing Company*, now known as the *St. Anne's Company*. The description of individual and common property resulted in confusion, so much so that the Webers questioned the wisdom of such an arrangement.

John was listening and seized control of the discussion. He began by describing the process in which property could be purchased, spending little time on particulars, since the *company* was already formed and nothing in the charter was likely to change. Land was held for sale by four principal buyers, including the railroad, and each purchase included a lot within the township site. Farmland carried title, and membership came with access to common property. John chose not to mention the requirement that homes within the township site must be of wood-frame construction, leaving that unpopular condition to his father-in-law. The newcomers still had a question or two, but decided that any plan acceptable to Meta was acceptable to them. They had followed her across America—why not one more step? All of this was somewhat premature since no action could be taken until the Neu-Warenburg party was accepted by the *Gemeinde*, but that action was virtually assured. The group adopted Meta Gerber in her time of need. The kindness was sure to be repaid.

John and Denzel Kalb met the newcomers just after daybreak to begin the process of selecting farmland. They were guided by a new map, which more carefully displayed access to water and the township center. The Baumann family chose a parcel on the far eastern perimeter of the 4,860 acre parcel, but one with good southern exposure. The Webers chose, then returned to the fields, and finally decided on their first selection. Christof Acker withheld his decision. He hoped to build a grist mill on the larger stream and make his home inside the mill, or on adjoining property. The Gerbers were destined for the fields and a soddy. The Baumann and Weber families planned on wood-frame homes within the township site. Elise settled on a lot that bordered the Schafer farm. The Webers had three unwed daughters, aged fourteen to eighteen—all eligible, attractive, and good wedding stock. The Schafers were a family of means with unmarried sons.

Late in the afternoon, Cyrus Larsen and four of his carpenters arrived on wagons heavily laden with lumber. Rather than waiting for Cyrus to visit St. Anne's, Peter had met the builder at his place of business to finalize construction plans. The workers expected to begin early the following day, working on both the Schafer and Austerlitz homes. Peter was riding with

Cyrus in the lead wagon. Before becoming a carpenter, Cyrus had farmed for three years. He confirmed the advice offered by Reinhart Muller and Paulus Richter. Corn should be the favored crop, planted at a rate three times that of spring wheat. He also recommended a horse-drawn planter given the size of the Schafer farm. Peter was already leaning in that direction, having watched others struggle with the hand-held alternative.

Upon arrival, he dispatched Albrecht to Nelson Feed to purchase the planter. It would be the second such device in St. Anne's. Gabriel Schuler, who hoped to plant at least fifty acres in corn, sent word through Anselm to ship a planter he saw at Mr. Leopold's Kansas Mercantile and Feed. Both devices required but one horse, and were capable of planting twelve acres per day. They also planted in orderly rows making cultivation far easier. There was some question whether the machine could be used for smaller grains, but if unsatisfactory, broadcasting by hand was an acceptable alternative.

Maria was sick for the second time in as many weeks. Her illness troubled John, but he was assured by Melina the *morgendliche ubelkeit* was a common queasiness associated with pregnancy and easily remedied by a day of rest. John's brooding depressed Maria. She told him to find something to do, suggesting he inspect the Lundeen Ranch and the narrow corridor of land leading to the soon-to-be purchased property. A few of the members had discovered a large bird the carpenters referred to as a "turkey." John saw four of these along the corridor, likely driven west by activity in St. Anne's. He also saw a very large deer, perhaps twice the size of that taken earlier by Hersh Schneider. Both the bird and deer were skittish, but a skilled marksman should have no difficulty making a kill.

Knowing the surveyor had not staked the property, he brought one of Anselm's original maps. At first, he saw nothing unusual about the thirty-acre strip of land. It was undisturbed and looked much like the remainder of the prairie. After traveling a short distance, John noticed a small stone outcropping, which traversed the property in a northwesterly direction, and continued as far as he could see. This would be the material Henry Bissing referred to as "limestone." In the distance, which he knew to be the Lundeen Ranch, the rise became a ridge, perhaps six to eight feet in height.

He reached a break near the westernmost boundary and saw to his right the remnants of a cabin, a corner of which had been burned. As he moved to the far side of the structure, his horse suddenly shied and backed away. John could do nothing to stop the movement. He carefully dismounted, thinking it might be a snake, then jabbed the ground with a stick. As he pushed the grass aside, John saw what appeared to be a cover made of tree branches, and lashed together with rawhide. The cover, long since overtaken by the prairie, was resting on rough-hewn limestone bricks. He forced a rock through the cover, and heard an unmistakable splash. A larger rock gave the same report. This was too deep for a cistern. John had found a "dug" well; unusual given water was commonly 200 feet or more below the surface.

His first instinct was to immediately return to the township and share the discovery, but he changed his mind deciding instead to continue along the western perimeter of the ranch. John could see an area of about thirty acres that had been turned under at some point in the past. He guessed it had been planted in corn, and since overtaken by prairie grass. The ground would be much easier to plow than virgin soil. He retraced his steps, crossing the limestone ridge and heading in a northerly direction. There was grass as far as he could see. If he decided to raise cattle, land for grazing was plentiful. The only area that had been disturbed was an acre or two which had been recently burned, likely the result of a prairie fire.

John returned to St. Anne's where he told Freidrich of his find. Peter, standing nearby, overheard the conversation and immediately asked where? He smiled when told the well was on Hermann's property. His brother had no end of good fortune—first, an unexpected inheritance, then a shipboard association with two successful American businessmen, and now a dug well. Peter sought out Felix Austerlitz, and the pair left immediately to investigate. They secured a wagon and grabbed a length of rope, scythe, and a bucket. Their plan was to determine the depth of the well and quality of water drawn.

Albrecht was assigned the task of dragging the harrow over ground broken by Mr. Olsen's sodbusters. As was his custom, he inexplicably stopped—not to rest horses or fetch water—but for reasons known only to himself. A shout from John brought him back to reality. Freidrich, now within a few days of leaving St. Anne's, came to his brother's aid taking the reins. Albrecht simply wandered away. Peter expected more from his eldest son, and he wished Albrecht was the son headed for the Dakota Territory.

Late that afternoon, John and Freidrich were able to experiment with the new corn planter. The device allowed three rows of seed to be planted at a constant depth and regular intervals. A weighted board was dragged behind to cover the newly planted seeds. In a few hours, a third of the harrowed ground was planted. The device had laid down more seed in an hour than ten workers planting by hand.

Peter and Felix took only minutes to confirm that John's discovery was indeed a well. The water tasted sweet and was very cool. The depth was thought to be 90 to 110 feet, shallow when compared to the depth that Anselm suggested necessary to reach water. Peter sampled only a small quantity given the accumulated debris. Some form of weighted screen must be devised, but that meant a cranking system was needed; hand pulling simply took too much time. John was excited about the well, more so than Peter or Felix, both of whom thought it too distant to be anything but a novelty. He liked the idea of another source for potable water, but for now several tasks assigned by his father-in-law took precedence.

John and the Schafer boys toiled each day from dawn to dusk. They spent all but a few nights in the fields returning to Hays City only when necessary. The schedule was unrelenting, and both Peter and the council were pleased by the growing number of fields planted, gardens seeded, and homes under construction. There were a few exceptions to the daily regimen. The periodic visitor or passing thunderstorm might lead to a short break, and every Sunday the members joined Father Lenkeit for celebration of the Eucharist.

By the third week of May, most in the party had relocated from the barracks to St. Anne's. The Schafer and Austerlitz homes were reaching the point of occupation, and Gabriel Schuler, using a different builder, was midway through construction. The Webers had solicited help in raising the roof, and were now working to enclose their structure. The Kunkels were behind the others. Luise demanded a larger home, and Gustav successfully resisted. Cyrus Larsen took time away from his larger projects to frame and roof the home, but it appeared that the Kunkels would begin their residency using tarps for a wall. Luise was beside herself. Hersh Schneider and Albert Wetzel had completed their soddies and taken up residence, as did their neighbor to the south, Eduard Hauer. The latter had first thought of building a frame house within the township site, but doing so would have exhausted his reserves. Finances suggested Eduard was better off using construction materials provided by nature.

The biggest surprise came from Denzel Kalb. He had more than enough money to build within the township, but had decided instead to build a soddy. The decision troubled Peter, who feared Denzel was likely to petition the council to build a permanent wood frame home on his farmland. Peter expected that some council members would be sympathetic to Denzel's request. If permission were given, others would follow and Peter's model township would be threatened.

The sea of prairie grass first seen by Henry Bissing, Nicholas Geist and Denzel Kalb now looked very different. Neat rows carved by professional sodbusters notched the prairie along with less precise cuts taken by those with one- and two-oxen teams. The latter tended to wander and lacked depth except where plowed again by horses. Tidy rows were not the concern, but rather the quantity of seed planted. Except for the smallest of plots, the horse-drawn corn planters had proven to be a wise investment. Adjustments to the planters were necessary for the smaller grains, but these were made without difficulty.

The hastily built corral had been replaced with a more substantial structure, including pens for smaller animals, and a fenced area for grazing. Perhaps two dozen cows were purchased, but only a few hogs. Cows were chosen since they provided milk, cheese, and ultimately meat. Hogs would be added after the first harvest, but for now feed corn was a problem. Hens and roosters were everywhere. Each home, whether in township or field, had its own vegetable garden, many with plants already beginning to surface. Water was painstakingly carried to gardens, and rodents nipped endlessly at new sprouts. The party was slowly winning its war against snakes, but without the reptiles the vermin flourished.

John had abandoned his plan to raise cattle in large numbers on the Lundeen Ranch. Planting the thirty acres previously turned would be enough, particularly given his commitment to complete that part of the Schafer home he and Maria would occupy. Peter saw his son-in-law as a replacement for both his lethargic eldest, and the now departed Freidrich. John's assignments grew daily. Peter had hoped to trap his son-in-law in a web of obligations, but John recognized the deceit. The longer he stayed in St. Anne's, the more he disliked its communal roots. He took solace knowing that he and Maria would be gone within the year.

Chapter Nine:
Merchants and the *Schullehrer*

---

*"For persons living on the nineteenth century frontier,
education was not something taken for granted. Maybe
saloons … blacksmith shops, and general stores came
first in most new settlements, but schools were never far
behind …"*

—Joe Zenther

The merchants of Hays City carefully watched the development of St. Anne's. The "*Rooshians*" transferred their skills well, and their determination suggested success was inevitable. Josef Pallitto made a decision. St. Anne's deserved its own general store and post office. He would become the exclusive provisioner, poised to take advantage of growth within St Anne's and the surrounding community. Josef had always been a favorite of the Schafer party and his proposal was quickly approved.

Within a week of Mr. Pallitto's decision, a second merchant arrived, an Irish blacksmith fresh from completing his apprenticeship in Ogallah. He wanted out of the raucous cow town. Mr. Nelson told him that St. Anne's might need a "smithy." He arrived in a six-wheeled wagon drawn by two oxen. The wagon carried his recently acquired tools and all of his personal belongings. The first to greet him was Elise Weber. Constance Doyle—he preferred Conn—announced that he was in St. Anne's to build a forge and find a wife—not necessarily in that order. Elise, always in search of a home for her daughters, was intrigued, but her questioning of Conn was interrupted by Nicholas Geist and Denzel Kalb, who invited the smithy to climb down and discuss his plans. Conn had learned some *Deutsch* in Ogallah, but it took sketching in the dirt before Nicholas and Denzel understood what Conn wanted. The smithy was willing to purchase commercial property, but he expected to be given a quarter acre of township ground for his residence and a garden. The request, more like a demand, came as a surprise.

Conn's proposal was beyond the scope of Nicholas and Denzel's authority, and required approval by the full council. Conn was told he was welcome to set up an overnight camp. Early the following day, the council unanimously decided against the blacksmith's proposal. A smithy was a useful addition, but did not justify exchange for residential property. Doing so would set an unhappy precedent—not in the best interest of St. Anne's. If he wished, Conn could build an extension on his forge to accommodate a personal residence, much like Mr. Pallitto's plan to build a loft above his general store.

Constance Doyle had a decision to make. He was new to his trade, but not naive. St. Anne's, by itself, could not keep him busy. With that in mind, he met, two days before, with the Fort Hays Quartermaster, another Irishman. He assured Conn that the Army could find work for him during the winter. The farms of St. Anne's, the military, and the occasional feed store job would be enough to keep him busy. Conn advised the council he could get by with living quarters adjacent to the forge.

The third proposal for a commercial enterprise came from a member of the Schuler party, Christof Acker. Since his arrival, he had been studying the possibility of a grist mill, but needed help from the council, railway, and *Gemeinde*. Christof believed that a strategically placed dam built on the larger stream could easily drive a wheel. He proposed construction of the dam above the pond rather than below. Christof's plan called for the council to deed 400 feet of stream front to the Acker family, and twenty acres immediately to the west. In exchange he would build, at his expense, both the dam and mill. The land belonged to the railroad and Mr. Randolph, like the council, was unwilling to gift the land. Christof next proposed a joint venture with Kansas Pacific, but the railroad had no desire to engage in milling.

Mr. Randolph had an alternative. He agreed to sell the land to Christof, with payment due on November 1, 1878—the price per acre determined by the last sale on or before that date. Title would be conveyed immediately based on a promissory note signed by each member of the party. If Christof failed to pay, the *Gemeinde* would settle the debt—each member obligated for an amount equal to their percentage of total land held. Ownership would then revert to the *St. Anne's Company*. New members would be similarly assessed. For their signature, St Anne's Company members were granted a reduction in miller's toll, good for five years.

John was aware of the discussion between the council, railroad, and miller, and petitioned his father-in-law on Christof's behalf. He wanted to build a second sluice gate running to a point below the dam, with the outflow designed to fill the water wagon purchased in Topeka by Elmer Klein and Gabriel Schuler. The water could then be transported to the township or elsewhere as needed.

Christof lacked the funds to start construction, but title to the land provided the necessary collateral to secure a loan. He found a willing lender in James P. Norton, president of the First National Bank of Hays City. Like his fellow merchants, Mr. Norton saw the potential in St. Anne's, and was looking for a way to introduce his bank to the community. After inspecting Christof's plans for the mill, the bank agreed to provide the loan. Within a few days, teamsters had delivered several large boulders purchased from the Kansas Pacific quarry. The boulders were placed in an arc from east to west leaving a small opening on either side. Cyrus Larsen then fashioned timbers to build the gate mechanism and flume. Christof planned on building the paddle wheel himself. The plan was to frame the mill before winter, perhaps with Mr. Larsen's assistance, then occupy the structure while building a permanent home.

John was slightly ahead of Christof, having already sketched the plan for his sluice gate. It would not disturb construction, and the miller had no objection. When he learned of John's woodworking skills, Christof sought to enlist his help in completing the hopper, stone casing, and trundle head. The work was new to John, but within his capabilities. Christof agreed to pay on a piece work basis, one-half in advance, and the remainder after the mill was complete. John trusted Christof to settle accounts, even if he and

PART I: THE GREAT AMERICAN DESERT

Maria left St. Anne's. The mill provided a welcome source of income, where his father-in law's endless projects did not.

Four days later, without notice, Hermann Schafer rode into St. Anne's. He was dressed in a well-tailored black suit, wide brimmed hat, and what appeared to be very expensive leather boots. A poorly concealed pistol could be seen beneath his jacket. He arrived by rail, and rented a horse from Mr. Nelson. Nothing in his appearance suggested his *Volga Deutsch* origin. Hermann dismounted near the center of the township site. A few women acknowledged his presence, but none recognized Hermann as a former neighbor. Even Melina, who passed within a few feet of her brother-in-law, thought him to be a stranger. Nicholas Geist, returning from the fields, was the first to acknowledge Hermann, and sent a young man to find Peter. Hermann did not attract a large crowd. He was neither well known, nor well liked in Pfeifer, but rather something of a curiosity.

Peter arrived, and the two awkwardly embraced. "You're spending the night?" he asked, hoping that was not the case.

"Can't," Hermann responded. "I have an early meeting with the railway and Hays City officials. My company is building a grain elevator."

Peter and his brother retired to the Schafer house, and were joined by John, Maria, and Melina.

"I'm now a vice president in Midwest Grain and Feed," he said, telling the family he left St. Louis six weeks earlier to investigate potential sites for elevators in Nebraska, Kansas, and Colorado. His journey had taken him along the tracks of the Union Pacific Railway in Nebraska and the Santa Fe, traveling as far west as Pueblo. He was now headed to Denver, courtesy of Kansas Pacific.

"I've a companion traveling with me to record transactions," Hermann said.

Melina flinched when she found out the clerk was a woman. Hermann seemed to be enjoying himself, and gave no indication of when he would return to his home in St. Louis, saying only that if his travels brought him to St. Anne's in the future, he would arrange an overnight stay. Hermann Schafer was a changed man—more like Mr. Randolph or Mr. Norton of the First National Bank, although a pistol was an unlikely addition to their wardrobe.

John asked, "Would you like to see Lundeen Ranch?"

Hermann declined, "Perhaps next time."

John was not surprised. He suspected the ranch would always be an afterthought. John told him of the surprise dug well, the limestone ridge, and the previously turned ground.

Hermann agreed with his nephew, "The well should be improved with a curb, well house, and pump—too valuable to leave as is." He agreed with John that running cattle on the property was not a good idea.

John told him of his plan to till the acreage already turned under.

"I'm not sure what to plant, perhaps corn or rye."

"Don't plant anything until you've heard from me," Hermann said. "A Mennonite community shared with me a variety of wheat called 'Turkey Red,' brought with them from the Alexanderwohl region. It's planted in the fall," he added. "They harvested sixteen bushels per acre with little in the way of soil preparation."

Hermann promised to send a quantity of Turkey Red for John to try in the fall, but cautioned the winter wheat was much harder and more difficult to mill. Finally, Hermann told his nephew an account would be established in his name at First National. Funds could be used for improving the well, preparing the ground for fall planting, or whatever John thought necessary. He was told to draw a reasonable salary from the fund. With that, Hermann was off to Hays City.

* * * * *

Turkey Red is the reason Kansas is known as the "Wheat State." A few acres of the original still remain, but successor cultivars, which produce greater yields, shun disease, and more effectively resist damage from wind and hail, have all but replaced the Heritage Wheat. In nineteenth century Kansas, corn was the predominant crop. Some spring wheat was planted, but settlers found it susceptible to drought and intense summer heat. The introduction of winter wheat, the so-called "Turkey Red," is attributed to the Mennonites who settled near Goessel, Kansas in 1874. They brought seeds with them from Crimea, having first imported them from Turkey. The winter wheat, planted in fall and harvested in early summer, was hardy and cold-weather tolerant. It was an immediate success when compared to its spring cousin, but introduction was slow. Few seeds were available, and the cloistered lifestyle of the Mennonite communities limited interaction with other farmers. It was not until 1890 that a large quantity of Turkey Red was imported. It took another twenty years before wheat production in Kansas surpassed that of corn.

* * * * *

Few in the Schafer party had noticed Hermann's brief visit. He was a stranger to most, and those who recognized him didn't care to associate. Peter was struck by how quickly Hermann had shed his *Volga Deutsch* persona. His brother bore no resemblance to the residents of St. Anne's, who were easily distinguishable as newcomers. Peter knew assimilation would come in time, but some degree of autonomy was good, if nothing else, to shield the members from those who preyed on immigrants. His biggest worry was not assimilation, but rather losing membership to the promise of America. Exposure outside of St. Anne's was exposure to independence—the wedge that threatened to shatter his dream. Cracks were already beginning to appear in the façade of his planned community. Some were obvious, such as Freidrich's departure for the Dakota Territory. Others were more subtle, like the incessant questioning of his leadership decisions.

It was not long before St. Anne's received its next surprise visitor, Amanda Lynn Geiser. Miss Geiser was a first-generation *Deutsch*, educated at Franklin and Marshall College in Lancaster, Pennsylvania. She spoke both English and her native language teaching for one year in Lancaster before accepting a position in Beatrice, Nebraska. There she tutored seventeen students in grades one through eight. She left when Protestant community leaders insisted that religious training be included as part of her daily curriculum. Miss Geiser had no objection to church-driven studies, as long as they took place outside the school day and were taught by a member of the congregation. A suitable agreement could not be reached and she resigned.

Miss Geiser recalled a handbill she had seen in early spring stating that there was a shortage of teachers in central Kansas. The handbill brought her to Hays City. She had visited the Hays City School, but all openings were filled. While there, she was told of St. Anne's, a new settlement. Rachel Austerlitz was the first to greet the young teacher when she arrived. Miss Geiser immediately asked for the *Vorsteher*. Maria, tending to the Schafer garden, overheard the request, and pointed toward the house where Peter and Albrecht were working. Rachel called for Peter. He emerged along with his youngest son, who took charge of Miss Geiser's horse and buggy.

Miss Geiser introduced herself asking, "Does St. Anne's plan a *Schulhaus?*"

Peter shrugged, which she interpreted as an invitation to proceed.

"The 1871 School Law of Kansas requires all children age eight to fourteen to receive twelve weeks of instruction in *lesen, schreiben, und rechnen*," she said. "That calls for a *Schulhaus* or equivalent."

Peter took a moment to study the young woman. Miss Geiser was not strikingly attractive, but impeccably dressed and very well proportioned.

"A community center is planned. That will be our school," Peter answered.

Miss Geiser then produced a letter of endorsement from the Kansas Superintendent of Public Instruction, her certification as a teacher, and several letters of recommendation. Two of the letters were written in *Deutsch*. Peter read these, and shared them with Albert Wetzel, who had joined the conversation. Miss Geiser provided an explanation for the other documents.

She advised Peter and Albert, "I seek employment for the school year and require a teaching desk, blackboard, a quantity of slates, map of the United States, and a full set of McGuffey Readers. I will also require lodging."

Albert had a question, but Miss Geiser raised her hand.

"*Warte bitte*," she said, stopping him in mid-sentence. "I assume your party has few English speakers," she continued. "One night of adult education will be provided."

Then, recognizing the audience, she referenced her baptism as a Roman Catholic, her devotion to Christ, and a lifetime of following the commandments. Miss Geiser handed Peter an envelope that included her required salary and stipend for once-yearly travel from Kansas to Pennsylvania and return. She would be staying at the Virginia House in Hays City for two more days, leaving at 4:00 p.m. on the second day.

Peter told Miss Geiser that the community would be meeting tomorrow evening, and schooling for the children of St. Anne's would be discussed. He, or a member of the council, would contact her before her departure. She thanked Peter, called for her buggy, and left for Hays City. Miss Geiser's reference to the school law, and possible non-compliance struck a chord. The council did not wish to start their city's first year with a violation of a Kansas mandate. Moreover, Miss Geiser stood before them as a credentialed answer to education in St. Anne's. Other topics were slated for tomorrow's meeting, but the school was sure to be among the first addressed.

The following morning Peter asked Albert Wetzel to visit First National Bank of Hays City and its manager, Mr. Norton. The purpose was to explore alternatives to financing the community center. Peter understood that Albert had no experience in banking, but Albert was a council member, and it was time he took a more active role in administration. Peter also recognized that Albert's opinion, because of his youth, was discounted among senior members. Funding for the community center was a chance for Albert to prove his mettle. Peter had calculated that more than half the work could be completed by volunteer labor. Materials would be the principal cost. There had been some discussion of using native stone of the type found on the Lundeen Ranch for the walls of the building. This would further reduce expense, and assuage naysayers.

Peter asked John to accompany Albert. Lacking an appointment, the pair were kept waiting for more than an hour. They were finally ushered into the president's office and immediately struck by its opulence. Mr. Norton was seated behind a very large desk with gold drawer pulls and a high-backed leather chair. The room was illuminated with crystal light fixtures, and the walls covered in embossed wallpaper. The office was designed to show substance, but also to intimidate. Albert, who had been expected to initiate the conversation, fell silent, fixated by the surroundings.

Recognizing his companion's dilemma, John sketched a building and referred to *geld, schule,* and *kirche*. Mr. Norton thought he understood, but recognized this would be a long discussion absent translation. He reached under his desk, poked at something, and suddenly a middle-aged woman appeared. She introduced herself as Hanna Bloomburg. She had come to the United States from Luebeck, where she worked for the *Hamburg-America Linie*. Albert now joined the conversation, explaining to Hanna that funds were needed for a *Schulhaus*. Mr. Norton raised a hand. He asked if funding for a school was the purpose of the visit. Both Albert and Hanna answered in the affirmative. Mr. Norton said a few words to his assistant, and she quickly left the room returning with a file.

A few months earlier, the Hays City School District had issued a bond, permissible under the 1871 school law. Mr. Norton saw no reason why St. Anne's could not do the same. The bank would assist, and he was sure the Superintendent of Hays City Schools would help in forming the district. Funds would be lent to St. Anne's, secured by the *Gemeinde*, and the state of Kansas. Hanna took a moment to explain the process.

"Payment would come on a date sometime in the future," she said. "Desks, blackboards, and other equipment could be treated as capital items and included in the funding."

Mr. Norton added, "Nothing can be done until a majority of landowners agree to funding. The community must approve."

Hanna escorted John and Albert from Mr. Norton's office, taking additional time to ensure the pair understood their obligation.

Albert suggested that they share the news with Miss Geiser. The Virginia House was just across the street, and she would almost certainly be somewhere on the premises. John anticipated the suggestion. Albert had not stopped talking about Miss Geiser since yesterday's meeting. He was obviously taken by the teacher. John argued against contacting Miss Geiser, since approval by the council and *Gemeinde* was required. Albert was disappointed, but agreed.

As the two left the bank, the enthusiasm of the moment was tempered by the sudden appearance of three cowhands. They were young men, still not weathered by the range, but dressed in buckskin vest, and chaps. At the sight of John and Albert, and their distinctive clothing, they blocked the boardwalk and muttered something in a disagreeable tone. John was able to pick up *dummkopf*. Cowhand and farmer stood for a moment facing one another just as Mr. Norton emerged from the bank. He quickly recognized the circumstance, and motioned with his head for the cowhands to move on. They did so, and what might have been an unfortunate confrontation was averted.

A similar event had taken place the week before at Mr. Nelson's feed store. The merchants of Hays City embraced the *Volga Deutsch* as willing buyers, while the townspeople looked upon them with indifference. Cattlemen were anything but indifferent. They plainly disliked sodbusters. Farmers meant fences—an unwelcome barrier to water and feed. Unfamiliarity also bred contempt. The newcomers spoke a strange language, dressed in a peculiar way, and had their own customs and traditions. For the cattlemen, the promise of America did not include the celebration of difference. John planned to suggest that the council recommend that women and children stay clear of Hays City, and men travel in pairs until the drovers headed south.

John and Albert returned to St. Anne's to share with Peter what they learned from Mr. Norton. The *Vorsteher* had scheduled a meeting for the following evening in the shadow of the Schafer home. Benches had been hastily put together using all manner of construction materials. The council expected almost every family to be represented—head of household, wives and children. Peter opened the meeting by thanking Gabriel Schuler and George Breit for having completed the last section of fence surrounding the common grazing land. A few small shelters and feeding stations were still unfinished, but most of the work was complete. Christof Acker then took a moment to discuss progress on his planned grist mill. He thanked the *Gemeinde* for supporting the effort, and told the members that he expected to complete the mill before next year's harvest, if not sooner. In the meantime, flour and cornmeal could be ground by hand, or in larger quantities at Mr. Nelson's horse-drawn mill.

Peter reminded the members that, in addition to the grist mill, two other merchants were expected to open in St. Anne's. Mr. Pallitto had promised a general store by midsummer and the blacksmith, Conn Doyle, was due to open his forge before harvest. The merchants were an important addition to St Anne's suggesting the community was something more than a remote collection of houses. Peter was quick to remind the membership that commercial expansion must be selective. St. Anne's did not wish to take on the characteristics of the frontier towns farther west.

John was next to address the group, discussing his plan to build a sluice gate near the top of Christof's mill pond, and using the outfall to fill the Klein-Schuler water wagon. The 400 gallons would then be pulled to the township site to be used for irrigation. He also discussed his plan to enclose the dug well on Hermann's property, and install a cast-iron hand pump. John had managed to remove the debris, and water drawn from the well was clean, but hand pulling was too difficult. Finally, he shared his intention to plant a new variety of wheat, called "Turkey Red," on the Lundeen Ranch. The seeds for fall planting would be shipped from Nebraska by his uncle. The change in variety of wheat created a stir among those gathered, far more than John's discussion of sluice gate and well. They understood that spring wheat often fell victim to drought and may not be well suited to the prairie. John's experiment with Turkey Red would provide insight on wheat as a cash crop.

Peter was eager to move on to the discussion of Miss Geiser and the school, but there were two projects that required attention—a common barn and centrally located community well. The first was already decided. The *Gemeinde* supported construction of a barn to begin in late summer and conclude after harvest. The party was aware of this schedule, but Denzel Kalb and Eduard Hauer sought confirmation. Both had recently purchased livestock—Denzel buying goats and a hog, while Eduard bought four cows. Their purchase was predicated, in part, on the availability of shelter. Peter's assurance that a common barn would be completed before the cold season seemed to satisfy the pair.

Denzel, holding the floor, introduced the second topic—a well in township center. The project had been rejected earlier, but John's discovery of a well on the Lundeen Ranch provided cause to reopen discussion. Two drillers had been contacted. Both used horse-drawn augers in combination with a tripod device that dropped a ram to break rock. No matter what the method, someone had to inspect the shaft from time to time. Even with brick lining, cave-ins were commonplace as was the accumulation of gas at lower levels. Most saw the project as foolhardy, and none shared Denzel's sense of urgency. Wells were expensive to dig, often $2.00 per foot, with no guarantee of finding water. Further discussion was put aside.

That left the final topic, and the one most in the party wanted to discuss—the *Schulhaus* and education. Three competing groups had formed since Miss Geiser's visit. The first was led by Elmer Klein and Philipp Weber. They supported lessons in catechism taught in various homes, but no secular education. Construction of the community center would be deferred. For this group, it was a matter of available resources. They had no funds to give, and believed that the children were needed for fieldwork. The second group, led by Wilfried Gerber, agreed with the first on postponing secular education, but favored building a community center as soon as possible. In their view, a central gathering place was necessary for meetings and to properly conduct mass.

Albert Wetzel stood for the third group, which included Peter and a majority of the council. He petitioned for immediate construction of the community center and a one room cottage for the teacher. Miss Geiser would be placed under contract at $221.00 per year—a salary recommended by Mr. Norton based on his experience as a member of the Hays City Board of Education. Albert went on to describe the bonding process. Funds were available following membership approval. There was no immediate out-of-pocket expense, and the state of Kansas would help with financing, but there were conditions. A school district must be formed. Mr. Norton's assistant thought it possible that the district could extend beyond the boundaries of St. Anne's. The law required that, within the boundary, education, "shall … be equally free and accessible to all children." Religious training was also constrained. The school law clearly stated that, "no sectarian doctrine shall be taught or inculcated in any public schools, but the scriptures without note or comment may be used therein."

Peter let Albert's final comments settle. Denzel Kalb, the only council member opposed to Albert's plan, argued that bonding meant the doors of St. Anne's School were open to all comers, and the state of Kansas, not the council, would control their children's education. Albert countered, reminding the membership that, absent the state's help, the burden of funding the community center fell entirely on the *Gemeinde*. Rates for borrowing were twice that of bonding, and St. Anne's could expect no help from the state with salary, training, or supplies. Under these circumstances, teachers with the credentials of Miss Geiser would be difficult to attract. Had they been in Pfeifer, there would have been no debate. Education was closed to anyone outside the community, but this was not *Russen*.

Albert, though he had no children, made an impassioned plea in support of the public option. Lessons in America were the pathway to assimilation, and ultimately to success. The children must learn the language of their adopted country and be given the same instruction as their peers in the secular world. Isolation had contributed to downfall in *Russen*, and would do the same in America. Hersh Schneider was quick to support Albert's argument. Religious instruction for the children of St. Anne's could take place in membership homes, or the community center after school hours. A more open community was critical to the future of St. Anne's.

Peter was conflicted. He understood the perils of isolation, but feared that exposure to the world beyond would someday bring an end to St. Anne's. The comments by Albert and Hersh set off a firestorm of debate, with the argument centered on public schools and intrusion by government. In *Russen,* the Crown and *Kontor* often worked against the *Gemeinde*. America was different. Here, the government was seen as a partner. Citizen and government worked together to the benefit of all.

After contentious debate, the three camps became two. Both wanted a church and school combination, but one wanted the school to become public, with Miss Geiser as the *Schullehrer*. The latter approach, supported by Albert, and all but one of his fellow council members, prevailed. Following the meeting, the intensely pious Nela Hauer accused Peter of violating the trust placed in him by the community. She considered opening the school to outsiders a mortal sin, one for which Peter must atone.

"You've opened our church and school to the heathens," she said. "St Anne's will be cursed."

Peter could only say, "It is the will of the *Gemeinde*."

Two questions remained—the first being where Miss Geiser would live if the cottage were not complete when she returned? This was resolved when Rachel Austerlitz offered a room in her home. The second question was who should manage construction? Albert and John were given this assignment. Early the following morning, Albert rode into Hays City to advise Mr. Norton that the community had approved construction and the bonding process. Then, making sure the trail dust was gone from what he considered to be his best shirt, he asked the Virginia House clerk to notify Miss Geiser that he was waiting in the lobby. She took one-half hour to respond. Albert told her she had both a school and position at St. Anne's.

Chapter Ten:
Summer: A Season of Tending

"It would tax the powers ... to portray the changes, the tree, yesterday laden with its heavy drapery of green, today denuded. The peach and apple trees, with luscious fruitage, withered as the fig tree accursed. Gardens ... lifeless, seared and fallen to decay. The cottage embowered, now exposed and blistered by ... burning heat."

—William Giles Frye

Corn, now the favored crop, was still being placed in the ground more than three weeks past the recommended date. Prairie sod had proven a formidable opponent, but members reasoned that a smaller yield was better than none at all. Peter Schafer and Felix Austerlitz, using commercial sodbusters, had bested the others, breaking one hundred five and eighty acres, respectively. Gabriel Schuler was just behind with seventy acres turned. He too had relied on Mr. Olsen's crew after his failed attempt to turn sod using horses. Most had fallen short of the acreage they planned to break, and spring planting was taking place in early summer. The crush of fieldwork had also delayed common projects, and left both families and their livestock exposed to the elements.

The St. Anne's school received preliminary approval from the Superintendent of Public Instruction, and Mr. Norton arranged to make funds available before all necessary paperwork had been completed. Albert and Miss Geiser had decided on 700 square feet as the size of the school building, with a separate 200-square foot cottage for the *Schullehrer*. Surprisingly, Miss Geiser made few requests, perhaps because the council had met her salary demands and agreed to all facility and equipment needs. She had her school, but understood that the building would also serve as a community center and temporary place of worship. The council took on the role of School Board, with the understanding elections must be held within six months.

Hays City was used as a model for curriculum, rules, and regulations. Albert was troubled by one standard for teachers that called for administrators to consider a woman's marital status before hiring. The "marriage bar" had largely been abandoned throughout the west, but Albert didn't like the reference. He harbored the unlikely dream of someday courting the *Schullehrer*. The provision, if included in the standards, would deny his fantasy. He was among the more substantial young men in St. Anne's, and could have his pick of young women, but imagined himself a lifetime partner of Miss Geiser.

The council, on the recommendation of John and Albert, had decided on limestone walls for the community center raised to a height of seven feet. The cottage would use the same construction. The native stone was available from the Lundeen Ranch, but George Bollinger, a Hays City stonemason, and a member of Father Lenkeit's congregation, already had suitable blocks cut and ready at his quarry. Cyrus Larsen had agreed to donate trusses and extend the best price on roofing materials—either tin or clay tiles. From that point on, completion was entirely dependent on volunteer labor.

Ground was broken the third Sunday in June, following Father Lenkeit's morning worship. The priest followed the congregation back to the township where he blessed the building site and became the first to put shovel to soil. Before returning to Pennsylvania for the summer, Miss Geiser made it clear she wanted the school term to begin on Monday, October 18 and extend through the first week in April. Thereafter, a six-week term would begin, attended by only the youngest children. The older *studenten* would be busy with fieldwork.

The end of planting season for field crops offered no respite for the women of St. Anne's. Every waking hour was spent making and mending garments, ironing, hauling water, gardening, preserving vegetables, maintaining cook fires, and caring for small livestock and poultry. For some, the endless drudgery was too much to bear. After moving to the family's soddy, Nela Hauer found it difficult to complete her daily regimen. She would sob uncontrollably, or slump to the floor in complete exhaustion. Nela displayed no physical signs of distress, but often spoke of the old country and life in *Russen*. A deeply religious person, she prayed for deliverance from her dismal existence. The women of St. Anne's struggled to understand Nela's condition. Some expressed sympathy, but her husband did not. Eduard attributed the malaise to the "fragility of woman folk." He had little tolerance for his wife's condition, and his frustration took form in the waning hours of the day. Nela saw the prairie as a "sentence." In time, she adapted to her punishment, but Eduard always saw his wife as failing to measure up.

The prairie wife was troubled by more than despondency and accompanying guilt. Snake bites, endless cuts and bruises, mild fever, and discomfort from spoiled foods brought everyday annoyances, but real tragedy was also commonplace—often the product of isolation and ignorance. Emma Heimler lost her first child less than an hour after birth. When it became apparent that the infant was failing, some prayed, while others turned to illusory cures, which hastened the child's demise. Midway through the ordeal a wagon was hitched to transport Emma and the baby to Fort Hays, but never left. Her child died in a soddy surrounded by a helpless community. The infant was buried in the area designated to become the churchyard—the unfortunate distinction of being the first resident entombed in St. Anne's. Father Lenkeit had been called to St. Louis, and Peter officiated in his absence. He could find no words to explain or console. Emma spoke briefly, thanking her neighbors for their prayers. After a day of mourning, she returned to her chores.

Two days later the nine-year old daughter of Gabriel Schuler was kicked in the head by a horse while helping her father feed the family's livestock. Marta was a beloved child with boundless energy—seemingly everywhere at once. She was taken to Fort Hays, but for reasons unknown the doctor took more than an hour to see the child. She died within a few minutes of his arrival. Father Lenkeit was available and administered last rites. He returned with the body, and on the following day, presided over a proper funeral for both children. In a span of two days, a like number of the community's most treasured resource had been taken. The members knew adversity, but only the most deeply pious could understand God's reason for taking a child.

Before the service began, Father Lenkeit took the unusual step of scolding Luise Kunkel for suggesting that their settlement was accursed. The priest told the assembled residents God had a reason for claiming his sheep, and to suggest otherwise was the work of the devil. Luise was banished from the ceremony, with an instruction to Gustav to silence his wife. It was a task that he struggled with in the past, but not so at the direction of the church.

Losing a child was deeply personal, but its impact was generally confined to the immediate family. Peter mourned the loss, but was more concerned for the effect of natural calamity. Merchant and settler alike talked of the grasshopper infestation just one year before, which drove thousands from the prairie. A few returned, but most simply abandoned their claim, often returning to their former home. Weather could be as devastating as insects. Prairie fires, extended drought, or a funnel cloud could easily leave the family or community with nothing for the winter.

In their short stay, the Schafer party had blessedly escaped both insects and adverse weather. A sudden downpour had done minor damage to the east bank of Christof's mill pond, and prairie fires were seen, but none threatened their community. The least understood and most terrifying events were the funnel clouds. John and Denzel rode out to inspect after one such event and found uprooted trees, and damage from large rocks hurtled through the air. The party had little understanding of the phenomenon, comparing it to a *staubteufel*—rotating pillars of dust often seen on the *Russische* Steppe. The damage observed by John and Denzel suggested the Kansas events were far stronger.

* * * * *

In late spring of 1874, swarms of Rocky Mountain locusts, more commonly known as grasshoppers, began a march across the prairie creating enormous devastation in the fields of Nebraska, Kansas, and the Dakota

Territory. The insects consumed everything in their path, arriving in numbers large enough to block the sun and contaminate the water supply. Even railroads were affected as insects settled on rails after sunset and denied traction to locomotives. When the onslaught finally ended, more than 500,000 acres had been reduced to stubble with an economic toll in excess of one million dollars. Efforts at eradication were late, primitive, and always ineffective. Farmers took to the fields with molasses-covered sleds, sought vengeance with flails, and turned under, or burned crops. One enterprising merchant even suggested that with proper dressing the grasshopper could be an edible delicacy.

The farmers, many newly arrived, were left without food for family and livestock or seed for next year's crop. Sadly, mortgages did survive, and the devastation left many settlers with no means to pay. Governor Thomas Osborn of Kansas issued bonds to aid in the relief effort, but the need was too great. He and others made a plea to the American people, who generously responded by sending carloads of food, much of it carried free of charge by the railroads.

Federal agencies joined in the relief effort providing seed, and relaxing occupancy requirements so homesteaders could leave the farm to find work. The Army, through its network of forts, dispatched soldiers to deliver military rations, clothing, and blankets to countless settlers all across the prairie. Their heroic effort came too late. Farms were already abandoned or foreclosed and, in a few cases, entire families froze to death or died of starvation. Well over half the farmers in Nebraska and Kansas were driven from the land. Westward migration slowed, then reversed with as many immigrants leaving the prairie as arriving. In the spring of 1875, just as the grasshopper larvae began to emerge, there was a late freeze. The devastation of the prior year would not be repeated.

* * * * *

Peter was experiencing a better than anticipated June. Even Freidrich's departure had a silver lining. Albrecht had shown some initiative, and John, assuming the projects once assigned Freidrich, was ensnarled in work enough to slow any plans he might have for leaving St. Anne's. Between the commercial sodbusters and the ground broken by John and the Schafer boys, the family had managed to plant near ninety acres, most in corn, with smaller quantities in spring wheat, oats, and barley. The corn was expected to do well, but Peter was less optimistic on yield for the smaller grains.

He shifted heavily to corn based on the advice of Mr. Nelson and counsel of Reinhart Muller and Paulus Richter. The approach seemed to be working. The corn planter laid down seed in a pattern that made cultivation easier, and the seeds the family had planted early were showing well. Peter had chosen his ground wisely. His fields fell off slightly to the east, providing some protection from the late afternoon sun.

The story was repeated across St. Anne's. Barring a major weather event, they would have their corn, but yield on the smaller grains may disappoint. The party understood what lay ahead. Their experience in the long *Russische* winter taught them the value of food preservation, and plans were made to put staples "by." Most purchased a cow since the animal provided both milk products and meat. A few of the members sketched maps showing movement of deer and antelope. Both were common and would be harvested as winter approached.

The early summer found Maria feeling much stronger. The *morgendliche ubelkeit* passed, and she had regained the energy lost in the early stages of her pregnancy. Her day began with household chores and light carpentry in the single room that she and John now called home. John had taught Maria how to use the tools of woodworking, and she had quickly taken to the profession. Her afternoon was divided between fieldwork—mostly cultivation—and tending the garden. The day ended with caring for livestock.

Whenever she could, Maria visited with Emma Heimler who had lost her baby a month before. Emma quickly returned to her tasks, but was unusually withdrawn, rarely initiating conversation. When she did engage her friends, she spoke of the past and family left behind. Like Nela Hauer, Emma was despondent and withdrawn. Her husband, Otto, purchased an elixir he saw advertised at Mr. Pallitto's Hays City store. Josef sold the product with the warning that it may produce momentary euphoria, but had no lasting medicinal quality. Now Emma seemed to display two divergent behaviors, bright and cheerful, or severely depressed. Worse yet, she became annoyed when the elixir was not available. Otto could not afford the potion and Josef, seeing its effect, had stripped the product from his shelves. Emma had no alternative, but to do without.

During the course of the summer, John was increasingly drawn to Mr. Nelson—an attraction not shared by many in St. Anne's. The feed store owner was a difficult man to like. He was short with members and more likely to growl than to greet. Few found fault with his business, but all disliked his behavior. John's association with Daniel Nelson began when he purchased materials to install a pump on Hermann's well. He saw beneath the gruff veneer, and found instead a shrewd *geschaftmann* able to link risk, resourcefulness, and personal gain.

Mr. Nelson's family was among the first homesteaders in the 1860s. He survived the early years and grew his farm to more than 200 acres. When the drovers appeared, he opened a trail supply business in Ogallah. Then came Nelson Feed in Hays City. Daniel Nelson was not one to shy away from opportunity. He had seen the well on the Lundeen Ranch, and admired John's work on the house, curb, and pump installation. The pair even discussed the feasibility of a wind-driven pump.

Mr. Nelson installed the area's first all steel, multi-blade windmill, now in use by Kansas Pacific, and was working on a similar pump south of Abilene. Wind-driven pumps meant a greater demand for wells, and Mr. Nelson had thoughts of using steam power to expedite the drilling process. John looked at Mr. Nelson and saw the promise of America. Risk taking, as opposed to risk aversion, was the key to success.

John had set aside time for work on the Lundeen Ranch, but not for his growing commitment to Christof Acker and the grist mill. Mr. Larsen, the primary contractor, was busy with home construction, and had advised Christof he would be late in starting the gate mechanism and flume, both of which must be roughed in before starting the foundation and framing the mill. Cristof asked John, with help from Hersh Schneider, to fill in for Mr. Larsen. John jumped at the chance and Mr. Larsen had no objection.

The Ackers still held out hope of moving inside the mill before the worst of winter set in. Christof paid a good salary, and the money increased the Schmidt nest egg, largely undisturbed since leaving Pfeifer. Peter was annoyed. He had intended to spend down his son-in-law's savings, making it difficult for him to leave. Instead, Hermann's ranch, and the Acker grist mill, were providing John and Maria with the one thing Peter feared most—flexibility. He complained, but John always managed to complete his chores on the Schafer farm, albeit sometimes late. John liked the additional money, but also enjoyed the distress contract work caused his father-in law.

The Schafer party traveled together each Sunday to the Fort Hays Chapel. As was their custom, John and Maria traveled in their own wagon purchased with funds from the Lundeen Ranch account. They were approaching the gate when they saw Mr. Pallitto waving frantically. Josef was given to excess, but he appeared to be even more animated than usual. He was shouting "from Anselm" and waving an envelope. John knew immediately it was the much-awaited letter from his father in *Russische*. Anselm had passed through Hays City on his way to Big Spring. Since time was short, he left the letter with Josef for delivery. The envelope included the notation, "Senta Schmidt on board the steamship *Baltimore*." The letter had been hand carried from Neu-Norka on the *Russische* Steppe to Des Moines and posted from there. Jacob had found a way to bypass the Eastern European postal service.

John and Maria contemplated whether the letter or Father Lenkeit's mass was more important. The letter won out. The couple had moved toward the back of the party then, at the last minute, stole away to the shade of a nearby hickory tree. The letter began with Jacob expressing excitement over the prospect of a grandchild. He asked if the couple had decided on a name, whether Maria had experienced any difficulties, and what sort of structure the family would be calling home. No doubt he had heard that many families were living in *semlinkas*. Jacob wanted his grandchild to have a permanent roof over his or her head. He was willing to pay using funds carried by a member of the Bruener party, scheduled to leave Pfeifer sometime in the next few months. John was uncertain how much wealth his father had accumulated, but his offer to pay for housing suggested that he was comfortable.

Jacob knew that Peter would be interested in the size of the Bruener party. They were currently twelve families, all but one from Pfeifer. Their destination was Topeka and a hoped for a rendezvous with the Schafer party. As of Jacob's posting, departure had been twice delayed, and two families were considering withdrawal from the party. Jacob gave no reason for their tardiness or possible reduced number.

He did say that the Schafer and Bruener parties made the right choice in leaving *Russen*. Alexander II, while professing sadness at the large number of *Volga Deutsch* leaving the Steppe, had continued to impose sanctions. Life was becoming increasingly difficult. The *Kontor* had made good on his promise to introduce *Russische* as the language of education, and was planning a *Buro* of the *Tutel-Kanzlei* in Pfeifer. After a century of amnesty, young men were being called to service, six from the nearby community of Kamenka.

Jacob's letter then turned to the Kansas prairie. What were the soil conditions? What crops had been planted? Did they have sufficient water, and was there any indication of what they could expect in the way of harvest? He asked how much land Peter had acquired, and whether John planned to put down roots in Kansas or perhaps elsewhere. Before closing, Jacob briefly mentioned his partnership with Stephan Haus, the blacksmith and long-time friend. Their newly designed plow had not sold in the numbers hoped for. Price, not design, was the problem. A similar plow was being mass produced in both Sevastopol and Saratov. Jacob and his partner could not compete, but the short-lived setback proved a blessing. Industrial fabrication, tool design, and woodworking left them with more work than they could handle. Their shop now employed four workers.

The letter was longer than expected, and John and Maria hung on every sentence waiting for word on Helena's condition. They got none. Jacob said only that "mother" was doing as well as could be expected. They had no idea what Jacob meant, but interpreted the vague reference to mean Helena continued to lose ground to her protracted illness. John and Maria read the letter once more, and slowly made their way back to St. Anne's. When Peter and Helena returned, they immediately asked why the young couple had not attended mass. John showed his father-in-law the letter. It was the first correspondence from Pfeifer, and Peter was anxious to learn of recent developments, particularly relating to the party led by Ludwig Bruener. John told him the party was late getting underway and smaller than expected. Peter was disappointed. He had written Arne Schwab soon after arriving in Kansas encouraging him to "talk up" the Bruener party and St. Anne's. He wondered if Arne had received the letter.

By not attending mass, John and Maria had missed Albrecht Schafer and Hilke Weber's first announcement of courtship. The declaration was read from the altar by Father Lenkeit. Elise Weber was obsessed with finding a suitable mate for her daughters, and in Albrecht, the *Vorsteher's* eldest son, she found a target. The effort at matchmaking was poorly disguised, yet the couple seemed to be genuinely attracted to one another. John was mildly surprised, but not so Maria. She knew that Albrecht's days as a single man were numbered the first time Hilke's mother set eyes on him.

A celebration would take place, but the cumbersome process attached to courtship was certain to be abbreviated. Tradition was less compelling in Kansas. There would be fewer pre-marital lessons, with ritual giving way to fieldwork and home construction. Hilke would also deviate from custom by joining her husband in a new home, rather than becoming part of the groom's household. As a principal buyer, Peter would either give land to Albrecht, or sell at a very attractive price. Albrecht and Hilke would spend a short time with the elder Schafers, if at all. Peter had insisted on a formal announcement of courtship as a means to preserve some trappings of Pfeifer. There may be no church and only a visiting priest, but *Volga Deutsch* convention must be observed.

Constance Doyle had also found a wife, but the union was unlikely to be announced from the altar. The blacksmith, soon to make his home in St. Anne's, was expected to wed Lucy Milbourne. Their marriage would not be impeded by tradition. Lucy was something of a mystery. She insisted their home adjacent to Conn's shop be constructed before any work was done on the forge. Lucy's initial visit to St. Anne's dominated conversation in the community. She was dressed fashionably and displayed a good deal of cleavage. In a community where "proper behavior" reigned, the soon-to-be Mrs. Doyle quickly became the topic of whispered innuendo.

Luise Kunkel immediately concluded that Lucy was a dance hall girl. Others had suggested far worse. As the first non-Catholic in St. Anne's, the more pious felt she, and her husband, must embrace Catholicism before taking up residence. Luise led the *Altargesellschaft*, a group of women that tended to the needs of the Sacristy. She imagined herself as a principal in church administration and approached Father Lenkeit with the suggestion. The priest had wisely deferred to the council. Peter and his colleagues favored Conn's smithing skills over what religion he practiced. St. Anne's had enough Catholics, but no blacksmith.

The last week of June marked the opening of Mr. Pallitto's St. Anne's General Store. The doors were open three days a week from noon until an hour before dusk. Josef planned to be there as often as he could, but hired Anna Schneider to manage the store in his absence. The stock consisted of flour, sugar, salt, coffee, cured meats, and other foodstuffs, along with soaps, medicinal supplies, chicken feed, nails, small tools, candy, bolts of fabric and sewing notions. There were a few dresses, and other non-essential items for women. Shirts, hats, boots, and overalls were available for men, and the store carried a small selection of farm implements. The counter had several catalogues, and orders could be filled from Josef's St. Louis mentor, or beyond, if desired.

The Post Office was located in the back of the store, along with an over-size stove. The location quickly became a gathering place. The enterprising Mr. Pallitto was also exchanging eggs, butter, and cheese for credit, and doing much better on meeting his commitment to the Army.

July was now upon the Schafer party and with it the intense summer heat. Temperatures, which had slowly risen through the spring, reached stovetop levels. Each day dawned bright and clear. A few clouds presented themselves, then disappeared, giving way to a persistent wind that gained strength as the day wore on. A combination of dirt, pollen, and chaff covered sweat-soaked bodies and became part of the prairie diet. Occasional wind-driven storms that bore this unholy combination reduced visibility and made fieldwork near impossible. The rain, which followed, was as much valued for cleansing the body as it was for irrigation.

The members continued to build shelter, cultivate fields, maintain gardens, water and tend stock, and pray for a good harvest. Mr. Nelson told John the season was "fair to middling." John was not sure what he meant, but thought he was referring to field crops. The corn planted in early May was now well above three feet—the only exception the late plantings by Felix Austerlitz and Gabriel Schuler. Even the spring wheat, barley, and oats looked better than anticipated. Mr. Nelson also understood, as well as anyone, the threat of insects that periodically ravaged the prairie. He was still recovering from the earlier infestation that drove homesteaders off the land, many still indebted to Nelson Feed. This year there was no sign of infestation—a late freeze, according to Mr. Nelson, had destroyed emerging larvae. John and the others could only hope that he was correct. The members knew prairie life was an ever-changing montage. Much needed rainfall today could easily give way to damaging hail tomorrow. Peter traded on the uncertainty, and preached the need for a stronger *St. Anne's Company.*

"God's will be done," he often said, "but only if we stay together as a village."

John was sure his father-in-law welcomed the occasional setback as an incentive to strengthen community.

In the early afternoon of July 9, a storm rose from the southwest. At first, it seemed that St. Anne's might be spared, but soon the dust-filled air became thick enough to cut. The storm was upon them in an instant, reducing visibility to a few yards. Wilfried Gerber had left home just before midday to engage in fieldwork on the northern edge of the settlement. His wife, Meta, left at the same time, her two children close behind. She set out for the home of Ida Kalb—the two women gathered each week to sew, while the children played. Meta planned on a short visit, but changed her mind deciding to wait out the storm. She was sure her husband would understand when he returned from fieldwork and found her and the children absent.

The storm seemed to abate and Meta, hoping to return before her husband, made a hasty retreat for home. When she arrived, Meta found their four sheep gone and the gate to their pen ajar. The Gerbers had just purchased the sheep—the first family in St. Anne's to do so. Meta's eldest had fed the sheep earlier, and perhaps left the gate open. The sheep could also have broken the latch to reach nearby prairie grass. Meta could see their path and sent her eldest in pursuit. She quickly returned frightened by what she thought to be a snake. The younger child was dispatched to the Kalb home for help. They joined the search, along with Eduard Hauer and two of his boys.

Darkness would soon be upon them and concern had shifted from finding sheep to locating Wilfried Gerber. The Hauers' youngest took a westerly course and located two of the sheep. He swung to the north toward the Gerber plot and came upon a large expanse of still smoldering prairie grass, the product of lightning strikes earlier in the afternoon. As he picked his way through the embers, he heard a noise ahead and to the left. He saw Wilfried, overalls and shirt charred, and his back and arms badly burned. He glanced down and saw a pool of blood. Wilfried had broken his leg and the bone pierced the skin. He was unable to escape the flames.

The young man fired his rifle calling out as he did. His fellow searchers quickly responded, but Wilfried had lost too much blood. He died with his wife looking on. The others shielded his children from the grisly sight, while Albert Wetzel went for a horse to transport the body. The next morning the missing sheep returned, one even reentering the pen. The youngest Gerber child was delighted, still unable to comprehend the gravity of her father's death. St. Anne's had lost its third resident. On his return to Hays City the following day, Josef Pallitto advised Father Lenkeit of Wilfried's demise. The mass was held two days later. His body was entombed alongside the two children already laid to rest.

The walls of both the community center and Miss Geiser's adjoining cottage had been raised to five feet, and Cyrus Larsen expected to have trusses on site within a few days. John and Albert had already formed two work parties. The first would extend the limestone by two feet, and the second lift and place trusses. Progress on the two structures had been discussed at a council meeting the night before. The fate of Meta Gerber was also addressed. St. Anne's now had a widow with two young children, a farm, and mortgage. The community would care for the family through the winter, but it was important that Meta find a husband before spring. Few single women succeeded on the prairie, and Meta was not a likely candidate. She was strong in spirit, but frail in body. She did have one redeeming quality. The years had been good to Meta, and she remained a very attractive woman. Felix Austerlitz agreed to contact Father Lenkeit. The priest was a good source for locating husbands, having buried the wives of several widowers, any one of whom would be happy to share a bed with Meta.

Word the Bruener party was in Topeka reached Peter in mid-July. It did not come from Mr. Randolph, although the railway still held property for sale within St. Anne's, but rather from Anselm. Mr. Randolph knew the Bruener party would find their way to St. Anne's, but wanted a chance to reach the party before Peter, hoping to sell property outside the *company*.

He believed the remaining parcels in St. Anne's were as good as sold, destined to fall into the hands of existing residents. Mr. Randolph's desire to catch the Bruener party first was thwarted by Anselm, who bypassed his superior sending word to Peter via the Hays City Station Master and Mr. Pallitto.

Peter received the note the following morning just hours before Ludwig Bruener and Jannick Wolfe arrived in St. Anne's. He was elated. Jannick was the eldest of three brothers and among the first families to arrive in *Russen,* perhaps pre-dating the ancestors of Peter Schafer and Jacob Schmidt. The Wolfe brothers had never been active in community leadership, but were known to have accumulated considerable wealth. The brothers would make ideal residents, purchasing a large block of farmland and building their homes on the township site. A small crowd assembled to greet Ludwig and Jannick. The Bruener party left only months after their own, but there was interest in what had taken place in *Russen* since their departure. Ludwig and Jannick were in no mind to entertain questions. They were more interested in what St. Anne's had to offer.

The crowd dispersed quickly leaving Peter, Felix Austerlitz, and Albert Wetzel to discuss, with Ludwig and Jannick, the Bruener party's plan for the future. Peter's hopes were soon dashed—Ludwig's party was smaller than anticipated, with only seven families, and one of those already working for the Atchison, Topeka and Santa Fe Railroad. The news did not get better.

"My brothers and I have scheduled a visit to a 700-acre parcel west of Hays City," Jannick said.

"Did Mr. Randolph arrange the visit?" Peter asked.

"Yes, along with two other parcels of similar size."

Jannick Wolfe listened to Peter's description of the *St. Anne's Company*, but expected to break with tradition. The brothers required no support beyond one another, and disliked building a home separate from farmland. Their decision was shaped long before they arrived in Kansas.

Peter drew some encouragement from Ludwig Bruener who planned a home in St. Anne's. He was sure the Hoch and Portner families would do the same. Ludwig intended to build on the township site, but was uncertain where the others may locate. A few days earlier, Karl Seigler, an original member who was forced into employment, contacted Nicholas Geist and told him his brother, still in *Russen,* sent enough money to buy sixty acres of St. Anne's farmland. Karl was committed to his employer for an additional thirty days, but would rejoin the party shortly thereafter.

A week earlier, the Mullers, who regularly attended the Fort Hays Chapel, announced the courtship of their eldest son and Carina Weber. Elise had again displayed her match-making acumen. Tradition called for the bride to join her in-laws in the family home, but Carina refused to live in a crowded soddy miles from St. Anne's. The couple instead planned to build adjacent to her parents, Philipp and Elise. The loss of the Wolfe brothers was disappointing, but any two-week period in which the *company* attracted five new families was a blessing.

Peter's good fortune continued into July. He and the council woke each day fearful that the crop would be lost to the unrelenting Kansas heat, but rainfall came as if some unseen hand recognized the need. The corn was growing tall and robust, and all signs pointed to an excellent yield. Oats and barley were doing equally well. Even the spring wheat looked strong and hardy. Joy was a term used sparingly in St. Anne's, but for the moment there was a sense of well-being. Mr. Nelson was particularly impressed by the condition of field crops. He told Peter corn and smaller grains appeared to be faring as well as any in the county.

Ludwig Bruener arrived with his party four days after his initial visit to St. Anne's. He brought word that the Wolfe brothers had purchased the 700-acre parcel shown them by Mr. Randolph. The Bruener party had no short-term housing, so each quickly erected tent-like structures on the township site. Rachel Austerlitz and Melina Schafer opened their homes to young children and their mothers until more permanent housing was available. The Brueners planned to construct a frame house—the Hochs and Portners, soddies. For the latter, housing would come quickly—the membership was accomplished at building earthen homes. In less than a week, the two families would have a roof over their head.

Apart from shelter, the first order of business was the purchase of land. The Bruener family bought seventy acres from Kansas Pacific. The Hochs and Portners each purchased fifty acres from Felix Austerlitz. The Hochs had been interested in a parcel belonging to Peter, but for reasons known only to himself, he made no attempt to market the property, even making excuses to avoid their scheduled meeting. All three purchases were sold at a five percent premium and included a share of the *St. Anne's Company*.

Ludwig Bruener had arrived with enough funds to support his family through the winter. He contracted for a wood frame home in the township, and began turning sod immediately. Rainer Hoch and Milo Portner planned on building soddies before taking on work as farmhands. Lacking funds, and a harvest of their own, both were dependent on the *company*, or outside employment, to survive. John saw the dilemma faced by the Hoch and Portner families as an opportunity. Hermann had sent several bags of Turkey Red, far more than necessary for planting on the Lundeen Ranch. If he could convince the newcomers to plant the excess, Rainer and Milo could work their own land, planting Turkey Red in the fall and harvesting in the summer. John would benefit as well. A larger planting provided a better test of how Turkey Red would fare on the Kansas prairie.

In Pfeifer, the elders had regularly assembled the community for meetings, although participants often complained that the gatherings lacked substance. The opposite was true in St. Anne's. There was much to discuss, but little time for meetings. The arrival of the Bruener Party, and progress on construction of the community center, gave the council good reason to assemble. After Father Lenkeit's mass, the banns for Michel Muller and Carina Weber were read for a second time. The members then returned to St. Anne's where the Bruener party was formally recognized and welcomed to the community. Ludwig was asked to say a few words before giving way to Peter and a discussion of the community center. The walls were now complete and trusses had arrived. John and Albert had constructed a triangular device for raising the supports, the first truss to be lifted by a work party that afternoon. Father Lenkeit blessed the construction—the third time the structure was so anointed. The assembled group sat down to a midday meal. By late afternoon, three trusses had been lifted and secured. Albert sought volunteers for the following week and, once satisfied that he had the requisite help, excused the workers. Typically, this would have signaled the beginning of a modest celebration, but the death of Wilfried Gerber still weighed heavily on the party. The members prayed for Wilfried, and for Meta, and quickly dispersed.

John and Hersh Schneider spent much of the next week plowing ground on Hermann's ranch in preparation for planting Turkey Red. He was beginning to shift more of the ranch projects to his friend, recognizing that commitments closer to home had begun to suffer. The shift was also expedient. Although he had said nothing publically, John was certain he would soon be leaving St. Anne's. Hersh was the perfect replacement as caretaker—conscientious and trustworthy.

Chapter Eleven:
In Death A New Life

"The best way to predict your future is to create it"
—Abraham Lincoln

Near midday John was surprised to see Mr. Pallitto making his way across the field. As he approached, he could see Josef was holding an envelope and shouting *Russen*. It appeared Josef had stopped first at the Schafer house as Maria was trailing some distance behind. His father could not have replied to the couple's last letter since the turnaround was at best twelve to fourteen weeks. This must be something new. John thanked Josef, who appeared exhausted, while Hersh, sensing this was a family matter, watered the horses. John and Maria opened the letter. All they needed to know was contained in the opening sentence; *"mutter ist tot."* John stared at the horizon as Maria read on. Helena was laid to rest on the day the letter was written. His sister Ada had come from Katharinenstadt, along with her husband, and planned to stay on for several days. Friends filled the church and community center. Everyone said Father Albin was at his best, praying over the body and citing Helena's courage and contribution to the community. She died peacefully during the night—her battle with the illness no one understood was finally over. Jacob assured the couple that he was doing well and would write again soon. Hersh had already tethered the horses and was making his way toward the township.

John and Maria came to a decision before they reached the Schafer home. Jacob must join them in St. Anne's. A letter was prepared and posted by Mr. Pallitto. They were not sure how Jacob would react. Emigration meant leaving his daughter behind, but Jacob had never visited Ada and she, until her mother's death, had never returned to Pfeifer.

He had also formed a successful partnership with Stephan Haus, the blacksmith, and would be reticent to abandon the newly formed enterprise. Helena's passing, and recent constraints imposed by the Crown made the decision easier, but the greatest attraction was the opportunity to spend his later years in the company of family, particularly his grandchildren. He could do the same with Ada in Katharinenstadt, but the city was too big and too busy, and he had always been much closer to John than his daughter. St Anne's was also home to many of his former neighbors.

A second letter arrived the same week, this one from Peter and Melina's second eldest son Freidrich. He and his friends had reached the Dakota Territory, and found work in or near the Red River Valley. Freidrich was a farmhand on 313 acres near Goose Creek, soon-to-be renamed Casselton. The property was owned by Karl Meyer, an early homesteader. He had lost a leg in an accident in 1872 and was having some difficulty managing the farm. Like others in the area, he had found it difficult to hire workers since the Custer expedition confirmed the presence of gold near French Creek in the Black Hills. As a result, the acreage now under cultivation had been cut by more than one-half.

Kurt Haus had signed on with the Cornellious Mann Company, a newly formed farming conglomerate created when the Northern Pacific Railroad, unable to service its debt, exchanged bonds for railroad land. Mann now held more than 3,000 acres. He and his absentee investors planned to double their holdings within the next year. Kurt was assembling a bewildering array of plows, harrows, planters, reapers and mechanical threshers. Close to 2,000 acres had been turned, but the Mann Company expected to increase that by 4,000 in the coming year—most in wheat, with some livestock and limited quantities of oats, barley and corn.

The last of the three young men, Klaus Schuler, stepped away from farming, and was employed by the NPRR. The company, despite bankruptcy and reorganization, was continuing its push westward hoping to reach Puget Sound in the Washington Territory. At last word, Klaus was working somewhere near the Missouri River crossing.

＊ ＊ ＊ ＊ ＊

In 1864, the Congress granted more than forty million acres to the Northern Pacific Railroad—a swath of land made up of alternating, odd-numbered sections extending for twenty miles on either side of the right-of-way. Even-numbered sections were held for distribution to small farmers through the Homestead Act. In the Dakota Territory, the grants amounted to 12,800 acres for every mile of track laid.

NPRR sold their grants to raise cash, or used the land as security for indebtedness. President Lincoln extended the grants hoping to create a second transcontinental rail link across the northern tier of the United States, but the soft ground of Minnesota, and difficult river crossings in the Dakota Territory, took a heavy financial toll. Bond sales in Europe fell short of expectations, and the panic of 1873, the "Long Depression," pushed the railroad toward collapse. Facing bankruptcy, the company exchanged land grants for preferred stock and bonds. Former debtors became land owners, many in the fertile Red River Valley. They were largely absentee owners, but understood the agricultural value of the land. Farms were created ranging in size from 3,000 to more than 30,000 acres—the so-called "Bonanza Farms." Their primary crop was wheat, though other grains and livestock occupied twenty to thirty percent of the acreage. The farms were often split into units of 3,000 to 5,000 acres with a farm boss for each unit.

Bonanza farms coupled the latest in farm machinery with the aggressive hiring of migrant workers during planting and harvest seasons. Good farming practices, technology, and strategically hired workers led to yields of spring wheat near twenty bushels per acre—numbers which startled the world. In the 1880s wheat production began to outpace demand. Overproduction, depleted soil, and drought led to the demise of most bonanza farms. The land was subdivided, and converted to small scale farming.

＊ ＊ ＊ ＊ ＊

Melina was disturbed by two comments in Freidrich's letter. The first had to do with the possibility of a Sioux uprising. Prospectors had overrun the Black Hills, an area considered sacred by the Lakota tribe, and within the boundaries of the recently drawn Fort Laramie Treaty. President Grant had reneged on the treaty sending the Army to forcefully relocate Sitting Bull. The Lakota chief refused to leave, instead gathering warriors from the Arapahoe and Cheyenne tribes. Melina had no idea of the distance between the Black Hills and Freidrich's place of employment, but envisioned Sioux war parties surrounding the Meyer farm.

A second comment was equally disturbing—Kurt Haus was ready to try his hand at prospecting. If that proved unsuccessful, he had plans to join a NPRR survey team pushing its way deep into Montana Territory. Kurt Haus was a free spirit, and Melina knew that her son and Klaus Schuler were sure to follow his lead. The young men had traversed Western Europe, crossed the Atlantic, and made their way to the northern prairie. Prospecting for gold and charting the wilds of Montana were simply one more step in the adventure. Melina began to wonder when she would see Freidrich again.

Since his mother's passing, John could not erase the thought that leaving Pfeifer hastened his mother's demise. He found work—multiple projects—helped assuage the guilt. The first was installation of the tin plate roof for the community center and Miss Geiser's cottage. He enlisted George Breit, Hersh Schneider and Philipp Weber to complete the roof on both. The interiors were still unfinished and John, with assistance from Albert, took that on as well.

Father Lenkeit made a number of suggestions designed to make the center look more like a church. The priest made sketches showing placement of the altar, and even proposed an assessment for statuary. Albert feigned interest, but did nothing. He was more interested in what Miss Geiser thought was necessary for the center's alternative purpose—St. Anne's school. Albert was interested in just about anything having to do with Miss Geiser, and his infatuation left Father Lenkeit's petitions wanting.

When his backlog began to lessen, John turned his attention to Christof Acker and the grist mill. He earlier committed to help Christof frame the mill taking the place of Cyrus Larsen, at least until the carpenter fulfilled

176

his home building commitments. Christof understood that John would be available only as time permitted. Fieldwork on the Schafer farm and, to a lesser extent, the Lundeen Ranch, took precedence. Christof was satisfied with progress on the mill. His family would have a roof over their head before winter set in.

One assignment John escaped was construction of the common barn. Coordination was left to Denzel Kalb, its primary advocate, though Denzel had helpers. With harvest close, and winter not far behind, others were fast becoming proponents of common shelter. Denzel's interest was cover for livestock, but there were other concerns. A clean dry space following harvest was also necessary for threshing, winnowing, and storage.

An acre of common ground had been set aside for the barn, and Peter offered an adjoining one-half acre he held as a principal buyer. Given the additional space, the council decided on two barns, one designed for grain processing and storage, and the other for livestock shelter. The first barn was to be raised in August and the second following harvest.

Albert and John once again set out to borrow funds from the First National Bank of Hays City. Mr. Norton was agreeable. The transaction was completed in less than an hour. Both principal and interest were due in three years. There was no labor expense, since both barns would be raised using volunteers. Albert signed for the community. A materials order was immediately placed with Cyrus Larsen. A new sawmill had opened in Hays City, but since Mr. Larsen donated trusses for the community center, his company was the preferred choice. Construction on the first barn was completed in just over a week, with one side and door left undone awaiting materials. There were no problems encountered aside from oppressive heat and Elmer Klein, who dislocated a shoulder when he fell from the loft.

Amanda Lynn Geiser returned from Pennsylvania on August 25. Albert was waiting at the station. The two proceeded directly to the newly-constructed community center where Miss Geiser declared the building would serve her *studenten* well, but adjustments were necessary. She brought with her a large quantity of teaching materials, and examples of others that must be purchased. Albert presented a list of twenty-one children ranging in age from eight to fifteen—most having received some education in *Russen*. Two families made the decision not to send their children to school. The

Portners, who believed education meant studies preparatory to the Sacrament of Confirmation and the Breits—the latter convinced their daughters had no need for education beyond that learned in the home.

Albert had intentionally left parts of both the community center, and Miss Geiser's cottage unfinished awaiting the *Schullehrer's* guidance. Adept at directing others, Miss Geiser did not disappoint. He soon found himself with a long list of suggested changes to "her" school and cottage. The interior still required work, which Albert welcomed as more time in Miss Geiser's company. He enjoyed every minute and hoped, at some point that their working relationship would blossom into some form of attachment. Albert was dreaming. Miss Geiser saw him as a council member meeting his obligation and nothing more. They worked well together, in large measure because Albert followed Miss Geiser's demands—a critical element in their relationship.

She used their work time together to further Albert's instruction in English, insisting that he identify objects in the language of his new country. This led to a noticeable improvement in language skills, and some humor as he struggled with pronunciation. Miss Geiser had returned to St. Anne's earlier than planned, but was happy she did. There were tasks to be completed, and she had come to enjoy the planning and work sessions with Albert and his occasional helpers.

Most of these sessions took place after Albert had completed his field-work. He was rarely late, but on a mid-September day was asked by the widow Gerber to make small repairs to the roof of her soddy. When he arrived at the *Schulhaus*, he found Miss Geiser buried in a box of writing slates, and other teaching aids just delivered by NPRR. She was obviously exhausted.

He stood frozen on the threshold until the *Schullehrer* finally asked, "Are you ill?"

His halting response came as a complete surprise.

"I was hoping that we could take a few of the materials, gather something to eat, and watch the sunset from Lundeen Ranch."

Now it was Miss Geiser's turn to be tongue tied. She had once before watched the sunset from that vantage point as it cast a different hue on each rise and fall of the prairie, but she had been alone. Albert's request created a good deal of trepidation. She was aware of his interest, if not infatuation, as were others in the community. Miss Geiser worried that her acceptance could easily be misinterpreted by both Albert, and the *Gemeinde*. The *Volga Deutsch* had rules regarding courtship. Was it acceptable for a young woman, especially the *Schullehrer,* to simply ride off with a young man, however innocent their intention? Miss Geiser quickly dismissed the thought. She was an independent, educated woman, and more than capable of making her own decisions regarding behavior.

Turning to her would-be suitor, she said, "I'd be delighted," adding, "We must return immediately following sunset."

Miss Geiser wondered if her decision to join Albert had been influenced by a discovery made shortly after her return to Pennsylvania. She asked about a young man she once courted, and found he had chosen a rival. Miss Geiser had ended the relationship herself by moving west, but his decision bruised her ego. Now she was riding toward what some might consider a romantic interlude. Had the end to courtship in Pennsylvania driven her to accept Albert's offer. She thought that to be unlikely. Albert was a kind person with a quick wit and pleasing manner, but fell short of her lofty standards for a partner.

One of the Miss Geiser's requests—or more properly demands—led to a confrontation between John and his father-in-law. Miss Geiser wanted a storage box for each child arranged in a shelf-like manner. Albert asked for John's help in building the boxes, and securing them to the wall. John agreed. Peter overheard John describing the project to Maria, and became agitated accusing his son-in-law of spending too much time on projects for others, and too little on the Schafer home and farm. Peter was upset by John's failure to complete the room especially set aside for the young couple. The room had not been touched for more than three weeks, and the baby would soon be due.

The challenge was not without merit. John was behind largely because of commitments elsewhere. The delay bothered Peter—as did anything that suggested independence or failure to comply with his demands. He saw the family, including John, as an extension of himself. They were to follow in lockstep at his direction. His son-in-law was errant.

Suddenly, Peter turned on his son-in-law.

"I don't think you're committed to St. Anne's," Peter said. "You intend to leave."

John saw no obligation to answer. What he did with his future was up to him, not his father-in-law. His failure to respond was answer enough.

Peter was livid. "After all I've done, you'll take my daughter and grandchild to some godforsaken outpost."

John had heard enough. "I've earned my keep," he said. "You and your fool's errand be damned."

Peter took a step toward his son-in-law, but Melina interceded. She was beside herself.

"Stop them, Albrecht," she pleaded, but her eldest was content to have someone else the subject of his father's abuse.

Finally, Maria, citing her pregnancy and need for calm, called for an end, and the two, face-to-face, separated. The tension between John and his father-in-law had been building since their departure from *Russen*. Maria's intervention resulted in a truce, but not a resolution. Peter was sure John was leaving, and John was now convinced he must. Any hope that Melina held for raising her first grandchild in St. Anne's was fading.

Peter's angst was rooted in a concern for the future of his experiment. He had just received a letter from Arne Schwaub who continued to meet with emigrants all along the Volga. Arne reported that interest in leaving the colonies had not declined, but there was evidence of greater dispersion. Kansas remained a popular destination, but so too did Colorado, the Dakota Territory, and even South America.

The greater concern to Peter was Arne's specific comments regarding the *St. Anne's Company*. His assessment was blunt. Many in his audience saw the *company* as a poorly disguised attempt to recreate the same conditions they desired to escape. The emigrants particularly disliked separation of home and farm. Arne suggested, as he had in the past, that members be allowed to build wherever they wanted.

It was Peter's second rebuff in as many days. The Wagner and Steyer families had visited St. Anne's the day before. Both were from a village south of Pfeifer and learned of Peter's colony from Anselm. Mr. Randolph sold them property some six miles north and west of St. Anne's. They were eager to become a part of the parish, and hoped to be included in community

180

events, but wanted no part of the *St. Anne's Company*. Both saw common holdings and the separation of village and farm as vestiges of the past. Peter did not take their rejection well, suggesting they were making a serious mistake. He now regretted the encounter. The families left abruptly, having learned nothing of St. Anne's, or the parish.

John was working at Christof's mill when Maria brought the letter. Jacob was coming to America. He made the decision immediately following Helena's passing. Social and economic conditions along the lower Volga were worsening. The jealously-guarded *Volga Deutsch* autonomy was threatened daily by the Crown. Some elements within the Czar's *coterie* maintained the colonies were a threat to *Russische* security. Alexander reacted by imposing even greater sanctions on village administration. The outlook was bleak and plummeting grain prices from growing worldwide production made matters worse.

Jacob was initially reluctant to leave his daughter, but that concern was eliminated when Ada announced her family was leaving Katharinenstadt for South America. She was against the move, but had little to say in the matter. Jacob no longer had an attachment to the Steppe. Leaving meant the sale of personal property and finding someone to purchase his interest in the joint venture with Stephan Haus. Neither was a problem. He expected to arrive sometime in the spring. John and Maria were elated and wrote back encouraging an early departure. They told Jacob it was possible they could be leaving Kansas. He would not be surprised. Father and son had discussed a break from the commune before John left Pfeifer. Maria suggested that they share Jacob's decision with Peter, but John was opposed. Better to wait until the departure date drew closer. Much could happen between now and then.

The following Sunday marked the dedication of the community center. Peter opened the ceremony thanking all in attendance and then turned to the introduction of invited guests—the Wolfe brothers, homesteaders, Reinhart Muller and Paulus Richter and the newly arrived families of Armin Wagner and Achim Steyer. Peter made a special trip to the Wagner and Steyer homes to invite the families and apologize for his earlier behavior. Next came the introduction of merchants—Josef Pallitto of Pallitto's General Store, Conn Doyle, the blacksmith, Cyrus Larsen, the carpenter,

George Bollinger, the stonemason, Mr. Nelson from Nelson Feed and a surprise visitor, Charles Norton the banker. Jeremia Olsen, the commercial sod buster, sent his regrets.

After a few brief remarks, Peter gave way to Albert, who traced the history of the community center, and how it came to be. He thanked all who contributed to the construction process. Albert then introduced Miss Geiser. She thanked the *Gemeinde* for their courtesy and invited all to visit what was today a church, but tomorrow would be a *Schulhaus*. Father Lenkeit acknowledged the comment knowing real control of the multi-purpose center rested with Miss Geiser. The dedication closed with the unveiling of a large monument given by Messrs. Pallitto, Nelson and Bollinger—the latter carving the stone. The inscription was simple; "St. Anne's Community Center 1875." Peter and the council members were listed below the inscription.

Father Lenkeit then invited the assembled group to join him in celebrating the inaugural mass. In his homily, he referenced the hardships endured by the Schafer party, and all those who sought to build a life on the prairie. He also expressed his admiration for what the community had achieved in just a few short months. The priest called for a moment of silence to reflect on those who had died since the community's inception.

Not wanting to miss an opportunity, he reminded the congregation that there was much to be thankful for, and the proper expression of gratitude was construction of a stand-alone church on the ground adjoining the community center. He paused briefly after his pronouncement to gauge reaction to this often made suggestion. He then surprised the congregation by telling them the bishop had assigned another priest to care for the spiritual needs of the surrounding communities. His duties were now confined to Fort Hays and St. Anne's, and he considered St. Anne's his home parish. Lastly, the priest again introduced, as tradition required, the two couples who planned to marry in the fall—Albrecht Schafer and Michel Muller to the sisters, Hilke and Carina Weber.

The mass now complete, the crowd moved to the reception area where the women of St. Anne's had prepared a sumptuous meal with *Bierocks* as its centerpiece. Food was plentiful, as was drink, though the latter was consumed less conspicuously. It was a joyous occasion, but something less than a celebration. Harvest was near, and the demands of fieldwork brought an early end to festivities.

The long days of harvest season quelled the simmering conflict between Peter and his son-in-law. John spent most of his time in preparation for the harvest, but devoted at least a few hours of each day working toward completion of the Schafer home—particularly the addition he and Maria occupied. He was also helping Melina build a larger door to the family's root cellar. The activities were close to home and seemed to satisfy Peter. John didn't care about his father-in law's state of mind, but he knew the women of the house were happy for the end to bickering. Maria was drawing ever closer to her due date, and much happier absent conflict within the family.

The growing enthusiasm regarding the harvest uniformly lifted community spirits. Mr. Nelson's prediction had proven correct. The grasshoppers did not return, and the weather cooperated. Spring wheat and the smaller grains looked good, but the real basis for the party's euphoric outlook was corn. The crop stood tall in every St. Anne's field and promised a good yield. Cellars were also near full with dried fruits and berries, along with onions, carrots, turnips and other root vegetables—enough to gird against the inevitable scarcity of winter. One last planting of radishes and lettuce was planned, and a few of the women hoped to experiment with potatoes. The party arrived in Kansas too late to plant the tubers in spring, but the Richter family enjoyed some success with late season potatoes, and that was enough to encourage the women of St. Anne's.

Along with traditional efforts to put foods "by," Mr. Pallitto introduced in midsummer a new form of preservation he referred to as "hermetic sealing." The term meant nothing to Josef, but he was told by his St Louis mentor that the process held great promise. He dispatched his wife to the kitchen of Catherine Schuler with the necessary materials and a basket full of tomatoes, beans, apples and wild blackberries. With eight women looking on, the tomatoes and small quantity of water were brought to a boil, ladled into glass jars, quickly cooled, then sealed with a zinc lid and threaded cap. The extreme heat was intended to purify both the tomatoes and the jar. Mrs. Pallitto repeated the process for the blackberries. She instructed Catherine Schuler to place the jars in the root cellar and proudly announced the contents would taste better than fresh, even after six months of storage.

Erna Klein had some unaccountable understanding of the process—the others none. Most were skeptical. Mrs. Pallitto was not sure if the women were impressed or just being polite. She got the answer when Catherine Schuler was the only taker purchasing just twelve jars. The process was interesting, but Kansas already offered more than enough learning experiences. This was simply one more for which there was too little time. Expense was also a factor. Jars would not fare well when compared to a new harrow or a bag of Turkey Red seeds. Perhaps this was an idea for next year, but not their first summer on the prairie.

Animals native to the prairie, deer, elk, and antelope offered another food source for the Schafer party. Their kill would be used to supplement hog and cow meat for sausage making and as a primary meat source during the winter months. Nicholas Geist and Elmer Klein were looked upon as skilled trackers. Both carefully studied the movement of game, and their feeding habits. Ludwig Bruener had done a great deal of hunting in his early years joining his grandfather whose duty it was to provide game for their village.

Ludwig had not hunted for years, but he was eager to display the skills learned from his grandfather years ago. He and his eldest son Heinz joined Nicholas and Elmer as they tracked a small herd of deer west of St. Anne's. The Brueners were sent ahead to make a kill. As Ludwig was stepping over a downed tree the Springfield .45/70 rifle, one of three purchased by the *company*, accidently discharged striking his son in the fleshy part of his left leg just above the knee. Heinz was in extreme pain with blood pulsing from the wound. Elmer set out for St. Anne's to secure help leaving Ludwig and Nicholas to tend to Heinz. Luckily, Elmer came across Albrecht Schafer and a wagon en route to make fence repairs. He gave the reins to Elmer who set for the accident site, while Albrecht ran to the Schafer house to advise his father. Peter dispatched John to Fort Hays to locate the doctor. After one-half hour of frantic searching, he found the Army physician. They intercepted the incoming wagon less than a mile from the Fort. It had been two hours since Heinz was wounded. He was ashen, unresponsive, and lying in a pool of blood. His father's effort to contain the bleeding had not been successful. Heinz was taken to the Fort Hays hospital. Several members of the Schafer party arrived and began the long vigil. Father Lenkeit joined them and all prayed together. After what seemed like an eternity, the doctor emerged from his operating space. He managed to stop the bleeding, but was unsure he could save the leg.

Two more hours passed with no word on the boy's condition. Finally, the exhausted physician completed the bloody task. He was able to save the leg, but Heinz would never have full use of the limb. Ludwig Bruener stayed by his son's bedside for more than a week. He was relieved from time to time by Nicholas Geist. After eight days, the two men returned Heinz to his home in St. Anne's.

The second week in August brought ideal conditions for harvesting. They had started, then stopped, the week before when a light rain had fallen midweek. Stalks bent to the weight of moisture making it difficult to cut grain without damaging the head. Oats were the first of the field crops to be harvested. The Schafer and Austerlitz families had ten acres each. Others in the party had two or less. The *Gemeinde* worked together knowing help for your neighbor today meant reparation tomorrow. The harvest for oats, and other small grains, took place in the traditional manner. Men cut the grain using cradles or a scythe while the women and children trailed behind gathering the stalks into sheaves. These were leaned against one another to build shocks, and left in the field to dry. The shocks would remain there for approximately a week, or until the threat of rain. They would then be collected by wagon and carried to the barn.

Mr. Nelson was among those on hand when the harvest began. He brought a two-horse reaper, and hoped that a demonstration would stimulate interest. Gabriel Schuler agreed to try the reaper on his field, but the blades were damaged by rocks. In their haste to plant crops, much debris still remained in the fields. No one questioned the reaper's potential, but obstacles must first be removed. Two days were required to harvest the oats. Late in the afternoon of the second day, several women left the fields to begin preparation of the evening meal. A small gathering was planned to mark the first field crop harvested. Miss Geiser, now an accepted member of the community, arrived an hour before to assist in meal preparation. The *Schullehrer* had struck a relationship with Maria, Emma Heimler and Anna

Schneider. The three women were interested in learning English and Miss Geiser was keeping a record of events in St. Anne's with particular attention to the ingenuity displayed by the prairie housewife. Both purposes were served by their association.

The *Schullehrer* took an early leave when some of the men showed signs of having too much to drink. Albert escorted her to the cottage, which was now complete. Miss Geiser appreciated his thoughtfulness, but quickly sent him on his way, not wanting to encourage anyone who saw evidence of a budding relationship. As a member of the council, Albert was the link between the *Gemeinde* and the *Schullehrer,* a working relationship that was best kept in that manner.

With shocks dried and stored, responsibility for threshing fell to smaller groups. The sheaves were opened and spread evenly over a clean floor, then beaten with a flail to separate grain from husk. The process involved more skill than the name implied. A novice could easily destroy as much grain as he separated. Philipp Weber had an alternative. He volunteered a home-built threshing sledge. A few sheaves were spread in a circular pattern on hard packed ground in front of the barn. A single horse then pulled the weighted sledge over the stalks to separate the grain. It was soon apparent the sledge worked no better than the flail, and had the disadvantage of dragging grain through the dirt. Philipp argued the sledge was more effective, but his argument was rooted more deeply in a defense of his creation than its performance. The remaining stalks would be put to the flail.

Winnowing was the final step and required a fresh breeze. The grain and chaff were swept into piles. With both sides of the barn open, the residue was cast into the air. The chaff was carried away and grain fell to the floor. The process was primitive, but effective. The product was then bagged, marked by grower, and set aside.

With small grains in the barn, John turned to planting Turkey Red on his uncle's thirty acres. He was surprised when his father-in-law directed Albrecht to assist. Perhaps it was an olive branch to mend feelings after their heated argument a few weeks earlier. John was glad for the help, although he would have preferred someone less inclined to wander off. The assistance was well timed since Hersh Schneider, his customary helper, was busy with the Acker's grist mill. The pair quickly completed their work with

Maria able to escape her mother's cocoon long enough to briefly take the reins of the planter.

The Hoch and Portner families planted their allotment of Turkey Red a few days before John. Mr. Nelson, always watchful for anything new in agriculture, had also taken notice of Turkey Red. He was able to acquire a small quantity, which was quickly purchased by Messrs. Austerlitz and Schuler. They expected to plant two acres each. Both would have liked to plant more, but winter wheat was scarce, and priced accordingly. John was glad for the additional planting. There was now enough of Turkey Red to accurately judge its success.

The yield for the small grains was too small to justify a communal set aside, and no help was required from outside the community. Corn was different. The Schafer, Austerlitz and Schuler families had planted at least sixty acres each using commercial sodbusters and horse-drawn planters. Contract labor was necessary. Neighbors were more than willing to help, but not when it put their own harvest in jeopardy. Notices soliciting fieldworkers were posted in both Pallitto's General Store and Nelson Feed.

Work was to begin on September 10. Pay was one dollar per day with two meals included. There was no provision for shelter. Able bodied sons and daughters of farmers in the surrounding area represented the best help, but they were likely to be occupied with their own harvest. Next came itinerant workers that moved north with the harvest. The Schafer party referred to these workers as *auslander*, an indication the *Volga Deutsch* saw themselves as more American than the transient laborers.

The apprehension so much a part of St. Anne's life for the past six months was cautiously replaced by a measure of elation. Late planting and stubborn prairie sod had given way to row after row of golden corn. The months ahead would see their staple boiled, roasted, or mixed with other vegetables. Ears would be joined with stalks as feed for livestock. Kernels would be ground for bread and cakes and shelled as feed for chickens. Nothing was left to waste, even the chaff used for thatch or chinking. Mr. Nelson stood ready to purchase excess or exchange for goods. For Josef Pallitto the harvest was welcome, but something less than a bonanza. The only movement of kitchen gadgets in his inventory was to lift, dust, and put back in place. It was far too early for extravagance. A good harvest meant another year on the Kansas prairie. That was enough for settler and merchant alike.

Fields of thirty acres or less were to be harvested by three separate work groups made up entirely of members of the *St. Anne's Company*. The first fields scheduled were those belonging to Hersh Schneider and Albert Wetzel. Family and neighbors made quick work of these. The larger fields belonging to Peter Schafer, Felix Austerlitz and Gabriel Schuler would be close behind. Twenty men responded to the call for help, but only sixteen were sent to St. Anne's. For reasons known only to the merchants, four had been judged unsatisfactory. Families relying on temporary help were responsible for feeding the workers.

The transients were assembled, fed and dispatched to the larger fields shortly after dawn. The process was less orderly for farms dependent on neighbors. Men, women and children were expected to participate in the harvest of these fields. Some demanded reassignment to a different work group such that friends were part of the same harvest team. The effort was quashed when Peter reminded the workers that bringing in the crop, and not visiting, was the objective. Then came a contentious discussion regarding whose field should be harvested first. The order had been decided two days earlier, but Gustav Kunkel, after inspecting his fields, believed that he should be moved up in sequence. Peter was again called upon to resolve the dispute, and the party returned to its original schedule, but not until one-half hour was lost. By midmorning, all community workers were dispatched, and a pattern quickly established. There was a short break at midday. Then in late afternoon several women left the fields to begin preparation of the evening meal which marked the end of the day—the exception a group who shared a small quantity of vodka or corn whiskey before retiring.

Mr. Nelson arrived early on the first day and let everyone know the feed store was a willing buyer of corn on the ear or shelled. His company also had the means to grind the product. He was something of an expert on estimating yield, and guessed the party could expect between twenty and twenty-four bushels per acre. This was a decided improvement over what central Kansas experienced the year before, when most fields were ravaged by grasshoppers.

The corn harvest was expected to take seven to ten days, with the approach similar to the smaller grains. A group of men cut the stalks, followed by women and children who piled them in an upright circular pattern. These were left in rows to dry. A few in the party left their corn standing for harvest later. Nicholas Geist and George Breit were among those. Their corn would be picked in the field and ears tossed against a "bang board" attached to a slow moving wagon. During these periods, the steady thump, thump, thump could be heard across the fields as picked corn was cast against the board and dropped to the wagon floor. Irrespective of approach, harvest was a task undertaken with a quiet mix of joy and gratitude.

By the end of the second day, it was apparent that the crop would reach the upper limits of Mr. Nelson's prediction, with even the least fertile ground producing a better-than-expected yield. The party's optimism continued to grow with each shock tied. The council, overtaken by the moment, took the unusual step of setting the date for *Kerbfest* well before harvest was complete. Their exuberance could be forgiven—the yield was better than anticipated.

The harvest was over in eleven days. A small amount of corn still stood in the fields and the Schuler farm had one day of work remaining. All but three of the hired hands had been released. John left the fields and had resumed work on the Acker grist mill, careful to devote some time each day to projects closer to home. He was making repairs to one of the Schafer wagons when Peter stopped by the barn. His father-in-law took full credit for the harvest and cast himself as something of a deity. John was grateful his father-in-law's visit had been brief.

Suddenly, the barn door swung open.

"Hurry," Anna Schneider announced. "The baby is coming."

John was stunned, "Right now?"

"Yes!" Anna responded, astonished by John's answer.

The two quickly covered the distance between barn and house to find Maria in her parents' bed tended by Melina. Maria appeared relatively calm. Her mother was frantic. Frida Geist arrived, and immediately began boiling water and gathering linens. She had delivered at least sixty babies in *Russen* and a few in Kansas. The throng of women, baking moments earlier, now surrounded the bedroom door.

"It's time you left," Frida said to the women.

Elma protested, "You'll need our help."

"I will not." Frida responded. "I'll need only Melina and Anna."

"Out!" she said, telling Emma Heimler to return following the baby's birth.

Some discussion had taken place the week before on whether to contact Doctor Himmelfarb, a newly arrived physician from Arkansas. He was *Deutsch*, said to be well educated, and very young. He was also a proponent of using chloroform to ease pain. John thought sedation was acceptable, but was alone in his view. Frida plainly stated she did not trust young doctors, or their methods. Maria and her mother agreed. John had protested, but was told to busy himself elsewhere. Advice from fathers was not valued. He did manage a wave to Maria, lying stoic and seemingly without pain. Peter arrived and was dismissed much as John. Father and son-in-law retreated to the kitchen, their differences forgotten for the moment.

After two hours, Frida emerged from the bedroom declaring that nothing would happen today. Her comments were made within earshot of Maria, and meant to disparage a first-time mother who succumbed to false labor. The terse remarks hurt Maria, but Frida was widely known for her skills as a midwife, not for her comforting manner. She was good at what she did. Frida had brought three children into the world since arriving in St. Anne's. Two were delivered without incident. The Breit baby died within minutes of birth, but absent Frida's intervention, Sibylle could easily have died as well.

Maria remained in her parents' bedroom. John resumed his chores checking on his wife from time to time before joining Maria in the early evening. He left for a brief period to feed and secure the animals, then returned an hour after sunset. Near midnight Maria woke John telling him it was time. His first instinct was to question, but he thought better and immediately woke Melina. He then roused Frida who arrived at the Schafer home and, after a brief examination, concluded the baby was ready. John waited by himself for an hour, his father-in-law still asleep. Maria's discomfort was becoming more apparent and Frida sent John to rouse Anna. The three women once again engaged in preparation with Frida giving instruction and Melina and Anna cajoling. Shortly before daybreak, Maria's muffled screams rose to a point where they could be heard throughout the township site. Her suffering tortured John and he could not help but think of Doctor Himmelfarb and his chloroform. A brief moment of quiet was followed by the unmistakable cry of a baby. John went straight to the bedroom to find Maria exhausted, but smiling—alongside lay a baby.

The John Schmidt family had grown by one, a healthy baby girl. Frida left for home promising to look in later in the day. Anna stayed on briefly giving way to Emma Heimler, whose task was to stay with Maria until early evening. Melina was slumped in a chair looking as if she delivered the child. John was allowed to briefly hold the baby and embrace his wife. Too excited to sleep, he returned to his work in the barn, but generally made a nuisance of himself checking every half hour on Maria and the baby.

The couple had decided to call the child Anna, if a girl, or Jacob, if a boy. He was surprised when Emma told him Maria changed her mind—the baby's given name was Morgan, *Deutsch* for morning. She would be Morgan Anne. John recalled Jacob asked if they had considered a name. It was time to write. He quickly penned a note to Jacob telling him Maria and Morgan Anne were doing well, and all were looking forward to his arrival. He posted the letter with Mr. Pallitto wondering if it would reach his father before he left *Russen*. Josef was excited by the couple's good fortune and sent John off with a small box of assorted hard candies for Maria.

Chapter Twelve:
Winds of Change

"What Dakota needs most, and first, is the addition to her population of active, substantial men, coming here to aid in developing the immense natural resources of this country."
—General George Hill

The council appointed Elma Wetzel to lead in planning for *Kerbfest*. She would be assisted by Ida Kalb and Nela Hauer, the latter still withdrawn and susceptible to long periods of melancholia. Melina suggested Nela, hoping that interaction would shake the young woman from her cycle of despondency. Specialties were attached to each household, and care was taken not to compete with a neighbor's recipe. The guest list included Hays City merchants and families the party had come to know through attendance at Father Lenkeit's Sunday mass. A good deal of advance planning was necessary, but not for the accumulation of spirits. Potato vodka, corn whiskey, and even beer surfaced from every corner of St. Anne's.

A mass of thanksgiving marked the beginning of the festival. Celebrants then moved to the Austerlitz home to salute the harvest and for Peter's introduction of guests. A variation on *Schwartzbarren kuchenen* and *grebble* were served. The evening meal came later. Elma, Ida and Nela chose *bierocks* prepared in the Schafer kitchen and relying on elk rather than beef. Dancing followed the meal. Saturday evening saw a repeat of Friday's activities with a smaller meal, but more dancing and late-night revelry. Miss Geiser attended Saturday's celebration escorted by Albert Wetzel. A few in the party—those more prone to gossip—thought they saw a warming in the relationship between the *Schullehrer* and Albert. He believed that to be the case, but Miss Geiser did not. She was fond of Albert as one might be fond of a neighbor or co-worker. She expected his escort as the council's liaison to the school.

The first frost had taken place a month earlier and the members turned their attention to the winter ahead. They knew cold from the *Russische* Steppe, but this was their first in Kansas. Mr. Nelson had told them the prairie winter was brutal and his predictions were most often correct. Women checked root cellars, took stock of winter clothing and met in shucking and shelling bees. The men checked roofs and roof supports, chinked cracks around doors and windows and supplemented fuel stocks with *mistholz,* a combination of compacted manure and barn scraps.

The council met to determine individual contribution to the common storehouse. Since the decision held the prospect of taking food from the family table, the meeting was well attended by the *Gemeinde.* Ten percent of harvested corn, exclusive of that set aside for seed, would be held by the *St. Anne's Company.* The purpose was to help those in need, service debt and fund common projects. Measurement was not exact since the corn was in various stages of processing. Self-reporting was the order of the day. Denzel Kalb, as a council member, was given the task of checking reported numbers against what he thought to be approximate yield. No discrepancies were noted. Families with relatively low production were excused, while larger farms were assessed against only one-half of their yield. At least six and perhaps eight families were likely to have a surplus. They had corn to sell, a remarkable achievement given their first year of harvest. The Schafer party had fared well. Peter was quick to point out careful planning contributed to their success, but so too did good weather and the absence of grasshopper infestation. John was surprised his father-in-law had not taken credit for these developments as well.

The start of the school year was now just one week away. To no one's surprise, Miss Geiser was more than ready for her *studenten.* All teaching aids and materials had been received, including twenty-five lightly used Noah Webster Blue-Back Spellers sent as a courtesy by Franklin and Marshall, her *alma mater.* The state of Kansas paid a visit and found the teacher, classroom, and curriculum met their standards. The contingent was led by

Kenneth Sloan, the Associate Director for the Kansas Superintendent of Public Instruction, and son of a state senator. Mr. Sloan seemed particularly taken by Miss Geiser and suggested she attend a conference of educators scheduled for the next spring. He promised to send additional information.

Adult classes in conversational English started a few days before the children began their studies. Miss Geiser referred to the sessions as *Englisch Zum Leben*. Maria, Anna Schneider and Emma Heimler, whom Miss Geiser had taken under her wing, were first to enroll. There was some initial reluctance among the older women, notably Luise Kunkel and Catherine Schuler, but that quickly changed. Luise was first, then Catherine. Soon others joined the weekly lessons. No real attempt was made to learn *Russische* in Pfeifer, which created an even greater distance between the native population and *Volga Deutsch*. The same mistake would not be made in America.

The council welcomed the *Englisch Zum Leben* lessons believing the members required at least a passing knowledge of the language. The classes were held two nights per week in the community center. Miss Geiser treated the adult learners as she would any student. Regular attendance was expected and there were lessons to be completed at home. The classes were less intimidating than the rules suggested. The *Schullehrer* made sure the women enjoyed their one-hour escape from what was often a twelve to fourteen-hour day.

Albert was returning from a meeting with Peter and Felix and looked in on Miss Geiser after her Thursday *Englisch Zum Leben* lesson. The evening had been filled with a healthy dose of laughter and Albert saw Miss Geiser was in a festive mood.

"May I help you straighten desks?" he asked.

"If you would like," Miss Geiser responded.

Their task was quickly completed, but Albert seemed reluctant to leave. He began to discuss courtship among the Volga Deutsch. Miss Geiser listened politely, but grew more apprehensive as Albert warmed to his topic.

Suddenly, he asked the *Schullehrer*. "Would you give me the honor of taking the first step toward espousal?"

"I'm tired Albert," she said. "Can we discuss this tomorrow?"

Miss Geiser had worried this day might be coming, but the suddenness of his proposal caught her off guard. Had she encouraged him to think of their relationship as something other than friendship? Perhaps she was naive. Their collaboration and her frequent requests for help could be seen as romantic interest. That was never her intention. She now regretted her decision to join Albert in watching the sunset a few weeks earlier. He saw her acceptance as far more than what it was meant to be.

Miss Geiser returned to the solitude of her cottage and immediately became angry with herself. In an effort not to hurt a friend, she put aside the inevitable and had likely made matters worse.

Albert was just leaving when she returned to the *klassenzimmer*. This time she was truthful.

"We will always be friends Albert—I hope dear friends—but nothing more."

Albert stood motionless. "I understand," he said, then quietly departed.

It was the last time they would work together. Early next morning Denzel Kalb told Miss Geiser there would be changes in the responsibilities of council members. He would now be the contact for matters relative to education.

In early September, John had sent a letter to Freidrich asking him about Dakota. He wondered if the land resembled Kansas, if homesteads were still available, and at what price railroad land was being sold. John had taken his time posting the letter, fearful that the correspondence would be discovered. Disclosure would fuel suspicion that he and Maria might soon be leaving. He finally wrote, but hand carried the letter to Mr. Pallitto, asking that any return correspondence be held for his pickup. Freidrich was quick to respond, but Josef had long forgotten John's request. Fortunately, Maria happened by the general store. If she had not, the letter could easily have been given to Peter or Melina for delivery. Correspondence from an errant son to a son-in-law with designs on leaving would rile Peter. When she returned home, Maria hid the letter in the couple's room. This was correspondence not to be shared with her parents, at least for the moment.

John had spent the afternoon with Christof Acker. His millstones just arrived from Ohio and the more difficult elements of construction could now begin. They were studying a sketch of wallower, face and pinion gears. John agreed to fashion these and help, when necessary, with framing the millhouse. He was looking forward to both the additional income and shelter that came with inside work.

When John returned to the Schafer house, it was apparent Maria had something to share. Her furtive glances suggested this should be done in private. The couple retreated to their room to read Freidrich's letter. He began by discussing what he knew of land that was available in the Dakota Territory. Some could be purchased for as little as $3.00 per acre, but the ground was barren, miles from the nearest town, and some without access to water. Good farm land near his location ranged from $5.00 to $7.50 per acre. The parcels were smallish, but with ground enough to support a family. John was busy calculating the cost of starting on unimproved land, while Maria read on.

What came next brought an audible gasp from both. Would John be interested in purchasing the farm owned by his employer, Karl Meyer? It was located less than a half-day's ride from Fargo and fewer than two miles from the Casselton rail yard. The farm encompassed 313 acres—most in wheat with some corn, oats, and barley. Less than ten acres was susceptible to flood and that contained a mix of alfalfa and prairie grasses. There were two frame houses in better-than-average condition, a barn and two livestock sheds—both needing work—but sturdy. The farm came with a small seed drill and several plows, including a sulky. There were two reapers, an early design, as well as a spike and spring tooth harrow. Other implements were scattered about the premises in various stages of repair. Water was plentiful, a stream and dug well. Finally, the Meyer farm included five horses, the same number of cows, two hogs, a goat, and blessedly few chickens. John was not sure he understood Freidrich's comment with regard to chickens, but seemed to remember his brother-in-law disliked the birds as much as he.

Karl's decision to sell was motivated by age and physical condition. The Meyer family had been blessed with three daughters—all married, two living in Minneapolis and one in Bismark. The youngest and her husband spent two years on the farm and built a home there. Freidrich was not sure why, but they abruptly left. The other daughters held no interest in farming. Freidrich was sure Karl was at least seventy years old or more. He was a stubborn, self-made man, but years of punishing physical labor on just one leg had taken a toll. Daily chores were increasingly difficult and the farm was beginning to show the effects of deferred maintenance.

The Meyers had taken a liking to Freidrich and treated him like a son. He and Karl spent late evenings together discussing the farm and what the future held for the Red River Valley. The Meyers offered Freidrich a partnership. He could buy in using the small amount of cash he accumulated, then build his equity based on labor and time committed. Terms of sale could be adjusted dependent on circumstance. Karl agreed to stay on providing guidance and whatever physical help he could muster. Freidrich was grateful for the offer, but like his friends Kurt Haus and Klaus Schuler, still believed there was much of America to be seen. The three young men decided Black Hills gold was a fool's errand, as was scouting for a bankrupt railroad. They now planned to travel by rail to San Francisco and from there by steamship to the Pacific Northwest. To what end he was uncertain, but that was part of the adventure.

When the Meyers offered the farm to Freidrich, he immediately thought of his sister and brother-in-law. He and John often talked of leaving St. Anne's and Peter's ill-conceived experiment. Freidrich told the Meyers of John's interest in striking out on his own. He knew John to be industrious and a man of character. In fact, John and Karl were very much alike—astute in a practical way and good with their hands. Freidrich was also sure John and his sister had the means to make a large down payment. They were committed to the earth and a lifetime of farming. The proposition appealed to Karl. The couple might be young, but it would take youth to return the farm to what it was. He also liked the down payment—personal investment was a sure sign of commitment.

Karl had been approached a few months earlier by the agent of an absentee owner new to the valley. He was the same owner that employed Kurt Haus. His 3,000 acres adjoined the Meyer farm. The agent made an attractive offer, but Karl disliked distant owners. They cared only for their enrichment, not for the valley. He wanted a buyer willing to put down roots and become a lifetime Dakotan. Karl's new neighbor came by his land by means of a debt settlement—not a desire to farm.

The Meyers planned on retaining ten acres of land where they would build a small retirement cottage. That left 303 acres at $7.25 per acre.

Freidrich was not an expert at pricing Dakota farms, but knew the Red River Valley and Meyer farm were both good choices. He warned John the farm would sell quickly. He should offer at least twenty percent down, and respond first by telegram followed by a letter.

Freidrich's letter then turned to his own future. Kurt Haus was committed to the Cornellious Mann farm through June 1. Klaus Schuler was similarly obligated. Until his friends fulfilled their contracts, Freidrich would stay put. That meant he would be in Dakota to help with spring planting. Beyond that he was not sure, but the Washington Territory looked attractive. The letter closed with a comment regarding other families from *Deutschland* or *Russen* living in or near the Red River Valley. He was aware of a settlement farther north, but the occupants were Mennonites who had emigrated from the Khortitsa area. He had also seen a small group in Fargo whose dress suggested they were *Deutsch*. They moved on before he could talk with them.

The young couple paused for a moment contemplating what they had just read. The contents were far too sensitive to discuss in the Schafer household. Maria suggested a ride in the cool fall air. John hitched the wagon and the two rode toward the Lundeen Ranch.

Maria told John, "I've worried about being miles from anyone," she said. "I know you can build a farm, but the isolation terrified me."

"We're not alone," said John, surprised by his wife's disclosure.

"I know," she said. "That's what makes the Meyer place so appealing. We have more than a working farm and ready-made home—we have neighbors."

Maria knew nothing of Casselton, but it was a community, and close to a railroad. They could start anew and do so in the company of others. The Meyer farm offered independence rather than exile to a far off and lonely homestead. Before they reached the Lundeen Ranch, a decision had been made. A telegram would be sent in the morning.

John left before sunrise the next morning to check on the availability of oak for use on the Ackers' grist mill, but only after stopping first at the Kansas Pacific station. He was hoping Anselm would be there to help send a telegram. He was disappointed to find Anselm was in St. Louis. The telegraph operator was able to start, but a *Deutsch*-speaking track supervisor saved the day. After an awkward three-way discussion, they managed to send "accept, 25 down, letter to follow." That evening he and Maria penned a note to Freidrich asking for a bill of sale identifying the precise acreage, description of buildings, list of equipment, livestock count, and terms of sale. The advance payment would be sent once the bill of sale was received. John had the feeling there was something else to be done, but trusted his brother-in-law to cover the details. He found it curious that, like St. Anne's, the Dakota purchase had been made sight unseen.

Chapter Thirteen:
Prairie Winter

"We lived in the little homestead house for five years ... Not having sufficient means to finish it all ... we slept in the upper rooms ... It was not unusual on awakening cold winter mornings to find the covers around our heads frozen and the bed white with snow driven through tiny cracks in the roof ... "
—Bessie Felton Wilson, Kansas Historical Society

The party was behind on construction of a second barn designed primarily to shelter livestock. The cause for their tardiness was not unwelcome. A larger than expected harvest had taken much longer to process. By mid-October, most crops were in and construction began. Mr. Nelson, always the prognosticator, told them snow sometimes fell in early November, but he expected that would not be the case this year—the first hard freeze was still weeks away.

Peter rarely took part in building projects, but had been asked to temporarily supervise a group of nine workers raising the west-facing barn wall. Denzel Kalb, whose task it was to coordinate the effort, had taken his youngest child suffering from high fever to see the doctor in Fort Hays. Just before the midday break, Peter noticed Melina walking deliberately toward the worksite. He could tell by her expression she was upset.

"You had better come," Melina said.

"Why now?" Peter responded. "Can't it wait?"

Melina ignored his plea, refusing to disclose the urgency. When they reached the house, Peter saw Albrecht seated dejectedly at the kitchen table. He averted his father's curious stare looking toward the floor.

"Hilke is with child," Albrecht said.

Peter took a moment to comprehend. "Say that again," he asked, hoping he misunderstood.

Albrecht, with head in hands said, "I think you heard me."

Peter hesitated, then slammed a fist on the table with such force Albrecht bolted upright, knocking an earthenware crock filled with berries to the floor. The Christmas wedding would produce a child a few months thereafter. Worse yet, Hilke could no longer disguise her condition. Melina made a hasty retreat passing through the addition where Maria was nursing the baby. She took her daughter and grandchild with her. Peter had contemplated discussing the dangers of intercourse before marriage with Albrecht, but given his son's lack of initiative thought him incapable of anything untoward. He quickly disavowed any blame in the sordid affair. It was Albrecht who disgraced the family and sinned in the eyes of God. He railed against his son until his voice began to fail, making it clear his eldest was a disappointment—a *schwarzes schaf.*

Peter then turned his thoughts to Elise Weber. She was the real villain. Elise pushed Hilke toward Albrecht. She was cunning. The Webers built a house next to the Schafers, and Elise made sure the couple spent time together. From the beginning, marriage under any circumstance was her purpose. He left the kitchen and proceeded directly to the Weber house.

He confronted Elise. "You planned this unholy event."

"What event?" she said. Elise was not aware of her daughter's condition, though she would admit later to being suspicious. Peter and Elise exchanged insult and accusation. He charged Hilke with promiscuous behavior, while Elise maintained Albrecht preyed on an innocent child. It was a scene not often witnessed in St. Anne's, and continued until Philipp Weber came in from the fields.

"Leave my house," Philipp demanded, adding, "You are an *arsche.*"

"And your daughter is a *hure*," Peter responded.

Philipp lodged the point of his scythe in the window frame, knocking the glass loose from its moorings. Peter left, but not without a passing vulgarity. Word of the dispute moved quickly through the community. Long hours and tedious farm work often left the members on edge and drove the inconsequential to more serious conflict. The confrontation between Peter and Philipp went beyond those rooted in fatigue, noteworthy because it involved the recognized leader of the community.

The wedding, once anticipated as a gala event, was now a shameful necessity. The ceremony was immediately advanced and the couple met with Father Lenkeit the following Sunday. The priest was no stranger to hasty unions, and accomplished at meting out sanctimonious abuse. Unlike some of his more senior parishioners, who paid no heed to a man of the cloth, this couple was trapped. After assigning a lengthy penance and assuring himself there was proper remorse, Father Lenkeit set a date for the ceremony two weeks hence.

Given the two heads of household did not speak to each another, it was left to Melina and Elise to plan the smallish wedding—only family members would attend. Melina was disappointed in her son, but recalled the joy Morgan brought to the family. She was also sure that John and Maria would soon be leaving. Another baby in the household was a delight, never mind the manner in which it came.

Elise Weber considered the entire event to be a minor transgression. She never suggested that Hilke engage in sinful behavior, but was pleased with the outcome. In a few weeks her daughter would become part of a wealthy family, and gain a position in St. Anne's not available absent the union. She was sure a resolution between Peter and her husband would come in time. The marriage would then work to her benefit.

Peter had planned to give Albrecht a wedding gift of sixty acres, drawn from the land he still held as a principal buyer. His son's "mistake" called for a change. Instead of gifting the land, Peter now intended to sell Albrecht forty acres, although nothing was to be paid in advance and no terms were set. The change in plan was just one more way to show his disgust. If that was Peter's intent, it was lost on Albrecht. He seemed indifferent as to how many acres he acquired, and on what terms.

Albrecht's forty acres allowed him to build on the township site, but he lacked the funds for construction. Peter was happy to consign his son to a soddy somewhere on the Schafer farmland, but Melina intervened. She did not wish to see her grandchild living in dirt. Peter acquiesced, purchasing enough lumber for a small frame house. He asked John to help with construction. At least Peter had asked rather than demanded. It was recognition, albeit tardy, that his son-in-law had his own commitments, and was not beholden to the V*orsteher*. John felt sorry for Albrecht, but dreaded the assignment. His brother-in-law was known to wander off, physically as well as mentally. John expected to build most of the home by himself.

Albrecht's hasty union meant another home in the township. He and Hilke would be joining Karl Seigler who purchased a small plot a few weeks earlier. The Seiglers expected to have a roof over their head before the onset of winter. Karl was resigned to at least three years of construction work on the ATSF line, but a generous gift from his brother in *Russen* allowed him to quit the railroad, buy sixty acres, and build a home in St. Anne's. The Seigler family was a welcome addition. Winter was not a time when new residents were expected.

The first snowfall came on the afternoon of November 12 and within an hour turned to rain. The early dusting served as a warning, and also signaled time for sausage making—something of a festival in itself. Within a few days, most everyone had teamed with at least one neighbor. Three residents of St. Anne's—Ludwig Bruener, Eduard Hauer and Burkhard Wetzel—were accomplished butchers. A fourth, Denzel Kalb, could be called upon if necessary, although it was said he was better at cutting fingers than carving hogs. Since there were relatively few swine in St. Anne's, the members slaughtered cows, and all relied on game kill. Nicholas Geist and Elmer Klein had taken an elk, three deer and several turkeys at the first sign of frost. The kill was widely distributed throughout the community and became an integral part of sausage ingredients. The meat was chopped and ground, then passed on to stuffers, with the unfortunate task of filling entrails.

All the implements used in the process were made of wood. Mr. Pallitto featured a cast iron grinder in his Fort Hays store, but like many of his gadgets it attracted attention, but not buyers. Each family or group of families had a unique recipe, which required some modification to fit the spices available from gardens or from Mr. Pallitto's limited inventory. John and Maria pared with the Schneider and Kalb families. They invited Albrecht and Hilke, but the couple declined. Peter saw the activity as beneath the *Vorsteher* and did not participate.

Albrecht and Hilke's marriage took place outside the sacristy on a wintry day befitting the somber mood of the participants. The muted celebration was attended by the Schafer family and Elise Weber, but not her husband, still bristling at the manner in which Peter treated his wife. Elise was disappointed. She hoped the two men could put aside their differences at least for this occasion. Father Lenkeit presided, rather stiffly, maintaining a disapproving look throughout. John thought it overdone, but the priest was somewhat of a *Darsteller* and enjoyed the opportunity to perform, even before a small audience. The newly wedded couple joined the Schafer family for their evening meal—neither Father Lenkeit nor Elise Weber was invited.

Albrecht and Hilke had decided to make their temporary home in a toolshed, rather than the Schafer home. They had only a small stove and the roof leaked, but the young couple tolerated the hardship rather than endure Peter's insensitive remarks. Perhaps it was the discomfort of the damp shed, but Albrecht displayed a zeal rarely seen as he and John worked toward completion of his small township home. His surprising diligence allowed John to quickly return to his work on the Ackers' grist mill. The gears were proving to be a test of John's woodworking skills. He had often observed his father engaged in intricate work, but observation was not practice. Christof understood the difficulty. Despite the occasional waste of oak, he was pleased with the progress.

Mr. Pallitto was surprised to see a letter postmarked in *Deutschland* and immediately left for the Schafer home leaving Anna to tend the store. This time he had not forgotten—letters meant for John and Maria were to be hand delivered. Within minutes of its arrival, Maria had the letter, and Josef a small cache of *kekse*, a reward for his trouble. Melina had seen Josef deliver the letter and knew her daughter and son-in-law were expecting a note from Jacob. Melina hoped her daughter would share the contents. Maria chose instead to wait for John's return. He arrived just before the evening meal and the two retreated to the privacy of their room.

The letter had been written weeks before and contained the message they had hoped for. Jacob would be leaving Bremerhaven aboard the steamship *Weser*. There were surprisingly few details. His description of travel was halting, and he wrote only of papers secured and fees paid. John recalled an earlier discussion with Armin Wagner and his experience in leaving *Russen*. The Wagners and their fellow travelers left the Steppe barely two months after the Schafer party, but their exit was far more difficult. The Crown, alarmed by the potential loss in farm output, had taken steps to make emigration more challenging, among them a levy on those departing for America.

The Czar's action left a confused landscape. The Second Edict pushed the *Volga Deutsch* away, but with so many leaving Alexander had second thoughts. Armin believed censors were intercepting letters. Their purpose was to locate and punish agents promoting the exodus. Perhaps this was the reason Jacob wrote only of conformance and said little of his travel plans beyond steamship passage. It made little difference. Jacob had secured passage, and God willing would arrive in Kansas sometime in late March. Nothing could be done to hasten his arrival. John expected to leave for the Dakota Territory sometime in early spring, probably before his father's arrival. Maria and Morgan would follow in Jacob's company.

Peter was aware of the letter, having been told of its receipt by Melina. He too assumed it was from Jacob and was anxious to hear what plans his long-time friend had for the future. With Helena gone, Peter was certain Jacob would be coming to America. He thought about asking John, but decided it was best to let his son-in-law volunteer the information. He did not have to wait long. Now that Jacob's departure was set, John was ready to disclose his father's plan to leave *Russen*.

Peter was delighted. Jacob was a friend and ally. The Schafer and Schmidt families were deeply rooted in *Volga Deutsch* heritage. He looked forward to the reunion, but wondered if Jacob's stay would be short-lived. He was increasingly certain John and Maria were leaving, possibly within months of Jacob's arrival. He couldn't be sure of his son-in-law's plans, but neither could he ask. Earlier inquiries led to conflict, and he learned nothing. John was not ready to talk. That displeased Peter, but not enough to reopen old wounds.

The party had an early taste of winter and already thought Kansas to be far colder than the *Russische* Steppe. Perhaps it was their imagination or memories of searing summer heat. Either way the cold was a dagger that pierced even their heavy wool coats. A stockpile of wood and mistholz was critical to survival. Wood was increasingly distant and the members, as in the past, turned to *mistholz*. Erna Klein was sickened by the smell of burning field scraps mixed with animal waste. Her husband had done his best to gather seasoned wood, but the demands of harvest slowed his progress and dry wood was hard to locate. He made several trips to a small creek bed north of St. Anne's, where he cut a large stock of green wood hoping to mix new with seasoned fuel—anything to lessen the stench of manure.

With less than a month of dry wood remaining, Elmer and his fifteen-year-old son set out for the Kansas Pacific woodlot hoping to buy enough dry wood to get him through the next month. Within the hour, a light snow began to fall and Erna huddled with her two girls, Christal, eight, and her newborn, Jutta. She glanced outside hoping their only cow was sheltered, but the animal was nowhere in sight. Erna secured the baby to a bench near the stove and instructed Christal to keep the infant warm. She found the animal with its tether entangled in a fence. Erna was able to free the cow, but in her haste to return the animal to its shelter, broke the locking mechanism on the gate. Two young goats escaped. She thought about letting the animals go, but knew Elmer would be angry.

Erna returned to the soddy repeating the instructions given to Christal a few minutes before. The cow had been quickly retrieved, but not so the goats. They were frolicking in the snow, and in no mind to return. Each time she got close they scampered away. It took the better part of one-half hour to secure the animals. Exhausted, she turned back and noticed smoke escaping from the window. She let loose of the goats and raced back to find the eight-year-old barely conscious and lying near the front door. She pulled Christal through the opening and, using the child's body as a wedge, went in search of the baby. The damper had swung shut on its own, or was closed by Christal in a mistaken attempt to carry out her motherly assignment.

The baby, struggling for breath, was still strapped to the bench, her face inches from the stove door. The soddy was filled with smoke. Erna fought to loosen the infant's restraint. By the time she reached the outside, the baby was no longer breathing. Christal had crawled free of the door and was sitting upright. Erna, holding the baby, ran the short distance to the Kalb soddy. Denzel took one look at Jutta and concluded the child was dead, but succumbed to Erna's plea to find a doctor. His wife raced to the

Klein soddy and found Christal sick to her stomach, but breathing regularly. Denzel harnessed horse to wagon. He and Erna started for Hays City, the distraught mother repeatedly crying out, "*bitte Gott, bitte Gott.*" They intercepted Elmer a few miles from Hays City and continued their frantic search for Doctor Himmelfarb. In a fleeting moment of good fortune, they found him in his residence above the office. He made an attempt to revive the child, but like Denzel before him, recognized the effort was futile.

The snow had begun to accumulate, but it made little difference to the solemn procession making its way back to St. Anne's. They found Christal to be fully recovered. Erna dressed Jutta in her best clothes and laid the child in her crib. Doctor Himmelfarb contacted Father Lenkeit. Not wanting to travel that evening, he reached St. Anne's the following afternoon. John and Hersh Schneider had built a casket, but Erna became hysterical when anyone approached the crib. Finally, Erna was forcibly taken by Elmer from the soddy and the child was placed in the small wooden box. Jutta's funeral was held three days later.

Tragedy was always on the doorstep of St. Anne's, but never seemed closer than when a child was lost. Erna mourned her daughter's passing, but quickly resumed her duties as wife and mother. To her neighbors she seemed a pillar of strength—her recovery said to be a gift from God. Elmer saw a different woman. Once behind the doors of the soddy, Erna fell to periods of despair, unable to escape her guilt.

Freidrich's answer to John's request for a bill of sale reached Hays City and, as directed, was delivered to Pallitto's General Store. From there it was transported to St. Anne's by Mrs. Pallitto and hand-carried by Anna Schneider to Maria. The letter assured John and Maria their trust in the Meyers would be rewarded many times over. Karl and Anneke were honest to the core. Before writing, Freidrich and Karl had again toured the property and found that conditions, as represented in Freidrich's earlier correspondence, were accurately reported. The Meyers held deed to the property and there were no liens. Karl had shown him a document that carried the Dakota Territorial Seal. He knew the property to be staked and there were no boundary disputes. Parts of the Red River Valley were prone to flood, but only a few acres of the Meyer property were susceptible. The ten acres the Meyers wished to retain were on high ground, but otherwise typical of the remaining property. Farm implements needed some attention, but no major repairs were necessary. He saw no need for additions. A neighbor joined Karl to contract for threshing and had done so for years. Work was underway on the two livestock sheds mentioned in his earlier letter. Repairs to the shed most in need should be completed by midsummer, the other sturdy enough to survive at least one more year. All other structures were in good condition. Finally, he listed the terms of sale—five years at five percent with one-quarter advance payment. John grasped Maria's hand and a simple nod affirmed what he was thinking—they had reached a decision.

Karl Meyer preferred the advance be sent by telegraph to Luther Ogden rather than mailed. Freidrich knew Mr. Ogden as a prominent business-man in Fargo. He owned a hotel, lumber yard, feed store, and was some-how involved in banking. Freidrich was emphatic—if Mr. Ogden was a friend of the Meyer family, he was trustworthy. John barely understood the telegraph, and could not conceive of sending money by wire. How could a stranger in Hays City send money to an unknown institution hundreds of miles away? The $550.00 represented much of what he and Maria had saved. Who held custody of the funds? John's only chance for enlighten-ment was Mr. Norton at First National Bank of Hays City. Perhaps he could explain how money was sent by telegraph, but first he must disclose the purchase of the Meyer farm to Peter and Melina.

John and Maria chose that evening to disclose the purchase. Albrecht and Hilke had joined the family at mealtime, but left quickly as did the boys. John could not think of a way to gently introduce the topic.

"Maria and I have news," he said. "We've bought a farm in the Dakota Territory."

Peter expected as much, but Melina—though suspicious this day might come—hoped the couple would put down roots in St Anne's.

"My grandchild," was Melina's tearful response.

Peter was livid. "So this is our reward for providing food and shelter," he said. "You steal away with Maria and Morgan."

Maria sharply rebuked her father. "John has worked tirelessly in the fields and brought respect to the family through his contribution to the *Gemeinde* and to 'your' *Company*."

His daughter's intensity surprised Peter.

"I have work," he said, and stormed from the house casting a chair against the wall as he did.

Melina was holding Morgan and began to weep. Maria tried to console her mother suggesting that there would be visits. Melina understood this to be possible, but the Dakota Territory was a long way off and commitments to the farm made travel unlikely. The thought of losing her only daughter and granddaughter was more than Melina could bear.

The next morning John paid a visit to the bank and James P. Norton. He was able to catch Hanna, Mr. Norton's *deutsch* speaking assistant, asking her to explain the practice of "wiring" funds. Hanna told John that Western Union was a very large company with representation throughout America. This allowed the company to take money in a Kansas office and dispense it in Dakota. The money itself would not travel from one city to the other. Since Western Union had offices in both cities, the money could be transferred in a request sent by telegraph. Funds would always be in the custody of Western Union. Hanna assured him that the bank had used the wire service in the past. His money was safe as long as he trusted the recipient. John had no real knowledge of Luther Ogden or Karl Meyer, but he trusted his brother-in-law. Hanna told John that the bank could handle the entire transaction for a small fee. Still somewhat confused, John handed his down payment to Hanna, still looking upon the process as something of a *wunder*.

An uneasy truce marked the next few weeks in the Schafer household. Peter said little to John or his daughter, and avoided time together with either. At first, Melina begged Maria to reconsider, but no longer did so—the subject too painful. John was careful not to antagonize Peter and did more than his share of chores. He also took time to meet with Denzel Kalb and Mr. Culp, who continued to assist with matters having to do with the *St. Anne's Company*. With John's departure, Denzel would assume responsibility for the *company* and manage common property for the *Gemeinde*. John worked as much as he dared on the grist mill. The additional income was welcome.

The birth of Christ, the most festive holiday on the *Volga Deutsch* calendar, was now but a few weeks away. The council was determined to make Christmas in St. Anne's as joyful as it was in Pfeifer. Catherine Schuler,

Elma Wetzel and Anna Schneider were directed by the council to arrange a two-week festival ending on New Year's Day. Emma Heimler was asked to help. She was thought to be pregnant again after losing her first born. Her assistance during *Kerbfest* had been welcomed and the activity seemed to lessen her grief. In addition to scheduled events, there would be the customary visits between member households and, if weather permitted, nearby *Deutsch* families.

Miss Geiser advised the planning group the children's choir would perform on Christmas Eve and she had another treat—a performance involving the younger *studenten*. She gave no hint of what was planned except to say that there was much excitement in the classroom. The children were learning *Englisch* and *mathematic,* but not to the exclusion of more practical education. She and her *studenten* could often be found in the fields or barn immersed in the study of what would soon be their livelihood. The *Schullehrer* had become part of St. Anne's. She was considered by the women to be a friend, if not a confidant. Her evening *Englisch Zum Leben* classes had expanded to include the more tradition bound and even included a few men.

The council had selected Elsa Bruener to play the role of *das Christkindche*. She would have the task of visiting each home bestowing gifts upon the children. Christmas Eve and Christmas Day were solemn occasions. Father Lenkeit inserted himself in the proceedings to ensure the meaning of Christmas was not lost. He planned to visit as many homes as possible, and welcomed a touch of vodka at each stop. The priest expected to stay at least four days in St. Anne's, spending the night with the Austerlitz family. His temporary residency was considered an honor.

The Sunday before Christmas brought an astonishing announcement from the pulpit. Father Lenkeit told a stunned congregation that Albert Wetzel and Meta Gerber planned to wed the first Saturday of the new year. Since his rejection by Miss Geiser, Albert had become something of a recluse. Meta understood his heartbreak. Three weeks before she made a late-night visit to Albert's home. She carried a proposition. Meta wished to be his wife and was there to carry out her desire. Albert was hesitant, but Meta was not. Multiple visits took place over the next several days leading to the announcement of the couple's union. Father Lenkeit suggested certain formalities be observed. Meta told him it was best they marry as soon as possible. The priest relented waiving the banns.

Given a moment to consider what they had just heard, the congregation erupted in applause. Meta was eleven years Albert's senior, but looked much younger than her age. She was widely respected for keeping family and farm together following her husband's untimely death. As for Albert, it was time he took a bride and all thought he had chosen wisely. Only Anna Schneider, to whom Meta confided, understood Albert's course had been defined by his soon-to-be bride. A line of well-wishers formed after the mass. Last in line was Miss Geiser. Albert had not spoken to the *Schullehrer* since she declined his offer of courtship. She never properly thanked Albert for his work on the *Schulhaus*, but could do so now as his step-children were *studenten*.

The party's first Christmas in Kansas was equal by any measure to their experience in *Russen,* perhaps more so given the events of the past year. The weather remained clear, though cool, with only flurries falling on Christmas Day. Elsa Bruener carried out her role as the *Christkindche* bringing the magic of Christmas to each child. Miss Geiser did not disappoint. The children of St. Anne's school sang for the assembled members and followed with a re-enactment of the events at Bethlehem. Father Lenkeit's homily was thoughtful and well prepared. He spoke of those lost over the past nine months assuring the party they were certain to be with the creator. He closed as he often did by expressing his desire that one year from now the community would have broken ground on a new church. The congregation listened politely to his plea, but most saw more pressing demands.

Two weddings took place immediately following the Christmas holiday. The first, the union of Michel Muller and Carina Weber, was originally scheduled for November, but delayed because of Father Lenkeit's obligations. The second, that of Albert Wetzel and Meta Gerber, was a far larger ceremony, including at least as many guests as attended mass on Christmas morning. Albert and Meta were well known in St. Anne's, and their roots extended deep into the old country. The crowd overwhelmed the community center, and two large warming fires were located in front of the building. Both the Schafer and Austerlitz houses were opened and the celebrants moved between the two. Albert and Meta planned on making their home in the Gerber soddy. The widow, who once feared she would never again marry, had successfully shaped her own destiny.

January saw the early snow all but gone, except for the north facing slopes. Members continued to gather wood, chink and re-chink soddies, and complete last-minute repairs to livestock shelters. The reprieve was short-lived. Winter made a return appearance the second week of the new year. Temperatures rose to slightly above freezing and the horizon was inky gray. A stillness set upon the prairie, and the members wondered how skies so heavily laden produced no precipitation. Snow came at last—at first reluctantly—then more heavily as if to cover the deficit left by weeks of dry weather. As the night wore on, temperatures plummeted and the wind freshened, lifting anything not secured and carrying it away. Even the most carefully chinked soddy felt the chill as inside temperatures reached near freezing, and overworked stoves fought back against the cold. This was the Kansas blizzard warned of by Mr. Nelson.

The snow fell through all of Wednesday and into the following morning. When it finally stopped, there were drifts reaching to the roofline of many of the earthen homes. The Weber family found their livestock shed collapsed and a prize calf dead. The Brueners lost two goats to the same cause. Younger animals were particularly susceptible to the cold and many families brought them into their homes. On Friday, St. Anne's began the slow process of digging out. Animals were fed and watered, and snow removed from windows and entrances. Roofs on earthen homes were cleared of their white blanket, and pathways to outbuildings were painstakingly dug. A few ventured out to check on neighbors and lend assistance as needed. Miss Geiser canceled school for the following week. The children would find it difficult to reach the community center and some would be kept at home to assist with cleanup.

When classes resumed, Miss Geiser noticed a few of her students complained of a sore throat and others exhibited signs of a mild fever. The symptoms were not uncommon for the season and she sent two of the younger children home for the day. She became alarmed the next morning when Erna Klein brought her daughter Christal to the *Schulhaus* early. Erna was deeply concerned and wanted the *Schullehrer* to see the swelling in her daughter's throat. Miss Geiser did not like what she saw. A few minutes later, Mary Acker brought in her daughter Elisabet who was also struggling to breathe. Christal and Elisabet were friends and spent much of the Christmas holiday together. Miss Geiser had seen this once before in Nebraska. It was almost certainly diphtheria. She sent one of the older children to find Denzel Kalb. Miss Geiser wanted to close the *Schulhaus*, but the council must first agree.

"It sounds like the croup," Denzel said.

Two other mothers arrived. Both were holding their children at home because of fever and sore throat.

Miss Geiser took Denzel aside.

"One of my Nebraska *studenten,* exhibiting like symptoms, died in a matter of hours."

"It's contagious then?" Denzel asked.

"Very," Miss Geiser answered. "It spreads like wildfire."

"Close the *Schulhaus*," Denzel said. "I'll advise the members to keep the children apart."

Although she considered it somewhat futile, Miss Geiser immediately began to scrub all common surfaces. Denzel asked John and Hersh Schneider to ride to Hays City and summon Doctor Himmelfarb. Two riders could alternate breaking a path through the heavy snow. They found the doctor who had just visited Nicholas Muller, the youngest son of Reinhart Muller. The boy's throat was raw making it difficult to breathe or swallow. John recalled the Muller family had visited St. Anne's for the wedding of their eldest son and spent a few days thereafter taking part in holiday celebrations. Doctor Himmelfarb advised John and Hersh he could not visit St. Anne's until early the following day. He gave them a small quantity of boric acid and swab to be inserted into the throat.

Their return trip was arduous. Snowmelt refroze on the surface and caused severe irritation to the forearm, knee, and barrel of their mounts. The pair arrived in St. Anne's just before dark and immediately sought the help of Frida Geist. She had no medical training, but her skills in birthing and knowledge of home remedies was widely recognized. Frida was all the community had. She was skeptical of the prescribed treatment, but had little choice. If Frida did not follow the doctor's suggestion and one of the children died, the blame would rest with her. Christal Klein, Elisabet Acker and Levin Bruener were selected to receive the acid wash. The application was difficult. In each case she reached the targeted swelling, and in each case the children became violently ill. Much of the application was now cast about the floor in a pool of vomit. A few hours later there were no signs of improvement.

Doctor Himmelfarb arrived the following morning. Elisabet Acker and the young Bruener boy had stabilized. Their breathing was labored, but no worse than the night before. Frida accompanied the doctor who admitted his only knowledge of acid wash came from a recent medical publication. There was no real proof of efficacy. The next stop was the Klein house where they found Christal's condition had worsened. Breathing was difficult and her temperature elevated.

Doctor Himmelfarb had a decision to make. He had read about intubation, but had never done it himself or witnessed the procedure. The doctor saw no reason to experiment further with boric acid, convinced the treatment was not responsible for the slight improvement in Elisabet and Levin's condition. Tracheotomy was his only option. Miss Geiser offered her cottage since the doctor was reluctant to operate in a soddy when other more sanitary environments were available. Christal's breathing had become more labored. Elmer Klein carried his daughter to the cottage. The procedure was carried out using only a small quantity of ether—the dosage limited given the child's condition. Christal Klein struggled for most of an hour before Doctor Himmelfarb could complete the tracheotomy. She died on a small table in Miss Geiser's cottage—her horrified mother witness to the death. The doctor stared blankly at Christal before leaving to check on Elisabet and Levin.

Near midnight Erna Klein left the family's soddy. She walked to the gravesite where Jutta was interred several weeks before. Erna was without coat or boots. She prayed briefly over her daughter's grave, then placed a wooden cross of her own making atop the small mound of earth. Elmer discovered his wife's absence an hour before sunrise. Thinking she might be tending animals, he checked the shelter. She was not there. When he returned, he noticed Erna's coat hanging by the stove. Elmer recalled his wife prayed the night before repeatedly asking guidance. Elmer had not questioned what guidance she sought, but it now occurred to him she might be contemplating her own demise.

He woke his son and both left for the cemetery, a frequent destination for Erna. His fears were confirmed when he saw the cross Erna held the night before resting on Jutta's grave. Elmer sent his son to the Schafer house. Peter immediately set out to wake others while John caught up with Elmer. The pair split following separate wagon tracks heading in a northerly direction. Elmer's son went back to the soddy on the chance his mother might return.

By midday, more than twenty residents were searching the area around St. Anne's. Armin Wagner, who purchased land outside the *company*, was hunting turkey with his son. They had wandered some distance to the south when they discovered Erna resting against the bank of a small dry creek. She had frozen to death, a rosary held tightly to her breast. The Wagners laid Erna's body over the larger horse and began the long walk toward St. Anne's, arriving just before dark. Along the way they encountered a few of the residents still searching for Erna and the small group formed a tearful procession. Elmer saw them approaching and knew by their pace his wife was dead. He simply said "*es ist das beste.*"

Erna Klein had lost two daughters in as many months—the first to her own negligence, and the second to a disease she did not understand. Erna and her daughter were buried together. Father Lenkeit told the members Christal was surely with the creator. He added Erna must be there as well. She had sinned, but a just God must grant forgiveness. Of the six members buried in the St. Anne's cemetery, three were Kleins.

Doctor Himmelfarb returned to Hays City deeply concerned for the condition of the young Muller boy. When he examined the child, he found him no better. Recognizing he waited too long to perform surgery on Christal, Doctor Himmelfarb immediately opened his throat, this time heavily sedating the boy. Nicholas began to breathe normally.

One life had been lost to diphtheria in St. Anne's and at least three in Hays City. There was talk of scarlet fever in Topeka, but no epidemic. Hays City and St. Anne's were spared. For the remainder of winter, the party saw only the usual chills and discomfort of the season. School resumed after a ten-day cessation. Miss Geiser's *Englisch Zum Leben* students again scrubbed the community center from floor to ceiling, all the while practicing the language of their adopted land.

In February, Miss Geiser received word of a surprise visitor. The

Associate Director for the Kansas Superintendent of Public Instruction had business in Hays City and planned to visit St. Anne's School—an unusual step. Small districts rarely saw state administrators, but Kenneth Sloan had made an exception. His effort was not lost on the *Schullehrer*. Mr. Sloan spent two hours in the classroom, even taking a role in lessons. He was much as Miss Geiser remembered him—a handsome, self-assured man. Before leaving, he again extended to Miss Geiser an invitation to the annual Conference on Teaching to be held in Topeka in April. She was surprised to find he included her on a panel discussing rural education. His office would arrange for travel, room, and board.

Peter had his own welcome surprise—a letter from Arne Schwab sent from Arne's home in Balzer. He told Peter there were at least six groups leaving *Russen* in the spring. Three listed Kansas as their destination. All were aware of St. Anne's. He reminded Peter the separation of household and farm remained very unpopular, particularly among younger families. Their reasons for leaving the old country were varied, but all mentioned tradition bound practices with no foundation in common sense.

Peter had begun to realize his desire to create a stand-alone village akin to Pfeifer was unlikely to succeed. Albert Wetzel and Hersh Schneider both openly talked of building permanent homes on their fields. Others in the *Gemeinde* would follow. Instead of a centrally located village or township site, the community would be spread over several hundred acres. The dispersion threatened Peter's vision, but his zeal to object was waning. Preserving tradition at the expense of new residents was not a good decision. He cringed at the thought his son-in-law was correct. A colony in the image of Pfeifer was doomed. Peter found encouragement in parts of Arne's letter, particularly the number of groups still planning to emigrate. He thought for a moment, then quickly made note to contact the railroad as soon as possible. He could afford to buy at least another 100 acres.

Eleven months had passed since the Schafer party stepped off the train in Topeka. Much had been accomplished. They had turned stubborn prairie sod, built shelter for themselves, and harvested food enough for table, spring seed and a modest surplus. One resident, Constance Doyle, was late to arrive. The blacksmith decided to remain in Hays City for the winter, having secured a contract with the Army. He planned to spend the next nine months in St. Anne's before again returning to Fort Hays in late fall. Conn's arrival was welcomed by the members, all with a backlog of "smithing" work. Conn and Lucy were now married, or so it was assumed. A few of the more pious struggled to accept the "sinners," but their cloistered view soon gave way to Conn's skills at the forge. Mr. Nelson was among the first on the smithy's doorstep. He made the trip from Hays City, having admired Conn's work for the Army. Mr. Nelson had designed a harvesting machine—a mechanical scythe and platform to catch cut grain. He needed help with fabrication.

Nelson Feed was also the sponsor of the first ever Hays City Agricultural Fair, an effort to stimulate sales lost to the prior year's grasshopper infestation. He managed to convince implement dealers from as far away as St. Louis and Chicago to display their products. The fair would feature the latest in farm technology, including gang plows, reapers, mechanical planters and even a horse-drawn steam traction engine. Mr. Nelson expected the event to restore some lost revenue, but he was also a realist. The fair was about the future. The equipment displayed was beyond the means of most of his customers, but innovation was coming. When it did, he wanted the farmers of Ellis County to know Nelson Feed stood ready to meet their needs.

Educators from Kansas State College, representatives from the Kansas State Board of Agriculture, and several politicians would be on hand, along with an assortment of booths selling everything from seed to salvation. Most everyone in St. Anne's planned to attend. John would not be among them. He refused to give Peter the chance to suggest his contribution had lessened in advance of departure.

John wrote Midwest Grain and Feed to advise Hermann he was leaving for the Dakota Territory and recommending Hersh as his replacement to manage the Lundeen Ranch. A prompt response was received from Louise Adams representing Hermann and the company. John wondered if Miss Adams was the woman traveling with his uncle when he last visited. She wished him luck and told John, effective March 5, Hersh would be the signatory on the account at First National Bank of Hays City.

A postscript asked if the Turkey Red had been planted and how it fared through the winter. The question was timely. John and Hersh inspected the thirty acres just two days prior. The winter wheat was resuming its seasonal period of growth. According to Mr. Nelson, this was a critical time since a sudden warm spell could easily reduce hardiness and result in damage if a late freeze occurred. As far as John could see the experiment was going well, but the answer was still weeks away. He wrote Miss Adams telling her all appeared to be in order, and future correspondence should be directed to Casselton Station, Dakota Territory, care of Karl Meyer.

The next day John received a telegram from the Meyers acknowledging receipt of his advance payment. They also asked when he planned to arrive, and if Maria and the baby were traveling with him. The Meyer cottage was still two months from completion. If John was traveling with the family, Karl and Anneke would move to the smaller house on the property. If he were alone, they assumed he would be comfortable in the bunkhouse with Freidrich. John wrote telling them Maria would follow in three to four weeks. He planned to leave in early March. His route carried him on Kansas Pacific and connecting routes with the Chicago, Burlington and Quincy rails. The final leg was on Northern Pacific. He had not heard from his father, but expected his arrival in St. Anne's sometime in late March. Given a week to rest, Jacob, Maria, and the baby would start north by mid-April. He told the Meyers the bunkhouse was fine.

John decided on March 4 as his departure date. He met with Mr. Culp and Denzel Kalb to be sure the accounts of *St. Anne's Company* were in order, then set aside a half-day to bid farewell to friends. The only remaining task was completion of two large trunks fashioned using scrap wood from the grist mill. These would ship north with Maria and his father. On the night before departure, Peter shook John's hand, wished him luck and quickly left the house. John appreciated the gesture, but understood it was taken at the behest of Maria. Melina planned to watch Morgan while Hersh and Maria drove John to the Kansas Pacific station. That changed on the morning of departure. Hilke was close to giving birth and experiencing difficulties. Melina decided to stay by her daughter-in-law's bedside and Maria, not wanting to expose Morgan to the elements, stayed with the baby. John and Hersh traveled alone to Hays City.

PART II: MARGIN TO MONOLITH

"How many names will be on the County Clerk's plat in fifty years? I might as well try to will the sunset ... to my brother's children. We come and go, but the land is always there ..."
—Willa Cather

Chapter Fourteen:
Casselton

Fargo and the Dakota Territory were the better part of three days from Hays City. John was well provisioned for the trip, having been supplied by Maria with a pack full of sausage, biscuits and dried fruit. He also had a large supply of hard candy supplied by his friend Mr. Pallitto. What he lacked for in variety, he made up in quantity. While changing trains in St. Louis, he caught sight of several immigrant cars on a nearby siding. He recalled the discomfort of these hastily converted cars, the uncertainty of what was to come, and the euphoria finding Maria was pregnant. His thoughts wandered back to the squalid conditions on the *Russische* trains. John was thankful for his second-class passage.

The train made a number of stops and John disembarked at each. He stared blankly at the terrain—his thoughts never far from his yet unseen farm. At three p.m. on the afternoon of March 7, John arrived in Fargo, Dakota Territory. He was surprised by what he saw. The town appeared to be slightly larger than Hays City and far less orderly. An assembly of tents laid out in military fashion bordered the tracks. John assumed it was housing for railroad workers. A large hotel owned by Northern Pacific stood next to the station. Most of the surrounding structures appeared to be temporary. John was not sure what a "frontier" town looked like, but from what he knew, Fargo fit the description—busy and disheveled. Their stay was brief with only time enough to walk a few hundred yards. When he returned, he found the car filled with railroad workers. Three additional freight cars had been added and carried timbers, rails, and various construction materials. He was now part of a work train. As the engineer signaled his intention to leave, another contingent of workers scrambled aboard, finding a place alongside and atop the material. All carried packs suggesting they would not soon return. The ride to Casselton took less than an hour. Ten to twelve workers left the train, but he was the only passenger. He found the station master and showed him the Meyer name.

The master studied him for a moment, "So you're the new owner," he said. "The Meyers are expecting you."

John wasn't sure he understood. The master pointed toward a wagon track headed north.

"Follow the track for two miles, then turn east at the split rail fence." He repeated "*osten*" to be sure John understood.

Aside from another tent camp, Casselton was a rail yard, a few buildings and not much else. A hand painted sign staked in an empty field read "Casselton *Skole*." Maria would be pleased a school was planned.

John had written Freidrich providing an expected arrival date, but was unsure if he or the letter would reach Casselton first. Freidrich had not received the letter and for the past three days had ridden to the station each afternoon. Now he saw John and began frantically calling out his name. After an enthusiastic handshake and embrace, Freidrich reversed course. His brother-in-law was full of questions, but John was consumed by what he saw around him.

After what seemed an eternity, Freidrich turned east. Immediately to their left was a well-maintained split rail fence and, some fifty yards beyond, an entry gate with "Meyer" carved in clapboard and suspended above. John could now see what he thought to be the main house. It was two levels, perhaps more correctly, a level and one-half with whitewashed siding and an attached log structure facing east, possibly the original home. John could see a freshly tilled garden and another, smaller house in the distance along with a few outbuildings. There was a look of order, but also evidence of deferred maintenance.

Karl Meyer fairly burst through the door as the wagon approached— his awkward gait a clear identification. He made his way down the two steps, stumbling at the bottom. There was another enthusiastic hand pumping. He thought Karl was speaking in *Deutsch*, but the dialect confused John. He recognized "*willkommen zuhause*," as Karl made a sweeping motion toward the home and property. Anneke Meyer emerged foregoing the handshake for an embrace. She immediately began a very animated conversation that no one, save Karl, could understand. Realizing she had lost John and Freidrich, she slowed her pace. Freidrich seemed able to follow what appeared to be a curious mix of *Englisch* and *Deutsch*.

Anneke announced, "I have smoked venison, corn, potatoes and dried apple pie."

"We'll inspect the property first," Karl said.

"Why inspect when there is nothing wrong?" Anneke responded. "The boy needs food."

John was eager to see the property, but it was clear Anneke had already won the argument. She had a special *kugelhopf* and suggested John, Freidrich, and her husband enjoy the pastry and a touch of corn whiskey on the porch while she finished preparing the meal. John was pleased with what he saw. Both the house and outbuildings were much as Freidrich described.

They had only been seated for a few minutes when two very blond girls, the oldest perhaps eight, the younger half that age, rushed through the door. They stopped suddenly and, remembering their manners, called back to Anneke.

"*Takk Amma*," both said.

Each of the girls had a pie in hand. John had no idea who they belonged to or why they were there.

"I'll explain later," Karl said, recognizing John's confusion.

Dinner was a welcome change from three days of sausage and too much hard candy. After the meal, Karl suggested another glass of corn whiskey and mentioned two changes to their agreement since John telegraphed his acceptance. The first was a purchase of two additional horses, bringing the total to seven. If John did not think the purchase necessary the horses could be returned. Freidrich caught John's eye and nodded concurrence. Karl left some ground fallow last year and was able to get by with five horses, one nearing an end to its working life.

The second change was a new family temporarily living on the farm. The Rasmussens had been in residence for a week, having come from Pembina where they homesteaded the year before. They were an Icelandic family from Lake Winnipeg. Colvis Rasmussen struggled there and had no better luck in Pembina. The farm was small and the ground poor. The family would never have survived the winter were it not for the generosity of their neighbors. His wife, Mary Etta, had no desire to suffer through another season. They abandoned their homestead, left what few implements they owned to satisfy debt, and set out for Minnesota where Mary Etta's brother owned a mercantile. North of Fargo, their wagon overturned when the bank of a swollen stream gave way. Colvis was able to save the wagon, but many of their possessions were lost. The family limped into Fargo where Colvis hoped to find short-term employment before resuming their journey.

Karl came across the Rasmussens as he was leaving Fargo, having purchased materials for his cottage. He was taken by the sight of the children looking hungry and forlorn. There were four—two young girls, a somewhat older boy who clung to his mother—and the eldest, almost as big as his father. He asked if they needed help. The older of the two girls responded. Karl didn't understand though he could tell the child was distraught.

The oldest boy, who spoke some English, explained.

"She's lost her favorite doll," pointing toward the stream.

Colvis told Karl they were bound for Minnesota and needed work to continue their journey.

"Do you know anyone in Fargo who is hiring?" he asked

Karl though for a moment, "Have you experience in farming?"

"We do." Mary Etta quickly responded.

"I could use a hand for at least a month." Karl said.

Colvis, who seemed hesitant at first, nodded agreement. With that, the two girls joined Karl and both wagons turned toward Casselton. Anneke was understandably surprised when Karl returned. Her husband had set out for lumber and came back with a family. When Karl mentioned the lost doll, Anneke disappeared for a moment and quickly returned with two penny wood dolls explaining, "These belonged to my daughters."

The girls were delighted and Anneke had made two forever friends. Karl hoped John would honor his one-month commitment to the Rasmussen family, but had told Colvis the final decision belonged to John. Freidrich again supported the decision, confirming an extra hand during planting season was more than welcome. The Rasmussens' eldest son was also capable and work could be found for him.

Karl was eager to end the evening with another glass of whiskey, but his dinner companions were not. John was surprised at his lack of anxiety. He hardly knew Karl, yet trusted him explicitly. The inspection was necessary, but tomorrow would be soon enough. Once complete, he and Karl would leave midmorning for Fargo to sign papers and pick up supplies for Anneke and lumber for the cottage. On their way to the bunkhouse, John commented on how well Freidrich understood Anneke. He expected an understanding of *Deutsch,* though her dialect was unfamiliar. What surprised him was Freidrich's ability to follow *Englisch.* When Anneke spoke slowly, Freidrich was able to keep pace. The answer was lessons. Since his arrival Anneke committed an hour each evening to language mastery, which she believed was a necessary step to succeed in America.

Early the next morning Karl, John and Freidrich rode through the Meyer farm. They inspected the barn and passed by the second frame house—much smaller—but well-constructed. John saw the livestock sheds and noted the repairs underway. Moving diagonally across the farm, he could see the cottage Karl and Anneke would soon call home. It sat atop a small rise protected by an orchard. With John, Colvis, and the Rasmussen boy available for planting, Karl and his helper would have more time for construction.

They watched Colvis as he and his son guided the two-horse harrow over ground plowed after last year's harvest. Karl had suggested more than 200 acres were ready to accept seed. In the distance, John could see livestock grazing. Freidrich's representation was accurate. If anything, he understated the farm's value. John was not surprised. Karl and Anneke kept a good farm. The three men continued toward the western boundary where the adjoining section on the north was held by an absentee owner.

Karl pointed that way and muttered, "Bad neighbor."

John looked at him quizzically.

Freidrich added, "He doesn't care about the valley or the people of Cass County."

"I've already clashed with the farm's superintendent," Karl said. "They're pulling too much water from the creek."

Turning south they rode along two quarter sections purchased from the railroad by Benjamin Erhardt just after Karl acquired his property. The eccentric farmer cobbled together a soddy, but he had not been seen for weeks. There was no evidence soil had been recently turned and Karl suspected Benjamin's debt to NPRR was past due.

When they returned to the main house, Anneke had an early lunch waiting. Karl had asked Freidrich to join them on the trip to Fargo. He wanted to discuss the farm's history and also cover what crops should be planted and when. Freidrich's translation would also be helpful when closing papers were signed. As they started toward the city, Karl handed the reins to John and began the discussion on how the Meyers found their way to the Dakota Territory. Karl and Anneke had immigrated from the *Deutsch*-speaking region of *Elsass Lothringen* when both were children and settled on farms north of Philadelphia. They were later married and built a small home on the property owned by Karl's parents. The two Meyer households enjoyed some success, but not enough to support two families.

Karl and long-time friend Rolf Neumann decided to move west. Minnesota was chosen and the pair found work in the timber industry. Two years later they became partners in a lumber brokerage. The business survived, but they had neither timber, nor mill, and sales declined in the face of stiff competition.

They left Minnesota for the Dakota Territory where both homesteaded. Karl was among the first to purchase land from Northern Pacific, buying a quarter section adjacent to his claim. Rolf did the same a mile west of the Meyer farm. Karl and Anneke raised three daughters. The two eldest had married and were now living in Minnesota. The youngest had married Rolf's nephew, taking up residence in the vacant smaller house.

Karl and his new son-in-law fought endlessly. After a short period, the young man took a job with a railroad survey crew and the family moved to Fargo, then on to Bismark. Karl lost his leg a few months later. There followed a series of hired hands or "farm bosses" as Karl preferred to call them with Freidrich being the latest. Karl paused for a moment as if engaged in self-examination. John understood. Keeping the farm in the Meyer family was important to Karl, but his decision to sell brought an end to that dream. Anneke felt the same and, like every mother, hoped to grow old in the company of her daughters and grandchildren. Both understood that would never take place, at least on the Meyer farm. Their obligation was now to the young man about to sign final papers. Karl continued to stare blankly ahead before turning to a discussion of fieldwork.

He told John, "If you can plant 200 acres, you'll be doing well."

John hesitated. He had hoped to do better.

Karl reminded him, "You have four men and a boy," then added, "And I'm not much good."

To bring all 300 acres under cultivation would be near impossible. The season was short. Wheat, oats and barley should be planted within fifteen days; corn would come next, perhaps a bit late. Freidrich and Colvis had already begun fieldwork, but even 200 acres might require additional help.

Karl paused for a moment then said, "That's what we'll do," speaking to no one in particular.

John had begun to notice fence posts tagged with the name C. Mann. There were three or four in succession, then none, then three or four again. He was about to ask the identity of C. Mann when a large four-axle wagon pulled by a team of eight horses approached. Karl was noticeably unhappy. He gave way, but growled "dummkopf" as the wagon passed. On board were eight logs and a quantity of dimensional lumber. John saw the name spelled out on a placard—Cornellious Mann company. There was a second, smaller wagon behind carrying what Karl identified as components of a reaper with some sort of rake attached. Freidrich reminded John that Kurt Haus was employed by Cornellious Mann, assembling equipment similar to what just passed.

Mann was the absentee owner Karl referenced earlier. He acquired 3,000 acres in a debt exchange with the Northern Pacific Railway and was said to be close to securing another large parcel. The company expected to plant at least 2,500 acres this year and double the next. There were rumors that even larger farms might soon be coming. John didn't understand how Mann acquired the property, but thought it best to leave the topic for later discussion.

They were now within sight of Fargo and John was again struck by the crush of activity. Karl told him there were 700 full-time residents that called Fargo home, but their numbers were swollen by railroad workers, prospectors, and the military. Wagons were everywhere and John struggled to find a path.

The first stop was the office of Luther Ogden—Karl's long-time friend and confidant. The office turned out to be a tent, though it had a cleanly swept wooden floor. A hotel directly across the street also carried the Ogden name. John discovered Luther was not a banker, at least not like Mr. Norton of the First National Bank of Hays City. He simply had the funds to act in that capacity. At first John was apprehensive. Mr. Ogden seemed much like his city—out of control. While they waited, the financier met with a riverboat captain, a lumberman, and two farmers. The more John observed, the more his respect for Mr. Ogden grew. There were three Ogden subordinates in the tent and all leapt at his command. One of them signed a credit authorization so Karl could purchase lumber, another Ogden venture. When it was John's turn, Luther spoke in *Deutsch* telling him he had done business with others from his country. John was happy to find someone with whom he could converse, and saw no reason to explain he had immigrated from *Russen*.

Luther could see John was uncomfortable with the frantic pace of activity.

"You'll find our business trustworthy," he assured John.

Karl added, "I can attest to that."

Luther placed a hand on Karl's shoulder. Turning to John, he said, "You've found a man of character."

An assistant brought a sheaf of papers, which John signed without reading.

"You're a lucky man," Luther said. "This valley will soon be the center of wheat production in the United States."

John wondered if the comment was something of an exaggeration, but noticed Karl agreed. Before John could say thank you, Luther Ogden was working with another client.

The next stop was the lumber yard where John and Freidrich loaded the last of the material needed to complete the Meyer cottage. Karl did his best to help, but was more of a hindrance. The three men started back toward Casselton. As they were leaving Karl told John that Fargo was a city divided—the one just visited, and the other Fargo in the Woods. The latter was known for its saloons and brothels. Luther Ogden had interests there as well. John was not surprised. There was much more to Mr. Ogden that met the eye.

Little was said on the return trip. John continued to weigh the options for planting, while Karl and Freidrich discussed whether Casselton would experience growth similar to that of Fargo. A few miles south of the city, they were overtaken by a contingent of Calvary. Karl explained the Lakota Sioux had been granted a large area of land under the Fort Laramie Treaty of 1868. The grant included the Black Hills where gold had recently been discovered. Prospectors had overrun the area and the Army had done little to enforce the treaty. Karl was sure gold, and not the treaty would prevail. The Sioux considered the Black Hills sacred ground and their warriors had engaged and killed several miners. The troop movement was intended to bring the Army closer to the growing conflict. Karl's friend, Rolf Neumann, had a son, Abe, riding with Lieutenant Colonel Custer, who had reportedly engaged the enemy in the Powder River area.

When they arrived home, Anneke was ready with an evening meal—the young Rasmussen girls, once again, in her kitchen. Karl wanted to talk after the meal, but Freidrich was not interested saying he needed to check on the animals. John also declined, borrowing a lamp and retiring to the bunkhouse to write Maria. He told his wife that, with careful management, the farm would be a good provider. John took extra time to describe the house and mentioned a school and general store were coming to Casselton. He knew Maria would see the school and store as evidence of community, though he wasn't sure when either would be completed. John did his best to describe the Meyers telling Maria they would make good neighbors. Finally, he told Maria to spend as little time in Fargo as possible.

The telegram arrived the afternoon of March 18. The station master noted the St. Anne's address, placed it in a sealed envelope and dispatched a worker to Pallitto's General Store. Achim Steyer, whose land was just north of St. Anne's, was in the store, having just visited Nelson Feed. He knew John and Maria Schmidt and agreed to deliver the correspondence to the Schafer house. Maria had been anxiously awaiting the telegram. Jacob was in Baltimore, or perhaps farther west. His arrival meant she and Morgan would soon be reunited with John. The wire was simple enough: "expect to arrive in four days." Maria was ecstatic. For reasons unknown, she was slow packing the two crates that John had built for their belongings. Now there was work to do. Even Peter, learning of the telegram, was excited. He looked forward to seeing his old friend, although he understood Jacob's arrival meant his daughter and granddaughter would soon be leaving.

Jacob's voyage had taken eleven days. He became ill on the sixth day. The cabin attendant had suggested *seekranheit*, but Jacob thought it was more likely something he ate. The *Weser* had experienced heavy seas just out of Southampton and he was not bothered. He fell ill after the seas quieted.

His above-deck cabin made interaction with steerage awkward, although he did manage to speak with Lutz Hoffman. Jacob recognized Lutz as a young man he had done work for a few months previous. The conversation took place on the steerage deck and Jacob realized the wisdom of his berthing choice. They were eight days into the voyage and the passage below reeked of unimaginable odors. The Hoffman party had relied on the Atchison, Topeka and Santa Fe to secure through passage from *Russen* to Kansas. They were forty-nine in all from the colonies of Kratske, Degott and Grimm. Two families, a total of thirteen, expected to move on to Colorado. The others hoped to settle in Kansas. Lutz knew of St. Anne's, but lacked any details. Jacob shared what he understood of the community and encouraged him to visit, "It is much like your colony in *Russen*."

Lutz seemed confused, "Like Kratske?" he asked.

Jacob immediately wondered if reference to the old country was a good idea. He did not see Lutz again, but caught sight of the party as they boarded their immigrant car. Jacob was glad for his second-class accommodations. Too little sleep and irregular meals were taking a toll. His transit across Europe and eleven days at sea were more taxing than he imagined. He reminded himself he would soon hold his granddaughter, something he thought impossible twelve months earlier. Sadly, the reunion was the product of his wife's death, but he was sure Helena would be pleased by his decision. She would have wanted father and son together.

Jacob arrived in Hays City the morning of March 22 and, as directed, made his way to the Pallitto's General Store. Recognizing John's father immediately, Josef shouted, "Jacob Schmidt," and embraced the newcomer. Josef had not planned a trip to St. Anne's, but quickly adjusted his schedule leaving his wife to mind the store. John was a good friend. If his father required transport, it was the least he could do. Their first stop was the rail yard. Jacob brought with him a trunk containing woodworking tools—undisturbed after crossing an ocean and two continents. He was told in Saratov there was little chance the tools would make it to America. They were now in Mr. Pallitto's wagon.

En route to St. Anne's Josef confirmed what Jacob had expected.

"Your son left for the Dakota Territory two weeks ago," he said.

"Maria and the baby are still here?" Jacob asked, although he knew the answer.

"They're at the Schafer house. We'll be there soon."

Josef did his best to carry a conversation, but Jacob was more interested in the countryside. He found it something of a surprise. He had expected few inhabitants and broad undeveloped grasslands, broken occasionally by tree stands. Instead, he saw a landscape dotted here and there with farms. Josef scanned the horizon and saw neither wall nor battlement. His fellow travelers on board the *Weser* told him Kansas was in Indian Territory and small farms were cloistered around military outposts to maintain security. Josef saw nothing but tranquility.

Maria was helping her sister-in-law plant early season vegetables when she saw the wagon approach. She fell to her knees.

"*Vater*, thanks be to God."

Jacob lifted her to his arms.

"*Mein enkelkin*," he said.

"She's with Melina," Maria responded.

They found Morgan asleep in the kitchen. Jacob reached for the hand of his former neighbor, then lifted the baby. Tears filled his eyes. He spent the early evening with his granddaughter before turning his attention to John's letter from Casselton, which had arrived two days before. Maria explained what she knew of the Meyer farm and described the events leading up to its purchase.

Peter was annoyed thinking St. Anne's and the *company* deserved as much attention as a distant Dakota farm. Jacob was exhausted, but agreed to take a short walk through the township.

"I'm disappointed our community is not growing faster," Peter said.

Jacob said nothing.

Peter told his friend, "The young members lack commitment."

"They may not like your rules," Jacob offered.

"The rules are for their own good," Peter responded.

Jacob said, "I don't think John felt that way."

Peter let the subject drop. He told Jacob he missed his son-in-law, having come to rely on John more than he realized. Albrecht was a poor substitute. They talked longer than Jacob wanted, discussing both the future of St. Anne's and the Crown's behavior in *Russen*. Jacob finally retired, but not before telling his friend,

"There is hope," he said, "The Hoffman party will pay St. Anne's a visit within the week."

"Is the party traveling with ATSF or Kansas Pacific?" Peter asked.

"I believe it's Sante Fe," Jacob responded, "But Lutz is intrigued by St. Anne's."

Jacob knew that to be an exaggeration, though Lutz had exhibited interest. He made the comment to encourage his friend. He spent much of the next day trailing Maria and holding his grandchild, an experience he could only imagine a few months before. The Schafer family consumed his every waking hour. He was, after all, grandfather, father-in-law and treasured friend. Peter knew others in the party were eager to talk with Jacob and arranged a meeting at the community center to renew acquaintances, and to meet those who joined the Schafer party en route. He introduced his long-time friend recognizing that he was a stranger to some. Jacob began with the subject foremost on the mind of the assembled group—conditions in *Russen* and recent actions taken by Alexander II. He confirmed their worst fears.

"The Crown is now active in Pfeifer," Jacob said. "A *Dorfburo* has been established by the *Kontor* and controls all administrative matters."

He paused for a moment waiting for the murmur of surprise and discontent to settle.

"What about the *schule*?" asked Felix Austerlitz.

"*Russen* is the language of education," Jacob said, "Teaching in *Deutsch* is forbidden and religion is not part of the curriculum."

The whispers continued among the crowd. Jacob paused again and Peter seized the opportunity.

"Tell them of the war," he said.

Jacob continued. "The Balkans are in turmoil and war is rumored.

They will come for the children." He looked toward Peter wondering if he should proceed. He did not wish to alarm the members, but it was time for an honest assessment of the perils ahead.

Peter said, "They deserve to know."

"There is no patience for the colonies," Jacob said. "Alexander has begun to question our allegiance." He then told the assembled group what they feared most—"the day will come when friends and family will face retribution."

Over the next few days, Jacob rested, visited with old friends, and spent as much time as he could with his granddaughter. He slowly recovered from his journey and even spent a day with Peter and Albrecht working the fields. Maria finished her packing and took full advantage of space in Jacob's trunk. They set May 2 as the date they were to leave for the Dakota Territory. John was advised by telegram.

Melina found it difficult to contain her emotions. Hilke's soon-to-be born child offered some consolation, but losing Morgan, her first-born grandchild, was a devastating loss. Peter struggled as well, but displayed his emotions in an unusual manner. As the departure drew closer, he became more distant, suggesting Albrecht should drive Jacob, Maria and the baby to the station.

Lutz Hoffman, whom Jacob had spoken with on board the *Weser*, arrived April 30, along with just three members of his party. Jacob expected a larger contingent and Peter was visibly disappointed. Lutz told him that two families were bound for Colorado and a smaller group led by two brothers decided to settle on Santa Fe land near Great Bend. Lutz and his associates were still considering St. Anne's, but leaning toward property farther west. Peter was faced with the possibility that no one from the Hoffmann party would join the *company*.

Peter became defensive. "You're not acting in the best interest of the party," he told Lutz.

"Consider your own actions," Lutz responded. "Your ways are too much like those of the old country."

Peter was angry. "St. Anne's will succeed and you will fail."

Whatever chance Peter had of convincing Lutz to join the *St. Anne's Company* was lost. Jacob understood the dilemma. St. Anne's embodied too much of what Lutz and his party wished to escape. Peter's colony was a poor imitation of Pfeifer, and the *Vorsteher* himself too much like the Czar. Newcomers found St. Anne's confining and those already committed were beginning to question their decision. Peter's dream was slipping away. The meeting was a crushing dose of reality on the eve of Maria and Morgan's departure.

The Schafer and Schmidt families shared one last meal together. Melina put Morgan down for the last time and remained at her bedside long after she had fallen asleep. Peter reconsidered his decision to have Albrecht take Jacob, Maria and his granddaughter to the Hays City Station. As patriarch, it was his obligation. Maria rose that evening and quietly walked through the township. St. Anne's would soon be a memory and she wondered when, or if, she would return to Kansas.

Melina chose not to make the trip to the station with her husband. She was worried her emotions would get the best of her upsetting both Maria and the baby. Instead, she watched from the porch as her daughter and grandchild departed. Melina was convinced she would never see them again.

Little was said en route to the station. Peter asked questions for which he already knew the answer.

"Are you sure you have food enough; do you have need for another blanket?"

"We're in need of nothing, father," Maria responded."

All were relieved when they arrived at the station. Peter confirmed the train was on time, quickly embraced his friend, daughter, and granddaughter. He left them on the platform never looking back. Maria hoped his abrupt departure disguised a deep feeling of sadness.

The train followed the same route taken by John a month earlier. It was a long and wearisome trip, but Jacob and Maria had seen worse. Morgan seemed to delight in rail travel lulled to sleep by the rhythmic sounds, and when awake, enjoying the full attention of her mother and grandfather. They arrived in Fargo just after noon on the fifth of May. John was waiting. Maria ran to her husband. Jacob stepped from the train and stood frozen by the sight of his only son.

"I am finally home," he said.

John let go of his wife and daughter and took a step back. A year had passed since he last saw his father. He looked much older than John remembered.

"Mother would be happy," John said. "She would have wanted us to be together."

Maria now understood her husband's admonition not to wander far from the Fargo Station. Everyone was in a hurry, teamsters shouted obscenities, and the most common appurtenance was a gun. Aside from the Northern Pacific Hotel, nothing appeared to be permanent. Maria also noticed a few women dressed in a manner that seemed unusual for the frontier.

Noting her discomfort, John quickly collected the trunks, declaring, "It's time we leave."

"Good!" said Maria.

John assured his wife, "You'll find Casselton and the farm more to your liking."

The conversation turned to the old country, St Anne's and the Meyer farm. With so much to discuss the trip seemed to be over in minutes. They encountered only one traveler, a lone rider aboard an empty Cornellious Mann wagon. This time the driver reined in his team and gave way to the Schmidts.

Maria said nothing, but was disappointed in Casselton. She had hoped for something more than a few buildings. Aside from construction materials piled near a future school site there was little to suggest community. Maria's anxiety grew as they approached the family's new home. Passing through the gate, she glanced up at a new sign that read "Farm of John Schmidt." Karl and Freidrich had replaced the "Meyer" placard. She asked John to stop, then took a long look at the farm spread before her. She was relieved. Casselton barely qualified as a town, but the farm was everything her husband said it would be. The Meyers were waiting on the front porch as Maria struggled to process all that was taking place. She was beginning a new chapter in the company of husband, daughter and father-in-law. A few months before, it was nothing more than a dream. Now they were together in Dakota. Anneke hurried to the wagon and embraced Maria as Karl waited on the porch to greet the newcomers. Freidrich was the next to arrive. He kissed Maria and shook Jacob's hand.

Karl told Anneke, "Be still woman," but Anneke could not stop talking, eager to show Maria her new home.

"You will love it," she said.

"*Es ist wunderschon,*" Maria said.

Compared to their small space in St. Anne's, the Meyer home was palatial. Karl and Anneke had moved to the small house the week before, but left enough furnishings behind to create a sense of belonging. A cabinet with four shelves stood in the corner with a curtain partially drawn across the front. A rough-hewn table with four chairs sat near the stove. There were two heavy benches fashioned from aspen trunks and a wooden bed with straw mattress. Finally, two trunks stood near the door, one containing a random collection of cooking utensils.

Maria asked, "Are these for us?" Anneke nodded, pulling the curtain back to reveal a set of tinware.

"You're too kind," Maria said.

John was eager to show Maria and his father what really mattered—the farm itself.

Maria hesitated, "But the baby?"

Anneke quickly intervened. "She'll be fine with me."

John steered the wagon toward the nearby outbuildings and Jacob immediately noticed the livestock shed which needed repair. He also noticed the smallish barn, but his cursory look suggested that expansion could be achieved with little effort. Jacob was ready to put his tools to work and the barn would be a good project. He also expected to do fieldwork as well. His transit from *Russen* consisted mostly of sitting. Getting his hands dirty was appealing.

John told his father, "We'll plant 220 acres, most in wheat."

"That much?" Jacob was uneasy.

"It can be done," he said. "You'll see."

At Karl's suggestion, there would also be oats, barley and corn, along with two gardens, one adjacent to the main house and a much smaller plot near the Meyer cottage. John and Karl met earlier with Rolf Neumann and decided, as they had in the past, to combine resources. Rolf and three of his sons would help with planting the Schmidt farm. John, Freidrich and the Rasmussens would reciprocate. Working together reduced the need for temporary help, at least for the planting season.

They found Colvis and his son harrowing and Mary Etta en route to the field with water. The two young girls were in tow, along with the family's second son, perhaps thirteen. Colvis had agreed to stay on temporarily, but it appeared he was in no hurry to leave. Using timbers from the repaired livestock shed, the family pieced together a shelter that would suffice through the summer and fall.

Karl spoke highly of Colvis as a worker. He was willing and required little supervision. Freidrich saw him in the same way. Neither understood how Mary Etta felt, but both suspected Colvis would prefer to stay put rather than join his wife's family in Minnesota. John hoped the Rasmussens chose to remain. He took a moment to introduce Colvis and his son to Maria and Jacob. Mary Etta arrived with two jugs of water. When her two girls learned there was a baby at the main house, they immediately wanted to see the child.

"Maria is busy," Mary Etta said. "Perhaps tomorrow, if there is time."

"Please," both said at once; the response drew a reprimand from their mother.

John noticed the Rasmussens youngest son clung to Mary Etta's dress. He made unusual sounds, but had no real speech and experienced difficulty walking, particularly in the freshly turned soil. The boy seemed lost and family members went out of their way to provide for his comfort.

John eased the reins heading in a westerly direction. The rundown condition of the adjoining Erhardt property was now in full view. John told Maria and his father what he knew of the farm. It was good land, but never received the attention it deserved. Jacob wondered why anyone would allow good land to turn bad. John then continued south passing by the Meyer cottage, now close to completion. Their circuit was complete.

Jacob said, "You've done well son."

Maria nodded in agreement, then added, "The baby will be fussy by now."

When they returned to the main house, Maria immediately began to question her host.

"Does Casselton have a doctor or church?" then added, "Are there nearby farms?" She continued to pepper Anneke with questions. "When will they start school construction? Is there a general store?"

Anneke patiently answered, "Doctor, general store, and mercantile are in Fargo. There is a church, but we don't attend services." She paused for a moment trying to remember all of Maria's questions. "The Neumanns are close, and there are a few Norwegian neighbors." Then, as an afterthought she added, "Karl and I are here, and Mary Etta is a good companion."

While Maria and Anneke spoke of community, Karl talked of the season ahead and the Army's presence in Fargo. He was careful not to mention Indians within earshot of the women. The three men retired to the porch where they discovered a shared appreciation for Karl's best whiskey.

The meeting on the porch threatened to go on forever.

"Let Jacob rest" Anneke said. "The family needs time together."

Karl reluctantly agreed.

"We resume planting tomorrow," he said, "Dawn to dusk with no time for family."

The next day brought heavy rain. They busied themselves with fence work and tinkered with equipment. Jacob enlisted the Rasmussens' eldest and set out to finish repairs on the livestock shed. He'd already sketched an addition to the barn and planned on starting by midsummer. After further discussion with Karl, John planned to seed 240 acres leaving some ground for winter rye. It was more ambitious than originally planned, but John believed the farm was ready. Karl had set aside much of the seed necessary and Colvis made one trip to Fargo to purchase a small quantity of spring wheat and barley. Rolf Neumann had a similar planting scheme, though not as ambitious.

The rain had passed by midafternoon. Work started on the Neumann farm with two hired hands assisting John, Freidrich, Colvis, his son and the Neumann boys. The plan was to move back and forth between properties beginning with wheat and ending with corn. Karl expected planting to be more efficient this year. He and Rolf jointly purchased a used Van Brunt force-feed drill. The device carved furrows, dropped seed, and backfilled before the birds disturbed the planting.

Jacob had made a decision to sleep in the loft, but abandoned his second-floor accommodations in less than a week.

"I'm intruding," he said, "And the ladder is too difficult in the dark."

"Take the small house when it becomes available," John suggested.

"I don't need all that space, just a bed and stove. The bunkhouse will be fine."

Jacob's decision meant the small house would be empty once the Meyer cottage was completed. John wondered if offering a more permanent home would encourage Colvis to stay on through harvest and beyond. He and his son had already shown their worth and the family made good neighbors. There were surely benefits for the Rasmussens as well—a roof over their head and stability. Maria had also begun to help with the son who took much of Mary Etta's time, and Anneke treated the two young girls as her granddaughters. John visited the family's makeshift shelter, something only Anneke had done before. Colvis mistakenly thought the visit meant his job would soon come to an end. Instead, John had a proposition. He was willing to put Colvis on year-round at $30.00 per month and pay his son sixty cents per day through harvest and one-half that amount for the winter. If the Rasmussens wanted, the small house was theirs as long as they stayed. Before Colvis could turn to Mary Etta, she was already nodding agreement.

Planting continued on the Neumann farm. A short-lived problem with the seed drill was quickly resolved and the crew worked dark to dark. Karl took on the role of overseer and Jacob left the fields each day in midafternoon. Maria and Mary Etta helped Rolf's wife with cooking for the combined crew. They lost one day to another downpour and finished planting corn on the Schmidt farm May 23. The next day was Sunday and John asked his father to read from the scriptures, giving thanks for their good fortune. Jacob chose "So neither he who plants nor he who waters is anything, but only God who gives growth." (1 Corinthians 3:7) The Schmidt family prayed alone. John knew the Rasmussens to be a God-fearing family and assumed they were doing the same. He wasn't sure about the Meyers.

Chapter Fifteen:
Seeds of Expansion

"The pursuits of agriculture [are] the surest road to affluence"
—Thomas Jefferson

The next morning brought a surprise visitor. Karl was helping Anneke with their small garden when Luther Ogden rode through the gate. His intent was to visit John, but an old friend deserved attention as well.

He told Karl, "Benjamin Erhardt paid me a visit. His debt is payable to Northern Pacific on June 15."

"He'll never pay," was Karl's response.

"Benjamin has no ambition," Luther said. "He wants me to settle with the railroad and carry the paper."

Luther knew Karl was right. Benjamin would almost certainly default. He had lived on the property for years and made no improvements. If Luther made the loan, the property would fall into his hands, but only after some unpleasantness. He decided on a different strategy, offering to buy the property at a small premium. Luther knew Karl once coveted the property and suspected the new owner, John Schmidt, would feel the same. But did John Schmidt have the money? If John was willing to pay what Luther paid, the property was his. He was also willing to finance all or part of the transaction. Unlike the unsavory Erhardt, Luther saw John as a good risk.

"Why not keep the property yourself?" Karl asked.

"Too small," the financier said. "I want a larger piece, not a few hundred acres here and there."

Luther had a feeling about John. He liked the young *deutscher mann* and expected him to be a long-time valley resident. A favor today held benefits for tomorrow. Karl and Luther set out to find John, but instead encountered Jacob. He told them his son left for the Neumann farm to retrieve equipment. Karl looked toward Luther and acknowledged it was acceptable to discuss the potential sale with Jacob. Luther explained the proposition.

"*Gut, gut,*" was Jacob's response. Pointing to himself he said, "*Kaufe jetzt.*" Jacob would pay in full.

"Are you sure?" Luther was not accustomed to dealing with wealthy immigrants.

Just as quickly as Jacob made the decision, he retreated. He must first talk with John. It was, after all, his farm. Luther agreed to hold the property for ten days, but no longer. That evening Jacob discussed the sale with his son and daughter-in-law. John's first reaction was negative. The purchase stretched resources too thin. Any calamity—the possibilities were end-less—could result in loss of the farm. Jacob also suspected his interven-tion was a threat to John's position as master. John should be the decision maker. Maria was annoyed. A false sense of pride was standing in the way of opportunity.

She told her husband, "You're behaving like my father."

"I didn't expect to grow the farm this soon." John said.

"It's good, adjacent land at an attractive price," Maria countered.

"More than that, it's an investment in our future," Jacob added.

John had never asked, but assumed his father left Pfeifer in better financial condition than most. His offer to buy the Erhardt property gave insight on the extent of his wealth—his partnership with Stephan Haus had apparently been profitable. A decision was reached. The Schmidts would purchase the Erhardt property.

Kurt Haus completed his contract with the Cornellious Mann Com-pany and was now staying in the bunkhouse. He told John the Mann prop-erties had grown to more than 4,500 acres with 2,600 under cultivation. He likened the farm to a regimented military operation. Management meticu-lously recorded every component of farm output including individual man hours, equipment usage, and even hours worked by each horse. Forty-three hands had been hired for planting. Twice that number was anticipated for harvest. Kurt expected the farm could reach 10,000 acres before next year's planting season with one-half the ground under cultivation.

Klaus Schuler was next to call the bunkhouse home, forfeiting a small bonus from NPRR by leaving his contract position early. The trio was now ready to undertake the first leg of their journey, a return to St. Anne's. They planned a short stay there before moving on to San Francisco and ultimately to the Washington Territory. Kurt was sure work could be found in the burgeoning timber industry, perhaps even a logging enterprise of their own. At least that was Kurt's latest plan.

John and Maria were saddened by Freidrich's departure. He was brother and good friend and the reason they found their way to Dakota. Karl and Anneke felt the same. Freidrich's stay had been short, but they had come to admire the young man—enough so to have offered to sell Freidrich the Meyer farm.

Maria gave Freidrich a letter for delivery to her mother describing their new home and the kindness displayed by Karl and Anneke. She mentioned their recent purchase, wondering how her father would react when told of the farm's sudden expansion. She told her mother Morgan was crawling, but declined to mention the child's fondness for Anneke Meyer, fearing it would bring sadness. Lastly, Maria shared a secret— one she withheld from John. She suspected Morgan would soon have a younger brother or sister.

On June 8, John drove Freidrich, Kurt and Klaus to Fargo. He questioned if they had the means to make their way to the Pacific Northwest, let alone start a business. If they had concerns, none was expressed. Adventure and uncharted ground were far more important than personal or financial security. Maria suggested to John that Freidrich and his friends were foolhardy. John reminded his wife they left *Russen* barely a year earlier and purchased a farm in Dakota sight unseen. He started to describe the risk taken by their ancestors, but stopped when told he was beginning to sound like a *Volga Deutsch* elder.

John left the three young men on the platform and began his journey back to the farm. Turning toward home, he saw a wagon approaching from the west pulled by two oxen. He could make out a woman at the reins and two children by her side. The father and young daughter walked ahead of the oxen. A boy walked alongside. A cow was tethered trailing some distance behind. The boy and cow appeared incapable of taking another step.

Once within shouting distance, the man waved and repeated *"vinur, vinur"* touching his breast repeatedly.

John did not understand, but interpreted the gesture to be a request for help. He took stock of their condition and signaled them to follow. Too exhausted to do anything but comply, they simply fell in line. The boy took a seat beside John and both wagons began a deliberate procession toward the Schmidt farm. They found Mary Etta, her son and the girls visiting Maria at the main house. The man again said *"vinur"* and Mary Etta recognized he was saying, "friend." The similarity between Icelandic and Swedish was tenuous, but enough to achieve understanding.

The family had been on the prairie for the past nine days traveling more than 120 miles. The nights were spent in the open except the last when they found shelter in an abandoned soddy. They left their claim after losing some of last year's crop to grasshoppers and much of this year's planting to a flash flood. The conversation was awkward, but the visitors understood they were welcome. The family planned on retracing their path of two years ago, stopping in Fargo then on to Sioux City to join relatives. In time, they hoped to return to Sweden—a task that seemed unimaginable to John. They had barely enough food and money to reach their relatives' homestead. Maria offered jerky, a few early vegetables and a small quantity of flour. They also replenished their supply of water. Jacob offered to move out of the bunkhouse, but the family chose to sleep in and under the wagon. The man spoke briefly with Colvis and John, admiring the farm. He was grateful for the courtesy.

"Beautiful farm," he said.

"Stay as long as you like," John answered.

"Thank you, but we'll be moving on early tomorrow."

The man bowed his head slightly and turned his gaze back to the fields. Beyond the expression of gratitude, the family kept to themselves. This was especially true of the mother. She sat motionless while the father and eldest son dealt with chores and cared for the younger children. The next morning the family was gone, having left well before daybreak. The Schmidt farm would have been happy to entertain a longer stay, but they seemed uncomfortable, particularly the mother, whom the family shielded from interaction. Jacob found only a walking stick he had admired the day before. "Vinur" was freshly carved near the top.

John believed he and the Rasmussens, along with one hired hand, could manage the farm until harvest. He did not consider his father or Karl as contributors and expected some help from Maria and Mary Etta. That outlook changed with the purchase of the Erhardt property. The farm had grown by 320 acres, most of which had never been planted. John would be happy if 100 acres were plowed. Any ground turned beyond that would lie fallow. Jacob had made repairs to the second livestock shed and shored up the barn anticipating its expansion—both projects completed a week before harvest. Karl and the Rasmussen boy pulled down what remained of the Erhardt soddy and moved on to turning ground. Benjamin Erhardt left nothing of value behind except a stove, which Jacob and Colvis moved to the bunkhouse.

Karl and Anneke shared a long-standing friendship with the Neumanns, but beyond that had little interaction with neighbors. When asked about nearby farms, both promptly responded "all Norwegian" and "keep to themselves." With regard to the latter, Maria suspected Karl and Anneke did the same. The Meyers and Neumanns were several years her senior and Mary Etta, closer to her age, was often occupied by her younger son. Farm life left little time for socialization, but she at least wanted the opportunity.

Colvis had noticed a new posting on the school construction site calling for a work party the third Sunday in June. All were welcome and participants were instructed to bring tools and food for a late afternoon meal.

Maria told John "It's a chance to meet neighbors."

"We have neighbors enough in the Meyers, Neumanns and Rasmussens," he said. "Meeting the Norwegians can wait."

Maria was adamant. "Colvis will want to participate. His girls will attend the school—in time, so will Morgan."

Maria prevailed. Four volunteer workers from the Schmidt farm, John, Maria, Jacob, and Colvis, arrived at the school site early Sunday morning. Maria left Morgan with Anneke. Mary Etta chose not to participate as her son was feverish and heavily congested. She did, however, prepare two traditional Icelandic dishes which she believed to have Norwegian origins. The work party was surprised to see newcomers, but happy for their assistance.

Eric Hansen, the unofficial leader, was quick to make assignments—John and Jacob to framing and Colvis to carrying materials. Jacob was immediately distracted by two men struggling to fashion a frame and double door.

"*Stoppen, stoppen*," he shouted. The men ceased their work, surprised by the stranger's command.

Colvis repeated the message in Icelandic. "He's a carpenter. You should listen."

Much to the surprise of the others, Jacob began a partial disassembly. In less than an hour he fashioned a sturdy frame and working door. Jacob was immediately whisked off to a new assignment. The Norwegians were delighted one of their helpers had more than a cursory understanding of construction. The women, though not discourteous, remained more distant. They had children in tow and were busy with food preparation. Lisa Hansen noticed Maria, introduced herself, and embraced their language difference as a challenge. Soon all were engaged in the sometimes humorous attempt to understand one another. Lisa told Maria she had four children, two girls ages one and three and two older boys. Maria managed to convey that her daughter, Morgan, would soon be two. They also discovered their homes were only a few miles apart. Maria was encouraged. The Norwegians were delightful companions.

When they returned to the farm that evening, Maria went directly to the Rasmussens' home to inquire on the well-being of their son. She found the boy with an elevated fever and having difficulty catching his breath. The couple planned to leave for Fargo at daybreak in the hope of finding a doctor. Karl agreed to join them. He knew a Doc Parsons who conducted his practice, like so many in Fargo, from temporary quarters. Karl possessed little knowledge of his skills, but suspected he knew more than any so-called "practitioners" in Casselton.

They left well before daybreak, arriving in Fargo only to find the doctor out of the office. A barely legible note said he would return by early afternoon. The Rasmussen boy had not traveled well.

"Please find the doctor," Mary Etta implored.

Karl went directly to the place where he first met Doc Parsons. He was seated at the same bar stool.

Colvis said, "We need help."

"A sick boy," added Karl.

Doc Parsons sensed the urgency, finished his drink, and left for the office. A quick examination indicated the Rasmussen boy had some nervous or behavioral infirmity which contributed to his agitation. He suspected "winter fever," although it was unusual for the season. Doc Parsons considered opening the breathing passage, but wondered if this would provide relief, even if the boy survived the process. "Bleeding" was an option in the past, but that remedy had been discredited.

The doctor turned to a drug he used extensively in the Civil War— morphine. This had the effect of settling the child. He next tried mercury to induce vomiting, suspicious there was an imbalance of body fluids. Cold damp towels were also applied and seemed to quell the fever. The doctor's treatment regime gave the impression it was dictated by accepted practice, but it was illusory. Doc Parsons was confused. After an hour of observation, during which the doctor came and went, the boy seemed to improve and was resting comfortably— the heavy dose of morphine having taken effect.

He told Mary Etta "The worst is over."

"You're sure?" Colvis was skeptical.

Doc Parsons seemed annoyed, "Go home. The boy will be fine."

Karl and the Rasmussens left for the Schmidt farm. Doc Parsons returned to the saloon. Before leaving, he gave Mary Etta what remained of the mercury, and recommended another dose when they reached the farm. Just after sunset, the boy's symptoms returned with a vengeance. Mary Etta suggested returning to Fargo, but Colvis decided that was a trip best taken during the day. His son died at midnight. Perhaps nothing could have been done, but Karl could not shake the memory of Doc Pardons bound for the saloon while a young man had been dispatched to his death bed. Burial took place the following afternoon in a glen near the Meyer cottage. Jacob read from Revelations 21:4 and noted the boy's life on earth had been a struggle. Perhaps now he was at peace. Karl and John enclosed the burial ground with a split-rail fence—its first occupant, Colvis Rasmussen II.

Maria thought it best to put some distance between announcing her pregnancy and the death of the Rasmussen boy. She kept the secret a week, but could wait no longer. The couple had finished their evening meal and Morgan had been put down.

"I'm going to have a baby." she said.

John sat in stunned silence, "When?" he asked.

"Probably in January," Maria said, smiling at the question.

John knew the answer, but could think of nothing else to say.

He embraced Maria and set off to find his father. He caught Jacob at the Meyer cottage, where he was helping Karl.

"Maria is pregnant."

"Congratulations son," Jacob said excitedly.

Anneke was ecstatic, "The farm is blessed."

"That's cause for celebration," Karl shouted.

He was already on his way to secure a bottle of store-bought whiskey, which he had saved for just such an occasion. They started back toward the main house, careful not to disturb the Rasmussens—still in mourning following the death of their son.

The evening was taken by Anneke's never-ending discussion of childbirth, while Jacob and Karl celebrated by drinking too much whiskey. John was more stoic. A few months earlier he might have hoped Maria was carrying a boy, but he was increasingly attached to Morgan. John also realized the past four months had been all about the farm. It was time to pay more attention to family.

If there were any respite in the planting to harvest season, it came in early summer. No one lacked for work, but the tasks were less urgent. Colvis and his son crisscrossed the Schmidt fields using a cultivator that fell into Luther Ogden's hands as satisfaction for an unpaid debt. The money for purchasing the device came from something of a windfall. John had received payment for his work on both the Lundeen ranch and the Acker grist mill. Hermann's payment included a stipend for the anticipated harvest of Turkey Red. Colvis quickly put the cultivator to use raking the neat rows laid down by the seeder.

John had studied other labor-saving devices, some with a much greater impact on productivity, but all were either unproven or too expensive. Mechanization on the Schmidt farm was a long way off. Jacob worked the fields, but only a half-day. He spent the afternoon on less strenuous work, typically with the assistance of the Rasmussens' eldest son. He had sketched an addition to the barn, but John thought the project too ambitious. The barn could wait.

Once a week, John dispatched his father and Karl to plow the Erhardt ground. The two had become close and spent as much time talking as turning soil. He chided the pair for their lack of progress, but was happy his father had found a companion. When not engaged in fieldwork, John focused on equipment repair. The past few years had seen too much deferred maintenance. John needed to begin harvest with every piece of the farm's equipment in working condition.

On July 3, Rolf Neumann slowly rode through the gate of the Schmidt farm turning toward the Meyer cottage. John did not see him leave, but learned from Karl the Lakota Sioux and Northern Cheyenne led by Crazy Horse and Chief Gall overran Lieutenant Colonel Custer and the five companies under his command. There were no survivors. Rolf's eldest son, Abe, had been riding with Custer and was listed as missing. The family was awaiting confirmation, but the outlook was not good.

Rolf had been opposed to his son's decision to join the military. The young man enlisted after a friend and his mother were dragged from their homestead by a band of renegade Indians. His friend was found dead a few miles away. The mother was never located. The same renegades later set fire to another homestead, killing a child and wounding the father before disappearing into the hills. The incident was troubling to everyone in the valley, but even more so to Rolf's son, who believed Indians should be forcefully driven from the territory. Abe struggled to put the incident behind him, but could not—the desire for revenge simply too great. In a decision his father thought impetuous, he enlisted and was assigned to the Seventh Calvary at Fort Riley, later joining Custer at Fort Abraham Lincoln along the banks of the Missouri. His latest correspondence had shown assignment to Company C, one of those lost at Little Bighorn.

Eric Hansen called for another school work party the first Sunday in August. Smaller groups had managed to erect three walls and work had begun on the roof. That left the interior, two outhouses and the soon-to-arrive windows donated by NPRR. Water would be supplied from a well ninety feet from the school. After making assignments, Eric took a moment to remind the workers of their purpose—not just a suitable building, but a quality education. They had relied in the past on volunteers, with the classroom moving from home to home. The teacher—always a male—selected the curriculum. The process was expedient. There were no standards, nor were there any expectations. Attendance was irregular, with many families choosing to conduct lessons at home.

The Casselton School would be different. An established curriculum set by the Territorial Superintendent of Public Instruction must be followed, with learning guided by educators trained in their profession. Eric had already talked with the superintendent and was told his office would help in locating a teacher, but could offer no financial assistance. Taxing for education was in its infancy and it would be at least two years before the Casselton School received any government support. Enrollment required subscription by each family.

The recommended supplies included McGuffey's Readers, slates and, if possible, maps of the United States and the world. Eric closed the meeting with a plea—a request for volunteers to serve on the School Board. The Superintendent of Public Instruction told Eric receipt of government funds was dependent on the existence of this body. Mary Etta understood the request and nudged John. He was not interested.

During the summer months, Karl made a regular trip to Fargo, stopping for supplies and visiting with his friend Luther Ogden. Rolf was a frequent companion, but the Neumann family had just received confirmation that their son died at Little Big Horn. Karl made the trip by himself. He stopped at the Casselton Station on the return home on the chance there was mail for one of the farm families. The station master received a letter the day before addressed to Maria Schmidt and posted in St. Anne's. Karl signed for the letter.

He found Maria in the garden. She had been expecting a response from her mother to the letter sent with Freidrich a month earlier. John, working near the barn, saw the exchange and set out immediately for the main house. The opening paragraph came as no surprise. Melina hoped purchase of the adjoining property was a prudent one and would not tax their resources. She reminded Maria there was always a home in St. Anne's. John resented the veiled suggestion they exercised poor judgment in buying additional land. He suspected Peter was behind the condescending passage.

Melina then turned to family matters asking if Maria was now sure of her pregnancy and if Morgan was able to stand on her own. She missed her granddaughter, but was thankful for Hilke's baby who, like Morgan, was a joy. Freidrich had come and gone, his visit cut short by Peter's insistence the decision to move west was irresponsible. She noted the tension between Peter and Albrecht had eased somewhat, a welcome change from the previous bickering. The two had even begun to collaborate on plans for the farm.

The letter also touched on developments in St. Anne's. Seven new families had visited, but only three joined the *company*. The reason was always the same—Peter was too deeply mired in elements of *Volga Deutsch* tradition and newcomers disliked the regimen. Melina confided that a few elders were beginning to wonder if the *company* could survive in its present form.

There was something in the letter for John as well. The grist mill he helped build was now functioning and ready for the upcoming harvest. Maria had assumed as much since Christof Acker had paid wages owed. She had also heard that Turkey Red, planted on the Lundeen Ranch, was expected to yield near one and one-half times that of spring variety. The same could be said for the seed planted on the Hoch and Portner farms. Everyone was scrambling to find Turkey Red.

Melina closed with a few surprises. The *Schullehrer*, Miss Geiser, had left her teaching post and was engaged to Kenneth Sloan—the state administrator who had twice visited St. Anne's during Miss Geiser's tenure at the school. Peter was struggling to find a replacement. In a second surprise, the *Schullehrer's* rejected suitor, Albert Wetzel, would soon be a father. He and the widow Meta Gerber were expecting in late fall. Melina's final revelation could be attributed to the Lord. Father Lenkeit would have his church. The foundation had been laid and completion was expected in one year. It would not be the cathedral the priest desired, but still a proud symbol of Catholicism in St. Anne's. John and Maria read and reread Melina's letter. The members of the Schafer party had put down secure roots, but the same could not be said for Peter's experiment—the *St. Anne's Company*. The commune's demise was inevitable, though Peter's stubbornness was likely to extend its tenuous existence.

Maria understood once the harvest began there would be little chance for her Norwegian friends to visit. Winter would be upon them with even less opportunity to nurture their friendship. She recalled the last work party. A friend of Lisa's brought four jars containing pears. She explained the fruit was packed six months earlier using a process which first boiled the pears, then quickly placed them in jars. The fruit was immediately sealed with a unique cap and lid and rapidly cooled. Maria thought the process similar to that demonstrated by Mrs. Pallitto in St. Anne's. Lisa Hansen had also seen it done and believed the jars would, in time, replace all types of food storage.

Maria knew Anneke had a large quantity of jars sent from Minneapolis by her eldest daughter, but had done nothing with them. The two had discussed experimenting with the jars, but Anneke seemed reluctant. Maria wondered if Lisa and her friends would be interested. Norwegian mothers, like the *Deutsch,* were more likely to socialize when coupled with some productive enterprise. The jars offered the perfect opportunity to put staples "by" while getting to know one another. Harvest would soon be upon them and time was running out. If there were to be an experiment, it must take place in the next few weeks. She made the proposal to Anneke who, much to her surprise, suggested it was a waste of time. Maria reminded Anneke the jars served little purpose standing empty in the barn. After a day of goading, Anneke divulged her real concern. She didn't understand the process, nor could she comprehend the instructions.

"I'll demonstrate nothing more than my ignorance," Anneke said.

"You're being silly," said Maria. "There are no expectations, just the chance to make new friends."

Anneke continued to protest, but finally agreed if her friend Gesine Neumann was invited, a familiar face to lend support.

The next morning the Rasmussen boy drove Maria and Mary Etta to the Hansen farm. They were struck by its appearance. Maria was told Norwegian farms were unusually clean, but the Hansen place looked much like a painting. Nothing was amiss and seemingly nothing in need of repair. The house was smaller than her own, but tidy with a large front porch surrounded by wild flowers. The barn and outbuildings sparkled. When Lisa saw the two women approach, she hurried to greet them, embracing Maria and taking Mary Etta's hand. Maria was uncertain how Lisa would react to the unexpected visit. Her response left no doubt. When told of the proposed experiment Lisa expressed delight.

"I'm ready anytime."

The response, coming in Norwegian, confused Maria, but she could tell Lisa was excited.

"Next Sunday at noon?" Maria said.

"May I bring friends?" asked Lisa.

Mary Etta answered, "As many as you'd like."

Lisa offered a *kjolid drikke*, but Maria declined since she had promised John the Rasmussen boy would be absent from his duties for only a short time. Upon returning to the Schmidt farm, she went directly to the Meyer cottage, telling Anneke that Lisa and at least two of her friends would soon be visiting. Anneke again began to fret, concerned there was not enough time to prepare. Maria left Anneke to her worries and set about to gather supplies, doing her best to recall Mrs. Pallitto's instruction. She contemplated a trial, but thought that might spoil the excitement. After all, this was a learning exercise and mystery would add to the fun.

A week later, Maria, Anneke, Mary Etta and Gesine welcomed Lisa and two of her friends to the Schmidt farm. Maria cleaned as never before and insisted her husband pick up around the barn. Anneke baked most of the week and prepared a *tee und beere punsch*. They ate quickly, turning to the task at hand. Soon two pots were warming on Maria's stove. They held hull peas, picked too early and green tomatoes. A third pot of freshly cut rhubarb was warming on the bunkhouse stove.

Maria began the process with the others watching intently. The tomatoes were brought to a boil and ladled into the jars using the illustrations as a guide. The jars and their contents were quickly sealed then cooled. The beans and rhubarb followed with everyone now participating. There were no mishaps. The experiment had gone better than expected. Lisa brought cherries, also simmering on the stove. Those were judged ready just as Lisa's father-in-law arrived for the return trip to the Hansen farm. Anneke and Gesine agreed to continue the process, delivering the cherries to the Hansen farm sometime in the future. The day had been a success. Lisa was particularly impressed and imagined a much larger garden providing fresh fruits and vegetables throughout the winter months.

John's concern was more immediate—how to approach the harvest. The reapers he inherited were old and Karl's injury had led to haphazard maintenance. Summertime repairs had them ready, but the chance they could fail midseason was real. Rolf also had two reapers, one an early McCormick "Old Reliable," which had not seen fieldwork in years. He could marry the machines, but the farm would still be left with tired equipment and too little capacity. A breakdown would delay the harvest with spoilage the likely outcome.

The Schmidt farm needed more dependable reapers. John favored the McCormick "Advance," which could handle wheat, barley, oats and, with a simple modification, hay. The machine also included a mechanical rake that periodically pushed grain from a platform leaving stalks neatly piled at regular intervals. The combination reaper-harvester meant fewer hours in the field.

John and Maria had the $135.00 necessary, but an outright purchase would stretch reserves too thin. He wondered if he acted too hastily in purchasing the cultivator. Maria suggested borrowing from his father, but John was reluctant to do so. He could also partner with Rolf. Sharing equipment worked to the benefit of both farms in the past, but John was thinking ahead. Within two years, the Schmidt farm could have 400 acres in small grains. There was only so much time to harvest and waiting his turn could result in crop damage. A new Advance was the solution.

An alternative to outright purchase presented itself on a trip to Fargo. McCormick had two of their Advance machines on display at the mercantile. Both were shipped directly to Fargo from the company's Chicago plant. Beneath the list of features was a line offering an industry first—financing by the manufacturer. John could have his Advance for $35.00 down and monthly installments beginning December 1. He did something out of character. He temporarily borrowed the down payment from Luther Ogden and ordered the Advance. Delivery was expected in three weeks. On the trip home, he rehearsed what he would say to his wife and father. The purchase, while not unexpected, was made without their counsel. He needn't have been concerned. Maria and Jacob, though somewhat startled, embraced the idea. Jacob was tempted to ask why John did not ask for help, but held his tongue. He already knew the answer.

John had similar concerns for threshing capability. In the past, the Schmidt and Neumann farms relied on Axel Moen, a custom thresherman always booked to the limit. He was aware the Norwegians formed a "ring," joining together to purchase and share a thresher. John and Rolf were only two and the high cost of thresher ownership was beyond their means. The payback was simply too long. The Schmidt and Neumann farms must rely on Axel. The trick was to get the thresherman on site before the crop was damaged by the elements and before supply began to drive prices lower. For reasons John did not understand, Rolf had a personal relationship with Axel and managed to get their farms high on the thresherman's list.

That left one obstacle—bindlestiffs for the harvest. John had little experience with transient workers. A few were hired in St. Anne's, but he had nothing to do with the selection process. He was told the bindlestiffs would begin arriving in mid-to-late July. Some were following the harvest from Texas north and others from Minnesota westward. Their first stop would be the bonanza farms, still in their infancy, but actively recruiting workers. The large farms had strident rules dictating behavior, and workers with a "history" were turned away. They often found their way to smaller farms. Karl warned John to be wary of bindlestiffs. They were a necessary evil, prone to drunkenness and theft.

The farm's new Advance arrived in Casselton on July 18. The machine was partially disassembled with the components resting on a flatcar. John gathered his father, Colvis, and two horses, assuming the device could be put together and pulled to the farm. One of Eric Hansen's neighbors had seen the Advance as it arrived. Eric had been considering a similar purchase. When he learned the machine was in Casselton, he left immediately for the station. He was pleased to find the Advance belonged to John Schmidt.

"When do you plan to start cutting?" he asked.

"I think we'll be ready by morning," John said.

Eric jumped aboard the flatcar to get a better look.

"I'd like to watch," he said.

John was pleased. Eric's interest offered conformation for his decision. "Come anytime," John said.

Early the next morning, Colvis put the machine through its paces cutting a mixed row of hay and prairie grass. The machine worked flawlessly. He was making a second pass when John heard Maria calling his name. He looked up to see three wagons. In the lead were Eric and Lisa Hansen followed by two Norwegian couples he remembered from the school work parties. Eric thought they might be too busy during harvest so he brought his neighbors to see the new Advance. John and the Norwegians studied each component of the machine as if they were conducting a pre-delivery inspection. The women gathered in the kitchen. Maria remembered the "sealed" cherries stored in the cellar, but Lisa told her to leave them be. It would give her a reason to visit again, or perhaps Maria could bring the cherries to the Hansen farm sometime after harvest.

The first of the bindlestiffs turned up at the Schmidt farm in early August. John was busy with fieldwork and they were promptly rejected by Jacob. All were dirty, displayed firearms, and the scent of alcohol was unmistakable. When Jacob related his experience, John began to wonder if this were the norm—the only applicants single men, all of them suspect.

His luck soon changed. A family came through the gate, perhaps attracted by the *Deutsch* surname above the entrance. Lukas Becker introduced himself, asking to speak to the master. He rode a work horse followed at some distance by a farm wagon. At the reins was a woman who John assumed to be his wife. There were two boys alongside the driver and two more in the back. Another person could be seen walking behind. He wasn't sure, but John thought she might be a girl. Lukas explained they had come from Yankton. The family had immigrated from *Sudrussland* two years before. They were Black Sea *Deutsch* who, like the Schmidt family, found their way to *Russen* decades earlier. Four brothers and one cousin shared two homesteads.

The Beckers remained in Yankton through midsummer, then started north to earn extra income as bindlestiffs. Last year's employer had been swallowed up by a bonanza farm and already had a full complement of workers. The Schmidt farm was the Beckers second stop. He told John they were willing workers and skilled in grain harvesting. They could also tend animals and the women were good in the kitchen. He continued to list the family's attributes, but John had already made a decision. A family was far better than what Jacob had seen of transients. Lukas dismounted and John saw he was a big man, a full head taller than himself. His skin was deeply weathered from too many years in the sun.

John asked "how old are your boys?"

254

"There are four, thirteen to sixteen and a daughter twelve."

Lukas noticed John's quizzical look.

"We both lost spouses."

John spoke with Karl earlier and knew what he should pay for help. He studied Lukas for a moment and looked back toward the wagon. He liked what he saw. Not wanting to seem anxious he hesitated.

"Ninety cents per day for you and the horse," John offered. "The two older boys get seventy-five cents and the youngest sixty. Your wife and daughter work in the kitchen without pay."

"What about meals?" Lukas asked

"Three a day and shelter included," John responded.

Now it was Lukas' turn. He paused, looking past John toward the farm—his wife and children watching intently. This was a decision Lukas would make without help from the family. He paused for a moment, turned his attention to John and extended a hand. Maria had been watching from the porch, hoping the two would strike a bargain. Like John, she saw a family as far better than a group of scruffy single men. Maria invited the mother and young girl to join her in the kitchen, while Lukas and the boys followed John to the bunkhouse.

Adele Becker found it difficult to disguise her envy. The Schmidts were living her dream. There were too many Beckers on the Yankton farm and not enough ground to sustain the extended family. She and Lukas talked often of homesteading in central Dakota, perhaps near the Missouri River, but, given their present circumstance, that was not likely. The marriage to Lukas had been one of necessity. Her husband died in a logging accident in Minnesota and Lukas lost his wife following the birth of the young girl who now stood in the Schmidt kitchen. Lizzie, as the young girl was called, was shy and said nothing. Maria suspected Lukas had little time for his daughter.

Rolf was ready to harvest. He had been tardy many years ago and lost more than half of his crop to a late season hailstorm. The grain that survived was damaged and found depressed prices. He had learned his lesson. They were in the midst of a dry spell—it was time to act. Rolf had pressed Axel Moen for an early start date. If the Neumann farm did not have grain ready to thresh when Axel arrived, his preferred status could be in jeopardy.

Rolf also managed to locate three bindlestiffs, two middle-aged workers he employed last year and their unknown companion. The trio worked the harvest together from Kansas north. Rolf had no knowledge of the new man, but knew last year's hires to be good workers. He suspected they drank a bit as did most of the men on the Schmidt and Neumann farms. As long as they bothered no one, a little drinking was acceptable.

Harvest on the Neumann farm began at daybreak on July 31. Wheat came first with Rolf hoping his often repaired reaper would hold together through the season. He fashioned, with Karl's help, a makeshift platform to catch stalks. The addition was meant to replicate modern reapers, but was a poor imitation. Rolf's youngest son tended the platform while the two older boys and the Rasmussens' eldest bound shocks.

Rolf had briefly considered the Advance, but rejected the idea, believing his machine had another season. He was proven wrong by midmorning. A corner of the ill-conceived addition caught a rise and separated from the reaper. Using scrap lumber and rope, the device was again lashed to the machine. The repair was unsuccessful. The stress from the dislodged platform had bent the cutter bar. Some stalks were cut, some torn from the ground, and others simply destroyed. Rolf immediately thought of John's old reaper, either as a source of parts or replacement for his damaged machine. He sent the Rasmussen boy to the Schmidt farm where the young man discovered his father and Lukas Becker using the old mower to make their second cut of hay. Rather than disturb the process, Colvis sought out John and the two harnessed the Advance. The machine would get its first real test on the Neumann farm. When John arrived, he found Rolf and the others moving through the field using grain cradles. John quickly lined up the Advance and began cutting. The new machine attacked the wheat, raking off perfectly cut grain at regular intervals. Jacob and Colvis were left with the near impossible task of patching together Rolf's broken reaper, hoping the damaged machine would be available as the harvest progressed.

The weather, as it had been for much of the summer, was near perfect. The season had been dry, or so John was told, but moisture fell when needed and without damage to crops. Karl had learned on one of his trips to Fargo that farms to the south reported a small grasshopper infestation, but the Red River Valley was spared. Speculation suggested a down year for wheat, but John was optimistic. He liked what he saw in the field. Small quantities of wheat had already made it to the elevators, and Karl reported prices near ninety cents per bushel. The goal was to bring his crop in before the larger farms. Once wheat from the bonanza farms reached the elevators, prices were certain to drop.

John cut eighteen acres the first day on the Neumann farm before the Advance was replaced by the older Schmidt reaper—Rolf guiding the mower. The new machine was then returned to the Schmidt farm. The Neumann boys and Rolf's bindlestiffs did the binding and shocking. The older Rasmussen boy was left temporarily with Rolf, but would return to the Schmidt farm within a day or two. Both farms must have enough shocks to keep Axel Moen and his threshermen busy the moment they arrived.

In the kitchen, Maria, Mary Etta and Adele Becker, along with her stepdaughter, prepared meals and continued to "put up" vegetables. Maria's garden had done well and she wished there were more jars. Anneke was excused from kitchen work. Her task was to watch over Morgan and the two Rasmussen girls. Occasionally, she would take Maria's place, whose *morgendliche ubelkeit* lingered as it had during her first pregnancy.

Within a week of the Beckers' arrival, Lizzie began trailing Mary Etta rather than her stepmother. She was becoming a young woman and uncertain of how to cope with the trials of adolescence. At a time when she most needed help, Lizzie got little from Adele and none from Lukas. Mary Etta had been raised in a blended family and recalled the difficult years. She took Lizzie under her wing and, in periods of respite, the two walked together, somehow bypassing the awkward language barrier.

Mary Etta asked Anneke to make Lizzie a dress, guessing it would be her first. Anneke chose instead to look through a trunk full of clothing, outgrown and left behind by her three daughters. She found a cotton dress with flounces and an apron skirt. Mary Etta and Anneke presented the dress to Lizzie who was reluctant, at first, to try it on. After some coaxing, she did so. Excited by the outcome she hurried to show Maria and ran headlong into the Rasmussen boy returning from the fields. The sight of Lizzie in a dress left him tongue-tied. Jacob, watching from the porch, said it best, "*es ist liebe.*"

That evening Colvis, thinking the animals were unusually noisy, left the small house to investigate. He immediately noticed an orange glow to the north and moved to higher ground near the Meyer cottage for a better view. He could see wind-driven flames racing across distant fields, the result of lightning strikes an hour earlier. Colvis roused John and shouted to Jacob to wake the others.

"We'll need tarps, shovels, anything to beat back the fire," he said.

Mary Etta called to Anneke, "Stay with the girls."

Tilman Becker had already hitched the wagon.

Lukas shouted, "Buckets," we'll need as many buckets as you can find."

A stream entered the property on the northern boundary and offered something of a natural fire break. Wetting down the fields might slow the fire's advance. They could hear voices from the Mann property. Their frantic calls suggested one of the men was lost.

"Where is Anders?"

"On the other side of the firebreak," was the muted response.

The Neumanns arrived along with Karl and it appeared all was lost. The flames grew in intensity and momentarily jumped the creek. John's heart sank, but the wind shifted, pushing the fire in a northeasterly direction. The orange glow persisted, but the threat had passed.

John and his father watched for two more hours until Colvis and his son relieved them. Twice during the early morning hours, embers set the wheat ablaze, but the wind favored the Schmidt farm and quick action extinguished the flames. The two stood watch for the remainder of the night. Karl learned on a subsequent visit to Fargo that the Mann farm had lost a worker and full section of wheat. Two adjoining farms farther to the west lost both crops and outbuildings.

Rolf finished cutting his small grains two days after the fire threat—John's patched-together reaper completing another season. On the Schmidt farm, Colvis finished cutting wheat and moved on to barley, while his son and Lukas Becker were dispatched to cut oats. They were making better progress than anticipated. The Advance cut wheat at a rate in excess of twenty acres per day and was doing even better on barley. John now expected to finish cutting all field crops, other than corn, by August 27. The harvest had gone so well he began to think something bad must happen, but that something never took place. The Schmidt farm harvested over 200 acres without incident. There were no major storms, no grasshoppers, and neither man nor beast had been injured. Their first season was beginning to look very good.

Axel Moen and his thresherman pulled on to the Neumann farm midway through the gathering of shocks. They came with two small ground hog threshers and a crew of four. Axel expected to work twelve hours a day, finishing the Neumann farm in less than five days. On the Schmidt farm, the Beckers continued to bind wheat and transport shocks to where they expected Axel to locate his thresher. Colvis and his son temporarily left the fields to assist Jacob, who borrowed anyone he could to help frame the addition to the barn.

The plan was to construct a large covered area one-half the size of the existing barn and then, before winter set in, enclose the structure. Karl was an occasional helper, but more recently accepted his role as transporting lumber and supplies between Fargo and the Schmidt and Neumann farms. John noticed Karl was slowing, and had lost much of the energy he displayed only months before. Rolf, who was perhaps as close to Karl as anyone, save Anneke, also noticed the change. Even the slightest exertion resulted in a shortness of breath. Karl stubbornly maintained there was no problem, but those close to him thought otherwise.

The Schmidt farm was ready to begin threshing, but Axel Moen was not. On the day he was expected to arrive, a young man was sent ahead to advise John the threshing crew would be a day late. John was disappointed. Threshing was a measure of progress and provided confirmation of just how good the crop would be. Maria saw it differently. The thresherman's delay was an opportunity for a break. Why not a late afternoon respite, a reward for those tedious hours in the field?

John did not like the idea. He saw the extra time as a chance to catch up on chores, but he was too late in voicing his objection. Maria and Mary Etta were already planning a mid-harvest festival. The kitchen was suddenly a beehive of activity with open fire, stovetop and oven all put to use. The meal would consist of pheasant, venison, stewed vegetables and a chokecherry tart. John feigned anger, but was quick to join his father and Karl when the latter turned up with whiskey. Everyone from the Schmidt and Neumann farm attended, including the Beckers and Rolf's bindlestiffs. Colvis and his eldest son combined fiddle and mouth organ to provide entertainment well into the evening. One of the bindlestiffs had too much to drink and John took that as an opportunity to end the festivities, reminding everyone there was still much work to be done.

The women immediately turned to clean up. Tomorrow the threshermen were scheduled to arrive and that meant more workers to feed. Mary Etta and Adele Becker were excused from the dirty work, turning instead to meal preparation. After an hour without conversation, Adele, who had been unusually quiet, suddenly engaged Mary Etta.

"We'll be done in three weeks," she said.

"Depends on the corn," Mary Etta replied.

"Either way conditions in Yankton will be the same—too much family and not enough farm."

Mary Etta said nothing.

Adele continued, "The children have no future, particularly Lizzie."

Her comment intrigued Mary Etta.

Adele paused then said quietly, "Lizzie would be better off with you as her mother."

"What are you suggesting?"

"Lukas barely knows his daughter," Adele said, "And she's not my flesh and blood."

Mary Etta was dumfounded. With no visible sign of emotion, Adele was suggesting her stepdaughter become part of the Rasmussen family. She was not thinking of a temporary placement. Adele wanted Mary Etta to raise Lizzie as her own. Her earlier comment was correct—Lizzie and her father could not be more distant. Perhaps Lukas blamed Lizzie for his wife's death or he was simply unable to cope with the trials of young womanhood. Whatever the reason, Mary Etta was being offered a twelve-year old, one she had met just weeks before.

She could only say "Did Lukas approve?" Mary Etta knew the answer—the idea was likely his to begin with.

The more important question was how Lizzie saw the proposed arrangement. Adele explained she had not asked her stepdaughter, thinking it best to determine first if the Rasmussens were willing. Mary Etta took a moment to regain her wits. At first, she was angry. Adele's proposal was made as if she were trading a bag of grain, rather than proposing a new home for a child. An already neglected young girl was about to experience further injustice. She began to ponder Lizzie's circumstance. She would never see the inside of a classroom. In two years, or perhaps less, Lukas would find his daughter a partner, a marriage of convenience. By contrast, the Rasmussens could offer love and security while she matured as a young woman. Mary Etta told Adele she would talk with her husband, and with Maria.

She woke Colvis at first light and told him of Adele's proposal.

"I like the child," was his response.

Mary Etta was looking for something more definitive. "Lizzie would be our daughter," she said.

Colvis rose and gazed out the window.

"Lizzie deserves better than what the Beckers and Yankton can offer."

"Then you agree with Adele's proposal."

"Yes," Colvis said. "We'll give the child a real home."

Maria was told just after breakfast. Her response could best be described as pure joy. Never was a child more in need of a mother and caring family. Maria pledged her support in any way possible. That afternoon Mary Etta told Adele they would provide a home for Lizzie on condition the Beckers return next summer. If the arrangement did not work, Lizzie could rejoin her family. Mary Etta knew this was unlikely. She doubted Lukas would ever return, and wintering on the Schmidt farm was sure to strengthen the bond between herself and Lizzie.

Mary Etta was aware of a Pembina mother who gave her newborn to a childless couple. The mother already had ten children and was too sick to care for the child. The family also faced their second foreclosure in as many years. Lizzie's circumstance was different. She was sure to face emotional neglect, but would always have food, clothing, and shelter. Mary Etta wondered how Lizzie would react. She was just twelve and the Beckers the only family she knew. When they completed the evening's work, Mary Etta took Lizzie aside and shared her stepmother's proposal. Lizzie's first thought was of rejection.

"He's my father. How can he abandon me?"

Sensing the hurt Mary Etta said, "Perhaps he thinks you'll be better off here."

Lizzie could only repeat, "But he's my father."

She asked to be alone and Lizzie's thoughts turned to the past six months. For the first time in her life, she was among people who cared for her and saw value in her as a person. Maria and Mary Etta treated her with compassion and understood the changes she faced as a young woman. To Adele, she was nothing more than an afterthought. Lizzie sat in front of the small house until well after midnight, then woke Mary Etta telling her "I want to stay with you and your family."

Axel Moen arrived just before noon, eager to begin his work. He brought with him one of the groundhog threshers from the Neumann farm and a much larger Case "Sweepstakes" thresher, the latter driven by an eight-horse team. Along with the threshers came two fanning mills and six seasoned workers. Each thresherman understood his role, and assembly began with the precision of a military exercise. Both machines were dug in and the arms attached to the "Sweepstakes" hub. Questions from curious onlookers were ignored. John began to wonder why Rolf liked the thresherman. He was both dismissive and rude with no time for anyone, his client included.

Axel expressed displeasure with the location selected for the "Sweepstakes." He gave John a look of disgust.

"Why here?"

"I thought it best," John responded.

"Far from it," Axel snapped, but accepted the placement since a large quantity of grain was already stacked. Axel's men required no shelter, but expected three meals per day and feed for their animals. The farm must also provide backup horses to relieve Axel's team as necessary. Axel forbade interaction between farm workers and threshermen. If there was a need for contact, it would take place between himself and ownership. He demanded more shocks be gathered, not wanting the threshers shut down for lack of grain. Jacob made the mistake of asking when threshing would begin. Axel responded, "When I'm ready."

The curt reply visibly annoyed Jacob who muttered a rare obscenity under his breath. John didn't like the response either, but was willing to accept boorish behavior in exchange for production. He sensed he and Axel shared a common goal—to complete threshing as quickly as possible. The unpleasant exchange had the immediate effect of breaking up the gathering. Some were afraid of the thresherman, while others were simply disgusted.

Axel then took John aside.

"I'm taking one-fourteenth of the cash proceeds for wheat sold in bulk," he said.

"What if I provide manpower?"

"Just gather shocks," Axel barked. "I've got crew enough."

Tolling made sense early in the season since wheat prices were still edging upward. Later in the year, with product more plentiful, prices would decline. Under those circumstances, Axel stood to fare much better charging by jute bag. For oats and barley, a bulk rate would apply. The same terms had been extended to Rolf. John asked no further questions. He dared not. The two men shook hands. John disliked Axel's gruff countenance, but appreciated his no-nonsense approach.

The Schmidt farm was up early the next day gathering shocks yet to be retrieved. Adele was among the field workers finding it awkward to work in the presence of Mary Etta and Lizzie. Meanwhile, Colvis and his son planned on two days of haying. At seven a.m. all hands, including kitchen workers, were gathered to watch the "Sweepstakes" spring to life. Noting the gallery, Axel took extra time to establish himself as the overseer. He checked the sweep, all harnesses and every significant fastener on the machine itself. Once assured he held everyone's attention, he raised an arm and, in dramatic fashion, signaled the start of threshing. Within minutes, the horses established a pace and the "Sweepstakes" quickly displayed its appetite consuming shocks at an astonishing rate.

John was pleased to see Karl on hand to observe the start of threshing, but it was clear the once capable farmer was failing. He was pale, unsure of his footing, and excused himself almost immediately. Karl no longer traveled and was rarely seen moving about the farm. Aside from Rolf and Anneke, Karl spent more time with Jacob than anyone, but the two had seen little of each other since harvest began. The same could be said of John and Maria who looked upon the Meyers as treasured friends—Anneke a surrogate grandmother and Karl a valued advisor.

The two wagons readied for transporting grain were filling quickly—much faster than Jacob anticipated. The yield would not be known until threshing was complete, but John was hoping for fourteen to sixteen bushels per acre. He spoke with both Karl and Luther Ogden on where he should take his bulk grain and decided on Valley Storage, a country elevator located on Northern Pacific tracks just east of Casselton. The product could be sold for cash or held, hoping for a better price later in the season. John looked upon storage as a gamble.

Two other options were available. The first was a newly constructed elevator in Fargo built in anticipation of output from the bonanza farms. He had no desire to be lost among these giants. A second alternative was Funding and Commission Merchants, new to the valley. They committed to purchase grain at some future date, then arranged for storage, insurance, and transport. John was likely too small for this approach to marketing. Even if the agents did show interest, he was suspicious of the process.

Valley Storage was known to Karl and recommended by Eric Hansen, who told John most of the Norwegian farms used the company. John appreciated the recommendations. Few standards existed for elevator owners, and rumors persisted of unscrupulous operators cheating on weight or grading. Immigrants were often the target. They had little insight on procedures at the elevator and struggled with the language. A season's worth of hard work could easily be compromised at the point of sale.

Axel Moen continued to work his crew at a furious pace. He had other commitments and understood the longer shocks stood in the field, the greater the chance for damage. He was perpetually unhappy and barked at anyone who disturbed his meticulously ordered routine. John kept his distance simply checking in each morning. If he received an affirmative nod, there was no need for conversation. Work was suspended on the sixth day of threshing much to Axel's chagrin. Wind was the culprit. Keeping sheaves together and feeding the machine became next to impossible. Reluctantly, Axel told his crew to stop work. John had no way to estimate wind strength, but was quite sure it was the strongest experienced since arriving in the territory.

John and the Becker family hurried to the barn and livestock sheds to help Jacob secure anything not tied down. Fortunately, the windward side of the barn expansion was complete and the few items scattered about were quickly retrieved. An hour after sunset, the sky cleared and the wind settled to a gentle breeze.

John took advantage of the full moon and, lifting his daughter from the cradle, walked through the farm to assess damage. He found none. Morgan fell asleep almost immediately and John continued toward high ground near the Meyer cottage. He saw Anneke inspecting their property, but stayed in the shadows until she completed her rounds. Taking advantage of a stump, he sat down to contemplate the immediate future. He could see much of the Schmidt farm. Threshing was nearly complete, but there was still corn to harvest, the barn to be completed, and if time permitted, more ground to be turned on the Erhardt property.

With Morgan resting comfortably his thoughts turned to next year and beyond. He recalled Axel's inquiry a week before. The thresherman asked how a young immigrant couple acquired 600 acres so quickly. He didn't know if Axel expected an answer and John offered none. Had he responded, he would have cited Freidrich's chance employment on the Meyer farm, the couple's frugality, his father's help, and Maria's willingness to follow her husband's dream. A wife was expected to oblige, but Maria had done so with a commitment that matched his own. John took a moment to thank the creator. He could be serving in the *Russische* military—or worse yet— toiling in his father-in-law's self-proclaimed *Duchy*. John took one last look at his new 600-acre farm. Morgan began to stir and he started for home.

Chapter Sixteen:
A Secure Winter

"Here on these northern plains wheat fields
become waves, beneath leaden skies ..."

—*Ghost Station*, Sue Hubbard

Two more days and the threshermen were gone. Ninety-four of the 135 acres planted in spring wheat were sold to Valley Storage at ninety-nine cents per bushel. Jute bags were piled in the barn, some for personal use and some for trade with merchants. Jacob took several bags of wheat to be processed at a new rolling mill near the large elevator in Fargo. Periodic trips to the city were now his responsibility as Karl was increasingly housebound. The mill used the "Minnesota" process, which relied on ceramic rollers and gradual reduction. The process was new to the valley and produced a high quality of flour free from bran, middlings, and dust. Jacob returned with two barrels of "purified" product. The Schmidt farm had closed the circle from seed to flour.

Jacob continued to work on the barn expansion, but helpers came and went dependent on field crop demands. There was now a greater sense of urgency since feed corn was coming and dry space was necessary for bedding stocks and for hay. John dispatched Colvis and his son to help Jacob, hoping to complete the project in three days.

The Beckers, including Lizzie and her stepmother, had already begun to harvest corn, soon to be joined by John, the Rasmussens and Neumann boys. They relied on wagon and bang board using Lukas' horse. The animal was adept at keeping pace, slowly moving ahead with the banging of corn against backstop.

266

With harvest behind them, John was faced with the decision of when to let the Beckers go. The Schmidts and Rasmussens could easily cull what little corn remained in the field and shucking would take place as time permitted. The alternative was to hold the family using them to turn more of the Erhardt ground. John had no idea what tomorrow, let alone the coming year, would bring, but the harvest, just completed, suggested the more ground planted in wheat the better. He decided to extend the Beckers stay sending them to the Erhardt property with two teams. The Rasmussens would join them with a third team once the barn was complete.

John expected three teams should be able to break sixty to eighty acres in ten days, given some of the Erhardt ground had been turned in the past. The farm had done well with its 135 acres of wheat—over 200 would be that much better. John also addressed the need for replacement equipment, but decided to postpone the decision until spring. He reached the same conclusion on horses, waiting for the March auction at the feed store with its better selection of livestock.

John and Maria talked of making a small advance payment on Karl's mortgage, and both agreed it was time to purchase store-bought clothing. The additions to wardrobe would come from the catalogue Maria often studied by lamplight. Necessities were purchased in Fargo and Anneke gave Maria a few hand-me-downs from her stash, but their threadbare woolen garments threatened to come apart with the next washing. The Schmidts, like most immigrants, could be identified by their clothing. John and Maria were a dead giveaway.

The Beckers surprised John by turning thirty acres of the Erhardt property in four days. The Rasmussens, father and son, joined the effort on day five and John's goal of eighty acres turned in ten days was easily achieved. On the last day, Colvis challenged Lukas to determine who could turn the most ground in an hour's time. Using his own horse and one borrowed from Rolf, Lukas was the clear winner. John watched the contest knowing he would miss the contribution Lukas had made to the Schmidt farm. His shortcomings as a father were not replicated in his work ethic. Since the Beckers decided Lizzie would stay with Mary Etta, Lukas had become far less withdrawn, even participating in a shucking bee. Maria noticed the change as well. Was it joy at having found a good home for his daughter or satisfaction an unwanted child was no longer underfoot? Not wishing to think badly of anyone, she chose the former.

A feeling of contentment settled over the Schmidt farm—the season was complete. They had staples to get them through the winter, grain to trade, and seed enough to begin a new cycle. The Schmidts had grown their reserves and, better yet, Maria was pregnant. John allowed himself a moment to consider what family and farm might look like in ten years, but dismissed the exercise as pointless meandering. Planning was good provided one understood the only constant on the prairie was change.

Maria received two letters immediately following the harvest. The first from her mother was expected. The second, from Freidrich, was somewhat of a surprise. The letter from St. Anne's was sent just as their season was drawing to a close. The Kansans had experienced a good year as well. Much of their crop was in corn, although the Schafer party and their neighbors were committing more ground to winter wheat. John's small experiment with his uncle's seed had proven successful. So much so that Hersh Schneider, still managing the Lundeen Ranch, planned a seventy-acre expansion of Turkey Red. The seed was difficult to come by, but not so for Hermann. He seemed to have an infinite supply.

Melina reported there were many new faces in the area, but most settled outside St. Anne's proper. Peter's dream was fading. She told Maria that young people saw little value in the *St. Anne's Company*. Dissolution was not far off. Melina reported many settlers were looking at property farther west. Lawless "cow towns" were becoming more tolerant of sodbusters and property was less expensive in Western Kansas and Colorado. As always, the newcomers stayed close to the Kansas Pacific Railroad.

In a reversal of his earlier stance, Peter made a half-hearted attempt to convince the railroad to build a spur to St. Anne's, but it was quickly rejected. Maria suspected all of this was a humbling experience for her father—his new world Pfeifer likely to collapse. But Peter Schafer was not one to give up easily. Those around him would suffer as his dream faded.

Melina had other news to share. Father Lenkeit's new church was taking shape and the faithful continued to grow in number. Parishioners now came from five and six miles away. The congregation crowded into the combination school and community center and the school now had two teachers. She made only a few comments on marriages, births and those who passed. Mrs. Pallitto died suddenly leaving Anna Schneider to run the general store. With the exception of Albrecht, her bothers were still single and Lucy, the blacksmith's wife, had given birth to twins.

Melina's letter then turned to a series of questions on how many acres she and John had planted, the yield, livestock count and whether they purchased any new equipment. Maria knew these were questions not of her mother's design, but rather prompted by her father. She wished the questions were asked out of concern for the couple's well-being, but suspected Peter would be just as happy if she and John failed. Any success they enjoyed simply diminished his own and proved opposition to their move was wrongheaded. Her mother asked about Morgan. Was she walking, who did she favor, and did she have the big appetite her mother once displayed? She also asked about the "surprise." If she was pregnant, who would deliver the baby? Melina closed with an unexpected comment. She was considering traveling to Dakota, perhaps in the summer, escorted by her youngest son, William.

Freidrich's letter was more lighthearted. The tone clearly suggested he and his two colleagues, Kurt and Klaus, were pleased with their move west. He assured Maria the rain craved by prairie farmers could easily be found in Washington Territory. In fact, it was a daily occurrence. He added it doesn't really rain—the sky leaks. The constant wet nurtures trees 200 feet tall and twelve feet through. These pillars, their crown often lost in the fog, provided raw material for Prairie Timber, the curious name chosen for their enterprise.

The three men had started a sawmill at the confluence of two rivers about fifteen miles east of Grays Harbor and the Pacific Ocean. They were cutting timber on 3,000 acres owned by Judge Lawrence Morehead II. In an agreement forged by Kurt, Prairie Timber and the judge shared receipts, but Prairie Timber owned the mill. Freidrich quickly corrected himself, telling Maria they would own the mill once the judge was paid back. The first load of dimensional lumber was transported to Grays Harbor by wagon on what Freidrich described as a trail rather than road. They expected to transport future shipments by scow down the Chehalis River.

Freidrich and Klaus ran the mill and supervised the logging operations, though Klaus was more closely aligned with cutting timber. Kurt was the one-man sales force. They had a crew of seventeen and hoped to double that in the spring. Transporting cut logs from the forest to the mill was their greatest challenge. There were times when logs could be floated to the mill and others where they were dragged by horses. The work was both difficult and dangerous. Kurt, always the entrepreneur, was bidding on nearby timber rights and contemplating opening a lumber brokerage. Freidrich and Klaus were content to leave the future to Kurt. He had a knack for being in the right place at the right time and was equally comfortable with bankers or the leadership of local Indian tribes.

Freidrich then mentioned something Maria might have anticipated. He was courting Judge Morehead's only child—at least he thought he was, though he believed Miss Morehead saw him more as a curiosity than a partner. They met when the judge came to visit the mill and brought Agnes with him. She had suitors throughout the territory and Freidrich was the most unlikely. Their relationship began with an invitation to afternoon tea at the Morehead home. Freidrich enjoyed the event and it appeared the family felt the same. Two weeks later he was invited to dinner. If anything, the invitation meant the money spent on the suit of clothes purchased for the afternoon tea had not been wasted. The invitation came from Mrs. Morehead, but included a note from Agnes encouraging him to attend. Sunday dinner had become a ritual and the pair were now seeing each other on a regular basis. Freidrich closed by asking if Maria had heard from St. Anne's. He wrote the family twice, but got no response. The mail was understandably spotty, but it could be his father was still annoyed by his decision to leave Kansas.

The Beckers left the Schmidt farm the last week in October. Maria and Mary Etta were concerned that Lizzie would react poorly to her father's departure. Staying behind seemed a good idea a month ago, but would she feel the same when the family left for Yankton? They needn't have worried. Lizzie accepted a peck on the cheek from her father and was the first to turn her back on the family. There was no hint of emotion and no wave goodbye. Lizzie sought the hand of Mary Etta and the two made their way to the small house to resume chores.

The Rasmussens decided Lizzie and their eldest daughter should both be enrolled in the Casselton School. Lizzie was a student twice while in

Yankton, but withdrew on both occasions. She had fewer than four months in the classroom. On a late September trip to Fargo, the station master told Jacob a male educator had been hired and was now on site. Mary Etta took time away from the farm to meet the teacher, bringing both her eldest daughter and Lizzie. They caught the school master, Mr. Johnson, just as he was leaving—packing books in his shoulder bag and stepping away from a very large desk. On the wall behind him were a number of official looking documents. Mary Etta's first impression was not good. He seemed annoyed by the intrusion. His reaction was such that Mary Etta made no attempt to introduce herself.

"We can come another time."

"Not at all," the school master said noting there were two children standing just outside. "This is a good time." He apologized, "I didn't expect anyone," then quickly changing the subject said, "Do you intend to enroll the children?"

"Yes," Mary Etta answered, eager to discuss Lizzie's lack of formal education.

"What are their ages and school experience?"

Mr. Johnson spoke in English, but spiked with enough Norwegian that Mary Etta understood. The Rasmussens' eight-year-old would be an easy placement, not so Lizzie. She would be among the least educated for her age. Mr. Johnson was quick to allay Lizzie's fears.

"You'll have company. Two other students of your age and experience just enrolled."

He assured Lizzie she would catch up within the year. Mr. Johnson then turned his attention to Mary Etta. He told her to return with Lizzie next week. A test would be administered to gauge the best course of study. He wrote two simple sentences on a slate asking Lizzie to read each. She recognized only two or three words. The school master again offered comfort. He advised Mary Etta to allow at least two hours the following week for Lizzie's evaluation. He would put together a study guide to help Lizzie prepare for the coming school year.

Mary Etta was also told to bring $1.90. The enrollment fee was $1.00 per family and the monthly charge forty-five cents per child. A five-month school year was contemplated with the possibility of two additional months in the spring for younger students. The Superintendent of Public Instruction for the Dakota Territory agreed to partially fund the Casselton School, but taxes levied on property fell short of the amount needed. Eric Hansen, the first Casselton School Board President, established the monthly stipend. Questions regarding payment should be directed to him. Mary Etta winced at the charge, but it was an amount she and Colvis could afford. Education was something the children required.

The first frost came the week following the Beckers' departure. John guessed a hard freeze was not far behind. Winter was closing in at least a month earlier than he recalled in St. Anne's. The prospect of cold and snow gave him pause, but he believed the farm was ready. The barn and livestock shelters offered security and protection for the animals. All but a few fence lines had been repaired and even the chickens, which he disdained, had cover for the winter. The Schmidt farm had sacks of grain hung in the barn and a root cellar stocked with fruits and vegetables, although Maria wished she had more greens. They could also use a better store of meat, but John was waiting for cooler weather. He planned on slaughtering a pig in mid-November and, with Jacob's help, trying his hand at sausage making. The process was new to him, but having watched others in both Pfeifer and St. Anne's believed he could add to their larder. Rolf Neumann also told him a small deer herd frequented a pond west of the Erhardt property. John planned on taking at least two before the snow fell.

If there was a flaw in his winter preparations it was sufficient fuel to warm the houses. Karl and Rolf warned him of temperatures cold enough to kill livestock. He wondered if the pair were telling tales, but understood extra fuel was a necessity. There was a small quantity of *mistholz* stored in a shed alongside the house and only enough dry wood to last perhaps two months. Seasoned wood was available, but some distance from the farm. Colvis and his son were scheduled to cut a six-month supply next week. When the real cold set in, the farm would be ready.

Maria shared John's optimistic view of the winter ahead. The harvest had been good and she felt secure in her new home. If this were *Russen* or even St. Anne's, the Schmidts and their neighbors would be preparing for *Kerbfest*. Maria wondered if the Norwegians celebrated harvest in a manner similar to the *Volga Deutsch*. The more she thought, the more convinced she was that some form of celebration should take place with the Norwegians included. John was less enthusiastic, but agreed a modest social gathering would be acceptable. He resisted using the term "celebration," thinking one afternoon with Hansens was enough merry-making. The following morning, with the young Rasmussen boy at the reins, Maria and Mary Etta set out for the Hansen farm. Lisa was excited to see the two women. Maria, with Mary Etta's help, explained the *Deutsch* tradition of *Kerbfest*.

Lisa told them, "We celebrate *Hosttakkefest*."

Maria was delighted.

"But this year Eric wants to combine the harvest celebration with the dedication of our new school."

"Is everyone invited?" Mary Etta asked.

"All of Casselton," Lisa responded. "I'm making a poster now."

Maria's plan to gather neighbors had turned into something much more. The three women discussed the festival and Eric's planned dedication. When she returned home, Maria shared the outcome with John who, if nothing else, was grateful not to be obligated as host. The upcoming event did suggest sausage making should be advanced so a selection could be brought to the festival. Just how much was dependent on the quality of sausage produced.

Maria had taken advantage of her husband's offer to purchase clothing and was patiently waiting for a Montgomery Ward mail order. Jacob had been sent twice to the station in the past week. On his third trip he found four parcels waiting. He signed for all and started back for the farm reaching the gate just as Maria and Mary Etta were returning from the Hansen farm. The women saw the parcels and hurried to the main house to examine the contents. Three of the parcels carried the Schmidt name with one addressed to the Rasmussens. Maria had two dresses, a shawl, and heavy winter coat. John had a Macintosh. Morgan received two pair of woolen pants, a coat, and one dress better suited for summer. Maria was disappointed her condition prevented her from trying on her dresses, but was able to drape them over her shoulders imagining how they might look. John gave an approving nod.

The largest of the parcels contained forty jars for putting "by" fruits and vegetables, the value of "air-tight" preservation now fully embraced by the Schmidt farm. The Rasmussens' parcel contained one pair of shoes and one dress for each of Mary Etta's daughters along with a surprise for Lizzie—a dress and very lady-like footwear. Lizzie had never received a mail order package and was not sure how to react. She dressed in hand-me-downs from her stepbrothers and Yankton neighbors. New clothes and shoes from some far off store were beyond imagination. Once adorned, she stared at her reflection in the window glass for a full minute finding the transition hard to believe. She thanked Mary Etta and asked if she might show Anneke. As she left the house she again came face to face with the Rasmussens' eldest son. Seeing Lizzie in a dress produced the same result. This time Lizzie reveled in the impression she created.

The excitement surrounding the mail order delivery was short-lived. Four days after the Schmidt farm joyfully opened their parcels, Anneke burst through the door of the main house pleading for help.

"Karl has fallen."

"Where?" Maria asked, starting toward the barn in search of John.

Jacob had seen Anneke hurrying by and correctly assumed Karl must be in some distress. He went directly to the cottage and found his friend collapsed on the threshold of the front door, his breathing tortured and shallow.

"Can you hear me?" Jacob shouted.

Karl seemed aware of Jacob's presence, but confused. He lost consciousness before John arrived. For a moment, his breathing settled, then a desperate gasp and nothing. Karl, against Anneke's wishes, had chopped a quantity of kindling that morning. Now John and his father stood helplessly as Karl took his last breath. Anneke returned to the cottage to find her husband expressionless, eyes open and staring upward.

She screamed at John, "Do something."

"He's dead Anneke. There's nothing I can do."

John realized his comment was unnecessarily abrupt, but the response stunned Anneke and she seemed to calm. Mary Etta closed his eyes as Anneke quietly watched.

Karl was laid to rest in the small cemetery where Colvis Rasmussen II had been buried a few months earlier. Jacob fashioned the casket. He also carved a large cross which carried the inscription "Karl Meyer, Beloved Husband,

Father and Friend." Two of Karl's daughters made the trip from Minneapolis, the third near the term of her pregnancy and unable to travel. Rolf Neumann was in attendance as was Luther Ogden and the Casselton Station Manager. Jacob presided over the ceremony, reading from *Romans* 6:23, adding the Schmidt farm had lost a treasured friend. Rolf also said a few words recalling the early days of his association with Karl and crediting his friend for much of their success in farming. John could not help but wonder if Karl's death would cause Rolf to rethink his commitment to the land.

The Meyers' eldest daughter insisted Anneke return with her to Minnesota for the winter months, but Anneke was not ready. She understood the wisdom of her daughter's suggestion, but it was too soon to leave the farm she and her husband had built together. John told Anneke he and Maria would care for the cottage and ten acres, but Anneke was steadfast. Perhaps next year she could winter in Minneapolis, but for now the small cottage Karl so loved would be her home.

The farm seemed very different without its founding patriarch. John missed his counsel and Jacob missed their frequent evening visits. Everyone missed his caring manner. Maria thought it best to skip *Hosttakkefest*, but changed her mind when Anneke insisted Karl would have wanted the Schmidt farm to attend. The school opening was important as was the sense of community. Maria insisted Anneke participate, and with her help she and Mary Etta set out to prepare a quantity of pound cake and various sweet breads. They would also bring cheese. John and his father concentrated on sausage making, which meant slaughtering the pig sooner than anticipated, but it was now cold enough that meat could be stored safely in the root cellar.

Karl had instructed Jacob on how to smoke certain cuts. This would be the Schmidts' first attempt at the process. With Karl's passing, no one on the Schmidt farm was a skilled butcher. Colvis seemed to have the best understanding so the task fell to him. He did an acceptable job carving several cuts of pork, leaving both waste and some good meat for sausage. The task of grinding was left to John using a wooden-geared machine borrowed from Rolf. Jacob was stuck with cleaning and stuffing entrails. The two Schmidts had the most experience in sausage making and both did their best to recall the recipes from *Russen*.

Maria chided her husband and father-in-law for their lack of imagination. She was able, using Anneke's selection of spices, to recreate an old Schafer recipe, noteworthy because of its fiery taste. The family stuffed and strung sausage for a full day, each string looking better than the one before. When they were done, the Rasmussens were called upon to judge the product—Maria's entry was the undisputed winner.

The Schmidt and Rasmussen families arrived at the festival earlier than most of the other guests. Maria was pleased to find Lisa had done the same. They were able to visit as tables were being set. Maria saw new faces she did not recognize from the work parties, testimony to the growing number of farms in the Casselton area. Eric Hansen opened the event by introducing Samuel Liam Johnson, the school master. He cited Mr. Johnson's education at Western Reserve College in Ohio, and teaching positions held in that state and in North Platte, Nebraska. He was certified in both states and recommended for the Casselton position by the Superintendent of Public Instruction for the Dakota Territory. Eric advised the assembled throng they were fortunate to have an educator with Mr. Johnson's credentials and experience.

The two men were standing in the back of a large freight wagon. Eric stepped down yielding the platform to the school master. He waited for absolute silence and spoke in English followed by Norwegian. John understood nothing and was somewhat disinterested. He thought the school master to be full of himself and trusted Mary Etta would let him know if anything of importance was said. The school master's initial comments were directed to the parents.

Classes would begin the first Monday in November, later than Mr. Johnson desired, and conclude in April, the exact date dependent on the demands of planting. The school day would begin at nine a.m. and conclude at three p.m. allowing enough time for morning chores and the trip home before darkness fell. Eric had prepared a map showing the location of each student's home, which he handed out as Mr. Johnson was speaking. The school master explained that tardiness would not be tolerated, nor would absence without good cause. In a tone that sounded much like a tyrant, he told parents to follow the lessons of their children.

"Learn with the students," he said.

"But how?" a Norwegian mother asked, "We have no education."

The school master was uncompromising. "Find a way," he said.

Mr. Johnson closed suggesting the possibility of late spring classes for the younger children and evening classes for adults. The school board would decide later if and when the classes would take place.

For the students, he had but one expectation—industry. They should come to class eager and ready to learn. Anything less was grounds for expulsion. The school master stood quietly for a moment, his gaze moving side-to-side. Confident he had made his point, he stepped down. Eric returned to the makeshift platform and advised parents the school was still in need of dry wood. He also encouraged attendees, if they had teaching materials, to make them available to Mr. Johnson.

With the school master's introduction complete, it was time for *Host-takkefest*. Eric asked his wife to open the festivities. Once again, Norwegian was the language of choice, which Colvis translated for John. Lisa's message was straightforward. Casselton and the valley had been blessed by a bountiful season, bothered by neither insect nor inclement weather. They had much to be thankful for. Lisa asked that all in attendance take the hand of the person alongside and, in a moment of silence, thank God for their blessings. She then announced the first School Board meeting would be held November 12 with a community meeting to follow. Finally, she invited all to enjoy the food and tour the classroom.

Parents who took advantage of the latter saw Mr. Johnson's oversize desk near the front of the room and to one side. The wall behind was adorned with framed certificates. The school master stood next to his desk, bored at entertaining anyone beneath his educational strata. The facing wall held a chalkboard and to the right a large stove and well-worn globe. In the common area were three rows of double desks with bench seating behind. The size and type of desk suggested younger students would be seated closest to the teacher. Boys and girls would be separated. Mary Etta pointed to a supply of McGuffey Readers and Blue Back spelling books, both of which she recalled from the school in Pembina. Texts and slates were neatly placed on each desk. While the parents wandered through the classroom, Mr. Johnson remained stoic, moving only when teaching materials were disturbed. When this occurred, the offender was admonished and the materials quickly returned to their place.

The classroom tour complete, families turned their attention to food. Most of that offered fell into the category of baked goods, pies, cakes, or more delicate pastries. There were a few main dishes, including cabbage rolls, meatballs and *lapskaus* as well as a large selection of cheese. The sausage brought by the Schmidt farm and served cold was very popular, especially that prepared using Maria's recipe. She made sure to point this out to John. As the festival was nearing its end, Maria heard her native tongue. She asked, "*bist du Deutscher?*"

"*Ja, Schwarzmeerdeutsch.*"

The two families had immigrated from Odessa, followed relatives to Yankton, then homesteaded south of Casselton. They heard of the school opening and *Hosttakkefest* from the Casselton Station Master and decided to attend. Gerhard Frank was the eldest and carried most of the conversation. They arrived in late April, but were able to get enough crops in the ground to feel secure for winter. The families built a common wood-frame barn and two soddies. Gerhard did not plan to send the children to school. The distance was too great. The conversation was brief since the Franks and their neighbors were far from home and the hour late. John, who now joined the discussion, circled the location of the Schmidt farm on the map provided by Eric Hansen. The two families parted company vowing to meet sometime after the snow was gone.

Late fall was a time of transition. For eight months, they had spent most of every waking hour engaged in fieldwork and tasks necessary to carry them through the planting to harvest cycle, but with crops in the barn, the anxiety eased. John focused on equipment repair while Jacob prepared houses and out buildings for the cold. Colvis and his son returned to the Erhardt property to "tidy up" the eighty-acres turned. Their previous effort, which included the Beckers, required a second pass. If time permitted, John hoped to build a livestock shed on the newly acquired land. Maria's attention was drawn to the food supply. She had a family to feed and held the same obligation to all those who called the Schmidt farm home. Her only deficit was vegetables. Maria must be careful in spreading these over the winter months. Next year, with a larger supply of jars, she could preserve more when the garden was overflowing. Thanks to Anneke there was plenty of cheese. She knew milk production would decline in the winter and had been busy throughout the fall. Using a press Karl brought from Pennsylvania, Anneke had at least ten blocks now aging in the root cellar.

Winter was also time to take stock of financial condition. The Schmidt family savings had grown slightly and John was eager to further pay down the debt owed Anneke Meyer. Maria was opposed. She reminded John the Erhardt property, with its additional 300 acres, must be sown next year without benefit of a preceding harvest. They needed a secure foundation— spending today what may be needed tomorrow was a mistake. She was adamant. It was the second time in as many days she snapped at John. The first came when he suggested her pregnancy had reached a point where physical activity should be avoided. Maria might have let the comment pass except it was followed by a recommendation she contact Doc Parsons. The suggestion was not well received. Mary Etta, within ear shot, was particularly disturbed.

"Your doctor did nothing to help young Colvis."

Maria joined the attack, "Will he deliver the baby in the saloon?"

Mary Etta added, "Parsons has no understanding of medicine," pointedly omitting any use of the term doctor.

John withdrew his suggestion and quickly retreated to the bunkhouse and his father's company.

School was underway and the two attendees from the Schmidt farm were adjusting well—not surprising for the Rasmussen daughter. She was bright, quick to make friends, and found herself among classmates of the same age. Lizzie faced a more challenging circumstance. She was far behind her peers, taking lessons with students four years her junior. The school master took a particular interest in Lizzie. Most parents thrust into a custodial function would have skipped education altogether, simply putting the child to work in the fields or kitchen, but not Colvis and Mary Etta. They valued education and anticipated their stepdaughter would be a student for at least two more years. The school master believed the family's commitment should be rewarded and he set about closing the gap between Lizzie's age and formal learning.

Mr. Johnson had taken the school master's position because he saw growth in the community. He imagined a much greater role for himself in territorial education, but this required something more than a country school. Casselton offered the potential for expansion and growth brought both income and the recognition he desired. For the moment, he must toil in the obscurity of a one-room schoolhouse. His school got little notice and faced a number of obstacles. Financial difficulties, poor health or disinterest were a constant threat to enrollment. Already he lost an older student to the demands of the farm. Two sisters with a round-trip of six miles would be next. There would be others. Enthusiasm for school waned quickly as parents saw farmhands become students.

Young women were the most likely to leave school. Their paradigm role required little in the way of formal education. For all but a few, the future was charted from birth and, at a very young age, they were ready for the rigors of womanhood. Mr. Johnson was tenacious. He had his eyes set on a position in the Superintendent's office. Taking his small school to a larger institution would draw the notice he sought. He insisted School Board members visit with each new resident, encouraging parents to enroll their children. When he suspected a family may withdraw a student, particularly a female, he publicly shamed parents, charging the farm meant more than their child's well-being. The population of Cass County was increasing and Mr. Johnson was committed, by whatever means, to a growth in enrollment.

The first snow of winter came on November 12. Balmy weather gave way to cold as temperatures plummeted and the Schmidt farm awoke to a shallow blanket of white. The event was short-lived, delighting the children and reminding the adults winter was not far removed. Jacob was glad for the snowfall. He had been working on converting one of the smaller farm wagons to a sled. Karl started the project by constructing four vertical arms. Jacob had reinforced those with struts attached to the wagon bed. The arms were fastened to four one-by-six slats, the leading edge notched and bent upward in the shape of a ski. The final step was to remove gate and sideboards to reduce weight. Jacob was quite proud of his project and tested the sled on straw used for livestock bedding. It pulled easily. Now with a light covering of snow, he tested again and found the outcome satisfactory.

November brought an end to the informal contract between John and Bjartr, the Rasmussens eldest son. According to their agreement, the young man was slated to receive one-half his summer pay through the winter months. Bjartr understood the reasoning, but decided to look for opportunities elsewhere. His first stop was the Northern Pacific Railroad. The station master told the young man the Casselton crew would be expanded by two workers in the spring. NPRR continued to push tracks westward and Casselton figured to be an important staging area. The hourly rate exceeded that paid by the farm during the summer months and also provided an opportunity for advancement. Bjartr applied and was immediately accepted, with the station master willing to place the boy on his temporary payroll until the position opened. One-half of his time would be spent in Casselton and the remainder in camps up the line. While in Casselton, the Schmidt farm would be his home.

The fall had been moderately cool, and both John and Maria wondered if the Dakota winter would be as ferocious as Karl suggested. Mornings were frosty, but by afternoon their heavier clothing was discarded. The children faced no weather related obstacles en route to school.

Maria, Mary Etta and the children continued their evening shucking bees, though the process was now more burden than social event. Late in the month Jacob made what was likely to be a last trip to Fargo and the general store. His list included items beyond the capability of the farm, among them coffee, sugar, spices, molasses and baking powder. There was also a pair of coveralls for John and two bolts of fabric, the latter to match a pattern Maria admired in her treasured Montgomery Ward catalogue. He carried with him a quantity of wheat and barley, hoping to barter for some of the goods.

Jacob told Oscar Niilsen, proprietor of the general store, that Karl had passed. He was deeply saddened. The proprietor took a moment to pen a short note to Anneke. With the help of Oscar's wife, Jacob filled his shopping list—the last purchase hard candy for the children. Oscar noticed the candy and placed it in a separate bag, refusing to accept payment. When Jacob returned to the farm, he was immediately subject to inspection by both children and adults. Each item was examined and judged to be satisfactory, even the two bolts of fabric. The children were delighted with the candy. Released from his obligation, he left to deliver Oscar's note to Anneke.

The second snowfall of the season came early in December. The flakes were large and wet, but fell with an intensity that made it difficult to see the outbuildings from the main house. Thankfully, it began in midafternoon so the children experienced no difficulty making it home, save some tardiness based on their own frolicking. A group of six reached the Schmidt gate where a sleigh from the Hansen farm was waiting to carry the Norwegian children to their respective homes. Jacob had been waiting as well. He found two coasters Karl made some years before. With a little cleanup they were ready for a try. He was waiting on the small rise near the Meyer cottage and everyone, even Anneke, gave the sleds a run.

The heavy snow also gave Jacob an opportunity to test the runners on his wagon, turned sleigh. The next morning, he set out for the Casselton School with Lizzie and her eight-year-old stepsister. Conditions were such that if his handiwork needed refinement, the two girls could walk the remaining distance. Jacob discovered the wagon was slow to turn, but otherwise performed satisfactorily. His greatest concern was the strength of the four uprights attached to the ski-like runners, but they held up well against the uneven road.

When Mary Etta learned of Jacob's excursion, she asked to ride along. The school master regularly sent Lizzie home with extra work designed to accelerate her progress. The extra assignments paid dividends, but the homework often confused Mary Etta. As before, a few minutes with Mr. Johnson resolved the problem. She took the opportunity to ask the school master about a planned Christmas celebration. Lizzie had told her there would be hymns sung by the younger children and recitals by the older students. Mary Etta wanted to know if parents were expected to contribute or assist in planning. The school master told her the School Board was in charge of the Christmas event and would soon be asking each family for some form of assistance. He was not sure what to expect, but thought the celebration would take on elements of *Jul*, since most of the students were Norwegian.

The following afternoon Eric and Lisa Hansen visited the Schmidt farm. They explained the Christmas celebration which Lisa called a pageant. It was to include an exchange of small gifts, the singing of hymns, and a few readings. Parents were expected to bring something sweet, perhaps their favorite Christmas recipe. Lisa was also preparing a basket of food for Mr. Johnson, and expected some parents may be giving the school master a small gift. Maria greeted the Hansens from the front porch just as Anneke was on her way back to the cottage, having left cookies for the children. Eric made it clear the invitation was for the farm, not just the parents. All were welcome. John then announced he was not sure Maria could attend given her condition.

"I'll be there," Maria said, ignoring her husband's comment.

"I'm sure you will," Lisa said—both women wondering how men could be so ill-informed.

The pageant took place on December 22. The night was cold, but the road passable. Maria and the entire Schmidt farm made the trek and were rewarded with an evening of entertainment, including a Christmas production featuring the first two grades, a hastily assembled choir, and a message from the school master. Mr. Johnson was delighted by his food basket and the many gifts from parents. He even became somewhat emotional while closing the ceremony—a surprise given his usual demeanor. The Schmidt farm planned its own Christmas Eve celebration. Jacob, dressed as Father Christmas, brought gifts for the children while the *Christkindche*, played by Lizzie, offered assistance. Morgan found safety in her mother's skirt, but warmed to the apparitions after discovering they bore gifts.

On Christmas day, Anneke joined the Schmidts and Rasmussens in the big house. Colvis had successfully located an eastern red cedar some distance from the farm and the children adorned it with Christmas cookies and paper chains. Jacob read the Christmas Story, followed by more gifts. Anneke and Jacob collaborated to carve and dress dolls for Morgan and the two Rasmussen girls. Hats and mittens were sewn by Mary Etta for each of the children. John purchased scarves for Maria, Mary Etta, and Anneke. He also purchased a bonnet for his wife, much like one she had admired earlier in the year while in Fargo. Bjartr was given long underwear, which brought giggles from the girls. Jacob secretly finished a cabinet started by Karl, but never completed. The sight of the finished product brought Anneke to tears. Last came a package of hand-me-downs from Minneapolis, sent by Anneke's daughters. There was something for everyone, including Lizzie who found a dress and coat in her size. Mary Etta could not help but notice Bjartr had difficulty keeping his eyes off Lizzie. He was growing up quickly in the company of the railroad workers.

Karl's often repeated prediction for winter took form in early January as temperatures fell to dangerously low levels. School was suspended and the Schmidts huddled around the stove wrapped in coat and blanket. The animals required constant observation and the short trip to the barn seemed like an eternity. John scanned the horizon every morning hoping for cloud cover and some break from the cold.

Each day, morning and afternoon, Anneke checked on Maria who, by any calculation, was beyond her due date. Then rather suddenly on Saturday January 6, Maria announced she was giving birth. Jacob was visiting in the main house and John sent his father to fetch Anneke and Mary Etta. The latter arrived with Lizzie in tow. Mary Etta concluded it was time. Lizzie was directed to boil water and gather clean linens. Jacob was dispatched to gather wood and John told to busy himself and keep his distance. He was somewhat confused. Morgan's birth had been more of a siege. Events were moving much faster. There was no false labor, no calls to heaven, and no screams. Barely two hours after her initial declaration, Maria had given birth. Compared to Morgan, Clara entered the world peacefully and with hardly a murmur. John and Maria long ago decided on a given name common to America rather than *Deutschland*. Clara was American. John was kept away from his wife and newborn child while Anneke engaged in post-birth cleanup. He was finally given access after complaining loudly. Maria looked very tired, but tranquil. The baby was resting comfortably.

He looked toward Anneke and she anticipated his question.

"Maria and Clara are both fine."

John kissed his wife and gently took the baby's hand.

"Out," Mary Etta said, "Maria needs rest."

John glanced back for one more look at the baby. He was hoping for a boy, but the thought passed quickly. Morgan was a joy and he expected Clara would be the same. A girl meant the Schmidt heritage would not be extended, but there were more children to come. Suddenly, John remembered his father waiting patiently in the bunkhouse. He found him close to the stove doing his best to respond to a letter received a month earlier from Stephan Haus, his friend and former partner in Pfeifer. Jacob looked up in anticipation as the door swung open.

"It's a girl," John announced. "Maria and the child are doing well."

Jacob was excited, but aware of his son's desire to continue the family name.

He assured John, "There will be a Schmidt son. Someday you'll have your boy."

Jacob insisted on seeing the baby so father and grandfather made their way to the main house. Anneke was watching mother and child—both were still resting comfortably. Mary Etta had retired to the Rasmussen home. Jacob wanted to hold the baby, but was discouraged from doing so in fear of waking Maria. He stood looking at Clara as long as Anneke allowed, moved by the sight of the newest Schmidt. The two men then left, returning to the bunkhouse to share a bottle of Karl's finest. Anneke, with no use for alcohol, left several bottles in Jacob's custody. John and his father talked for an hour in freezing temperatures, recounting the season passed, and wondering what the Schmidt farm would be like when the next child entered the world.

The cold persisted through the second week in January. Maria recovered nicely and the baby seemed happy and content. The Rasmussen girls were fascinated by the newborn and became Maria's constant companion. The dolls Jacob and Anneke collaborated on for Christmas were no match for the real thing. John and Colvis busied themselves puttering in the barn and keeping a watchful eye on the animals. For Jacob, it was a time to build and repair furniture and hand tools. He was also called upon to transport the children to school, often acquiring other riders along the way. Temperatures rose toward the middle of the month and the air, still close to freezing, felt almost spring like. Jacob moved his woodworking out of the barn to enjoy the sunshine. John and Colvis cleaned livestock pens, moved wood to a more accessible location and cleared ice from pathways. Everyone found some reason to get out of the house. Maria even sat briefly on the porch with Clara and was surprised one morning to see the Hansens. They stopped to see the baby after taking their two boys to school. The families visited for an hour.

The unusual spell of good weather lasted for almost ten days, a welcome respite from the usual cold. On the last Thursday of the month, Lizzie and her stepsister set out for school under broken clouds on what appeared to be another beautiful day. By midmorning, the sky had darkened and the wind freshened. A light snow began to fall. Another hour and they were experiencing blizzard conditions. The wind blew roofing materials from the barn and snow covered the interior of livestock sheds. Mary Etta became concerned for the children. She trusted the school master's judgment, but worried he may have dismissed the students early. They could easily be trapped on an impassable road. Her agitation drove Colvis to harness a pair of horses to Jacob's sled. John saw the activity, grabbed two blankets and jumped aboard. Visibility was poor and the horses fought every command, unhappy at leaving the security of the barn.

They had traveled less than a mile when they encountered Lucia Johansen, a young girl John recognized from the Christmas pageant. She was attending school half-days while her mother recovered from a particularly difficult childbirth. The school master, concerned about the weather, dismissed her younger brother at the same time thinking it better if she had company. The pair left in light snow with instructions to stop at the first house if conditions worsened.

"I've lost my brother," Lucia called above the wind.

"Where?" John asked.

She pointed back toward the school. John could see nothing but blowing snow. Lucia could not stop shaking. John was sure the temperature had dropped at least fifteen degrees since early morning. The two men decided to continue south toward the school hoping to locate Adam along the way. If not, they would enlist the help of the older boys and any workers available at the Casselton Station. There was no sign of Adam. The station master was already at the school when John, Colvis and the Lucia Johansen arrived, having brought blankets from a stash held for winter track crews. Mr. Johnson was preparing to keep the children overnight. He was deeply disturbed by Adam's disappearance, recognizing the children should not have been released. When the station master heard the young boy was missing, he quickly volunteered his workers—one of those Bjartr Rasmussen.

There were now six men available to conduct the search and no reason to rely on any of the students. They set out for the point where Lucia was found, marked by a tree limb Colvis dragged across the road. Time was not their ally. The farm wagon was abandoned and John and Colvis mounted the horses. They continued north, while the railroad workers split—two following John and Colvis—the remainder retracing their steps, faces already marked by a sharp red hue.

Visibility was near zero and the track made less than an hour before barely discernable. Ten yards ahead, Colvis saw the young man face down behind a stump and nearly covered in snow. He had apparently wandered off the road, finding it again after John and Colvis passed. At first, the two men thought the boy to be dead, but there were signs of shallow breathing. John stripped off his outer garment and passed him to Colvis, still mounted, who enclosed the boy in his heavy Icelandic coat. The pair started toward the Schmidt farm. The two railroad workers headed back for the school to advise Mr. Johnson that Adam had been located. The drifts were at least three feet and the passage took far longer than John and Colvis anticipated. They reached the farm just as Einer Johansen was arriving. He had started for school hoping to intercept his daughter. Instead, he was carrying his near lifeless son toward the warmth of the main house.

"Where is Lucia?"

"Safe at school," John said.

Einer was relieved, but terrified by the condition of his son.

"Get him out of those wet clothes," shouted Maria, pulling the clothes from the Johansen boy. She placed Adam directly in front of the stove, wrapping him in blankets.

Colvis studied the boy's extremities.

"I've seen this before in Lake Winnipeg."

The fingers on Adam's left hand were pale and waxy as were the toes on both feet. He was unresponsive and unable to speak.

"He needs a doctor," said Colvis.

"But how," John said. "The storm shows no sign of abetting."

Colvis knew, as did John, leaving the Schmidt farm with darkness approaching was foolhardy.

The boy drifted in and out of consciousness. During the night he began to experience severe pain. By midmorning the skin was darkening and blisters were forming on his left hand. A strange quiet settled over the farm. The children were safe at school, but the adults understood there was a boy in their midst in danger of losing limbs or perhaps his life. The snow showed signs of letting up and John decided to test conditions. As long as they carefully chose the path, progress could be made. He knew travel would be even more difficult tomorrow. The snow was sure to crust, tearing at the body of their mounts.

A decision was made to transport Adam to the Casselton Station. John and Einer set out immediately with the boy astride the horse and seated ahead of his father. The two-mile ride consumed as many hours. When they arrived, they saw a locomotive standing on the siding still making steam. It had two flat cars loaded with rails and lumber, and one passenger car. The train was headed west. Ten men were milling about the station. Two of them came forward when they saw the child wrapped in a blanket. Einer gently exposed the boy's feet. Both turned away at the sight. John quickly located the station master who told him the train had arrived just before midnight. Twice they had found it necessary to break through drifts. The blankets were opened again this time showing the hands.

Someone called for the engineer. He studied the boy for a moment.

"We're backing to Fargo," he announced.

The station master reminded him, "The lines are down; we have no communication with westbound trains."

The engineer paused, then shouted, "All aboard."

The trip was made without incident, although the passage was slow. Except for a few saloons, Fargo was dark. John had learned en route that Doc Parsons left the city and a new doctor opened an office in his home east of town. Two of the workers offered to secure a NPRR wagon and, with some difficulty, John and Einer drove the boy to the doctor's home. There were no lights when they arrived, but pounding on the door brought a young woman with a lantern. She glanced at the boy and told them to wait in the parlor. A few minutes later the doctor entered the room. He introduced himself as Ethan McKellar. John thought him to be speaking English, but with an accent that tested his limited understanding. The blanket was opened to expose the toes. The doctor motioned to remove the blanket entirely and saw the discolored fingers. He took the boy from Einer and placed him on a table in his office. The young woman furiously stoked the fire while the doctor examined the extremities, moving from toes to fingers and back again.

John was not sure if the young woman was a wife or assistant.

"I'll need morphine," he said, passing his hand over the toes on the left foot.

"Can they be saved," Einer asked.

"Two can be saved?" He lifted the boy's left arm and, looking toward his father, made a sawing motion above the thumb and index finger.

"I'm sorry," he said. "I have no choice."

Surgery began within the hour. He immediately injected morphine and told Einer the boy must stay with him. Einer should stay as well. They could take up residence in what had, at one time, been a wood shed. It was attached to the house and accessed through a small door. Though barely large enough for two people it, did have the advantage of being close to the stove. John left the doctor's home that evening and spent the night with the track crew in the Fargo Station. He returned to Casselton the next morning with the unfortunate task of telling Adam's mother her son was likely to lose toes and fingers. She had been expecting worse.

February was a kinder month. The school master and students kept track of Adam Johansen's progress by telegraph, a service volunteered by the NPRR. The young man returned to Casselton in mid-February, having recovered nicely from his surgery. The blizzard was behind them, but there was more inclement weather to come. A late season ice storm tested the strength of both tree and structure. Jacob's recently repaired livestock sheds and expanded barn escaped without damage, but not the bunkhouse, where a section of the roof collapsed.

Late in the month, Anneke Meyer surprised the Schmidt farm by announcing she had seen enough of Dakota winters. The farm's adopted grandmother was leaving for Minneapolis. Dakota was not the same without Karl—better she spend her last years in the company of her daughters and their children.

Anneke was treasured by all who knew her. She made a decision to gift the Meyers' ten acres to John and Maria, but wished to retain the cottage hoping to visit from time to time. John offered to buy the land, but the suggestion was summarily rejected. She suggested Jacob occupy the residence, rather than leave it empty. John was not sure his father would leave the bunkhouse, but assured Anneke, occupied or not, he would care for the cottage, as well as Karl's gravesite. Anneke wished to quickly carry out her decision, rather than prolong the agony. A hastily planned dinner was set for two days hence. It would include the Schmidt, Rasmussen, and Neumann families. John and Maria had seen little of Rolf and wondered what the future held for Karl's former partner. The dinner went nicely until Lizzie mentioned summer was not far off and the farm's grandmother would soon return. The comment was intended to be uplifting, but had the opposite effect. Everyone, even Colvis, had difficulty controlling their emotions.

Anneke left two days later. John watched as she knelt at the foot of Karl's grave seemingly engaged in conversation. Raising herself, Anneke looked across the fields that she and Karl had nurtured for so many years. John helped her to her seat in the wagon, wrapping a blanket around her legs. They drove toward the gate passing Maria standing on the porch. She was holding Clara—Mary Etta just steps away. The youngest Rasmussen daughter ran to the wagon and briefly grasped Anneke's hand. The older children had walked to school and would be in the classroom by now. It was just as well. Watching the woman they called "grandmother" leave the farm would have been difficult.

Little was said on the way to the station. Anneke commented on the pile of lumber near the school wondering if Casselton would finally get its general store. The train was alongside the platform when they arrived. The station master saw Anneke and they embraced. He and Karl had been friends for many years. Anneke did not want John to wait. They said their goodbyes. John expressed his gratitude for the kindness shown his family, then turned for the farm. He had driven about a mile when he slowed his pace. His thoughts were still with Karl and Anneke. It had been a year since he first laid eyes on the Meyer farm. The couple had welcomed him and Maria, treating them as they would their own children. Karl offered advice and counsel and worked the fields. Anneke embraced Maria as a daughter and the children as granddaughters.

Karl and Anneke would soon fade from memory. Perhaps that was the way of things. Change was inevitable as old gave way to new. They had completed a successful season and had no reason to believe the next would be less so. Maria had blessed him with a second child and his father escaped *Russen* to join the family. A new season was upon them and signs of spring could be seen in every direction. Blackbirds flew overhead, prairie crocus pushed through the dampened soil and the crabapple were already budding. Suddenly, he snapped the reins causing the horse to momentarily bolt. The prairie held no countenance with melancholy. There was work to be done.

Chapter Seventeen:
The Great Dakota Boom

*"Capitalists and lesser souls acquiring Northern Pacific
Railroad lands established bonanza farms and small
homesteads. The prairies of the Red River Valley lay ready
and waiting, without stone, stump or tree to hinder
the plow. The locusts left, the rains came. The prairie
entered a period of unprecedented economic growth."*
—University of North Dakota Scholarly Commons

John had been part of two successful seasons, one on the Schafer farm in Kansas, and the other his own farm in the Dakota Territory. His experience in farming the valley fell short of Rolf and the Norwegians, but it was enough to spark both optimism and confidence. This year 450 acres would be sewn. Some ground must still be plowed and some, turned under in the fall, required harrowing. Colvis had been devoted to this task since early March and was now joined by three recently hired Norwegian boys, ages twelve through sixteen. Their family immigrated in 1875, finding their way to Casselton in late fall after a brief stay with relatives in the Minnesota River Valley.

The boys were recommended by Eric and Lisa Hansen. Their addition meant fewer bindlestiffs—a godsend. The eldest was a good worker with some experience in farming. John hoped to retain him beyond planting. The boys returned each evening to their temporary home on the Hansen farm. If the eldest stayed on through harvest, he would take up residence in the bunkhouse. John was sure the Rasmussens' son would not be returning. He was recently assigned to a survey crew in eastern Montana. Lizzie was also lost. She was scheduled to assist the school master with the education of younger children, a task that would occupy much of the spring. Mr. Johnson was correct. Lizzie caught up with her peers and was engaged in studies beyond her grade level—the session with younger students evidence of her progress. Colvis was pleased with his adopted daughter's achievement, but felt Lizzie should return to the farm. He was quickly overruled by Mary Etta and Maria, both of whom voiced support for the opportunity.

The division of labor was set for the season ahead. John was the master and filled in wherever needed. Colvis took on the role of farm boss, setting the daily schedule and directing his newly acquired subordinates. Maria and Mary Etta were busy in the kitchen and garden and already beginning to plan what fruits and vegetables could be put "by," their capacity enhanced with a larger cache of "airtight" jars. Lizzie watered and fed animals before leaving for school and again upon her return. She was helped by the older Rasmussen girl. This year would follow the same pattern as last. Colvis and the others would join Rolf and his sons planting the Neumann farm, then reverse the process to work the Schmidt ground. Noticeably absent from the combined work crew was Rolf, no longer capable of fieldwork.

Just prior to planting, John and his father traveled to Fargo to acquire additional seed and replace essentials consumed during the winter months. They found the city alive. Row after row of immigrant cars occupied the NPRR siding and the yard itself was at least twice its former size. The tents, once so prevalent when John first arrived in Fargo, had given way to several wood-frame structures.

With their errands behind them, John and his father sought out Luther Ogden. They found him in his office surrounded by a group of Swedish immigrants. Luther stepped away from the gathering when he saw the Schmidts.

"Fargo is growing!" Jacob said.

"The same throughout the western half of the territory," Luther answered. "Population has doubled in the past two years."

The financier was momentarily interrupted by an associate, then turned back to the Schmidts.

"Is Anneke still on the farm?"

"Back in Minnesota," was the answer.

He was surprised. "Are you working the Erhardt property?" he asked.

"Should have 150 acres planted this season," John replied.

The response confirmed Luther's assessment. John Schmidt was one with the valley and would, in time, grow his farm. Luther then shared his view of what lay ahead for the territory. Statehood was not far off and he believed there would be a north and south division. The next decade would see a substantial increase in population, as well as wheat production. There were too many variables to speculate on what this meant to individual farms, but there was sure to be one constant—increasing land prices. The Schmidts purchased wisely and should do so again if the opportunity presented itself. With that Luther excused himself and returned to the Swedish immigrants.

Not much was said on the way home. John contemplated Luther's advice, but had no plans to acquire additional land. Irrespective of means, he barely had time to manage the ground he held. His father, who could possibly finance expansion, knew his place. John was the master and, until his son was ready, the Schmidt farm would stay as it was. As they passed through Casselton, Jacob noted the changes taking place closer to home. A general store would soon open; there was talk of a school addition; a blacksmith was coming in midsummer; and the rail yard had grown to twice its original size. Evidence of Luther's prophecy could be seen in every direction.

Seeding began on the Neumann farm in late April. Barley was first in the ground, followed by oats and then wheat. Corn was scheduled for mid-May. Good progress was made, and after four days two of the Norwegian boys were sent to the Schmidt farm. Jacob accompanied the boys and before leaving decided to check on the health of Rolf and his wife. He found both doing poorly. He expected as much. Maria visited Gesine Neumann whenever possible and rarely found her up and around. With three boys in the home, she and Rolf were well cared for, but age and lack of activity were taking a toll.

The outlook for the Neumann farm was not good. The boys worked hard and kept the farm going, but often spoke of Freidrich's exploits or some other far-off adventure. Rolf expected at least one of his sons would stay, but only as long as he and Gesine remained on the farm. Freidrich wrote the boys, extolling the opportunities in timber. Rolf saw the letter as unwelcome encouragement, fueling his sons' wanderlust. He wished Freidrich had not written, but suspected the boys were destined to leave, if not for the Pacific Northwest, then somewhere else.

* * * * *

Eighteen Seventy-Seven marked the leading edge of the Great Dakota Boom. In the ten years to follow, the population of what is now North Dakota swelled by a multiple of at least seven, surpassing earlier migrations to California and Oregon. Hundreds of immigrants arrived each week and by the end of the period, one-half of Dakota residents were foreign born. Bonanza farms and improved milling procedures skewed agriculture toward wheat to the exclusion of livestock, poultry and the other grains. Summer wheat production over the ten-year period increased from 2.8 million bushels to near 38 million. The wheat made its way to Minneapolis, where barrel after barrel of purified flour was shipped throughout America and to every corner of the world. Grasslands became wheat fields and crossroads became towns with mercantiles, schools, hotels and newspapers. To carry immigrants and transport product to market, railroads laid thousands of miles of new track throughout the territory. The two largest contributors were NPRR and the St. Paul, Minnesota and Manitoba.

The expansive growth led Dan Scott, a Dakota pioneer to write:

"Have seen wild flowers on the broad expanse of virgin prairie nodding to the breezes one week and on the next have seen the sod dotted with homesteaders' cabins, church spires and school houses looming up in a new settlement."

The boom reached its peak in early 1884 and began to fade a few years later, but not before the foundation was laid for the new states of North and South Dakota.

* * * * *

The planting season gave way to a cooler than average summer. Rain-fall, by mid-August, according to Eric Hansen, was two and one-half inches above normal. John was not sure of normal, but thankful rain came gently and when most needed. He and his father were also good learners, and in their second year had begun to better understand farming on the northern prairie. With any luck the yield per acre should exceed the prior year by at least one-quarter. Two of the Norwegian boys had agreed to work the season—the eldest now a full-time employee.

Five bindlestiffs were also hired and Axel Moen was under contract for threshing. John and Rolf were among the first on the thresherman's sched-ule, which meant less potential for damage to crops standing in the field. Their favorable position in the threshing queue mitigated, to some degree, Axel's unpleasant demeanor.

John considered purchasing his own thresher, but it made little eco-nomic sense. Until the farm was much larger, he was subject to Moen's periodic rants. As expected, the Beckers did not return. Lizzie gave no indication they were missed. She was living a dream with a family that cared deeply for her well-being. Lukas was her father in name only and Adele long since forgotten. Colvis and Mary Etta were her parents now and offered a far brighter future than imagined a year before.

John's guess on expected yield proved to be optimistic, but bushels per acre still came in twenty percent greater than the prior year—price per bushel dropped slightly averaging eighty-five cents. The harvest had gone smoothly with only minor complications—a brief hail storm just before wheat was cut, and cuts and bruises when the youngest of the Norwegian boys toppled from a wagon. John knew he would be looking at a surplus and his thoughts immediately turned to new equipment. He was particularly intrigued by self-binding harvesters. The machines took one important step beyond the Advance—they bound stalks. No one need rake or tie. The device did it all. John and his father spent hours debating the balance between man-hours saved and entry cost. The discussion included the potential for a second gen-eration of harvesters which could easily render the new equipment obsolete. Already there was talk of twine to replace wire as a binding material. The latter found its way into feed with dire consequences for livestock. John decided to wait. Maria liked his decision, reminding her husband building reserves was essential given their recent expansion. New machines were of little value if next year's harvest was destroyed by locusts or some other natural calamity.

John did reward Colvis with a bonus and allowed Maria to make a few purchases for herself and for the girls. The family's woolen clothing was gradually giving way to more colorful attire and Maria had replaced her snug woolen scarf with a small selection of cotton bonnets. She did not, however, lose sight of the practical. Among the purchases made were more jars for "canning" and metal tools for sausage making.

Canning and sausage making had become important components of the Schmidt farm's winter food supply, but Maria valued them for another reason. They were also social events that drew together the women that called "Meyer Farm Road" their home. Maria's circle of Norwegian friends was expanding. The women came together at planned events, as in canning and sausage making, or more casually at school or the newly opened Casselton General Store. They bridged the language gap using a curious dialect borrowed from English, *Deutsch* and Norwegian, precisely what the school master, Mr. Johnson, wished to avoid. His goal was to advance the mastery of English. Progress was noteworthy, but the confused mix of overlapping language often worked to frustrate his objective.

Kerb and *Hosttakkefest* were again combined and hosted by Eric and Lisa Hansen. The festival consumed a full day, with most participants Norwegian. The exceptions were the Schmidts, the Neumann boys and one Swedish family new to the valley. Maria could not help but recall the school work parties. Building a community then seemed a long way off. Now visits among the women were commonplace. The men were not as close, but John knew he could rely on Eric and the others should he need help.

Maria saw Lisa and her Norwegian friends at the school's Christmas pageant, a ritual Mr. Johnson considered equal to the award of diplomas in the spring. The event was held on the day before students were excused for the holiday and the building filled to overflowing. The Schmidt farm was well represented with Lizzie organizing a short play, relying on the younger students she taught in the spring. She then read a prepared text citing her adoption by the Rasmussens as a miracle guided by the hand of God. She was born again—a message the school master thought appropriate for the season.

Father Christmas and *Christkindche* did not make an appearance on the Schmidt farm, but their spirit was represented beneath the tree. A bountiful year led to a loosening of purse springs though John and Maria tried not to spoil the children. The biggest offender was Jacob who was grandfather not just to Morgan and Clara, but to the Rasmussen girls and Lizzie as well. Jacob promised to exercise frugality, but it was a promise soon forgotten. Maria did not have the heart to scold her father-in-law, who maintained grandparents were obliged to spoil their offspring. He took great delight in gift giving.

Winter slowed the pace of immigration, but the seeds of expansion were sewn. Yields on bonanza farms captured attention throughout the world, and grain from the Red River Valley made its way to Minneapolis where advanced milling technology produced an exceptional flour recognized for its purity. John and his father were simply observers, beneficiaries of events beyond their control. Weather cooperated while a drought in Europe brought a decline in wheat production on the Continent. Immigrants flocked to the Dakota Territory, and population in the valley and farther west grew exponentially. With the growth came rampant speculation, but John had no desire to participate. Gambling was better left to Luther Ogden.

Chance again forced John's hand in January of 1878. Jacob had visited Rolf Neumann and his wife a few weeks before Christmas. He found Rolf barely able to walk and struggling to sit erect. He was in constant pain. The boys helped where they could, but their father was failing and their mother worried and frail. Rolf saw Doctor McKellar in late November, but refused to see him again, calling him a sorcerer—the designation preceded by a few words that drew a reprimand from Gesine.

Rolf's eldest walked with Jacob as they left the cabin. He was certain his father had lost the will to live and would not see another planting season. His brothers were eager to leave for the Washington territory. He hoped to do the same, but would stay on if his mother so desired. Rolf lasted until January 13, quietly passing during the night. To everyone's surprise, including the boys, Gesine decided to join her sister in Colorado where the family had been growing sugar beets for more than eight years. A part of the farm was still undeveloped and Gesine planned on building a modest home and investing in the family business. She saw practicality in the move. Her younger sons had designs on leaving and her eldest considered the Dakota farm an unwelcome anchor. Colorado and her sister provided security. If the boys chose to move on—a near certainty—she would have family close at hand.

John offered the Schmidt cemetery for Rolf's burial and Gesine accepted. Jacob again presided. He read from a letter Gesine had written for her husband a few weeks before his passing. The letter recalled the early years and the lifetime friendship with the Meyers. It included a note, witnessed three years before by Luther Ogden, directing that Karl and Anneke should have right of first refusal in the event the Neumann farm were sold. Karl had passed and Anneke was now in Minnesota—farming the last thing on her mind.

In the Meyers' absence, Gesine believed Rolf would have wanted the farm sold to their successors. John expected as much. Expansion was not on his mind, but like the Erhardt property, it was an opportunity too good to pass. He had been reluctant to accept his father's help a few years before, but not today. He understood the Schmidt farm was a family business and welcomed his father's assistance. John and Gesine Neumann quickly came to terms at $10.75 per acre. The price reflected recent speculative bidding, but was still below what similar properties had sold for in the Casselton area. The final papers were signed on February 7. Gesine and her three sons left for Colorado a week later.

No matter how often John repeated the number, he still had a hard time believing his farm had grown by a multiple of three. The Schmidts now turned more soil than any of their neighbors, save the bonanza farm of Cornellious Mann.

The purchase agreement with Gesine called for one-half down with the balance due in five years, interest to be paid annually. John knew the Neumann farm must be brought online as quickly as possible. Additional workers would be necessary, but it was early for bindlestiffs and his experience with the transients gave him pause. He again sought help from his friend Eric Hansen and was promptly rewarded. Eric was aware of at least three Norwegian families intending to move farther west in the spring and wintering with relatives in the Casselton area. The Haugens were one of those. They spent the fall living out of a wagon, but on cold winter nights retreated to the cabin of their host. Four adults and nine children shared one roof.

John's acquisition of the Neumann farm provided relief for the Haugens. They had both a home and employment. Two days later, Albert, his wife Marit and five children, arrived at the Schmidt farm. There were three boys, ages eleven to sixteen and two girls, three and nine. The family planned to homestead on the Missouri plateau, but just how and where were uncertain. The opportunity extended by John and Maria was a godsend. Their move west would be delayed, but the Schmidt farm offered security while they decided on a course of action.

The Haugens also understood they had been a burden to their host. Marit's sister provided food and shelter during the winter, but crowding was taking its toll. Albert was out of money and his sister-in-law short on patience. John proposed to pay Albert eighty cents per day and his three sons sixty cents each. Marit would be paid nothing, but was expected to work alongside Maria and Mary Etta. Albert's salary began immediately—the boys with the start of planting season. The Haugens would be provided foodstuffs to get them through the winter. The Haugens were not hard to please. The family committed to delay the move west, at least through planting season.

John's plan for the season included seeding 200 acres of the Neumann farm. The task would fall largely to Albert and his sons. The plan was ambitious. Rolf's horses were tired and his equipment old, but John believed in his new hire. Albert was a tireless worker, took directions easily and understood farming. Marit also proved a good fit. Where Albert was quiet and contemplative, Marit was spontaneous and never stopped moving. She took less than a day to find her niche. The three women of the Schmidt farm got on well as did the children. The Haugens' youngest provided a playmate for Morgan. Maria was happy for that. Morgan struggled to keep up with the Rasmussen girls and had taken, over the past few months, to trailing her father. If John was engaged in fieldwork, that's where Morgan wanted to be. If he was tending stock, she was helping. She was also true to her name, rising with her father each day before sunrise.

The Schmidt farm saw more than 650 acres planted in 1878. Spring wheat was sewn on 450, corn on 100 and remainder divided between oats, hay and barley. The task was accomplished in twenty-six days using fifteen bindlestiffs in addition to John, Colvis, Albert Haugen, and two of his sons. Most of the hired hands were of Norwegian descent with a few Swedes. The ever-increasing demands of bonanza farms made hiring a challenge, but John paid a premium and was rewarded with committed workers.

The Schmidt farm matched the growth in acreage with an increase in livestock. The farm now had thirty-one horses, seven cows, the same quantity of goats, and three hogs. The additional livestock required cover and feed. John had two barns and five shelters, but got no help from his purchase of the Neumann farm. Rolf had maintained his home, but not the outbuildings. Sometime in the next two years repairs must be undertaken.

Most of the feed came from the farm itself. John traded for what was lacking. Given his dislike for chickens, there were only a few in evidence, just enough to satisfy the needs of three families. In midsummer, he was annoyed to see Morgan and her sister return from a visit to the Hansen farm with four chicks.

"We don't need more chickens," John protested.

Maria was concerned Morgan and Clara would be hurt by her husband's caustic remark.

"They're a gift John," she said. "Leave it be."

Jacob sided with Maria and the girls. "Four chicks will hurt no one," he said.

John was outnumbered and returned to the barn. Soon Jacob had constructed a new coop—predictably, the population grew. Within five months, the Schmidts, taking advantage of their proximity to the general store, were trading eggs with the proprietor on a regular basis.

The Haugen family settled in quickly thankful for employment and their new home. Albert and his sons immediately adapted to the farm's work routine and Marit brought new energy to the kitchen. She was constantly in motion and a favorite of the children. Both men and women saw enough of one another during the workday and were content to go their own way at day's end. On Sunday afternoons, all three families came together in the main house to share an evening meal. They were near twenty in total. The Schmidt farm was now its own neighborhood and offered the perfect complement to the fifteen nearby Norwegian families Maria called friends. All shared the same road and all were known to one another. Children were the thread which held the families of Meyer Farm Road together.

Lizzie continued her work with the younger children, and Mr. Johnson was increasingly convinced she had the qualities of a natural born teacher.

"You should consider further studies in education," Mr. Johnson told Lizzie.

"I'm happy working with the younger children," she answered.

The school master continued. "You're very good," he said. "I know the headmaster at Mankato Normal in Minnesota."

"No thank you," Lizzie responded politely.

"Arrangements could be made to defer some costs." He persisted.

Lizzie was simply not interested. Even the newly appointed Superintendent of Public Schools for the Dakota Territory, on a visit to Casselton, was unable to convince Lizzie to advance her schooling. She was flattered by the attention, but unmoved. The school master turned to Mary Etta hoping that she might encourage Lizzie. The effort was futile. Lizzie saw her beginnings as too humble. She could not envision herself a college student, an abandoned waif among people of means. Maria tried to convince Lizzie as well, but to no avail. The more cajoling, the more adamant Lizzie became.

Lizzie did agree to help Lisa Hansen with a fundraising campaign designed to erect a new building for secondary education. Land had been set aside by the territorial legislature in the 1860s to fund common school construction, but not in a quantity sufficient to meet demand. Population growth simply outpaced the funding source. Construction was dependent on contributions from the community. Fundraising was a challenge given more than half the decision makers were foreign born and many families saw a day's work on the farm more valuable than book learning. The task fell to Eric Hansen as School Board President. He asked his wife Lisa to guide the effort. Lisa immediately turned to Lizzie, who began her campaign by contacting those she knew best—parents of the younger students she taught each spring.

She also joined Lisa in contacting Northern Pacific Railroad, the Casselton General Store and the soon-to-open First National Bank of Fargo— the latter expected to break ground in Casselton within the year. Among the larger individual contributors were Jacob Schmidt and Eric Hansen. Luther Ogden gave an in-kind contribution of building materials. Four letters were sent to Cass County bonanza farms. One responded with a modest contribution. Cornellious Mann ignored the request. Before the summer break, the campaign secured commitments to fund one-half the construction and provide for three new teachers.

The harvest of 1878 produced a yield per acre slightly less than the preceding year. Machinery breakdowns, a dry spell in June and hiring difficulties contributed to the mildly disappointing output. Many of the newly arrived Norwegian immigrants had moved on during the summer and John faced intense competition from the bonanza farms in recruiting temporary help. He was at least six men short for harvest and forced to pay more than the going wage. To compound matters, Axel Moen was two days late. Where Rolf Neumann had some control over the frequently belligerent Axel, John had none. His reason for tardiness was a pair of new Case "Eclipse" threshers—no-apron engineering marvels which exemplified the pre-eminent role Case held in threshing manufacture. Equally surprising was the power source, a pair of steam traction engines.

Axel now had two sons in the business with two others to follow. Expansion was on his mind and he needed faster state of the art equipment. The traction engines also gave him the flexibility to engage off-season work, notably well-drilling. Axel Moen and Sons could now be found throughout the Red River Valley, elsewhere in the territory and in Minnesota.

Instead of offering an apology, Axel complained he was spending too much time on the Schmidt farm. He told John he needed wood and water for his machines and would not begin until both were available in quantity. John was annoyed, but had few alternatives. The farm was too large to join a threshing ring, and machines, such as the Eclipse, were simply too expensive. The pace of technological development was also a factor. A thresher purchased today could easily be obsolete tomorrow. Like it or not, John was stuck with Axel Moen. The last of the wheat crop was carted off to Valley Storage early in September. John did not expect to use the country elevator again. Next year most of the farm's wheat production would be sold to a newly formed association of Minnesota millers. Jacob was skeptical, but John liked the idea. The small stipend paid in advance was appealing.

Corn was the only crop still standing. All but two bindlestiffs had been released and the farm harvested the larger grain on the strength of its own work force. Three weeks later they celebrated *Hosttakkefest,* now a Meyer Farm Road tradition—the *Deutsch Kerbfest* simply absorbed in the festivities. Sixteen families attended—all Norwegian save the Schmidts and Rasmussens. The young Swedish couple attending the year before lost their farm to the bank. Eric and Lisa Hansen took part in the celebration, but only for an hour. Their daughter, a playmate of Morgan's, was thrown from a horse in August and killed. Morgan struggled with understanding her death. On the morning of the *Hosttakkefest,* she asked if Isabel would be there. Maria could not find the words to explain. She considered leaving Morgan with Jacob, but decided against it. Morgan was unusually quiet throughout the day, spending most of her time with Maria.

Winter came early and the Schmidt farm set about in earnest to prepare for the cold. Outbuildings, winter stores, feed and fuel were checked and checked again. Maria saw a need for one last trip to Fargo for kitchen supplies and she dispatched Jacob. On his return trip, he happened by the NPRR yard and found the station master waiting on a telegram that involved the Rasmussens' eldest, Bjartr. He was in Montana and second in command of a NPRR scouting party. The master received word earlier there had been an accident and he was awaiting confirmation. Word came within the hour. The telegraph operator read the wire.

"Ice injured on Bozeman Pass, rescue party en route."

Jacob was confused "Ice?" he asked.

The master explained, "No one can pronounce Bjartr. The men call him 'Ice' owing to his birthplace."

He told Jacob he would send word to the farm as soon as additional information was received. Jacob hurried to the farm and shared the telegram with Colvis and Mary Etta. Colvis thought about leaving immediately for the station, but the master had told Jacob there would be no update until tomorrow. Colvis was at the station early the next morning and learned the rescue party was en route and expected to return to Livingston late afternoon of the following day. Ice had broken his leg and sustained other unspecified injuries.

Colvis and Mary Etta worried about the term "unspecified," but decided against further inquiry. Another wire was received—Ice was out of danger and under doctor's care in Livingston. He was expected to return to Casselton in three to four weeks. The Rasmussens were looking forward to a visit at Christmas, but not under these conditions.

Updates were periodically received and, three weeks later, Ice arrived on a work train bound for Fargo. The crew had fashioned a bed so the leg could be fully extended. He was carried off the train where Colvis, Mary Etta and John were waiting.

The heavy splint was expected, but not the bandage which covered the left side of the young man's face. There was a depression in the area of the cheekbone covered by a six by six-inch mass of gauze and tape. Traces of blood shown through the bandage and ran down the neck. It was obvious the face had been disfigured. He was placed in the wagon using the make-shift bed from the train. Fighting back the tears, Mary Etta rode beside him. Bjartr seemed confused by his whereabouts. The engineer told Mary Etta he was heavily sedated. He also advised NPRR would arrange for a doctor's visit within two days. When they arrived at the farm, John, Colvis and two of the Haugen boys carried Ice to his parents' bedroom. He slept for more than fourteen hours. When he awoke, the confusion had passed and he was very hungry. Against his objections, Mary Etta helped him bathe, finding it necessary to remind Bjartr she was still his mother.

Both father and mother were surprised to see how much their son had filled out since leaving the farm. He was now the measure of Colvis and perhaps more muscular. While Ice was resting, Jacob fashioned a half-bed, half-chair so Ice could be closer to the stove. Doctor James Clarke found him there two days later. Clarke was a former intern of Doctor McKellar's and scheduled to staff the office in Fargo. McKellar preferred country "doc-toring" and would soon open a second office in Casselton.

Doctor Clarke's short time in Fargo had left him with enough Norwe-gian to communicate. Ice did not want his mother or father in the room during the examination. After some discussion, it was decided Colvis would remain since it was necessary to move the patient. Mary Etta protested, but quietly left not sure how she might react when confronted with her son's injuries. The doctor began by raising Ice to a standing position and forcing him to put some weight on the broken leg. With the help of his father, he was able to take a few painful steps. He was returned to a sitting position and the splint removed. The doctor was pleased with what he saw.

"The splint can be reduced in length," he told Colvis.

"Our Jacob can easily do that."

"He should begin walking short distances," the doctor advised. "He'll need support, then crutches, and maybe a cane."

The doctor turned to the face studying the bandage as if reluctant to see what lay beneath. He slowly began its removal, each tug causing Ice to wince. Colvis did not have a clear view, but it was apparent from the doctor's expression the damage was abhorrent. From what he could see, the flesh had been torn away below the cheekbone and again just above the chin. The practitioner had sewn the gaps shut in a somewhat crude manner pulling the left side of the face together. Ice was badly scarred. The only good news being the wound was healing and free of infection.

The doctor applied salve and started a new dressing.

"You may have to do this if weather interferes with my next visit."

"I can do that," Colvis answered.

Jacob was immediately called upon to fashion a new splint. Within the hour, Ice began testing the leg, leaning heavily on his father for support as he hobbled through the house. A week later, he was getting around on his own using crutches assembled by Jacob.

Colvis and Mary Etta had not questioned their son on how the accident occurred. They expected Bjartr, the name they used exclusively, to breach the topic when the time was right. That came with the evening meal two weeks later. Ice, hesitant at first, described the events. Some came from his own recollection and some from the remembrances of his railroad companions.

He and two surveyors were investigating an alternative route down the western flank of Bozeman Pass that separated the Bridger and Gallatin mountain ranges. Ice stepped out on a ledge to gain a better vantage point and somehow lost his footing, tumbling down a sixty-foot wall to a stream below. The survey crew was forced to retreat more than two miles to access the stream bed and make their way to the site. They found Ice with a broken leg and what they suspected to be a dislocated shoulder. He was bleeding profusely from the head. They managed to slow the bleeding, but two surveyors could not move Ice without help. One of the men stayed with Ice while the other set out for Livingston. A party of six men returned to the location late the next day. Morphine was administered and the group began the two-day journey, resting briefly during the night. They intercepted a locomotive for the final leg to Livingston.

Bjartr had no response when asked by Colvis if he knew anything of the doctor who treated him. He was unsure of his experience or training. The doctor had seen him only once following surgery and then only to change bandages. Colvis was thankful someone was there to help, but wondered if a more skillful surgeon could have better restored his son's appearance. Ice was relieved to have told his story and realized, during the telling, how much he was indebted to his rescuers. He left Montana without thanking the men who saved his life.

A captive of the small house, Ice was often entertained by his much younger sisters. He barely knew the girls, but his lack of mobility made him an easy target for conversation and all manner of diversion. The girls were excited by Christmas and did their best to convince Ice he should attend the school's holiday pageant. He resisted having no desire to appear in public. As the holiday approached, the girls became more insistent. When Colvis and Mary Etta joined the chorus, Ice gave in. The station master had told many of the Casselton residents the story of the young man's rescue and he was something of a celebrity. Lizzie arranged to have Ice and the Rasmussen family introduced at the beginning of the pageant. Once by the introduction, Ice enjoyed himself.

Mr. Johnson made sure every student participated in some capacity. There was a short Christmas play and a selection of mostly Norwegian carols. The children exchanged small gifts and Mr. Johnson was presented with a handsome overcoat and large world map. Gifts were also exchanged on the Schmidt farm. Maria and Mary Etta had done most of their shopping before Bjartr arrived. His last-minute gifts were taken care of by his mother. Once again Jacob spent too much making sure all the children were included. John and Maria took leave to visit briefly with the Hansens, then returned to the farm to host the Christmas supper. All the families of the Schmidt farm were represented. Jacob offered a prayer of thanksgiving. Another season had passed, families were intact and Ice had shown good progress recovering from his injuries.

Maria had come to expect letters from both her mother and Freidrich during the holiday season. They were much anticipated as a means to catch up on events taking place during the year. Her brother's letter came first. It was unusually long and began with the announcement that he was now married. He had won the hand of Agnes Morehead, against what he considered overwhelming odds. Freidrich was not sure why he won Miss Morehead's hand, but was delighted with the outcome. He was equally sure his new father-in-law was baffled by his daughter's decision.

The couple was married in September and temporarily living with the Morehead family while building a home in the small community of Montesano in the Washington territory. He got on well with his wife's mother. His father-in-law, the judge, remained more distant, still wary of a farmer turned lumberman. Prairie Timber now had three mills and was considering a fourth north of Grays Harbor. They had over sixty employees and several thousand acres of timber rights. He corrected himself, saying the rights were held by Prairie Timber and the judge.

Kurt still handled sales and was something of a "dandy." He had an office in Grays Harbor and one in the city of Tacoma. Freidrich ran the mill operations and interacted with his father-in-law and benefactor. Sadly, the third member of their enterprise, Klaus Schuler, who spent most of his time in the woods, was killed in a logging accident. Freidrich offered no details except to say a sum of money was sent to the Schuler family in St. Anne's. He also told Maria that Rolf's two youngest sons found their way to Washington. Both were now employed at the company's Satsop mill.

A few days later she received her mother's letter. Melina began with news of the *St. Anne's Company*. The system of governance and land tenure that lasted more than a century in *Russen* could not find traction in Kansas. The *company* had been dissolved and common property divided among the members. The community no longer had a mayor, nor was there a council. St. Anne's existed in name only. No additional businesses had opened and a planned expansion of First National Bank of Hays City was abandoned. Growth was all around them, but not in St. Anne's township.

Melina guessed more than forty outlying farms had been added in the past year alone. Most were doing business in Hays City which continued to push its boundaries to the south. The barn was the only structure available for common use with a portion now occupied by the Grange. Peter had become active in the Granger Movement and held a leadership position at the state level. Maria was not surprised. Her father was never far from the seat of power. The group and its objectives were known to Maria. John participated in a meeting of Norwegian farmers to discuss the Grange, but a competing group—the Farmers Alliance—was more active in Casselton.

Maria assumed the Schafer farm was doing well. Her mother offered no specifics saying only that Peter retained all of the property he had purchased as a principal owner. She wanted John to know the farm was equally spread between corn and the smaller grains with Turkey Red gradually replacing spring wheat. The latter was a seed much sought after, but difficult to acquire. The biggest surprise was Albrecht's behavior. Perhaps it was fatherhood or Peter's occupation with the Grange, but he had noticeably matured, assuming day-to-day management of the farm. They escaped the year without major calamity and the farm was on good footing. With that Melina lapsed into the usual questions about Morgan and Clara, mentioning that Hilke was again pregnant and Albrecht's house required expansion.

She knew Maria would be interested in the welfare of Anna Schneider, a long-time friend. She was recovering from a difficult childbirth. The baby died and Anna had come close herself. Anna had just now returned to work at Pallitto's General Store. There was no mention of visiting the Dakota Territory and Maria wondered if her mother's once expressed desire to visit Casselton was forgotten. A postscript was included. As she was closing the letter, Peter's brother, Hermann, arrived. He was again headed west on company business. Hermann had continued to purchase property near St. Anne's and now held close to 600 acres of prime farmland. Hersh Schneider managed the properties, along with a full-time crew of three. Hermann spent two hours with Hersh, but only a few minutes with his brother. He was aware of Peter's involvement with the Grange, an organization which sought to reign in alleged price fixing exercised by firms such as Hermann's Midwest Grain and Feed. The two argued and Hermann abruptly left. Melina closed telling Maria her uncle had not returned to his home in St Louis for over three months, and still traveled with the same female associate.

Colvis and his son made the trip to see Doctor Clarke the second week in January. They took the train planning to spend at least one night in Fargo. The doctor turned immediately to Bjartr's leg removing the splint.

"Walk as often and as long as possible," he told Ice, but cautioned, "Use a cane until sure of your balance." He next turned to the facial injuries. The wound was healing nicely, but the scars and distortion were even more noticeable.

Ice studied himself in the mirror, but said nothing.

"There are surgeons who can remove the scar tissue," the doctor offered.

Ice remained silent. The doctor applied two small bandages just below the cheekbone.

"Unless the leg gives you trouble, there's no need for further visits."

Ice thanked the doctor and father and son moved on to the general store, where they filled Maria's list before taking a room at the Headquarters Hotel. Colvis noticed his son pulled up the collar of his heavy jacket so as to cover much of his face. He did the same as they waited for their evening meal.

They were leaving the restaurant when someone called, "Is that Ice?"

When he turned, Ice saw two of his former co-workers hurriedly coming toward him.

"It's time your vacation ended," the taller of the men said.

"James, Robert, it's good to see you," then recalled, "I left Montana without thanking you."

"Buy us a drink then."

Ice introduced Colvis who, knowing the young men had much to discuss, quickly excused himself.

It was four hours before Ice joined his father. The "catching up" had taken longer than expected. During the discussion, Ice discovered his friends were leaving early the next morning on a westbound NPRR work train. The men were sure space could be found for the Rasmussens. Ice accepted since it saved a full day. Colvis listened as his son recounted the evening's conversation, hoping his son understood there were many who, like his co-workers, valued the person more than his appearance.

Jacob was waiting in Casselton, having been notified by the station master the Rasmussens were aboard the work train. He intentionally avoided even a glance at the now exposed facial wounds, commenting instead on the discarded splint and tawdry cane. Jacob committed to carve something better. When they arrived at the farm there was little discussion of the doctor's visit. Bjartr was met with an embrace from his mother and both Maria and Marit. The children showed no interest in the scar, focusing instead on the bag of hard candy Ice purchased in Fargo.

Colvis was encouraged by the change in his son's behavior following the visit with co-workers. On the return trip, he made no attempt to conceal his face and discussed the need to rebuild his strength after weeks of inactivity. Colvis was sure his son had taken the first step in refusing to let his appearance define the future. Ice asked Jacob if he could fashion barbells similar to those seen in one of Maria's catalogues. Jacob was sure he could carve a hand hold in a piece of fencepost, hollow the ends, and have the blacksmith fill them with lead. Within two days' time, Ice had his barbells. He also took to the porch stairs, using the hand rail to steady himself climbing up and down several times a day.

Lizzie had only limited contact with Ice while he recuperated on the Schmidt farm. She had always been attracted to him, fantasizing about intimacy and imaging romantic encounters. There were times when she thought Ice might feel the same, but he was a quiet man, adept at concealing his emotions. Lizzie kept her distance. Ice was an intimidating presence. He had experienced the wilds of Montana and possessed the chiseled body one might expect from a mountain man. He also fixed an unnerving stare on anyone who engaged him in conversation. In their few conversations, Lizzie found the stare disconcerting.

Ice had taken to walking three times each day. He circled the house then made several rotations around the barn. He finished by climbing up and down the porch stairs. He did so even in the worst of weather. His father sometimes accompanied him and, if unavailable, Mary Etta filled in. On a particularly soggy day, Colvis was tending to a sick calf and Mary Etta busy with meal preparation.

She told Lizzie, "Bjartr needs a companion—walk with him."

"I have to check on the hens," Lizzie answered.

That was all the opportunity Mary Etta needed.

"Then he'll keep you company."

C'mon," said Ice already standing in the doorway.

The next morning Ice suggested, "Time to get out of the house." He asked his mother, "Can you spare Lizzie?"

Lizzie answered before Mary Etta could respond, "She can."

Within a week, Lizzie and Ice were walking together almost daily— their sojourns often extending beyond the barn. Colvis was thankful for the break and saw Lizzie's help as a commitment to family. Mary Etta saw much more. Ice said little and Lizzie was content to simply walk. Mary Etta was increasingly convinced her son and stepdaughter were falling in love.

By the end of January 1879, Ice was taking on tasks which caused his mother to cringe. He was in the barn loft, on the porch roof and again riding horses, but he never missed his daily walk with Lizzie. Ice was an active participant when fieldwork began, most often in the company of his father. He was easily recognized, having developed a curious hop to cover ground. With or without the strange gait, he was the equal to any man on the farm. John had more than once offered to pay Ice, but he refused any remuneration. Ice was happiest when busy, but John knew the young man's heart was not in farming.

John's assumption proved correct. On a spring morning, after taking the children to school, Ice took the opportunity to visit with his friend the station master. A few weeks of fieldwork had convinced him it was time to return to NPRR. He understood the attachment John Schmidt and others had to the land, but missed his co-workers and the adventure of cutting a path through the wilderness. He told the station master he was ready if the railroad would have him.

A telegram was sent to Fargo. A day later he had an offer to supervise the forward-most track crew working toward central Montana. The offer was tendered by Alfred Marlow, Director of Western Track Construction, and delivered by one of the Casselton Station workers. Ice signed the note accepting the position. When the Rasmussens sat down for supper that evening, he told the family. Colvis knew from the beginning it would be difficult to keep his son on the farm. He had been exposed to a world where each mountain crest or bend in the river unveiled a mystery. He was young and the lure of adventure too great.

Mary Etta was deeply disappointed. She expected him to return to railroading, but in a less dangerous position. His new job once again placed him in harm's way. The two Rasmussen girls were also saddened. Ice had proven to be a good companion. They would miss their brother. As Ice discussed his plans for the future, Lizzie sat with head bowed fighting back tears. Mary Etta saw the heartbreak. Bjartr saw it as well. He stood walking slowly to where Lizzie was seated.

"Please come with me to Montana as my wife."

Lizzie bolted straight from her chair to the arms of the young man she had come to love.

"I think that was a proposal," Maria said.

"It was," said Lizzie and the answer is "Yes."

Colvis immediately sent their eldest daughter to find the other families. The mood changed from sadness to joy for all except Mary Etta. She had seen it coming, but the reality of her son's departure tempered her zeal for celebration. Ice was due in Livingston in one week. He was committed there until late July, returning to Casselton for the wedding. He and his bride would leave shortly thereafter for Montana. Before the night was out, Mary Etta shed her melancholy and was making plans for the ceremony. John, along with the men of the Schmidt farm, dipped into Karl's greatly diminished private stock. Lizzie and Ice were lost in the evening.

The winter of 1879 passed without incident. The days were consumed with caring for animals and providing a modicum of warmth for their keepers. Tools and equipment were checked and repaired. There was the occasional school event and neighborly visit. All prayed for the early arrival of spring. A February blizzard closed schools for six days. Wind-driven snow found its way through every break in clapboard, but the farm was ready. The snowfall was heavy enough to suspend rail traffic for three days from Brainerd to the Missouri crossing. The school closure was the second of the new year. The first came in January when "winter fever" reduced Mr. Johnson's student count by more than half. Diphtheria ravaged Minnesota and rumors held some families lost all their children. A few cases were reported in Fargo and many feared the disease would continue its westward march. Blessedly, Casselton escaped the scourge. Marit was pregnant with her sixth child, somewhat of a surprise. Maria and Mary Etta were excited—the expectant mother less so. Letters from Montana suggested Ice was doing well. He spoke of Montana's beauty, the challenge of laying track in rugged terrain, but mostly of his eagerness to return to Lizzie and their marriage in July.

Immigrants continued to pour into the Dakota Territory, but in numbers that fell short of the staggering demands for seasonal workers. Bonanza farms grew in size and number, many reaching 20,000 acres or more. Unwilling to risk their investment on the vagaries of transients, larger farms took the unusual step of sending trains south to recruit workers in advance of the season. The decision fueled a simmering discontent in the valley. Locals saw the larger farms as distant and detached monoliths with no interest in agrarian reform or civic betterment. The influx of dark-skinned workers created even more unrest. Mexican workers were considered by some as beneath the mythical standard of the steadfast prairie farmer—an unwelcome blight on the community. Colvis was particularly vocal in this regard, once publicly voicing his displeasure at a meeting of the Farmers Alliance.

The recruitment scheme by the bonanza farms worked to the benefit of the Schmidt farm. Suddenly, bindlestiffs from the local population were much easier to find. John selected his workers carefully knowing the wrong choice could bring unwanted disruption. For the most part, he turned to recent Norwegian immigrants. Eighteen were hired to join Colvis, Albert and the Haugen boys. They set to work in March and by the end of May all crops, save corn, were in the ground.

Word reached the Schmidt farm early in June that Anneke Meyer died, having never returned to the farm and cottage she and Karl so lovingly built. She would return now. Her wish was to be buried next to her husband on the homestead once known as the Meyer Farm. Maria was deeply saddened by the news. Anneke had welcomed the Schmidts to the Dakota Territory and treated the children of the farm as if her own. Her eldest daughter, Monika, would bring the casket in a week's time. In the telegram, she asked John to arrange for a minister. Monika was Methodist, but left John to make the choice. He turned to Luther Ogden who recommended the pastor of the Scandinavian Evangelical Lutheran Church. He was new to Fargo and happy to preside over the burial service.

Anneke's daughter and her husband arrived on June 7. John and his father were waiting. In addition to the casket, Monika brought a four-foot obelisk inscribed with the words "In Loving Memory of Karl and Anneke Meyer." The station master agreed to bring the casket and monument to the Schmidt farm. Monika and her husband stayed at the Meyer cottage. The service took place two days later. The pastor arrived well before the ceremony. He spoke with Monika and Maria and, having ridden with Luther to the Schmidt farm, learned much about the Meyers and Anneke. He delivered a brief, but moving eulogy. Monika and her husband spent one more night on the farm. In the morning she told John her mother wanted the cottage to be given to the Schmidts. Her only request was to preserve the structure in its present state. John suggested some value be established. Monika refused. John and Maria looked after Karl and Anneke in their later years. The gift was the family's way of saying thank you.

Ice returned to Casselton on July 24. Lizzie wanted to be the only one at the station when he arrived. She knew Colvis and Mary Etta were eager to see their son, but believed the bride-to-be deserved some preferential treatment. The Rasmussens agreed. Lizzie took one of the farm wagons and was there three hours before his expected arrival. Ice had a surprise. He purchased a home in Livingston from the owner of a nearby mining company. The purchase was a revelation to Lizzie. Their new home was about the size of the main house on the Schmidt farm. The mine owner lost his wife thirteen months before and the home had since been neglected. Ice had made repairs, but there was still much to be done. Lizzie was delighted, but would have been happy if their new home was a tent.

When the couple reached the Schmidt farm, they were warmly greeted by all three families. There were stories to tell, questions on what lay ahead, and a good deal of catching up. Ice had reclaimed his muscular body and lost the unusual gait. The facial scars were still in evidence, but long forgotten. Maria and her helpers prepared an evening meal for eighteen. John talked of farming, Ice of NPRR, and Lizzie and Mary Etta discussed wedding plans. Ice planned on staying with Jacob in the bunkhouse until the newlyweds spent their first night together in the Meyer cottage.

Mary Etta had come to realize that Lizzie, because of her work with the school, was acquainted with almost everyone in Casselton. Ice also had a number of railroad friends and Mary Etta knew many of the families along Meyer Farm Road. Invited guests reached numbers well beyond what the Rasmussens anticipated. Maria saw Mary Etta's trepidation. She contacted Mr. Johnson, the school master and her friend Lisa Hansen. Soon a planning group formed to help with food and drink. Mary Etta was both thankful and relieved. The Meyers' eldest daughter provided another unexpected gesture of kindness. When Anneke's daughter returned to bury her mother, she asked if Lizzie had a wedding dress. When told she did not, Monika offered her store-bought dress and veil. The dress arrived a few weeks before the ceremony. Marit could make the necessary alterations.

The wedding day dawned with the threat of thunderstorms. Since there was no choice but to conduct the wedding outdoors, the sky was as closely watched as the bride and groom. Two hours before the ceremony, rumblings were heard far to the north and the threat was gone. The nearly 120 guests began arriving in midafternoon. Mr. Johnson had arranged for the older school children to manage horse and buggy and NPRR sent benches from the Fargo station. Jacob built an arch for the recital of vows and the Norwegian community brought food and drink to supplement that provided by the Schmidt farm.

Two days before the wedding, amidst all the confusion, Marit gave birth to a baby girl. She was concerned the delivery might be difficult given her age, but there were no complications. Barely forty hours after childbirth, Marit was in the kitchen helping Maria and Mary Etta. Bjartr's sisters, followed by Morgan and Clara, preceded the bride and, at Lizzie's request, John and Maria stood for the couple. Colvis asked the Lutheran pastor to officiate and he spoke as if the couple were lifetime members of his congregation. He talked of hardships faced by each, citing Lizzie's early childhood and Bjartr's accident and recovery. He reminded all it was a union made of God's will.

The ceremony was over in less than one-half hour and the guests turned to food and drink. Most were gone by dusk. Ice and Lizzie had long since retired to the Meyer cottage. The newlyweds spent two more days on the Schmidt farm. Lizzie rose early on the day of departure purposely avoiding Morgan and Jacob as they tended the chickens. She wanted one last walk through the farm she would always consider home. Lizzie came to the valley a neglected waif cowling behind a work wagon. She was leaving on far better terms. Her life began when Adele Becker suggested she become part of the Rasmussen family. She had been exiled from bondage. Colvis and Mary Etta had taken her in as a daughter. In a twist of fate, she was now married to her stepbrother. Lizzie had much to look forward to, but much to remember as well.

The Rasmussens were ready to drive the couple to the Casselton Station. Before leaving, Lizzie embraced each member of the farm family.

"A part of me will always be here," she said.

Lizzie took one last look at the golden fields now ready for harvest.

"My life began here."

Finally, Ice lifted her to the wagon and they set out for Casselton. Lizzie looked back once and was struck by the fear she would never return. The train was late. Colvis held up well, but not Mary Etta. She was saying goodbye to a son and young woman, now far more than a stepdaughter. The couple boarded and moved to the last car. Lizzie was still waving as Casselton faded from view.

With Lizzie's wedding a memory, the farm turned its attention to the harvest. Colvis had the workers he needed and the weather cooperated. Crops were brought in without a single disruption. Even Axel Moen was caught up in the moment, giving a nod to John as he and his threshermen left the farm. The gesture, coming from Axel, was high praise indeed. The Schmidt farm had planted 670 acres which returned seventeen bushels per acre. The price per bushel, although somewhat lower than the previous year, never fell below eighty cents.

Chapter Eighteen:
Prosperity Means
One More Year

"You crown the year with a bountiful harvest. Even the hard
pathways overflow with abundance. The
grasslands of the wilderness become a lush pasture
and the hillsides blossom with joy."

—Psalm 6: 11-13

The new decade began much as the prior ended. The Minnesota millers came to rely more heavily on wheat from the Red River Valley, and railroads extended their tentacles in every direction to meet the insatiable demand for "purified" flour. There were dry spells without drought, strong winds without funnel clouds and rain without damaging hail. Conditions held throughout the 1880 harvest, leaving the farm with its highest yield ever. With each year John's understanding of the northern prairie grew and with knowledge came productivity. Trains brought both European immigrants and Mexican labor, the latter destined for the bonanza farms. The growing immigrant population meant the farm was no longer dependent on transients moving north with the harvest, a development which pleased Maria. Threshing was still left to Axel Moen. He was belligerent as ever, but John had no alternative. The pair conferred briefly at the start of threshing, then avoided each another—Axel's skill the salve that tempered conflict.

The expanded Casselton School opened its doors on September 13, 1880. Lisa Hansen, with Lizzie's help, raised enough funds for the additional school building and Mr. Johnson had both an elementary and secondary program. He also had six new teachers, thanks to help from the Superintendent of Public Instruction. The school was now much closer to meeting the needs of the community it served. Along with the expanded Casselton School District, the First National Bank of Fargo had broken ground on a Casselton branch in July and there were rumors of a feed store and hotel coming in 1881.

Morgan was still too young to attend school, but kept busy as her father's constant helper. She was every ounce a farm girl, taking the reins of seeder and farm wagon and doing her best to keep pace with the older Rasmussen and Haugen children. She developed a real affinity for animals, particularly horses. John enjoyed his daughter's company and took pride in her farming instincts. His only source of displeasure was the chicken coop, which now extended along the back side of the barn for most of its length. He was powerless to resist. Morgan had the support of her mother and grandfather. To their credit, all three proponents took an active role in caring for the malodorous fowl. The coop was clean and eggs were delivered each day to the Casselton General Store. The Schmidts were dependable and the proprietor came to rely exclusively on the farm for his egg supply, sending a quantity four times a week to Fargo. John could not deny his eldest daughter was learning responsible behavior.

Morgan's most unusual relationship was her friendship with the irascible Axel Moen. He went out of his way to befriend Morgan while others on the farm barely earned a glance. Their unlikely association had begun the year before when she and her grandfather came to watch Axel's thresher start the work day. Instead of waving her off—as he did with most observers—he took time to explain the process, even discussing the future integration of harvesting and threshing. The pair moved on to the traction engine where Axel and Morgan studied its connection to the thresher. When he was sure Morgan had no further questions, he announced, for all to hear, that there was at least one farmer among the Schmidts.

Clara had also come with her grandfather to watch the start of threshing, but chose to keep her distance. She was the polar opposite of her older sister. Clara never wandered far from her mother's skirt and embraced everything having to do with homemaking. The Schmidt daughters were still very young, but John already saw the distinction—Morgan the farm boss, and Clara the perfect wife.

Land value in the Red River Valley continued to appreciate—the product of record yield on bonanza farms and improved milling techniques. Success fueled further speculation with prices growing much faster than the bushel price of wheat. Buyers were not deterred. Assets were excessively leveraged and modest setbacks led to collapse. John and his father simply watched. Land was too expensive, as were the human and technological resources to support expansion. Those who settled farther west found lower prices, but less fertile ground. Most were homesteaders who settled on unforgiving land. They came with little and left with nothing, save debt. Albert Haugen watched the rush to buy land play out. He and his family came to the Schmidt farm in 1878 expecting to stay just one season before moving on. Two years later, the Haugens were right where they started. Albert could not afford land anywhere in the valley and saw immigrants heading east, having failed on the Missouri Plateau and beyond. He was still tempted, but the attraction grew less as each pitiful caravan passed through Casselton. Marit had no desire to leave. The Schmidt family was generous and she was surrounded by trusted friends. John and Maria hoped Marit's contentment overcame Albert's wanderlust. Like the Rasmussens, the Haugen family was valued both as friends and workers.

The 1880 holiday season was especially noteworthy for the Schmidt farm. As part of the annual Christmas pageant, Lisa Hansen was feted for her successful effort to raise funds for school expansion. Before accepting the commemorative plaque she asked John and Jacob Schmidt, along with Lizzie Becker, to step forward. The Schmidts made a contribution early in the fundraising drive, then followed with another two months later. The combined donation pushed the drive beyond its goal. Lisa then turned to Lizzie, telling the audience her tireless effort brought in more funds than any other participant. Fully one-half of total funds raised came from Lizzie's individual contacts and those made in company with Lisa. Unaccustomed to the attention, the three could not sit quickly enough. Mr. Johnson rose and shook the hand of John and Jacob and embraced Lizzie. It was a proud moment for the Schmidt farm and came just three weeks after Maria told her husband she was pregnant. John could not imagine a better holiday season.

On January 10, Maria lost what would have been the couple's third child. The miscarriage came some fourteen weeks into pregnancy. Early that morning, she experienced a small amount of vaginal bleeding, but said nothing. An hour later, she was doubled over in pain and calling to Morgan,

"Get your father," she said.

Mary Etta had just sent the girls off to school when Morgan jumped from the porch of the big house.

"Auntie" she pleaded, "It's mother. She needs help."

Marit Etta found Maria kneeling on the floor in obvious pain. She immediately noticed the water.

"My God, it's the baby."

John arrived, but struggled to understand what he saw before him. His efforts to comfort Maria were useless.

Marit had noticed John running toward the house and quickly followed. She understood the circumstance, having tended to her sister while in premature labor some years before. Within minutes, Maria gave birth.

"Take Morgan outside," Mary Etta told John.

Clara had wandered into the kitchen.

Morgan looked toward her father.

"I'll take sister," she said. "We'll feed the goats."

Marit recalled Lisa Hansen intervened when a Norwegian friend miscarried. The concern was not for the lifeless child, but for Maria who continued to bleed profusely. Albert was sent to locate Lisa and she promptly returned within the hour with two of her neighbors. They stayed with Maria through the night and into the next day. By evening, Maria was out of danger. The bleeding had stopped and the pain eased, though even the slightest movement caused Maria to wince.

Doctor McKellar arrived the following morning. Miguel had tried to find the doctor earlier, but was told he was in Fargo. He administered morphine and left a small quantity of laudanum, suggesting the most important thing for Maria was rest. The bleeding would continue for at least a week. He told John the bed should be regularly changed. If there was any sign of fever, he wanted to know.

Maria drifted in and out of consciousness for the next two days, then slowly began to regain her awareness. Lisa visited each day and after a week became concerned for her friend's mental condition. Maria was devastated by the loss. A newborn was a gift, not just for the parents, but for everyone on the farm. Jacob carved a small cross which carried the inscription, "Baby Schmidt - March 1881." Only John and Maria watched as he placed the cross at the eastern edge of the cemetery. Maria showed no emotion before retreating to the main house.

John was increasingly troubled by his wife's behavior and insisted she visit with the doctor at his new Casselton office. Maria acquiesced although she considered the visit a waste of time. After a cursory exam, he advised Maria there were no lasting physical effects, but suggested she avoid pregnancy for two years. The doctor offered no support for his recommendation, and Maria wondered if he simply felt obliged to proffer some medical opinion, regardless of worth.

He told Maria, "You have much to be thankful for. Embrace your blessings—your husband, children, and the farm."

John studied Maria trying to gauge his wife's reaction.

"Miscarriage is commonplace," the doctor continued. "There's no reason for melancholy."

The parting comment stung Maria. Losing a child was a travesty. To Doctor McKellar, it was merely a bridge to be crossed. Others had made the crossing, she could as well. The scolding tone brought Maria to tears. John thought about defending his wife, but said nothing. Maria's despondency impacted their marriage and troubled the children, particularly Clara, who wondered what happened to her kitchen companion. John saw wisdom in Doctor McKellar's lecture.

The farm provided support as Maria recovered. Mary Etta entertained Clara in the Rasmussen kitchen while John and his father kept Morgan occupied. Maria put the loss behind her, but never forgot. When asked about her children, she often included, "one taken by the angels." Maria visited the cemetery every Sunday and prayed over the small cross, careful to leave her sadness at the gravesite. There were moments when she still grieved, but always alone. She sought relief in diversion. It was Morgan's first year of education and she became active in the Friends of Casselton

School, quickly assuming a leadership role. She also entertained more than twenty of her neighbors at a gathering to "put up" fruits and vegetables. By the beginning of harvest, Maria gave every appearance the miscarriage was behind her.

John wondered if the yield for 1881 could possibly measure up to the prior year. Was 1880 a harbinger of years to come or an anomaly? Planting had gone well enough. The farm was ready and all crops were in the ground before the recommended date for seeding had passed. By midsummer, John was convinced the wheat crop might be their best ever, but his optimism was dashed. The normally dependable Advance failed with four days of harvest remaining. The two older reapers were unable to fill the void. Before the Advance could return to the fields, a hailstorm laid waste to wheat still standing. Threshing was delayed and shocks hopelessly saturated. Axel Moen pulled one of his machines to meet prior commitments. His son arrived the following day with a smaller ground hog thresher, but the damage was done.

John's hoped for increase in year over year output was not to be. Jacob reminded his son that falling short of a record season was not cause for disappointment. They could not expect every year to be better than the last. Reserves were strong and the farm could easily sustain a reduction in yield. Maria was more caustic, telling her husband if she could recover from a miscarriage, he could get along with fewer bushels of wheat. John quickly forgot the misfortunes of fall, immersing himself in the tasks necessary to prepare the farm for winter.

Christmas followed the pattern established when the Schmidts arrived in Casselton six years earlier. The farm family all played some role in Mr. Johnson's holiday pageant and celebrated together on Christmas Eve and again on Christmas day. The *Christkindche* tradition returned and Jacob spoiled the children. Mary Etta's sister from Pembina and her five children spent the week, adding to the excitement.

The best gift for the Rasmussens came three days after Christmas. Ice sent a two-word telegram announcing, "we're pregnant." Mary Etta was ecstatic. Lizzie had earlier confided despite considerable effort she was unable to conceive. Their prayers had been answered. She anticipated the birth in July. If a boy, the child would carry the name Colvis Rasmussen

III. Lizzie had little knowledge of her deceased stepbrother, but understood him to be a special child. Mary Etta was delighted, but immediately began to fret. What about Lizzie's care? She was sure Lizzie needed help, but who was there to assist? In her mind all things having to do with Montana were primitive. Care for expectant mothers was surely the same. Lizzie anticipated her stepmother's concern. A letter arrived two weeks later telling Mary Etta there was a competent doctor in Livingston and she had more than enough support from friends who often assisted in deliveries and after-birth care. Mary Etta was still not convinced, but travel to Montana was put on hold.

Maria was excited by Lizzie's good fortune, but more so by what she thought to be her own pregnancy. John wanted more children. Her role was to oblige, although she remained troubled by the specter of miscarriage. She waited three weeks to be certain of her condition before telling her husband. On a quiet evening in January, after the children were settled, Maria shared the news. John was cautiously happy, but concerned given Maria's recent experience. He insisted on a visit to Doctor McKellar. Maria agreed though she held an intense dislike for the man. To the surprise of both, the doctor displayed a kindness notably absent in her earlier visit. He told the couple miscarriage, given Maria's history, was a possibility and suggested bed rest each day for a period of not less than two hours. Physical activity must be limited. Maria disliked the doctor's regimen and was quickly admonished by John when she voiced an objection. She was pregnant. If that meant an upset in daily routine, then upset there would be. Mary Etta, Marit and the girls could fill in.

Freidrich's Christmas letter came two weeks after the holiday. He surprised his sister by announcing he and Agnes planned a business trip to Chicago in early spring with a stop in St. Anne's en route and one in Casselton on the return trip. Freidrich was eager to see his sister and revisit what he once knew as the Meyer farm. John and Maria had difficulty understanding a trip to Chicago. They knew from Freidrich's correspondence that Prairie Timber had done well, but traveling across the country for business was beyond their imagination.

His stop in Casselton would be an interesting contradiction. Freidrich sent photographs of the wedding and the reception that followed. Clara immediately concluded Agnes was a princess. She wore a sparkling gown and was attended by a court of young women dressed much the same. The scene had a storybook quality. Given the apparent opulence, princess was an apt description. Maria could not help but wonder how Agnes would react to the comparatively primitive conditions of the Schmidt farm. She mentioned her concern to John. He was unfazed. It was the only farm they had. If Agnes was uncomfortable, she'd have to find other accommodations. Maria expected as much. It would be easy to entertain Freidrich. Her task, entertaining a young socialite of means, was far more difficult.

Melina's letter was also late, arriving the first week in February. The letter was unusually short with no mention of St. Anne's and little discussion of how the farm was doing. She did say Peter was less active in the Grange and considering a run for the Kansas State Senate. Mr. Norton of the First National Bank of Hays City would be managing his campaign. She knew little of politics except Peter was gone for long periods of time, which left Albrecht to run the farm. Her mother promised to write again soon. Maria promptly responded with news of her pregnancy, confiding this time she hoped it was a boy. She said nothing in earlier correspondence regarding her miscarriage and chose once again to do the same. Instead, she described the Christmas just passed, how quickly the girls were growing up and the differences between the two. The Rasmussen and Haugen families were also mentioned along with their role on the farm and her fondness for both.

Albert Haugen told John in mid-February he no longer planned on homesteading. He and Marit would stay as long as John would have them. Marit was content and moving west was likely to result in hardship rather than happiness. The division of labor, once tentative, was now set. John was master; Colvis the nominal farm boss; and Albert responsible for equipment and livestock. All three men were capable of taking the other's task. Jacob filled in as necessary and also took responsibility for recruiting help during the planting and harvest season. John was fortunate. The confluence of chance and design left the Schmidt farm with an enviable group of overseers.

The spring also saw Maria hire permanent help for the kitchen. Feeding family and workers, caring for small animals and tending gardens had become too great a burden. Juanna Martinez joined the Schmidt farm in

March. She had been a seasonal worker on the Cornellious Mann farm where her husband enjoyed full-time employment. Juanna expected to be hired again, but learned there were no positions available. Seasonal positions had already been filled by workers soon to arrive by train. The Schmidt farm was her first stop. The timing could not have been better. The kitchen needed help and Juanna appeared. She had one son and five daughters. John said nothing, but was certain Maria liked the children as much as she did Juanna.

Early in March, John and his father attended an agricultural fair in Fargo. Their purpose was to acquire two McCormick harvesters. The farm's Advance had failed the prior year and crops suffered. His backup machines had been purchased by Karl Meyer and Rolf Neumann many years before. McCormick's just-introduced machine bound stalks on its own which meant fewer workers. The machines also lashed stalks with twine, a significant improvement over wire binders that left behind jagged ends. John purchased two harvesters scheduled for delivery in July. He paid one-half in cash with the balance due in November 1884. That left the new machines to work three harvests before final payment.

Jacob suggested spending a moment with Luther Ogden before returning home. The financier knew the territory as well as anyone and offered trusted insight on what the future held.

Luther told them, "Speculation is nearing its peak and property values will fall. Your neighbor, Cornellious Mann, will find himself in bankruptcy court."

John expressed surprise.

Luther continued. "Mann and his partners have used the bonanza farm as collateral for other ventures."

"What ventures?" Jacob asked.

"Railroading," Luther answered. "One of his lines is rumored to be struggling."

Luther congratulated the Schmidts noting the value of their 900 acres had increased significantly over the past two to three years. They should remain financially nimble and ready to pounce when the distressed Mann farm inevitably collapsed. Jacob was excited by what he saw as opportunity. John saw nothing more than an invitation to join Cornellious Man in financial ruin.

In addition to upgraded machinery, John was making other changes designed to increase productivity. He was slowly beginning to replace stock horses with Percherons, a much larger dray animal. The conversion was slow at first, but had accelerated over the past year. His Norwegian friends had already made the conversion with favorable results. The Percherons were stronger, less likely to tire and generally more docile. They were known to be slower, but overcame the deficit by working longer without rest. The Schmidts chose Percherons simply because they were bred locally. Angus McFarland did the breeding. The bloodlines were not pure, but the horses were everything John required in a dray animal.

A second change had to do with the mix of field crops and rotation. It was a preliminary topic at a meeting attended by John and his father sponsored by the Farmers Alliance. The subject caught John's ear. A young man from Iowa Agricultural College chastised the assembled farmers for their near exclusive planting of a single crop—wheat. His message was clear. Relentless planting of the same crop led to depressed yield. The earth needed time to recover and farmers in the Red River Valley were forsaking the ground they were dependent upon. John recalled slowly declining yields in Pfeifer with a few visionaries suggesting overworked land might be the cause. The young scholar used terms which, at times, confused John, but he understood the concept. He was convinced some acreage should be left fallow or a different crop introduced. In fact, he had done so in the spring, leaving 100 acres as pasture and replacing wheat with oats and barley on another seventy-five. John left the meeting convinced crop rotation deserved more attention.

The 1882 planting season began poorly. A week of heavy rain was followed by a hard freeze. John started as early as possible, but quickly found himself behind the recommended planting date. To make matters worse, the stream which entered the property on the northern boundary overflowed its banks. The torrent had taken with it a bridge and several acres of newly planted ground. John suspected an ice dam upstream, but was reluctant to investigate. The dam would have formed, almost certainly, on the Mann property—patrolled by an unpleasant cowboy carrying a sidearm. He had once told Jacob to stay clear of the fence line or face the consequences. His comments were riddled with insult.

The washout was disappointing, but the farm would survive. Needless confrontation would do nothing to repair the bridge or replant damaged ground. Jacob hired four additional workers and by mid-May planting was back on schedule.

Maria did not receive the promised follow-up letter from her mother until early August. Melina apologized for the tardiness citing family illness. Albrecht's second oldest had fallen sick in early March to a mysterious disease the doctor could not define. He was feverish and lost control of his extremities. Lack of definition did not slow a plethora of remedies. Albrecht and Hilke watched helplessly as the child was exposed to foul smelling ineffective potions. His condition worsened until Hilke finally called for an end to experimentation. The priest was called, but the child began to improve and was now on his feet, though very weak. She also reported that Peter had become listless, particularly over the past three months. He was perpetually tired and his usual interest in the farm all but lost. At first Melina thought it might be his ill-fated run for the Kansas Senate. The campaign ended almost before it began. He faced a native Kansan and civil war general that frequented the halls of the statehouse. Peter was a relative unknown, underfunded, and naïve. Melina used farming terminology to describe the outcome—a thrashing.

She also mentioned Maria's four brothers whose future on the Schafer farm was very much in doubt. The youngest was attending Kansas State University. She believed he would stay in farming, though perhaps not with his father. The others got on well with Albrecht, but not with Peter. Melina expected at least two would soon leave. Freidrich's success could not be denied. They saw the farm as drudgery and often spoke of following in their older brother's footsteps. Maria waited to respond to her mother's letter knowing her father would be interested in the outcome of this year's harvest. Two weeks later she reported field crops were robust. Barring an unforeseen calamity, John expected a slightly better yield on the 640 acres planted in wheat.

The Casselton Station Master brought news from Montana on August 8. Mary Etta saw him as he passed through the gate, snatching the telegram before he had taken ten steps. She had a grandson. Colvis Rasmussen III was introduced to the world just after midnight. Mother and child were doing well. She was relieved. No matter how often Mary Etta was told good care was available in Montana, she continued to fret. Now the delivery was behind them.

Two weeks later to the day, Maria delivered the Schmidts' third child. John had his boy, Calvin Jacob. Given Maria's earlier experience, he was understandably anxious, pacing endlessly between front porch and barn. No one seemed interested in his plight. Even Clara told him to sit down. Mary Etta and Marit were by Maria's side and Calvin came easily. Doctor McKellar's admonition to avoid strenuous work and take daily bed rest had been ignored without penalty. John had been mildly disappointed a few years before by the birth of a second girl. The recollection brought pangs of guilt. Every child was a blessing. His two daughters had proven that many times over.

Though careful not to play favorites, John was especially fond of Morgan. She took an interest in all things farming while Clara was her mother's constant companion. A few hours after Calvin's birth, Clara had already taken her customary place in the kitchen and Morgan, once assured that mother and child were doing well, had ridden out with her grandfather to inspect the footings on the repaired bridge. The actions of each daughter offered testimony to their differences.

Morgan and Jacob were now returning. She was astride the largest of the Percherons, a horse she called "Chipper." She appeared small, but within that demure body was a true farm girl, one who loved the prairie and its rich dark soil. He thought of Calvin and wondered if his newborn son would someday become master. That was the way of things. The son took on the farm while the daughters married and followed their husbands. Morgan may prove to be the exception.

The much-anticipated visit of Freidrich and his new bride was twice delayed. Scheduled to arrive in late spring, the couple now expected to reach Casselton in early September. The first delay was business related. The second had to do with the completion of the Northern Pacific route from Minneapolis to Puget Sound. The connection was completed in late August with the celebrated last spike driven in Gold Greek, Montana. Freidrich's return trip would now be exclusively on NPRR from Chicago to Puget Sound although the final leg was circuitous. The route skirted the North cascades following the Columbia River to Portland before turning north toward Tacoma.

Maria's anxiety grew with each passing day. She was aware Freidrich and Agnes purchased a part-time residence in Tacoma, one that included indoor plumbing and a housekeeping staff. Maria could never match the luxuries so much a part of her sister-in-law's life. She found some relief in a letter from her mother discussing the couple's stay in St. Anne's. Melina said Agnes was a delight and had no difficulty adjusting to her surroundings. John was not concerned about amenities. He trusted Maria and the children would make Agnes comfortable, irrespective of conveniences. He did wish that Freidrich held to the original schedule rather than arriving during harvest. There would be little time for conviviality, but he expected Freidrich to understand. He knew farming and the demands of the season.

Freidrich and Agnes arrived in Casselton on September 10, aboard a specially designed car with just two compartments, each with its own water closet, sleeping quarters and lounge area. Two porters were centrally located, one for the occupants at either end of the car. As the train arrived, Freidrich jumped from the steps of the forward compartment embracing his sister, John and the children. He remained there as Agnes was helped to the platform. Her appearance brought a stop to all activity in and around the station. She was the instant center of attention and comfortable in that position. John saw her as attractive, but something more. She possessed a compelling intrigue, striking in her attire and aristocratic manner. Maria's impression was much like Clara's. She looked and acted like royalty. The distinction between Agnes and those gathered on the platform could not have been more pronounced. She took Maria's hands then knelt embracing Morgan and Clara saying as she did "I have gifts." That brought a gleeful response from the girls and noticeably eased the tension. They were ten minutes on the platform when John noticed the couple had six trunks and at least twenty large boxes. Agnes, tapping on trunks and boxes with her parasol, selected those she wanted transported to the Schmidt farm and those best left at the station.

John was happy one of the Haugen boys brought a second wagon, but wondered if a carriage would have been more appropriate. He was making arrangements with the station master to borrow a hansom when he saw Agnes and the two girls headed away from the station in the smaller of the farm wagons. He looked toward Maria whose affirming nod made it clear Agnes asked for and received permission for the early exit. That left himself, Maria, the baby and Freidrich in the second wagon piled high with baggage.

Freidrich was taken by the change he saw all around him. The train had stopped in Fargo for less than an hour, but he guessed the city's growth at tenfold. Casselton had grown as well, though at a lesser pace. There was a blacksmith, general store, and recently completed hotel. John told him there was more to come, including a newspaper. Freidrich admired the school, which was nothing more than a dream when he left and noted every inch of ground from Casselton to what he knew as the Meyer farm was now under cultivation.

Freidrich and Agnes took up residence in the Meyer cottage. Agnes immediately expressed a desire to see the farm, having changed to what she considered work clothes—a hand tailored riding outfit that Marit termed "exquisite." Morgan offered to serve as guide and held Clara ahead of her on Chipper. Agnes mounted one of the other Percherons. They rode through the fields visiting with Colvis and the Haugen family, found Jacob with the chickens, and spent time in the barn. Agnes was very much at ease on horseback. She frequently visited the stables of Prairie Timber, which held a large number of dray horses used in logging operations. Agnes had taken it upon herself to ensure the animals were well cared for, including a log of hours worked and frequency of rest periods.

Agnes spent her mornings observing fieldwork and entertaining Morgan and Clara before joining Maria, Mary Etta and Marit in the kitchen where she helped with meal preparation. They were busy dawn to dusk feeding the harvest crew. Agnes knew little about cooking, but entertained with tales of travel, logging and the Pacific Northwest. The stories were not meant to self-aggrandize, but simply to share her experiences with new friends. For his part, Freidrich returned to his farming roots, spending most of his day in the field. John had been concerned Freidrich would be a distraction, but his brother-in-law quickly proved him wrong. He attacked every task with a contagious enthusiasm.

On the second night, all four families gathered in front of the big house for the evening meal. As promised, Freidrich and Agnes had gifts—two dresses for Morgan along with a stylish coat, a dress and doll for Clara, and a rocking horse for Calvin. There were also small gifts for the Rasmussen and Haugen children. The adults were not forgotten. Maria received a full set of dishes and cookware and John a case of fine whiskey.

The couple's visit ended two days later. Freidrich was overdue at Prairie Timber and Agnes had social commitments. What had been seen as perhaps an uncomfortable stay turned instead to a joyful reunion. Far from impeding harvest work, Freidrich had contributed to its completion and Agnes was a delightful companion in the kitchen and elsewhere. If she missed the luxuries of her home, it was not evident.

On September 14, John and Maria drove the Freidrich Schmidts to the station. The children said goodbye at the farm and were deeply saddened by the departure—Clara unable to hold back tears. Freidrich donned his business suit, and Agnes again looked the part of a wealthy socialite. The trip to Casselton seemed to pass in an instant. There was a brief embrace and Freidrich and Agnes were gone. They had made a lasting impression, especially on Maria. She marveled at how easily the couple embraced farm life and how quickly they returned to the trappings of wealth. Agnes changed only in external appearance. She maintained the same persona whether in soiled apron or latest fashion. They had become friends. Before leaving, Agnes told Maria she delayed having children much to Freidrich's disappointment. Her experience on the farm and time spent with Morgan, Clara, and Calvin changed her outlook. She now looked upon motherhood in an entirely different light.

The unfortunate circumstances that plagued spring planting had no impact on harvest. By any measure, it was a good year. The new harvesters worked flawlessly, and the farm used the least amount of temporary help since expanding to 900 acres. Conservative management, timely purchases and a healthy dose of luck was beginning to amass a comfortable nest egg. The Schmidts, father and son, had become important depositors at the Casselton Branch of First National. The family's modest success caused John's name to surface as a candidate for various civic appointments. He politely refused although happily contributing funds in support of the Casselton

School. Maria, because of her association with Lisa Hansen, was far more active, participating in various school projects and serving on a woman's club, which focused on social welfare in Cass County.

The year ended with a reversal of fortune and left Christmas a season of contradiction. The Haugens' second youngest, barely five years of age, became ill the third week in December. She developed a high temperature which Marit could not break. Fearing the likelihood of "winter fever," Albert and Marit set out for Casselton. En route she developed seizures and lost consciousness. Doctor McKellar was conflicted. Traditional treatment such as induced vomiting had been called into question and he was left with few options. He tried cold compresses and a tepid bath, turning at last resort to willow bark. Nothing worked and the child died the following morning. Ilse Haugen was buried in the Schmidt family cemetery. At Marit's request, only the immediate family attended. The specter of death hung over the farm as the families prepared for the Christmas holiday. The Schmidt and Rasmussen families participated in the school pageant and returned home to open gifts, most from Jacob and the Freidrich Schmidts. *Christkindche* did not visit the Schmidt farm in light of the Haugen's loss.

The somber mood became less so when Ice and his family surprised everyone arriving unannounced at the Schmidt farm on December 27. The trip was part business and part pleasure. Ice was traveling with a NPRR team called upon to address persistent roadbed problems in Eastern Minnesota. Lizzie suggested they extend the trip to include a stopover in Casselton. Colvis and the Casselton Station Manager were the only ones that knew the family was bound for Dakota. The Schmidts and Rasmussens celebrated the return of Bjartr, mindful of their neighbor's loss.

The Haugens took no part in the holiday, choosing to remain in their home. Maria brought food and small gifts for the children. Albert accepted, but with the admonition the family would prefer to be left alone with their grief. The loss was difficult for both Albert and Marit, but more so for the grieving mother. She could not reconcile the birth of Christ and the cruelty of her child's death. On Christmas Eve, she repeatedly called out to God condemning him for his senseless act. Albert was finally able to contain his wife, but John faintly heard the call on his way to the woodshed. In the main house, the Schmidts and Rasmussens had just sat down to supper.

John called for a pause and the family prayed that Marit be delivered from the depth of her agony.

The years 1883 through 1885 saw few changes on the Schmidt farm. Morgan reached ten years of age and her interest in farm operations grew stronger with each passing year. When not engaged in schoolwork or tending chickens, she was her father's constant companion. Clara split her time between the kitchen and helping her mother care for Calvin.

The Rasmussen girls were both at home—the eldest betrothed to the son of a Norwegian family. A summer wedding was planned. The youngest was now twelve and, like Clara, very much a homemaker. Only one of the Haugen boys remained on the farm. He was a full-time employee and gave every indication he would stay on. John had worried in the past one or both of the families might leave the farm—the Rasmussens to Pembina or Minnesota and the Haugens to homesteading. That was no longer a concern. Both Colvis and Albert were paid well. Profits were shared and both displayed a sense of ownership, although neither held a proprietary interest. If the farm prospered, they did as well. The three families were united by friendship and the bond between them grew with each succeeding year. The elders were referred to as "aunt" and "uncle" with Jacob grandfather to all. John and Maria had a hard time imagining the farm without the two families.

John and his father carefully followed technological changes in farming, but saw nothing in the immediate future that would affect profitability. Combines were gaining favor on the west coast and the southern plains, but the integrated machines took to the fields later and required heads to be dry. A later harvest meant exposure to hail and morning dew was not uncommon in Dakota—even in August. Neither John nor Dakota was ready to embrace the new technology. Entry cost was also prohibitive and outstripped promised gains in productivity. Payback was simply too long. The price of combines was expected to drop with improved manufacturing techniques. Until then, the Schmidt farm was content to rely on their new harvesters, increasing use of draft horses, rigid crop rotation, and sadly, Axel Moen.

John continued to sell most of his wheat to the Minnesota Milling Cooperative, although for the first time he seriously considered selling to a

Funding and Commission Merchant. He liked the idea of risk aversion, but remained skeptical of the process. One autumn constant remained. Axel Moen and his thresherman returned to the Schmidt farm. The two were now speaking. After nearly a decade, Axel apparently decided John held some promise as a Dakotan farmer. The two could even be seen in friendly conversation before the day's work began—unlikely in prior years.

By 1885, farm values had begun to stabilize. The period of unbridled prosperity, which gave rise to wild speculation, was drawing to a close. Luther Ogden was proven correct. Those who came last to the valley were the first to leave—doomed from the beginning, having paid too much for land and ill prepared for the lean years. Prices for wheat were trending downward, while foreclosures and tax sales moved in the opposite direction. A few saw a quick return to prosperity, but not John. He was in Luther's camp—hard times were ahead.

On November 6, 1885, Maria experienced her second miscarriage. The event stood in contrast to what had been the celebration of another successful harvest. Maria said nothing to John of her pregnancy, instead making plans to join Mary Etta on a trip to Casselton to purchase forgotten essentials for winter. The real intent was an appointment with Doctor McKellar. Two days before the visit, she lost the baby. With the exception of Mary Etta, no one on the farm was aware of her condition.

The unfortunate event passed with far less bleeding and discomfort. Her Norwegian friends were again called, but dismissed by nightfall. John was as disappointed in his wife's decision not to share the pregnancy as he was in the loss of the child. Maria offered no excuse saying only that something didn't feel right and she wanted to talk with the doctor. The loss saddened Maria, but she quickly recovered. She had miscarried before, then gave birth to her first son.

The miscarriage had a curious effect on Marit. Following the death of her daughter, she closed herself in the house—her only exception to complete chores and walk late in the evening. Marit's unusual behavior placed a strain on Albert and the one Haugen son still on the farm. Following Maria's loss, Marit offered assistance with the children and some companionship. She drew strength from Maria's resolve. A miscarriage could not be equated to the loss of a child, but Marit saw in her friend a woman who shouldered the burden of tragedy without punishing those around her. To the contrary, Maria's steadfast response lifted the spirits of all. Marit stopped walking at night and began to engage her husband and son. What began as a dutiful response to a friend ended in an epiphany. The change was immediate and within a week Marit once again took on the task of wife and homemaker.

Maria also anticipated a quick return to matriarchal duties, but Morgan would have none of it. She told her mother a longer period of rest was necessary. She dispatched Clara to the kitchen to help Juana and Calvin to the Rasmussen home under the watchful eye of Mary Etta. John was sent to field and barn—anywhere to keep him from underfoot. Morgan deftly assumed her mother's role with only limited guidance from Mary Etta and Marit.

Maria soon found herself immersed in holiday planning, and thoughts of miscarriage gave way to the excitement of Christmas. Her mother, Freidrich and Lizzie all wrote. Peter and Albrecht were troubled by declining wheat prices, but otherwise pleased with the harvest in Kansas. Prairie Timber saw no evidence of economic stagnation. Freidrich acknowledged rumors of a slowing economy, but demand for timber remained strong. The Rasmussens of Montana announced Ice had accepted an "executive" position with NPRR and the family would soon be moving to Tacoma. His new title was Assistant to the General Superintendent of Western Operations. Mary Etta was proud of their son, but troubled by the distance between Casselton and the Pacific Northwest. She thought Livingston a long way off—Tacoma was beyond imagination. Colvis reminded her Freidrich spoke highly of the Washington territory, suggesting Seattle and Tacoma were more advanced than Fargo. Mary Etta was not concerned about development, but rather with seeing her grandson.

Chapter Nineteen:
The Lean Years: Harvesting on Credit

"If one hopes to profit from farming on the prairie or from the purchase of plains real estate, one must be nimble or lucky."
—David Danbom

The spot price for wheat fell by more than ten percent early in 1886 and never recovered. The effect was too much for highly leveraged dirt farmers whose ill-timed speculation meant certain failure. Even the Schmidt farm, with ten years of successful operation, began to feel the economic pinch. John was troubled more by the trend—a decade of falling prices—than he was the year-over-year decline. Markets were no longer local. Worldwide production affected the market for grain. He had little knowledge of what the next year, let alone ten years, would bring. The farm curtailed expenditures, buying only that necessary to maintain operations. He was glad much of the farm's wheat was committed, but wished more of the harvest was covered by a "forward" contract.

Yield reached eighteen bushels per acre on some sections and price held at seventy-one cents. John counted himself fortunate, but was still apprehensive. Earlier in the year, Gunnar Renstrom, an acquaintance of John's, asked to borrow a small sum of money to get through planting. John contacted Eric Hansen and found Gunnar had approached him as well. Eric advised his friend the Renstrom farm carried a mortgage of eighty percent, more than the property was worth. The bank was sure to come first. John respectively declined Gunnar's request.

337

Midyear brought a ray of sunshine to the farm when Morgan and Clara received awards for their educational achievements, and Maria was recognized by the Norwegian women for her contribution to the Casselton community. A week later the youngest Rasmussen girl, barely fifteen, was married. The shy, endearing girls John and Maria met ten years before were now both gone. The wedding was as much ceremony as festival, with the groom's family spending three days on the Schmidt farm.

John scaled back the number of bindlestiffs for harvest and still managed to bring in the crop on a timely basis. Colvis pressed for more help, citing the possibility of spoilage and the large number of workers available at daily rates ten cents below last year's fare. Both sought protection—John for his income and Colvis for his crop.

John told Maria to spend less on Christmas gift giving. He asked his father, the biggest offender, to do the same. The children would understand. Morgan and Clara had friends driven from their land by foreclosure and there was evidence of hardship throughout the valley. In the weeks preceding the annual holiday pageant, Mr. Johnson quietly asked the more fortunate to help those in need. The Schmidts gave both food and money. On Christmas Eve, Jacob offered a much longer prayer of thanksgiving. With tragedy on the doorstep of so many, the Schmidts, Rasmussens and Haugens would see another season of planting.

In St. Anne's, the Schafer farm faced both a slowing economy and the failing health of their patriarch. Melina reported Peter was found in November stumbling through the fields and confused by his whereabouts. He had since regained his faculties, but his left arm hung limp and he struggled to walk even with a cane. The doctor thought improvement unlikely. He was found by a worker on a plot some three miles removed from the original farm. The land had been purchased in better times and left fallow. For reasons Melina did not understand, Peter took it upon himself to prepare the ground for spring planting. She was sure his decision to take on the heavy work contributed to his apoplexy.

For a man accustomed to being in control of all things, Peter was frustrated by his condition. He took out his anger on Albrecht and the farm's four permanent workers. Peter and his eldest, having once struck an accord, were again at each other's throat. Son number three had left for California unable to contend with the never-ending abuse. The youngest Schafer boy, William, was a student at Kansas State Agricultural College, choosing what Peter called senseless book learning. Melina thought it unlikely he would return to the farm. There was little in the way of other news. As in Dakota, her mother reported farm prices generally down and a drier than normal year. She was excited for Hilke's latest pregnancy, and the two families planned to trade homes—the smaller house easier for Peter to negotiate and the larger best for Albrecht's growing brood.

Freidrich also wrote. He and Kurt Haus had sold Prairie Timber and acquired controlling interest in Chehalis Wood Products, a much larger company with holdings throughout the Washington and Oregon Territory. Maria gathered the sale brought a small fortune to her brother. He mentioned new investments in Columbia River fishing and a firm which manufactured equipment for the logging industry. The couple planned to sell their Montesano home and move permanently to Tacoma where a new home was in the planning stage. Travel was next on the agenda, but Agnes must deliver their first child. The baby was due in June. The note included a postscript. Agnes assured Maria whatever their travel plans it would include a stopover in Casselton. Maria was pleased. She felt a kinship with Agnes far greater than what might be expected from their brief association.

Last to be heard from was Lizzie—her letter arrived a few days after the holiday. The couple had settled in their new home, but she was having some difficulty making friends. Ice, though maintaining an office in Tacoma, preferred the field and was often away for days at a time. Lizzie confided she had only a few acquaintances in Tacoma. In Bjartr's absence, her life began and ended with Colvis III. Ice encouraged his wife to get more involved in the community, but the few times Lizzie had done so she felt out of place. The couple had paid a social visit to Freidrich and Agnes, but Lizzie was intimidated by the sophistication and wealth. The problem was not with Agnes, but with herself.

The 1886-87 winter had come early and long-time valley farmers predicted a sharply colder season. They were proven correct. The worst blizzard in memory struck the Dakota Territory on January 9, 1887. Temperatures plummeted to forty degrees below zero and the unrelenting cold held for days. Cattlemen, particularly on the Missouri Plateau, were caught off guard. A decade of mild winters had led to substantial growth in herds. Ranchers were convinced their experience over the past few years would continue. Complacency left them with inadequate shelter and too little feed. Cold and starvation took tens of thousands of cattle. When the weather finally broke, carcasses floated in rivers and cluttered pastures. Many ranchers lost more than half their herds.

For wheat farmers, the disruption brought by the cold and snow came later when rivers and creeks breached ice dams and sent acres of topsoil downstream. For many, the loss was simply too great to overcome. The steady stream of farmers and cattlemen leaving the territory grew to a torrent in late spring. Wagon after wagon descended on Casselton. Most were eastbound, casting aside their dream and hoping to find security with once abandoned family.

Their travels brought them to First Lutheran Memorial Church established by the Norwegian community in 1884. The church was always a sanctuary for local families, but now found itself overwhelmed by desperate transients. John and Maria gave to the relief effort since Eric Hansen was an elder in the church. The travelers sought employment as bindlestiffs to fund their journey, but there were few opportunities. Bonanza farms planned cutbacks in production and were committed to trainloads of workers from the south. Those unable to find gainful employment took what was given, then moved on culling the land for sustenance.

Like many of his neighbors, John had come to believe long growing seasons and tepid winters were the norm. The preceding fall and winter months offered a stark dose of reality. Mother Nature and the market place gave no quarter to the Dakotan farmer. John decided to plant less than 400 acres in wheat and told his father to hire only eight bindlestiffs for planting. Even Axel Moen, who was accustomed to choosing rather than soliciting customers, approached John early in the season to ensure the farm would be using his services.

The blizzard had taken Chipper, Morgan's favorite, along with three cows and a number of stock horses. More shelters were needed as were with larger feed stores and additional fencing to allow quick retrieval of livestock. The freezing temperatures also took more than one-half the chickens. The old coop offered too little protection from the elements—the stove unable to maintain fire through the night. At the height of the storm John forbade Morgan from making the near impossible trek to restart the fire. When her grandfather offered, he was told to stay put. The outcome was a significant loss of hens. A new coop was constructed with two stoves, both capable of heating for twelve hours. The structure represented more than a concession to Morgan and her grandfather. The egg business was now providing a steady source of revenue to the farm. John still disliked the birds, but his disdain was tempered by their contribution to income.

The summer of 1887 saw homesteaders continue to pass through Casselton. The more intrepid were heading west—the majority following an easterly course, crushed by the unforgiving prairie. As they passed one another, the American dream came face-to-face with reality. The newcomers were confident of success, their eastbound predecessors content to end the unpleasant experience.

The Schmidt farm's decision to scale back led to an easily manageable harvest. Yield per acre was good, but total revenue and profitability suffered. By year's end, the price for wheat was near the cost of seeding and supporting the crop. John could only hope conditions would improve the following year. In early December, Lisa Hansen and friend paid a visit to the Schmidt farm. Their church was caring for a German family who spent two hard years on a homestead north of Dickinson. Determined to succeed, the Fischers tried one more season, but abandoned their claim in September knowing it would never carry them through the winter. They headed east and made Casselton before a horse turned up lame. First Lutheran Memorial took them in providing food and arranging shelter. They were eleven in all. Their current host put them up for six weeks, but the housing was not suitable for cold weather. Lisa mentioned the family's plight and John and Maria offered the bunkhouse. Jacob had partitioned his space and was content to have visitors.

"The Fischers are welcome to stay through the winter," Maria told her friend.

Lisa was grateful. "The congregation is sympathetic, but it's hard to find space for eleven."

Damien worked at the church and did the occasional odd job for its members. In exchange, the Fischers were provided with food and clothing. Lisa brought these contributions to the Schmidt farm at least once each week.

The addition of two adults and nine children made for an unusual Christmas. Damien helped Jacob fashion over forty gifts from dolls to housewares while his wife worked in the kitchen and entertained with games, crafts and storytelling. The Fischers joined the farm family in the celebration of Christmas and New Year's. Not wanting to overburden their benefactors, the church made other arrangements for the family in early January.

Melina's annual letter arrived a few days after the holiday. The note was short. Albrecht, Hilke and their children were doing well. Only one Schafer son remained on the farm and his tenure was in question. She mentioned the farm had also scaled back operations, but provided no detail. Her only reference to Peter was the suggestion he was doing as well as could be expected. Maria took that to mean her father's health was failing.

Freidrich's note carried an entirely different tone. He made no mention of the dismal farm economy, but rather spoke of progress on their new home and travel, perhaps to Europe, sometime in the next two years. Agnes penned a short note and apologized for not sending gifts. She was busy decorating and commitments interfered with holiday planning. Instead, she sent six freshly minted Morgan silver dollars, two for each of the children, and a $50.00 Montgomery Ward gift certificate for the family. She closed with the words, "Hoping to see you."

January 12, 1888 saw another epic blizzard—one that rivaled the massive storm of just one year before. Unseasonably warm temperatures gave way to sub-zero readings and winds in excess of fifty miles per hour. The sudden change, which took place over a period of a few hours, came with blinding snow, leaving much of the territory buried under massive drifts. Dakotans were trapped by the unexpected onslaught. The Sioux called the unholy combination "*Waziyati*", meaning its touch resulted in death. Mr. Johnson understood the meaning. Recalling the experience of Adam and Lucia Johansen, he kept the children at school. NPRR brought additional firewood and collected enough food to last through the following morning. Others school masters were not as wise, choosing to dismiss their students. Over 200 Dakotans died, many of them children trying to find their way home. The Meyer Farm Road had but one casualty. Janne Nilsen, a single mother of two, left her home in search of the family's only cow. She was found the following morning frozen to death twenty feet from her front door.

John picked a wintry morning in late February to assess the farm's readiness for planting. The weather matched both his mood and the outlook for the Schmidt farm. On a similar ride a decade earlier, he dreamt of leaving a much larger farm to his children, but conditions over the past two years had shaken his confidence. The farm was still on solid footing, but if bad weather and declining wheat prices persisted, the depth of their resources would be tested. He reached the Mann fence line and wondered how long the colossus would endure. Luther suggested no more than two years. John once coveted the ground, but not today. His focus was getting through the year—the farm would take no chances. Perhaps someday expansion would again be considered, but the farm economy must first improve.

John swung away from the Mann property riding south. As he did, his thoughts turned to family. The girls were growing up quickly. Morgan was a young woman and Clara not far behind. Age did nothing to mitigate their differences. If anything, each passing year saw less similarity. His eldest was sure of herself and at times bossy. Clara was proxy to Maria, a steady hand in the kitchen and her brother's caretaker. As a four-year old, Calvin was something of a mystery. He was a happy child and content with the world around him. Even at this stage it was clear he was more Clara than Morgan. He wondered who among his children would take up the yolk of farming. Morgan was the farm girl and already had thoughts on management. Clara wanted nothing more than motherhood and family. He expected an early marriage for his second daughter. John smiled when he thought of Calvin's destiny. He was perpetually distracted and Maria was sure he lived in a world all his own. Conversations with Calvin were decidedly one way. He had a habit of cocking his head when spoken to and often wandered off midway through the discussion.

John reached a small rise and could see the farm in the distance. Two fence repairs had extended his ride and Maria would be concerned. She was the center of child-rearing and household, the hub around which day-to-day farm life revolved. Her paradigm role was too often ignored. A week before, he had acknowledged her contribution when she announced there would be a fourth Schmidt child. John was apprehensive about the birth recalling her history of miscarriage and wondering aloud how the farm could exist without its matriarch. She quickly reminded him three children were carried to term—there was no reason to believe the next would be any different.

Maria's announcement rekindled one of two subjects Jacob would not let go. Whenever the first was mentioned—an addition to the main house; the second—acquisition of the Mann property, inevitably followed. Both John and his father believed the main house was too small, but neither saw the project as a necessity. There was no such middle ground on purchase of the Mann farm. Jacob had become obsessed with its acquisition.

John scolded his father, "Neighbors are losing their farms and you talk of expansion."

"Cornellious Mann will fail," Jacob replied.

"We may as well," John answered. "There's a glut of wheat."

"Someone, not the Schmidts, will get the best property in the valley," Jacob countered.

John left his father still mumbling about opportunities wasted. Over the past year, Jacob's demeanor had become less docile and more argumentative. Even small disagreements had the potential to become hostile. John thought his father's behavior was simply a byproduct of age. Maria saw something more. She noticed Jacob had become increasingly forgetful and there were periods when he seemed lost. Lisa Hansen mentioned an uncle who became more belligerent with loss of memory. John might have dismissed his wife's concern were it not for an incident a month earlier. He sent his father to retrieve Colvis who was working in the fields, but instead Jacob rode to Casselton. Marit found him at the general store. He was talking about Pfeifer and Helena.

In early March, John gathered Morgan and set out for Fargo. He purposely left his father at home since he intended to visit Luther Ogden. The Mann farm would surely be discussed and Jacob would likely disrupt the conversation. Their first stop was a meeting of the newly formed Populist Party, an extension of efforts to politicize common grievances among Dakotan farmers. The party espoused an increase in the money supply, an end to private ownership of banks, and nationalization of transport services. John had no debt so money supply and banking were not significant issues. He was interested in the relationship between railroads and elevator operators. Collusion had long been recognized in the movement and storage of grain. Railroads, working in consort with the elevator operators, manipulated price, often to the detriment of growers. Ranchers also suspected wrongdoing. They too were dependent on forces beyond their control to move, feed and accumulate product.

After an hour of speechmaking absent substantive discussion, John left the meeting and set out to find Luther. En route to the financier's office, he was struck by the number of empty storefronts. The city seemed eerily quiet compared to the frenetic activity of the early eighties. Fargo in the Woods had largely disappeared along with the crowds, chaos, and confusion. Even Luther's office, which now occupied a quarter-block, looked orderly and restrained. When he saw John, Luther immediately broke from his conversation. He was planning a trip to the Schmidt farm, but was now spared the task.

He told John, "Mann and his partners have purchased the right-of-way for another railroad."

"Was the farm used as collateral?" John asked.

"I believe so," Luther answered. "My sources are checking now."

"Too many railroads," John said. "Maybe it's the grant money he's after."

"If the railroads fail, your neighbor will be forced to liquidate at least part of the farm."

Luther did not believe failure was imminent, but the situation bore watching. Mann had another problem. When the farm was created, it resembled a checkerboard. The land grant extended NPRR gave the railroad every other section. The effect was a patchwork quilt which required farmhands to work one section then skirt a series of small farms to work the next. To increase efficiency, Mann purchased many of the intervening sections, but did so near the pinnacle of the speculative boom. Declining wheat prices meant the newly purchased ground was not earning its keep. Luther expected Mann to be gone in two years or perhaps sooner. John told Luther to keep him apprised, but for the moment he would be interested in only a fraction of the 13,000 acres, if any.

While John and Luther discussed the Mann farm, Morgan was dispatched to purchase needed supplies. She filled her mother's list at the general store and moved on to the mercantile to purchase seed, nails and wire. The two were on their way to Casselton and the farm by midafternoon and Morgan was unusually talkative. John thought he understood. When he arrived at the mercantile, he found his daughter behind the store talking with Gunter Stockman, the owner's son—her shopping list unfilled. Morgan knew Gunter from an award ceremony for scholars hosted by the Cass County Superintendent of Public Instruction.

Morgan blushed when playfully asked "Why did shopping take so long?"

"It just did," Morgan said, quickly changing the subject.

Her interest in the young man gave John pause. The thought "his" girl could someday find room for another man in her life was disquieting.

Maria's pregnancy brought only mild discomfort and she remained active during spring planting. She was sure this delivery would be much like that of Calvin—without complication. Marit suggested she contact Norah Madden, a cousin to Lisa Hansen. Norah immigrated six months earlier and was known to have practiced midwifery for several years before coming to America. Maria earlier declined a visit to Doctor McKellar. She felt the same regarding Lisa's cousin. Mary Etta and Marit were the only attendants necessary. The first signs of labor came at daybreak on July 9 and began in earnest just after noon. The baby was progressing nicely through the birth canal until the shoulder contacted Maria's pelvis. Both Marit and Mary Etta tried to free the baby and, after twenty minutes of less than skillful maneuvering, the delivery was complete. Maria was exhausted, but mother and child gave every indication all was well.

During the ordeal, Albert Haugen was dispatched by John to find Doctor Clive Austin, a retired Army physician, who now made his home in Casselton. Colonel Austin, as he preferred to be called, no longer practiced, but offered consultation. John and Maria had met the colonel at the Casselton School where he sometimes volunteered. In their conversations, they learned he had considerable experience as lead surgeon at both military and private hospitals. Failing eyesight forced retirement and he came west to join his brother who owned a nearby farm. The colonel arrived two hours later. He conducted a perfunctory examination concluding there were no complications. Maria was up and about within twenty-four hours. Three days after the birth she felt slightly nauseated and feverish. On the morning of the fourth day Maria began to experience severe abdominal pain and the fever was elevated. The colonel and Norah Madden were summoned. Colonel Austin was the first to arrive with Norah just behind.

"It's childbed fever," he said. "I saw two cases in Virginia."

"My God," said a terrified Norah.

John was confused, but knew from the look on Norah's face his wife was facing a serious challenge. Norah erased all doubt, reaching for John's hand.

"You should prepare for the worst," she said.

John had another son, but at what cost? Tavendar Patrick Schmidt could be facing life without his birth mother. Maria's condition steadily worsened. She was often delirious and when lucid suffered intolerable pain. A feeling of helplessness and inevitability settled over the main house. Colonel Austin slept in the bunkhouse. He rejected Norah's old-world suggestions as likely to worsen Maria's condition. A Norwegian wet-nurse known to Norah was called upon to feed Tavendar. Cold compresses were used to manage the fever and a small dose of morphine to ease pain. He suspected infection caused by unclean hands attempting to dislodge the baby. Whatever the cause, Maria would have to wall off the illness on her own.

Five days after Tavendar's birth, the fever broke. Maria awoke and immediately asked for the baby. Clara lifted the newborn from his crib and placed him adjacent to his mother. Maria looked at John. His reassuring nod suggested the baby survived the ordeal without complication. The crisis had passed, but not without consequence. It would be two months before Maria regained her strength. Colonel Austin was uncertain of the after effects, but advised against too much exertion. For once, Maria took the doctor's advice. She turned to her neighbors, children and Juanna to complete her chores. For John, it was an experience not soon forgotten. He could have easily lost his wife. There would be no more children for the John Schmidt family.

While Maria faced the near unthinkable delivering her fourth, Agnes had given birth to Sophia Alden Schmidt, the middle name that of her grandmother's family. Sophia came into the world July 15 in her Tacoma home attended by the family's physician and two nurses, one of whom took up residence three days prior. According to Freidrich, Agnes bore up well throughout the ordeal. There was already a nanny in place and the family was planning travel to begin next spring. Freidrich assured Maria any excursion would include a stopover in Casselton. Maria wondered who suggested the nanny, probably Freidrich. She smiled thinking young Tavendar had a nanny as well—his sister Clara.

John stayed true to his conservative approach, leaving more than a third of the farm without crops. Yield per acre was good, but output reflected the lesser ground under cultivation. Farms in the valley continued to fail as did homesteads and cattle ranchers to the west. He could plant more wheat, but to what end? Better to focus on maintenance, particularly projects that required little or no expenditure. Colvis spent his days removing stumps and other obstacles to plowing while Albert turned to equipment repair and shoring up outbuildings. John had long since given up on predicting when the price of wheat might rebound, but when it did the farm would be ready.

December was marked by an unusual number of snow events, the last of which took place just before the Christmas holiday. The result was a more subdued pageant—one more in keeping with the hardship faced by many of the students and their families. The Schmidts gathered together in modest celebration as did neighbors lucky enough to escape the bank or County Tax Collector. Offering thanks for their deliverance became as important as gift giving.

Wheat prices had steadily declined over the past two years, but recently indicated some sign of leveling. The reversal, albeit slight, provided hope for the coming season and a reprieve for the bonanza farm of Cornellious Mann. Jacob closely monitored Mann's tenuous financial condition and gave his son little rest. He had demanded following the harvest that Luther Ogden contact the beleaguered owner offering to buy three sections north of the Schmidt farm. John was unwavering. The Schmidt farm was not ready for expansion. John had created something of a cocoon. If he avoided rash decisions of the type his father advocated, the farm's security was assured. His scaled-back operation provided little for surplus, but also meant freedom from indebtedness. Success was no longer defined by the size of the farm, but rather the ability to put crops in the ground next spring.

The Kansans faced a similar circumstance. Melina characterized the year as a struggle given the dismal market for agricultural products, particularly wheat. She reported that Peter's left side had begun to atrophy and his role in managing the farm grew less significant with each passing day. He was master in name only. If there was any good news, it was that Peter and Albrecht were getting on better. The younger sons were all gone. Save Albrecht, the exodus was complete. Their departure angered Peter, but health tempered his response. Gone were the outbursts of the past. He was now reduced to sulking.

Freidrich also wrote. The baby was doing well and Agnes eager to have another. He was no longer engaged in day-to-day management and missed the give and take of direct supervision. The "club," which Freidrich visited each day, offered little in the way of stimulation. Boredom was behind plans for travel to Europe. He was ready, but Agnes thought pregnancy should come first. The correspondence gave no indication how the debate might end, but Maria suspected Agnes would prevail.

Lizzie wrote from Tacoma as well. She was adjusting to her new home and reported Ice and the baby were doing fine. Maria knew from conversations with Mary Etta that Ice continued to advance in the NPRR hierarchy—his last promotion leading the couple to consider a new and larger home. The same correspondence referenced Lizzie's difficulty in conceiving. She had consulted with a doctor, but came away with the opinion she knew more than the supposed specialist. Lizzie was tired of advice, professional and otherwise. She closed saying, dependent on pregnancy, the family hoped to return to Casselton for the Christmas of 1889. Ice had time coming and his position allowed free travel.

In the midst of family correspondence came an unexpected letter from Jacob's former associate in Pfeifer, the blacksmith Stephan Haus. The correspondence had been in transit for more than three months and showed signs of tampering. The first stop was St. Anne's where it was forwarded to Casselton by Anna Schneider, still working at Pallitto's General Store.

Stephan spoke of change in the village, but not of its source or motivation. The *Kontor* had completed the takeover of schools, judiciary, and public works. No daughter colonies had been established and the number of Pfeifer youth serving in the military grew daily. Stephan never mentioned the Czar, perhaps fearful of censorship, but the message was clear. The Crown had dealt a crushing blow to *Volga Deutsch* autonomy. *Russification* was near complete. The note closed with a plea. Stephan had not heard from his son in fourteen months. His last correspondence had Kurt contemplating a voyage aboard the steamship *Malaga Sami* bound for the South Pacific. Stephan asked that his letter be forwarded to Freidrich on the chance his former partner knew something of Kurt's whereabouts. The ship and his son had both gone missing. A similar request had been sent to the Schafers.

On February 22, 1889, Grover Cleveland signed an omnibus bill providing entry of North and South Dakota to the union of American states. Mr. Johnson asked the students of Casselton Secondary to write an essay on what the territory's ascension to statehood meant to its citizens. Morgan's essay was one of those chosen to be read at the Casselton's celebration, even though she devoted a paragraph to the inconvenient fact the Sioux owned, through treaty, three-quarters of what would soon be South Dakota. John had not planned to attend the event, but changed his mind with the selection of Morgan's essay. He intentionally kept a good deal of space between himself and politics, occasionally participating in meetings of the Farmers Alliance, but nothing more. His reticence to engage was resented by some of his Norwegian neighbors, who believed the farm and its 900 acres should be an active participant in their cause.

The year saw few changes on the Schmidt farm. John followed the tepid acceptance of steam tractors and the more widespread use of combines in the western states. The savings in manpower were noteworthy, but he understood most innovation was beyond his reach and would remain so until conditions in the marketplace improved. Wheat prices were stuck at fifty cents per bushel, leaving him with little or no tolerance for risk. Only essential purchases would be made. He did find some comfort in knowing the farm stared down the worst of conditions and was still on solid footing.

Cornellious Mann had no time to contemplate the future. His effort was devoted to escaping the past. The first of his ill-timed railroad ventures was on the edge of collapse and the others a significant drain on resources. Lower prices for wheat taxed his shrinking resources. In June of 1889, Luther Ogden wrote the attorney representing the Mann property offering to buy several sections of the bonanza farm, a few of which bordered the Schmidt farm. The attorney thanked Luther, but indicated they were not interested. Luther was not fooled. He believed a sale was more imminent than counsel let on. John was aware of Luther's contact, but told the financier he was not ready. Jacob got wind of the discussion and threatened to contact the Mann creditors directly. John was tired of his father's interference.

"We're not ready to buy," he told Jacob.

"If not now, when?

"When I'm ready," John answered. "Stay clear of Luther and his negotiations."

Jacob was surprised by his son's intensity. He sought a reprieve from Maria, but got none.

Earlier in the year, Colvis had told John there were no workers in the Mann fields. Even the armed guard was missing. John was to learn that Mann had reduced cultivated ground by one-half and canceled a trainload of workers from the south. His farm boss had trouble finding bindlestiffs and the farm was in disarray, barely qualifying as a bonanza enterprise. Some of John's neighbors took delight in Mann's travails, but not John. His neighbors' struggles were exacerbated by poor decisions on farming and finance, but the real problem was the depressed price of the farm's predominant crop—the same problem faced by the Schmidt farm. Conditions did not improve in the fall. The harvest was met by prices largely unchanged from the year before.

Morgan's secondary education was fast coming to an end and many of her friends had already left school. Dire economic conditions had driven families to withdraw their children, particularly daughters. John and Maria never considered an early end to Morgan's secondary education, instead insisting she complete her full complement of studies. For the past two years, she had taken a keen interest in the science of agriculture. Her school kept a small cache of publications offered by the Farmers Institute of Minnesota and by a similar organization in South Dakota. Morgan often brought the publications home and used them to question her father's decisions. Some discussions turned confrontational with her father taking the contrary position based on nothing more than his age and experience. John knew farm machinery and the marketplace, but not the sciences. Their kitchen table disputes worked to the benefit of both—John kept abreast of plant structure and genetics while Morgan learned practical farm management.

Morgan's intense curiosity in all things farming did not escape the notice of Miss Amelda Sutherland, a first-year Casselton teacher. She saw Morgan as a candidate for further studies and suggested advancing her education at Fargo's soon-to-open North Dakota State Agricultural College. Morgan would be close to home yet able to hone her skills in what Miss Sutherland was sure to be her lifetime pursuit. Morgan was ambivalent. The learning appealed to her, but not the environment. She saw college students as children of privilege. Miss Sutherland herself came from a wealthy family in Minneapolis. Morgan wondered how a farm girl would be looked upon. Her only exposure to wealth was Aunt Agnes. A room full of students with her sophistication was intimidating. Miss Sutherland approached John and Maria to bolster support for her proposition. Maria embraced the idea; confident Morgan could do the work and adjust, in time, to college life. John was less enthusiastic. He was an advocate of education, but trusted as much in experience as classroom tutelage. Although unsaid, he was also bothered by the experience of the Schafer family, whose youngest had left for college and never returned.

Clara quietly watched the discussion. She had grown accustomed to Morgan as the center of attention. John Schmidt was a farmer. So too was his first born. Father and daughter had much in common. Clara understood and held no resentment. Her chance at homemaking was fast approaching. Until then she was content to be her mother's helper and surrogate mother to Calvin and Tavendar.

The two sisters were the perfect complement to each other, creating an orderly division of labor which favored their skills and interest. Calvin simply watched his sisters, an indifferent observer who rarely demanded attention. Lack of purpose, rather than order, characterized his daily life. Maria was sure he lived in two worlds— one he shared with his family and the other known only to himself. John often found Calvin staring blankly at the horizon.

"What are you looking at?" his father asked.

"Nothing," Calvin answered The query never jarred his son to action. He simply returned his gaze to emptiness. Like Morgan and Clara, the Schmidt brothers were a world apart in behavior. Tavendar was both angel and black sheep, although the latter seemed a more apt description. He was easily the most disruptive of the children. His entry to the world was discordant and his behavior as an infant the same. He was demanding, endlessly fussy, and stubborn. Both John and Maria expected their youngest would be a handful.

The decision on whether to enroll in college proved difficult for Morgan. Her mother embraced the idea and Miss Sutherland was convinced she was the perfect candidate for further education. John avoided the discussion, all the while hoping she would stay on the farm. Miss Sutherland managed to convince Morgan to visit the college, which planned to accept its first student in December. She would provide the escort. The pair traveled to Fargo near the end of school year where Morgan, on her own, visited with Kendal Lehmann, Dean of Agricultural Studies. The office was somewhat intimidating with its books and large desk, but not the dean. He was a kindly gentleman, whose weathered features suggested he spent as much time in the field as in the classroom. Morgan sat quietly as he discussed the proposed course of study.

"A revolution is coming in agriculture," he said. "Its impact will be felt on both small and large farms alike."

Morgan understood, but wondered how her education would make a difference on the Schmidt farm.

The dean provided the answer. "Those with the knowledge to successfully apply science and technology will endure. The others will find it difficult to survive."

Morgan asked, "Will small farms continue to exist?"

"A few, but larger farms, like AMG, will dominate."

Morgan said nothing of her father's deep dislike for corporate farms.

Near the end of their discussion the dean asked Morgan if the Schmidt family might be interested in setting aside land for an experimental station. The college was developing its own farm, but wanted space, distinct from academia, to ensure studies matched prairie conditions.

"We'll need sixty acres," he said. "Faculty and students will direct activities."

He explained the Schmidt farm would be reimbursed for use of the land at one and one-half times the earnings per acre for the farm's predominant crop. Morgan thought that unnecessarily complex, but said nothing. Plans called for three buildings—a research center, housing and a small equipment shelter. The structures would accrue to the host farm if and when the college closed the station. The professor expected Deere, McCormick, Champion and others to bring their equipment to the station. Educators specializing in agronomy would be on hand as well. All of this equipment and research would be available to the host farm. The college hoped to have a working station within eighteen months. A contract specifying the respective roles of each party was now being prepared.

Morgan answered before the dean finished his sentence, "Father would be happy to participate."

"Your farm would be perfect."

Morgan wondered if she had spoken too soon. John Schmidt may be less willing than his daughter to share the farm.

That evening Morgan told Miss Sutherland she was leaning toward enrollment. By morning, she was already beginning to waiver. Morgan found the course of study intriguing, but fears on how a farm girl would be seen by fellow students resurfaced. John was waiting at the station when the pair arrived in Casselton. They left Miss Sutherland at school and started toward home. Morgan told her father the college was looking for a farm to host an experimental station. She was chagrined to learn he did not share her enthusiasm. The plan for reimbursement was confusing and he disliked giving up land. Morgan did her best to explain that ownership was not affected and the farm would be left economically whole. Her father had no interest in allowing "intruders" on his farm—particularly when the sum of their experience consisted of turning pages in an unintelligible text. He saw enough of that at county fairs. Morgan continued to push for the station and, before they reached home, John agreed to at least entertain a proposal.

Morgan believed Kendal Lehmann was correct. The future belonged to those who could exploit the coming change in agriculture. She had also reached the conclusion that college life was not for her. Perhaps her father would see the experimental station as an opportunity to continue her education without the need to leave home. John was thinking the same way, but said nothing, believing it was a choice best made by Morgan. A week later, Morgan told Miss Sutherland she would not enroll. She hinted at attendance in the future, but knew this to be unlikely.

John Schmidt was delighted. Morgan's decision to stay close to home left him with a new partner and the two became inseparable. She was a proponent of his scaled back planting scheme and her contagious enthusiasm for all things farming did much to mitigate the harsh reality of difficult times. Colvis worried a second master might lead to confusion, but soon learned John and his daughter spoke as one. Morgan not only left him to his work, but thanked him for his contribution. A step John, by his nature, rarely took.

A week before harvest, John, Morgan and Colvis took one last survey of crop conditions, particularly the acreage acquired from Rolf Neumann. Wheat had been slow to develop there and it was decided to give the crop ten more days before cutting. The farm boss left the pair as they were returning to the main house. Morgan took the opportunity to ask her father a question—one she wanted to ask for weeks, but was afraid to do so. Near the end of planting season, she had noticed her father sometimes sought an anchor for his left hand. Even today the hand was not on the reins, but tightly gripped the saddle horn.

Morgan took a deep breath and asked, "What makes your hand shake?"

"My hand isn't shaking," he answered.

Morgan smiled, "It will, when you let loose of the saddle."

John dismissed the query. "It's temporary, comes and goes."

Morgan knew that to be a lie. She sensed her father shared her concern, more so than he let on.

Morgan told her mother of the conversation and she in turn asked the same question of her husband. She was rewarded with a less civil retort.

"We begin harvest in a week, and you worry about an imaginary ailment?"

"And why not?" Maria answered. "Without you there would be no harvest."

Maria allowed the matter to drop, but planned to confront her husband again, perhaps with the help of Morgan and her father-in-law. Her concern was rooted in the experience of a long-term acquaintance, Ingrid Dahl, whom she met at a gathering to can fruit and vegetables. Ingrid exhibited behavior similar to John's, but more pronounced. She was now housebound. Maria had no understanding of the tremors or what treatment regimen, if any, was recommended. She only knew John was unlikely to take action and she must.

The holidays saw a new family join in the Schmidt Christmas celebration. In the spring of 1890, Clara had begun a courtship with Aaron Bergmann, the eldest son of Aaron and Priscilla Bergmann. The family had been living with relatives in Sioux City before opening an apothecary and emporium in Casselton. The latter included an "elegant" woman's department called *Marche de la Mode*—nothing more than a few catalogs.

Clara and Robert met at school and were often seen together at community gatherings. He had since become a frequent visitor to the Schmidt farm. John expected Clara to beat her sister to the altar, but her relationship with Robert was proceeding faster than he liked. Robert was two years older than his naive daughter and far more worldly. He talked incessantly, not of farming, but of clothing—an unusual topic for a young man. John had been told by Mr. Fenwick, owner of the Casselton General Store, that the Bergmanns were heavily in debt. He took this with a grain of salt as the Fenwicks and Bergmanns were competitors.

John was concerned the courtship would result in marriage, a prospect he abhorred. He shared this thought with Maria and was told not to intervene. Standing in the way of the budding romance would only make the attraction greater. The Bergmanns talked with John and Maria following the Christmas pageant and were invited by Maria to visit the Schmidt farm sometime following the holiday. They did so the second week in January, much to John's disappointment. Aside from their children's relationship, the couples shared nothing in common and conversation was strained. Mrs. Bergmann spoke of fashion, while her husband said nothing.

In the three weeks leading up to the holiday, the Bergmanns gave Clara her first taste of working off the farm when she agreed to part-time employment in the emporium. Clara was excited. John was livid. Her salary was generous for retail, but traveling to and from the store proved a burden for all involved. Clara would later confide to her mother that Mr. Bergmann was a difficult man to work for and her salary was yet to be paid. Maria concluded her husband's less-than-flattering assessment of the Bergmanns was correct. Clara was finally paid a month later, but there were deductions she didn't understand. She said nothing to her mother or father.

The holiday also brought an unwelcome surprise to the Rasmussen family. The long-planned visit by Ice, Lizzie and the baby was postponed. Construction delays on NPRR's two-and one-half mile tunnel high in the Cascade Mountains were the cause. Lizzie advised her stepmother rock slides were wreaking havoc and Ice did not feel he could leave the Tacoma office. Lizzie sent her apologies and told Colvis and Mary Etta the family would try to visit in late spring. The Rasmussens' eldest daughter surprised the family, deciding at the last minute to spend the holiday on the Schmidt farm. Their arrival on Christmas Eve did much to ease the sadness of Lizzie's change in plans.

A few weeks before Christmas, Melina wrote with news of the Schafer farm and St. Anne's. Her father was much the same though he had recently taken to driving one of the smaller farm wagons to observe fieldwork. The drive became a ritual and served to lift his spirits. Melina was glad to have him out of the house. Albrecht was proving to be an effective manager and the Schafer farm was holding its own, while hoping for some improvement in the price of grain. Hilke was endlessly fertile, turning out children at an astonishing pace—six boys and two girls. Her mother thought there were as many children as chickens, but enjoyed the circumstance.

Freidrich also included a note with gifts sent from Tacoma. He had convinced Agnes that travel should come before pregnancy. The couple had decided on Europe as their destination. Stops were planned in London and Paris. He did have one sad note. An investigator discovered his friend Kurt Haus had gone down with the "*Malaga Sami*" in a typhoon north of the Marquesas. There were three survivors. Kurt was not one of them. Just after selling Prairie Timber, his former partner prepared a will and named Freidrich as executor. The task was proving difficult and each day brought a new revelation, including unknown investments, and the likelihood of a wife on the Island of Hawaii. Kurt's life was far more complex than Freidrich realized.

Late in February John slipped out of the house before daybreak. His solitary ride was intended to assess the farm's readiness ahead of spring planting, but there were other reasons for the excursion. The persistent tremors had begun to affect his daily life. He suspected no one was fooled by his often repeated contention things were getting better. He managed to sidestep inquiries from his wife and daughter, both of whom feared his response if the subject were breached. John wanted time to think. He needed advice, but had no idea where to turn. In a few minutes, he managed to convince himself to leave well enough alone. His condition would improve.

The other issue on John's mind was expansion, an unlikely consideration given the depressed state of the farm economy. The Clerk of the Cass County Court told Luther two liens had been filed on the Mann property in December of 1890. Cornellious Mann was running out of options. The second of his three railroad ventures had fallen into receivership, borrowing was next to impossible, and banks were growing weary of his deception. Economic conditions were dire. Europe was on the cusp of recession and financial collapse on the Continent often foretold what was in store for the United States.

For John, the timing could not have been worse. If the Mann empire collapsed, he would be faced with an unpleasant decision—purchase some part of the bonanza farm and jeopardize his security, or watch as someone else, perhaps AMG, captured the distressed property. Even in these dire economic times, John knew good land was sure to be snapped up, leaving him to wonder what might have been. He disliked the timing, but felt his hand was being forced.

Maria had long since lost patience with her husband's decision to ignore what she plainly saw as tremors. She fabricated an excuse to visit Casselton and sought the counsel of Colonel Austin, thinking he knew something of her husband's condition. He did. While serving as medical director for the Soldiers' Home in Bath, New York, he had diagnosed several cases. The colonel identified the condition as Parkinson's disease, named for an English surgeon who first described the malady in 1817. He was relatively sure of his diagnosis, having seen John in Casselton just before Christmas. His symptoms mimicked the cases he had seen in New York. Parkinson's affected the nervous system. There was no cure. The rate of progression was the only unknown.

Maria expected as much given Ingrid Dahl's experience, but the stark reality of the diagnosis left her deeply saddened. Her husband would not take well to confinement. Colonel Austin suggested a visit with Horace

Saalberg, a Minneapolis research physician experimenting with treatment of the disease. He offered to write the doctor describing John's symptoms, but only after John visited the colonel for a brief examination. Maria expected resistance, but found her husband willing. Doctor Saalberg took over a month to respond. He confirmed the diagnosis, but recommended any visit be postponed. He was working with patients whose symptoms were far more advanced. The treatments relied on belladonna and electrical stimulation, both experimental and with uncertain outcomes. He told Colonel Austin he preferred to see John in perhaps six months. It was not what the colonel expected and not what Maria hoped for. They were left to watch and wait.

The Schmidt farm received a letter from North Dakota State Agricultural College announcing plans for the experimental station had been temporarily placed on hold. Kendal Lehmann cited the flagging economy and a smaller than anticipated enrollment. Morgan was disappointed and expressed that sentiment in the return letter written for her father. She also affirmed the farm's interest in meeting with the dean if and when the college decided to go forward. Since the subject was first introduced, Morgan had convinced her father the station would be an asset. John still saw the arrangement as something of a bother, but if it kept Morgan close to home, he was amenable. The dean's letter closed with the notation "hoping to see Morgan in the fall."

Miss Sutherland had obviously spoken with Professor Lehmann. It was time to put an end to the discussion. Her first thought was to write Miss Sutherland, but upon reflection thought it best to speak with her in person. Two days later she rode to the school and told the teacher she would not enroll. She gave no reason and Miss Sutherland asked for none. Morgan considered using her father's condition as an excuse then quickly reconsidered. She thought the tremors to be worse, but he was still very much in control of mind and body. If her father learned of the ruse, he would be angry.

The season was upon them and farmers, who often found it necessary to borrow against the harvest, planted fewer acres. The Schmidt farm bucked the trend. Based on nothing more than a hunch, Morgan convinced her father to reject convention and add acreage in wheat. Planting had gone well and by mid-June Morgan's plan was looking very good. Prices ticked upward and the farm dared hope the market might be improving. John was not sure what motivated his daughter's decision or why he agreed, but he was glad for the outcome.

His euphoria suddenly dimmed when faced with the proposal he had been dreading for months. On June 19, Robert Bergmann asked for Clara's hand in marriage. The proposal took place on the front porch of the big house. John suspected this day would come and was prepared. Robert tentatively approached and made his request. As he spoke, Maria quietly listened, while John simply studied the young man.

"It's far too soon," he said.

Maria, rather than scold as he expected, simply looked at him quizzically.

Clara stared at her father then tearfully cried, "Speak to him mother."

Robert tried to say something, but simply babbled.

John told the couple to wait on the porch and taking Maria's hand retired to the house.

"Clara is too young," John told his wife.

"I agree, but I'm afraid of what will happen if you forbid the union."

"I'm not forbidding, just delaying," John answered.

The couple returned to the porch.

"I'll approve as long as Clara completes one more year of schooling," John announced. "You can marry in June of next year."

Robert, having found his voice said, "What good is school for a shop-keeper's wife?"

The comment riled John. It was tacit admission of what John long suspected. The Bergmann family was looking for an inexpensive clerk. Clara's dream of becoming a homemaker would come sometime, but not until she completed her servitude. Clara appealed, but John stood firm. A wedding date of June 10 the following year was set. The Schmidts hosted a small celebration in early August to commemorate the engagement. Clara's school-mates attended along with Mr. and Mrs. Bergmann. Robert's parents left in less than an hour, claiming commitments at the apothecary.

Maria wrote to her mother in late July. She was eager to share news of Clara's marriage and John's illness. She received a prompt reply. Melina said only that Clara's betrothal was "nice." Maria interpreted that to mean that her mother, like John, thought Clara was too young. With respect to

John's illness, she mentioned a neighbor who also suffered with tremors. A sentence following was partially erased. Her mother had written something about the neighbor's condition, then thought it best stricken.

The Schafer farm was holding on and it looked to be a better year for corn. Albrecht, Hilke and the children were well. Peter had once again entered the political arena, this time as an activist rather than candidate. He joined the Populist Party advocating a familiar agrarian theme—nationalization of railroads and a fiscal policy which encouraged inflation. The movement had secured a foothold in the nation's capital and appeared to be gaining momentum. Melina did not fully understand the party's goals, but was delighted her husband found a cause.

Albrecht was pleased as well. Peter's new-found interest in politics meant his meandering through the farm would cease, along with his endless critique of Albrecht's farming skills. Melina also included a paragraph on the whereabouts of Maria's younger brothers. Given her father's behavior, she was not surprised to learn they were scattered from California to Alaska. All were a source of constant worry, but apparently doing well.

Following on the heels of her mother's letter, Maria received a note from Agnes. She was pregnant. Freidrich was delighted though he received the news while traveling on business. Agnes only knew her husband was "realigning" investments. She was uncertain what that meant, but knew Freidrich was deeply concerned over the state of the economy. The couple's planned trip to Europe had been canceled. She suspected money was an issue, but Freidrich told her successive years of recession on the Continent had created unrest. Safety was a concern.

The uptick in wheat prices led to a modest improvement in profit, but not enough to escape what increasingly looked to be a decade of stagnation. John met with Luther, but was told Cornellious Mann, against all odds, negotiated a settlement on liens and was looking toward yet another planting season. The northern prairie was mired in a five-year drought, but weather played only a minor role in the hardship suffered by Dakotan farmers. Price was the culprit. For the past several years, wheat had traded in a narrow range, spiking on occasion, but trending downward. In the spring of 1892, the price per bushel threatened to fall below fifty cents. The Schmidt farm again scaled back production.

Chapter Twenty:
Economic Collapse

"Many agreed on a date when the good times ended. One relative optimist wrote, 'farming has at times returned a profit and at times a loss'... Most agreed with his blunt conclusion, there has been no profit in farming since 1885."

—Solender, Department of History,
Columbia University

M aria was determined not to let the angst surrounding a depressed market affect Clara's wedding, particularly since her husband never warmed to the union and his indifference grew with each passing day. Finally, Clara sarcastically asked, "Will you be attending the wedding?"

Coming from his typically demure daughter, the comment pierced John's psyche. He started to offer an excuse, then decided there was none.

"I'm sorry," he said apologetically.

Maria never expected her husband to take an active role in wedding plans and she had long before enlisted the help of Mary Etta and Marit. The planting season slowed their effort, but as June approached, the pace quickened. Priscilla Bergmann was asked to participate, but declined. The recession had taken its toll on the family business and she was content to let the Schmidts bear the expense of her daughter's wedding. She told Maria the Bergmanns invited just five guests beyond the immediate family. The Schmidts were planning on more than 100. The farm family would attend along with friends and business associates. Clara expected all of her classmates and a few teachers. The biggest surprise came when Maria received a note from her mother. She would be making the trip from St. Anne's with her youngest son, who was temporarily excused from his teaching duties. They expected to arrive two days before the wedding and leave four days after.

Peter would not be traveling with his wife and son. No reason was given. Earlier in the year it was thought Agnes and perhaps Lizzie would be attending. That was no longer the case. Agnes had given birth in January and she had no desire to travel with two young children. Maria also suspected there may no longer be a nanny. The tone of Agnes' letter suggested Freidrich was likely in financial trouble. Lizzie decided against the trip as well. She was finally pregnant with her second after seven years of trying. Her doctor recommended she stay close to home. Ice was glad for the excuse. Northern Pacific was locked in competition with the rapidly expanding Great Northern Railroad and facing yet another financial crisis. Leaving the office, given the circumstance, was not a good idea.

One guest of particular interest to Maria was Gunter Stockman, the son and heir apparent to the family's successful mercantile. Morgan and Gunter were seeing more of each other. Maria suspected Gunter was interested, but Morgan less so. John saw the relationship as a good match, facetiously suggesting marriage would result in better pricing from Gunter's father. The relationship had recently seemed to intensify with Gunter scheduling unnecessary deliveries to the Schmidt farm, then spending the better part of the afternoon in Morgan's company. Most of Morgan's school friends were married and Maria feared she might be drawn to Gunter out of fear of becoming a spinster. She tried to engage her daughter on the subject, but Morgan promptly dismissed both the subject and her mother.

Despite his apology, John did his best to stay clear of wedding plans. His only real assignment was to ensure the new leader of the Fargo Diocese, Bishop David Williams, would conduct the ceremony. In mid-April, the Schmidts attended their first mass in years and returned twice thereafter. The diocese was raising money for a cathedral and John and his father contributed, thus securing the bishop's participation. Maria was excited by the prospect.

The wedding party consisted of Morgan as maid of honor while a classmate would stand for Robert. Clara's wedding gown and Morgan's dress were ordered through Bergmanns' emporium. Maria was sure Priscilla agreed to provide both at her expense, but her husband thought otherwise. When Aaron made the delivery, he seemed reluctant to leave. Maria concluded he was waiting to be paid. Afraid to tell John, she took money from egg sales accumulated over the past few years.

The train from Fargo carrying Melina and her youngest son arrived on June 8 at five p.m. Maria had not seen her mother in eighteen years. She was gray and heavier than she remembered, but judging by her exit appeared to be in good health. The two embraced, Maria in tears. Melina then turned to John and each of the children spending the longest time with Clara, the bride to be. They were on the platform for more than a half hour before Tavendar pulled his grandmother toward the wagons. John took the reins of the first with Tav and the youngest Schafer, William, alongside. Morgan guided the other.

In less than a mile, Melina had already assessed what the future held for the Schmidt grandchildren. Morgan was the farmer, every bit the measure of John, and Clara like her mother, but more passive. Calvin, the heir apparent, was reclusive—a follower without leadership skills. Tavendar, though very young, was the cowboy—his personality already too big to be fenced in. She expected neither of the boys would see their twentieth birthday on the farm.

Mary Etta, Marit and Juanna helped with last-minute wedding details allowing Maria and her mother time to visit. They were up half the night catching up. Melina shared with her daughter events not contained in her letters. A funnel cloud had touched down last year destroying a barn and damaging the home she and Peter now occupied. It was since rebuilt. Her father was still somewhat active, touring the farm on occasion and attending meetings of the Populist movement, but Melina saw interest and activity waning.

She had encouraging news as well. Albrecht's skills as a farm manager had grown with each year. He expanded ground under cultivation and was negotiating for commercial property west of Hays City. She was proud of her eldest son. The Schafer farm was as secure as any in central Kansas. Melina was also quick to mention Albrecht's hastily planned wedding to Hilke had blessed her with eight wonderful children, all of whom were attentive to their grandparents.

Clara rose early to watch the sunrise on her last day as a single woman and her first as wife and homemaker. Maria, already in the kitchen, gave Clara a few minutes then joined her on the veranda. The moment was bittersweet as mother and daughter talked of the future and recalled their years together. The pair stood beside an altar built by Jacob and Javier. Bishop Williams sent word he would not be attending due to illness. John wondered if his smallish contribution to the cathedral fund had affected the bishop's health.

A young missionary priest bound for Bismark was sent in his stead. He was a delightful substitute. More than one hundred twenty-five guests attended, and the women of the Schmidt farm set out a buffet, supplemented by their Norwegian neighbors. Luther Ogden provided the spirits—his contribution arriving well before the ceremony. Clara and Robert received a handsome array of gifts, most of them practical and well suited to newlyweds. By five p.m., only a few adults remained, but it looked to John and Maria that several of Clara's friends might be spending the night in the bunkhouse.

There was one early departure. Shortly after the ceremony Marcella Stockman told Maria her son was anxious to leave and the family would be joining him. She gave no explanation, but Maria guessed Gunter made a proposal of courtship to Morgan and her response was not what he desired. Maria took a moment to look for her eldest, but she was nowhere to be found.

Clara and her new husband spent the night in the Meyer cottage. She was due at the Bergmanns at nine a.m. with Robert scheduled to begin his first day of farming much earlier under the tutelage of Albert. The Bergmann stores were suffering financially and Robert was the first casualty. His father, Aaron, correctly assumed Clara could impose on her father to hire Robert until conditions at the emporium improved. Robert would be replaced by his new wife who, as a family member, was expected to contribute to the Bergmann enterprise, with or without pay. Robert knew little of farming and John saw it more a charitable donation than employment contract. He wanted to assign his son-in-law to Colvis, but Maria intervened. Colvis had no tolerance for tenderfoots.

The Bergmanns were amiable, staying on until most of the adults were gone. Priscilla complained of a nervous stomach, but seemed to recover after learning the Schmidts would not be cleaning up until the next day. John noticed Aaron spent a good deal of his time "inspecting" gifts, even opening one to examine the contents. John told Maria he would not be surprised to see Robert and Clara's gifts on display at the Bergmann's emporium. He was promptly scolded by Maria.

John was not sure what to make of the coming year. The harvest of 1892 represented the highest per-acre yield in the farm's sixteen-year history—more than a third the prior year, yet there was only a modest increase in profit. Conditions in the valley were increasingly dire. Each week brought news of another foreclosure as farms hanging by a thread were seized by the bank. Two long-time friends of Eric Hansen, caught up in the speculation of the early eighties, lost their farms to tax sales. The non-farm sector was on better footing, but conflicted by signs of both strength and weakness. Uncertainty, as always, led to retrenchment.

* * * * *

The Panic of 1893 surprised many economists. The preceding year had shown some strength—a reduction in negative balance of payments, lower unemployment in manufacturing and growth in unfilled industrial orders. Yet there were worrisome signs. Production of fossil fuels began to decline as did railroad mileage and employment in the building trades. In February, the Philadelphia and Reading Railroad declared bankruptcy, followed by the Northern Pacific, Union Pacific and Atchison Topeka and Santa Fe. Many smaller railroads also collapsed. The failures crippled industries heavily dependent on rail transportation.

Mining companies also experienced a reversal of fortune. In 1890, Congress, bending to the demands of farmers and mining interests, passed the Sherman Silver Purchase Act, which allowed bank notes to be backed by silver as well as gold. With the United States Treasury a willing buyer, silver production rose algebraically. Overproduction led to falling prices and a flight to gold. Reserves fell to dangerously low levels, at one point threatening the gold standard. Americans began to lose faith in their financial system and bank runs were commonplace. By year's-end, more than 500 banks had failed. In October of 1893, Grover Cleveland managed to repeal the Silver Purchase Act, but the damage was done. Hundreds of mines were shuttered and workers joined their industrial and railroaded brethren among the unemployed. Nearly one in six American jobs were lost and 15,000 companies filed for bankruptcy protection.

The family farm, particularly in the heartland, saw widespread fore-closure and tax sales. The prairie farmer was heavily in debt and borrowing next to impossible.

* * * * *

Cornellious Mann was ensnarled in a web of deceit. He was destitute and facing the prospect of indictment for misrepresenting his assets. Mann's attorney had made contact with Luther Ogden in June of 1892, ostensibly to discuss sale, but a planned meeting was canceled without explanation. The Mann farm had planted less than 5,000 of its available 13,000 acres. The recent history of deferred maintenance and twice failing to meet pay-roll made even that modest objective difficult. The harvest was late and yield per acre less than two-thirds of that experienced in the eighties.

Luther was contacted again in February of 1893. The investors were ready to sell, but if Mann was facing financial disaster, it was not reflected in the price. He wanted $16.80 per acre. Two homes on the property were included in the price, but equipment and livestock were valued separately. Luther penned a two-word response, "too high." The following day he con-tacted the Schmidts to apprise them of his answer.

John agreed with Luther, "Two dollars less, $14.80, is more realistic."

Jacob, as expected, was annoyed. "We should have made a counteroffer."

"There will be no takers at $16.80," Luther answered. "Mann has exhausted his sleight of hand. He's in trouble."

Luther's assessment was correct. The recession was deepening and Mann himself faced the likelihood of prosecution. The farm would soon be available on better terms. Three weeks later Luther's patience was rewarded. A second, hand-carried offer was received. Ezra Bell of the Minneapolis firm of Bell and Lancaster was now representing the Mann investors. The price had fallen to $15.00 per acre with equipment and livestock subject to negotiation. Luther immediately sent a messenger to the Schmidt farm asking John and his father to meet with him in Fargo the following day. He also sent a telegram to Bell requesting a tour of the property as soon as possible. He received an immediate response suggesting an inspection could be arranged, but only on condition the buyers agree to a minimum purchase of 10,000 acres. If such a commitment were not made, Bell would seek other buyers. Luther anticipated the purchase requirement. Mann and his investors needed money and a single buyer was the quickest way to access cash. Finding multiple buyers was time consuming and could be difficult given economic conditions.

John and his father arrived at Luther's office just before noon and were advised of the minimum 10,000-acre purchase. John was thinking more in terms of 2,000 acres. Any purchase beyond that was outside his comfort zone. Luther told them he would purchase one-half the minimum and finance the Schmidts' additional purchase of 3,000 acres. Luther was proposing a more than fivefold increase in size of the Schmidt farm. John wanted time to consider, at least a few days. Luther pushed for a decision. Mann's financial distress was fast becoming common knowledge. Others would soon learn of the sale. After some discussion, John agreed. Luther telegraphed Ezra Bell, "Agree to minimum, subject to inspection."

March 3 was set as the inspection date. Levi Andersen, a Mann farm boss turned caretaker, was assigned the task of escorting John, Jacob, Luther and Mann's counsel. Three days before the inspection, John advised Colvis and Albert of the purchase. The Schmidt farm was beginning preparations for the season, and John's two associates would otherwise wonder why he chose this time to be absent. Both were excited by the prospect, but concerned with the magnitude of the task. Taking on 5,000 acres represented an unimaginable increase in ground under cultivation. The pair peppered John with questions on timing and whether the purchase came with manpower, horses and equipment. He had few answers. Morgan knew of the purchase and trusted her father and Luther to broker the best possible terms.

The day before the inspection Luther received a telegram. There were complications. Three of the Mann investors objected to the manner in which the farm was being sold. They wanted a more public listing. Bell also advised the federal government recorded a lien and others were sure to follow. The inspection was on hold until Bell was sure the property was available. John felt a strange sense of relief. The sale came quickly and he was still processing its implications. Luther expected as much. Mann had countless secured creditors—all maneuvering to ensure their place in line.

News of the pending sale spread quickly. Luther was aware of at least three offers, one for the entire 13,000 acres. In early May, the National Cordage Company, the nation's most actively traded stock, had fallen into receivership. The failure had a chilling effect on investors. Within days, all offers were withdrawn. For the moment, Luther and the Schmidts were alone as buyers, but John was hesitant. An additional 5,000 acres demanded a viable market and the bushel price for wheat had just fallen to forty-eight cents. Luther discounted his concern. The business cycle was the natural order of things. Prices were sure to rebound and the Schmidt farm would be better positioned when they did.

To his surprise, Luther received a telegram from Ezra Bell on May 27. His legal team found a path through the quagmire surrounding the Mann title. The inspection would be conducted at nine a.m. on June 5. John's first inclination was to tell his father he was not welcome. Jacob was sure to interrupt negotiations, almost assuredly at the wrong time. Instead, he took a few minutes the night before to lecture his father, telling him questions during the inspection were acceptable, but negotiation fell to Luther.

When the pair arrived the following morning, they found Luther, Ezra Bell and Levi Andersen, the Mann caretaker, in heated debate. The attorney had just been advised by Mr. Andersen that lack of manpower left the farm with an uncertain accounting of livestock and equipment. An unknown quantity of horses, cattle and machinery had gone missing. Livestock could have wandered off and equipment could be anywhere on the 13,000 acres, but Levi suspected theft, probably by Mann employees still owed a paycheck. Bell was visibly annoyed. The morning of an inspection was not the time to be advised of losses. After some discussion, it was decided the inspection would continue. A full inventory of livestock and equipment would begin immediately and steps taken to ensure the farm's security.

From the entrance, John could see two homes, a cookhouse and what appeared to be sleeping quarters. One of the homes was very large. Bell characterized the design as a "Queen Anne." The second home was a traditional gabled farmhouse. The attorney was eager to show the homes, thinking them to be important to the sale. The buyers were not interested in housing, but rather field conditions and working elements of the farm. Homes produced no income and were incidental.

The neglect in fieldwork, equipment and outbuildings was immediately obvious. A large expanse of wheat had been left to rot in the field. Equipment was scattered here and there as if a sudden work stoppage had been called. Outbuildings fared somewhat better as did the equipment stored within, but disregard for maintenance could be seen in every direction. John and his father cringed at the sight.

Most of the buildings were located on the 5,000 acres John hoped to purchase: five large barns, a granary, three equipment sheds, and four livestock shelters, two occupied by hogs. From their vantage point, they could also see four windmills. The group set out in a clockwise pattern slowly at first then more quickly as the day wore on. After five hours, the group came upon a series of ponds. They saw horses, but fewer than necessary to manage the farm. According to Levi, they were likely to find another grouping to the north and west, on property that would fall to Luther. As they approached the ponds, Bell and the caretaker fell back engrossed in conversation.

The attorney rode forward and announced, "The inspection is over. We'll pick up again at noon day after tomorrow."

"There's still much to be seen," Jacob protested.

"We need a better handle on livestock and equipment," Bell answered. "I need to contact ownership."

Luther feigned a half-hearted objection, "Your clients are here— why not complete the inspection?"

"We're done for the day."

John and his father were disappointed, but not Luther. He understood why Bell canceled the inspection. Conditions on the farm did not support the asking price. When John returned home, he sought the counsel of his daughter. He agreed with Luther's assessment. The asking price was coming down, but the inspection indicated the cost of bringing the farm online was going up. Father and daughter spent most of the night discussing how long before the Mann farm paid dividends. Both understood that may never happen with wheat priced below fifty cents per bushel.

When Luther, John, and his father returned to the Mann property, they found an entirely different Ezra Bell. The smug confidence the attorney had displayed earlier was no longer in evidence. He was both shaken and annoyed the farm had been misrepresented, knowingly or otherwise. Several telegrams had been exchanged with the bonanza farm ownership, and he advised Luther equipment and livestock were now included in the asking price. He turned to mount, but Luther took his arm.

"The Schmidts are willing to pay $13.50 per acre, as is, where is," he said. "There is no need for further inspection."

Bell started to object, but Luther interrupted.

"You'll have the payment in forty-eight hours."

The offer surprised everyone. John said nothing. The amount tendered was more than $3.00 below the original asking price. Bell started to counter, but Luther interrupted the attorney.

"Hell will freeze over before you find a buyer at $15.00 per acre."

Bell took a moment to gauge Luther's intensity, deciding further negotiation was futile.

"Not my decision. I'll forward the offer and press for action before noon tomorrow."

Luther set out for Fargo. John and his father turned for home. Little was said as both tried to assess how the Mann investors would react. Cornellious Mann and his colleagues were in trouble. Buyers were scarce and the once proud bonanza farm in disrepair. Was there any choice? John shared the day's events with the family, Colvis and Albert. He spent much of the night contemplating various scenarios for bringing the Mann farm back to life. He considered the strengths of Colvis and Albert and his own infirmities. Morgan must play a greater role in farm management. She consistently displayed the necessary acumen and her views on the farm and farming were widely respected. He finally checked himself knowing the offer could be rejected and his planning for naught.

Shortly after sunrise, Jacob amassed a series of tasks which kept him close to the front gate. Luther had said a rider would be sent to the farm as soon as the Mann investors responded. The senior Schmidt was rewarded just before noon. Jacob met the courier at the threshold, but the pouch he carried was marked for John. Morgan also saw the rider and called to her father who was working behind the big house. The shout brought not just her father, but Maria and Colvis as well. John opened the pouch which contained an envelope. Scrolled across the front was the word "Bonanza" and beneath, "sign and return." John read the first few sentences and handed the letter to Morgan. She nodded affirmatively. The Schmidt farm had grown by 5,000 acres.

Jacob was ecstatic—the others more reflective. They were pleased, but filled with trepidation for the task ahead. The packet included a preliminary acceptance of terms. There were no changes. The property was being sold "as is, where is" with no guarantees, expressed or implied. The Mann investors had but one obligation—to deliver clear title. John signed the document and sent the rider on his way. Final papers would be executed within one week.

Maria had a premonition the night before. She told Mary Etta that by afternoon the Mann property would be theirs. Now she suggested the three families celebrate their good fortune. John was still experiencing buyer's remorse and suggested they pray first—a step he rarely took. It was a signal to the assembled group the next two years would see the Schmidt farm on the precipice. He was quite sure of his abilities and those of his associates, but there were variables beyond his control. Help from any quarter was welcome.

John gathered Colvis, Albert and Morgan early the next day to discuss how to best approach Mann's neglected 5,000 acres. Over the past few weeks, John allowed himself to consider various options for staffing his now much larger farm. Craig Duffy, widely recognized for his management skills, divided his bonanza farms into parcels—each subdivision run by an autonomous farm boss. The Schmidt farm would take a different approach. For the past eighteen years, John had placed his trust in Colvis Rasmussen. He was not about to change now. Colvis would be assigned all fieldwork. Only 3,000 acres of the newly acquired ground would be planted next spring. The remaining acreage would be used as pasture or left fallow, a well-deserved rest after too many years of wheat production.

Albert would care for the equipment, animals and any structures on the property assisted by his son and Juanna's husband, Javier. The latter joined the Schmidts six months earlier, having served as a farm boss on a 700-acre farm south of Casselton. Luther was one-half owner of the property and recommended Javier, knowing he was eager to rejoin his wife and family. Levi Andersen would also be joining the Schmidt farm. John was impressed by the caretaker's honesty during the short-lived inspection. His knowledge of the Mann farm would be an asset going forward. John thought briefly about dividing the farm, leaving Colvis and Levi with their own parcel, but uncertainty regarding Levi's skills gave him pause—better to have Levi schooled by Colvis. The addition meant a change in Morgan's role. She was less companion and more co-manager—admission she was the future of the Schmidt farm.

The Mann acquisition brought two new homes to the farm. The largest, the Queen Anne, would be home to John, Maria, Jacob and the Schmidt children. Colvis and Mary Etta had no desire to move, nor did the Haugens. Levi, his wife and seven children would occupy the big house on the original Meyer farm. That left the gabled farmhouse. Maria assigned that home to Javier and Juanna. The additional acreage meant much larger work crews and the need for more help in the kitchen. Juanna would be close to both the cookhouse and Maria, who was now dependent on her to manage the household. Colvis suggested it was unusual to assign preferential housing to a Mexican family, but John's icy look brought an end to the discussion.

John still had crops to bring in and told his father to hire twenty men beyond that required for harvest. He planned to dispatch the additional force to prepare ground on the Mann addition. The best of the new hires would be retained until the first hard freeze. Morgan suggested they be given a small bonus in exchange for the promise to return in mid-February. The farm would then have a core of qualified workers when the ground softened and fieldwork resumed.

Four of the workers were allotted to Albert and dispatched to gather equipment scattered throughout the new acreage. In Albert's estimation, there was enough machinery left on the Schmidt and Ogden parcels to meet the needs of the season ahead. In mid-harvest, John shifted ten more workers to the Mann property. As a result, wheat came in late, but the farm suffered no significant penalty. Weather cooperated and yield per acre was marginally improved, though price remained depressed.

The thirty men working the newly acquired property continued through early December. All but two agreed to return in exchange for a bonus conditioned upon their return early next season. John was pleased, but troubled by the knowledge the farm would begin the new year with far less cash in reserve.

The specter of 5,000 new acres so consumed John he almost forgot the holidays. He enlisted the support of Clara to help fill his modest shopping list. Planning for the holiday was left to Maria and Juana. They were joined by the women of the Schmidt farm who understood this was not the year for extravagance—even Jacob behaved himself. The family stayed close to home and the celebration was more intimate.

Melina wrote with the usual update from Kansas. Conditions there were no different than what the Schmidts were facing in North Dakota. Maria responded, but chose not to share news of their recent addition. She was in no mood for a lecture from her father on buying land in the midst of a recession. Maria did not hear from Freidrich. There had been no news from Washington State for some time and she feared the recession had finally caught up with her brother.

January was uneventful. By midmonth, all was in readiness for the planting season. Fieldwork resumed before the last frost with more than sixty bindlestiffs including those released in December. All of those who committed to return did so. For the first time since his arrival, John was afraid of what the future might bring. He had been apprehensive in the past—now he was simply scared. The farm was spending down reserves at an alarming rate, while wheat prices continued to hover in the fifty-cent per bushel range. Something had to give or the Schmidt farm would find itself in serious financial difficulty.

The die was cast and spring planting, at least for the year ahead, would proceed as planned. By season end, 2,900 acres, slightly less than half the 6,000 available, had been seeded. John hoped for more, but could not bear the cost of the additional manpower. Employment was scaled back for the summer, but sixteen men were retained to continue work on restoring the Mann property. Most who helped with spring planting tended their own ground, but working for wages brought more income.

The summer had been good to the Schmidt farm. There were a few weather related problems, but nothing threatened the crop. Each morning

John rode through fields. He was accompanied by either Morgan or Colvis. What they saw was encouraging. By the end of July, the fields were turning a golden yellow, and seed heads, when broken open, revealed a grain which passed the bite test. Within a few days the heads were bowing on the stem. It was time for harvest.

Jacob assembled 112 workers for the harvest of 1894. The number did not include Juana's kitchen staff, which included five cooks and three servers. Albert's diligence over the summer left the farm boss with access to twelve harvesters, four working threshers and more than enough horses to satisfy demand. If more threshing capacity was necessary, Axel Moen would be called upon. Albert and the farm were also the beneficiary of Luther's generosity. He had no plans to work his land, instead leasing the ground as pasture or to small farmers and taking a percentage of the proceeds. The horses and equipment that came with Luther's 5,000 acres were available for use, if necessary, on the expanded Schmidt farm.

What looked to be a positive start to the harvest season turned bad early on the third day. Work crews were being assembled and a number of wagons had gathered alongside the central barn. One team bolted and struck a freight wagon, leaving a dray horse with a broken leg. Only John, Colvis or Albert had authority to put down a working animal. Albert was closest and responded to the call. As he pushed his way forward, he was kicked in the midsection by a younger horse. He doubled over and was kicked again, this time in the temple. Albert was dead before he reached the ground. The workers stared down in stunned disbelief. Javier glanced at the body and immediately concluded there was no sense of urgency. Blood poured from every orifice and Albert's face was disfigured. The workers draped the lifeless body across Javier's saddle and started toward the Queen Anne.

Albert had recently taken to wearing a wide brimmed hat which now rested on the saddle horn. Marit was returning from the root cellar and was attracted by the commotion. Her view was momentarily blocked. Suddenly, she saw the hat. She cast her basket aside and ran toward the motionless body. Kari Andersen, coming from the barn, quickly assessed the circumstance and tried to intercept her friend. She was unable to do so. Marit dropped to her knees and caught sight of Albert's face.

"Do something," she demanded.

Javier could only say, "There is no life *senora*."

Colvis was next on the scene. He took a moment to study Albert.

"Return to your wagons," he told the workers. "There is nothing for you here."

A worker had been sent for Meier, Albert's son. He lifted his mother carrying her from the scene.

Albert was laid to rest alongside the newborn buried by the family ten years earlier. Marit was slow to put the baby's loss behind her. She would never recover from the loss of her husband. John said nothing at the graveside. His speech was halting and he had no desire to stumble through a eulogy. Morgan spoke on his behalf. She recalled Albert's arrival on the Schmidt farm, calling him "uncle" as did all children of the farm. He was looking for temporary work before the family continued their journey west to homestead. A few months turned into a year and Albert soon became a trusted friend and associate. His quiet dedication and commitment would be missed.

After the service John told Meier he would assume his father's role and like his father, share in year-end profits. Meier was thankful and assured John his mother would always be secure. Marit left immediately following the ceremony speaking to no one. Her son, who had taken up residence in the bunkhouse, moved back to the family home. The women of the Schmidt farm made it a point to visit Marit, but over time the visits became less frequent and she even more reclusive.

The expanded farm's first harvest brought in 2,300 acres of wheat and 650 acres of corn, oats and barley. Weather, which had cooperated through the summer, plagued the harvest and drove crews from fieldwork for the better part of four days. Yield for wheat was eighteen bushels per acre— less than expected. John had severed his relationship with the Minnesota millers and made no attempt to presell the wheat crop hoping prices would edge up in the fall. They did not and the crop was sold to Valley Storage. The Schmidt farm finished 1894 having achieved nothing—save spending down reserves. Two of the four Eclipse threshers had broken down and Meier, lacking his father's experience, struggled to bring them online. Thankfully, Levi knew the machines well enough to return one to service.

The excitement of a much larger Schmidt farm had given way to the burden of working 5,000 additional acres. John was thankful that their contract with Luther called for interest to be paid with mortgage settlement. He told Morgan he was beginning to question the wisdom of their purchase. Morgan reminded her father the Mann property was an investment in the future. They had come close to breakeven and wheat prices would not remain depressed forever. She chided him for his lack of optimism. A 5,000-acre increase was testing their resources, but better days were ahead.

The Christmas holidays were subdued. John and Maria did their best to create a celebratory mood, but economic conditions and Marit's tragic loss made it difficult. Calvin and Tavendar were still enrolled in school and the Schmidts dutifully attended the holiday pageant. The burden of a dismal farm economy was etched in the faces of attendees. The Hansens and Bergmanns visited the farm though not together. Eric disliked Aaron Bergmann and John assumed the feeling was mutual.

Clara now spent hours alone in the emporium. Priscilla came only at closing. Clara confided to her mother the outlook for both the emporium and apothecary was not good. She still hoped her father would find a more responsible position for Robert. If he were something other than a farmhand, she could make a fresh start as homemaker and mother. John was not sympathetic.

Circumstances were similar 2,000 miles to the west. Maria had been correct. Freidrich did his best to shelter cash before the panic, but much of his fortune was lost. Agnes sent one small gift for each of the children—a far cry from the extravagance of the past. In the short note accompanying the packages, she apologized for not writing. The couple had been forced to sell the Tacoma home and was now living with her mother in Montesano. In November, Judge Morehead died unexpectedly. The inheritance she shared with her mother included a large stand of virgin forest. Prairie Timber, which had collapsed after Freidrich and Kurt sold the firm, was soon to be reborn, though economic conditions were anything but favorable.

The news from St. Anne's was not much better. The Schafer farm managed to stay profitable, but only by the narrowest of margins. Melina was worried for the future. Albrecht scaled back production and suspended negotiations on the property west of Hays City. The anxiety was not good for Peter. Her father no longer attended Populist meetings, but was still active in the movement contributing broadsides to party activists. The *Topeka Daily Capital* had taken note of his attack on the railroads and their allies in Congress. Melina thought the rhetoric became even more savage as his condition worsened.

Recent gains in both state houses and the election of a Populist senator provided some satisfaction in an otherwise banal existence. There had also been a scare involving a grandchild in late fall. The fifth of Hilke's durable brood was stricken with "winter fever." White hot temperatures and dehydration twice left the child near death. There were complications, but Melina offered no explanation.

Lizzie's note was the only correspondence to offer a token of happiness. She had given birth to a girl, Alice Valla Rasmussen, her middle name owing to Mary Etta's family. Maria was aware of the birth, but pleased to hear mother and child were fine. Given the times even good news carried a pinch of bad. The NPRR had filed its second bankruptcy in October and was now in receivership. Ice and his position were secure for the moment, but there were no assurances for the future.

Late in January, John asked Javier to harness horse and carriage, the latter one of two included in the Mann purchase. Morgan caught sight of her father just as he prepared to leave.

"Where are you off to?" she asked

"I'll be back soon." John was annoyed that his every move was closely watched.

"Morgan should ride with you," Maria called from the veranda.

John glanced at his wife, but rode off without responding. Morgan started toward the barn, but her mother intervened.

"Let him go," Maria said. "Trailing behind will just make him angry."

John rode south toward the original Meyer farm purchased nineteen years before. He still wondered if growing the farm from 900 to near 6,000 acres was a wise decision, but quickly dismissed the thought. Luther and his daughter called that "backward thinking." Both would accuse him of dawdling in the past. The economy would improve—maybe not tomorrow, but better times would come. As he crossed the threshold to the Mann addition, he was encouraged by the work completed by Colvis and his crew following last year's harvest. John guessed several hundred additional acres had been readied for planting. He allowed horse and carriage to drift east toward the pond that bordered Luther's property.

He wished now he had invited Morgan to join him. Crops to be planted and in what quantity were decisions which begged her input. As he cleared the berm marking the pond's end, John caught sight of a horse and rider. The horse was unmistakably "Cloud" which meant the rider was Morgan. He reined in and watched as she closed the distance. She brought biscuits, jerky, and a blanket, but none were accessible until he listened to a lecture on riding off alone. He instructed her to tether Cloud to the buggy and the pair continued in an easterly direction.

John told his daughter it may be possible to plant 3,000 acres on the Mann addition alone. Some ground had already been prepared; they had the necessary horses and equipment and, given circumstances in the valley, experienced manpower was plentiful. Morgan was skeptical. She had devised her own planting scheme, 3,200 acres, including both old and new properties. It was more conservative with 2,500 acres in wheat. There was plenty of pasture in the 3,000 acres left fallow, some unturned to allow fields to recover and some because Morgan saw no market for additional grain. The pair continued the debate until deciding Colvis should have the opportunity to offer his opinion.

Morgan made a small fence repair while her father inspected a windmill. Cloud was put to work pulling a harrow to one of the small barns. None of these actions were particularly urgent, but they served to extend the day, something both enjoyed. Turning for home, there was a period of silence, each lost in their own thoughts.

With the Queen Anne coming into view, John reined in.

"I'm drafting a will," he announced.

Morgan was surprised. Her mother had suggested, following Tavendar's birth, it was time to begin planning for succession. She had reminded him again after the Mann purchase. Neither effort drew a response.

"I'm glad," Morgan said. "What changed your mind?"

"I'm afraid," her father answered.

"Afraid of what?" she asked.

"I fear for my health and your future as master of the farm." Morgan was confused.

"Your sister is gone, Calvin will never make a farm boss, and Tav—he'll won't be happy with Casselton, even North Dakota."

John paused for a moment. "You're the farm's anchor," he said, "Without you there is no Schmidt farm."

Morgan was honored by her father's expression of trust, but saddened by the discussion of his mortality.

John recognized the distress. "We'll talk about this later," he said.

The spring was marked by persistent cold and endless rain. Colvis was concerned. Levi had told him it was not uncommon for the pond bordering Luther's property to swell, but this year it threatened to breach the top of the berm. A small break on the southeastern end created a rivulet which meandered through the fields, finally reaching a distant creek bed. The rogue stream had washed away a half-acre of soil, but also provided relief to the growing body of water. The greater concern was saturation of the berm wall.

The heavens opened the third week in April bringing a halt to field-work. The rain continued through that day and into the next. With no end in sight Colvis and Levi set out to inspect the pond. They anticipated erosion, but found devastation. The berm had given way sending a torrent of water racing across 200 acres of just-planted wheat. The torrent had breached the creek bed destroying 50 acres of pasture and sending a wall of water downstream. An equipment shed and thresher stored within were damaged. Too late to plant wheat, John and Morgan considered planting at least some of the acreage in corn, but the bushel price of corn had reached a point where planting was busy work and nothing more. They decided on an additional 50 acres of barley leaving the rest fallow.

The stress of managing the expanded Schmidt farm along with a string of bad luck had begun to wear on John. His motor skills were diminished and speech increasingly difficult. He did his best to maintain an even demeanor, but was easily angered. No one was exempt—not Maria, not Morgan. John even berated Colvis for what he considered a bad decision on repairs to a windmill. The verbal attack was uncalled for and unfair.

Maria had seen enough. She asked Morgan to contact Colonel Austin. He dutifully responded knowing Maria would ask him to again contact Horace Saalberg, an effort he considered futile. She was hoping for the impossible, a cure or at least treatment to arrest progression of the Parkinson's. The Colonel knew Doctor Saalberg had neither. He summarized John's condition in a telegram which drew a surprisingly quick response. The doctor would be happy to examine John, but cautioned his motives were selfish. The clinic needed more patients for study and experimentation. John would be poked and prodded and leave precisely as he arrived. Maria was shattered. She was prepared for bad news, but not Saalberg's brutal conclusion. John had agreed to the correspondence to placate Maria. He now forbade any further discussion of treatment. The episode confirmed what the family knew all along. The time had come to assess the future of the Schmidt farm and its leadership.

The harvest held no surprises. Fewer than 2,800 acres had been planted and prices for both small and large grains continued to disappoint. Their second full season on the Mann addition had been even worse than the first. Morgan told her father the early season flood was responsible for their second loss in as many years. John appreciated the kind words, but knew the real cause for their dismal year was the falling price of wheat.

Jacob shared his son's angst. In a mind beginning to falter, he saw his early obsession with the Mann property as cause for the farm's current economic hardship—perhaps the family would have been better off staying at 900 acres. Jacob was included in family functions and never wanted for attention, but his role in planning had long since passed. Morgan was now her father's advisor and confidant. Jacob simply watched the day unfold from his perch on the veranda.

Maria did her best to bring a modicum of joy to the holidays, a challenge given events of the past twenty-four months. The family participated in the usual celebrations. The Hansens visited as did the Bergmanns. Clara's husband, Robert, now had more than three years of farming under his belt. He left following harvest each year, but sadly, for himself and John, he returned. Clara and Robert spent Christmas Eve in the Meyer cottage, then joined the family for a gift exchange Christmas morning. A midafternoon holiday meal followed.

Melina's Christmas note from Kansas was brief and did nothing to lift the spirits. Her father experienced a second angina attack and, except for short periods, was confined to bed. To compound matters, Albrecht's daughter, stricken the year before by "winter fever" was in her words "slow." Melina described the family's condition as "dug in." Albrecht had nothing planned until the farm economy showed some signs of life.

News from Washington State was more encouraging. Agnes and Freidrich were settled in Montesano and Prairie Timber was again up and running. Milled lumber was being produced from the timberlands of Agnes' inheritance. In Tacoma, Lizzie reported Ice survived the NPRR reorganization. He was assigned a new position with even greater responsibilities. Their newborn was doing well as was Colvis III.

John was deeply concerned for the year ahead. One more year of loss would further deplete cash reserves and jeopardize their ability to repay Luther. He gathered Morgan and Colvis and told them to ride every inch of the farm. John could not erase the specter of last year's flood. Nothing should escape their review. The pair rode the farm once, then rode again. The season ahead included enough unknowns without a surprise borne of poor planning. Morgan knew any setback, occurring naturally or because of negligence, could easily threaten their existence. John knew this as well. Readiness became their singular focus.

On the morning of February 2, Juanna and her children returned from their pre-dawn gathering of eggs. Jacob often met them when they reached the kitchen, making a game of counting their take. After a time, the girls wondered why grandfather did not join them. Maria wondered as well. She sent Javier to check on her father-in-law. There was a muffled scream as Javier tumbled down the stairs crying *"abuelo no respira."* Maria knew enough Spanish to understand. She and Juanna raced to Jacob's room while Javier went in search of John. They found Jacob lying peacefully, death having visited hours before.

John was helped to his father's room. He asked everyone to leave.

"Without you there would be no bonanza farm," he said, taking his father's hand in both of his own. He closed Jacob's eyes and whispered, "The children will never forget their grandfather."

John returned to the kitchen where the family had gathered. Maria was in tears. Morgan repeated the thought expressed by her father moments earlier.

"He was always there for us," she said.

Calvin gave voice to his innermost feelings. "Grandfather, more than anyone, understood."

John was not sure what Calvin meant, but realized his son was much closer to Jacob than previously thought. Javier was sent to Fargo with a note for the bishop. Was he available four days hence at two p.m.? He was. In the intervening period, Levi and a few helpers expanded the perimeter of the Schmidt family cemetery. A large stone was dragged by sled to the newly opened space. John liked the simplicity of granite and intended to inscribe "Jacob Schmidt, Grandfather to All."

The service was well attended. Among the mourners were Luther Ogden, T. Fergus Jenkins, Chief Financial Officer of First National Bank of Fargo, Axel Moen, mercantile owners James and Marcella Stockman, Eric and Lisa Hansen and several neighbors Jacob met while carrying children to and from school. Based on conversations with John, the bishop recounted Jacob's early years on the *Russische* Steppe. He had also spoken with the children, asking them to recall special moments. Their stories became part of his eulogy. When the bishop raised his hand to extend a final blessing, Calvin suddenly rose. John reached for him, but the bishop acknowledged the young man and encouraged him to speak. In the past year, Calvin had spent more time with Jacob than any of the Schmidt children. The often misunderstood eldest son visited his grandfather for one-half hour each day, patiently listening to the same stories unfazed by the repetition. Now it was his turn to speak, but he was overcome with emotion. A prepared text was abandoned for a simple expression of thanks.

The spring of 1896 saw 3,700 acres planted, nearly 2,900 acres in wheat. The expansion of ground under cultivation placed the farm in a precarious position, having been funded by increasingly depleted cash reserves. Both John and Morgan understood the significance of the year ahead. Planting was completed without incident and weather cooperated. By early July, all signs pointed to a good year. Even the market began to tick upward. Spurred by industrialization, workers had begun to flock to the cities. Demand for cereal grains matched the growth in urban centers.

The farm economy stirred, then slowly came to life. John and his daughter watched cautiously as expected yield and price grew in unison. By mid-harvest, Morgan assured her father the farm's disappointing performance in the past two years would soon be forgotten. Yield averaged twenty bushels per acre and price reached sixty-nine cents. John and his neighbors were on the leading edge of the second Dakota boom. The Red River Valley awakened. Foreclosed property—long ignored—was carefully studied by eager buyers and tax sales drew large crowds. The Schmidt farm rejoiced. When the last of the crop was in, John asked Morgan to help him to the cemetery. He guessed Jacob was aware of their good fortune.

"You were right all along," he whispered. "The Mann addition paid handsomely."

John nodded as if acknowledging Jacob's response. Morgan allowed her father a few minutes at the gravesite before returning to the Queen Anne.

November 17 was an otherwise forgettable day. A driving rain changed to sleet and falling temperatures suggested snow sometime during the night. A single rider approached the farm just after sunset. He hesitated at the gate, then proceeded to the Queen Anne. Morgan answered the knock and recognized a young railroad worker new to the Casselton Station. He carried a telegram for Colvis. Morgan offered to deliver the wire, but the young man insisted on making the delivery himself. Maria joined her daughter and could tell by the carrier's somber mood the wire contained bad news. She waited a few minutes before wrapping herself in John's oilskins and made her way to the Rasmussen home. She found Colvis slumped in a chair and Mary Etta at his knees.

"Bjartr is missing," she said, "Swept away in a slide west of the NPRR Cascade tunnel."

"Are you sure?" Maria's asked.

"I'm leaving for Tacoma tomorrow. The wire said there were no survivors."

It was a stunning reversal of fortune coming on the heels of the farm's first profitable harvest in years. Two days later, Colvis was handed a second telegram confirming his son's passing and briefly describing the events which took his life. The railroad had experienced a series of rockslides near the western terminus of the soon-to-be completed tunnel. Ice accompanied two surveyors and a blasting crew to investigate. He and four of the workers were approaching the tunnel entrance when a large section of mountain gave way. The slide passed across the entrance taking 200 yards of track and all five men. Two members of the blasting crew returning to the handcar witnessed the event. Ice and his companions were buried beneath tons of rock and debris. No attempt would be made to recover the bodies. The railroad planned to erect a monument in Skykomish, a small town near the tunnel entrance.

Mary Etta left for Tacoma the following morning. The trip consumed three days. When she arrived, she found Agnes sitting with Lizzie. Agnes had read the account of the accident in the *Tacoma Daily Ledger*, recognized the Rasmussen name and insisted Freidrich take her to Lizzie's home. The three women closed up the house, arranged for its sale, and shipped a few pieces of furniture to Casselton. Maria offered the Meyer cottage to Lizzie, Colvis III and Alice for as long as she wished to stay. Taking John's lead, Colvis dragged a second large stone to the cemetery. It was placed adjacent to the grave of Colvis II. The inscription awaited consultation with Lizzie.

The year held one more tragic, though not unexpected loss. Like his friend Jacob, Peter Schafer died peacefully in his sleep. He would be remembered as the titular head of St. Anne's and for his contribution to the Populist movement. In the span of eleven months, John and Maria both lost a parent, and the Schmidt farm lost a beloved son. The farm family dutifully observed the birth of Christ in an apathetic daze driven by a desire to preserve tradition for the children. There were gifts for the youngest, but no Christmas dinner—the Schmidts and Rasmussens preferring to be alone with their grief.

Chapter Twenty-One:
Golden Age of Agriculture

"The changes that occurred in American agriculture during the 20th century exceeded in magnitude all of the changes that had occurred during the 10,000 years since human beings first converted themselves from hunters and gatherers to herdsmen and cultivators."

—Don Paarlberg, Philip Paarlberg

A solitary thread of optimism wove its way through the tragic events of 1896, its path obscured by painful loss. The Schmidt farm had regained its footing. John and Morgan, with the able assistance of Colvis, Meier and Levi, began the year with a renewed passion driven by recent success and the understanding hard work was the best elixir for tragedy. Just under 3,900 acres had been planted without incident. By midsummer, all indications suggested a bumper crop. Spring wheat occupied nearly three-quarters of the ground under cultivation and Colvis expected an average of twenty bushels per acre. John disliked selling in advance of harvest and suspected manipulation by railroads and elevator operators, but he worried that Valley Storage was fast becoming an afterthought in the marketplace for wheat.

The question of how and when to sell the wheat crop created some debate within the family. Curiously, Calvin took an interest. Working with the few publications the Schmidt farm received and other source data from school, he began to chart wheat futures, tracking everything from world markets to weather patterns. He scanned the newspapers for articles on the Populist movement and price-fixing. It was the numbers that intrigued

Calvin. He charted, graphed and moved calculations from one page to the next with little interest in how the outcome may or may not affect the Schmidt farm. After a few months of study, he grew weary of the project—his only conclusion that nature and intermediaries, not growers, controlled supply and demand.

Casselton's non-farm economy had also realized the effects of an improving agricultural sector. The Bergmanns' struggles were far from over, but receipts had improved to the point where Robert was able to rejoin the family business. His tenure on the Schmidt farm did not change John's opinion of his son-in-law. He was no better or no worse than the other farmhands, but insisted on making recommendations on how the farm should be managed. John never understood how a failed dress salesman became an expert in agriculture. He was glad to have Robert out from underfoot. He could only hope an improved business climate meant Clara could finally escape the emporium and realize her dream of becoming mother and homemaker.

Tavendar was the only member of the Schmidt family who saw value in Robert. John didn't understand why. Perhaps he was too young to know better, but Tav could be a contrarian, taking a different view hoping to start an argument. He enjoyed the confrontation—probably because he often won. Teachers who recalled Morgan saw the same traits in her brother, every bit as bright, but perhaps more caustic. Like his sister, he saw industry as an end in itself, but lacked the patience for farming and was too fond of attention to toil in the fields. John and Maria had no idea what the future held for their youngest, but thought him well suited to a career in public service.

The Schmidts received a surprise letter from Professor Lehmann in midsummer. North Dakota State Agricultural College had survived the panic and was now ready to initiate its joint educational venture. Plans remained the same with three buildings including space for faculty, students, and representatives of the private sector who wished to participate. The search was underway for an on-site manager. They planned to scrap the earlier, somewhat confusing, reimbursement scheme in favor of a simple lease with all production accruing to the host farm. A stipend was added, recognizing their host would contribute labor and equipment. Given the expense involved, 150 acres and a three-year lease were mandatory. Professor Lehmann asked if the Schmidt farm was still interested. Morgan was ecstatic. Within the hour, she responded by telegram. "Yes—whenever the college is ready." Ten days later the contract arrived; Professor Lehmann advised the on-site manager would arrive in October.

Both John and Morgan expected a period of transition following Albert's untimely death, but there was none. Meier Haugen had proven to be a seamless replacement for his father. He quickly assumed Albert's role managing equipment and the farm's working stock. As a temporary concession to his mother, he had moved from the bunkhouse to the family home, a circumstance suggesting what many believed—Meier was a confirmed bachelor. A chance meeting between Maria and her long-time friend Lisa Hansen changed that outlook.

Lisa was just leaving the Casselton General Store as Maria was arriving. During the course of their brief conversation, Lisa mentioned Oleanna Kupp and her three children were living with the Hansens in a small shed adjoining the barn. She lost the family farm in July and her husband ten months before. The two families were friendly and Lisa agreed to take Oleanna in. Her temporary quarters were not suitable for the winter. Lisa wondered if Maria knew of any trustworthy bachelors among the farm's permanent work crew. Meier Haugen came to mind. Maria knew nothing of his past relationships, but recognized him as a good worker and fine young man. Lisa was eager to bring the two together and Maria, while not enthusiastic, was agreeable.

When Lisa returned home, she mentioned Meier to Oleanna.

"Once your time of grieving has passed, perhaps you would like to meet Meier?"

"My children need a father more than I need time to grieve," Oleanna responded.

Maria arranged a dinner to include Marit, Meier, the Rasmussens, Hansens, and Oleanna. Another Norwegian couple was included in an attempt to disguise the event as a gathering of neighbors. Meier was not fooled. He enjoyed the company, but gave no indication he was taken by Oleanna. John, who disliked the matchmaking, told his wife Meier would never marry. Four days later, to everyone's surprise, Meier stopped by the

Hansen farm. Two successive Sunday visits followed. On the second, Meier, or perhaps Oleanna, proposed. The couple was married the last week in September and joined Marit in the Haugen home. Maria was delighted by the union. Oleanna was a good companion. She had seen too much tragedy in the past twelve months and considered her new circumstance nothing short of a miracle.

The on-site manager for Professor Lehmann's experimental station passed through the Schmidt gate on October 15. Britton Lowry was met there by Kari Andersen and asked for either John or Morgan Schmidt. Kari sent him in the direction of the Queen Anne. Maria had noticed the young man as he approached and knew immediately he was not an itinerant looking for a temporary position. He was dressed for work, but his clothing appeared tailored, rather than purchased from a catalogue or general store. The manner in which he carried himself complimented his attire.

Britt Lowry was twenty-eight and the eldest son of a doctor. He was raised in Yankton, South Dakota. His father wanted Britt to follow in his footsteps, but it was not to be. In 1878, the family acquired 800 acres on the Nebraska-South Dakota border. At the time, the land was thought to be a future railroad terminus, but the planned development never materialized. One-half the property had since been leased to a distant cousin and was now a working farm. Britt spent many hours there as a youngster and secretly hoped to someday call the property his own. He had no interest in assuming his father's practice.

Britt managed to convince his father to allow him to attend Iowa State Agricultural College, an institution that included a model farm. He left the college after two years and joined his uncle, a member of the Chicago Board of Trade. Britt found office work far too confining. His next stop was the Champion Machine Company, a competitor of McCormick and manufacturer of farm implements. His casual manner and clean-cut appearance landed him a position demonstrating Champion products at agricultural shows and county fairs. While attending a show in Peoria, he learned North Dakota State Agricultural College was seeking to fill a position as manager of an experimental station. He immediately applied, but his age, experience and education placed him near the bottom of eligible applicants. He did manage to qualify for an interview with Professor Lehmann, after which his stock rose dramatically. Two more interviews and the professor's impassioned plea to his superiors secured the position.

Britt took the four steps to the veranda in two and nearly overran Maria as she emerged from the house. He introduced himself and asked for John or Morgan. John was resting after spending the morning with Colvis. Maria asked Calvin to escort Britt to the Mann addition where his sister was bringing in the last of the threshers. Morgan saw the pair approach and correctly assumed he was the new station manager. Even at a distance it was apparent he was neither stodgy educator nor common farmhand. She immediately began fidgeting with her hair. They shook hands with Morgan apologizing for her appearance, not sure why she did so. Without acknowledging the comment and paying little heed to Morgan, Britt started toward the thresher, "Who made this engine?"

Morgan found herself staring at the lithe body as he effortlessly vaulted over a wagon tongue.

"I'd like to see where the station will be located."

"Not until we've reviewed the contract," she replied rather sternly.

Morgan had the unfamiliar sensation of being drawn to Britt, but annoyed he paid more attention to machinery than to his host. When they returned to the Queen Anne, Morgan surprised her mother.

"Mr. Lowry should stay with us," she said. "He can take the third-floor room."

"Have you made other arrangements Mr. Lowry?"

"The Casselton Hotel, and please call me Britt."

"You'll stay with us," Morgan responded. "Javier will return the horse and secure your belongings."

Over the next two weeks Britt spent most of his time with Peder Soderstrom, a carpenter recommended by John, staking and laying foundations for the three buildings on the college property. Britt also cleared an area for access to the buildings and constructed a trench from the college property to a well 100 yards to the north. With that behind him, he began to spend more time observing fieldwork. Britt would be comparing yield on the Schmidt farm to the ground managed by the experimental station. Before any distinction could be made, he must first understand the Schmidts' farming methods.

Britt took his evening meals with the family and then spent a few minutes with John, careful not to overtire his host. Morgan often joined the pair and when John took his leave the two were left alone. The conversations were about farming and Britt's family and work history. After a few weeks, Morgan found herself behaving in a manner she found distasteful in others. She was becoming flirtatious. She told her mother she was attracted to Britt in a manner not experienced before, but was uncertain of his feelings. Maria cautioned against forcing the issue, recalling her own actions twenty years earlier in a Pfeifer shed. She could easily imagine her headstrong daughter and a young man eight years her senior in a similar circumstance. But there was a difference. She and John were in love. Maria sensed Morgan had fallen, but Britt was not ready to make a commitment. If something were to come of the relationship, it must be on his initiative.

Britt was scheduled to return to the college in early December, then spend Christmas with his family. On the night before his departure, Morgan and Britt again found themselves alone on the veranda.

"We should discuss the future," Morgan ventured.

"We've made good progress," Britt answered.

"I'm talking about our future," Morgan countered, somewhat annoyed.

Britt had been thinking of the relationship between farm and college. Morgan was focused on something quite different. He listened politely until Morgan took his hand.

"I'm not ready for that discussion," he said. "Perhaps someday, but it's far too soon."

"Are you sure?" Morgan was uncertain how to respond not accustomed to being rebuffed.

"We'll talk when I return." Britt then excused himself.

Morgan was hurt and embarrassed by what she now saw as a serious miscalculation. Their relationship, if any, had been jeopardized by clumsy aggression. In matters of the heart, Britt preferred to make decisions on his own. The next morning, Maria was surprised to see Levi escorting Britt to Casselton. He said goodbye to the family the night before, but Maria expected her daughter to take Britt to the train. Something was amiss, but Maria chose not to question Morgan.

Two weeks later John received a letter from Britt. He would not be returning in January as planned. Instead, the college was sending him to California and later to Washington State to study the growing use of combines and their potential application to the Midwest. Holt Manufacturing was the developer and the company had accumulated considerable data over the past three years. He expected to complete his work and return to the Schmidt farm before a student work crew arrived in the spring. The letter closed by wishing the family a happy Christmas. Morgan wondered why the letter was not addressed to her as well as her father. Was it simply sent to the titular farm master or was her omission intentional?

She shared with her mother the outcome of Britt's last night on the farm. Maria suggested she write, apologizing for her transgression. Morgan did so, but took the added step of telling Britt she was sincere in her expression of feelings. She wondered about the wisdom of the latter, but decided it best to clear the air. Britt's return thanked her for the note and closed with "best to the family." He included a few handbills on the Holt Combine and his thoughts on the machine's use in the Dakotas. Britt's response fell short of what Morgan had hoped for.

Christmas 1897 saw a partial return of the traditional celebration set aside the year before by the death of Jacob, Peter Schafer and Ice. The three were not forgotten, but a year had opened enough distance to allow a more joyful observance. The farm's financial condition also contributed to a more festive mood. The price of wheat edged upward by fifteen cents while non-farm goods stabilized, leaving the Schmidts and their neighbors with a substantial increase in purchasing power.

The women of the Schmidt farm saw an opportunity for a Christmas more akin to those of years past. Children would be the center of attention. Their ranks had grown by the addition of Colvis III, Alice, and Meier Haugens' three stepchildren. A much larger farm family attended the school pageant where Tavendar played the lead in the Christmas play and also presented gifts to the principal and his staff, the first child ever to do so. John watched Tavendar and saw something of Peter Schafer in his willingness, if not intent, to take center stage.

The joy of Christmas had also returned to Kansas, although Melina's note began on a melancholy note. She believed her husband, even in death, still walked the ground that was once St. Anne's. Her comments turned more cheerful as she listed the number and ages of grandchildren and their excitement over the coming holiday. She reported the family and farm were both doing well. Albrecht was again discussing the purchase of property west of Hays City and the formation of a real estate company. She also believed one, if not two, of Maria's younger brothers may be returning to take part in the new venture.

From Agnes came word that Freidrich had just completed construction of a second sawmill. The note included his picture standing in snow along with several workers. The inscription read "Prairie Timber, Plant Two." The more things changed, the more they stayed the same. Freidrich was apparently on the move again with the eager support of his mother-in-law, an entrepreneur in her own right.

Britt Lowry returned to the Schmidt farm the last week in February. Maria saw him dismount and met him before he reached the steps of the veranda. She surprised him with a peck on the cheek.

"We've missed you," she said.

"Welcome home," John shouted from the parlor.

Britt called out in return, "Glad to be back."

From her second-floor room Morgan hurried downstairs then checked herself remembering their last encounter. She stepped across the threshold and found herself in Britt's embrace. Maria left the couple alone. Morgan waited most of three months wondering what would happen when Britt returned. She had her answer in seconds.

Britt whispered, "You were right, it's time we discuss the future."

"Tonight," said Morgan.

The veranda was suddenly crowded. Colvis and Meier had come from the barn and Tavendar arrived from school.

Later that evening Britt apologized.

"In three months of travel, I've come to realize what I left behind. I won't make that mistake again." Within the hour, Britt had proposed.

Morgan immediately woke Maria.

"Britt has asked for my hand in marriage," she said, careful not to disturb her father.

Maria embraced her daughter, "He's a fine young man."

John was asked for his permission the following morning.

"I knew it all along," he said, delightfully giving his blessing.

Maria thought a large wedding was in order, but Morgan preferred just family and close friends. Her mother wondered if that were possible. The engagement was celebrated four days later and included the farm family, Clara, her husband and the Hansens.

Against Morgan's wishes, Britt took up residence in the experimental station. He was the manager and obligated to be available. Full-time faculty and students would not arrive until the fall, but there was much work to be done. The station's first crop was to be planted using Schmidt farm workers and a temporary cadre of students. Buildings must also be readied for the first full year of operation. With few exceptions, Britt spent his evenings with Morgan. John sometimes joined them, but found it increasingly difficult to keep up with the conversation. He required help to reach his bedroom and was often asleep before sunset. Tav participated as well until run off by Morgan. For his age, he had a surprisingly good grasp of farming issues.

Morgan had begun to press her father on what farm management would look like with Britt as a member of the family. John's health had made it more difficult for him to act as master and decisions increasingly fell to Morgan. Now Britt would be a part of the process. Three managers were too many. In April, John announced he would take on the mantle of adviser, leaving management to his daughter and future son-in-law. Morgan appreciated the gesture, but knew her father could never be just an observer. She was not concerned—his continued participation was welcome. Morgan was eager to start a family. Her father's availability to counsel Britt provided for continuity.

Britt was under contract with the college for a period of three years, but the agreement could be terminated by either party at their discretion. He submitted his resignation in March to be effective May 1. The college appointed Stanton McDowell, the young man who filled in for Britt during his winter absence. Professor Lehmann was saddened by Britt's departure, but delighted he would play a key role in farm management. Studies had been largely confined to the station. The professor hoped Britt's new position meant experiments could be expanded to include more of the Schmidt farm.

Colvis watched the change of guard with passive interest. His role as farm boss was secure. He had great respect for John Schmidt, his daughter and Britt. Colvis was delighted to work with any one or all three. He had but one problem—that being arthritis or what he called gout. An hour in the saddle brought excruciating pain as did too much time on a wagon seat. He had come to rely on Levi as his eyes and ears.

Like her daughter, Maria was not sure John was capable of stepping down, but delighted he agreed to a diminished role. Her husband often claimed "duties" as the reason for taking on projects beyond his capability. With Morgan as master, John would no longer have that crutch. Maria understood it was John's illness that defined the future. Periodic improvement always gave way to a setback. She was most concerned with his fading spirit. He remained driven, but Maria feared the Parkinson's was sapping mental acuity.

Maria had begun to experience her own troublesome malady. In the past year, seasonal congestion morphed to shortness of breath punctuated by bouts of uncontrolled coughing. Morgan had finally convinced her mother to consult with Colonel Austin. He recommended a cherry pectoral which resulted in giddiness, but nothing more. He then encouraged inhaling stramonium powders or smoking asthma cigarettes obtained from the Bergmanns' apothecary. She hated the cigarettes, although they did provide a modicum of relief. The Colonel worried at first it might be consumption, but there was no history of exposure save contact with animals, an unlikely source. He concluded it was late onset asthma accentuated by years of inhaling dust and chaff. The Colonel's remedies were almost as bad as the affliction. In desperation, he suggested a coastal climate might offer relief. Maria accused him of drinking too much of her cough syrup.

Morgan and Britt, with input from Colvis, decided on planting 4,600 acres in the spring of 1899. Two-thirds would be sewn in wheat. That was increased slightly when the price touched $1.00 early in the year, dropped a bit, then held near ninety cents a bushel. John had pushed for closer to 5,500 total acres, but the resources were simply not there. For the first time in several years, the farm struggled to find help. Small farms were crawling out of indebtedness and owners no longer found it necessary to supplement their income to pay the banker or tax man. Instead, they stayed at home and took advantage of the steadily rising grain prices. On the Schmidt farm, children not otherwise engaged, were sent to the fields as were women whose help was not required in the kitchen. The farm still required 138 bindlestiffs. Ten of those came from Javier's friends in the Mexican community. A mid-season exodus of temporary help led to a shortfall in acreage planted. More than fifteen temporary workers were lured away by the 9,000-acre Hobart farm twenty miles to the north. The newly formed bonanza was desperate to get crops in the ground and paid a third again the Schmidt wage, plus a bonus for workers who stayed through harvest.

Stanton McDowell, expanding on Britt's effort, continued to make improvements to the experimental station. Under his guidance, the capacity for faculty, students, and visitors had been increased. Stanton recruited a friend of Juanna's and Juanna's daughter, Margarita, to cook for the station and provide housekeeping as necessary. Professor Lehmann had not been as successful in attracting private sector participation. Several companies expressed interest, but none would be on site in the station's first full year of operation. The college planned to devote seventy acres to wheat, half from the same seed stock used by the Schmidt farm and half using a hybrid. Experiments with in-bred corn, hybrid barley and superphosphate fertilizers would also take place. Schmidt farm equipment would be used to plant, cultivate and harvest—labor would be provided by the students.

Stanton McDowell was not a social person and interaction with the Schmidt farm was limited to Colvis and occasionally Morgan or Britt. On one of his infrequent visits to the Queen Anne, Stanton asked if he could plot the Schmidt farm by section and conduct studies within each. His intent was to record soil quality, irrigation, fertilizer, and exposure to sunlight, charting the effect of each variable on production. Morgan heard of the study and asked if Calvin could participate. Stanton welcomed the assistance. John also got wind of the project and thought his son's time was better spent on fieldwork, but was pleased Calvin had found something on the farm that piqued his interest.

Calvin poured himself into the task. Much like his study of wheat futures, it was the numbers, graphs, and charts that intrigued the young man—he had no real interest in the outcome of the study or what impact it may have on farm production. The station manager was happy for the help and saw something of himself in Calvin's behavior. He only wished the farm boss exhibited as much interest. Colvis tolerated the study, but saw the effort as busywork.

Stanton had also taken notice of the farm's egg production. Selling or trading surplus eggs was not uncommon, but the Schmidts took it a step further, contracting with the Casselton General Store to provide eggs on a daily basis. Stanton was interested if Morgan intended to expand their commercial egg venture. She did not. Casselton was too far removed from Fargo and others, closer to the city, were expanding to meet the demands of the larger market. With the Mann addition, wheat was king and eggs were now a distraction.

Midway through the planting season, Maria began to focus on Morgan's wedding. Morgan again expressed her preference for a small gathering, but attempts to pare down invitees were futile. Britt was no help, announcing the number of Lowrys attending was twenty-three and growing. Melina would also be on hand along with Hilke, at least two of her sons, and an unknown number of children. The farm could accommodate the Schafers, but not the Lowry clan. Britt had the answer. The June 26 wedding date fell during the two-week period when faculty and students left the experimental station and returned to campus. Melina, Hilke and her boys would stay in the Queen Anne along with Britt's father and mother. The rest of the Lowry clan would make the experimental station their temporary home.

A month before the wedding, Britt received an unexpected letter from his father. William Manchester Lowry planned on gifting the family's 800-acre leasehold to his son and new bride. The decision on what came next was up to Britt. He could sell, continue to lease the ground or—the outcome his father desired—take up residence there. The senior Lowry hoped Britt chose the latter since it brought his son much closer to Yankton. The couple thanked Britt's father, but told him they were committed to the Schmidt farm. "It's yours" was his response.

Britt and Morgan had a decision to make. The pair had discussed building just north of the Queen Anne, but now had an option. The nearby LeMaster farm was rumored to be for sale, but John was disinterested and Morgan saw no reason to press the issue. Selling the Yankton leasehold meant Britt and Morgan could purchase the property for themselves—a place of their own. It was 320 acres, less than a mile from the original big house, and included a prairie four square home and three outbuildings. As prime Red River Valley land, it would take all of the proceeds of the gifted farm. Luther Ogden was called upon for advice and recommended an immediate purchase.

Using funds from cash reserves the Schmidt farm purchased what Richard LeMaster called "Sunset Ranch." Britt planned on reimbursing the Schmidts upon sale of the Yankton property. Once the transaction was complete, the ranch would be treated as part of the larger farm, with one-half the harvest proceeds accruing to Britt and Morgan.

Britt's family was also responsible for a second surprise gift. His uncle, who gave Britt his first job after college, was unable to attend the wedding. As an alternative, he sent two round-trip tickets to Chicago, along with two nights' lodging at the Palmer House. After the hotel stay, the couple would join the Lowrys for three nights. A number of events were planned entertaining family and friends. Morgan was both excited and apprehensive. A visit to Chicago was appealing, but associating with wealthy socialites was not. What to wear, rather than casual conversation, was her concern. Morgan's wardrobe hardly matched that of Chicago's elite. Two days later Morgan visited the Bergmanns' emporium, selecting four rather conservative dresses. One, with some adjustment, would serve as a wedding dress. Priscilla Bergmann was the first to offer help, but her suggestions were extravagant. Morgan made her final selections with the help of her younger sister. She left satisfied with her purchase and wondering how anyone could work with Mrs. Bergmann.

Morgan had one more visit with her sister before the wedding. She was running errands for the farm and had reason to visit the apothecary. Clara immediately pulled her sister aside.

"Robert must return to work on the farm," she said. "Our rent has been increased again."

"We can always use another hand," Morgan replied.

Clara snapped at her sister, "Not a bindlestiff; Robert deserves a position in management."

Knowing John's dislike for his son-in-law and the similar view held by Colvis, Morgan responded in the only way possible.

"Robert will never hold a supervisory position."

"You don't understand," Clara pleaded. "I'm trapped here."

Clara became even more agitated accusing Morgan of enriching herself at the expense of her siblings. To placate her sister, Morgan agreed to speak with their father and Britt, but immediately regretted reference to the latter.

Clara was now shouting, "Why is your husband treated differently than Robert? Father has an obligation to treat his children equally and consider their needs before those of an outsider."

Morgan left the apothecary having forgotten what brought her there to begin with. A few days later Robert returned to the Schmidt farm and was again assigned to Meier.

Britt's family arrived in Casselton with the force of a small tornado. They were twenty-five in all—his father William, his mother Elizabeth, a grandmother, two of his brothers, Quentin and Charles, one aunt, two uncles and seventeen cousins. All made their home in or near Yankton. With the exception of Britt's father and Uncle Alexander in Chicago, the family was linked in some way to rail transportation, most recently with the Sioux Falls, Yankton and Southwestern Line. Britt told Maria to expect a great deal of energy, but nothing could have readied the Schmidt farm for the onslaught. Within an hour the Lowrys were riding, tending animals, and trailing Colvis, eager to experience life on the farm. John likened them to a swarm of locusts spreading uncontrolled in every direction. The wellspring of energy was Britt's mother, who proceeded directly to the kitchen apron in hand, ready to work. Britt's father visited with John each afternoon, careful, as a doctor, not to discuss Parkinson's, he understood the disease, but had attended only one patient. Instead, the pair discussed the farm, the Populist movement, and agricultural innovation. Britt asked his father to assess John's condition. Doctor Lowry told his son John was doing as well as could be expected, but nearing the point where the pace of decline would accelerate.

Melina, Hilke, her two sons, and four of their children arrived one day after the Lowrys. The younger Schafers were immediately caught up in the Lowry whirlwind, while Melina sought shelter in the kitchen. She visited briefly with John and was surprised by how securely the Parkinson's had taken hold. Maria and Morgan were understandably preoccupied and, when not in the kitchen, Melina found herself in the company of Tavendar. Nothing had changed since her earlier assessment of the Schmidt children. The youngest was mature beyond his years and very comfortable in conversation with those older than himself. Maria had once told her mother that Tav bore traits similar to Peter, but Melina saw more of William Jennings Bryan. Tav might even be smarter and every bit his match as an orator.

Freidrich and Agnes were unable to attend. Agnes sent her regrets, including a note for Morgan telling her to expect a package not to be opened before the wedding. The package turned out to be a very large crate. With her mother's permission and promise never to tell Agnes, it was opened two days before the ceremony. The crate contained a full set of china. Agnes no longer had need for the dishes as she would inherit an even larger set from her mother. Included in the crate were several Marshall Field boxes containing dresses, shoes and assorted women's wear. A few boxes appeared never to have been opened. A note was attached that simply read "a time and size long since passed." The gift could not have been more opportune preceding Morgan's trip to Chicago. Maria was pleased she allowed her daughter to open the crate early, but both agreed her aunt's generosity should never be mentioned to Clara. Her sister was sure to see the gift as further evidence both family and friends favored Morgan.

The number of guests soared as the wedding day approached. Clara and Quentin stood for their elder siblings. Bishop Williams presided. Maria was sure he chose to preside because of the family's growing stature in the valley. John thought it had more to do more with the bishop's desire for another contribution for his cathedral, now nearing completion. He had promptly reminded John of the building fund upon his arrival.

The post-wedding celebration lasted well into the night fueled by the Lowrys and Luther Ogden's customary gift of spirits. Britt and Morgan snuck away before sunset, spending their first night together on the third floor of the Queen Anne. Two days later, the newlyweds were off to Chicago. The Lowrys departed eight hours later still in a festive mood as they boarded the train. Melina and Hilke stayed with the Schmidts for two more days—the extra time gave mother and daughter space to visit quietly together.

Morgan would recall their two nights at the Palmer House as the quintessential honeymoon experience. Britt's uncle made sure the newlyweds saw the best of the city, arranging special dinners and escorted tours. The remaining four days were also noteworthy, but for the wrong reasons. The Chicago Lowrys were far different from Britt's immediate family. As wealthy socialites, their days were spent entertaining or being entertained at upper-crust venues and magnificent lakefront homes. Morgan was uncomfortable throughout. She was often cast with women who discussed fashion, art and world travel. Most of all they discussed their neighbors. She found the experience distasteful, knowing it was her that became fodder for gossip whenever she left the room. Finally, it ended. She was gracious in her farewell, but happy to exchange the shallow and surreal for the prairie she loved.

The Schmidt farm harvested near 3,100 acres of wheat in 1897— most selling at a per bushel price of seventy-two cents. Average yield reached twenty-one bushels per acre and, in some sections, as much as twenty-five. Insatiable demand and consistently good crops were fast making the depression a memory. John, Morgan and Britt even looked at the purchase of a 200-acre parcel some four miles from the eastern boundary of the farm. They never considered themselves serious buyers, but it felt good to look. Innovation promised further gains in productivity and the farm dollar stretched more with each succeeding year.

The Schmidts had reached a position of relative comfort. The family never forgot the early years of the decade. Although occasionally guilty of extravagance, they required little of the excess others sought to display wealth. Britt was the more likely to deviate, suggesting at one point the family make an effort to engage North Dakota's elite. His suggestion was ignored. Maria and Morgan were content with boredom.

The purchase agreement on Sunset Ranch left the LeMasters on their farm until the first of November—enough time to complete the harvest and ready their belongings for the trip to Des Moines where they planned to live with their eldest son. Their home had been somewhat neglected in recent years. Richard did his best, but advancing age meant deferred maintenance. Britt and Morgan, eager to leave their temporary lodging in the Queen Anne, began work immediately upon the LeMasters' departure. The stairs, porch and fireplace attached to the summer kitchen were all repaired, while Morgan and her mother concentrated on furnishings.

The couple moved to Sunset Ranch in mid-November and Morgan insisted on celebrating Christmas in their new home. Maria was reluctant to break with tradition. The pair reached a compromise. Christmas morning would be spent with Britt and Morgan with dinner for the farm family at the Queen Anne. Clara and Robert joined the family, but the Bergmanns sent regrets. Maria insisted she, Morgan and Britt visit the Hansen farm. The two families had seen less of one another, a development Maria regretted. Success had its advantages, but the seemingly endless demands of the larger farm left a chasm between friends.

Maria asked Oleanna and Kari to plan the Christmas celebration for the greater farm family. They happily did so. Beyond the Christmas dinner, the pair arranged for decorations and coordinated travel to the Casselton school pageant, where the Schmidt farm made up the largest contingent of adults and children. Gift giving was left to the discretion of each family except for an exchange two days before the holiday. Oleanna and Kari purchased two gifts for each child, including those of full-time and temporary workers. The children kept one for themselves and, in the spirit of the season, gave the other to a child previously selected by Oleanna. The event was held in the barn and drew virtually every adult.

The first year of the new century saw a disciplined, well-ordered system settle over the Schmidt farm. Colvis, Meier and Levi went about their duties and required little or no direction. Their movements exuded a calm not seen a decade earlier. Anxiety was replaced by the knowledge the Schmidt farm would persevere, no matter what the season brought. Morgan gave credit for stability to Colvis who knew every inch of the farm and understood the responsibilities of each work crew. He planned on something over 3,500 acres in spring wheat with a total planting of near 5,100 acres—the largest ever. Britt and Morgan's Sunset Ranch would see 160 acres planted. The LeMasters had left their fields in relatively good condition, though twenty-five acres of last year's crop was left standing in the field.

The experimental station had begun an investigation of new hybrid seed that produced a shorter, stronger stalk, better able to withstand inclement weather. The seed was originally developed and planted on the Fargo campus with remarkable results. Stanton had secured enough of the

new seed the year before to plant fifty acres on both the experimental station and the Schmidt farm. The new seed had bested the farm's average
yield by two and one-half bushels per acre. Britt took an interest. When
applied to the current planting, the experimental seed amounted to almost
$7,500.00 in additional revenue. He hoped to plant more of the hybrid as
it became available. Britt's scrutiny was precisely what Professor Lehmann
desired—the opportunity to extend experiments beyond the small amount
of ground allotted the college.

Calvin's interest in charting output by section soon began to fade. Morgan was disappointed, though she expected as much. Whether by design or
nature, Calvin liked to start projects, particularly those having to do with
mathematical calculations, then quickly became bored. He was better at
completing assigned tasks on the farm, but often required a nudge.

Spring brought completion of his secondary education and Morgan
was uncertain what to do with her brother. She asked if there was an assignment that appealed to him.

"Perhaps the station," he answered.

Morgan was surprised. "You didn't finish your last project with Stanton."

"Then I'll work with Meier," he responded.

Calvin's tenure with Meier was satisfactory, but average was something
less than expected from the owner's son. While the family pondered his
future, Calvin announced he had accepted a position at the mercantile. He
apologized to his father who had a hard time coming to grips with his son's
decision. Losing a daughter to marriage was one thing, but his eldest son
leaving the farm?

"I need to get away," Calvin told his father.

John was disappointed, but upon reflection decided a look at the world
beyond the farm would be good for his son.

"Perhaps it's better," he said, then added, "You'll always have a place
on the farm."

Morgan was both surprised and relieved. She expected her brother to
leave, but his departure came sooner than anticipated. She was tired of
finding something for Calvin to do, then making excuses for his failure to
complete the task. Morgan was looking forward to life without her brother
and his quirky behavior.

Calvin came by his new position on a visit to the mercantile. He had a long list of harvest needs, but found the shelves stripped bare. Mr. Stockman was perplexed, bemoaning the condition that left him with too many slow-moving products and too little of those in demand. Calvin found Mr. Stockman's dilemma interesting, and the pair discussed seasonal demand, off-season pricing, and lead time for delivery. The mercantile owner was impressed. He planned an expansion and told Calvin there was work at his store should he decide to leave the farm. He could be both roustabout and supply chain manager.

Mr. Stockman meant the offer as a compliment thinking Calvin was committed to his father and the farm. In something of a surprise, Calvin accepted, but the mercantile owner imposed a condition. John Schmidt must approve. Calvin took a full month to ask his father's permission, but on September 1 he left the farm with a horse and thirty dollars for room and board. As he rode away, John wondered if somehow he had failed his eldest son, although he knew Calvin's heart was never in farming. Maria was saddened as any mother would be when a child leaves the home. Morgan was delighted her brother was gone.

Professor Lehmann was making some headway in his effort to entice manufacturers to trial their equipment on the Schmidt farm. The Champion Machine Company, which briefly employed Britt, planned on fitting one of its gas engines to a Schmidt thresher. The company would also bring a stand-alone engine for demonstration purposes. An inquiry was received from the C&G Cooper and Company. C&G was ready to make one of its self-propelled steam tractors available for either planting or harvest. The device was far too large for the station so the machine would be put to work on the Schmidt farm. Morgan saw steam tractors as dangerous and Colvis disliked the leviathan plodding through his fields. The company withdrew its offer. Negotiations were also underway with two California combine manufacturers, although both were reluctant to ship given the machines were not often seen on the northern prairie. Britt was disappointed. Stanton was not. The college was gradually shifting its attention from machinery to seed genomics and hybrids. A colleague of Professor Lehmann's was now in residence at the station. He and other academicians were engaged in plant breeding. Their work was drawing attention throughout the Midwest.

Calvin's departure left John and Maria with two children still on the farm—Morgan, who was unlikely to leave, and Tav already straining to break free. Tavendar was a good student and, for his age, displayed an unusual understanding of issues important to the farm lobby. For him, farming was more about politics and less about working the land.

Tav began to follow John Burke, a former Democratic Senator who ran for the United States Congress and a local judgeship, but was defeated on both counts by a heavily Republican majority. Burke was a tireless defender of the farm community and denounced the relationship between prominent political figures and the railroads. Tavendar and Britt attended a Burke rally in Casselton. Moved by Burke's forceful attacks on collusion, Tav wrote the attorney. He received a prompt response and an invitation to meet Burke following a speech in Fargo. He was accompanied by Britt and Morgan. The three met with Burke for an hour. He was impressed by the Lowrys, but more so by the young man whose grasp of the farm movement far exceeded his age. He saw like-minded constituents in Britt and Morgan, but a protégé in Tavendar. He told Tav to complete his secondary studies and contact him upon graduation.

The farm finished 1900 much as it had the year before. Yield held constant with price drifting between sixty-five and seventy three cents per bushel. Britt turned his attention to all things mechanical. At least two threshers were in need of extensive repair or perhaps replacement and he was considering a trip west to study combines. Morgan thought the latter frivolous.

Britt had begun to refer to the Schmidt farm as an "agri-business," a term gaining favor in journals of the day. John and his daughter preferred to be looked upon as a small business although output and receipts were beginning to suggest otherwise. The farm drew attention from the USDA, large grain buyers and agricultural schools interested in research conducted by the college. Morgan disliked the notoriety, but Britt enjoyed every minute, often acting as tour guide when the experimental station had visitors.

Oleanna and Kari volunteered to manage Christmas festivities. They did so cognizant of Maria's concern the farm's celebration was gradually becoming more about gifts and less about giving. Progress had been made the prior year when the exchange of gifts was extended to include all farm workers, but

Maria felt more could be done. Their recent good fortune should be shared with the greater Casselton community. With help from the Hansens and their church, Kari located three families who had fallen on hard times—their debt so great there seemed to be no escape. Two lost farms after the Panic of 1893. One of those, after five years, was still trying to finance a return trip to Pennsylvania. All were living in borrowed shelter and faced a bleak holiday. The children of the Schmidt farm were each tasked with providing two gifts for the beleaguered families—the first drawn from their own toy box and the second, something new of their own creation. Meier and one of the older Andersen boys helped with the latter. John, Maria and Morgan donated a small gift of cash. Oleanna and Kari gathered the farm family and delivered the gifts on three successive days. They came with cider and cookies and something more, the real meaning of Christmas.

Colvis again planted over 5,000 acres in 1901, swinging his crew in late spring to help Meier Haugen with construction of a small pond. The idea was Stanton's and part of his studies on the effect of irrigation. He was able to convince Colvis additional yield would more than make up for the few acres lost to the pond. The Champion gasoline engine would be used to pump water to a closely managed half-section. The ground was crisscrossed by a series of irrigation channels and a few acres also treated with a fertilizer under development by the college.

Britt had spent much of his winter studying threshing machines deciding on the Case "Agitator." Morgan thought it too early for replacement, but not Colvis. The prior year saw the failure of one machine leaving the farm short of threshing capacity. The "Agitator," featured steel components and a new tubular return elevator. It could also be adapted to accept a gasoline engine. There was little question gasoline was the power of the future. Britt was able to convince Case to discount one of the machines, including it as a working component of the experimental station.

His deliberations took him away from the farm and Morgan seized the opportunity to put her touches on the interior of their new home. Both disliked Victorian era design, but Britt embraced something called "Art Nouveau." With her husband gone, she was able to decorate in a manner more to her liking—Dakotan farmhouse rather than Britt's "modern" furnishings. She enlisted the help of one of the Hansen boys, an accomplished carpenter, to redesign the living area. There were concessions to the future. The home now included a water closet, tub, expanded kitchen and a battery-operated telephone—the latter a novelty installed by Cornellious Mann to connect the Queen Anne to the main barn. Levi told Britt it was rarely used because of its tendency to shock the user. Colvis managed to overcome the problem with a better system of grounding. The device now connected the Sunset Ranch and Queen Anne.

Calvin was beginning his second year away from the farm and had returned only twice to visit. With two of her children gone and Tav sure to follow, Maria became obsessed with finding some means to bring the immediate family together. She settled on a monthly dinner. Morgan promptly reduced that to every other month. Clara and her husband were supportive, but Calvin missed the first gathering. He had no idea his sisters were expecting.

The announcement had come during the inaugural dinner. Morgan told the family she was pregnant while Clara quietly observed the attention given her sister. She too was pregnant, but reluctant to disclose her condition until there was no doubt. Finally, her emotions gave way and she told the family. Maria was ecstatic. Both of her daughters were expecting. She had been suspicious of Morgan, noting signs of the sickness that plagued her own pregnancy.

Clara's pregnancy was more of a surprise. Robert favored waiting, but Clara had different thoughts. Britt had also noted a change in Morgan's behavior. Thinking it was related to the burden of managing the farm, he spoke with Juanna about hiring one of her daughters, Rosa, to assist Morgan with household tasks. The pregnancy meant Rosa would become a permanent addition. Upon hearing of Morgan's new helper, Clara glanced at her mother with a look of disgust. Nothing was said, but Maria understood her daughter's message. Where was her maid and what of a redecorated home helped along by the family farm?

Colonel Austin called on the farm twice during the last quarter of the year. He was not asked to visit, but felt an obligation to check on John and replenish Maria's stock of asthma ministrations. On the second visit, he told Maria that John was closing on the final stages of the Parkinson's. Falls would become commonplace; he would require bathroom and bathing assistance; and may even experience hallucinations. The family must encourage interaction and some form of exercise. The latter was a struggle. Simply getting John to his feet required the assistance of two people. The Colonel encouraged Maria to find someone to sit with John. Aspiration was likely to be a problem, particularly during the night.

As to Maria's congestion, the Colonel offered little relief.

"Continue the stramonium regimen and leave the farm when you can."

"Leave the farm?" Maria was incredulous.

"Yes," he said, angry at being challenged. Maria found his recommendation amusing, but twice during the harvest Morgan sent her mother to Clara's for an overnight stay. Once removed from the suffocating dust of fieldwork, Maria began to breathe more easily.

The Schmidts had not seen Luther Ogden for some time and Maria was delighted to learn he would pay a call just prior to harvest. John looked forward to his friend's visit recognizing the financier had his finger on the pulse of the valley. On this occasion, Maria suspected he had something else in mind. He requested Morgan join in the conversation and she in turn asked Britt to attend.

When Luther arrived, he found both the Schmidts and the Lowrys waiting. He immediately turned to the purpose of his visit. He wanted to sell the 5,000 acres acquired from Cornellious Mann seven years earlier. His proposal drew surprise, then silence. Luther allowed his comment to settle. He then explained there was an opportunity to invest in a venture significant to the future of agriculture. Luther offered no details, only that he needed to convert hard assets to cash. Most of the 5,000 acres he acquired from Mann had been leased, but contracts on 1,500 acres had been restructured to end in January of 1902, the coming year, with another 600 available in March. That left 2,900 acres still under contract—900 acres accessible in February, 1903 and another 2,000 in November, 1904. He would like to advance the latter, but the ground was leased to Anderson-Middleton Grain, a Chicago-based corporate farm. The company was unwilling to negotiate.

Luther needed an immediate commitment for a cash buy on the 2,100 available in January and March. The remaining properties, as they became available, could be purchased or leased. He preferred the former. Luther had a bad experience with a lessee who charged him with misrepresenting property. If he must lease again, he wanted someone who knew farming. No decision on the 2,900 acres available in 1903 and 1904 need be made today, although Luther wanted to know if the Schmidts were interested in the property. Luther repeated the initial buy, 2,100 acres, must be cash.

Maria was the first to speak. She simply said "John," expressed more as a plea than question. The family was comfortable and times were good. Purchases of the size Luther was discussing could mean a return to the hard scrabble days of the early nineties. John said nothing, but rather turned toward Morgan.

Before she could speak, Britt asked, "Are all parcels contiguous?"

"They're accessible," Luther assured him. Sensing his answer did not satisfy Britt, he added, "You can easily reach them from the Schmidt farm."

Britt asked, "How much?"

"Twenty-two dollars per acre, buildings and equipment included." Luther knew the price was slightly below comparable properties, including that paid by the Lowrys for Sunset Ranch. All eyes turned to Morgan. She sat quietly staring at Luther, but her focus was not on the financier. She was looking through him considering both the offer and what the future might hold. The harvest looked good—3,300 acres of spring wheat at an expected bushel price near ninety-one cents. Hybrids had pushed the yield to near twenty-three bushels per acre.

By any measure the farm had enough reserve funds to make the initial 2,100-acre buy. The price was competitive, lower than she might have anticipated. Other benchmarks made Luther's offer attractive. Markets were strong and gave every indication they would remain so. Good land had increased by more than fifty percent in the past ten years and technology promised gains in productivity in the years ahead. Morgan struggled to find a negative, but could not. The bigger threat was looking back in five years knowing the family passed on a lucrative opportunity. Seven years before her father had purchased 5,000 acres while the economy was mired in a depression. Why not do the same in a period of relative prosperity?

Morgan studied Luther for a moment longer then nodded her agreement. John smiled and Maria shrugged. Britt and Morgan shook Luther's hand. Luther was first to his feet, happy for the sale, but mostly to escape Morgan's unnerving gaze. There were two conditions—an inspection of the property and first right of refusal on the 2,900 acres available in 1903 and beyond. Both were acceptable.

A cursory inspection was conducted two days later and took only a half-day. The property was known to the Schmidts and there were no surprises. The 1,500 acres were divided among six different families and, once vacated, a few structures would need razing. The second piece, available in March, included a bridge that required replacement. Neither was a significant issue. Of greater concern was how the additional 2,100 acres would be managed. Colvis wanted to discuss that immediately, but Morgan was not ready. She needed time to think. A week before, Colvis confirmed what now gave her pause. He planned on returning to Pembina in two years, perhaps even sooner. His arthritis had progressed to the point where the cure, a never-ending dose of salicylates, was bothering his stomach. Colonel Austin told him it was time to leave his daily regimen behind. Morgan was not surprised, but saddened by losing a trusted worker who was considered part of the family. The farm without Colvis seemed unimaginable, but planning to fill the void must begin immediately.

Morgan's estimate of the 1901 harvest proved remarkably accurate. Wheat held at ninety cents per bushel and yield exceeded twenty-two bushels per acre—confirmation the farm had made the right decision in deciding to buy Luther Ogden's property.

Christmas of 1901 was celebrated in customary fashion though Britt and Colvis were preoccupied with expansion and John and Maria with the birth of their first grandchildren. Maria did not like Morgan's active participation in preparing for the year ahead, but was reminded she did the same when pregnant herself. Oleanna and Kari assumed their role as planners, steering the farm family through a myriad of holiday activities. The newest tradition—including the farm's children in charitable giving—was extended. John and Maria limited their time away from home, instead entertaining a small group of Norwegian friends at the Queen Anne. News from more distant family and friends was uniformly good. The Kansas farm economy had improved, and Freidrich's second pass at Prairie Timber was gaining momentum.

The first of two very special gifts came on December 28 when Clara gave birth to Alecia Anne. The baby was delivered in Doctor McKellar's office. John and Maria made the arrangements and covered the doctor's fee. Two and one-half weeks later Morgan introduced Spencer David Lowry to the world. The birth took place in the Queen Anne and Doctor McKellar was again the attending physician. There were no complications with either birth. Clara hoped to spend time with Alecia, particularly in the first few months, but it was not to be. She was back at work within two weeks—the baby's grandmother spending more time with Alecia than did Clara. The opposite was true at the Schmidt farm. Morgan was eager to return to work and insisted a spare bedroom in the Queen Anne be converted to an office so Spencer, when not cared for by Rosa, remained at her side.

Calvin did not visit the farm over the holidays, spending Christmas with the McCutcheon family in Fargo. John and Maria were aware of his decision and also the reason. Calvin had been seeing Victoria, the daughter of Claire McCutcheon, also employed at the mercantile. James Stockman, Calvin and Victoria's employer, had told Britt the couple spent most of their free time together. Britt shared the news with John and Maria. Victoria's father was known to the Schmidts having once been employed on the farm. By all accounts, he was a good worker and now employed on the Concord bonanza farm.

Victoria waited tables at the Riverfront Hotel and had done so for the better part of three years. The Schmidts got their chance to meet Victoria the last week in February. Calvin borrowed a mercantile wagon and, taking advantage of a warm spell, visited the farm to introduce Victoria. It was also an opportunity to see, for the first time, the newest additions to the family—Alecia and Spencer. Victoria was three years older than Calvin and very much in charge of the couple's relationship. After some prodding by his companion, Calvin announced they planned to marry, perhaps in early summer.

John and Maria were not surprised, but disappointed that Calvin had not advised them earlier. They anticipated an announcement of courtship. Instead, they were introduced to a soon-to-be daughter-in-law. Why had Calvin kept it a secret? Maria had questions, but feared inquiry would be seen as objection. Instead, she disguised her sorrow and offered the Queen Anne as a venue for the wedding. Victoria was reticent though offering no alternative. John was losing focus and Calvin, as was his habit, drifted away from the conversation intrigued by his niece and nephew. Victoria was left with Maria, Britt and Morgan.

Morgan asked, "Where do you plan to make your home?"

"Calvin and I expect to live here."

"Here, not in Fargo?" Maria was confused.

Victoria's response startled all three. If it were Calvin speaking, the remark would have been difficult to fathom. Coming from Victoria, it was offensive. A relative unknown had carved out a space on the Schmidt farm. The off-hand comment was made with resolute assurance—Victoria expected a home and a role for her husband in farm management. Morgan was incredulous. She contemplated sharing her less-than-civil thoughts, but decided it was a topic best discussed with her brother.

Morgan took Calvin aside, "Opportunities exist on the farm, but only as a laborer," then added, "Victoria is confused."

Her brother simply shrugged.

"There's no housing here for you or your bride-to-be," Morgan said.

Clara heard Victoria's brazen remark and pulled her mother aside.

"Robert should also be given a supervisory role. He's family, not a farmhand."

"That's unlikely," Maria answered. "Your father would either deny the request or defer to Morgan."

"It's always Morgan. Have you forgotten you have other children?"

Maria was stunned by her youngest daughter's comment and immediately left the room. Calvin and Victoria were already out the door. Clara and Robert followed immediately behind. Maria's plan to bring the family together had come to an unfortunate end.

Britt, Morgan and Colvis had met several times in December to discuss how best to manage the soon-to-be 8,000-acre Schmidt farm. Nothing would be done with the 600 acres scheduled to come into their possession March 1, since acquisition came far too close to planting. The remaining 7,400-plus acres would be divided between Colvis and Levi, with Colvis as the nominal farm boss. Levi was to be included in substantive decisions on fieldwork. All property once owned by Cornellious Mann fell to Colvis. Levi was assigned the remainder, which consisted of the original Meyer farm, Sunset Ranch and the Erhardt and Neumann purchases.

The allocation left Colvis with more than five times the ground, a condition Morgan planned to balance as Levi gained experience. In a year's time, Levi would become a managing partner joining Colvis and Meier in profit sharing. Britt was formally installed as co-manager, a position he already occupied, except in title. His appointment recognized Morgan's desire to reduce her role, albeit modestly, in farm management.

Colvis had earlier petitioned Britt and Morgan to move a relative newcomer, Chez Schouffle, to a position of greater responsibility. He was eager to groom future managing partners knowing his own years on the farm were numbered. Chez first turned up as a temporary worker three years earlier and quickly became a regular. He was a favorite of both Morgan and Britt—always first in the barn and last to leave. At just twenty-nine he displayed knowledge of livestock and equipment well beyond his years. He was assigned to Meier Haugen which left time for the livestock and equipment manager to expand his knowledge of fieldwork.

Forty additional workers were needed to prepare and seed the 1,500 newly acquired acres—all would be retained through the summer. Meier thought the number of horses was adequate and the same could be said for plows, seeders, and harrows. Threshers were also sufficient in number and their conversion to gasoline power would continue. Axel Moen's son was placed under contract for a two-week period beginning August 15. Harvesters did present a problem. The farm was short by at least two and those on hand were showing their age.

Britt preferred the harvester/binders produced by Champion, his former employer. Colvis and Meier liked the recent McCormick design which included several improvements on the original. Britt asked for and received permission to study a McCormick harvester/binder in use on a 2,000-acre Anderson-Middleton farm in Minnesota. After the visit, he sided with Colvis and Meier. While conducting his study Britt noticed AMG had two steam tractors. He made one more pass at convincing his wife to allow Case to demonstrate their latest sixty-five horsepower model. Morgan was not interested.

In the fall of 1896, Marit Haugen had graciously opened her home to Meier's new bride and her three children. Since that time, Oleanna brought her fourth child into the world and was again pregnant. Soon there would be five children and three adults in what by any measure was a small home. Marit loved her grandchildren, but space was becoming an issue. Her older sister had just become a widow and asked if Marit was interested in joining her on the original homestead, now managed by her nephew. The farm was less than seventy miles from Casselton and Marit would have her own room. She seized the opportunity. Her departure left room for Meier's growing family and she was still close enough to see the grandchildren. A move was planned as soon as weather permitted.

John was saddened by the news. He rarely saw Marit, but fondly recalled Albert's contribution to the farm before his untimely death. John had provided for Marit by elevating Meier to his father's position as a managing partner. The decision meant Marit's future was secure. Had Meier not been an employee of the farm, John would have found some means to help Marit, but he wasn't sure how.

Albert's death raised two questions—what, if any, action should be taken when a spouse was widowed in a farm-related accident, and did the farm have any obligation to a long-term employee whose age or failing health meant they could no longer contribute?

John must first address a more compelling query—succession planning for the Schmidt farm and family. John was aware Clara and Calvin felt they deserved some role in farm management, as did their spouses. He believed something must be done, but the last thing Morgan needed was her two siblings underfoot. Neither had any interest in farming and both had chosen to leave the farm in the lean years. Prosperity had suddenly made the farm more attractive.

John had twice before tried to engage Morgan in planning for the future, but she withdrew unwilling to face the specter of her father's death. Procrastination could no longer be tolerated. They had reached a point where management of the farm must be codified. John knew this, as did Morgan. The opportunity for orderly succession would soon be lost.

On a balmy February morning, against Maria's wishes, Morgan bundled up her father and the pair started toward what they now called the Ogden addition. Before the day was out, she hoped to set the foundation for a Last Will and Testament. Morgan understood something of her father's intent, but several questions remained. Rather than press for answers, she allowed her father to guide the conversation. He began by acknowledging that she and Britt represented the future. Their secure leadership was necessary to carry the farm into the twentieth century. He next turned to the managing partners suggesting some form of compensation when they left the farm, possibly a lump sum payment dependent on years of service. He offered no details except to say Mr. Jenkins, by virtue of his position at the bank, may have some ideas.

He paused for a moment and Morgan asked, "How will you treat Clara and the boys?"

"There is no role for your siblings as a principal," he answered. "The potential for conflict is too great. Tav is a possible exception, but he's unlikely to stay in farming."

Morgan had long known she and her father agreed on not including the siblings in a leadership role, but was pleased by the confirmation.

"Clara and Calvin lack the necessary acumen," he continued. "Their spouses would enrich themselves at the expense of the farm."

Having expressed his misgivings, John still believed the children deserved, to some degree, to share in year-end profits. Clara and Calvin had already expressed their dissatisfaction with Morgan's selection as farm manager, but John believed an annual payout would go a long way to mitigate unhappiness.

He motioned to his daughter to rein in. He wanted her to understand two conditions that must be contained in the will. Neither was open for discussion.

"The Schmidt farm must never fall into the hands of a corporate farm such as Anderson-Middleton Grain," he told his daughter. "AMG and their ilk take no interest in the community—Casselton and civic betterment be damned."

"I understand," Morgan said.

John paused before turning to the second non-negotiable condition.

"The will, once completed, must provide funding for the cemetery. Those who now rest in peace and all who follow deserve no less." Two hours had passed and her father was tiring. Morgan had the outline she needed and was anxious to summarize his wishes while still fresh in her mind. She planned on contacting Luther Ogden for help in selecting counsel to prepare a will, preferably before crops were in the ground.

Colvis and Levi planted 6,300 of the 8,000 acres available, eighty percent in spring wheat. Luther's half of the Mann purchase included several gang plows, most manufactured by John Deere. Since Luther had no intention of farming his ground, they ended up with the Schmidts, but were never put to work. Now the farm needed the plows, but the equipment suffered from neglect. Meier and Chez brought most online in advance of planting. Britt ordered harvesters and continued his effort to convince Morgan a steam-powered tractor should be purchased or at least trialed. Morgan held her ground. For the moment, horses would provide the necessary power. Stanton and Colvis expanded their hybrid planting to more than 600 acres and, for the first-time, the college had a large-scale test for the rapidly evolving seed. The station had also expanded its studies to include research on cold weather fruits, varietal corn and synthetic fertilizers. Stanton now saw himself as a working partner. Even Colvis, who once questioned the station's value, agreed.

Luther recommended Silas Reed as an attorney to prepare John's will. Silas was the owner of Fargo's first legal firm, whose history predated the city's incorporation. Morgan recorded the thoughts expressed by her father and sent those to Reed, directing him to codify John's intent. She received a response indicating Xander Adams, a junior partner, would outline a tentative will. The document arrived the second week in March and closely followed the pattern outlined in Morgan's notes. She was designated as the executor and exclusive farm manager upon her father's death. A co-manager may be appointed at her discretion and Britt was designated as Morgan's successor.

Xander suggested a careful review by John, Maria, Britt and Morgan followed by a meeting on March 29. He included a provision for a trustee to act as an arbiter and to ensure conditions identified in the will were carried out according to John's instructions. The provision was not included in Morgan's February notes and proved contentious. John thought appointing a trustee was absurd while Morgan sensed a more fundamental problem—loss of control. The document provided for partial distribution of profit among the children. Virtually all decisions affected profit. Morgan asked what would stop siblings from using the trustee to endlessly challenge decision making? Xander had considered that prospect. Expenditures need only be reasonable and enhance the value of the farm. Morgan was correct. All decisions could be challenged, but her discretion was broad enough to render most allegations moot.

There was additional value in the process as it offered the illusion of fairness and participation. Morgan understood "illusion" and dropped her objection. The appointment of a trustee held other advantages. John did not want the children to return to the farm. In the event something happened to both Britt and Morgan, the trustee would appoint an experienced farm manager—a far better choice than Clara, Calvin or even Tavendar in his later years.

To further insulate Morgan from any hostile takeover, Xander proposed shares would be created for each of the family members. Maria would be awarded twelve shares; Calvin, Clara and Tavendar nineteen each; and Morgan thirty-one. Morgan held the largest number recognizing her position as farm manager and Maria less, assuming she would be cared for by the family. Only shares allotted to Maria and Morgan held voting rights. Upon Maria's death, her shares would be divided equally among the children. Morgan's shares went to Britt or the trustee until the children reached the age of sixteen. The voting provision meant operating control of the farm, even after Maria's death, remained with Morgan or her successors. In the event the property was sold, proceeds would be divided among voting and non-voting shares according to participation.

Xander also made an attempt to address separation pay for managing partners. He suggested it be granted only if the employee had fifteen years of service. John wondered if Marit Haugen would have qualified following Albert's untimely death. Xander pondered the question. Separation pay was unusual. Mr. Jenkins had told Xander he knew of no other farm, bonanza or otherwise, that offered a similar benefit. Perhaps separation pay was better left to the discretion of ownership. All reference to the concept was removed. Xander's draft also addressed prohibition of sale to a corporate farm and perpetual funding for maintenance of the cemetery. The discussion had already run some two hours and John was exhausted. Britt helped him to his room while Morgan and Xander continued their discussion. Xander asked how family members were paid.

"We let father take what he needs, but it's very little." Morgan said. "Mother leaves purchases for the kitchen and incidentals to Juana. We settle with the general store, mercantile, and the others each month."

"What about you and Britt?" Xander asked.

Morgan told him their salary changed from year to year.

"We look first to the farm. Then, it's whatever we need. Colvis made more last year than Britt," she added.

Xander cringed at the response, "You need a more careful accounting of revenue and expense, particularly for salaries. Does anyone on the farm pay for food or shelter?"

"The farm owes us that," was Morgan's response. Then, as an afterthought she told Xander, "Britt receives a monthly payment from the Lowry family trust."

Morgan's response to his question on salaries troubled Xander. Too much of the farm's accounting practices were left to happenstance—carried in Morgan's head or in a portfolio which contained everything from shopping lists to contracts with funding merchants. The Schmidt farm was more orderly than most, but its bookkeeping left something to be desired.

The attorney had one final question. "Did John wish to disclose terms of the will prior to his passing?" Xander explained, "A prior reading can have the effect of reducing conflict after death. If beneficiaries question the contents, the testator is there to answer."

"I like the idea," Morgan said, "but I'm not sure how father will react."

Both agreed a prior reading of the will was a decision to be made later. Xander was directed to revise the document for review in June.

Tavendar Schmidt completed his secondary education graduating with honors. He wrote to John Burke offering to join his staff in whatever capacity the former state senator desired. Burke had temporarily stepped away from politics after his stinging defeat in the race for congress and district judge. He was, for the moment, committed to the practice of law. Burke recalled Tavendar from their meeting in Fargo. He was a bright young man and one whose origins mirrored his own. The Schmidts started with very little, suffered through hardship, and built a successful enterprise. He offered Tav the opportunity to clerk in his Devil's Lake office with the goal of becoming a legal practitioner. Burke still had political aspirations and his offer included the possibility of campaign work.

The offer was far more than Tav expected. He jumped at the chance. The Schmidt farm reacted with enthusiasm and sadness. It was an exceptional opportunity in a field for which Tav was well suited, but the farm was losing its favorite son. Maria was particularly chagrined. He was a happy, loving child. Clara and Calvin were gone and Morgan increasingly occupied with the farm. Tavendar filled the void spending time almost every day with his father. The visits were short, but he rarely missed.

On the day of his departure, John gave Tav a horse and a sum of money far greater than offered Calvin. Tav would soon be in a law office and needed appropriate clothing. The two visited for close to an hour before John fell asleep. Tav sat with him for another one-half hour. He recalled his father in earlier years behind the plow or seated at the kitchen table, but could not escape the inevitable. Tav knew this might be the last time he saw his father alive.

Maria sent a note to Calvin in early June asking if he and Victoria still planned on a midsummer wedding. She learned a week later the date had been changed to December 1. No explanation was given for the delay. Calvin also told his mother the couple planned to visit the farm the following Sunday. The exchange of nuptials could be discussed at that time. They arrived to find John in the throes of a difficult period, heavily congested and feverish. Colonel Austin and Doctor McKellar both visited and feared pneumonia, a common cause of death among those suffering from Parkinson's. Calvin looked in on his father, but there was no recognition. Not wanting to further disturb her husband, Maria sent Juanna for Morgan. She could not be found. Her daughter's absence was not entirely circumstantial. Morgan knew her brother was coming and found reason to be in the fields. Maria again offered help with the wedding, suggesting the Queen Anne as a venue. She also asked if the couple would consider waiting until spring when travel would be much easier.

Victoria interrupted, "Calvin and I will be married by Judge Kennedy. We don't want guests beyond immediate family."

Maria was dismayed. "Weddings have always been celebrated on the farm."

"Then celebrate with a gift," Victoria said. "Perhaps what you and your husband spent on Morgan's wedding? We'll put it toward a home."

Victoria's tone was demanding. Maria glanced toward her son, but he was transfixed by a dust devil spinning in the distance.

"That's a decision for Morgan," Maria said, trying to remain civil.

"Why isn't your daughter here?" Victoria asked angrily.

"She has a farm to run," answered Maria.

That was the opening Victoria had hoped for. She pressed Maria.

"How will you manage the property purchased from Luther Ogden?"

Maria was now angry. "That's none of your business." She was disturbed by Victoria's rude behavior—and even more annoyed with Morgan for leaving her alone. She again looked toward Calvin, but he was transfixed by the dust devil. Finally, Calvin grew weary of studying the whirlwind and turned toward his wife and mother.

"It's time we leave," he told Victoria.

Xander Adams returned to the farm in late July with a revised will for John's signature. It included the appointment of a trustee and clarification of Morgan's role as executor. Separation pay was left to the discretion of management. John's desire to prohibit sale to a conglomerate was also noted along with a plan to maintain cemetery grounds. The will codified the distribution of stock and affirmed only Maria and Morgan held voting shares. Distribution of profit to siblings was addressed with discretion as to manner and amount left to the farm master.

Xander included a note encouraging Britt and Morgan to establish a formal salary schedule. Morgan had written counsel earlier in the month asking him to prepare power of attorney. She wanted authority for any and all decisions affecting the farm transferred from John to herself. The ascendancy took immediate effect. Xander asked John if he understood the documents to which he responded affirmatively. Meier was called to witness the signature. Morgan was now in complete control. The meeting, which she expected to consume most of the day, had taken less than one-half hour.

Britt's parents arrived on August 4 to spend two weeks with their new grandson. They brought gifts for the baby and stayed at Sunset Ranch, spending most of their time with Spencer. Elizabeth Lowry did make several trips to the Queen Anne to briefly visit with Maria. John was feeling somewhat better and managed an hour-long visit with Britt's father. Doctor Lowry again avoided any discussion of John's illness. There was nothing he could offer by way of diagnosis or remedy. John was happy the subject was avoided. The Lowrys took their leave as harvest was just getting underway. They stayed long enough to see the farm fully engaged. As they left, Britt's father suggested the family visit Yankton sometime after Christmas. Britt was excited by the prospect, Morgan less so. Traveling with an infant was not attractive and her father's condition suggested they stay close to home.

Chapter Twenty-Two:

Lost Homestead: The Final Years

> *"In 1900, the average value of the American farm was $3,563.00. By 1910, the same farm was valued at $6,444.00. Farm value increased, in a single decade, more than it had from the landing of Columbus to the end of the nineteenth century. During the same period, the value per bushel of corn, oats and wheat increased by seventy-four, ninety-one and seventy-eight percent, respectively. Price increases for farm equipment and goods in the non-farm sector rose by a fraction of that amount."*
>
> —J. L. Coulter

The farm required less temporary help than usual for the harvest of 1902. Morgan and Colvis encouraged workers to stay on after planting, shifting their effort to the Ogden property. More than half took advantage of the offer. The new harvesters continued to perform well as did the machines repaired by Chez Schouffle. Midway through harvest Colvis realized the farm would fall short of threshing capacity. Morgan immediately contacted Axel, who convinced his son to swing another steam-powered thresher from the AMG fields. The younger Moen was much like his father, a good thresherman with an uneven temperament—pleasant and surly all at once. He arrived two days later, quickly set up his machine and just as quickly was gone, but not before extending best wishes from his father to John. When it was over, the Schmidt farm recorded its largest output ever, near 120,000 bushels of spring wheat. The average yield was twenty-four bushels per acre with the last uncommitted grain selling for seventy-one cents per bushel. At John's insistence, the farm continued to sell its grain to Valley Storage. He considered Funding and Commission Merchants, but recalled the small country elevator had been a willing buyer when times were not as good.

The farm's success earned a column in the *Casselton Reporter,* which quoted Morgan giving credit to her father, the farm family and North Dakota State Agricultural College. The Fargo press took note as well. Newspapers kept close watch on Luther's business activity and those in contact with the financier. The *Fargo Forum* went so far as to suggest Luther and John Schmidt were allied. Morgan was repulsed by the coverage, preferring privacy to trivial mention in local tabloids. Britt liked the attention telling his wife social connections were important to the farm's future. The couple were invited to a number of gatherings with civic and business leaders and selectively attended. The list of invitees, a who's who in Cass County, was regularly cited in the *Cass County Reporter.* Their participation did not escape Clara's notice. The attendees frequented the more expensive section of Bergmanns' emporium and knew Clara was John Schmidt's daughter. When the conversation turned to Morgan, as it often did, Clara painted a less than flattering picture. She characterized her sister as something of an ogre who seized control of the farm at her siblings' expense. Morgan was aware of her sister's caricature, but cared little about how she was seen by the county's elite.

While the Lowrys flirted with notoriety, Calvin and Victoria's marriage got only one line in the *Forum* Journal of Record. As requested, only immediate family attended. John was too ill to travel and Maria was escorted by Britt and Morgan. Clara was absent with no reason given and travel difficulties kept Tav in Devil's Lake. The Schmidts were invited by the McCutcheons to attend a small celebration following the wedding sponsored by Victoria's employer, but declined citing John's poor health. On the return trip, Maria could not help but contrast Calvin's stark wedding to that of her daughters. Her eldest son was customarily detached and the ceremony was over in minutes. No one, including the bride and groom, showed enthusiasm for the union.

Calvin and Victoria had visited the farm two weeks before the ceremony to collect their monetary gift, an amount roughly equivalent to the cost of Morgan's wedding. The figure was somewhat elusive since much of the food and drink was donated. Knowing Calvin planned to use the money to build a home, Morgan asked Britt to estimate the cost of materials for a two-bedroom cottage. Land was not included, nor was construction labor. Britt came back with $600.00 as a good approximation. The amount was close to Morgan's estimate of the wedding cost and a check was drawn. She handed the check to Calvin who glanced at the amount, but said nothing.

Victoria abruptly snatched the check. "You've abandoned your brother," she said angrily, "And not for the first time."

"It's more than you deserve," Morgan responded.

Maria had been quietly observing, still disturbed by Victoria's last visit to the farm. "It's quite generous," she added.

It was obvious Victoria expected a much larger amount. She stared disgustingly at the two Schmidt women, grabbed Calvin's arm and left.

Colonel Austin paid a courtesy visit to the farm a few days before Christmas and was alarmed by John's condition. His fever was elevated and breathing labored. Maria told the colonel her husband seemed confused, particularly when he became overtired. She had withdrawn from any role in planning for the holiday, leaving that to Oleanna Meier and Kari Andersen. The two women were sensitive to John's condition, but determined to protect the children's celebration. Activities were planned including a gift exchange, sleigh rides, and even a variation on the traditional Christkindche—the recently forgotten *Volga Deutsch* ritual. John watched some of these activities, but there were times when the purpose seemed to elude him. Gift giving took place on Christmas Eve. Robert and Clara joined the farm family, which for the first time included Lizzie. Her children attended in the past, but she avoided the gathering fearful her grief might spoil the celebration.

The farm heard from Freidrich and Agnes. The couple sent an assortment of Christmas treats all prepared by Agnes. Maria marveled at the change in her far-away friend, from socialite to homemaker. Agnes sent a special gift—a broach admired by Maria years before when she and Freidrich visited. Melina also wrote from Kansas. Her health had improved, but she now stayed close to home, venturing out only in the company of her grandchildren. She was thankful for their help and support. Albrecht was bitten by the expansion bug, adding near 400 acres of farmland in two purchases over the past year, probably in recognition the Schafer family was growing much faster than the farm. Melina admitted there was a time when Albrecht's action would have troubled her, but the family was secure and her son a good businessman. Tav did not make the trip to Casselton. He sent his regrets citing distance and weather, but promising to visit in late March. The Calvin Schmidts spent the holiday with Victoria's family. A terse note was received suggesting they could exchange gifts when time permitted. Maria was saddened not to see Calvin, but relieved at not having to contend with her new daughter-in-law. There was enough stress surrounding John's condition without introducing Victoria's confrontational behavior. John continued to pass in and out of consciousness and Doctor McKellar, early on New Year's Eve, told Maria to prepare for the worst. Morgan was certain she was pregnant with her second, but decided against an announcement before Christmas. John was on his deathbed and the holidays were about the children, not her. After some thought, she decided her father would be pleased by the news. She told her parents, but no one else knew, save Britt.

Early on the morning of January 3, 1903, Juana, working in the kitchen, heard Maria's frantic call.

"Come quickly, I need you now!"

Juana raced toward John's room to find Maria shaking her husband.

She refused to stop, "Wake up John, wake up," she pleaded.

A glimpse of the beloved master's face and Juana understood John Schmidt could not comply—the patriarch of the family was dead. Maria knew that as well, but was unwilling to face the reality of her husband's passing.

"Find Morgan," she told Juanna, "And have Miguel fetch the doctor."

Juana hurried to the veranda. Her husband was nowhere in sight, but she was able to get Levi Andersen's attention.

"Maria needs Morgan, hurry," she shouted. "Send Miguel for the doctor."

Levi sensed the urgency and immediately began a search for Morgan, while a rider was dispatched to Casselton.

Juana returned to John's bedside where Maria was still engaged in the impossible. She gently pulled Maria away. Britt and Morgan were at John's bedside within minutes. Morgan thought sure her father held the same faint smile she had seen a few days earlier when advised of her pregnancy. By the time Doctor McKellar arrived, a small crowd had gathered in front of the Queen Anne. He went directly to John's bedside. No examination was necessary. John Schmidt had succumbed to Parkinson's disease, the underlying cause pneumonia.

All but a few of the workers were sent home. The day would be one of mourning. Clara and Calvin were notified and arrived in midafternoon. Both planned to spend the night. A telegram was sent to Tav. He received the wire while in Bismark traveling with John Burke. He set out immediately for the farm. Maria spent the afternoon at her husband's bedside, finally leaving after Clara promised to maintain the vigil. She was greeted in the parlor by Colvis. The long-time farm boss told her he would stay on as long as needed, postponing his return to Pembina. He had conveyed the same message to Morgan a few hours before.

John had made a sketch of how he envisioned the cemetery following his demise. The lines were erratic, but Maria understood. It showed an extension into the field opposite the obelisk erected after Karl Meyer's passing. John wanted a monument of the same size and type. The two founders would face each other with members of the farm family laid to rest between them. Maria kept the drawing to herself, but now shared it with her daughter. Morgan asked Britt to arrange for the cemetery extension and begin the arduous task of breaking frozen ground. A stonemason in Fargo would be contacted later to shape the obelisk.

The burial took place on a bitterly cold January 6 with John's children and their spouses in attendance. Victoria was the only exception. Tav arrived the day before and told his mother he would stay on for at least a week. Eric Hansen led a large contingent of neighbors, mostly Norwegian. The service was attended by more than one hundred past and present farm workers. Luther Ogden was there along with Colonel Austin, Xander, Doctor McKellar, Robert Bergmann and the Moen family. The editor of the *Cass County Reporter* was a few minutes late. His paper planned a story on John to be published later in the month. The Schafers in Kansas, Freidrich and Agnes in Washington State and Britt's family in Yankton were notified by wire. All sent regrets.

Morgan had sent a note to Bishop Williams describing her father's time in Dakota and the years before in Kansas and *Russen*. The cleric had studied the contents of the note and arrived early speaking with Morgan and others on the farm. He deftly combined a summary of John's past with more recent achievements delivering a poignant, but blessedly brief eulogy. The group watched John's interment and quickly set out for their respective homes just as a light snow began to fall. The temperature had dropped below zero and only a few stayed on for the small luncheon prepared by Mary Etta and the others. Maria dutifully accepted condolences, wrapped herself in several layers and returned to the gravesite. Tav stayed with his mother until her black veil was covered in white, finally responding to Morgan's plea that both return to the Queen Anne.

The following day found Maria working alongside Juanna in the kitchen. She knew her husband would not approve of mourning if it meant cessation of activity. The best way to honor his legacy was to return to work. Colvis and the managing partners, taking their lead from Maria, did the same. John Schmidt had grown a homestead to a bonanza farm. Work was not just an elixir, but an obligation.

A week following John's death, Morgan completed paper work on the 900 acres the farm would acquire from Luther in February. The price was $22.90 per acre. She also confirmed the right of first refusal on the 2,000 acres now under lease to AMG. That lease would terminate in November of 1904. Colvis worried what impact the near 3,000 acre expansion would have on equipment and working livestock. He brought together Britt, Morgan, Meier and Levi to assess the farm's readiness to take on new ground.

Seeders represented the only issue for the spring. Most were single harness machines planting four rows and dating from the early days of the Mann farm. Hench and Dromgold, Superior, and Von Brunt had introduced better equipment with much broader coverage. Chez studied the machines available and believed the Hench and Dromgold seed drills were the best alternative. Colvis planned to talk with Morgan on the number the farm should purchase. Meier thought there were plenty of horses, perhaps too many. He also believed harvesting capacity was adequate. He and Chez brought one more salvaged harvester online during the summer and another could be made ready if necessary. The threshing contract with the Moen family was renewed with an option to add one more machine in 1904. Contract threshing was an expensive alternative, but it provided immediate backup when necessary.

Morgan could not shake the thought there would soon be a division of profit among siblings. In the past, purchase decisions were made after the books were closed. Cash available went to operating expenses with some amount set aside for the future. A new accounting entry was on the horizon—distribution of profit. Like it or not, this category would be closely watched by Morgan's sister and brothers, particularly Clara and Calvin. Operating expenditures during the year, as well as commitments at year-end, could easily reduce surplus, leaving the siblings with a lesser piece of the pie. If this were to happen, Britt and Morgan would be subject to criticism. Morgan disliked extraneous forces limiting her decision making, but that was sure to happen. Clara, Calvin, and their spouses were changing how the farm did business.

The reading of John's will was set for Sunday, February 3, 1903. Britt and Morgan disagreed on the timing. He felt it too soon creating the appearance of scavengers fighting over spoils. Morgan simply wanted it over. Maria settled the matter siding with her daughter. Each family member and spouse was invited. Xander was to make the presentation and act as moderator. The reading began with the decision to appoint a trustee followed by John's desire to have the children share equally in year-end profit. There was a noticeable drop in tension.

Victoria was especially pleased and the first to speak.

"We can finally access the farm's bounty," she pronounced.

Xander responded, "You'd best wait until the will has been read in its entirety."

He continued his review discussing the cemetery and prohibition on sale to a conglomerate.

The reference to sale piqued Victoria's curiosity.

"If the farm were sold, how would proceeds be distributed?"

Xander was annoyed. Sale was not the intended topic, but he knew

Victoria would persist until the question was answered. He listed the allocation of stock to family members and noted only Maria and Morgan held voting shares. Victoria was angered by Morgan's superior position, but calmed somewhat after learning Calvin would own shares enough, after his mother's death, to provide a handsome payout in the event of sale. Her contentment was short-lived. Xander's reading made it clear Morgan controlled the purse strings and could easily manipulate decisions, notably those affecting funds for distribution.

"Do the siblings have any control over expenditures?" Victoria asked.

Xander's answer was "None."

Robert joined the fray. "Is our share of profits influenced by expenditures during the course of the year or would the farm summarize its books then make deductions?"

"Both," was Xander's response. "Purchases will continue to be made as necessary, but prior to closing profits may be used to pay down debt, replace equipment or make any reasonable expenditure."

Clara was confused, "What does the trustee do?" She was advised his role was limited to judging whether expenditures were "usual and customary," which Xander defined as contributing to the well-being of the farm.

Victoria was visibly angered by Xander's explanation.

"Morgan will 'improve' the farm to the point where Calvin and I get nothing," she charged.

"You have no evidence that will occur," Xander answered.

"Look no further than John Schmidt. Morgan influenced a sick man to our detriment."

Maria struggled to her feet pointing toward her daughter-in-law, "This family doesn't need a lecture from a waitress. If it were up to me, you'd get nothing." She turned toward Calvin expecting him to intercede, but he was folding the cover page of the will into unusual shapes.

Clara glanced toward her husband, gently shaking her head as if to say "not now." The Bergmanns' apothecary was in its usual cash-poor state. She knew at some point, sooner rather than later, she would need her family's help.

Xander was beginning to lose control of the meeting and they had yet to breech the topic of distribution—a subject whose outcome was sure to anger the siblings. A meeting had taken place in early December which included John, Morgan, Britt and Xander. The purpose was to discuss the farm's chart of accounts. Xander knew that John's will, particularly his desire to share profit in some form, meant the farm's books would be subject to careful scrutiny. Scribbled notes in a portfolio or box of receipts on Morgan's desk would no longer suffice. For some reason, Britt had insisted that expense related to the 1,500 acres acquired in January of 1902 and the 600 purchased in March of the same year be accounted for separately. Neither Morgan nor Britt recalled the purpose, but the decision left accounts in disarray. Morgan could put her hands on sought after documents, but the process was cumbersome and required reconstruction—expense in one place, receipts in another. There was no evidence of chicanery, but that would be hard to prove given the farm's recent bookkeeping practices. The longer Xander studied the farm's chart of accounts, the more convinced he became—distribution of profit in 1903 could not proceed when the foundation—receipts and expenditures for 1902—were incomplete, if they existed at all. The process must be defensible and based on comprehensive records.

Xander also knew Clara and Clement, once they heard the conditions of the will, would expect an immediate payout. A year's wait would not be well received. Britt argued a distribution should be attempted based on the books as they existed. The others favored a delay. Morgan sided with council. Xander now had the unfortunate task of sharing the news with the assembled group.

"There's one more item to discuss," he said, struggling to get everyone's attention. "The first distribution will not take place until 1904."

"Damn you," Victoria shouted. "We have to wait one more year?"

"Yes," said Xander, "For the distribution as stipulated in the will, but John signed an addendum providing $90.00 to each of the children payable immediately."

Xander produced the addendum which Victoria swept from the table.

"Was he sane," Victoria shouted.

Even Calvin cringed at the comment.

Britt and Morgan had seen and heard enough of Victoria's angry rhetoric. Taking Maria's hand they left the room. Xander moved for closure making sure each family member had a copy of John's final wishes, including the addendum. Clara signed the document; Victoria did not. She refused when asked a second time, but took the $90.00 check, as did Clara.

Xander was disappointed the meeting ended as it did, though not surprised. He discovered two weeks later Victoria investigated a challenge to the will, but abandoned the effort when told reversing the intent of the deceased was difficult and expensive. Undaunted, she wrote to Britt and Morgan demanding to know if the recent 600-acre Ogden purchase was paid for with cash or financed. When Morgan learned of the correspondence, she insisted on responding. She told Victoria the response was a courtesy—one she didn't deserve. The farm would not open its books to non-voting shareholders until the first distribution of profits in February of next year. Perhaps the response was too harsh, but it was precisely what the situation warranted. There was no further contact with Victoria.

Morgan had been a youngster when the first Dakota boom took place. She was now witness to the second. Urban population soared as did income on the farms of the Red River Valley. Prosperity had returned. More efficient manufacturing meant once novel, labor-saving technology was now commonplace. Morgan was content to observe, leery of the cost and pace of innovation. Change carried a heavy price and today's machines could easily become tomorrow's relics. That's precisely how Morgan saw steam tractors. She was convinced traction engines would replace the horse, just as the horse had replaced manpower, but gas, not steam, would drive the machines. Luther felt the same, investing much of his fortune in gas-powered tractors. To date, acceptance had been slow. Tractors of any kind were expensive and gasoline models lacked the power to be anything more than a novelty.

Britt remained a fierce advocate of steam.

"One machine can replace forty horses," he maintained.

The debate raged between husband and wife. Morgan saw fields cluttered with rusted steel monsters and reminded her husband horses provided their own replacements. Britt saw less manpower and pasture converted to cash crops. Morgan prevailed.

"There are few steam tractors in the Dakotas," she said. "Twenty years from now, there will be even less."

* * * * *

The agricultural revolution put food on the table of an increasingly industrialized nation. Machines replaced the horse, cities grew exponentially and the farm population declined. More efficient manufacturing opened the floodgates of innovation and brought labor-saving technology within reach of even the smallest of farms. The revolution was not confined to a few years or even a decade, but rather spread over much of the nineteenth century. The rate of adoption was dependent on the innovation. Some enjoyed immediate acceptance while others provided a foundation for further advancement and yet another iteration. The steel plow was first introduced in 1830 by John Lane and made commercially available by John Deere. Steel proved stronger than cast iron and sliced through deep roots with less accumulation of soil. Lane's invention, unlike some of its successor developments, was quick to gain acceptance.

In the same decade, Cyrus McCormick and Obed Hussy introduced competing reapers which relied on a wheel and reciprocating knives to cut grain. Before the reaper's introduction, one man using a back-breaking scythe or cradle was lucky to harvest two acres per day. The reaper could neatly cut ten or more. McCormick's design eventually won out and by 1860 reapers were commonplace throughout the Midwest. Further gains in productivity came with incorporation of a platform and rake which periodically swept cut grain, leaving the stalks in tidy rows ready to bundle. Next was the addition of a binder. One farmhand, operating what was now called the reaper-binder or harvester, could cut, gather and bind sheaves. Crops spent less time exposed to the elements, and ten farmhands were replaced by one.

The 1830s also saw the development of the first threshing machine (a European version predated the U.S. model by seventy years.) Prior to its introduction, heads were separated from chaff and straw by pummeling with a flail or trampling by horses. Both methods achieved the desired objective, but led to considerable waste. J.I. Case and others developed a machine which achieved separation by shaking or agitation. Early models were driven by horse power, but Case, building on the Watt-Boulton invention, introduced the first steam-powered thresher in 1869. The machines were expensive and gave rise to thresher teams that followed the harvest or threshing rings consisting of small farms that pooled their resources to purchase a shared device.

The first patent for the harvester-combine was secured by Hiram Moore in 1836. Once again Moore's invention trailed the European entry. Combines brought together reaping, threshing and winnowing. Evolution continued through the late 1800s, but widespread use was limited to the bonanza farms of California and inland Washington State, with Daniel Best and Charles Holt leading the way. Their appearance in the Midwest did not take place until after World War I. Cost was a factor, but early combines also required the grain to be free of moisture before harvest, a condition not always possible in the prairie states. Early combines were pulled or pushed by horses. Draft animals gave way to steam-driven tractors, but these behemoths were heavy, hazardous and expensive to operate. Even at their zenith, they were rarely seen on Midwest farms. It took the gasoline engine to send horses to pasture for the last time. The first self-propelled gasoline tractor was developed by Iowan John Froelich in 1892. J.I Case developed a similar machine in the same year, although it was not commercially available. Not until Henry Ford introduced the Fordson did tractors become commonplace. By 1930, even the most steadfast supporter of the horse admitted a gallon of gas was far cheaper than pasture and feed.

Last in the chain of agricultural developments was the self-powered combine first introduced in 1911 by the Holt Company—a modification of their horse-drawn combine introduced decades before. Large-scale production by Massey-Harris and others would come much later. The "revolution" had finally run its course taking nearly a century to complete. During the period, the cost to produce a bushel of grain had been reduced dramatically with one man able to do the work of twenty or more.

Labor-saving machinery is most often cited as the paradigm of the Agricultural Revolution, but science played an equally significant role. In 1862, Congress passed the Morrill Act, which established land grant colleges for the exclusive study of "agriculture and the mechanic arts." Access to higher education was now more broadly available. The institutions so created developed hybrid plants resistant to drought, synthetic fertilizers, pesticides that eradicated plant and animal disease, and cultivars that grew faster and stronger

* * * * *

Morgan had been plagued by morning sickness for most of early 1903 and she was late in taking her contemplative ride to assess the farm's readiness for the season. More than 5,800 of the farm's 8,900 acres would be planted in wheat with the remaining ground in oats, barley, hay and corn. Near 1000 acres would be left fallow. Britt offered to join his wife, but Morgan declined, preferring solitude to companionship. What she saw pleased her. The winter had been easy on the farm. Spring floods took only a few acres and much of that repaired and ready for planting. Evidence that Colvis rallied the managing partners following John's death was everywhere. The fields were alive with activity and all equipment in working order. When she encountered a work crew, their activity was well guided and purposeful. Faculty and students from the experimental station were similarly engaged, their projects an integral part of operations. Morgan was concerned her father's death might somehow affect productivity. In fact, the opposite had taken place. The Schmidt farm was perhaps better prepared for the planting season than ever before.

Colvis dispatched Chez to the mercantile in May to buy fencing materials and feed supplies. He carried with him a note from Maria inviting her son and Victoria to visit the farm after Morgan gave birth to her second—probably in early August. Maria's plan to bring the family together at bi-monthly dinners had long since been abandoned. Maria didn't expect a miracle, just some degree of reconciliation. Morgan counseled against the gathering, but acquiesced knowing her mother was troubled by the discord. When Chez arrived at the mercantile, he was told by James Stockman that Victoria had given birth two days earlier. There were complications and Calvin was not expected to return until tomorrow. Chez had no knowledge of the pregnancy, but such matters were not commonly shared with workers, even those close to management. He filled the list and reversed course. He told Maria he was unable to deliver the note as Calvin was tending to the birth of his child. Maria gave him a quizzical look and retreated to the parlor. She was dumbfounded. Why would Calvin keep the birth of a child secret, saying nothing to his mother? Morgan had been outside with Spencer. When she entered the Queen Anne, she heard her mother softly crying. Before she could ask the reason, Maria said, "Calvin is a father."

Morgan was at a loss for words. The couple was married just five months earlier. There was, of course, an answer. The child was conceived prior to the marriage—a deceitful effort to ensnarl the son of a wealthy land owner. Maria did not recognize the abbreviated term of pregnancy, still dismayed by her son's decision to keep news of the birth from the family.

"What should I do?" Maria asked,

"There is no choice mother. We must wait for Calvin to announce the birth."

Six weeks after learning Calvin was a father, Morgan gave birth to Alexandria May Lowry. Doctor McKellar was in attendance supported by Mary Etta and Juanna. Britt announced the arrival of Lexi in a letter to family and friends. Calvin's letter included a follow-up note from Maria inviting him and his wife to attend a family gathering to celebrate the newest addition to the Schmidt family. She purposely avoided any reference to Calvin's newborn. Maria was pleased to learn Calvin and Victoria would attend and bring their own new addition, Gavin.

The first few moments after Calvin's arrival on the farm were awkward. Calvin was apologetic—Victoria surly. Maria went straight to her new grandson, commenting that he looked much like John. Calvin explained that he withheld the announcement of Gavin's birth because the child had come much sooner than expected. He was also sickly and Calvin did not wish to burden the family. Maria was content to accept her son's explanation. Morgan knew Calvin was lying, but saw no point in exposing the falsehood. Her mother had found a way around the hurt of not being advised of the birth. It served no purpose to challenge Calvin's story.

The gathering began amicably with Alexandria and Gavin taking center stage. They were briefly forced to share the attention when Tav made an unexpected appearance. He was on his way to join John Burke in Sioux Falls and rearranged his schedule. Tav was an appealing presence; a combination of his mentor's leadership with a dash of Freidrich's devil-may-care. He briefly held sway, but the focus soon returned to the newest additions to the Schmidt family. Morgan began to think the babies would be enough to push any discussion of the will aside. She was wrong. Less than an hour after Tav's arrival, Victoria, who had maintained a look of contempt throughout, asked if the farm would purchase the last of Luther's property—2,000 acres—when it became available next year. Britt interrupted, "Not now, Victoria."

His curt response simply fueled Victoria's ire. Changing the subject, but not her tone, she asked Britt, "How much are you and Morgan paid?"

Absent a response she provided her own, "Too much."

Morgan glanced toward her sister-in-law before turning to her brother, who was doing his best to stay clear of the confrontation.

"You and your wife are a disgrace to this family," she told Calvin. "Take your family and get out of this house."

Maria protested, but withdrew when Tav sided with his sister. It was his first exposure to the simmering conflict. He was stunned by Victoria's behavior and Calvin's feckless effort to control his wife. Tav tried to take his mother from the room, but Clara blocked their path. She had just learned the emporium was closing and there would only be one position available at the apothecary.

"Robert and Calvin deserve a responsible position on the farm."

"That's not my decision," Maria answered, finally managing to escape.

Following the confrontation, Tav changed his plans spending a day comforting his mother and spending time with Morgan studying the plan for distribution of profit. He had no suggestions for the latter, but did express his sympathy for anyone with the unfortunate task of interacting with Victoria.

Over the course of its near three decades of existence, the Schmidt farm had somehow eluded significant crop loss. Maria was certain it was the unseen hand of Jacob and John guarding against calamity. Morgan saw it as luck and nothing more. Their good fortune ran out in mid-August. Lightning, or perhaps an open cook fire from a bindlestiff camp, sent windswept flames over soon-to-be harvested wheat. The fire raced across a small adjoining farm under Ogden lease and scorched 1,500 acres of Schmidt ground, taking with it a barn, windmill and thresher, the latter just put in place by the Moen family. It was a major setback laying waste to more than thirty percent of the anticipated wheat production.

Britt and Colvis surveyed the damage, but there was nothing that could be done given the proximity of harvest. In the early nineties, a similar crop loss would have sent John in search of a lender or worse yet, cast the farm into bankruptcy. The Schmidt farm was now more secure. The loss was disappointing, but one the family could easily absorb. Work proceeded with the remaining acreage yielding over twenty-five bushels per acre driven by hybrids which occupied an ever-growing percentage of ground. Blessedly, the market cooperated as well. A fall uptick in the bushel price for wheat not already committed provided some mitigation.

Christmas 1903 was the first without the farm's patriarch. John's absence saddened Maria, but she found comfort in knowing the holiday would be the first for two new grandchildren. She contemplated the juxtaposition. A beloved family member had passed, while two others entered the world. Maria had known for some time John was failing, but the human condition is such that hope springs eternal and no one is truly prepared for the passing of a loved one. Now she saw her husband everywhere. He was the morning zephyr and the gentle afternoon rain. His countenance could be seen daily in the children she cradled to sleep. Maria grieved for her husband, but found consolation in these constant reminders.

She had suffered through much of the fall troubled by asthma. Late summer was difficult—the fall unbearable. She endured bouts of sneezing, shortness of breath and fitful sleep. Colonel Austin had no answer and Doctor McKellar experimented with bizarre remedies, none of which provided relief save the disgusting stramonium powder. Finally, an early onset to winter gave some reprieve.

Maria had been looking toward the holidays determined to bring her children together absent the ugliness that marked their August gathering. She sent a letter to each, imploring them, for John's sake to put differences aside until the season had passed. Victoria was the biggest concern. She was eager to confront Britt and Morgan and Calvin had little control over his wife. Calvin assured his mother this time would be different. Victoria would abide by the rules. Maria was buoyed to learn Tav was planning to attend and stay on for at least a week. Her youngest had learned a great deal from John Burke, not the least of which was how to deftly reign in confrontation.

Tavendar's skills were never required. The children knew their mother's first Christmas without her husband would be difficult and carefully avoided any topic that would lead to conflict. Christmas Eve was spent together and on Christmas day the larger farm family gathered for an exchange of gifts. In the days before the holiday, Norwegian neighbors left enough *krumkaker* to fill a small barn, and Maria entertained the Hansens who brought an entire *ribbe* dinner. Well wishes were received from business associates in Fargo and Casselton, including Luther who sent his customary gift of whiskey. He told Maria he would miss sharing the holiday cheer with his friend.

The family also heard from more distant friends and family. It was a good year for all with the exception of Melina. Albrecht sent word from Kansas that his mother was doing poorly, having experienced an event not unlike that of her husband. He asked for their prayers. The Schmidts traveled to Casselton where children of the farm family were again actively involved in the school's holiday pageant. It was particularly noteworthy for Lizzie's participation. While visiting the school in the fall, she renewed an acquaintance with an administrator who convinced her to volunteer a few days each week. The chance meeting had given way to an unpaid position in the school's office and a role in planning the annual Christmas pageant. Since the tragic loss of her husband, Lizzie had stayed close to home, rarely venturing beyond the farm. Colvis and Mary Etta were delighted their stepdaughter had emerged from her cocoon. For Maria, the most precious gift was family reconciliation. She prayed the relative calm would continue through the year ahead.

On January 9, 1904, Melina Schafer collapsed in her kitchen. She had been confined to bed for ten days and apparently decided that was long enough. Without asking for assistance, Melina rose from her bed, fell, and could not be revived. Albrecht was uncertain whether the fall or heart failure ended her life. She left behind seven children and twenty-nine grandchildren. Maria was notified by telegram a few hours later. She had recently discussed visiting Kansas knowing her mother was failing. Melina was gone, but her legacy could still be honored. Morgan was reluctant to travel with the baby and suggested Britt provide the escort. The funeral service was planned for five days hence—time enough to reach Kansas.

Maria and Britt arrived at the Hays City Station midafternoon on January 13. Albrecht and Hilke were waiting. Maria had not seen her brother in twenty-six years. She was not sure what to expect and mildly surprised by his appearance. He wore a broad brimmed hat, white shirt, western bow tie and stylish tweed coat. Had it not been for the boots, he could have easily passed for a banker or prominent cattle rancher. Hilke was every bit his equal. She wore a stylish "tailor-made" utilitarian suit, and like her husband, expensive boots. Maria stole a look at her own attire, happy she borrowed two dresses from Morgan. They moved quickly to the carriage and began the trip to St. Anne's. Maria scanned names on gates, but saw none she recalled.

"Is Anna Schneider still in St. Anne's?" Maria asked.

"Hersh lives north of here and Anna died several years ago," Albrecht answered.

"And your parents?" Maria inquired, turning to Hilke.

"Both are dead."

Britt studied the countryside, while Maria continued to search for anything remotely familiar.

She recognized the Austerlitz name. "Is that the family that came with father?"

"It is, Felix is gone—his son Helmut makes his home there."

"Have you seen Uncle Hermann?"

"He sold his land and Midwest Grain and Feed no longer exists." Maria didn't recognize the business name, but saw no reason to continue the discussion.

The land began to look more familiar and Maria saw a sign that released a deluge of memories, "Pallitto's General Store." She learned Josef was gone, but the new proprietor retained the name. Three small businesses surrounded the general store and in the distance a church. The carriage turned at a well-worn intersection. As it did, she saw the sign—St. Anne's Crossing. Maria fought back the tears.

A half-mile later Albrecht guided the two-horse team through the entrance to the Schafer farm. In the distance, she saw the main house she and John shared with her parents many years before. She recalled Morgan's birth and the angst her decision to leave St. Anne's caused the family. This was also the home where she and her beloved father-in-law Jacob were reunited. Her time in St. Anne's was short, but filled with memories. They passed over a small rise and Maria could see what she thought to be the original barn and at least three newer homes.

The Schafer farm looked to Britt like a Currier and Ives reproduction. Outbuildings were freshly whitewashed, equipment neatly arrayed in a large shed, and fencing straight and unbroken.

He asked, "How many acres?"

"Just over 2,100 here and 1,900 two miles south," Albrecht answered. Britt would learn in subsequent conversations the family had also purchased sixty acres of commercial property adjoining the railroad west of downtown Hays City, all of which was under lease. The commercial enterprise carried the name Schafer Brothers Land Development.

Four Schafer families made their home on the farm—Albrecht, two of his brothers and a cousin, the latter having arrived from Pfeifer the year before. Albrecht guided the entire enterprise. One brother was master of farm operations, the other, along with the just-arrived cousin, managed the commercial property. Britt and Maria were escorted to a guest house by two very polite youngsters, part of what appeared to be a small army of children. Leaving Maria to reminisce, Britt sought out Edward Kantor, the Schafer farm boss, hoping to learn something of his methods. Like the Schmidts, Albrecht was a student of technology, but still relied on horses to complete much of the farm's work. The farm did have one steam tractor now located on leased land.

Maria spent the remainder of the day helping prepare for tomorrow's service, which was expected to draw as many as 100 mourners. She peppered her host with questions and was slowly beginning to piece together thirty years of St. Anne's history. Hilke did her best to answer, but clearly had other things on her mind. Finally, when one of the grandchildren was asked to deliver baked goods to the church, Hilke encouraged Maria to ride along.

They took what appeared to be a shortcut angling through fields before approaching a school situated just inside the Schafer property. They were almost past the building when Maria caught the name, "Amanda Lynn Geiser Elementary." Under the name was the year, "1892." The young woman told Maria the school was built by her grandfather and named for the first teacher in St. Anne's. She was about to continue when Maria said, "I knew Miss Geiser."

That was more than the young woman could process and the conversation turned to another topic. Maria later asked Hilke what happened to Miss Geiser and was told after leaving St. Anne's she became an elementary school principal and later superintendent of Topeka schools. She returned to St. Anne's when Peter died and spoke at his funeral. Hilke thought she was now in Pennsylvania.

If there was any question the Schafers of St. Anne's made a lasting impression on central Kansas, it was quickly erased the following day. Melina's service was held in the church Maria had first seen when they arrived. It was small, but the seating adequate given the time of year and difficulty in travel. The foyer was filled with baskets of flowers from farm friends as well as dignitaries who met Melina through her husband's active participation in the Populist movement. Two priests, both from Hays City, officiated. The speakers included the Lieutenant Governor, a representative from the First National Bank of Hays City and a young woman from the office of William Jennings Bryan. Melina was laid to rest beside her husband on ground purchased by the Schafers in 1894 and subsequently donated to Ellis County. The cemetery was open to the public, but the Schafer family had its own section and separate access.

Freidrich and Agnes hoped to reach Kansas in time for the ceremony, but encountered bad weather in the Columbia River Gorge. They reached Hays City a day after the funeral. The couple's first stop was the gravesite. Freidrich spent more than an hour, while the cold forced Agnes to the farmhouse. The couple returned to the cemetery early the next morning before attending mass with Hilke and two of her sons. Maria noticed religion was more central to the Schafers. Perhaps it was the proximity of the church, but it was clear the family was diligent in their practice of Catholicism.

Agnes was eager to speak with Maria and the reverse true as well. They kept in touch, but it had been twenty years since Agnes visited Casselton. Age and childbirth had scarred her previously petite figure, but she was still very much the center of attention. With the ritual of mourning behind her, Agnes was ready to talk and to see as much of the farm as possible. She had lost none of her childlike exuberance and quickly wore out her chaperone, the wife of the youngest Schafer son. Maria and Agnes spent the afternoon catching up in the Schafer parlor. Agnes surprised Maria telling her Prairie Timber had once again sold, this time for good, or so Freidrich said. The business had done well on its second outing with six sawmills and contracts for dimensional lumber scattered throughout the Western United States. Agnes and her mother also owned or held harvest rights on over fifteen square miles of timber—Freidrich managed the land under the name Morehead Timber Resources.

Agnes had another surprise. She and Freidrich had recently visited California's Sonoma Valley and were captivated by its beauty. Freidrich knew the area from a business trip years before and often suggested the valley as the ideal place to retire. After one visit, Agnes agreed. She was taken by the picturesque setting and chance to escape the dank winters of Washington State. The big question was how to convince her mother to leave the ancestral home and her husband's burial site. Freidrich was able to persuade his mother-in-law by committing to build a cottage in Montesano where she could spend her summers if desired. A second trip was made and the couple purchased one hundred-twenty acres. A main house was under construction with an adjoining space for Mrs. Morehead.

Maria stared blankly at Agnes admiring her willingness to adapt to change, no matter what the circumstance.

"I sometimes think Britt is impetuous," she said. "He's a novice compared to Freidrich."

"I'm just along for the ride. I did insist on acreage to keep Freidrich busy."

"What will he do?" Maria asked.

"Grow grapes," I suppose. "He already has a planting scheme."

Agnes shrugged at the thought—timber to grapes.

She paused for a moment then took Maria's hand.

"You should join us."

"Perhaps a visit," Maria answered.

That evening Freidrich shared the same news with Britt and Albrecht.

Both men exhibited surprise, particularly Albrecht. He was sure his brother had become detached from reality. Why would anyone make a conscious decision to abandon a successful enterprise? He was unable to make sense of the decision. Britt was more charitable. He was familiar with the valley, having visited there while managing the experimental station. Britt also understood his brother-in-law was driven by an insatiable demand for change. He was always up to something. If risk were involved, the task had even more appeal. Britt gave it a year before Freidrich's 120 acres grew by fivefold.

Morgan met twice with Xander while her mother and Britt were in Kansas. The first distribution of year-end profits was just a few weeks away and she was apprehensive. A chance encounter at the general store led to a brief conversation with her sister. Clara was unusually pleasant. Morgan feared the change in behavior was based on the expectation of a large payout. Clara hinted as much saying she was excited for the February meeting. Morgan had not seen the final distribution, but from conversations with Xander, she was certain her siblings were in for a disappointment. The late season prairie fire affected profit as did salaries and the ongoing conversion of threshers to gasoline power. Morgan was also sure Britt and Meier had other equipment purchases in mind.

Among the more factious of decisions affecting year-end distribution was profit sharing for the farm's managing partners. Morgan expected the bonus to Colvis and the others to exceed the year-end distribution for Calvin, Clara and Tav. The distinction was justifiable to Morgan. Her siblings would not understand. The real hostility would come with disclosure of salaries paid herself and Britt. Xander had installed, along with extensive revisions to the farm's accounting procedures, a fixed annual salary—simply good business practice.

Pay levels for private sector owner-managers were difficult to come by. This was not the case for managers on large corporate farms. In reviewing those, Xander found comparable pay in the range of $1,200.00 to $1,900.00 per year. He settled on $1,400.00 for Morgan and sixty percent of her salary for Britt. Xander spoke with T. Fergus Jenkins, Chief Financial Officer of First National Bank of Fargo. As trustee, he found the numbers reasonable based on his own research.

Following the ugliness of last year's reading of the will, Morgan had decided not to participate in any meeting on distribution of profit. That duty, should it be necessary, would fall to Xander. A certified check, in the amount of $105.00, had already been mailed to each of the siblings, along with an invitation to review supporting documents. Morgan knew the amount was far less than Clara and Calvin anticipated. She had no idea what Tav was thinking. The documents available in Xander's office included year-end statements of income, along with a summary of assets and liabilities. Xander had recommended against absolute transparency, but Morgan, with Britt's agreement, decided on full disclosure. She believed her father would have done the same and the farm had nothing to hide. Xander saw transparency as a trigger for conflict. Morgan argued no more so than keeping books in confidence.

The mailing included a note on purchase of Luther Ogden's last parcel. The right of first refusal must be acted upon by August. Luther had already agreed to a price of $24.50 per acre. Morgan knew if there was any hesitation, the property would go to the existing tenant, AMG. The ground was simply too good to pass up. The question was not whether to buy, but how much of the purchase price should be financed. The larger the down payment, the less funds available for distribution. Xander included the note hoping the siblings would realize each year brought a different set of circumstances. The one constant—the farm always came first, not distribution of profit.

Victoria was first to react to the February payout and Xander's offer to review financial documents. As Xander had anticipated, she did so in the company of an attorney. Austin Moore was barely in his twenties and moved to Fargo just weeks before. His education in the law consisted of a two-year tutelage with a less than prestigious Minneapolis firm. He was inexperienced and brazen. Xander thought Victoria had found the perfect match. The pair visited the office a few days after receiving the payout. Moore carried a note from Clara saying the firm also represented her and Robert. Xander asked counsel, "Are you representing Tavendar?"

"Not yet," the attorney responded.

Xander knew the siblings could not afford a retainer and was equally sure Moore was not donating his services. His fee was likely dependent on an increase in payout or some other yet to be determined settlement. Moore poured over the books, but was particularly interested in the salary paid managing partners and that paid Britt and Morgan. There had been much speculation regarding how much the Lowrys took from the farm. The real numbers were now before them.

Xander understood from Morgan that Clara earned $390.00 per year—a good salary for a store clerk, but Xander knew there were weeks when she was paid much less. Robert's salary was also variable and, when paid, roughly equivalent. Calvin and Victoria's combined salary was unknown, but thought to be less than $900.00 per year. Austin Moore's investigation quickly seized upon an entry titled "Profit-Sharing, Managing Partners." Simple division told him the share of year-end net income paid managing partners represented at least twice Calvin's monthly salary. When Victoria heard that, she mumbled a one-word response not commonly used by women. Moore then asked where individual salaries were shown. Xander told him they were not disclosed on the Statement of Income, but rather lumped together under the category "Wages Paid Managing Partners" and "Wages Paid Ownership." Victoria cringed at the proprietary reference.

Moore demanded to see the salary breakdown. Xander complied. The numbers disclosed the farm boss, Colvis, was paid twice Calvin's salary and Morgan three and one-half times that of her brother. Victoria was enraged. The farm boss and managing partners held positions that rightly belonged to Calvin, Robert and Tav, arguing the latter would have chosen the farm over John Burke if offered a salary anywhere near that paid Colvis. Victoria stormed from the room dragging Austin Moore behind her. Xander offered a justification for Morgan's salary, but Victoria interrupted, "There is none." Another obscenity was hurled at the attorney.

Morgan advised her mother of Xander's meeting with Victoria and her council. She omitted her sister-in-law's crude language, but did mention salaries had created much of the discord. Maria was deeply disappointed. She hoped the year-end distribution would reduce tension. Instead, it made matters worse. The thought that two of her children had hired an attorney to contest the will was abhorrent. The family was being torn apart and she felt powerless.

For the first time, Maria wondered if Clara and Calvin were being treated fairly. She was uncertain of Morgan's salary, but guessed she was doing far better than her siblings. Britt had recently suggested they buy an automobile and she overheard the couple discuss investing in electrification in Casselton, a light tower similar to what Fargo recently constructed. Maria thought these ideas frivolous and was pleased when Morgan quashed the expenditures. They did nothing more than rub salt in festering wounds. Calvin and Clara were struggling to put food on the table, while Britt suggested the whimsical. She wondered if John would approve of his daughter's distribution of profit, and then recalled it was her husband who put Morgan in charge. She was sure of one thing. John would disapprove of any effort to interfere with his appointed master.

Chapter Twenty-Three:
A Less Troubled Path

"People have to snatch at happiness when they can in this world. It is always easier to lose than to find."

—Willa Cather

Colvis and the managing partners held no interest in disputes within the Schmidt family. Their obligation was to get crops in the ground, more than 7,900 acres in 1904 with 6,500 in wheat alone. It was the last season for Colvis. He, Mary Etta, Lizzie and her children were moving to Pembina in July to join family. The departure of the long-time farm boss meant a change in roles. Britt would assume the reins from Morgan who wanted to spend more time with Spencer and Lexi and was hoping for another child. Levi had more than proven his worth and would take on most of the ground assigned to Colvis. He would also be the farm boss. The newcomer, Chez Schouffle, would then take on Levi's responsibilities and become a managing partner. He and his family would occupy the Rasmussen home. Meier continued to manage working livestock and equipment. He was content in that post. A decision was yet to be made on the position vacated by Chez. The position was a stepping stone for advancement. Two offspring of the managing partners were potential candidates. Morgan must tread carefully in picking one over the other.

Maria was still disturbed by the conflict among her children.

She asked Morgan, "Is there a chance a place can be found for Calvin or perhaps Clara's husband."

Maria got the answer she expected, "There's no place for either."

"Is that what John would have wanted?"

"Father invested his life in this farm," Morgan answered. "Its care deserves better than Calvin and Robert."

Colvis struggled through his final planting season. Arthritis wracked every inch of his frame and even the smallest movement brought excruciating pain. His final days offered testimony of his devotion to the Schmidt farm. Maria believed his years of commitment deserved recognition and the family itself a proper goodbye. She held Mary Etta and Lizzie dear, and John had always seen Colvis as much more than a farm boss. Morgan agreed and a gathering was proposed to honor the Rasmussen family. The preponderance of attendees would come from the Schmidt farm.

Colvis had few friends in the community and Maria insisted all of her children attend, if nothing else to recognize the Rasmussens' long-standing service to John. Though left unsaid, Maria hoped for a modicum of civil discourse. She had spoken with Clara once since the holidays and had not seen or heard form Calvin. Maria and Morgan felt obliged to honor Colvis, but both were also concerned his tribute could easily turn sour. Victoria was almost certainly mounting a legal challenge to the will and not beyond exploiting the Rasmussen tribute to advance her case. She needn't have worried. Calvin was never close to Colvis and quickly sent his regrets. Tav, who briefly visited in March, was unable to get away. Only Clara and Robert attended—their motivation the need to maintain ties to the family in the event the apothecary closed.

The Rasmussens were celebrated with a healthy dose of sadness. The farm would simply not be the same. Colvis was gracious in his remarks, remembering his first meeting with John. What was intended as temporary work while the family regained its footing had turned instead to more than twenty-five years of service and the opportunity to provide for his wife and children. His youngest son, Colvis II, was buried in the Schmidt cemetery. He vowed, no matter what his physical condition, to make a yearly pilgrimage to the gravesite. Mary Etta was unable to finish her remarks giving way to tears. Lizzie also spoke. To her, the farm represented unconditional love, a rebirth and new life. Lizzie planned to join her stepfather in his yearly pilgrimage.

A second goodbye took place three weeks later when Morgan and Britt drove the family to the Casselton Station. They were bound for Fargo then on to Pembina via the Duluth Manitoba Railway. Two farm hands set off at the same time to deliver household goods overland to the Rasmussens' new home.

Throughout the planting season, Maria experienced difficulty catching her breath. With the onset of summer, the asthmatic-like symptoms, once held in check by Colonel Austin's remedies, began to worsen. A wind storm the second Sunday in June prompted Morgan to send Rosa to the Queen Anne. She was instructed to relieve Juana who in turn would assist Maria as she dealt with the suffocating dust. The storm subsided a few hours after dark and Juana sent her daughter back to Sunset Ranch. Britt noted Rosa's absence the following morning and assumed she spent the night at the Queen Anne. When he arrived there, he was told she left the night before. He quickly retraced his steps, but Rosa was nowhere to be found. Levi joined the conversation and dispatched two men to search the area between the two homes. As he was forming daily work crews, Levi noticed Raul Lopez was missing.

The young Mexican worker was hired in early March on the recommendation of Miguel, Juanna's husband. Raul was a good worker, but something of a loner, sleeping under the stars and prone to wander at night. He had more than once startled both Lizzie and Morgan. Britt told him if he was up after dark to stay well clear of housing. Now Raul and Rosa were both missing. Levi immediately formed three five-man crews and assigned search areas. All returned to the farm before noon, having seen nothing of Rosa. Miguel and two others were directed to continue the search.

A few hours later an Ogden lessee came through the gate. He was at the reins of a heavily used wagon. Rosa's body was under a blanket in the wagon box. Coyotes had been bothering his cattle and he had just set a trap line when he noticed women's clothing and found the body under a pile of brush. Britt tried to restrain Juanna, but she rushed to the wagon. Her daughter had been beaten on the upper torso and her face badly bruised. Levi suggested Chez return with the farmer to the location. Mexican horses were shod differently. An examination would indicate if Raul's horse had been at the scene. Chez returned within the hour. The shoes were almost surely Mexican. The Cass County Sheriff was notified and a wanted poster issued. Four days later, a farmer near Madison, South Dakota reported scaring off an intruder who fit Raul's description. Miguel set out with his second oldest. He knew the camps followed by Mexican workers as they headed south. He vowed to find Raul.

Morgan was pleased with Levi's seamless assumption of his role as farm boss. He was a gentle soul who made it a point to know his workers. By contrast, Colvis had always kept his distance, a big man who sometimes used size, manner and years of experience to intimidate. Their approach to supervision could not have been more different, but both achieved the desired result. Chez, the youngest of the partners, had also adapted to his new assignment confirming the trust shown him by Britt and Morgan. He was the picture of sartorial elegance, dressing as if he were an overseer on a southern plantation rather than a Dakotan farmer. His attire was the brunt of good-natured ribbing, but Maria noticed the others were beginning to take his lead. Even Meier, whose shirt often resembled a rag, began to pay heed to appearance.

Before his departure, Colvis sat down with Britt and Morgan to discuss the purchase of Luther's last 2,000-acre parcel. Far too much of the land included "Islands"—the product of having purchased intervening sections from NPRR. The sections had been broken up and were now occupied by small farms. Colvis believed the land was good, but thought it wise to buy less ground and redirect funds to "square-off" the eastern boundary. He estimated 500 man-hours were lost each year in steering around the islands, not to mention the disputes that arose when the property was inevitably damaged in crossing. Better to create, to the extent possible, a straight north-south boundary. Existing owners were likely to drive a hard bargain, but Colvis thought it worth the effort.

Britt and Morgan were eager to settle on the Ogden property in advance of the original purchase date. Land values in the valley were increasing and any delay was sure to result in a higher price. They expected Luther to be agreeable, but instead found him reluctant. Britt had tried on three occasions to reach the financier, but got no response. Farms were appreciating by as much as ten percent per year and Britt wondered if Luther had decided to hold on to his property rather than sell. On the fourth try, he was successful. Luther was still interested, but not at $24.50 per acre as previously agreed. He wanted $26.70. At that price, Luther was willing to sell as much or as little as Britt and Morgan wanted.

The note from Luther was uncharacteristically terse, suggesting if the Schmidts were not willing to pay, others were. The response surprised Morgan. This was unlike the Luther Ogden she and her father had come to trust over the years. Britt and Morgan decided on just 1,400 of the 2,000 acres available Their purpose was to eliminate the "checkerboard" problem. Terms were one-half down with the remainder financed over five years by First National Bank of Fargo. Once again Luther took his time, leaving Britt concerned the purchase might be an all or nothing proposition. Then on August 9 he accepted.

Britt and Morgan now faced another decision. A few months before, Xander suggested Sunset Ranch should be sold to the Schmidt farm. The existing lease was awkward and made no real economic sense. Both properties were controlled by the same ownership which effectively left the farm both lessor and lessee. A cash sale was the best course, but an outright buy meant less funds available for year-end distribution. Once again the decision, even one arguably in the best interest of the farm, must pass through the filter of sibling reaction. Morgan followed good business practice—damn the siblings. The LeMaster property would be purchased from operating funds. Under terms of the agreement, she and Britt retained the cottage and twenty acres. The remaining ground passed to the farm for $1.25 more than paid for Luther's 1,400 acres. Morgan argued the property's historical yield justified its higher value.

Maria's asthmatic condition turned much worse with the start of harvest season. She was often late to the kitchen in the morning and stopped reading to Spencer and Lexi in the afternoon. When told there was a new litter of kids, she nodded passively rather than share the event with her grandchildren as she often did with new arrivals to the barn. Morgan finally sent for Doctor McKellar. He arrived two days later and noticed Maria's poor coloring and deep cough. He was aware of Colonel Austin's treatment options and questioned their value. The cough and weight loss were more symptomatic of tuberculosis, yet there was no exposure. A few studies suggested the disease could spread from cattle to humans, but he quickly rejected the thought. Instead, he encouraged Maria to visit a colleague in Fargo with more experience in respiratory illnesses. Maria resisted which drew an unusually sharp rebuke from her daughter.

Doctor Leland Ray was waiting when Maria and Britt arrived. He received a note from Doctor McKellar a few days earlier suggesting the possibility of consumption, but was skeptical. Doctor Ray was a general practitioner and well-versed in congestive disorders. He made a cursory assessment as Maria entered the examination room. She was thin, pale and looked to be exhausted. She also cleared her throat each time before speaking. Mrs. Schmidt obviously did not want to be in the office and was evasive when responding to questions. He was finally able to enlist her help to induce coughing and immediately noticed signs of pain which she attempted to disguise. He ruled out acute asthma although her environment could be a contributing factor. Maria Schmidt was suffering from something much worse. Her hollow look, weight loss and pain suggested lung carcinoma, unusual, but consistent with her symptoms. He decided against sharing his diagnosis until their next visit in four weeks.

Doctor Ray told Maria, "You must rest for two hours every afternoon. No more asthma cigarettes or stramoniun powder."

"My wife and I will see to it." Britt answered. He knew, if left to Maria, the treatment plan would be ignored.

"She needs to put on some weight," the doctor said. "A healthy farm diet—three meals a day."

In late October, Morgan received an unexpected letter. The correspondence was addressed to John Schmidt and carried the embossed return address of Anderson-Middleton Grain. Inside was an offer to buy the Schmidt farm. No price was given, but the letter suggested AMG had a tradition of paying well above market. Terms could be set by the seller—cash or periodic payments over the life of the contract. A prospectus on the company was included along with three testimonials, each of which discussed farmers who recently sold to AMG and were now enjoying the fruits of their labor. The company planned to have a representative in Fargo in November and desired to visit the Schmidt farm at the owner's convenience. Morgan immediately thought of her father's intense dislike for absentee owners. She discarded the letter, quite sure the correspondence caused John to stir in his grave. Selling to a corporate farm was beyond imagination. Morgan did not mention the offer to her mother or Britt.

October also saw the return of Juanna's husband and second eldest, having spent thirteen weeks in pursuit of Rosa's killer. They found Raul Lopez in the Texas valley which shared the same name as its Dakotan counterpart. He was traveling with a female companion. She was killed instantly in a nighttime ambush while Lopez suffered a gut wound. Miguel offered few details, but Britt learned some time later the killer was staked and left to die among the nocturnal vermin. No attempt was made to inter either corpse and the authorities were never advised. Miguel had acted as judge and jury and issued a speedy verdict.

The argument over the utility of steam tractors simmered through much of the year with Britt advocating his support and Morgan opposed. Stanton joined the fray on Britt's side. The college wanted to trial one of the machines on their Fargo campus and Stanton suggested the Schmidt farm offered a far better test. He appealed to Morgan who reluctantly gave her permission. The tractor was scheduled for delivery in December. Morgan's acquiescence was shaped, in part, by field conditions on the most recent Ogden purchase and the knowledge the farm must soon plant near 10,000 acres. Perhaps there was a place for steam. The tractor would be pressed into service as soon as ground conditions permitted, probably in late February. Britt was excited and immediately wrote Case. He expected the trial to be a success and the Schmidt farm sure to purchase at least one tractor in the year ahead.

Christmas 1904 marked the second time in as many years an elder Schmidt was gravely ill. Conflict was put aside as Maria's children rallied around their mother. Calvin and Clara, their spouses and children spent Christmas Eve on the farm. Tav was there as well. His employer knew of Maria's condition and insisted he take time off. Upon his return, he would officially join the Burke and Associates as an attorney, although his recent activities suggested a role more political than legal. Burke's name increasingly surfaced in newspapers as a gubernatorial candidate and Tav often made appearances on his behalf.

Morgan kept her mother's illness close to the family. The Schafers in Kansas were told as were Colvis and Mary Etta in Pembina and Freidrich and Agnes in the Sonoma Valley. Lisa Hansen also knew, but Morgan wanted no contact with other neighbors. She tried to send word to Luther, but heard nothing in return. Because of their involvement with John's will and the distribution of profit, Xander and Mr. Jenkins were advised. Albrecht Schafer spoke of his father's respect for the Schmidt family. Mary Etta was heartbroken, recalling the early days on the farm and the memories shared with her best friend. Agnes' letter expressed disbelief. Maria had seemed fine on their joint visit to St. Anne's. Freidrich added a post-script sending his prayers.

Morgan was especially concerned her mother's illness not dampen the holiday for the children of the Schmidt farm. A few of the youngsters suspected the unfolding tragedy, but knew little of the circumstance. Oleanna again managed the celebration saying only that Grandmother Maria would be joining them later. Britt assisted Oleanna and the farm family made its annual trek to the school pageant. Morgan was just as happy not to attend. She had begun to avoid such gatherings knowing the conflict within the family was common knowledge in Casselton. Some couldn't resist questioning Morgan on the status. She found their shallow concern boorish, particularly those who suggested that wealth often precipitated family conflict.

Maria never returned to Doctor Ray's office. Something always got in the way. If not weather, it was fatigue, which inevitably appeared on the day of her scheduled visit. At wit's end, Morgan implored Doctor Ray to make a house call. He chose to travel to Casselton by rail, visiting first with Doctor McKellar before Britt escorted him to the Schmidt farm. Doctor Ray believed he made a mistake in failing to share his findings on Maria's first visit. Lung cancer was a rarity, but he was now certain of his diagnosis. Morgan was in the room when he told Maria,

"You have a disease of the lungs, carcinoma. It has not progressed since our last visit, but it will."

Morgan asked, "What can we do?"

Maria started to question the prognosis, but the doctor intervened. "I have no answers. All I can do is make your mother more comfortable. There is no cure."

"How much longer?" Maria asked.

"Maybe six months, maybe a year."

The doctor could not predict the pace of decline, only that the condition was sure to worsen. "You should advise the family," he said.

Maria knew she was seriously ill, but the doctor's abrupt assessment surprised even her. Later that evening, with her daughter's help, Maria wrote Calvin, Clara and Tavendar. The Schmidts were left with a contradiction. The farm was blessed by a record harvest in the just completed season, but economic success bore no relation to happiness. Their matriarch was threatened by a life-ending illness and the family, who should have been drawing closer, was instead more distant. Calvin had not shown his face for months and his wife was contemplating a lawsuit. Tav was absent owing to location and desire to avoid conflict. Clara did visit on occasion, but for the wrong reasons. The Bergmanns abruptly left Casselton, transferring ownership of the apothecary to Robert. The terms were onerous, with two-thirds of monthly proceeds going to contract payments. Clara continuously asked for money and her mother wondered which Bergmann family she was supporting.

Maria began to withdraw beset by a feeling of helplessness. She saw no resolution to family turmoil and illness was sapping her strength. The period of rest and near force feeding had done nothing to improve her condition. Maria told everyone she was feeling better. It was a lie. Within a few weeks of her visit with Doctor Ray, she began to cough up blood. She told herself the condition would take care of itself, but the episodes became more common and efforts to disguise them difficult. Juanna was suspicious, finding droplets of blood on bedroom linens and handkerchief. Finally, she confronted Maria who begged Juanna not to say anything. She could not in good conscious comply.

Juanna showed Morgan one of Maria's linens. "This belongs to your mother."

Morgan went directly to her mother's room, "How long?" she asked.

Maria shrugged.

Juana answered, "*Dos senanas*," counting ten days with her hands.

A note was sent to Doctor McKellar, who in turn sent a courier to his colleague in Fargo. Three days later Doctor Ray was at Maria's bedside. His diagnosis was confirmed. Maria was in the latter stages of lung cancer. Literature suggested an array of drugs were available, but all had been debunked. The only answer was surgery, a lobectomy or perhaps a pneumonectomy. He was not capable of such a procedure, nor was he aware of any surgeon in the Midwest with the requisite skills. It meant a trip halfway across the country. Morgan immediately suggested they begin planning. Maria shook her head and the doctor agreed. Surgical removal of all or part of the lung was in its infancy. Even if the process could be confined to one surgical procedure, the operation was brutal and the outcome far from assured. Maria's suffering would be for naught. The answer was to provide the best quality of life in what was surely her last months on earth. In the next week, Morgan twice decided on surgery. Maria sensed what her daughter was thinking and forbade it. She was not afraid of death, but rather dying in some far-flung hospital room.

Doctor Ray believed palliative care was more than the comfort of one's own bed and nearby family. When restorative treatment was unavailable and pain constant, there were drugs. Before the Christmas holidays he started Maria on tinctures of opium and laudanum. The effect was notable. Maria experienced less suffering and fewer bouts of coughing. The drugs and perhaps the season had allowed her to spend more time than expected with the family.

Britt and Morgan decided before the holidays to spend their nights in the Queen Anne. They would be close to Maria and able to provide relief for Juanna. The move was completed on New Year's Day. She also asked Lisa Hansen to occasionally sit with Maria. Her presence seemed to bring comfort. Very little was said, but the two prayed together and Maria looked forward to the visits.

The Schmidt farm began 1905 with close to 11,000 acres of exceptional ground and a market poised to consume every bushel of wheat produced. Urban centers were growing exponentially as was the demand for agricultural products. Good weather, stable prices and a wave of technology saw a farm economy that easily outpaced the retail, service and manufacturing sectors. The Schmidts found themselves with an uncommon companion—affluence. Xander spoke of wealth management and the bank was eager to discuss investment opportunities. By any measure, the farm was better off than it had ever been, but Britt and Morgan felt no elation. Maria was slipping away and the brief respite from sibling conflict would soon come to an end.

Despite these concerns, Britt was excited for delivery of his long-sought steam tractor. The machine arrived by rail, partially disassembled, on January 13. The tractor had spent its early life in demonstrations throughout the Midwest. Assembly required two full days, and the one-hour trek to the experimental station laid waste to the Meyer Farm Road. The college had the first crack at the machine, picking at the device as if it were a cadaver there for examination, not work. Britt was eager to test its capabilities.

Following a week of dry weather, the tractor was moved to the acreage just purchased from Luther. On softer ground, the machine crawled forward for 50 yards, buried itself in muck and required rescue by the horses it was designed to replace. Two days later the tractor was moved to higher ground where its staggering power was on full display drawing sixteen plow bottoms with no difficulty—one man, one machine and no horses. Britt nodded his approval, but had few supporters. Meier was the most critical. The tractors tore at the ground and all too often sank in a trench of their own making. He found himself shifting from tractor to horse and back. Even when the tractor stood idle, the fire must be maintained.

Morgan was ambivalent. She was impressed by the machine's strength, but concerned steam would soon be replaced by lighter gasoline models. More than anything, she feared the potential for injury. Barely four days after the tractor's arrival, a pressure fitting failed, leaving a worker badly burned—skin peeling off with his clothing. Morgan and Meier prevailed. The tractor assigned to the Schmidts was scheduled for return, but not without controversy. Britt's unbridled enthusiasm was interpreted by Case as an order for a new tractor. Britt contended he was simply advising the company an order might be forthcoming. Case saw it differently and began production. After some interrogation by Morgan, Britt conceded he may have "unintentionally" misled the company. The farm paid Case $400.00 for the misunderstanding.

Maria's health delayed work on calculation for distribution of profit based on the calendar year 1904. The books were still open and Morgan yet to discuss the subject with Xander. Victoria wrote in mid-January asking when the siblings could expect their check. She was told it would be late owing to Maria's illness. She voiced displeasure, but less than Morgan expected. The farm had done well in 1904 as had most in the valley. Clara asked in early December if the farm had recorded its best harvest ever. The question troubled Morgan. Clara saw only revenue, not operating costs and capital expenditures. Meier was convinced another thresher was in the farm's best interest and Levi was anxious to add a windmill, pond and gas-powered pump. Colvis had been awarded a year's salary with his departure, and managing partners deserved an increase in profit sharing. Whether equipment purchase or salary expenditure, all were decisions that influenced the payout to siblings.

Morgan suspected a larger distribution of profit would blunt what she now saw as an almost certain legal challenge to the will. She was faced with a twofold question. How much was too much and what did John mean when he suggested the children share in profits. She believed her father saw each of his children as a part owner. Equity meant a payoff, but also reinvestment and planning for the future. The farm should be run as a business, not a wellspring to be run dry when the season ended.

Morgan was facing her second year of distribution and already despised the process. Clara and Calvin—more so their spouses— anxiously awaited news of the distribution. Morgan understood their expectations would always outdistance reality. What Clara and Calvin really wanted was instant wealth. She voiced her disgust to Xander who offered a surprising escape.

"The farm could be sold."

His matter-of-fact comment caught Morgan off guard. Sale was antithetical to the family legacy. "Father would have never given up the farm."

Xander reminded her, "John would see endless family conflict as no less repugnant. Sell today and the never-ending fight over how much your siblings deserve is over. You and Britt are left with a lifetime income."

Morgan's stare was unnerving. Xander was unsure if his argument reached his client or she was angry.

He continued, "As master, you possess the absolute authority to create a pension providing even greater security."

Xander expected a prompt rejection. Instead, Morgan shrugged her shoulders, "Perhaps someday." She ended the discussion directing Xander to increase payout by fifty percent over the prior year.

The distribution, $158.00, was sent by courier to Calvin and Clara and mailed to Tav. It included an invitation to meet with Xander in his office when convenient for the siblings. Morgan did not expect the larger payout would put an end to hostility, but was cautiously optimistic the inevitable dispute would be less confrontational. She again chose not to attend and was told by Xander the meeting, which included Victoria, Clara, Robert and Austin Moore, was remarkably civil. Moore noted the separation pay for Colvis and contended the increase in profit sharing for managing partners was excessive. He studied the most recent 1,400-acre addition, telling his clients without his engagement the purchase would have been greater and their distribution less. Xander ignored the claim even though it had no foundation in fact. Moore also cited the price paid to Britt and Morgan for Sunset Ranch was more than recently paid Luther. Victoria was particularly disturbed contending the price was inflated to benefit the Lowrys. Xander argued it was productivity—bushels per acre—that influenced price. He offered to show Victoria supporting documentation, but she was suddenly disinterested. There were no further questions. Morgan was shocked when told Victoria left the meeting issuing a perfunctory "thank you."

The tenor of the meeting troubled Xander. He was still new to his profession, but wondered why the sudden change of heart. Morgan shared his concern and worried that Austin Moore had something else planned. She discussed the meeting results with her mother, who embraced the larger payout and less contentious outcome. Maria believed a middle ground, albeit tenuous, had been reached. Morgan started to caution against an early judgment, then decided to leave well enough alone. Her mother had little exposure to joy. There was no reason to spoil the moment.

Two weeks passed and none of the Schmidt children questioned the distribution of profit. Morgan had not seen or heard from her siblings. Even Xander, ever the cynic, began to think the conflict was behind them. On a visit to the mercantile, Britt learned Calvin was now part of the management team and he and Victoria had started construction on their new home. Perhaps her husband's circumstance had tempered Victoria's greed. Robert and Clara were quiet as well, although Morgan expected as much. She discovered in January her mother had been giving money to Clara from a small stash she kept under the bed. Morgan confronted her sister, but allowed the payments to continue. Her mother would never approve of suspending the monthly stipend and, absent the payments, the apothecary would be lost.

Early in March, Maria asked her daughter to take a brief tour of the farm. Morgan responded midway through her request. The answer was no. Maria pleaded with her daughter, but Morgan was adamant. A few days later, she asked Doctor McKellar his opinion. He agreed with Morgan noting the cold air could trigger a coughing spell and further discomfort. Then he reconsidered. Maria had surprised him showing unusual resolve. Why not allow this simple pleasure?

The next morning Maria, Britt and Morgan left the Queen Anne in a four-place carriage just renovated by Meier—the first time the carriage had been put to use. Maria was positioned with her back resting on her daughter's shoulder, dressed in wool, and covered by three heavy blankets. They started toward what had been the original gate to the Meyer farm. Maria periodically raised her arm and Morgan would signal Britt to rein in. Morgan was uncertain what caught her mother's eye, perhaps something new or recollection from an earlier time. Another signal and Britt would move to the next vantage point. At one stop Maria made a broad sweep with her arm which Morgan interpreted to be a question on size of the farm. Morgan told her it was near 11,000 acres. Maria seemed puzzled by the response, then returned her gaze to the fields.

Britt chose a circular route touching on both the Mann and Ogden addition before ending at the cemetery. Maria asked to leave the carriage and Morgan refused. An appeal brought the same response. Britt drove a short distance to a small rise where the obelisk erected to honor Karl Meyer and its counterpoint honoring John Schmidt could easily be seen. Morgan had difficulty containing her emotions. Maria was stoic. She simply stared at the hallowed ground as if in touch with those entombed. She took Morgan's hand and nodded in the direction of home. Britt turned for the Queen Anne.

Maria suffered no ill effects from her sojourn. Beginning in January, Doctor Ray had increased his dosage of laudanum and also permitted limited use of Mrs. Winslow's Soothing Syrup. The latter was billed as a cough suppressant, but used sparingly since it also contained morphine. Morgan thought her mother was resting more comfortably. Doctor Ray and McKellar saw a heavily sedated patient moving in and out of consciousness, but free of significant pain.

Early on the morning of April 9, Morgan awoke to the sound of her mother's cough, punctuated by a muffled cry. She hurried to the bedroom and found Juanna, who arrived seconds before, holding a blood-soaked bed sheet. Her mother was in obvious pain and unable to speak. Her feeble attempts resulted in a gut-wrenching cough and more blood. Maria's expression begged for help, but she understood none was coming. Morgan sent Miguel to find Doctor McKellar while Juanna tried to get Maria to swallow Mrs. Winslow's elixir. Most returned to the bed sheet in a sickening combination of blood and syrup. In time, there were fewer coughs and Maria fell unconscious. Doctor McKellar arrived noting the blood and Maria's pained expression. He fixed his gaze on Morgan. She understood immediately and penned a note to her siblings. Riders carried the note to Calvin and Clara and to the telegraph in Casselton to advise Tavendar.

Robert and Clara reached the farm in time to see their mother alive, though it was unlikely she was aware of their presence. Maria Schafer Schmidt died just before midday. At her bedside were Britt, Morgan, Robert, Clara and Juana. Blessedly, Clara's daughter Alecia was not in the room. Earlier in the day Clara insisted her daughter visit Maria's bedside one last time. The child was traumatized by the sight of bloodstained sheets and clothing. Morgan found Clara's decision to expose a child to death in its most gruesome form to be abhorrent.

Calvin came three hours after his mother's passing and a runner brought a return telegram from Tav advising he was on his way. Calvin stayed on for the night. The family gathered when Tav reached the farm late the next day. Morgan shared three requests made by her mother a few months before. She wished to be buried as close to her husband as possible. Aside from family, she wanted only the Rasmussens, Hansens, Xander, Luther Ogden, Juana and the managing partners in attendance. Finally, she asked that Pastor Donavan Beall preside. Pastor Beall led the First Lutheran Memorial Church of Casselton and, at the behest of Lisa Hansen, visited Maria three times before her passing. Maria found those visits comforting and requested he conduct the funeral service when it came time for interment. He was delighted to do so.

In his remembrances, the pastor focused on Maria's devotion to friends and family, noting she took far greater pride in the blessings bestowed upon her by children and grandchildren than she did in the achievements of the farm. Tav closed the brief ceremony thanking the pastor and those in attendance. He also took a moment to share his thoughts when, for the first time, he rode through the gate knowing there was no father or mother eagerly awaiting his arrival. The farm looked precisely as it had on his Christmas visit, but, in fact, there had been a sea change. John and Maria Schmidt no longer cast their shadow on the land.

There were notes of sympathy from friends and business associates in Fargo and Casselton. Colvis, Mary Etta and Lizzie were unable to attend. The Lowrys and Bergmanns sent their condolences. Albrecht and Hilke arranged for a special mass to honor Maria at the church in St. Anne's. They were especially thankful for the memory of her recent visit. Freidrich and Agnes wrote a long letter addressed to Morgan and family. The poignant note was penned by Agnes and expressed her disappointment Maria was unable to visit the Sonoma Valley.

Shortly after the ceremony, Clara asked her older sister, "Will the monthly stipend continue?"

Morgan was annoyed, "Your mother's grave has not been closed and you worry about money." She told Clara, "The stipend will continue until mother's cache is exhausted. I will not pay beyond that."

The Casselton Reporter devoted two columns to Maria's passing, noting her husband John died two years before. The newspaper mentioned the family's history, the recent growth in acreage and the farm's noteworthy record of production. Survivors were listed and the paper noted Morgan Schmidt Lowry would continue as master of the farm, a position she held since her father's death. There was also mention of Luther Ogden's relationship to the Schmidt farm. The scribe noting Luther had a hand in every purchase made by John and Maria. The financier had facilitated the initial purchase of the Meyer farm, sold John the Erhardt property, counseled the family on the Neumann and LeMaster properties, was instrumental in the first Mann purchase, and more recently sold 5,000 acres of his own holdings—the last addition to the Schmidt's 11,000 acre bonanza farm.

Maria's passing had no effect on farm operations. Levi knew it was a difficult time for the family and simply took charge. He understood his limits and both Morgan and Britt trusted his judgment. Unlike his predecessor, Levi embraced the workers—a fierce advocate of those toiling in the field. At first, Morgan questioned his tactics, but soon came to appreciate an approach which resulted in both lower turnover and increased productivity.

Under Levi's tutelage, the farm attracted workers from throughout the valley. His first harvest had been good. The first full year promised to be even better. He was meticulous, leaving no ground unturned. More than 8,600 acres had been prepped for wheat and sooner than ever before. Morgan was pleased, but felt a strange detachment. Levi, Meier and Chez required almost no direction, often beginning projects before she made the assignment. Britt had also become more aggressive, pre-selling crops and taking a more active role in farm purchases. Morgan told herself that Levi and her husband acted within their authority following the example set by herself, and before that by her father. She was happy for the additional time spent with her children, but missed the challenge of daily farm management.

A few weeks before her passing, Maria asked Morgan to gift a quilt to Lisa Hansen. A quilter herself, Lisa had often admired the heirloom, which had been in the Schafer family for as long as anyone could remember. Morgan and Alexandria were returning from the Hansen farm, having carried out Maria's wish, when they noticed an unfamiliar carriage alongside the Queen Anne. She would soon learn it belonged to Silas Reed, Xander's senior partner.

Morgan entered the parlor and immediately knew something was amiss. Britt was seated head in hands while Silas was making notes in a document that looked like a deed or government decree. A step closer and she understood. Clara and Calvin had challenged John's will. Morgan was chagrined. She had allowed herself to believe her siblings were content. She was wrong. The challenge was filed in the Court of Cass County—Clara Schmidt Bergmann and Calvin Schmidt v. Morgan Schmidt Lowry, Executor. The family was destined to face one another in a court of law. Both Silas and Xander agreed Morgan should be represented by the senior partner. Silas was a fixture in the courthouse and Xander could be called as a witness. He could not do both—offer testimony and act as counsel.

The challenge included two fundamental charges. The first addressed the mental state of John Schmidt at the time the will was drawn. Maria had told Calvin that John was occasionally subject to hallucinations. The episodes ranged from seeing long deceased friends to imagining travels in a strange country. Colonel Austin told Maria such actions were not uncommon among those suffering from late-term Parkinson's. Austin Moore had learned of the hallucinations and now claimed John signed his Last Will and Testament while mentally incapacitated. As part of the allegation, Moore charged that Morgan and counsel knew of John Schmidt's condition and chose a period of cognitive impairment to execute the will. As evidence, Moore cited Morgan's steadfast denial of access to their father in his final days. Morgan shrugged. She had, in fact, shielded her father from Clara and Calvin simply because her siblings were more interested in money than his well-being. The visits would have distressed her father.

The second challenge targeted the executor's interpretation of John's directive regarding distribution of profit. Claimants charged Morgan had twisted their father's intent. The will stated that profits be shared equally among the children. Instead, Clara, Calvin and Tavendar received only a "dividend." The arbitrary scheme left Morgan and her husband with a disproportionate share of profits. The executor justified her actions as necessary to protect the future of the Schmidt farm. In fact, she, not the farm, was the beneficiary. Moore cited Britt and Morgan's annual salary, excessive by any measure, the price paid for Sunset Ranch, well above market, and the frivolous purchase of a steam tractor and subsequent penalty. Finally, the farm provided food and housing for the Lowrys, a benefit not accessible to claimants. Morgan listened as Silas continued to recite a litany of capricious actions allegedly taken by Morgan and her husband. She recalled Xander cautioned against opening the books. He was right. Transparency cleared the path for Moore's challenge.

She sat quietly for a few minutes and envisioned a courtroom with her and Britt on one side, Clara and Calvin on the other. At least her mother was spared the indignity. Maria would have been mortified. Morgan rose and walked to the window staring at the fields ready for planting. In the distance a work crew, likely directed by Meier, was making repairs to a windmill. It was time to replace the machine, but Meier believed he could fix anything.

Silas continued on. He told Britt it would be difficult to prove John was not in full possession of his faculties when he signed the will. The hallucinations were an anomaly. Answering the second challenge could be more arduous. Just how much profit John intended to be set aside for improvements or reserves, vis-a-vis distribution to his children, was open to debate, but he had repeatedly demonstrated the security of the farm and not personal gain was paramount. Morgan's treatment of distribution of profit as a dividend was consistent with her father's decision making. John would always look to the farm first, before withdrawing funds for salary. Morgan was simply following her father's desire for a better, stronger farm. In addition, the trustee had never questioned Morgan's judgment, save the ill-advised purchase of the Case steam tractor. Reed suggested some adjustment in distribution may come from the proceeding, but the change, if any, would be small. The executor and the farm would survive the challenge.

Morgan had missed much of Silas's discussion with Britt, but his next comment caught her attention.

"Neither Clara nor Calvin expect a significant revision to the will," he said. "They simply want to make Morgan's life miserable."

"They've succeeded," Morgan responded.

Silas continued. "A change in distribution, at best, yields a modest increase. If the farm is sold, your siblings have immediate access to John's wealth—a windfall. I believe that to be their objective."

Morgan thought for a moment, "I need some time alone," she said.

"I'll have Juana feed the children," Britt answered.

Morgan penned a note and asked Silas to carry it to Xander. Her gaze returned to the fields. Meier and his crew were making their way back to the barn—the windmill repaired. As Morgan watched, she envisioned her father toiling late into the night while her mother begged him to come in from the cold. John and Maria Schmidt could not have given more to family and farm. She wondered how her parents would see the challenge to her leadership. She and her father had always been in lockstep when it came to management. Would he agree with her approach or favor a more generous distribution? If only she could ask.

It was after midnight when Morgan finally retired. Britt checked on his wife early in the evening, but he had long since fallen asleep, flanked by the couple's children. They had joined Britt earlier, frightened by the unusually strong winds. The Queen Anne was imposing, but hastily constructed. A fresh wind gave rise to unusual sounds.

Morgan had spent much of the evening reminding herself there were blessings amongst the disquiet. After weeks of grieving for her mother, she was at peace recognizing it was cruel to sustain life without quality. Maria was in a far better place, free from pain and reunited with her beloved husband. She had other reasons to be thankful. The transition from Colvis to Levi Andersen was seamless. Both she and Britt had feared a period of instability, but there was none. Levi had aggressively taken control. Barely six months into his tenure, the farm was running better than ever. Her children were also a blessing. Both enjoyed good health and were a constant source of joy. With luck, there would soon be a third child. She said nothing to Britt, but was relatively certain she was pregnant. One more week and she planned to make the announcement.

The revelation never came. Five days following counsel's visit to the farm, Morgan lost the baby. She experienced cramps early in the day followed by an unusual discharge and menstrual bleeding. Juanna found Morgan on her knees clinging to the bed. She asked for Kari Andersen or Oleanna. Juanna ignored her plea and instead called for Britt before sending Miguel to find the two women. He hurried to the bedroom and recognized what had taken place. Kari and Oleanna arrived and Morgan was moved to her mother's room. Juanna sent her husband for the doctor and another worker to the Hansen farm recalling Lisa had assisted Maria after she miscarried. The doctor arrived two hours later and was annoyed by the army of attendants. He promptly dispatched all but Britt, telling him the only prescription necessary was bed rest. He assured Morgan her ability to bear children would not be affected. She found little comfort in his words.

May 26 was set aside to review the draft answer to Clara and Calvin's legal challenge. Silas prepared the response leaving the document with Britt and Morgan for their study. Two witnesses were ready to testify that John was of sound mind when the Last Will and Testament was signed. Xander was one of those. He expected the attorney would be allowed to testify despite having served as counsel to Morgan. Silas also planned on calling T. Fergus Jenkins, the farm's banking contact and now trustee. Jenkins spoke with John at length regarding the will and found him intellectually capable of understanding its contents. Jenkins would also be called upon to defend Morgan's decision on distribution of profit. As the farm's banker, Jenkins knew how the former master approached management. Morgan's decision to equate distribution as a dividend was precisely the action her father would have taken. Silas hoped to elicit a similar response from Luther Ogden, but to date was unable to connect with the financier.

Silas left the draft with Britt and Morgan. He told them the fee for Moore's services was dependent on the outcome of the proceedings. If Morgan prevailed, Moore would not be paid. The attorney had virtually no income while the case wound its way through the court. Silas planned to exploit Moore's meager bankroll by filing a number of challenges. If he and his clients survived, Moore would then turn to discovery. Clara and Calvin's day in court was months away, perhaps as much as a year. Silas surprised Morgan telling her she and Britt should "get away." Morgan's response was instinctive.

"Leave in the in the midst of planting season?"

"Yes," Silas answered, "Just for a few weeks."

"That's not possible."

Britt glanced at his wife with a look that suggested otherwise.

"Levi is doing fine as farm boss", he said. "Perhaps he'd do even better if given free rein."

That evening Morgan looked toward Britt across the table.

"Where would we go?"

Britt expected the query. "Agnes and the Sonoma Valley," he answered. "You need the rest and nothing will happen in the next three weeks." Morgan studied her husband, but said nothing.

Britt left early the next morning with Meier to inspect a newly constructed roadbed. Morgan took the opportunity to open Xander's response to the note sent counsel via Silas Reed. She had asked Xander to summarize their financial condition assuming the Schmidt farm was sold. He had done his job well. In his estimation, the farm could bring somewhere between $350,000.00 and $400,000.00. The price was above market, but Xander believed the farm's productivity, structures, and equipment supported the valuation. Outstanding debt was minimal and there was some worth in the farm's long-standing relationship with

Stanton McDowell and the college. Xander doubted any farm in the valley had a better reputation. According to John's will, the designated share participation would leave Britt and Morgan with close to one-third of the sale price or near $140,000.00. If they decided to sell what remained of Sunset Ranch, they could expect another $1,200.00. The Lowrys had cash reserves of $30,000.00 from the initial sale of the Sunset Ranch and from their personal bank accounts. Xander anticipated these funds would generate an annual return of five percent. There was also the $1,500.00 Britt received each year from his family trust. Xander recommended that Morgan, exercising her powers as farm manager, create a pension in the amount of $1,344.00 per year or sixty percent of Britt and Morgan's existing salary. As long as the pension came with sale of the farm, there would be no objection from the siblings. They may be unhappy, but their annoyance would be short-lived. Proceeds from the sale would provide salve for any discomfort. Lastly, there was the matter of Britt's inheritance following his father's passing. Absent any real knowledge, Xander guessed the couple could receive as much as $30,000.00 from the family estate producing an additional $1,500.00 to $2,000.00 annually. Xander had answered Morgan's question. If the farm were sold, she and Britt would be very comfortable.

Three weeks later Britt, Morgan and their children arrived at the Sacramento Valley station on tracks laid three decades earlier by Central Pacific as part of the cross-continent rail corridor. Their departure came shortly after crops were in the ground. Morgan had taken several days to make a decision, but eventually agreed with her husband—a break would be good for them both. She prepared a multi-page list of projects for Levi, each with its own benchmarks and what action to be taken if anything went awry. "Wire with problems" was scribbled on the final page. The list was the product of countless nights and too many meetings with the farm boss. Levi complained to Britt and was told the family would soon be on its way and the tedium would end.

Britt was still uncertain why Morgan agreed so quickly to the trip, but he had wasted no time making arrangements. Morgan did impose conditions: the children must be included; Levi, Meier and Chez must approve; a means of regular contact must be established; and their absence could be no more than three weeks. Britt objected to the latter, but acquiesced fearing he may lose the trip altogether.

Morgan's first wire to Agnes was met with an effusive response. They would be delighted to entertain the Lowrys. Her mother was spending two months in Washington State and the cottage was available for their entire stay. Morgan followed with a letter explaining she had miscarried and asked their first day be one of rest. They were traveling by Pullman coach, but thought the quiet would be good for herself and the children. Thereafter, she was ready for anything. Agnes agreed to the former and was eager to fulfill the latter.

On the second day, she hosted an afternoon event with twelve friends. Some cultivated vines as a casual diversion while others grew, bottled and distributed wine, and had done so for many years. Morgan was surprised at how quickly Agnes had become part of the community. Her friends were mostly Italian with some of Spanish descent. No one made an effort to flaunt wealth, nor did anyone try to be something they were not, a refreshing change from her limited social experience in Casselton. The most striking characteristic was their casual, spontaneous behavior. They were uniformly enthusiastic, relaxed and happy. Morgan contrasted that with her own circumstance over the past several months.

All of the women brought young children save two whose offspring were grown and long since left the home. They questioned Morgan about farming in North Dakota and marveled at the challenge posed by weather and the sheer size of the Schmidt farm. When the gathering dispersed, Morgan felt as if she had known the women for years.

Freidrich's approach was more businesslike. He took Britt through his newly acquired acreage explaining it would be one more year before his vines bore fruit. The neighbors were "schooling" him on pruning, a critical element in the growing process. The pair visited two other farms, both operated by husbands whose wives Morgan met a few days before. Britt learned that farming in Sonoma, as often the case in North Dakota, was a family affair with several generations working together. The *vigneron* was often the great grandfather. There were also notable distinctions. Farmers on the northern prairie were constantly on edge waiting for the next spate of bad weather or precipitous drop in prices. If Freidrich's associates had similar concerns, they disguised it well. Everyone in the Sonoma Valley seemed to go about their tasks with a sense of light-hearted enjoyment. Freidrich also took time to show Britt available real estate, some undeveloped land and a few with established farms. One property even included a winery in business for over fifty years.

Freidrich knew Britt was taken by the Sonoman landscape and culture.

He told his friend, "Farming is farming, whether grapes or grain."

Britt responded, "You can't mow grapes."

"Nor can they be logged," Freidrich said. "Nurture the soil and you can grow anything."

The pattern established in the first few days of their visit continued throughout Britt and Morgan's stay. The only disruption came early when Morgan insisted on contacting Levi far more often than necessary. Each trip meant travel to and from the telegraph office, which played havoc with the daily routine. The trips were an annoyance even though made in Freidrich's newly acquired "Daimler" automobile. After the fourth wire, Levi sent a poorly disguised "leave us be." Morgan began to relax and decided the Schmidt farm was doing fine. She also discovered something lost for the past several years—time to focus on herself and her family. The farm and its many complications in the past year had consumed her being, so much so there was little else to give.

During the second week of their visit, Freidrich introduced Britt to a joint winemaking venture, which involved his Sonoma Valley friends. Two members of the group were currently producing a highly acclaimed Cabernet and a third produced a prize-winning Zinfandel. That left two participants, Freidrich and another novice. Both had vines, but no history in winemaking. What they brought to the table was venture capital. Construction was to begin on two wineries before the end of the year. The first, modeled after a French country estate, would be home to the Cabernet and Zinfandel. A second, more pedestrian facility would produce blended wines for broader consumption. Fine wine had a mercurial quality. Consumers were finicky. Less expensive wines were always in demand, could be bottled under various labels, and provided a more consistent source of income.

Chapter Twenty-Four:
Duplicity

"Each betrayal begins with trust."

—Martin Luther

That evening Britt and Morgan shared a bottle of Zinfandel given Britt by one of the winemakers. They were discussing Freidrich's new venture when Morgan suddenly left the porch. She returned a few minutes later and handed Britt an envelope containing Xander's statement of financial condition if the Schmidt farm were sold. The heading was "Income Following Disposal of Assets."

He stared at his wife in disbelief. "Are you seriously considering selling the farm?" Britt carefully studied the numbers—his only correction the sum he expected to inherit from his father's estate.

"I expect twice that amount," he said still unable to grasp the moment. Perhaps it was the wine or the Sonoman culture, but the conversation turned to the lifestyle experienced over the past few weeks. Neither could recall a more pleasant interlude.

"I've never felt I could make a home anywhere but on the farm," Morgan said.

"And now you've changed your mind?" Britt ventured, hoping his wife had reached the same decision he reached soon after their arrival.

"Perhaps—a winter retreat—some respite from the cold."

Britt responded before his wife completed the sentence.

"A seasonal home is another arrow in Austin Moore's quiver—a frivolous expenditure. The trustee may not approve. If you're serious, California must be our permanent home."

Morgan faced a conundrum. She rose an hour before daybreak staring into the darkness. Selling the farm was attractive for many reasons, but is that what her father would have wanted? Was the farm his legacy or was his goal something larger—a life for his children free of uncertainty? Britt did not share in his wife's confusion. The more he considered the options, the more certain he became—leaving North Dakota provided security for the family and offered the only sure way to put conflict among the siblings behind them.

Morgan remained conflicted, but agreed to further discussion. She had but one request. The decision should be made on North Dakota soil, far from the intoxication of the Sonoma Valley. Twenty-four days after their arrival, the Lowrys boarded a Southern Pacific train bound for Casselton. Their stay proved to be far more than a "getaway." Family ties were renewed and friends made. They had been exposed to a new and very attractive lifestyle.

Before leaving for California, Morgan questioned the length of stay. She left thinking the opposite. A week earlier, without Britt's knowledge, she wrote Xander asking him to arrange a meeting to include Britt, Luther Ogden and himself. She preferred the meeting take place within two weeks of their return. She said nothing of purpose, but assumed Xander would guess that sale of the farm would be discussed.

After a longer than expected return trip marked by interminable delays in Colorado, the Lowrys finally crossed the threshold of the Schmidt farm. Levi had done just fine absent Morgan's sometimes suffocating management. She was prepared for a long list of problems, but got nothing from the farm manager except "nice to have you back."

The siblings and Austin Moore had been busy as well. Clara failed to receive her promised stipend from Maria's cache and accused her sister of intentionally reversing her mother's deathbed wish. While Morgan and Britt were absent, Calvin borrowed a wagon telling Levi permission was given. Neither Morgan nor Britt had authorized the action and the wagon was still in Calvin's possession.

Austin Moore filed a deluge of interrogatories seeking background information on virtually every financial decision made in the past five years, including working papers supporting distribution of profit. Several of these were piled on Morgan's desk. She had hoped to return to farming, but instead found herself embroiled in litigious conflict. Moore was also demanding to question Colvis, Colonel Austin, Doctor McKellar and the managing partners. Silas left a note advising Morgan he expected much of the discovery effort to be dismissed, but she should begin to compile whatever documents were available and advise potential witnesses. He also admitted to misjudging Moore's tenacity. He had long believed the challenge to John's will was harassment, designed to encourage sale of the farm. He still believed that to be the case, but was surprised by his adversary's tenacity.

Xander had also responded to Morgan's note sent from California. As directed, a meeting was tentatively set for August 29. Xander had some difficulty finding Luther and advised Morgan that the financier was facing bankruptcy. The prototype gasoline tractor he invested in was a major disappointment, with fewer than ten purchase commitments, most of those already canceled. He was awash in debt and liquidating assets in advance of almost certain liens—one reason for the delay in selling the last 2000 acres to the Schmidt farm. Xander told Morgan that Luther was a desperate man. She understood the warning. Advice from Luther should be carefully evaluated in light of his financial demise. Morgan acknowledged the risk, but believed her father would have still relied on his friend for assistance.

Morgan left California vowing not to discuss sale of the farm until they reached North Dakota, but the subject was breached on the first day of travel and quickly became the exclusive topic of conversation. By the third day, a decision had been reached. Britt and Morgan would list the Schmidt farm as soon as possible following their return. If there was any doubt as to the wisdom of their decision, it was erased by the events of the past few weeks. Clara, Calvin and their attorney had made their position clear. They were committed to make Morgan's life miserable and would not rest unless provided a role in farm management or equivalent remuneration. Even if Silas and Xander prevailed in the courtroom, the unpleasantness would continue. She found the thought repulsive.

The cemetery was among Morgan's first stops upon returning. She visited on several occasions and came away from the last believing her father, if he were alive, would have embraced the decision. Xander's earlier remarks remained paramount. John was committed to the enterprise he built, but equally so to his children. His first dream had been realized, that of building a successful farm. His second, providing security and happiness for the family had not. Sale of the farm would bring closure. She asked herself if the decision was simply a means to escape conflict designed to benefit her and Britt, irrespective of what John may have desired. Perhaps it was, but she still believed her father would approve. Morgan thought of the inscription on her mother's small stone. Surely her parents would "Rest in Peace" knowing there was an end to turmoil. Morgan reached one other decision. Sunset Ranch should be retained. The cottage would provide a temporary home on return trips to visit her parents' resting place. She planned on asking Juanna to occupy or, at least, maintain the home.

Silas Reed and T. Fergus Jenkins were asked to join Britt, Morgan, Xander and Luther for the late August meeting. Xander told Morgan Luther had been located the day before—the once proud Fargo merchant living with a former confidant. A few minutes before the meeting began, Morgan told counsel the Schmidt farm would be sold, then shared the decision with Mr. Jenkins and Luther. Xander and Silas anticipated as much. Mr. Jenkins was surprised. Luther was not. The discussion turned immediately to the farm's value and how best to market the property. Luther was central to this discussion. His ill-fated tractor enterprise had taken him away from real estate, but Morgan believed he still possessed a keen understanding of value. She recalled Xander's admonition regarding Luther's financial distress. Ten additional pounds and the strain of facing financial ruin had taken a toll. He looked disheveled, the self-assurance so much a part of the Ogden persona apparently lost.

Morgan turned toward Luther speaking to him directly.

"There's no reason to give the property away," she said, "But a quick sale would be better for our circumstance. The longer the farm stays on the market, the more likely Clara, Calvin and their counsel will find some way to interfere."

Luther acknowledged the comment, but said nothing.

Xander asked, "What will the property bring?" Luther paused, then began a random discussion of the farm's attributes comparing them to properties sold in years past. Most of his comparisons were dated.

Xander pressed for an answer, "Today, what's the property worth today?"

Luther seemed preoccupied, staring at the floor and tapping his fingers together.

"The bank has been a party to several agricultural sales this year," Mr. Jenkins offered. "I'll compile those for comparison."

Suddenly, Luther interrupted. "I have a buyer."

Morgan was dismayed. A price had yet to be established and Luther had the property sold. No name was given, but Luther described his potential client as a long-time friend drawn to the Dakota Territory by Black Hills gold. He found none and eventually settled on the Missouri Plateau, building a successful cattle ranch. The homestead was lost to the panic of 1893. He made his way to Oregon to work in the fishing industry before once again succumbing to gold fever. This time luck was on his side. Three weeks after arriving in the Klondike, he became one of the few prospectors to stake a successful claim. He returned to North Dakota in 1899 and settled in Bismark. On a recent visit to Fargo, he told Luther he might be interested in property in the Red River Valley.

Morgan was skeptical, "At what price?"

This time Luther responded. "Near $29.00 per acre is possible," he said. "Perhaps more if this year's harvest is good."

Morgan was not sure, "Prices have increased by forty percent in the past few years. I like to see $31.00 per acre."

Britt and Xander agreed. After some discussion, a price of $30.50 was set.

Mr. Jenkins committed to research comparable property, while Xander continued his work correcting errors in recording the first Mann purchase. The latter would take at least three weeks to complete. Luther was advised to contact his mystery buyer, whom he now identified as Michael Aiden O'Connell. No one in the group recognized the name.

Morgan reminded Luther, "The buyer must not be a conglomerate."

"I understand," Luther answered.

Morgan had one more condition, something of a surprise.

"The positions held by Meier Haugen and Chez Schouffle must be protected for one year and they occupy their housing without charge for the same period."

"That's a bit unorthodox," Mr. Jenkins said.

Morgan was adamant, "Either those conditions are met or the buyer pays each the equivalent of six months' salary."

No such provision was made for Levi. Morgan understood ownership would unquestionably want their own man as farm boss. Levi would be taken care of independently by Britt and Morgan,

The following day Silas Reed made inquiries regarding Mr. O'Connell and learned he was something of a recluse, married to an Asian woman who suffered from a serious illness. He occasionally dabbled in the purchase and sale of cattle and was rumored to be heavily invested in other businesses. These were not defined. One thing was certain—O'Connell was very wealthy. The attorney's source estimated a net worth in excess of one million dollars.

For Britt and Morgan, preparing for harvest was lost in the confusion of court proceedings and sale of property. Levi was both farm boss and manager, carrying out his duties as if he held both positions for a lifetime. He met briefly each morning with Britt. From that point on the farm was his. The first week of harvest suggested a solid wheat crop though unlikely to be a record. When time allowed, Britt and Morgan joined Levi and his crew, happy to put distractions aside. Fieldwork was far more satisfying than time behind a desk contemplating Austin Moore's next move.

Morgan spent her evenings answering interrogatories, compiling documents and trying to make sense of the boundary issues recently discovered by Xander. Britt set about updating the contract with the college and experimental farm. A number of changes had been made since the original agreement. All were confirmed by a handshake, but new ownership was certain to require codification.

Midway through harvest, Austin Moore discovered Britt and Morgan planned to sell the Schmidt farm. As expected, he became a nuisance, demanding to see the listing and raising questions on how price was determined. Silas had little time for the attorney. He penned a sharply worded response reminding Moore the decision was Morgan's exclusive right. Only she determined when and how the property was to be sold. Silas characterized the decision as both tentative and fragile. Continued intervention could result in a decision not to sell, an outcome injurious to Moore and his clients.

He went on to advise council the lawsuit represented an impediment to sale and further litigation must be abandoned. Silas had already told Moore the listing meant an end to further distribution of profit. The process could easily interfere with the sale. Moore's response arrived a week later. He called the decision on distribution of profit arbitrary and inconsistent with the will. Silas relented and removed the condition. Moore did commit to withdraw the lawsuit if proceeds from the sale followed the assignment of stock. Within days, Calvin had also written. The correspondence was obviously the work of Victoria and asked how Morgan planned to distribute the family's personal items. He and Victoria had a new home and their need was great. Calvin told his sister he would return the borrowed farm wagon after furnishings had been transported from the farm to his Fargo home. Morgan did not respond.

T. Fergus Jenkins contacted James Buskirk, an appraiser in Minneapolis with experience in the valuation of large-scale farms. Mr. Jenkins had steadfastly maintained the need for a professional opinion on value and Buskirk's name was suggested by Luther. He had worked with the appraiser in the past and thought him to be the best judge of farm value on the northern prairie. Silas Reed had some knowledge of Buskirk and had no objection. With Levi's help, Luther sent the appraiser a list of buildings and equipment along with the Schmidt farm's record of production. Financial statements were sent by Britt under separate cover.

Buskirk's response was disappointing. Comparable sales suggested the price was too high. The appraiser concluded there were no buyers at $30.50 per acre save those with a long view of the market and the means to absorb short-term losses. He recommended a price of $27.50. Xander was worried. Too low a price would dissuade Morgan from selling. The appraiser also recommended any and all conditions of sale be removed, including the prohibition of sale to a corporate farm and Morgan's insistence managing partners be retained or receive separation pay. The appraiser called the conditions ludicrous. Both Xander and Mr. Jenkins suggested a second visit and on-site appraisal. Morgan was opposed. A contentious debate ensued with Morgan insisting the conditions be retained, but to everyone's surprise she was amenable to a price reduction. The new price was $28.00 per acre.

Britt and Morgan shared their decision to sell with Levi, Meier and Chez and with the farm's business associates, including Stanton McDowell. Formal notice to Clara, Calvin and Tavendar was left to Xander who wrote the siblings and met briefly with Austin Moore. The Schmidt children and Moore knew of the sale and the contact was seen as a courtesy. Xander was also hoping for a civil dialogue to prevent disruption, if and when offers were received.

Xander and Britt believed Luther's buyer was something of a long shot and determined broader exposure was necessary. Midwest Farm and Land, a Minneapolis firm, was selected as the listing agent and bought advertising in the *Farm Journal, Progressive Farmer* and newspapers in Minneapolis, Chicago and St Louis. Negotiations with Mr. O'Connell, Luther's contact, were outside the agency agreement.

With the announcement made, Morgan received notes from well-wishers and a visit from two old family friends, Lisa Hansen and Axel Moen. Lisa was saddened by the family's departure and Axel spoke of his respect for the Schmidt farm and its ownership. Tavendar also wrote saying he understood the decision, but was sad the family farm, which held so many memories, would soon be gone. He offered legal assistance, but Morgan declined.

An encouraging flurry of interest followed the listing. Two visits took place. The first visit came from an agent representing a South Dakota buyer. He toured the farm spending fewer than three hours on the premises. The second spent even less time and tendered a bid well below the asking price.

Curiously absent was any word from Luther who seemingly vanished. Morgan thought his behavior in their recent meeting was odd, as did Britt. Both began to wonder if Luther's mystery buyer was a myth. They were pleasantly surprised when Luther sent word O'Connell had been located, having spent the past three weeks in Cleveland seeking treatment for his wife. He was prepared to pay the advertised price. Xander remained skeptical. He sent a note to Luther asking for confirmation from O'Connell or his legal representative. An immediate response was received. Chance McCown of the firm McCown and Senk would be in Fargo within two days to review preliminary documents. He would carry an offer of $28.00 per acre, subject only to on-site inspection and a complete inventory of assets. No other conditions were imposed.

Silas knew little of the Minneapolis firm, but could find no evidence of inappropriate behavior. He drafted the agreement of sale and was ready when Chance McCown arrived. The meeting was brief. Mr. McCown took two hours to study the documents and had no questions. Britt was making last-minute adjustments to the farm's inventory, but the attorney was content to accept the list "as is," a move Silas thought unusual. McCown planned on leaving the next day to carry the draft agreement to Bismark for review. Adjustments were to be made via telegram with the final document sent by courier to Bismark for Mr. O'Connell's signature. The attorney then planned on returning to Fargo to arrange for an inspection. Thereafter, McCown would record the sale with the Cass County Assessor.

McCown made it clear the buyer did not wish to leave his wife's bedside. An inspection was tentatively set for two days hence. McCown noted it was a formality. Both he and his client trusted Luther's judgment and the farm's reputation spoke for itself. He apologized for the frantic pace, but O'Connell's decision came as a surprise. If the sale were not finalized in the next few days, McCown would not be available for at least three weeks. He and his firm were occupied with other business.

Maxwell DeSalle spent an uncomfortable night in Casselton's only hotel and was taken to the Schmidt farm by carriage the following morning. He was a slight, bespectacled man often employed by McCown and Senk to evaluate the real worth of property or business enterprise. Most of his work was commercial or industrial. This was his first farm, a circumstance unknown to the seller and one he was told not to share. Among his various goals was a desire to spend as little time as possible astride a horse, although he understood it might be necessary to keep up appearances. The farm's current books had already been studied, along with three years of prior financials. There were deviations from accepted accounting principle, but nothing to trouble McCown's buyer. His purpose was to ensure assets were accurately represented. DeSalle thought the entire transaction was odd, but so was most everything associated with Luther Ogden.

The inspection was more symbolic than investigatory. Apparently, Chance McCown's client had already made a decision and simply required confirmation, or at least, the appearance of confirmation. He was impressed by the farm's pristine look and even more so the farm manager, his host for the inspection. He knew her to be the eldest daughter of the original master, John Schmidt, who had taken the farm from a few hundred acres to 11,000. She answered questions without hesitation and, in most cases, backed her answers with supporting documentation. Her husband was eager to show the farm. Both were surprised when he declined, choosing instead to inspect only the Queen Anne, barn and equipment shed. He feigned interest in a thresher and seed drill, then asked a few "farm-like" questions provided him by Mr. McCown. DeSalle was sure his host believed him to be well versed in agriculture. The "inspection" took fewer than three hours. Upon leaving, the accountant told Morgan he saw nothing to jeopardize the sale.

Britt and Morgan should have been giddy. In the span of a few weeks, marginal interest had turned to imminent sale, but there were issues. Chance McCown wanted to sign final papers as quickly as possible, but there was still much to be done—too much. Britt was struggling with the college to secure final approval on the experimental farm contract. The parties were in agreement, but the college was hopelessly bureaucratic, requiring multiple levels of acceptance. Morgan had also assured Xander that all equipment would be in working order before papers were signed. She had since discovered a thresher, two harvesters and a windmill turned up in need of repair. Morgan was unsure if Meier could meet her commitment. To compound matters, Xander's clerk was still mired in the resolution of boundary problems dating back more than ten years. Most had been resolved, but the county was proving to be more deliberate than the college. Finally, there was the question of moving. Travel arrangements were yet to be made, nothing was packed, and Freidrich was searching for temporary housing in Sonoma. Morgan's desire for a quick sale had been achieved, but at the expense of an orderly departure.

A week before the signing date, Morgan made a decision that rekindled the dispute between herself and Victoria. The furnishings in all four homes would remain in place. There was one exception, a chair painstakingly carved by her grandfather, which she had transported to Xander's office. Victoria was furious believing that she, and perhaps Clara, should have access to whatever furnishings they desired. Calvin arrived with the borrowed wagon to lay claim to Maria's bed, a settee and several chairs. He left with John's saddle and one-half the set of dishes given Maria by Agnes. Clara took a few inexpensive trinkets and hand-carved onyx jewelry box of unknown origin. Tavendar arranged a business trip and visited the farm the same week. He sent a note to Morgan asking that his father's watch, a Union Pacific timepiece given him by his stepbrother, be set aside, along with any papers relating to immigration. Tav took one last ride through the farm telling his sister she made the right decision. Morgan was grateful. The comment was unsolicited and came from outside the circle of conflict.

Chance McCown was due in Fargo on November 28 to sign papers, but Britt and Morgan were still struggling to complete the agreed upon tasks. McCown was unwilling to change the closing date. After an exchange of telegrams, it was decided to transfer ownership as planned. McCown would simply allow Britt and Morgan to extend their occupancy by two weeks. The Agreement of Sale was signed on the appointed date and filed the following Monday, December 1. Britt and Morgan were joined by Austin Moore, Silas, Xander and Mr. Jenkins of the First National Bank of Fargo. The latter was in attendance to settle outstanding debt and to begin the allocation of funds between Morgan and her siblings.

Upon returning to the farm, Morgan went directly to the cemetery. She knelt at the obelisk asking for her father's blessing, but confident she had done the right thing. Morgan felt both a sense of sadness and relief. The farm was gone, but so to were the trappings that tore the family apart. She glanced again at her mother's headstone. John and Maria could indeed rest in peace.

Britt, Morgan and counsel took full advantage of the extra time to complete their tasks. By the second week of the extension, the family was ready to move. Chez finished all equipment repairs, a new contract with the college was in place and boundary issues had been resolved. Agnes had also wired advising the couple temporary housing had been located.

Britt was helping Chez move a recently repaired harvester when he noticed Levi Andersen leading a group of six men and two wagons toward the Queen Anne. He was immediately struck by their appearance. All were clean shaven and wore similar heavy wool coats. The wagons were either new or freshly painted. The group paused at the gate. Levi and one of the men rode forward.

Cade Upzinger was confused. Levi had just told him the new owners had given Britt and Morgan two weeks additional occupancy. Cade was told by his superiors it was just one. Expecting to see only a caretaker, he saw instead fifteen men and considerable activity. Britt was now on the veranda and listened as Cade sheepishly asked if his work crew arrived too early. Britt offered to show him closing documents, which specified a two-week extension. The young man was apologetic and told Britt there was no need. His group was hastily formed, Cade being the only prior employee. In their rush to put a work crew together, the date was obviously confused. Cade told Britt he would return to Casselton, contact ownership and make other arrangements as necessary.

Morgan had been listening and called to Britt.

"They can occupy the experimental farm," she said. "The students will be returning to the college for the holidays."

"That's generous of you ma'am," Cade said, glad to avoid the finger pointing sure to take place when ownership discovered the mistake.

"The place is yours," Morgan answered, realizing her comment was, in fact, the truth.

Cade tipped his hat to Morgan and promised not to be a nuisance. Britt and Levi escorted the group to the experimental farm. En route, Britt mentioned Michael Aiden O'Connell. Cade could not place him among ownership, but told Britt he had only passing knowledge of the firms' executives.

From the beginning of negotiations, it was understood Levi Andersen would not be retained as farm boss. Chance McCown had confirmed this decision and Levi was given six months salary as severance. The payment came from Britt and Morgan's personal funds. He was now in search of employment.

Levi spent the day before on the 4,600-acre Jason Seequest farm located fifteen miles north and east of Fargo. Jason learned of Levi's availability on a visit to the mercantile and sent his son to the Schmidt farm to talk with Morgan and arrange for Levi to visit. The interview took place two days later. Levi carried a letter of recommendation from Morgan. Jason was impressed and immediately hired the former Schmidt farm boss.

Rather than make the long return trip in one day, Levi spent the night in Fargo with a cousin leaving early the next day. He returned on a less traveled path approaching the Schmidt farm on its southeastern edge. When he reached the point where the Steven Norsen property met the Schmidt farm, he noticed a sign—a red triangle posted on white background. Within the triangle were the letters AMG. Levi knew John Schmidt did not want his property to fall into the hands of a corporate farm, but assumed Morgan's view was less strident. The following morning while discussing his interview with Britt, Levi mentioned the sign.

Britt was stunned, "That can't be."

He wanted to see for himself and quickly saddled a horse. Before reaching Norsen's corner, Britt encountered Cade and his crew. He pointed to the signs on the floor of the wagon asking "Your employer?"

Cade, a bit confused, answered, "Yes, for eight years." Britt had assumed Cade's earlier reference to ownership referred to Luther's buyer, Michael Aiden O'Connell. He was wrong. Cade's employer and the new owner of the Schmidt farm was Anderson-Middleton Grain. When Britt referenced O'Connell, Cade simply assumed he was a principal in AMG. Britt told Cade to return to the experimental farm. He in turn reversed course and rode directly to the telegraph office. His note to Xander read, "AMG signs posted on Schmidt property." When he returned to the farm, Britt found his wife seated at her desk, head in hands. She had spoken with Levi.

Morgan told her husband, "We've been deceived by Luther and perhaps others."

Late in the day, Xander sent a timeline of events by courier. Forty-eight hours after final papers had been signed, O'Connell sold the property to AMG for $30.10 per acre. The difference between the amount paid O'Connell and that paid by AMG provided the incentive for duplicity. Luther Ogden had betrayed the family's trust and collected more than $22,000.00 in the process.

"I've sold to a corporate farm," she told Britt. "Tell Cade and his AMG crew they're no longer welcome."

Britt reminded her, "Its AMG's property. We're the interloper," he said. "Cade was not involved," he added. "Punishing an innocent achieves nothing."

Morgan knew he was right. She dismissed her husband and sat alone in the parlor retracing each step of the sale still disbelieving what had taken place. She wondered if her father would have been as easily deceived.

The next morning Levi reported AMG signs now covered much of the farm's southern boundary. Xander saw them as well. He arrived just after noon. His time at the courthouse the day before convinced him there was no recourse. John's desire to avoid sale to a corporate farm was clearly stated in his will, but not formally recorded as a condition of sale. Any attempt to reverse the unfortunate turn of events would be both expensive and unlikely to succeed. He was apologetic. The warning signs were there, but he missed them. O'Connell kept his distance and Luther recommended Buskirk as the appraiser. The accelerated closing and sham inspection were also harbingers of things to come. The Lowrys and their counsel missed them all. No doubt AMG, O'Connell, James Buskirk, and Chance McCown had some knowledge of the ruse. Xander would later discover the common thread was McCown who had ties to all the parties. The transgressor, Luther Ogden, was nowhere to be found.

Morgan made one last trek to her father's gravesite. She was angry with Luther, but equally so with herself. Due diligence had not been practiced and the farm was in the hands of AMG. She stared blankly at her father's monument even as a light snow began to fall, a necessary catharsis. Britt had told her John would understand. The sale was grounded in a desire to bring peace to the family. She could not have seen a trusted friend would turn on them.

December 13 had arrived and Morgan, Britt and the children were leaving their home of twenty-eight years. She spent the morning reviewing travel plans, discussing care of Sunset Ranch with Juanna and simply walking through the Queen Anne. Every room held memories. She recalled her mother toiling in the kitchen, her father resting on the veranda, Jacob holding his grandchildren, and her fateful meeting with Britt.

Morgan was finally at peace with the events of the past six months. Eric and Lisa Hansen would arrive in a few hours to transport the family to the Casselton Station. She still owed Cade Upzinger a note listing items that should be checked before the planting season began. He was capable of developing his own checklist, but Morgan felt an obligation, if not to Cade, then to the farm. Morgan was preparing the list and caught sight of the AMG foreman coming through the gate at the reins of a small wagon. She and Cade were now friends. He had joined the Lowrys twice for dinner in the past week. Cade had been advised of the deception, but was innocent of wrongdoing.

As Morgan stepped onto the veranda, Cade called to her, "Would you like to keep this placard? The crew found it yesterday in a pile of barn wood near the entrance to the old Meyer homestead."

Morgan saw the heavily checked sign, "Farm of John Schmidt." Almost three decades had passed since Karl Meyer and Freidrich hung the sign. The entrance had been abandoned after the first Mann purchase and the sign forgotten. She had passed beneath it many times as a young woman, before the farm became an 11,000-acre collossus. Morgan turned her gaze toward the snow-covered fields—the stark landscape a perfect reflection of her thoughts. Sensing his mother's distress, Spencer came to her side.

"This could have been yours," she whispered.

Cade asked again, "Morgan?"

Britt answered, "We'd be obliged if you leave the sign at Sunset Ranch."

List of Characters—Continued

Christian Berg
—Herta
George Breit
—Sibylle
Nicholas Geist
—Frida
—Werner
Wilfried Gerber
—Meta
Eduard Hauer
—Nela
—Franz
Kurt Haus
Denzel Kalb
—Ida
Elmer Klein
—Erna
—Christal
—Jutta
Gustav Kunkel
—Luise
Sander Metz
—Anja
Karl Seigler
—Ella
Burkhard Wetzel
—Elma
—Albert

Members of Schuler Party

Gabriel Schuler: Leader
—Catherine
—Klaus
Henry Bissing
Otto Heimler
—Emma
Gotthold Sumas
—Mari
Emil Zimmerman

MEMBERS OF PARTY FROM NEU-WARRENBURG

CHRISTOF ACKER
—MARY
　—ELISABET
SAMUEL BAUMAN
PHILIPP WEBER
—ELISE
　—HILKE
　—CARINA

MEMBERS OF THE BRUENER PARTY

LUDWIG BRUENER
—ELSA
　—HEINZ
　—LEVIN
RAINIER HOCH
MILO PORTNER
JANNICK WOLFE

MEMBERS OF BECKER FAMILY

LUKAS BECKER
—ADELE
　—LIZZIE
　—TILMAN

MANAGING PARTNERS

COLVIS RASMUSSEN: FARM BOSS
—MARY ETTA
　—BJARTR (ICE)
　—LIZZIE (ADOPTED)
　　—COLVIS RASMUSSEN III
　　—ALICE
　—COLVIS RASMUSSEN II
LEVI ANDERSEN
—KARI
ALBERT HAUGEN
—MARIT
　—MEIER*
　　—OLEANNA
　—ILSE
CHEZ SCHOUFFLE

Merchants

Aaron Bergmann: Proprieter, Hays City Apothecary
——Priscilla
  —Robert
George Bollinger: Hays City Stonemason
Conn Doyle: Hays City Blacksmith
——Lucy Milbourne
T. Fergus Jenkins: Fargo City Banker
Cyrus Larsen: Hays City Carpenter
Axel Moen: Casselton Thresherman
Daniel Nelson: Proprieter, Hays City Feed Company
Jeremia Olsen: Hays City Contract Sodbuster
James Norton: Hays City Banker
Joseph Pallitto: Proprieter. Hays City General Store

*Becomes Managing Partner After Albert's Death

James Stockman: Proprieter, Fargo Mercantile
——Marcella
  —Gunter

Others

Louise Adams: Assistant to Hermann Schafer
Xander Adams: Attorney for Morgan Schmidt Lowry
Father Albin: Pfeifer Priest
Colonel Clive Austin: Retired Army Physician, Casselton
Anselm Baten: Assistant to Mr. Randolph, Kansas Pacific
Ezra Bell: Attorney for Mann Investors
Gisa Berger: Leader of Outlaw Band
John Burke: Mentor to Tavendar Schmidt
James Clarke: Fargo Doctor
George Culp: Topeka City Official
Maxwell Desalle: Accountant for Chance Mccown
Craig Duffy: Bonanza Farmer
Benjamin Erhardt: Sells Adjoining Land to John Schmidt
Amanda Lynn Geiser: Teacher, St. Anne's
Erik Hansen: Friend of John and Maria Schmidt
——Lisa
  —Isabel
Himmelfarb: Hays City Doctor
Johann Houfner: Knowledge of Immigration
Einer Johansen: Norwegion Homesteader
  —Lucia
  —Adam
Edward Kantor: Schafer Farm Boss
Valentin Krause: Mapmaker

488

KENDAL LEHMANN: DEAN NORTH DAKOTA STATE COLLEGE OF AGRICULTURE
RICHARD LEMASTER: OWNER, SUNSET RANCH
FATHER LENKEIT: ST. ANNE'S PRIEST
CORNELLIOUS MANN: ABSENTEE OWNER OF BONANZA FARM
JUANA MARTINEZ: MARIA'S HELPER
—MIGUEL
CHANCE MCCOWN: ATTORNEY FOR MICHAEL AIDEN O'CONNELL
ETHAN MCKELLAR: DOCTOR, FARGO, CASSELTON
KARL MEYER: PRECEDES JOHN SCHMIDT AS OWNER OF DAKOTAN HOMESTEAD
AUSTIN MOORE:ATTORNEY FOR SCHMIDT SIBLINGS
LAWRENCE MOREHEAD: JUDGE
—AGNES
REINHART MULLER: HOMESTEADER
—MICHAEL
—NICHOLAS
ROLF NEUMANN: HOMESTEADS WITH KARL MEYER
FATHER NICHOLAS: PFEIFER PRIEST
MICHAEL AIDEN O'CONNELL: WEALTHY BUSINESS OWNER AND SHILL
   FOR LUTHER OGDEN
LUTHER OGDEN: FARGO FINANCIER
DANIEL RANDOLPH: LAND SALES, KANSAS PACIFIC RAILROAD
LELAND RAY: FARGO DOCTOR
PAULUS RICHTER: HOMESTEADER
HORACE SAALBERG: MINNEAPOLIS RESEARCH PHYSICIAN
C.B. SCHMIDT: LAND SALES ATCHISON, TOPEKA AND SANTA FE RAILROAD
CHARLES SENK: ATTORNEY
ARNE SCHWAB: EXPERT ON AMERICAN PRAIRIE
KENNETH SLOAN: KANSAS ASSISTANT SUPERINTENDENT OF PUBLIC INSTRUCTION
AMELDA SUTHERLAND: TEACHER
CADE UPZINGER: EMPLOYEE OF ANDERSON-MIDDLETON GRAIN
BISHOP DAVID WILLIAMS: FARGO DIOCESE

Made in United States
Orlando, FL
09 March 2022

15582230R00274